MORE CLARIN

By the same author

Clarinet Virtuosi of the Past

The Clarinet Teacher's Companion

Clarinet Virtuosi of Today

Yesterday's Clarinettists: a Sequel

More Clarinet Virtuosi of the Past

PAMELA WESTON

First published in London England 1977
Reprinted 1982
Reprinted 1992
Reprinted 2002

ISBN 0-9506209-4-7

Printed in Great Britain by
The Panda Group · Haverhill · Suffolk CB9 8PR

Contents

	Page
Preface	11
Acknowledgements	13
Introduction	15
Abbreviations	19
Biographies	23
Locations	287
Compositions	333
Bibliography	371
Index	375

Illustrations

PLATES

Between pages 96 and 97

1 Georges Bachmann
Heinrich Backofen

2 Franz Bartolomey
Aloysius Beerhalter

3 Bellison Clarinet Ensemble

4 Simeon Bellison. Signature
Valentin Bender. Signature

5 Berr in group

6 Dantan's caricature of Berr

7 Dantan's caricature of Blaes

8 Frédéric Blasius
Ferdinando Busoni

9 Busoni's Vinatieri clarinet
Louis Cahuzac

10 Cavallini as a young man. Signature
Cavallini in later years

11 Haydn and Mendelssohn Draper in group
Charles Duvernoy

12 William Egerton
Carl Ehrenreich

13 Joseph Faubel
Anton Friedlowsky

14 Maximilian Gabler
Karl Goepfert

15 Gustav Heinze. Signature
Gustaf Hessler

16 Johan Kjellberg
Thomas Klein

17 Jacob Kleine
Johann Kotte

18 Lazarus in Kneller Hall group

19 Henry Lazarus with clarinet
Henry Lazarus

20 Lazarus' Fieldhouse clarinet

21 Adolphe Leroy
Müller's Schuster clarinet

22 John Maycock. Signature.
Ralph McLane

23 Mimart by Nadar

24 Franz Otter

25 Henri Paradis. Signature
Mozart Petersen

26 Joseph Proksch. Signature
Antonio Romero. Signature

27 Rose by Nadar

28 Adolphe Sax
Louis Schindelmeisser

29 Oskar Schubert
Henri and Alexandre Selmer

30 Robert Stark
Friedrich Wilhelm Tausch

31 Cadwallader Thomas
George Tyler

32 Leopold Wlach
Miguel Yuste

LINE FIGURES

		Page
1	Letter from Demnitz to Marhefka	84
2	Concerto by Duvernoy	93
3	Letter from Kotte to Kranklin	144
4	Concert invitation from Iwan Müller	183
5	Concert programme of Caroline Schleicher	227
6	Letter from F.X. Wolf to André	276
7	“Der arme Spielmann an seine Clarinette”	280

Preface

Response to the original volume of *Clarinet Virtuosi of the Past* indicates that clarinettists of today have a more than healthy appetite for information on their forebears. Finding their appetite unappeased I hasten to offer a second course and hope they will enjoy its consumption as much as I enjoyed collecting the ingredients.

In writing the first book my object was to give the story of a select few of the really great clarinet players. There was never any doubt that those chosen were of the élite, for each had made a contribution of lasting importance to the saga of the clarinet. However, there was a doubt that there might be others whose achievement had been as great, but who lay unjustly forgotten. The doubt could only be resolved by investigating on a wide scale the lives of a very much larger number of players. Such an investigation I have carried out and my conclusion is that those in the first volume do reign supreme. Exclusion from the ranks of the élite does not mean the lesser players are of no account. On the contrary, their story is equally worth the telling, for the amount of interesting material gleaned from their activities makes them as important collectively as were the great ones individually.

Acknowledgements

To the following descendants, who so generously provided information on their forebears: Franz Bartolomey, J.H.P. Draper, the late W.B. Draper, Michael Egerton, Reginald Egerton, Harold Gomez, Jean Selmer and Lawrence Tanner CVO.

To the following for help of diverse kinds: Elie Apper, Thomas Ayres, Herman Baron, Kalman Bloch, James Brown, David Cairns, Oliver Davies, Guy Deplus, Georgina Dobrée, Dr. Ehrmann, Yona Ettlinger, Richard Gilbert, Jane Harrington, Paul Harvey, Dr. Karl-Heinz Köhler, Señora Laureiro, Charles & Judy Mackerras, Richard Macnutt, Peter Makings, Douglas Matthews, William Maynard, Graham Melville-Mason, Ronald Moore, Elizabeth Nussbaum, P.C. Roscoe, B. Schott's Söhne, Mrs. Taylor-Stach, Graham Turner, David Weber and Dr. L. Wenzel.

To the staff of the British Library and to Mrs. Gleed of the Royal Society of Musicians. And finally, to Mr. Polacek of Jerusalem for the loan of the late Dr. Fritz Marcus' collected notes, which were a source of inestimable value, particularly with regard to the players of German origin.

Introduction

The biographical section of *More Clarinet Virtuosi of the Past* contains information on nearly a thousand players at three levels of importance. Firstly, all top-level players from the original volume have been listed again for the ready location of dates, etc., and for the recording of new information, some of which is considerable. The reader should refer to the original volume for their full lives.

Second-level players, some of whom made a brief appearance in the original volume, now come into their own and are given detailed treatment. Their ranks are swelled by several hundreds and lest the reader should be at a loss where to begin, I would like to recommend to his particular attention the following: Heinrich Backofen, the Bänder brothers, Barth of Leipzig, Beerhalter, Simeon Bellison, the Bender family, Blasius, Boufil, Ferdinando Busoni, Cahuzac, Canongia, Cavallini, Dacosta, David, Duvernoy, Farník, the Faubel brothers, Gambaro, de Groot, Heinze father and son, the Kleine family, Kotte, Landgraf, Langenus, Meissner, Mimart, Friedrich Müller, Oehler, Pisařovic, Gaspard Procksch, Georg Reinhardt, Romero y Andía, Rose, the Roth brothers, Rummel, Sax, Schindelmeisser, the Selmer family, Sobeck, Solère, the two Springers, Stark, F. Tretbar, Vanderhagen, Joseph Williams, Wlach and Yuste.

As I delved into the lives of third-level players, scarcely any of whom appeared in the original volume, I became aware of one striking and significant feature. This feature, which fully justifies the players' inclusion in the present study, was the appearance of particularly interesting and unusual music in their programmes. The reason for this occurrence is not far to seek, for here was a struggle for existence against more successful and popular artists for which a counter-attraction of this nature was essential. Third-level research yielded a number of other interesting items such as the fact that Messrs. Freudenfeld and Rosenburg had a Benefit in Hickford's Great Room, in London, on 25th March 1726, thereby pre-dating Mr Charles' first known performance on the clarinet by over a decade. Mr Charles may however have been the subject of the following notice in *The Daily Post* of 31st June 1722: "RICHMOND-WELLS . . . . . on Mondays will be a select Band of Musick from the Opera . . . . . N.B. There will be several Concerto's every Evening on a new Instrument from Germany call'd *The Shalamo*, never play'd in Publick before." In the 1790s two players emerged well in advance of their times: Francis Schaffer, who demonstrated "spiccato" (undoubtedly this was staccato from the reed turned underneath) and Georg Nason, who demonstrated "double sounds". It is probably also worth mentioning the pranks of Franz Schalk, the charlatan basset-horn player, who set most of Europe and St Petersburg a-laughing in the 1820s and 1830s.

As with the previous volume, so with the present one, many problems had to be sorted out before it could be written. Outstanding amongst these was the disentangling of the activities of two sets of brothers – the Bänders and Benders – both of German origin and both flourishing in the first half of the nineteenth century. As with Josef Bähr and Joseph Beer, so with the Bänders and Benders, the latter have been credited with activities belonging to the former. Conrad and Ludwig Bänder were renowned as virtuosi in St Petersburg, Paris and throughout Germany, and were said to rival Heinrich Baermann. Jakob and Valentin Bender were not travelling virtuosi, but military bandsmen, who from early in both their lives became distinguished bandmasters in the Netherlands.

In assessing the virtuosi as a whole, it is interesting to note that roughly one in twelve were basset-horn players, a high proportion by present-day standards. Of the new virtuosi, several approached the stature of a Baermann or Hermstedt. Many fine partnerships existed, notably that between de Groot and Georg Reinhardt, who played under Spohr at Frankfurt. There are several instances of brothers playing the instrument, of father and son, and occasionally of three or four in the same family. Like Hermstedt and Mühlfeld, there were some who, through experience on other instruments and/or the ability to compose, became Kapellmeisters. Others became fine teachers, and the reader will note how often these would allow a talented pupil to perform a double concerto with them in public.

The biographies, besides dealing with each player's life, give all known details of his concerts and works, including sources for the latter. The biographical information is confined mainly to what is of interest to clarinettists. This means that where a performer changed his instrument or became principally a composer or music director, the ensuing part of his life is given only briefly and the reader wishing to know more should consult other sources. Likewise in works lists, only those for clarinet(s) or members of the clarinet family are included. Tutors are given, but not studies, unless these are of special significance. The biographies are followed by lists of locations and compositions compiled from information in both volumes. These lists are pertinent only to the present study and do not constitute a complete record of court lists or clarinet compositions. In the list of locations every player mentioned who is known to have been in regular employment at a court or town for a year or more is given, together with dates.

In the list of compositions every performance mentioned where both date and composer's name are known is given. This list provides a guide to the relative popularity of composers and of specific works. It will surprise nobody to see that Mozart, Weber and Spohr top the polls. Mozart's "Parto!" was played more than any other work and it is noticeable how many performers "discovered" his Concerto and Quintet in their later years. Weber's Concertino proves to have been the favourite solo work. The compositions of Brahms are not played as often as might be expected, but this may be due to their late arrival in the period under survey. Of the lesser-known composers, Krommer, Lindpaintner, Reissiger and Winter appear frequently. Of the clarinettist-composers, Crusell is by far the most popular, with Heinrich Baermann and Iwan Müller coming second, and Franz Tausch third. Krommer's concertos for 2 clarinets were extraordinarily popular and Iwan Müller's one double concerto was also often played. Of the chamber works, Beethoven's Septet takes pride of place.

Abbreviations

General:

(B-H)	Basset-horn player
BBC	British Broadcasting Corporation
CBS	Columbia Broadcasting System
NBC	National Broadcasting Corporation
OV	Original volume

Libraries and Collections:

AaS	Aarhus, Statsbiblioteket
AKVM	Antwerp, Koninklija Vlaams Muziekconservatorium
BarBM	Barcelona, Biblioteca Musical
BaU	Basel, Universitätsbibliothek
BDS	Berlin, Deutsche Staatsbibliothek
BIM	Berlin, Institüt für Musikforschung
BoLM	Bologna, Liceo Musicale
BrBC	Brussels, Bibliothèque du Conservatoire
BrBR	Brussels, Bibliothèque Royale
BSPK	Berlin, Stiftung Preussischer Kulturbesitz
ChiNL	Chicago, Newberry Library
CSL	Carlstad, Stifts-och Läroverksbibliotheket
DHLH	Darmstadt, Hessische Landes-und-Hochschulbibliothek
DiBC	Dijon, Bibliothèque du Conservatoire
DoFB	Donaueschingen, Fürstenburgische Bibliothek
DrSL	Dresden, Sächsische Landesbibliothek
EdBHC	Edgware, Boosey & Hawkes Collection
EiKEM	Einsiedeln, Kloster Einsiedeln Musikbibliothek
ERC	Edinburgh, Rendall Collection
FSU	Frankfurt a. M, Stadt-und-Universitätsbibliothek

HGM	The Hague, Gemeente Museum
LBL	London, British Library
LeK-MU	Leipzig, Karl-Marx Universität
LHM	London, Horniman Museum
LiBN	Lisbon, Biblioteca Nacional
LRAM	London, Royal Academy of Music
LRCM	London, Royal College of Music
LuMS	Lübeck, Musiksammlung auf der Stadtbibliothek
MaCSM	Madrid, Conservatorio Superior de Musica
ManPL	Manchester, Public Library (Henry Watson Collection)
MarPKS	Marburg/Lahn, Preussischer Kulturbesitz Staatsbibliothek
MasSL	Massachusetts, Smith Library
MBS	Munich, Bayerische Staatsbibliothek
MiAUL	Michigan, Ann Arbor University Library
MiBC	Milan, Biblioteca del Conservatorio
MuUB	Münster, Universitäts-Bibliothek
NBN	Naples, Biblioteca Nazionale
NCM	Naples, Conservatorio di Musica
NYPL	New York, Public Library
OBC	Oxford, Bate Collection
OSB	Örebo, Stadsbibliothek
PBN	Paris, Bibliothèque Nationale
PhFL	Philadelphia, Free Library
PrNM	Prague, Národní Museum
ProPL	Providence, Public Library
RBC	Rome, Biblioteca del Conservatorio
RTTH	Regensburg, Thurn & Taxis Hofbibliothek
SBS	Stockholm, Börgarskola
ScML	Schwerin, Mecklenburgische Landesbibliothek
SKB	Stockholm, Kungliga Bibliotheket
SKMA	Stockholm, Kungliga Musikaliska Akademiens
SKTB	Stockholm, Kungliga Teaterns Bibliotek
SpPLM	Speyer a.R, Pfälzische Landesbibliothek Musikabteilung
TBMAM	Tokyo, Bibliotheca Musashimo Academia Musica
TwKHL	Twickenham, Kneller Hall Library
UUB	Uppsala, Universitetsbibliotheket
VGM	Vienna, Gesellschaft der Musikfreunde
VNB	Vienna, Nationalbibliothek
WLC	Washington, Library of Congress
ZAM	Zurich, Allgemeine Musikgesellschaft

Periodicals & Reference Books:

AMZ	Allgemeine musikalische Zeitung, Leipzig
BMZ	Berlinische musikalische Zeitung, Berlin
DMDZ	Deutsche Musikdirektoren-Zeitung, Leipzig
DMMZ	Deutsche Militär-Musiker-Zeitung, Berlin
DO	Das Orchester, Nuremberg
GSJ	Galpin Society Journal, London
LZ	Luditzer Zeitung, Luditz
M	Metronome, New York
MGG	Die Musik in Geschichte und Gegenwart, Kassel
MISM	Mitteilungen der Internationalen Stiftung Mozarteum, Salzburg
MJB	Mozart-Jahrbuch, Salzburg
MM	Music & Musicians, London
MT	Musical Times, London
MTe	Music Teacher, London
MY	Music & Youth, London
MZ	Musik im Zeitbewusstsein, Berlin
NACWPI	National Association of College Wind & Percussion Instructors, Washington
OM	Österreichische Musikzeitung, Vienna
PMM	Penguin Music Magazine, Harmondsworth & New York
SM	Süddeutsche Musikzeitung, Mainz
TC	The Clarinet, New York
WM	Woodwind Magazine, New York
WN	Woodwind News, New York
WW	Woodwind World, New York
WYB	Woodwind Year Book, London
ZI	Zeitschrift für Instrumentenbau, Leipzig & Breslau
ZM	Zietschrift für Musik, Stuttgart

Biographies

Works lists at the ends of articles use the following order: solo concertos, multiple instrument concertos, unaccompanied works, sonatas, miscellaneous solos with piano or orchestral accompaniment, duets, larger chamber ensembles, works for clarinet and voice, bass clarinet works, bassethorn works, methods. Unless otherwise specified, the word 'duet' denotes a work for 2 clarinets; 'quartet' and 'quintet' denote works for clarinet with 3 and 4 strings respectively. Information in parentheses uses the following order: date of composition, earliest publisher(s) known and date of publication, copy locations (see list of abbreviations for libraries and collections).

ABEL (APEL). He worked at Frankfurt a.M., probably as a member of the theatre orchestra. He played in the Mozart Wind Quintet for the Frankfurt Museum Concerts on 19th February 1872 and 23rd November 1874.

ABRAHAM(E). 1760-1805. French. In 1788 he was playing in the orchestra at the Paris Opéra. By 1790 he had moved to the Théâtre des Délassements Comiques. He was a teacher of the clarinet and of solfège.

Works: Recueil d'Air choisis, Walses, Marches etc.

(Frère c.1790 – LBL). Petite Méthode de clarinette (Frère c.1780 – DiBC).

(B–H). **ADAMI, Giuseppe.** Italian. He was engaged as the first teacher of clarinet and basset-horn at the Milan Conservatoire in 1808 and held the post until 1815.

ADAMI, Vinatier (Viantier?). Piedmont, ? – ? Italian. He was a well-known clarinet teacher at Turin at the beginning of the 19th century.

Work: Méthode pour la clarinette (Reycend c.1800).

ADDNER, Anders (André). Linköping, 26 Oct 1799-1876 Sept 14, Linköping. Swedish. He was Crusell's most distinguished pupil and like him became a chamber musician at the Swedish Court. It was said that he had an extremely beautiful tone, that "singing was his aim and with this he opened all hearts." He undertook several concert tours abroad and in 1837 was engaged as first clarinet at the German Opera in St Petersburg. After Crusell's death he came back to Sweden to take over his master's directorship of the First Life Guards at Linköping, and remained in this post until 1859. The library of the Royal Musical Academy at Stockholm has the following works by Crusell which were hand-copied by Addner: "Potpourri for clarinet, horn and bassoon" (signed and dated 25th May 1817); Grand Concerto op.5 (signed and dated 19th August 1818).

Addner's concerts abroad included the following: 1827 – 6th October at Hamburg, a solo by Weber in a concert given by Ferdinand David. 1828 – May at Berlin's royal opera house, an entre'acte concert. 1833 – autumn in Vienna. 1834 – October at Prague's Dauscha Hall, Rossini's Fantasie, Pastorale (from op.5) by Crusell, variations by Blatt and Franz Lachner's "Das Waldvöglein" for Nanette Kratky. His success here was exceptional, they said his playing had a magical effect and they had never heard such control of dynamics.

AGNER, Karl. ? – 1874 July 17, Vienna. Austrian. He was a member of the Vienna Philharmonic Orchestra from 1830 to 1874.

(B–H). **AGTHE, Johann August.** 1795 – 1864. German. He also played the violin and viola, and composed. He was a member of a large musical family and was court clarinettist and chamber musician at Weimar from 1821. Berlioz heard the orchestra in 1841 and remarked on the excellence of Agthe's playing. There was no cor anglais player available at the time and it was Agthe's transposition of a part for this instrument that particularly won the composer's admiration. Agthe was pensioned in 1850 but was still playing in the orchestra in 1855. He was a fine teacher, Nehrlich being his most famous pupil. His daughter Rosa Agthe von Milde was a well-known singer.

He played in the following concerts, at Weimar unless otherwise stated: 1821 – concerto by Crusell. 1825 – Lindpainter's Concerto. 1826 – Concerto for clarinet & horn by Theodor Müller. 1832 – concerto (probably no. 1) by Weber. 1833 – Jena, he introduced Weber's Second Concerto and played Variations by Franke, his colleague at the Weimar Court. Later in the year, Weber's Second Concerto at Weimar. 1834 – Jena, Weber's Concertino and one of the concertos. 1835 – Jena, his own compositions. 1839 – Maurer's Concertino at a court concert. 1841 – Mozart's "Non più di fiori" for Sabine Heinefetter. 1842 – Jena, compositions by Täglichsbeck and Weber.

AHL. German. He played soprano and bass clarinet in the court orchestra at Mannheim from about 1809. He was very popular as a soloist and one report speaks of him as "the darling of the public." At the first performance in 1813 of a Mass by Vincent Maschek, which had several important clarinet solos, his playing was so outstanding that the composer made him take a bow.

Work: Variations.

ALBES, Karl Wilhelm. Northeim, 1793 – ? German. He was music director to a battalion of Grenadier Guards and then became second clarinet in the court orchestra at Hanover in 1821. He resigned from this in 1844.

ALBESBY (ALBESPY). French. In 1795 he was in the orchestra of the Théâtre de la Cité, Paris.

Work: Concerto no. 1 in E flat (Sieber, c.1790).

ALBRECHT, Julius Bruno. Grimma 24 July 1825 – ? German. He played second clarinet in the Leipzig Gewandhaus Orchestra from 1850 to 1863 and then became their librarian and archivist.

ALEXANDROV, A.M. 1895 – 1962. Russian. He studied under Rozanov at the Moscow Conservatoire. Later he became a member of the Bolshoi Theatre Orchestra and taught at the

Gnesinykh Music Teachers Institute.

ALLEGRA, Edmondo. Swiss. He lived at Zurich, where he gave the first performance of Stravinsky's Three Pieces on 8th November 1919. Busoni dedicated his Concertino op.48 of 1919 to Allegra and in 1922 supplied him with a cadenza with orchestral accompaniment for the Mozart Concerto. In 1925 Allegra toured the United States of America, when he played twice with the Boston Philharmonic Orchestra.

(B–H). **ALT.** Austrian. He taught the basset-horn at Lilienfeld, near Vienna, at the beginning of the nineteenth century.

AMBROSI, Carl. ? – 1776 Aug 22, Forst. Czech. He studied philosophy and theology at Prague, but did not attain the priesthood; instead, he became an excellent clarinet player and teacher.

AMELANG. In 1849 he was a member of the court orchestra at Dessau.

AMME. German. He was a town musician at Heinichen. On 15th February 1833 he played Iwan Müller's double concerto with Kunze at Merseburg.

ANDERSON, George W. 1867 – 1951 Dec 2. English. He was a pupil of Lazarus. Early in his career he adopted the Boehm clarinet, producing on it a peculiarly sweet and delicate tone. As an ex-student, he gave the first performance of Coleridge-Taylor's Quintet op.10 on 10th July 1895, at the Royal College of Music. From 1904 to 1943 Anderson played in the London Symphony Orchestra, with which he served as a director for 20 years. He was also principal clarinet for the Beecham Opera Company, played in the Scottish Orchestra for the 1908/9 season, and was a member of the BBC Military Band. He was a fine teacher and from 1941 to 1951 was a professor at the Royal Academy of Music.

ANDRÉ. French. He was a clarinettist in the orchestra at Kassel in 1823. In 1834 he had moved to Fulda, where he played in the military band as well as the court orchestra. He was probably one of the clarinettists who took part in a performance of Schindelmeisser's Symphonie Concertante for 4 clarinets at Fulda in 1835.

ANTON, Friedrich. ? – 1850. German. He was also a

violinist, and began as a teacher of military bandsmen. In 1813 he became a Chamber Musician at the Darmstadt Court and in 1850 received the Gold Medal of Ludwig for his services in this capacity. He was probably related to Ludwig Anton.

ANTON, Ludwig. ? – 1842. German. He was probably related to Friedrich Anton and like him also played the violin. In 1804 he became a court musician at Darmstadt.

(B–H). **ASSMANN, Guillaume Ernest.** 2 Nov 1742 – ? In 1773 and 1774 he played clarinet and basset-horn at the Paris Opéra. He was appointed a teacher of the first class at the Institut National de Musique in 1793 and kept the post when the Institut became part of the Conservatoire in 1795. He also taught drums and solfège and was active in the administration, retiring in 1802.

AUGARDE, August (Wells). 1865 – 1946 Mar 18. English. He was the father of Edward Augarde. August's father was Edwarde Augarde, who came from a family of French musicians who fled to England during the French Revolution. Up to 1936 there were members of this family in the Grenadier Guards, one of them being solo clarinettist in 1860. August was bass clarinettist in the London Symphony Orchestra from 1904 to 1916. He joined the Royal Society of Musicians in 1906.

AUGARDE, Edward (James). 13 Dec 1886 – ? English. He was the son of August Augarde. He studied at the Royal Academy of Music and in 1913 when George Clinton died Sir Alexander Mackenzie, the Principal, offered him the professorship. This was in preference to Charles Draper, who had applied for the post. Edward held the post until 1923. He played in the London Symphony Orchestra from 1913 to 1933.

AUGARDE, Gustave. English. He belonged to the same family as the above. From 1881 to 1887 he played soprano and bass clarinets for the Richter Concerts.

AUROUX. French. From 1861 to 1863 he played first clarinet in the orchestra for the Concerts Populaires, with Grisez playing second. Elwart describes him as "le clarinettiste par excellence" and, after a performance of the slow movement of Mozart's Quintet, says "il obtint un succès éclatant en exécutant avec sentiment exquis ce sublime *adagio* (sic)." Auroux appeared frequently as soloist for the society and on two occasions movements were repeated at the following concert because he received so much applause. His principal performances were: 1862 – 16th March, Beethoven Septet. 26th October, Mozart Quintet. 1863 – 1st February and 29th March, Beethoven Septet.

Bibliography:

ELWART, Antoine: *Histoire des concerts populaires*. Paris 1864.

AVÉ-LALLEMENT, Louis Johann Gottfried Ernst Sigismund. Magdeburg, 1782 – 1823 Nov 19, Greifswald. From 1805 to 1815 he was a clarinettist and piano teacher in the town of Lübeck. He then went to Greifswald to become town music director.

AVONI, Petronio. Italian. From 1797 to 1826 he was first clarinet at the Teatro Communale in Bologna. In 1812 he succeeded the oboist Giuseppe Casa as clarinet teacher at the Conservatoire. This was the first time separate appointments had been made for the clarinet and oboe.

BACHMANN, Franz? He was first clarinet to the Brunswick Court in 1865. He may be the Franz Bachmann of Prague whom Branberger cites as a pupil at Prague Conservatoire from 1840 to 1846.

BACHMANN, Georges Chrétien. Padeborn, 7 Jan 1804-1842 Aug 28, Brussels. German. See OV. He spent his professional life in Brussels, where he was principal and bass clarinet player in the court orchestra and also a member of the royal wind band. During the time that he was teacher at the Conservatoire, from 1832 until his early death ten years later, he established a reputation of very fine teaching. His most illustrious pupil was Blaes, with whom he performed Späth's double concerto at the Church of the Augustins on 10th April 1836. He opened an instrument factory and was joined in this for a short time, until 1836, by Charles Mahillon. In 1839 Bachmann was awarded a medal for wind-instrument construction. His speciality was Müller-type clarinets, a pair of which was used by Blaes.

About 1838 Bachmann had the misfortune to come up against Sax, who was just starting out on his stormy career. Sax wished to introduce his improved bass clarinet to the royal wind band and gained permission to play it at a rehearsal. Bachmann, no doubt wont to use an instrument of his own manufacture, was incensed at the intrusion and cried: "I shall no longer play!" Seconds later, regretting his outburst, he added: "If miserable students like Monsieur Sax are allowed to play in such a distinguished orchestra as this." Sax's reply was: "I should be very sorry, Sir, if the public were deprived of your fine talents through my invention, but I will not retract at all." "What do you propose to do then?" "Let you play first and then play myself. The public shall decide whether the great master or the miserable student wins the fight." Bachmann accepted the challenge, muttering under his breath: "I shall crush him like a fly!" In spite of the esteem in which he was held, Bachmann's solo received no special recognition, but Sax was greeted with a storm of applause. This was a severe blow to Bachmann who henceforth had to yield all bass clarinet solos to the young inventor.

BACK, N. ?-1816, Darmstadt. German. He also played flute and violin. From 1795 until his death he was a court musician at Darmstadt.

BACKOFEN, Gottfried. Durlach, 1771-? German. He was the brother of Heinrich Backofen (q.v.) and of the bassoonist Ernst Backofen. In 1780 the family moved to Nuremberg, where Gottfried and Heinrich had clarinet lessons from H. Birckmann. In 1803 Gottfried became a member of the town orchestra at Nuremberg, playing violin as well as clarinet. He was probably the Backofen who travelled with Weber in the Nuremberg area from February to July 1807. They visited Bayreuth, Erlangen, Ansbach and Amburg. In 1820 Gottfried performed a concerto by Crusell and he was a soloist again in 1822. He was still at Nuremberg in 1825.

(B–H). **BACKOFEN, (Johann Georg) Heinrich.** Durlach, 6 July 1768-1839 July 10, Darmstadt. German. See O.V. He also played the flute and harp. He was the brother of Gottfried Backofen (q.v.) and of the bassoonist Ernst Backofen. The singer Mlle Backofen (Mme Steinert) may have been their sister. In 1780 the family moved to Nuremberg, where Heinrich learnt the clarinet with H. Birckmann and composition with G.W. Gruber. He also learnt portrait painting and languages, at which he did well. In 1789 he left Nuremberg and travelled as a clarinet virtuoso. He stayed for some time in France and Spain and later toured through Italy. On returning to Nuremberg in 1794 he was made a member of the town orchestra and at this period took up the study of the flute.

In May 1802 Backofen set off on a second tour, this time with basset-horn and harp. He travelled first to Hildburghausen and then spent considerable time at Gotha where he performed for

Prince August. In November he visited Halle, Magdeburg and Merseburg. By December he was in Leipzig where he played harp solos for a private society, and on 9th basset-horn solos and a quintet (probably his own op.9) at the Gewandhaus. He returned to Nuremberg and was there for most of 1803.

In 1804 he performed on both basset-horn and harp at Munich, but neither his playing nor compositions were appreciated. In December 1804 he was appointed director of wind music at Gotha, becoming Chamber Musician in 1806. Spohr came to Gotha as general music director in 1805 and, not long after, became affianced to Dorette Scheidler, one of Backofen's harp pupils. On 16th December of that year Dorette played Backofen's Harp Concerto at the Leipzig Gewandhaus. Backofen was instrumental in obtaining a fine Naderman harp for her first concert tour, undertaken with Spohr the following year, shortly after their marriage. At the end of November 1808 Backofen played basset-horn at Frankfurt, but there was only a small audience to hear him. In 1811 he moved to Darmstadt as court musician on basset-horn and harp, and by 1820 had been made a chamber musician. Backofen founded an instrument factory at Darmstadt in 1815, making flutes, oboes, clarinets and basset-horns. Clarinets by him were used by Niebergall, Georg Reinhardt, Reitz and Th. Schmidt. There is a 12-keyed clarinet, made by Backofen c.1825, in the Rendall Collection, Edinburgh, which is similar in construction to those made by Carl Bischoff, another Darmstadt maker. Backofen continued to direct his manufacturing business until 1837 and it was then carried on by a son. This son, also called Heinrich, was a talented painter like his father and court harpist at Darmstadt from 1828. He went with a group of other young Darmstadt men to Texas in 1847, taking instruments with him. This attempt at colonisation did not succeed and Backofen returned to Darmstadt in 1850 to carry on the family business. Backofen senior wrote numerous articles for music periodicals, including a report on music in Spain, which he made after his early visit there. The archives of Breitkopf & Härtel contain many letters from him.

Works: Concerto op.3 in B flat (Breitkopf & Härtel. Simrock). Concerto op.16 in E flat, dedicated to Alexander I of Russia (Breitkopf & Härtel 1808 – RTTH, VGM). Concerto op.24 in E flat (Breitkopf & Härtel 1824 – DoFB VGM). Concertante op.10 in A for 2 clarinets, dedicated to Alexander I of Russia (1804. Breitkopf & Härtel 1810? – LBL, VGM, VNB). 3 Duos op.13 (1804. Breitkopf & Härtel. Haslinger). 3 Duos from the Method (Cappi). Quintet op.15 in B flat for clarinet, violin, 2 violas & cello (1803. Breitkopf & Härtel 1805? – BoLM, LBL). Concerto (Fétis says he wrote 3) for basset-horn (Ms. – DHLH). Variations for basset-horn (Peters). Concertante op.7 for basset-horn, harp & cello, dedicated to the Hereditary Princess of Saxe-Gotha (Brietkopf & Härtel c.1800 – BrBC, LBL). Quintet op.9 for basset-horn & strings (Breitkopf & Härtel 1803). Numerous works for wind band. Anweisung zur Klarinette nebst einer kurzen Abhandlung über das Basset-Horn (First edition for 5-keyed clarinet, Breitkopf & Härtel c.1802 – LBL. Second edition for 13-keyed clarinet and 15-keyed basset-horn, 1824 – BrBc, LBL). Neue theoretisch-pracktische Klarinettschule nebst einer kurzen Abhandlung über das Basset-Horn (An entirely different method, Cappi c.1812 – VGM, VNB. Cappi and Witzendorf both published the Kurze Abhandlung as a separate item).

Bibliography:

KIEFHABER, Johann C.S. – *Nachrichten zür altern und neuern Geschichte der Stadt Nürnberg.* 1804.

ZINGEL, Hans J. – "Heinrich Backofen." MGG Supplement 1971.

BÄHR, (Franz) Josef. 19 Feb 1770-1819 Aug 7. Austrian. See OV. The dates of his employment with the Prince of Öttingen-Wallerstein were from 1787 to 1794. The Prince sent him to study the clarinet with the great teacher Meissner at Würzburg.

Bibliography:

RAU, Ulrich – "Johann Joseph Beer." MGG Supplement 1971.

SCHIEDERMAIR, Ludwig – "Die Blutezeit der Öttingen-Wallerstein'schen Hofkapelle." (*Sammelbände der Internationalen Musikgesellschaft*) Leipzig 1907/8.

WESTON, Pamela – "Beethoven's Clarinettists." MT, December 1970.

(B–H). **BÄNDER (BENDER) (Johann) Conrad.** c.1787-1859, Feb 12, Kassel. German. He was the younger brother of the bassoonist Johann Heinrich Bänder (born 1785 at Röhrenfort) and elder brother of Ludwig Bänder (q.v.). Conrad and Ludwig were magnificent clarinettists and won glowing reports during their tours of 1816 to 1822. They were frequently heard in the same halls as Baermann and by many considered the latter's equal. At the age of fourteen Conrad was a fife-player in a Grenadier Guard regiment belonging to the Prince of Hesse-Philippsthal-Bergfeld. The Prince recognised his talent and had him taught various stringed and wind instruments. From here he progressed to employment in the King of Westphalia's Life Guards and saw service in Russia. The King had him taught the clarinet by Iwan Müller. Conrad then returned to Germany and obtained his discharge from the army. The earliest concert report of the brothers comes from Lübeck in 1805, when they both performed on the basset-horn.

By 1816 Conrad, Ludwig and Ludwig's wife Charlotte, who was a singer, were living in St Petersburg with appointments at the Imperial Court. In the autumn of that year they set out on their travels together. The next report comes from Leipzig, where Conrad is hailed as another Baermann. On 31st October they gave a concert in Berlin, when Conrad played a concerto by Crusell and earned praise for the sweetness of his tone and "rare pianissimo in the Adagio." The brothers performed a double concerto by Mess, who was a violinist in the court orchestra at St Petersburg. Charlotte sang an aria with chorus and obligato clarinet by Catterino Cavos. They stayed on in Berlin, for Charlotte was engaged to sing Julia in performances of Spontini's *La Vestale* during November.

Early in 1817 the party moved to Frankfurt and on 10th January gave a concert similar to that of Berlin. Conrad was again given exceptional applause. They stayed a considerable time in Frankfurt, where Charlotte had an engagement at the theatre. In 1818 the brothers performed at Aachen on 11th and 16th January, also on 27th October and 7th November. After this the trio moved to Paris and when the brothers were heard at the French Court the critics took delight in announcing that they had beaten Baermann in receiving this honour. Early in 1819 the brothers gave a subscription concert with the Bohrer brothers, who played the violin and cello. Few subscriptions were received and the audience included only a duke and a handful of ambassadors. In order to attract a better audience for a second joint concert to be held at the Théâtre Favart on 1st April, much publicity was resorted to. This succeeded and the concert was very well attended. Paris was fully appreciative and reported that the Bänders were "wonderfully talented." They expressed sadness that lack of pecuniary reward in the French capital had forced them to move on. Conrad performed a concerto by Iwan Müller on 14th May at the Frankfurt Museum Concerts. Berne was the next to hear the trio and by December they were at Strasbourg, where they gave a concert on 6th. Charlotte surpassed herself, and the brothers were received with "ecstatic applause" when they played a double concerto by Ludwig, an Adagio and Polonaise by Krommer, and a Fantasie "with echo" on Swiss & Tyrolean Songs (probably also by Ludwig). Echotone, or the art of *mezzo voce*, was a feature of their playing. Strasbourg was truly delighted and considered them better than either Baermann or Müller, both of whom had played in the town recently.

In April 1820 the Bänders played at Berne again and the next report is from Munich, where they gave a concert on 21st May. They then visited Stuttgart and by the autumn were in Zurich, where they gave two concerts in the large concert hall, which was filled to overflowing. The Swiss wished they could have given three concerts, one each and one together, for they found their playing "magnificent." The Bänders moved on to Vienna, where they performed to the Music Society and gave concerts on 3rd and 6th December in the Small Ridotto-Room. The brothers were called "a true phenomenon" and Charlotte "a northern Catalani." Billed still as from the Russian Court, the clarinettists played "two concertinos by Danzi, a Rondo by Mees (sic), Alpen Song with Echo, and a Potpourri of Russian National tunes."

The Bänders now retraced their steps to Russia, taking their journey in easy stages. During 1821 they were at Königsberg and gave a private concert in the hall of the Kronen Lodge. They also gave two public concerts which were sold out. Charlotte did not sing, it was the brothers alone who displayed their talents on a brilliantly lit stage, the audience being seated in the dark. They each performed a solo concerto, and then "double concertos by Danzi and others." The most popular item was Variations on Tyrolean and Swiss Songs for 2 unaccompanied clarinets by Ludwig. The applause was deafening, their playing marvelled at and these two concerts declared the best of the year. In 1822 when they played at Mitau their reception was no less good; they were called "perfectionists" and "heroes on their instrument." From Mitau they went to Riga where they were pronounced to be, with Baermann, the three finest living virtuosi. By the winter the three Bänders were back in St Petersburg and employed once more at the Russian Court.

Ludwig and his wife probably remained in Russia, but early in 1823 Conrad and his elder brother Johann Heinrich returned to Germany and both secured appointments in the court orchestra at Kassel. (A report that Conrad had an engagement in this orchestra in 1816 would seem to be unfounded). Conrad performed twice as a soloist during 1823, first for the Euterpe Society, when with Egling he gave them a double concerto by Krommer. For his second concert he tactfully played a concerto by Spohr, who had recently been made music director at Kassel. It must therefore have been a shock to him when later in the year de Groot arrived on the scene to take over the position of first clarinet. The inhabitants were enraged and complained in print about the insult to Bänder. Spohr either did not appreciate Bänder's talents or it is possible that a contract with de Groot, who had been under him earlier at Frankfurt, had been drawn up before Bänder's arrival. Whatever the reason and in spite of ill feeling, Bänder was forced to step down to second clarinet. When de Groot moved away in 1827 Bänder once more became first clarinet. In 1829 Bänder performed a concerto by Iwan Müller, his former teacher, who had stayed in Kassel for several months in 1823. On 14th January 1830 he introduced a light-hearted arrangement of a folk song for bass and contra-bass clarinets to a Subscription Concert: he played the contra-bass and Deichert the bass clarinet. On 18th March of the same year he took part in Lindpaintner's Concertante for wind. In 1835 he played two works by Iwan Müller: a solo concertino and, with his son F. Bänder, a double concerto. In 1841 Conrad Bänder, like Blaes, had the thrill of playing with Liszt; in a performance at the court theatre on 22nd November two of Spohr's Six German Songs op.103 were sung by Johann Derska, a tenor at the Kassel Court, accompanied by Bänder and the great Liszt. In 1845 Conrad played an Introduction and Rondo by his son Heinrich Bänder, and was heard for the last time as a soloist in February 1846.

Conrad had three sons who all did well musically. The eldest, August, was a cellist who learnt from Bernhard Romberg and made his debut at Königsberg in 1832. The second was the clarinettist F. Bänder (q.v.). The third, Heinrich (1816-1838), was a violinist and composer of great promise who died young. He learnt the violin from Spohr and made his debut at Kassel in 1832.

BÄNDER (BENDER), F. German. He was the second son of Conrad Bänder. His first public appearance was with his father in June 1836 at Kassel, when they played Iwan Müller's double concerto and earned much applause. In 1837 Bänder went to St Petersburg, where his uncle Johann was then first bassoon in the theatre orchestra. His tone was said to be beautiful, but thinner than they remembered his father's to have been. Early in 1839 he was back at Kassel as a member of the court orchestra and played in the Beethoven Septet on 19th May and a Potpourri for 2 clarinets by Späth with Griesel in June. He performed the obligato to Mozart's "Parto!" for Betty Pistor on 15th November 1839 and for Mlle Stegemüller in 1841. By 1850 he had become first clarinet in the orchestra.

(B–H). **BÄNDER (BENDER), Ludwig.** German. He was the younger brother of Conrad Bänder and like him was probably a pupil of Iwan Müller. He married a singer named Charlotte Rambach, whose father was a double bass player at Berlin. She was a singer at the Russian Imperial Court in 1816. Ludwig travelled considerably with his brother (q.v.) from 1816 to 1822, when his compositions were often performed. He probably remained at St Petersburg from 1822, as there are no further reports of him after this date.

Works: Concerto for 2 clarinets. Variations on Tyrolean

& Swiss Songs for 2 unaccompanied clarinets. 3 Duos op.3 (Simrock). 3 Duos op.12 (Schott c.1827 – MasSL). 3 Duos concertants op.14 for clarinet & bassoon (Schott 1830 – LRAM).

(B–H). **BAERMANN, Carl.** Munich, 24 Oct 1810-1885 May 24, Munich. German. See OV. He was the official basset-horn player from 1839 and bass clarinettist from 1840 for the Munich court orchestra. With his father he played at Lübeck in 1828 and then went with him to Sweden and Denmark. On 13th February 1836 Carl played on his own at Hamburg and early in April 1837 gave a big concert at Munich at which he performed some of his own compositions, including his 'newest' concerto.

During the Parisian tour which he and his father undertook in 1838/9, Carl kept a diary. In it we learn that Meyerbeer arranged lodgings for them both near to his own house and invited them to partake of all meals with him. But for this generosity their tour would have meant a financial loss, for in spite of their concerts being well advertised and their extraordinary talent acknowledged, their concerts received little support. The Baermanns arrived in Paris on 14th December and until their first concert made music frequently at Meyerbeer's house. On 1st January they went with Meyerbeer's wife to the Opéra for a performance of *Les Huguenots* and Carl was particularly struck with the new gas lighting, which he says gave such a good effect of daylight on the stage. Writing to his wife Barbara on 4th January, Carl extols Meyerbeer and says he is not the pretentious person many people think him to be. He mentions that Meyerbeer is going to write a piece for him and his father, to include a voice part. (There is no record that Meyerbeer carried out his promise). On 10th, Meyerbeer gave a large dinner to which many celebrities came. When the meal ended at 10.30 pm. the Baermann's were asked to play Carl's "E flat Duo." The result of this was an invitation by Habeneck to perform for the Société des Concerts on 13th, with Sontag. On 21st January the Baermanns gave a recital at the Opéra, and on 17th February a public concert at the Conservatoire. On 22nd February, they ate at Meyerbeer's with Rosenhain and Adolph Schimon (probably the "M. Simon" who accompanied them for their Conservatoire concert on 13th January). Afterwards, Carl played a concerto of his own composition which he dedicated to Meyerbeer. Meyerbeer was extremely pleased with it and said he liked it better than the concertos by Weber.

Carl kept a diary again when he travelled on his own in 1843. This tour took him to Leipzig, Weimar, Dresden and Berlin. He arrived at Berlin on 16th March and Meyerbeer gave a dinner for him on 21st, to which many important people were invited. Meyerbeer took 12 tickets at a ducat each for Carl's first concert in April. Carl performed his own Variations on an Original Theme (op.8?), also Ein Abend auf dem Berg, and was well received. He gave a second concert with the mezzo-soprano, Mlle Brexendorff.

Like his father, Carl was a big handsome man and Kotte's little son thought him the biggest man in the world. Kotte was on friendly terms with both Baermanns, especially Carl. He must have known of the disillusionment felt by Carl through having such a famous father and when in September 1844 he heard via the Berlin clarinettist Tamm that F.W. Tausch had been unable to play at Court for three months because of a broken collar bone, he wrote urging Carl to apply for the post. There had been negotiations between Carl and the Berlin officials at an earlier date, for when AMZ reported Carl's concert of April 1843, they said he had come to receive a post at the Court. Tausch was consumptive and it is likely that the court officials were already trying to find a suitable substitute for him. Carl, however, did not accept the Berlin post. Berlioz reports seeing him amongst the clarinettists (Blaes was also in the lists) for the Beethoven Memorial celebrations at Bonn in August 1845. Carl was a member of the Munich Subscription Concerts from 1828 to 1880 and gave his own concerts under their auspices on 12th April 1845, 22nd April 1850 and 17th April 1858. The only report we have of his playing with his own son Carl, who became a famous pianist, is at Hamburg on 7th May 1857.

Works: Concerto militaire op.6 in E flat (Schott 1875/6 – LBL). Concerto in C minor (1839? This may be the one dedicated to Meyerbeer). Concerto op.10 in B flat minor. Conzertstück op.44 in D minor (André 1880 – BoLM, LBL. Hofmeister). Conzertstück op.49 in E flat (André – BoLM). Duo concertant op.33 in A flat for 2 clarinets (Ms. – MBS. André. Schott). Divertimento, ein Traum op.47 (André). Divertissement op.2 (Joubert. Schott). Ein Abend auf dem Berg op.25 (Schott – BaU). Fantaisie brillante op.7 (Joubert. Schott. Troupenas – PBN). Fantaisie op.15 (Schott). Fantaisie brillante, Sternenhelle Nacht op.17 (Schott – BaU. Troupenas – PBN). Fantaisie, Souvenirs de Bellini op.52 (Schott). Fantaisiestücke und Lieder ops.84 to 87 (André 1875 – BaU, LBL). First Travesty, Introduction & Polonaise op.41 (with instructions for comedy-style playing) (André 1880 – LBL). Funfzehn Schubert Lieder op.88 (André – LRAM). Gnomenklänge op.38 (André c.1867 – LRAM). Impromptu, Erinnerung am meine Kinderjähre op.34 (André). Introduction & Rondo op.36, dedicated to Heinrich Möseler (André 1873/4 – LBL). Melodische Schwärmereien op.53 (Schott c.1853 – LRAM). Phantasiegebilde. Scène brillante, Die kleine Bettlerin op.14

(Joubert. Schott – BaU. Troupenas – LRAM, PBN). Second Travesty, Grand Fantaisie op.45 (André 1880 – LBL). Seliger Schmerz op.37 (André). Variations brillantes op.8 (Schott 1839 – LRAM). Verlorenes Glück op.30 (Schott – BaU). Duo concertant op.4 (Joubert. Schott – BaU, LRAM. Troupenas – PBN). Quartet op.18 (Schott). Vollständige Clarinett-Schule ops.63 & 64, dedicated to Duke Ernst of Saxe-Gotha (André 1864 to 1875 – LBL).

Writing:

"Erinnerungen eines alten Musikanten." (*Münchener Neueste Nachrichten*). Nov 1882.

Bibliography:

BECKER, Heinz – "Carl Baermann." MGG Supplement 1971.
BECKER, Heinz – *Giacomo Meyerbeer: Briefwechsel und Tagebücher.* Bk. 2, Berlin 1970; Bk. 3, Berlin 1975.

BAERMANN, Heinrich (Joseph). Potsdam, 14 Feb 1784-1847 June 11, Munich. German. See OV. Although he allowed his son Carl to take over first clarinet in 1834 he remained in the court orchestra at Munich until his death. He played for the Munich Subscription Concerts from 1811 to 1843. It has now been discovered that the Introduction, Theme & Variations said to have been written for Baermann in 1815 by Weber is by Joseph Küffner. Georg Weixelbaum, a tenor at the Munich Court, wrote a Grand Septet with an obligato part for Baermann. It was well received when performed by Baermann, some time prior to 1816. There is a copy of Meyerbeer's *Gli Amori di Teolinda* which indicates that it was performed at the Munich court theatre, presumably by Baermann and Harlas, in October 1817. This pre-dates the only other confirmed public performance, at the Munich Court on 9th November 1817. During his stay in England Baermann performed a Concertino by Riotte for the New Musical Fund on 29th April 1819. Baermann was closely associated with Lindpaintner during the time that the latter was music director of the Isarthor Theater, from 1812 to 1819. Lindpaintner dedicated his Concerto in E flat to Baermann, and he undertook to write the orchestral accompaniment to Baermann's own Concertino op.29. Lindpaintner's *Der Vampyr* has a big clarinet part in the aria for Count Port d'Amour in Act I. After a performance of the work at Munich on 19th October 1828 the *Münchener Theater-Zeitung* said it "allowed our unsurpassed master Baermann to shine in full glory." Carl Blum dedicated his Air Polonais varié op.126 to Baermann. Touring gave Heinrich Baermann very little time for teaching, but enthusiastic young players did manage to catch him between whiles; amongst these were Joseph Albanus Link, Adam Schott (some time before 1816), Joseph Faubel (1818) and Friedrich Hummel (1820).

Works: Concerto op.28 in D minor (Richault – PBN. Breitkopf & Härtel 1824 – VGM, VNB, ZAM). Concertino op.32 in E flat (c.1820. Breitkopf & Härtel – VGM, VNB). Concertino op.24 in F (Breitkopf & Härtel 1822. Costallat. Richault – PBN). Concertino op.27 in E flat (Richault – PBN. Breitkopf & Härtel 1824). Concertino op.29 in C minor (1818 – Ms. in MBS. Lindpaintner scored this for Baermann. The opus no. being the same as the Andante & Variations in F suggests this Concertino was never published). Sonata op.31 in F minor (Breitkopf & Härtel – PBN, VGM). Sonata op.33 in F (c.1827. Breitkopf & Härtel – VGM). Exercises amusants op.30 for solo clarinet, dedicated to Mr George Key (Breitkopf & Härtel 1826. Wessel – LRAM). Andante avec variations et polonaise op.20 (Gambaro. Hofmeister c.1819 – LRAM). Andante & Variations op.29 in F (See Concertino in C minor. Ricordi – VGM. Breitkopf & Härtel). Andante & Variations op.37 in A flat (Falter 1842. Hofmeister). Divertissement op.34 in A flat (Breitkopf & Härtel 1829). Divertissement op.35 in C (Breitkopf & Härtel 1829 – BaU, VGM). Divertissement op.38 in E flat (1843. Hofmeister. Stift. Allg. Musikhandlung – DoFB). Drei Var. Lieder op.12 (Gambaro. Simrock – VGM. Breitkopf & Härtel). Exercises op.36 for clarinet with ad lib piano (Breitkopf & Härtel 1838 – BoLM). Fantasia op.26 (Breitkopf & Härtel 1824 – ZAM). Introduction & Polonaise op.25 (Richault – PBN. Breitkopf & Härtel 1822. Schott). Nocturne op.21 (Hofmeister). Quartet op.18 in B flat (Gambaro. Breitkopf & Härtel 1818/19 – clarinet part only in LRAM. Schott c.1820 – LRAM). Quintet op.19 in E flat for clarinet, zither & 3 strings, with 2 horns, 2 bassoons & bass ad lib (Breitkopf & Härtel. Hofmeister). Quintet op.22 in F minor (Breitkopf & Härtel. Costallat). Quintet op.23 in E flat for clarinet & strings, with 2 horns ad lib (Breitkopf & Härtel 1821 – FSU. Costallat c.1821).

Writing:

"Anerbieten." AMZ, Intelligenz-Blatt. May 1832.

Bibliography:

BECKER, Heinz – "Heinrich Baermann." MGG Supplement 1971.

BECKER, Heinz – *Giacomo Meyerbeer: Briefwechsel und Tagebücher.* Bk.2, Berlin 1970; Bk.3, Berlin 1975.

KROLL, Oskar – "H.J. Baermann." MZ, VII, 1934.

KROLL, Oskar – "Weber und Baermann." ZM. 103, 1936.

BÄTTENHAUSEN. German. He was a member of the

court orchestra at Kassel. In 1839 he played Iwan Müller's double concerto with Curth and in 1841 took part in Schindelmeisser's Symphonie Concertante for 4 clarinets with Curth, Kollmann and Wenderoth.

BAGEARD, Alphonse. 1873-? Belgian. He was a pupil of Poncelet's at the Brussels Conservatoire, where he himself was a professor from 1904 to 1911.

BAISSIÈRE, François. French. He was a clarinettist and general music teacher at Rheims, where in 1822 he resided at no. 60 "sous les loges de la Couture." He is probably related to Charles X's trumpet-major, Baissières-Faber, who wrote a clarinet method which he dedicated to Monsieur Germain of Rheims (Schonenberger c.1830).

Works: Sonatas op.3, 2 bks.. Air varié. 36 Caprices. Variations on "Ma Zétulbe" for clarinet & strings. Variations on "Rien tendre amour" for clarinet & strings. Variations on "Sexe charmante" for clarinet & strings. (These were all published by Janet between 1810 and 1825).

BANGER, Adam. German. He first played in a military band and then from 1819 was a court musician at Darmstadt. He also played the cello.

BARBANDT, Carl. Hanover, 30 Apr 1716-c.1776, London? German. See OV. He was probably the son of Barthold Barbandt, who was a Chamber Musician at the Hanover Court from 1705 until he died in 1764. Carl joined the Hanover orchestra in 1735, probably as an oboist doubling on clarinet. In 1752 he travelled to London and on 14th January had a Benefit in Hickford's Great Room at which he performed oboe and organ concertos of his own composition. He remained in London, calling himself "the music king of Hanover," and was not surprisingly dismissed from his German post. From 1753 to 1763 he organised subscription concerts at the Little Theatre in the Haymarket. At one of these, on 25th March 1756, his oratorio *Paradise Regained* was given and "A Great Concerto with Clarinets, French Horns and Kettle Drums," also by him, was performed in one of the intervals. Pohl says he performed on the clarinet in 1756 and that his playing was very expressive. Barbandt was employed as court organist to Count Haslang, the Bavarian Ambassador, and later to the Portuguese Ambassador. His pupil Samuel Webbe succeeded him in the latter post in 1776.

BARBAY. French. He was a member of the Swiss Guards band. At the Concert Spirituel he performed a concerto of unknown authorship on 11th April 1786 and a concerto by Yost on 27th May 1787.

BARBIER. In 1779 he played for the Comédie theatre at Port-au-Prince.

BARGHEER. He also played the violin. He was a clarinettist at the Schaumberg-Lippe Court from 1828 until 1855. He used Müller clarinets and was a devoted friend to Müller during the latter's last embittered years at Bückeburg. After Müller's death Bargheer tended his grave with loving care. His son Carl, born at Bückeburg on 31st December 1831, became a famous violinist and Kapellmeister.

BARNARD. He also played the violin. On 8th December 1779 he performed a clarinet concerto at Mme Marchetti's Benefit in Edinburgh.

BARTH, Joseph (Johann August). Grosslippen, 29 Dec 1781-? Czech. He played and taught clarinet, flute, trumpet and violin. For three years he was clarinettist to the theatre orchestra in Linz. He then returned to Bohemia and formed an instrumental group with which he toured the country. In later years he became well-known as a tenor singer, with an appointment first at the Bohemian Court and later at Vienna. (see Sedlak).

(B–H). **BARTH, Wilhelm (Leberecht).** Grimma, 10 May 1774-1849 Aug 22, Leipzig. German. He was a distinguished clarinettist in the Leipzig Gewandhaus Orchestra from 1802 to 1829. He was also a remarkably fine teacher and numbered amongst his pupils Ferdinand Heinze, F. Tretbar and Wieprecht. Before he came to Leipzig Barth was employed by the Prince of Dessau. During this time it was reported that because of poor quality compositions he did not get the applause he deserved. When he came to Leipzig he put this to rights and only played works of good quality. He was one of the first to play the Mozart Concerto. In his early Leipzig years Barth made a speciality of the concertos by Krommer; in later years he turned more to Crusell's compositions, which he obtained as soon as they were off the press at Peters' shop in the town. In 1814 Barth became the official town musician of Leipzig in place of Gottlob Maurer, who had recently died. In this position he had from 20 to 26 apprentices under his care. This necessitated having a large house and here he held musical evenings at which many local and visiting artists performed. In 1829 Barth resigned his post of first clarinet in the Gewandhaus Orchestra to his pupil Ferdinand Heinze and until 1835, when he retired, took a back seat in the second violins. Although he is said to have composed, no works have come to light. His eldest son, Wilhelm, became a flautist and composer at Leipzig.

Barth's solo performances at Leipzig were as follows: 1804 – 7th October, a "new concerto" (op.52?) by Krommer. 23rd December, Krommer's Concerto op.35 with Maurer. 1805 – 24th October, "two agreeable concertos" (probably op 36 and op.52) by Krommer. 1806 – "a difficult and interesting" concerto in E flat major (op.52) by Krommer, in which he substituted an Adagio in C minor "by another master" for the "inconsiderable" Andante. 29th September, Krommer's E flat concerto. 1807 – 1st January, Mozart's "Parto!" and Winter's Concerto. 8th January, Krommer's double concerto op.35 with Claus. 1808 – a solo concerto by Krommer. 1809 – 5th January, a double concerto by Tausch with Claus. 1810 – 6th December, a "new concerto" by Friedrich Schneider; AMZ's critic remarked that the influence of Hermstedt, who had recently been heard in Leipzig, was clearly detected. 1812 – 19th November, a "new concerto" (op.5?) by Crusell. 1815 – 9th February, Krommer's "newest" double concerto (op.91 in E flat) with his pupil Ferdinand Heinze. 9th November, Mozart's Concerto. 1816 – May, Crusell's Symphonie Concertante. 1817 – concerto by Friedrich Schneider. 1818 – 11th October, concerto by Crusell, obligato to Poissl's "Se in liberta pot" for Mme Neumann-Sesse. 1821 – 22nd October, a concerto by Crusell. He played clarinet solos on numerous other occasions and basset-horn solos on 10th January 1811 and 20th February 1812.

BARTOLOMEY, Franz. Smichow (Prague), 1 Mar 1865-1920 Nov 20, Vienna. Czech. He first learnt the violin and at the age of ten took up the clarinet, which his father Mathias Bartolomey taught him. His first concert tour was undertaken with the pianist Grünfeld and viola player Ruzicka. This brought him to Vienna and here in 1890 he was appointed first clarinet to the court opera. Shortly afterwards he became a member of the court orchestra itself, just in time to play at the Imperial Court balls during the last remaining years of the illustrious Johann Strauss. He also played with the Vienna Philharmonic Orchestra from 1892 onwards. From 1898 until his death he taught at the Conservatoire, his most illustrious pupil being Leopold Wlach. The Golden Employment Cross (second class) and Silver Jubilee Medal were given him for his court service.

Work: Method.

BARTON. Irish. He was the brother of the violinist James Barton and played in the Hawkins Street Theatre orchestra, Dublin. He also composed, conducted and taught singing. About 1824 he was living in Baggot Street.

BASSI, Luigi. 1833-1871. Italian. Hans von Bülow called him a "valentissimo artista." He was first clarinet at the Scala Theatre, Milan and is best known as the composer of the popular "Rigoletto Fantasia." Quite early in his career Bassi made an edition of Lefèvre's tutor, which Ricordi published.

Works: Fantasia on Verdi's *Rigoletto* (Ricordi). Nocturne (Ricordi – LRAM). Many other Fantasias.

BAUER, Adolf. He was employed first by the Prince of Hohenlohe-Öhringen and then at Berne. On 29th April 1840 he played compositions by Emil Vogt, Iwan Müller and others on a 13-keyed clarinet at Strasbourg; they liked his tone and said he had extraordinary dexterity. He had recently been employed at Amorbach and had an appointment at Paris in view.

(B–H). **BAUER, E.** German. He performed as a soloist at the Leipzig Gewandhaus on 27th January 1876. In 1881 he became a member of the Gewandhaus Orchestra.

(B–H). **BAUERSACHS, Carl (Friedrich).** Schnabelweid (near Pegnitz), 4 July 1767-1845 Dec 14, Sömmerda. German. He also played the cello. He was employed at one of the smaller courts on the Rhine until 1790 when the appointment ceased as the result of war. He then visited England where, according to Mendel, he bought a new sickel-shaped basset-horn and was commissioned to introduce this to Germany. In 1796 he went to Vienna, Hungary and Venice. In 1798 he travelled through Germany looking for a post but failed to find one and took to the study of mining in the Harz mountains. By 1802 he had settled at Clausthal where he became well-known in the world of mineralogy. He composed much for the basset-horn but none of it was published.

BAUM, Joan. He was second clarinet in the Elector of Bonn's orchestra in 1783.

BAUMGÄRTNER, Joseph. German. He played clarinet in the theatre orchestra at Frankfurt and also taught the instrument. His performance of Mozart's Quintet in 1805 is one of the earliest recorded, apart from those of Anton Stadler. His solo performances at Frankfurt were as follows: 1805 – 1st March, Mozart's Quintet and a double concerto by Tausch with J.G.G. Hoffmann. 1811 – 20th March, Variations by Westerhoff. 1813 – 29th March, Mozart's Symphonie Concertante. 1814 – 1st April, a double concerto by Tausch with Schecker, who was billed as a "young unknown" and was possibly one of Baumgärtner's pupils. 1815 – 25th March, concerto by Bösinger. 1816 – 3rd April, concerto by Kleisner. 1817 – 17th March, Winter's Concerto.

BAZIN (BASIN, BASSIN). French. From 1821 to 1825 he was first clarinet at the Théâtre de la Gaité in Paris. From 1827 to 1829 he held the same office at the Théâtre de S.A.R. Madame. His various addresses were as follows: no. 23 rue de Lancry in 1824, 80 rue du Temple in 1825, 24 rue de Bondi in 1827.

BEATE, Hermann. Bernburg, 27 Apr 1825-1899 Aug 1, Hanover. German. He was a member of a Guards band until 1850, when he was appointed first clarinet in the court orchestra at Hanover. In 1856 he was made a Royal Court and Chamber Musician, and retired from playing in 1884.

BECHT, Carel Julius. The Hague, 2 Mar 1826-1902 Mar 28, the Hague. Dutch. He was a pupil of Philipp Faubel, with whom he played at the age of twelve in the court orchestra at the Hague. He had extraordinary talent and Letzer reports that his playing of the famous solo in Adam's *Le Postillon de Longjumeau* and of an arrangement of one of Spohr's violin concertos sent his audience into ecstasies. He played for more than 50 years for the French Theatre and for the Diligentia Concerts. In 1852 he was appointed clarinet teacher at the Royal Music School in succession to Faubel. He was also conductor of the National Guard, and a member of the Toonkunst Society.

BECKAU, Joseph. c.1742-1792 Nov 18, Ehrenbreitstein. German. From 1783 until his death he played in the court orchestra for the Elector of Trevès at Ehrenbreitstein castle, Coblenz.

BECKER, Anton Joseph. German. He is first heard of in Turkish music circles and then from 1788 to 1802 or later he was a member of the court orchestra at Mainz.

BECKER, Karl Friedrich Wilhelm. Berlin, 4 Nov 1811-? German. He learnt the clarinet from Nehrlich and in 1837 became an assistant in the Berlin court orchestra. In 1858 he was made a Royal Chamber Musician and was still playing in the orchestra in 1886. He performed Iwan Müller's double concerto with Nehrlich at a concert given by Jenny Lind in 1845.

BEER, (Johann) Joseph. Grunewald, 18 May 1744-1812 Oct 28, Berlin. Czech. See OV. The year of his death has now been established as 1812 and not 1811. After his concerts at Warsaw in April 1781 he evidently went back to Paris, for his name appears as chamber musician to the Prince of Lambesc again for 1781 and 1782. It was not until May 1782 that he definitely took up residence in St Petersburg. During his original Parisian stay in 1773, Bernhard Schott, the founder of the publishing firm, came to him for lessons. In Beer's performances for the Concert Spirituel the instrument's potential was realised for the first time; his 26 concerts for the society between December 1771 and November 1779 made a great impression. Detailed information on the works he played is lacking, except for his concert of 2nd February 1772 when he chose Karl Stamitz's Concerto no.1. Apart from this, 2 performances of unspecified concertos by Stamitz are recorded, 7 of concertos by himself (4 billed as "new") and the rest have no details at all.

Works: Concerto no.1 in E flat (Breitkopf & Härtel 1785). Concerto no.2 in B flat (Breitkopf & Härtel 1787). Concerto (Berlin, 1794). Concerto op.1 in B flat (Kühnel 1807. Peters – LBL). Concerto in E flat, with Karl Stamitz (Berlin 1793). 3 Concertos for 2 clarinets (mentioned in the 1st edition of Grove's *Dictionary of Music & Musicians,* but not located). Adagio & Air with Variations (1782). Fantasia. Royal French Hunting Song. 6 Duos concertants (Naderman 1802). Sonata for clarinet & bassoon (Mad. le Marchand 1775). Quintet for clarinet, horn & 3 violas d'amour.

Bibliography:

(*Berlinische musikalische Zeitung*). 1793, ps.156 & 193.
RAU, Ulrich – "Johann Joseph Beer." MGG Supplement, 1971.
WESTON, Pamela – "Beethoven's Clarinettists." MT, December 1970.

(B–H). **BEERHALTER, Aloysius.** Merckingen, 1800-1852 Mar 21, Stuttgart. German. He was very much a musical factotum until in his 20s he heard one of the Reinhardts play the basset-horn at Stuttgart and decided to make this his main instrument. His father, a humble village musician, sent Beerhalter at the age of twelve to nearby Neresheim to be an apprentice to the town musician, Sauerbrey. At fifteen he was moved to Tübingen to be under Hetsch, the town musician there. At seventeen he became a trumpeter in the Stuttgart mounted guard and at nineteen was engaged as flautist in the Court of Thurn and Taxis at Regensburg. At twenty one he was engaged as a cellist for the court orchestra in Stuttgart and at the same time as a trombonist in the Royal Würtemberg 3rd infantry regiment. After this amazing display of general musical proficiency he turned to the basset-horn, which he taught himself. He made such a success of this that he was called a "second Paganini." In 1828 he became first clarinet and basset-horn player for the Stuttgart orchestra.

His principal concerts at Stuttgart were as follows: 1828 – Mozart's "Parto!" for Catherine Canzi. 1829 – concerto by Molique, Stuttgart's concert master. 1830, 1831 and 1832 – Theme & Variations on "Im Kühlen Keller sitz'ich hier" for basset-horn, composed by himself. This was always popular and generally encored. 1832 – December, "Der Kritikaster und der Trinker" for basset-horn, almost certainly of his own composition.

Beerhalter toured in later years and was at Augsburg for some time in 1836. On 9th May 1842 he performed at the Theatre in Frankfurt and in 1843 had a successful season in London. In 1844 he performed the basset-horn obligato to Proch's "Schweizer Heimweh" for Emma Basse at a public concert in Strasbourg. This had to be repeated and the critics raved about his playing on both clarinet and basset-horn.

Works: Fantasie op.1 (Hallberger. Deutsche Verlags-Anstalt). Divertissement op.2 for basset-horn (Hallberger. Deutsche Verlags-Anstalt). "Der Kritikaster und der Trinker" for basset-horn. Theme & Variations on "Im Kühlen Keller sitz'ich hier" for basset-horn.

BEHRENS, Franz. He played in the Vienna Philharmonic Orchestra from 1903 until 1910 or later.

BELETTI. In 1860 he was first clarinet at the Théâtre Italien in Paris.

BELKE, M.F. German. He was a Chamber Musician in the Berlin court orchestra early in the nineteenth century.

BELLISON, Simeon. Moscow, 4 Dec 1883-1953 May 4, New York. Russian, becoming naturalised American. He had enormous energy and strength of purpose and the sheer mass of his activities – he boasted of more than 10,000 concerts – is amazing. During his later years in America he had a tremendous following and for the annual recital he gave in New York clarinettists would travel hundreds of miles to hear him. He used Oehler system clarinets, choosing a very hard reed, which he tied on, and produced a vibrato by finger movement over the holes. He gave the first performance of the Khachaturian Trio and provided Prokofiev with the themes for his Overture on Hebrew Themes op.34. His dignified and benign personality made him an impressive teacher and he was described by a pupil as "an artist and a gentleman." He edited the Klosé and Baermann tutors and made a large number of transcriptions. He was also an authority on Hebrew music and possessed a valuable and extensive collection of ancient songs and instrumental compositions.

Shortly after Bellison's birth his father, who was a military bandmaster in Moscow, was sent to the garrison town of Smolensk and took his family with him. Simeon learnt to play the clarinet from his father and before he was ten was performing in the bands which his father conducted. In 1894 it happened that Wassily Safonoff, then director of the Moscow Conservatoire, was forced by a train crash to spend an afternoon in Smolensk on his way through to Moscow. He wandered into the park to listen to the band and heard young Bellison execute a series of dazzling cadenzas. He was so impressed that he immediately offered to arrange a scholarship for him at the Moscow Conservatoire. Simeon's father gave his consent and Safonoff placed him in the clarinet class of Joseph Friedrich.

In 1901 Bellison graduated from the Conservatoire with honours and a Bachelor of Music degree. In 1902 he formed the Moscow Quintet with which he toured Russia, Poland and Latvia. He was called up for military service in the Russo-Japanese War of 1904-1905. When this ended he became first clarinet in the Moscow Opera and Symphony orchestras, and in 1908 undertook an extensive tour of northern Europe with a chamber group. Besides these playing activities he taught at the principal schools in Moscow from the time of his graduation. In 1915 he won a competition for the post of first clarinet in the Imperial Opera Orchestra at St Petersburg, but conscription for army service once more interfered. Then came the turmoil of the 1917 Revolution and when this had subsided he set about organising a new chamber music ensemble, under the auspices of the Russian Zionist Organisation, which he called Zimro. From 1918 to 1921 this group toured through the Urals to Altay and other large Siberian towns to China, Japan, India, Dutch East Indies, Canada and finally America.

Bellison was offered the post of first clarinet in the New York Philharmonic Orchestra in 1921 and decided to settle in America. He retained the post until 1948 and during this time also played as a soloist with nearly every chamber music organisation in the United States. In 1927 he formed the unique Bellison Clarinet Ensemble which consisted of 50 clarinets (some of them women), brass, percussion, harp and harmonium. The Ensemble toured under the patronage of the New York Philharmonic Orchestra, playing music specially arranged by Bellison. After retiring from the Philharmonic Bellison continued to teach and to perform chamber music. He gave his last concert on 26th April 1953 at New York's City Hall, just a week before he died.

Writings:

Jivoglot (or *Eat 'em Alive*), a novel about the hardships of life as a musician in Old Russia. (Ms.).

"Vibrato in Wind Playing." TC, Fall, 1953.

"Weber's Variations." TC, Spring 1952.

Recordings:

Khachaturian – Trio. Classic 1002.

Mozart – Quintet K581. Columbia SET293.

Bibliography:

KING, William G. – *The Philharmonic-Symphony Orchestra of New York*. New York, 1940.

BENDER, Adam. ?-1873 Sept, Hasselt. Belgian. He was the son of Jakob and the brother of Constantin Bender. He was a distinguished clarinettist and also directed the Galeries St Hubert Orchestra in Brussels, the Royal Wind Society of Vilworde and the 11th regiment of Grenadiers.

BENDER, Constantin. Belgian. He was the son of Jakob and brother of Adam Bender. He was a fine clarinettist and also conductor of a Grenadier regiment.

BENDER, Herman. Belgian. He was a performer and teacher of the clarinet, chiefly notable for his pedagogic works. He edited Lefèvre's tutor, making some sweeping changes.

Works: 4 Duets op.30 (Cochrane). Der Solo Clarinettist und Virtuoso op.14, 2 vols. (André 1878). Die jungen Klarinettisten op.15 (André 1877 – LBL). Praktischer Lehrgang für das Klarinetspiel op.26, 3 vols. (Litolff 1879).

BENDER, Jakob. Bechtheim 1798-1844 Aug 9, Antwerp. German. He was the brother of Valentin Bender and father of Adam and Constantin. At five he began to learn the piano, at nine the violin and then went on to other instruments, including the clarinet, on which he showed especial aptitude. Jakob taught his brother Valentin to play the clarinet and they went on tour together. In 1819 Jakob was made director of the 31st Infantry Regiment of the Netherlands. In 1829 he became director of the Wind Society of Saint-Nicolas and also founded a Philharmonic Society. Four years later he was called to Antwerp to take over his brother's conductorship of the Royal Wind Society. In 1843 this society presented him with a splendid ebony clarinet with golden keys, as a token of their gratitude.

BENDER, (Jean) Valentin. Bechtheim, 19 Sept 1801-1873 Apr 14, Brussels. German, becoming naturalised Belgian. He was the brother of Jakob Bender. He was a notable clarinettist and director of military bands. He began studying flute and violin at six and later took up the clarinet under the tuition of his brother Jakob. The brothers made a concert tour together and in 1819 both went into the Netherlands 31st Infantry Regiment, Valentin as solo clarinet and Jakob as conductor. After eighteen months Valentin was offered a directorship of the 51st Regiment of the Line and with them he took part in the Spanish Campaign of 1823. As the regiment was then being drafted to the Colonies he changed to another, the 59th. He relinquished this post when he was called to Paris to discuss the formation of a band for the Viceroy of Egypt. He was not prepared to accept the terms offered by the Viceroy and returned to the Netherlands. From 1826 to 1833 he conducted the Royal Wind Society at Antwerp. He then gave up this post to his brother and moved to Brussels where he was made director of the 1st Infantry Regiment. He changed to the regiment of Guides and was finally made director of military music for the King's household. For a considerable time he conducted the concerts of the Brussels Philharmonic Society. Valentin Bender was an excellent teacher, numbering Sax and Wuille amongst his pupils. Iwan Müller dedicated his Scène Romantique to him. Bender's wife was a singer.

Works: Concertino no.1. Concertino no.2. (Rivière & Hawkes 1877 – LBL). 3 Airs variés for clarinet & wind orchestra (Petit). 4th & 5th Airs variés for clarinet & piano (Rivière & Hawkes 1877 – LBL). Introduction & Theme with Variations (Chappell 1858 – LBL).

BENDLEB, Karl. Sondershausen, 1808-1841. German. He was probably the son of the Sondershausen bassoonist Siegfried Bendleb. From 1828 he was first clarinet in the wind band at Sondershausen and in 1835 became director. Shortly after this he suffered a haemorrhage as the result of over-exertion and on learning he could never again play the clarinet he lost the will to live. The Duke showered him with kindnesses whilst he was in hospital and in gratitude Bendleb began to study composition and when recovered made a successful career as a composer of music for wind band.

BENOÎT, Christofle. From 1785 to 1787 he played in the orchestra for the Société du Concert at Neuchâtel and also in the band of the royal cavalry.

BERANGER. French? He performed his own concerto at Starck's Long Room in Baltimore on 25th November 1793. He then moved to Philadelphia where he played an unspecified symphonie concertante with Lullier in a Benefit at the Oeller Hotel on 3rd March 1795, and Pleyel's Symphonie Concertante with Dubois on 24th April 1798.

BERENDT. On 1st June 1825 he played a double concerto by Krommer with Pfaffe at Berlin.

BEREZIN, Anatoly Vasilievich. 1889-? Russian. He was a fine clarinet teacher in Leningrad, numbering Gensler amongst his pupils.

BERGER. German. He played in the Leipzig Gewandhaus Orchestra from 1798 to 1807.

BERGER, Julius. He was the son of David Berger, the music director at Stavenhagen. In 1883 he was a clarinettist at the Mecklenburg-Schwerin Court.

BERGEVEL (BERGEVAL). In 1823 he was playing second clarinet to Berr at the Vaudeville theatre at Paris. From 1824 until 1829 he was first clarinet. His address was no. 42 quai de la Grêve.

BERNER, Friedrich Wilhelm. Breslau, 16 May 1780-1827 May 9, Breslau. German. Weber, when he was music director at Breslau, held him in high esteem. Berner played clarinet in the Breslau theatre orchestra from 1797 to 1805. Later he became better known as an organist, composer and writer of didactic works.

Works: Divertissements. Variations.

BERR, Frédéric. Mannheim, 17 Apr 1794-1838 Sept 24, Paris. German. See OV. In 1819 Jean Jacques Selmer, grandfather of the famous brothers, asked Berr to be godfather to his son, who was named Frédéric after him. Information on Berr's theatrical appointments has been found to be incorrect. His first appointment was as principal clarinet at the Vaudeville theatre in 1823. He did not play at the Théâtre Italien until 1825, when he became second clarinet to Gambaro. On Gambaro's death in 1828 it was Loudelle who took over the post of first clarinet and Berr did not become principal until 1830. When Berr was appointed to the Conservatoire staff in 1831, he was an assistant for 7 months first without pay and in 1832 became official professor. Compositions by Berr were set for the annual competitions in 1836, 1837, 1838, 1869, 1873 and 1876. Dacosta dedicated his Concertino to Berr.

Berr was the editor of a *Journal d'Harmonie*. He had a close association with the military band conductor Alexandre Charles Fessy and collaborated with him in a series of 28 Fantasias for clarinet and piano. He began a 29th, but died suddenly and this one was completed by de Groot. The association of Berr and Fessy has been immortalised in a double head sculpture (see illustrations) by Jean Pierre Dantan. This head was previously thought to be of Joseph Beer and Fessy, but as Dantan always modelled from life and the sculpture is dated 1833 this rules out Beer, who died in 1812. Berr's association with Fessy and the cruel likeness in the caricature give further proof that he is the subject.

Works: Concerto no.1 in E flat, dedicated to "son ami Mr Estabel" (Leduc – PBN. Gérard – PBN. Meissonnier c.1870 – LBL). Concerto no.2 (Leduc). 11 Airs variés (Lemoine – PBN. Schott – no.5 in MiAUL. Lafleur 1881 – nos. 2, 3, 5 to 11 in LBL). Divertissement (Leduc). 28 Fantasias (Schott – LRCM, Lafleur 1887 – nos. 2, 3, 5 to 11 in LBL). Mes Loisirs (Wessel 1857). Petites soirées dramatiques, 4 books (Breitkopf & Härtel c.1837). 11 Solos (First Solo in B flat: Richault – BoLM. Lafleur 1847 – LBL. Third Solo: Ms. – BarBM). 20 Petits duos (Costallat). 3 Duos concertants op.38 (Schott c.1828). Overture to Rossini's *Siege of Corinth* for 2 clarinets (Troupenas c.1827). 6 Quartets of Rossini arranged for flute, clarinet, horn & bassoon (Lemoine. Schott 1827). Traité complet de la clarinette à quatorze clefs (Duverger 1836). Méthode complète de clarinette (Meissonnier c.1845 – BrBC, LBL, PBN).

BERR, Phillipe. 1804-? German. He was the younger brother of Frédéric Berr, who taught him to play the clarinet. He became conductor of the 14th Light Infantry Regiment.

Work: Méthode de Clarinette d'après celle de Vanderhagen (Lemoine). Ditto, with an appendix on the Boehm clarinet by

V. Blancou (Aulagnier – BrBC). Recueil (Petit – MiAUL).

BESSMERTNOV, P.S. 1879-1942. Russian. He was self-taught and became a brilliant clarinettist in the Bolshoi Theatre Orchestra in Moscow.

(B–H). **BETZ.** German. He played in the theatre orchestra at Strasbourg. His solo concerts were as follows: 1814 – 19th November, Mozart's "Parto!" 1815 – a double concerto by Krommer with one of his pupils. 1818 – 15th April, "O Salutaris," a trio for 2 cor anglais & basset-horn by Gossec. (Gossec originally wrote this as an additional vocal number to his oratorio *Saul*).

BEUSCHEL. When a student at the Vienna Conservatoire in 1833 he took part in a concertante for oboe, clarinet, horn & bassoon by Gyrowetz. When he left the Conservatoire in 1834 he took up an appointment at the Theater an der Wien.

BIANCHINI (BIANCANE), Francesco. Italian. He taught at the Liceo in Bologna during the second half of the nineteenth century. His pupils included Maccagni and Magnani.

Work: Popular Method (Ricordi – RBC).

BICHE. French. About 1785 he was clarinettist to Prince Louis François Joseph of Conti in Paris. He was also active as a teacher.

(B–H). **BIČIŠTĚ, Josef.** 1749-1802. Czech. He was active as a basset-horn player in Poland from 1775 to 1780.

BIMBONI, Giovanni. Florence, 1813-1892 May 28, Florence. Italian. He taught at the Conservatoire in Florence. He was the brother of Giovacchino Bimboni, trumpet and trombone teacher at the same institution, who wrote some variations on a theme from Donizetti's *Lucrezia Borgia* for clarinet, trombone and piano.

Work: Método (RBC).

BINFIELD. ?-1840, London. English. He played second to Willman for the Philharmonic Society in London.

BIRCKMANN, H. German. He taught the clarinet at Nuremberg. Heinrich and Gottfried Backofen became his pupils in 1780.

BLAES, (Arnold) Joseph. Brussels, 1 Dec 1814-1892 Jan 11, Brussels. Belgian. See OV. He was made first clarinet to the King of the Belgians after his first Russian tour. His concert for the Société des Concerts in 1846 at which he played a work by Hanssens, described by Elwart as a "concerto fantastique," was on 8th, not 2nd, of February. On 13th October 1862 he performed a transcription of a Phantasie-Caprice by Vieuxtemps at Wiesbaden and they said it was appropriate for him, because he certainly handled his instrument like a violin. He was a soloist again at Wiesbaden in the summer of 1865. His pupils at the Brussels Conservatoire included Vandenbogaerde (1852) and Van der Gracht (1867-1871). Joseph Snel dedicated a Fantasie de Concert to Blaes.

Works: 2 Concertos. 2 Airs variés. 3 Fantasias. 2 Salonpieces. Carnival of Venice. Meyerbeer's "Ranz des vaches d'Appenzell" arranged for soprano & clarinet (1847). Méthode de Clarinette (1848).

Writing:

Souvenirs de ma vie artistique. Brussels 1888 – BrBC, BrBR.

BLANCOU, (I.) V. (A.). French. He trained at the Paris Conservatoire, gaining a First Prize in 1840. Working with the instrument-maker Buffet-Crampon he produced in 1845 a *clarinette omnitonique,* an improved model of Müller's 13-key system, which incorporated keys and rings borrowed from the newly-invented Boehm. He supplied an appendix on the Boehm clarinet for Phillipe Berr's edition of the Vanderhagen tutor.

(B–H). **BLASCHKE.** German. Mendel lists him as a well-known basset-horn player.

BLASIUS, (Matthieu) Frédéric. Lauterbourg, 24 Apr 1758-1829, Versailles. Alsation. During his lifetime he was held in high regard as conductor of the Opéra Comique. Today it is by his compositions that he stands. He was the son of a master-taylor, Jean Michel Blasius, who gave him the elements of music. He became a violinist and clarinettist of the front rank, a good flute and bassoon player, and a prolific composer. About 1782 he went to Paris and after playing in the first violins at the Comédie Italienne for some years he became music director in 1790. From 1793 to 1795 he played in the National Guard. When the Conservatoire was opened in 1795 Blasius was made a professor of the first class for wind instruments, but at the reorganisation in 1802 he lost the post. From 1799 to 1804 he was director of the Consular

Guard. At the Restoration he became a member of Louis XVIII's private orchestra and was made conductor of the 5th regiment of the Imperial Guard. He retired from both these posts and as conductor of the Comédie Italienne, which had become the Opéra Comique, in 1816 and went to live at Versailles. Boufil dedicated his 3 Grand Duos op.3 to Blasius.

Works: Concerto no.1 in C (Cochet 1802 – PBN. Leduc). Concerto no.2 in C (Cochet 1802. Leduc). Concerto no.3 in F (Nägeli 1805. Girard – NBN, PhFL. Frey). Concerto no.4 (Leduc 1805). 6 Sonatas op.55 (Magasin de musique – AaS. Frey). Duos op. 18 (Sieber). 6 Duos op.20 (1794. Ozi 1802. Schlesinger). 6 Duos op. 21 (1795. Ozi 1802. André. Schlesinger.) 6 Duos op.35 (Petit). Duos op.38. 6 Very easy duos op.39 (André, Leduc, Breitkopf & Härtel 1798). 6 Duos faciles op.40 (Leduc 1800. Cochet). 6 Duos op.46 (1805. Naderman). 6 Very easy duets from the *Méthode* (Sieber). 6 Sonatas op.55 for clarinet & viola (1805). 3 Trios dialogués op.31 for various combinations (Gaveaux, Sieber c.1800 to 1810 – LRAM). 3 Trios op.2 in E flat, F & B flat for 2 clarinets & bassoon (Porthaux – VGM). 3 Trios for clarinet, violin & bassoon (Sieber. Gaveaux). 3 Trios for clarinet, horn & cello (1805). 3 Quartets in G,F & B flat (Breitkopf & Härtel 1782/4). 3 Quartets concertants op.1 in F,E flat & B flat (Sieber 1782 – VGM). 6 Quartets op.13 (Sieber 1788?). Méthode de Clarinette (Michel c.1795. Sieber). Nouvelle Méthode pour la clarinette (Porthaux 1796 – PBN).

Bibliography:

RAU, Ulrich – "Matthieu Frédéric Blasius." MGG Supplement, 1971.

BLATT, (Franz) Thaddäus. Prague, 1793-1856 Mar 9, Prague. Czech. See OV. Letters of 1850 and 1853 from him to Moritz Bermann, who had asked for a biography for a new lexicon, reveal him to be living at no.855 Herrengasse. (Bermann's *Oesterreichisches biographisches Lexikon* was published to vol. 3 only and did not reach an entry on Blatt). Amongst his pupils at the Conservatoire were Gustav Farník, Mauermann and Pauer.

The following are details of his concerts in Prague, the first two of which were at the Conservatoire: 1816 – 19th March, Cartellieri's Concerto. 1817 – 28th February, Spohr's Variations on an Alpine Song. 1820 – Andante & Polonaise by Tausch. Variations on an Alpine Song by Spohr. 1824 – April 13th, Adagio & Polonaise by Tausch. 1827 – Variations on a Theme from Rossini's *Barber of Seville* by himself, a concertino by Lindpaintner and the obligato to Mozart's 'Parto!' for Mme Zomp. 1828 – he shared a Benefit with two other members of the Conservatoire staff and played some "new" variations of his own composition.

Works: Amusing exercises op.26 for solo clarinet (Costallat. Breitkopf & Härtel 1832). 12 Caprices in the form of studies, 2 bks. (Breitkopf & Härtel). Introduction & 5 Variations brillantes op.14 (Costallat. Simrock). Introduction & brilliant Variations op.18 (Hofmeister. Ryba 1834). Introduction & brilliant Variations on a Theme from Rossini's *Barber of Seville* op.28 (Costallat. Breitkopf & Härtel 1832). 3 Duos concertants op.29 (Costallat. Breitkopf & Härtel 1832. Richault – LRAM). 6 Elementary duets (Rivière & Hawkes 1885-LBL). Trio op.3 (Berra. Hoffmann). Trio op.27 (Costallat. Brietkopf & Härtel 1832). 8 Variations concertantes in C & G minor for clarinet & string quartet (Simrock). Méthode complète de clarinette, dedicated to his Conservatoire pupils (Schott 1828 – BrBC, HGM, RBC).

Bibliography:

CULKA, Zdeněk – "Franz Thaddäus Blatt." MGG Supplement, 1971.

BLÈVE. French. He was a clarinettist at Le Havre. Amongst the first to experiment with ring-keys, in 1826 he commissioned François Lefèvre to make an instrument incorporating this feature.

BLIESENER, Friedrich August. 1780-1841 Dec 21, Berlin. German. He was a pupil of Franz Tausch and in 1801 embarked on a distinguished career as a soloist. In 1805 he became first clarinet at the Berlin opera and later was made a Royal Chamber Musician. He was also a fine teacher, his most notable pupil being Ebert. With his brother Ernst, a horn player, he founded in 1800 a Music Institute, which was particularly designed to give opportunities to students and dillettante to play orchestral works. Yearly subscription concerts were given at the Stadt Paris Hall. The standard these set during their best period of 1810 to 1820 was such that they were considered amongst the best in Berlin. In 1823 Friedrich was pensioned from the Court, but continued to instruct at the Institute until 1837, when his son Louis took over direction.

His principal concerts were as follows: 1804 – a solo concerto by Krommer, Krommer's double concerto op.35 with Georg Reinhardt. 1810 – 2nd April, double concerto by Franz Tausch with F.W. Tausch. 1814 – 25th February, concerto by G.A. Schneider for clarinet & bassoon with C.G. Schwartz. 1817 – 19th December, Weber's Variations op.33 with Mme Heinike.

BLIESENER, Louis. ?-1880 Aug 22, Berlin. German. He was a well-known clarinettist in Berlin, the son of Friedrich August Bliesener. In 1837 he took over his father's Music Institute, continuing this for a few more years only. He is mentioned in a performance of Beethoven's Septet in 1840.

BLIZZARD, John. English. He was first clarinet in the band of the 1st Life Guards and fought at Waterloo. Later he became bandmaster at the Duke of York's School. From about 1825 to 1829 he taught Lazarus at the Royal Military Asylum in Chelsea. He used a 12-keyed clarinet in B flat made by Thomas Key which he gave to Lazarus in 1838.

BLONK-STEINER, (Felice) Umberto. Sermoneta (Rome) 15 Nov 1881-? Italian. He learnt first from his father, Carlo, who was a music teacher in Sermoneta, and at sixteen entered the St. Cecilia Academy in Rome to study under Magnani. He gained his diploma and silver medal in 1901 and in the same year became first clarinet at the Costanzi Theatre, retaining this post until 1905. In 1903 he was appointed to teach at the Academy under Magnani. From 1905 to 1912 he was principal clarinet in the orchestra of the Augusteo, except for the season of 1909/10 when he played at the Buenos Aires Colon. He gave solo recitals at the Adriano Theatre, Costanzi Theatre, Pichetti Hall and Verdi Hall. In 1913 he undertook a tour to Heliopolis, Egypt and then returned to live at Milan. From 1914 to 1918 he was first clarinet at La Scala and in 1915 was made a professor at the Royal Conservatoire.

BLÜMEL, Franz. He was a student at the Vienna Conservatoire, completing his training in 1896. He then had a post at the Carltheater.

BLUM, Stephan. He was in the Würzburg court orchestra from 1760 to 1790. On 20th April 1778 he performed at Frankfurt.

BOCHSA, Karl. ?-1821, Paris. Czech. He also played the flute and oboe. He was the father of Charles Bochsa, the harpist and composer. His first occupation was as a regimental musician. He then settled at Lyons as general wind player at the large theatre there and later moved to a similar appointment at Bordeaux. In 1806 he took his family to Paris and opened a music shop at no.19 rue Vivienne. Amongst many interesting items he published was Tausch's Thirteen Pieces for 2 clarinets, horn & bassoon. The Bochsa firm was taken over by Dufaut & Dubois after Karl's death.

Works: Concerto no.1 op.33 in B flat (Dufaut & Dubois. Simrock – solo part only in AKVM). Concertante for flute

& clarinet. Duos ops.10, 15 & 20 (Simrock). 3 Quartets ops.1, 2 & 3, dedicated to his pupil L. Aimé Dubourg (Momigny 1805? – LBL. Op.1 was also published by Janet, op.3 by Sieber). Quartet op.30 (Dufaut & Dubois). 3 Nocturnes ops.14 & 24 for clarinet & string trio (Dufaut & Dubois). Romances de Gilles variés for clarinet & string trio (Dufaut & Dubois). 12 Petit airs op.12 for wind quartet (Bochsa – PBN). Airs variés for clarinet & string quartet (Dufaut & Dubois. Gaveaux. Omont). 2 Quintets op.post for clarinet, horn & strings (Dufaut & Dubois). Diagolo brillante for basset-horn. Fantasia on "Cease your funning" for basset-horn. Méthode de clarinette (Omont c.1810).

BÖGEL, Christian V. ?-1824. German. He also played the violin. In the 1790s he played in a military band, next he became a bandmaster in Spain and then spent some years in England as a successful singer. From 1815 to 1824 he was a clarinettist in the court orchestra at Darmstadt and for his services in this was decorated with the Order of Ludwig second class.

(B–H). **BOEHMER, Johann Sebastian.** ?-1819 May 23, Dresden. German. In 1793 he played at the Bentheim-Steinfürt Court and later at Utrecht. When he played basset-horn solos at the Beygang Museum at Leipzig on 5th July 1802 he was hailed as from Amsterdam. In 1808 he gave a concert on the basset-horn at Lübeck. He became music director at Bentheim-Steinfürt and from there went to perform again at Leipzig on 10th March 1812. This time he was joined by his eleven-year-old son Karl who showed considerable talent on the violin and flageolet. Boehmer's tone was reported to be clear and pleasant, though somewhat weak and effeminate.

Work: Concerto(s) for basset-horn.

BOFINGER. German. In 1806 he was first clarinet in the Stuttgart orchestra.

BOLLAND, Hermann. Olbersleben, 27 Feb 1861-1944 Mar 3, Harleshausen. German. His first appointment was as a clarinettist in the Bilse Orchestra at Berlin. In 1886 he became principal clarinet in the court orchestra at Hanover and two years later was made a Royal Chamber Musician. He retired in 1926.

BOLM, Carl. He was first clarinet in the Imperial Opera and Ballet orchestras at St Petersburg in the early twentieth century and made some recordings about this time.

BOLSIUS. He was a pupil of Tamm at the Friedrich Charitable Institute in Berlin. In October 1824 he performed Weber's Concertino and on 9th September 1825 a concertino by Cramer (J.B.?)

BOUFIL (BOUFFIL, BOUFFILS, BONFIL), Jacques Jules. Muret, 14 May 1783-1868. French. From 1801 he was a pupil of Lefèvre at the Paris Conservatoire, gaining a First Prize in 1806. In 1807 he became second clarinet at the Opéra Comique, from 1821 shared first with Duvernoy and from 1825 to 1830 was principal clarinet. He is also said to have been a member of Napoleon's private orchestra. Boufil played in a brilliant wind quintet consisting of Joseph Guillou (flute), Gustave Vogt (oboe), Antoine Henry (bassoon) and Louis Dauprat (horn). They performed all the Reicha wind quintets in a series of concerts at the Théâtre Favart during 1818 and 1819. In reporting these performances for AMZ, G.L.P. Sievers singles out Boufil as having a more seductive tone than the others. Spohr was enthusiastic over the group when they took part in his Nonet at a concert of his compositions in December 1820, also when they performed his Quintet op.52 with Moscheles in January 1821. In 1828 Boufil was present at the convocation ceremony for the Société des Concerts, and became a member of the orchestra then formed. His compositions for clarinet duet and trio are some of the most worth-while written for the medium. They are full-scale works of considerable substance and were doubtless intended for performance by professionals. Boufil lived at no.73 rue de Cléry in 1822 and no.11 rue Gaillon in 1828.

Works: 3 Grand Duos op.2, dedicated to M. Martin, conductor of the Imperial Guard & Member of the Legion of Honour (Jouve 1815/16 – LBL). 3 Grand Duos op.3, dedicated to Blasius, composer for the huntsmen of the Imperial Guard, etc. (Jouve 1815/16). 3 Duos op.5 (Gaveaux – PBN. Joubert). Duo for piano & clarinet (Garaudé). 3 Trios op.7 (Petit c.1810 – BrBC, PBN). Grand Trio op.8 (Petit c.1810. Schott 1827 – BDS). Trios for 2 clarinets & bassoon (Petit).

BOUTRUY, K.I. French. He was a pupil of Klosé at the Paris Conservatoire, gaining First Prize in 1852. He played in the orchestra for the Colonne Concerts.

BOVE, S. Italian. He was professor at the Milan Conservatoire and made some disc recordings c.1908-1910.

BOWLEY. English. He performed the obligato to

Panseron's "Tyrol, my Fatherland" for Miss E.J. Smart on 22nd December 1840 at the Third Subscription Concert of the City of Westminster Literary, Scientific and Mechanics Institution.

BOYMOND. French. He was first clarinet in the theatre orchestra at Strasbourg from about 1835 to 1846. He had a beautiful tone and considerable finger dexterity but was criticised for not putting light and shade into his playing. As he seems to have performed only the compositions of Berr it is probable he was at one time Berr's pupil. His concerts at Strasbourg were as follows: 1835 – concerto by Berr. 1839 – Variations on the Polonaise from Bellini's *I Puritàni* by Berr. 1846 – Variations by Berr.

BOYNEBURGK, Baron Friedrich (Carl) von. German. He held an administrative post at the Court of Weimar and was also a talented clarinettist, pianist and composer.

Works: Introduction & Variations on a Theme of Weigl op.10 (Simrock 1823 – LRAM). Variations (Breitkopf & Härtel 1827).

BRATTOLI, Giacinto. Italian. From 1795 to 1802 he taught at the Naples Conservatoire.

BRAUN, Johann Baptiste. In 1792 he was in the court orchestra at Donaueschingen. He also played the violin.

BREKKER, Vasily Fedorovich. 1863-1926. Russian. He received his training in Germany and then returned to Russia where he was made first clarinet in the orchestra of the Kirov Theatre, Leningrad. He was also a fine teacher and was on the staff of the Leningrad Conservatoire from 1897 until his death. His pupils included P.P. Vantroba and D.I. Raiter.

BRETONNEAU. French. He played at the Paris Opéra. In December 1891 he gave a recital on the Fontaine-Besson contrabass clarinet in London.

BRETSCHNEIDER. German. He was first clarinet in the Frankfurt theatre orchestra from 1821 until 1834. His solo performances, all for the Museum Society except for December 1823, August 1825 and December 1826, were as follows: 1821 – 16th November, quintet for clarinet & strings by Krommer. 1822 – 22nd February, Hummel's Septet. 1st November, Beethoven's Septet. 1823 – 14th March, his own variations. 7th November, Weber's Concertino.

December, Variations (probably Gerke's) on a Romance from Spohr's *Zemire.* 1825 – 14th January, double concerto by Tausch with Philipp Faubel, his colleague in the theatre orchestra. August, double concerto by Krommer with Faubel. 1826 – December, concerto for clarinet & bassoon by Gustav Düring, with the composer playing the bassoon. 1829 – 30th January, Mozart's Wind Quintet. 1831 – 4th February, Trio (probably C.R.N. Bochsa's) for harp, clarinet & horn. 22nd March, Mozart's "Parto!" for Mlle Reich. 1833 -11th October, concerto by Aloys Schmidt. 1834 – 5th December, a divertimento, composer unspecified.
Work: Variations.

BROCA y Casanovas, Pedro. Barcelona, 26 June 1794-1836 Sept 22, Havana. Spanish. He was the elder brother of Ramón Broca. Pedro Broca began to learn music from the town musician at Cuenca where his father, director of a military band, was posted. In 1805 the family moved to Madrid and Pedro studied the clarinet under Andréas Martinez, doing so well that in 1808 he was made first clarinet in the Zafra regiment of huntsmen. He transferred to the 2nd regiment of Badajoz and Valencia, until 1816 when he was made first clarinet of both the Royal Halberdiers and of the court orchestra. He also played oboe and cor anglais and in 1818 took on an extra post as first oboe at the Teatro del Principe. At the end of July 1829 he and Magin Jardin were made professors at the newly opened Madrid Conservatoire. Jardin taught flute as well as clarinet, so it is likely Broca took pupils on oboe and cor anglais as well as clarinet. Broca remained in the army all this time, steadily rising to the rank of captain, and benefitting much from the friendship of his patron, General Vincente Quesada. In 1836 during an uprising General Quesada was set upon and massacred by the crowd. Because of his part in attempting to protect his old commander, Pedro Broca had to flee the country. He settled in Havana as first clarinet in the Italian Opera and also as first clarinet and music director for an artillery regiment, but did not long survive the move.

BROCA, Ramón. Madrid, 19 Nov 1815-1849 Jan 30, Madrid. Spanish. He was the younger brother of the famous Pedro Broca and like him also played the oboe and cor anglais. In his short life he not only made a fine reputation as a player but won esteem from his colleagues and pupils as a person. He studied under his brother Pedro at the Madrid Conservatoire and when Pedro fled the country, took his place in the court orchestra and at the Teatro del Principe. From 1839 until 1849 he taught at the Conservatoire. His home where he died was at no.10 calle de Valverde.

BROEU, Jean François de. Brussels, 1766-1834 Jan 27, Brussels. Belgian. He was solo clarinet to the King of the Netherlands and concert master for the Church of St Nicolas.

BROUGH, L. English. He played fourth clarinet in the Hallé Orchestra at Manchester from 1901 to 1906 and then moved up to third place until 1915. From 1921 to 1929 he was third clarinet in the London Symphony Orchestra.

BRUNNER, George. ?-1826 Feb 10, St Petersburg. Czech. He became second clarinet in the court orchestra at St Petersburg in 1779. His salary in 1791 was 500 roubles and in 1800 it was raised to 700 roubles.

BUCH. He was in the Anhalt-Dessau court orchestra in 1849.

BUDINSKY, Franz. Born Kamenitz? Czech. He was a distinguished pupil at the Prague Conservatoire under Farník from 1825 to 1831, but it is not known what happened to him in later years. He played at the following Conservatoire public concerts: 1829 – 13th March, Variations by Heinrich Baermann. 1831 – 11th March, Variations by Joseph Faubel. 18th March, Iwan Müller's double concerto with Pisařovic.

BÜHRMANN. German. In the 1840s he was a member of the court orchestra at Kassel. At the Subscription Concerts in 1844 he played Maurer's Concerto and in 1848 a Fantasie by Gerke.

BULTOS. In 1795 he was second clarinet in the theatre orchestra at Hamburg. (Hamburg was one of the earliest towns to employ clarinets on a permanent basis, doing so first in 1738).

BUM, Michael. From 1781 to 1783 he was second clarinet in Prince Joseph Bathyány's orchestra at Pressburg. He also played the violin.

BUSONI, Ferdinando. Spicchio, 24 June 1834-1909 May 12, Trieste. Italian. He spent most of his life as a touring virtuoso because his sight reading was not good enough for an orchestral post and his temperament unsuited to it. He modelled his style on that of Cavallini and had considerable success as a soloist in spite of an erratic sense of rhythm. His son, the composer Ferruccio Busoni, described his playing as "combining the virtuosity of a violinist with the beauty and sensitiveness of the old Italian *bel canto*." Ferdinando taught himself to play to begin with and then had lessons from Gaetano Fabiani, director of the town band at Empoli. When he was about twenty he joined the Banda Carini at Leghorn and in 1862 moved to the municipal band at Novara. Here he became a professor at the music institute, but only for five months, leaving on the grounds of ill health. In 1863 he played at Milan and in 1864 at Bologna, where he was made an honorary member of the Accademia Filarmonica. In 1865 he married Anna Weiss, a talented pianist who lived at Trieste and who accompanied him at a concert there in May. Their only child Ferruccio was born the following year. In 1868 Ferdinando and Anna made an extensive tour, playing at Laibach, Trieste, Venice, southern Styria, Stuttgart and Nancy. They reached Paris in December and on New Year's Eve played to a large gathering at the house of M. Kugelmann, the proprietor of *Le Gaulois*. Ferdinando was "vigorously applauded" and called "a great virtuoso." Anna too had a great success. They stayed on and in May of 1869, after a third public concert, they were reported to be "decidedly the heroes of this musical season, which is now at its last gasp." The Busonis remained in Paris for a further year and then returned to Trieste. In the following summer months they played at Gorizia, Abano and Recoaro as well as Trieste itself.

Ferdinando travelled on his own for most of 1871 and 1872. He then returned home and started his son's musical education. He ruled the boy with a rod of iron and subjected him to dreadful fits of temper, but divined his great talent and determined to make him a fine pianist. This bad temper was due to chronic dyspepsia which gave Ferdinando considerable pain and insomnia. He tried many remedies including mud baths, but all without result, and his irregular life did not help matters. His son was deeply appreciative of his father's schooling and always said that his love of Bach was due to his father's influence. In 1879 it was decided that Ferruccio must have the specialist tuition his talents required and the family moved to Graz for him to study with Wilhelm Mayer. To meet the big expense both Ferdinando and Anna gave piano lessons. In the summer months of 1881 Ferdinando went off with his clarinet again for a tour of the Styrian baths. In the autumn the whole family commenced a concert tour. Their performances at Bologna in March and Empoli in April 1882 were particularly successful. Ferdinando and Anna played Carl Baermann's Gnomenklänge, Cavallini's Scherzo from *Don Pasquale*, "Casta Diva" and Fantasia on *Il Trovatore,* whilst Ferruccio played piano solos and improvised. Ferdinando played at Vienna, Milan and Arezzo in 1884, Leoben and Frohleiten in 1886. There are no further reports of him after a concert in Gorizia in 1890.

The instrument Busoni used was one of boxwood made by Vinatieri of Turin c.1860. It had 4 rings and 16 keys, including an improved form of speaker key which Rendall describes thus: "The orifice, pierced on the top, is controlled, by means of a ring contrived in a groove in the wood, by a lever at the back." In his method, Busoni advocates playing with the reed on top and makes the surprising announcement that he does "not agree with those who contend that the tone-vibrations depend more on the under lip than the upper. The lower jaw is stronger and less flexible by nature than the upper one. According to this method a tone is produced, which .... is powerful, but at the same time raw, less vibrating and often unpleasant."

Work: Scuola di perfezionamente per il clarinetto (Cranz 1883 – LBL).

Bibliography:

DENT, Edward J. – *Ferruccio Busoni.* London, 1933, 1974.

BUSSE. Born Berlin. German. He also played the violin and trombone, and conducted. For twenty years he played clarinet in a military band and was active as a soloist in Berlin. By 1828, when he performed at Leipzig, he had gone blind.

BUTEUX (BUTTEUX), Claude François. Paris, 15 Oct 1797-1870 Jan 8, Paris. French. He also played the bass clarinet and cello. He learnt the clarinet from Lefèvre and then Duvernoy at the Paris Conservatoire, gaining a First Prize in 1819. He next played for the Opéra Buffa and from 1821 to 1824 was second clarinet at the Théâtre Italien. On 1st January 1825 he became second clarinet at the Opéra, moving up to first when Dacosta retired in 1842. He played for the Société des Concerts for many years from its foundation in 1828, appearing four times as soloist. As a bass clarinettist Buteux was well known, though he came in for much criticism through using a poor instrument. At the first performance of Meyerbeer's *Les Huguenots* at the Opéra on 29th February 1836 he played the famous bass clarinet solo that comes in the fifth act. The instrument he used on this historic occasion was said to be one of Lefèvre's. When Donizetti wrote a special part for Sax's new bass clarinet in his opera *Dom Sébastien* Buteux, seeing his pitch queried, wrote a letter to the *Gazette des Théâtres* attacking Sax. Sax was enraged and, hoping to topple another head, as he had done Georges Bachmann some years earlier, sent a letter to the same paper challenging Buteux to a public contest. Buteux declined to answer the letter, refused to let Sax play the part, and the opera was given its first performance on 13th November 1843 without the instrument which Donizetti had intended. Buteux lived at no.9 rue de Crussol in 1821 and at no.24 faubourg du Temple from 1822. He edited Lefèvre's tutor, adapting it for Müller's instrument (Troupenas c.1830 – BrBC).

Work: Method (Heugel).

CAHUZAC, (Jean) Louis (Baptiste). Quarante, 12 July 1880-1960 Aug 9, Luchon. French. He was one of the finest clarinettists of the twentieth century and has been honoured by his countrymen with a plaque on the house where he was born and by having a street named after him. Early in his career he did much to make Brahms' works known in France, and later made a speciality of Stravinsky's Three Pieces. When he first played the Pieces to Stravinsky the composer found his interpretation too romantic, so Cahuzac spent considerable time studying them under the composer at his own home in order to get them exactly as wanted. Cahuzac took the same trouble with Debussy's Rhapsodie and rehearsed it carefully with the composer playing the piano reduction before performing it in public with him. He collaborated also with Ravel and Roussel, and gave first performances of Honegger's Sonatine, Jean Rivier's Concerto and of Milhaud's Sonatine, the latter being written for him. His playing was sensitive and very inspired. His tone was full and rich on Boehm clarinets made by Buffet. Pupils came to study with him from all over the world, and could be accommodated in his house at Luchon which was divided into apartments for them. Cahuzac was active as a union member and when for a time he was personnel manager for the Opéra he strove vigorously to improve working conditions, disregarding the consequences to his own personal relationships in his fight for justice. Short of stature and with legendary good health, he put great vitality into everything he did.

Cahuzac first learnt from his father, an amateur musician in the local band. He then went to Toulouse Conservatoire and finally to the Paris Conservatoire, where he was a pupil of Rose. He was awarded Second Prize in 1898 and the following year First Prize, the test piece for the latter being Messager's "Solo de Concours." Two years later he became a member of the Opéra orchestra and then was for many years first clarinet at the Théâtre Colonne, the Concerts Symphoniques Touche and the Luchon Casino concerts. In 1920 he gave up orchestral playing to conduct and travel as a soloist. He conducted the Luchon Casino concerts and many of the provincial radio orchestras in southern

France.

His principal engagements were as follows: 1921 – Brahms & D'Indy trios with D'Indy in a tour of the Rhineland, sponsored by the Ministry of Fine Arts. 1923 – Stravinsky's Three Pieces at the Stravinsky Festival in Paris; these were very well received. 1924 – February, Mozart Quintet at the Colonne Concerts; this gained him an ovation. April, Schumann's Phantasiestücke at Lisbon. May at Barcelona. 1925 – Debussy's Rhapsodie with piano, at Venice in March and Rome in April. 1927 – Berezowsky's Sextet at Amsterdam and London. 1928 – February, Mozart Quintet at San Sebastian and Bilbao. April, Stravinsky's Three Pieces at Berne for the Society of New Music; a report said that the "ultra modern" work would not have had the success it did without such an artist to carry it off. 1931 – December, Mozart Concerto for the Concerts Colonne and La Société d'Études Mozartiennes; *le Monde Musical* said "you could not play the clarinet better." 1933 – January, Mozart Concerto at Basle; as an encore he played the Stravinsky Pieces. October, Mozart Concerto at Saint-Gall and Zurich. 1934 – January, Mozart Concerto and Recit. & Rondo from Weber's Second Concerto at the St Cecilia Academy in Rome and at Salzburg, sponsored by the Ministry of Fine Arts. December, Mozart Concerto at the Palais des Beaux-Arts in Brussels.

Some of Cahuzac's finest work was done when he reached his 70s, particularly recordings of the Mozart Concerto in 1952 (he had already made one in 1929) and Nielsen Concerto in 1954. In 1955 he gave a performance of the Mozart Concerto with the Lucerne Festival Orchestra which was reported as more than ordinarily inspired. In 1957 when he performed Hindemith's Concerto under the composer's baton at Frankfurt, Hindemith was so impressed that he exclaimed: "Where has this clarinet virtuoso been hiding that I have not met him before," and the following year invited Cahuzac to record the work with him. Cahuzac met his death as the result of an accident on his moped in the Champs Elysées.

Works: Arlequin for solo clarinet (United Music Publishers 1975). Cantilène (Ditto). Fantasie variée (Hansen). Pastorale Cevenole (United Music Publishers 1975). Variations sur un Air du Pays d'Oc (Leduc 1953).

Recordings:

Cahuzac – Cantilène. Columbia CCX 1310. Re-issue: Grenadilla GS – 1006.

Hindemith – Concerto. Columbia 33CX 1533. Angel 35490.

Honegger – Sonatine. Columbia CCX 1273.

Jeanjean – Arabesques. Columbia CCX 1309.

Migot – Quartet. Deutsche Grammophon Gesellschaft W 872/3.
Mozart – Concerto K622. Haydn Society HSL 1047.
Mozart – Quintet K581. Columbia LDZ 7003.
Nielsen – Concerto. Columbia 2219.
Pierné – Canzonetta. Columbia CCX 1274.

Writings:

"Mozart's Message to Clarinettists." TC, autumn 1953.
"The Mozart Clarinet Concerto." WW, April 1959.

Bibliography:

WIENER, Hilda – *Pencil Portraits of Concert Celebrities.* London, 1937.

CALDES. He was second clarinet at the Porte St Martin theatre in Paris in 1828.

CALVIST, Enrique. Spanish. He was a pupil of Gonzáles. He became well-known as a teacher and composed some clarinet studies.

CAMPBELL, Robert. Irish. He taught the clarinet, as well as flute, flageolet and piano at New Ross in County Wicklow about 1809.

CAMPOS, Gaspar. Barcelona, 1790-1854 Dec 1, Lisbon. Spanish. One of many foreign musicians to join the Portuguese army after it's spectacular successes of 1812, he returned with them to Lisbon. Here in 1816 he joined the Brotherhood of Saint Cecilia. The following year he was selected to play in a band of musicians accompanying the Princess Leopoldina to Brazil, where she was to marry Dom Pedro (q.v.), heir-presumptive to the Portuguese throne. The Portuguese royal family were at that time living in exile at Rio de Janeiro and Dom João, Dom Pedro's father, invited the musicians to remain in the country. Thus Campos became a member of the court orchestra. In 1824 he returned to Lisbon and was made second clarinet at the San Carlos Theatre. When Canongia died in 1842 Campos became first clarinet. He was given the task of reforming the Brotherhood of Saint Cecilia in 1838. In 1834 he was one of the founders of the Montepio Philharmonic and in 1842 of the Music Association. He lies buried in the Alto de San João Cemetery.

CANONGIA, Ignacio. Born Manresa. Spanish. He came from a silk-making family and was the father of José Avelino and Joaquin Ignacio Canongia. In the 1780s he moved to Oeiras in Portugal. When the San Carlos Theatre at Lisbon was opened in 1793 he was made first clarinet.

CANONGIA, (José) Avelino. Oeiras (near Lisbon), 10 Nov 1784-1842 July 14, Lisbon. Portuguese, of Spanish origin. He was a virtuoso of the spectacular type, achieving fame and a large following through extreme technical brilliance. In his early years he had the patronage of Count Farrobo, at whose expense his compositions were engraved in Paris and London. In later years he employed an impressario and did very well financially. Avelino was the son of Ignacio Canongia, who sent him to a school run by Paulist brothers. Here, at some time after 1799, he had the benefit of clarinet lessons from Wisse, and also learnt singing, piano and violin. Soon after leaving, he obtained a post in the theatre orchestra at Salitre. From 1806 to 1808 he lived in Paris and then spent some time in Nantes. Next followed some brilliant concerts in Paris and London. On returning from these he was made principal clarinet to the King of Portugal, about 1816. In the Spring of 1818 he played at Genoa and Bologna and in 1819 went to St Petersburg. He returned via Italy and in Lent 1820 played at Turin, showing his prowess in his own arrangement of a set of violin variations by Rode. AMZ's critic reported that "he is master of his instrument, ... has great fluency, but not enough rounding of the phrases, in which it seems his fourth finger (of both hands) is at fault." In the summer of the same year Canongia played at Gotthard and Zurich, where the reception was excellent. He then went to Dresden and Weimar, where he played his own Fantasia with Variations in the theatre and was favourably compared to Baermann and Hermstedt. On 29th September he played his own Nocturne and an Introduction, Adagio & Variations by Mme Müller-Bender for the Frankfurt Museum Concerts with Mme Müller-Bender herself. At Berlin's theatre he gave a concert on 18th November in which he played a Concerto in G minor and Thême Varié, both by himself. The critics remarked that he played easily up to g'''; they said his middle register was soft and pleasant but that the low notes did not have sufficient resonance. Canongia gave Berlin another concert of his own compositions on 4th December. In May 1821 he performed at Munich for the Museum Society and then went to Paris, returning to Lisbon in August. He was then made first clarinet at the San Carlos Theatre, a post he held until his death. On 25th March 1822 he gave a star concert at the theatre, to a packed house, at which it was estimated he made 600 escudos. The programme included a wind quintet by Reicha, and a concerto and variations of his own composition. In 1824 Canongia was appointed professor at the Patriarchal Seminary and retained this post when the Seminary became the Conservatoire. Amongst many fine pupils he trained was Croner. He had a younger brother, Joaquin Ignacio, who was also a clarinettist but did not achieve celebrity.

Works: Concerto no.1. Concerto no.2. Concerto no.3, dedicated to Dom Fernando II, King of Portugal (Schoenenberger 1834 or later – LiBN). Concerto no.4 (Schoenenberger 1834 or later – LiBN). Fantasie with Variations. Introduction & Thême Varié (Pleyel. Simrock). Nocturne. Variations in G after Rode.

CARLOS. Spanish. He was first clarinet at the Italian Theatre in Madrid. A report of 1799 says: "Whoever thinks of the clarinet as a limited instrument should hear Carlos," adding that he can transpose anything and has a fluent tongue. This praise is tempered by criticism of miserable tone and lack of taste.

CARULLI, Benedetto. Olginate, 3 Apr 1797-1877 Apr 8, Milan. He was principal clarinet at Milan's La Scala until about 1840, when his pupil Cavallini took his place. He received his training at the Milan Conservatoire, graduating in 1816. Spohr was at his graduation concert on 19th September, when a sextet by Agostino Belloli was performed; Belloli played horn, with Carulli on clarinet, Giuseppe Rabboni (flute), Carlo Ivon (oboe), Angelo Savinelli (bassoon) and Giuseppe Schirolli (cor anglais). In later years Carulli belonged to a quartet with Rabboni, Ivon and the bassoonist Cantu which had considerable success playing works by Bellini, Donizetti and Rossini. The year after his graduation Carulli was appointed professor at the Conservatoire and held this post until 1873. He was an excellent teacher and numbered amongst his pupils Cavallini and Orsi. Ricordi published an edition by him of Lefèvre's tutor.

Works: 2 Potpourris (VGM). Variations (VGM). Divertimento for flute, clarinet & orchestra (Carulli – VGM). Trio (Ricordi). Trio op.1 for 2 clarinets & bassoon (Carulli – VGM). Quintet for wind & piano.

CASALI, Domenico. Italian. From 1818 to 1839 he was first clarinet in the court orchestra at Lucca.

CASTRONOVO, Lorenzo. Madrid, 1766-? Spanish. He was considered unequalled for his time, in Spain.

CATANEO, Tomaso. Italian. From 1797 to about 1801 he taught clarinet and violin at the Conservatorio della Pietà de' Turchini in Naples.

CAVALLINI, Ernesto. Milan, 30 Aug 1807-1874 Jan 7, Milan. Italian. He became a pupil at the Milan Conservatoire at the age of ten, under Carulli, who had just been appointed clarinet professor. Both he and his brother, the violinist Eugenio Cavallini, performed at the Conservatoire concerts in the Canobbiana Theatre in 1830, their final year. Shortly after this Ernesto was made solo clarinet at La Fenice in Venice. He then played in a Piedmontese band for a short time and returned to Milan where he was made second clarinet at La Scala, with Carulli playing first. In 1837 he performed at Cano and the following year did an extensive tour, part of it with his brother, who was now leader at La Scala, and the flautist Rabboni. He played at Trieste, Florence, Parma, Leghorn, Genoa, Turin, and returned once more to Milan where he took over principal clarinet at La Scala. He became friends with Mercadante at about this time, writing an Andante and Variations on a theme of the composer's and also dedicating Six Grand Duos to him. Rossini was a great admirer of Cavallini and so was Verdi, who wrote all his big clarinet solos with Cavallini in mind, the most notable of which is the obligato and cadenza in the third act of *La Forza del Destino.*

In August 1839 Cavallini performed at the opera and gave a private concert in Vienna. The Viennese were surprised to see that he was using a primitive boxwood clarinet of six keys. On 23rd January 1842 he performed a Fantasia of his own composition for the Société des Concerts in Paris. Commenting on this concert, Elwart writes: "An artist of skillful and mellow performance, his quality of sound was extremely beautiful. He was very well received by the Conservatoire public, who do not like instrumental solos much." Cavallini then travelled to London and was invited to play for the Philharmonic Society, on 2nd May. The directors objected to his choice of work, a Fantasia of his own composition, but Cavallini refused to play anything else and they had to give in. The audience found his technique marvellous and were amazed at his apparently inexhaustible breath. Lazarus heard him and some years later told Sir George Grove that "although his tone was not of the purest, he might well be called the Paganini of the clarinet for his wonderful execution." He thought Cavallini's intonation was poor, but Fétis commends both intonation and tone. In December 1842 Cavallini was in Paris again and was made an honorary member of the Académie des Beaux-Arts. Other titles he received were: "Virtuoso di Camera" to the Duchess Maria Luigia of Modena and Parma (1846), Member of the Philharmonic Society of Rome, Member of the Philharmonic Society of Bergamo. On 23rd June 1845 Cavallini again played a Fantasia for the Philharmonic Society of London.

Towards the end of 1851 he gave a concert in Barcelona. The following year he gave up his appointments in Milan and travelled via Vienna and Pesth to St Petersburg, where he made his home for eighteen years. He played in the court and theatre orchestras from 1852 to 1867 and achieved immense popularity as a soloist. Anton Rubinstein founded the St Petersburg Conservatoire in 1862 and invited Cavallini to become its first clarinet professor, a post he held until 1870. Cavallini also taught singing while he was in Russia and composed for the voice. In 1870 he left St Petersburg and returned to Milan. He was made deputy professor at the Milan Conservatoire and trained some fine pupils. A noteworthy pupil from his earlier Milan years was Labanchi. De Groot dedicated his Grand Fantasia on Russian Themes to Cavallini.

Works: Concerto in E flat (Bertuzzi – MiBC). Concerto op.4 in C minor (Carulli – MiBC). Concerto for flute & clarinet (Tagliobo & Magrini). Adagio e Tarantella (Ricordi). Adagio, Theme & Variations with Coda (Ricordi). Andante & Variations on a Theme of Mercadante (Ricordi). 30 Caprices (Ricordi – LRCM). Casta Diva. Chant grec varié (Ricordi). Elegie (Ricordi). Fantasia on an original theme (Ricordi). Fantasia on *Il Trovatore.* Fantasia on motifs from Bellini's *Sonnambula* (Ricordi). Fantasia, Souvenir of *Norma* (Ricordi – BoLM). Fiori Rossiniani, dedicated to Giovanni Ricordi, founder of the publishing firm (Ricordi – LRAM). Potpourri on themes from *Robert le Diable* (Ricordi – LRAM). Rêverie Russe (LRAM). Scherzo from *Don Pasquale* (Ricordi). Serenata (Ricordi). Variations on a theme from Bellini's *Straniera* (Ricordi). Variations on motifs from Donizetti's *L'Elisir d'amore* (Ricordi). Variations on the Carnival of Venice (Schlesinger). 2 Duos for clarinet & piano (with Pietro Bona); no.2, on melodies from Donizetti's *Lucrecia Borgia*, dedicated to "Madame Fanny de Capitani D'Arzago de Balabio" (Ricordi c.1850). 6 Grand Duos, dedicated to Mercadante (Ricordi). Trio for flute, oboe & clarinet.

Bibliography:

CERMINARA, Napolean – "Ernesto Cavallini." TC, Spring 1950. Reprint, Winter 1956/7.

TENNEY, Wallace – "Ernesto Cavallini: Paganini of the Clarinet." WM, December 1949.

CHARDON, Jean. Metz, 9 Nov 1786-1867. French. He was the son of David Chardon, director of music at Metz, and for many years played in the theatre orchestra there.

CHARLES, "the Hungarian." See OV. Mr Charles' place as the first known virtuoso on the clarinet has been usurped by Messrs Freudenfeld and Rosenburg, who performed on the instrument in London during 1726. Mr Charles was nonetheless in London earlier than was originally thought and on 1st April 1735 performed on the clarinet and horn at the Swan Tavern in the City. On 11th March 1737 he gave a concert at Stationers Hall when he played the chalumeau as well as clarinet and horn. Two of his horn pupils also performed on this occasion, "an English Gentlewoman" and a negro boy of ten. In 1739 he performed on the horn again and was advertising for pupils. He was in Dublin during 1756. In the library of Sir Samuel Hellier at Wombourne Wodehouse there is a "Concerto in D" by "Sig. Charles" for horns or trumpets; Dr Horace Fitzpatrick dates this between 1753 and 1756.

CHELARD, André. ?-1802 May 18, Paris. French. He was a member of the National Guard in 1793 and taught at the Institut National. In 1795, at the opening of the Paris Conservatoire, was made a solfège professor of the second class. In 1800 he was made a clarinet professor and as such was a member of the committee appointed in 1801 to discuss the official tutor which Lefèvre had been commissioned to write. Chelard played second clarinet to Ernest for the Concert Spirituel in 1790 and later to Lefèvre at the Opéra. His son was the composer Hippolyté Chelard.

CHIAFFARELLI, A. He was first clarinet in the New York Philharmonic Orchestra in 1917.

CHRISTIANI, Philippe (Xaverius). Amsterdam, 1787-1867, Amsterdam. Dutch. He was the son of a prosperous musical instrument maker, but his parents were against his making music his career and he did so in opposition to their wishes. He taught himself to begin with and then after lessons from the elder Planke and Vincent Springer his talent developed quickly. At the age of fourteen, in 1801, he became a member of the orchestra at the French Opera in Amsterdam. He soon became first clarinet and remained in this post until 1840. From about 1813 to 1850 he played in the court orchestra. He played for the Felix Meritis Society for forty years and was popular throughout the Netherlands as a soloist. He was also a good teacher, one of his best pupils being Van der Finck. In his early years Christiani was much involved with army life: 1801 as a bandsman in a Batavian Republic regiment, 1805 as music director to a band under King Louis-Bonaparte, 1811 as conductor of Napoleon's National Guard, and 1812 as a participant in the Battle of Naarden. He retired in 1850 and was made a *Chevalier de l'ordre de la Couronne de chêne.* Christiani married in 1806. His daughter, Cornelia Helena Anna, became the wife of the painter Lambertus Johannes Hansen.

Christiani's principal concerts in Amsterdam were as follows: 1816 – concerto by Crusell; concerto by Wilms, the composer of the Dutch national anthem; Variations with Turkish Music by Benucci, Amsterdam's music director. 1817 – concertos by Benucci, Röhner (probably a misprint for Boehmer – q.v.) and Schneider (probably G. Abraham Schneider). 1820 – double concerto by Krommer with a pupil. 1823 – double concerto by Krommer with J.C. Kleine. 1825 – Lindpaintner's Concerto.

CHRISTMAN, H. He was second clarinet in the New York Philharmonic Orchestra in 1917.

CHRISTOPH, Wilhelm. Berlin, 1810-1859 Feb 25, Berlin. German. At eighteen he was a clarinettist in the Emperor Franz Grenadier regiment. Later he was made conductor of this and of a choir used for religious services in the army. He became an important member of the Prussian military staff and in 1853 accompanied King Friedrich Wilhelm IV to Vienna on a visit to examine the standard of Austrian military music, which was said to be the best in Europe. The Prussians did not find it better than their own and no major reforms were carried out as a result of the visit. Christoph died of small-pox in 1859. He composed a small amount of military music.

CIMETTA. Italian. He played in the orchestra of Venice's La Fenice theatre in 1823 and 1824.

CLAUS (CLAUSS). German. He also played bassoon and violin. In 1803 he became a member of the Leipzig Gewandhaus Orchestra and took part in the following performances as clarinet soloist: 1807 – 8th January, Krommer's double concerto op.35 with Wilhelm Barth. 1809 – 5th January, a double concerto by Tausch with Barth. 1810 – 1st March, works unknown. 1811 – 31st January, concerto by Carl Heinrich Meyer. After this he left the orchestra to go into a regiment band – possibly the Highland Regiment at Clausthal, of which Meyer was the conductor.

CLAUSÉ. French. He was the only clarinet player in the orchestra of the Cirque Olympique at Paris in 1822 and 1823.

CLERMONT. French. He was first clarinet at the Porte St Martin theatre in Paris from 1822 to 1826. From 1828 to 1833 he held a similar post at the Théâtre des Variétés. In 1822 he lived at no.28 rue de Lancry and the following year moved to no.354 rue du faubourg St Denis.

CLINTON, Arthur. English. See OV. He was a clarinettist and bandmaster, the father of George and James.

Works: Fantasia on Bellini's *La Somnambula* (Hawkes). Fantasia on Donizetti's *Lucrezia Borgia* (Hawkes). Fantasia on The Keel Row, dedicated to his son James (Lafleur).

CLINTON, George (Arthur). Newcastle-on-Tyne, 16 Dec 1850-1913 Oct 24, London. English. See OV. His Clinton-Boehm clarinets, which he played from 1890 until his death, are in the Boosey & Hawkes Collection at Edgware. A pair of Barret-system instruments made by Buffet-Crampon which he used before this are in the Rendall Collection, Edinburgh. Clinton taught at Trinity College of Music from 1892 to 1912. In 1909 he made a revised and fingered edition of Berr's tutor, which was published by Boosey & Co. His address from 1886 until his death was no.15 Devereux Road, Wandsworth. His solo performances, for the Philharmonic Society except where otherwise stated, were as follows: 1876 – 1st April at the Crystal Palace, Spohr's Concerto op.26. October at the Crystal Palace, Weber's Concertino. 1877 – 25th June, Cherubini's "Ave Maria." 1885 – 28th May, Spohr's "The Maiden & the Bird." 1887 – 24th March, Mozart's Symphonie Concertante. 1892 – 10th March, Mozart's "Parto!" 1898 – May, for the Clinton Chamber Concerts, Walthew's Trio for clarinet, violin & piano, and obligato to his song "The Song of Love and Death." 1899 – 4th May, Mozart's "Parto!"

CLINTON, James. Newcastle-on-Tyne, 18 Sept 1852-1897 Feb 4, London. English. See OV. He founded the Clarinettists' Society of London. An example of his Combination-Clarinet can be seen in the Boosey & Hawkes Collection, Edgware.

COMPAGNON. He and Lankammer were reported as

"two clever clarinesttists" who in 1759 were going to be engaged for the court orchestra at St Petersburg. There is no evidence that Compagnon ever played in the orchestra, but Lankammer did.

CONRAD. He played first clarinet at the Théâtre des Variétés in Paris from 1821 to 1827. He lived at no.27 rue Poissonnière.

CORMAN, Giuseppe. Italian. In 1788 he was playing in the orchestra at Santa Croce, Florence.

CORTESI. Italian. He played second clarinet in the Hallé Orchestra at Manchester from its inception in 1858, until 1860.

CRÉMONT, Pierre. Aurillac, 1784-1846 March 12, Tours. French. He studied clarinet and violin at the Paris Conservatoire from 1800 to 1803. He then travelled in Germany with some itinerant comedians and went on to St Petersburg where he became music director at the French Theatre until 1817. He returned to Paris and played in the first violins at the Opéra Comique until 1824. After this he made a successful career as a conductor.

Work: Concerto no.1 op.4 in E flat, dedicated to "son ami Dacosta, Premier Clarinette de l'Académie Royale de Musique" (By 1808. Gambaro 1817 or later – AKVM, BoLM, LRAM, WLC. Breitkopf & Härtel).

CRÉPIN (CRESPIN), Théodore Nicolas Charles. French. He was a pupil of Lefèvre at the Paris Conservatoire, gaining First Prize in 1821. In that year he played second clarinet at the Théâtre de la Gaité, but does not appear in the theatre lists for subsequent years. He is said to have played at many concerts in Paris.

CRISPIN. ?-1854, Darmstadt. Originally a drummer-boy in a bodyguard regiment, he then became a clarinettist. From 1819 he was a court musician at Darmstadt. He also played the violin.

CRONER, Antonio (Raffaello) José. 1828-1884. Portuguese. He learnt the clarinet from José Avelino Canongia and became a well-known performer. He also played the oboe and saxophone.

CRUCIANO. Italian. He was a well-known clarinettist in Rome. On 13th June 1834 he shared a concert in the theatre with the singer Dionilla Santolini. On 15th December 1836 he was the principal soloist at a concert given by Duke Alessandro Turlonia, which was attended by a brilliant gathering of princesses, cardinals, bishops and members of the diplomatic corps.

CRUSELL, Bernhard (Henrik). Nystad, 15 Oct 1775-1838 July 28, Stockholm. Finnish. See OV. In his autobiography Crusell says that when he went to Berlin in the Spring of 1798 to have lessons from Tausch his ego was considerably deflated because the great teacher took him back to the beginning with fundamental scale exercises. Crusell was given leave for this visit until October and towards the end of his stay he gave a recital in Berlin. This was well attended and the receipts were good, but Tausch kept most of the money in payment for lessons, allowing Crusell only enough for the first stage of his journey back. Crusell gave two concerts with Hurka, the Berlin court singer, at Hamburg and these raised the necessary funds to get him to Stockholm. The appearance in Crusell's concert programmes in later years of a duet for horn and clarinet by Tausch, which is not known to have been published or played by any other artist, suggests that Crusell possessed the manuscript of this.

In the autumn of 1799 Crusell married Anna Sofia Klemming. Theirs was a happy union, blessed with six children. Two sons and an unmarried daughter only survived their father. Crusell visited Finland in the summer of 1801 to see his own father, who died the following year. He was already becoming well known through his solo performances in Stockholm and also sought after for private gatherings. One of his patrons, Count Trolle-Bonde, at whose manor Crusell was a frequent guest, was the dedicatee of the Concerto op.1. Crusell composed this concerto in 1803, probably before his Paris visit.

In April or May 1803 he travelled with M. de Bourgoing to Paris. This time he wanted to study with Lefèvre and gained entrée to the Conservatoire, normally barred to foreigners, through the good offices of Gossec. Crusell entered heartily into the musical life of the city and would dearly have liked to stay to the following Spring but, as before, his leave expired in October. As he had been offered the post of first clarinet at the Théâtre Italien he journeyed to Carlsruhe where his King, Gustavus Adolphus, was on a long visit, to ask for an extension of his leave. The extension was not granted, but Crusell was invited to play before the Court and presented with a beautiful gold box by the Elector of Baden.

Back in Stockholm, Crusell resumed his duties as first clarinet in the court orchestra and also became assistant conductor. On the resignation of Haeffner in 1808 he was made temporary director for a year, but the post was then given to Du Puy. Du Puy died in 1822 and Crusell again applied for the post, but his favourite daughter Sofia died suddenly and he withdrew his name from the list of candidates. Crusell was most unwell himself at this time, with an attack of vertigo and the recurrence of a nervous disorder he had had since childhood. This made him withdraw also from playing for a time. By adhering to a strict diet his condition gradually improved and in 1824 he was able to take up his playing again. His solo performances were now infrequent and he gave his last public concert in 1830. His last private concert was at the castle for the Queen's birthday on 8th November 1831.

Crusell's music was the spark that ignited Glinka's flame to life. In 1814 the 10-year-old Glinka heard one of Crusell's clarinet quartets (probably op.2) played by serf musicians at his uncle's estate in Smolensk and many years later wrote in his autobiography: "This music produced an unbelievable, novel and quite delectable impression on me . . . . . indeed, from that time I passionately loved music." Crusell was reported to be a kindly, warm-hearted and unselfish man, unassuming in character. He was much sought after as a teacher, the following being his best known pupils: Andreas Addner, K.F. Böhme, G.G. Gerlach, Kellman, Kindgren, Carl Köbel, Wetterström, possibly also Carl Ehrenreich and J.A. Fabian. In 1830 Peters asked him to write a method, but he declined.

Crusell's performances in Stockholm included the following: 1795 – 19th April, an unnamed concerto. 1797 – 15th January, concerto by Johann Friedrich Grenser (oboist to the King of Sweden and cousin of Heinrich Grenser, maker of Crusell's clarinet). 25th March, concerto by Michel (Yost). 12th July, unnamed concerto. 1798 – 24th March, concerto by Tausch and variations by Du Puy. 1799 – 20th February, concerto by Tausch. 13th April, Winter's Concerto and unnamed aria with clarinet obligato. 1800 – 8th February & 15th March, ditto. 22nd December, unnamed aria with clarinet. 1802 – 18th April, duet for horn & clarinet said to be by himself but more probably by Tausch – see 14th May 1805 and 4th January 1807. 18th May, concerto by Lebrun and obligato to an aria by Winter. 13th November, Mozart's Concerto (this is the earliest known performance after the work's publication) and a vocal duet with clarinet & bassoon obligato by Reichardt. 1803 – 2nd & 23rd March, Lebrun's Concerto. 20th November, Adagio & Rondo by Grenser. 1804 – 4th March, Mozart's Concerto and Variations by himself. 25th March, his own variations and an aria with clarinet & bassoon obligato by Righini. 8th April, Grenser's Adagio & Rondo. 15th April, Lebrun's Concerto. 27th May, Winter's Concerto. 20th October, his "Variationer på visan: Goda gosse, glaset töm M.M." (op.12?). 1805 – Prologue for clarinet, violin &

orchestra by Oxenstierna. 20th January, a double concerto by Krommer with Schatt. 1st February, Grenser's Adagio & Rondo. 24th February, his Adagio & Variations (op.12?). 25th March, Mozart's "Sextet" (Quintet?) and Beethoven's Septet. 14th May, a concerto by himself and duet for horn & clarinet by Tausch. 10th October, Beethoven's Septet. 16th November, Grenser's Adagio & Rondo and his own "Var. på en svensk national-melodi." 23rd November, trio for clarinet, horn & bassoon by "Jarden" (probably Louis Emmanuel Jadin). 1806 – 8th March, a concerto by Krommer and a duet for horn & clarinet by Skapelsen. 30th March, Mozart's Trio K498 (this is the first known performance). 20th May, Beethoven's Septet. 26th November, a double concerto by Krommer. 10th December, Winter's Concerto. 1807 – 4th January, duet for horn & clarinet by Tausch. 20th February, Mozart's "Quartet" (Quintet?). 27th February, his own Adagio & Variations. 2nd March, concerto by himself. 20th March, his Concerto op.1. 2nd April, Winter's Concerto. 10th April, Lebrun's Concerto. 25th April, Beethoven's Septet. 29th April, Winter's Concerto. 9th May, a concerto by Krommer. 14th May, Sextet for clarinet, horn & strings by Eggert. 2nd September, Grenser's Adagio & Rondo. 24th October, a concerto by Krommer. 28th December, Winter's Concerto. 1808 – 4th January, concerto by himself. 5th February, Grenser's Concerto. 27th February, an aria with clarinet & bassoon obligato by Stenborg. 19th March, his own variations. 2nd April, a concerto by Krommer and his own Symphonie Concertante op.3 (this was probably the first performance). 9th April, his op.3. 8th May, Winter's Concerto. 1812 – 17th November, Beethoven's Wind Quintet and his own "Variations in B flat" (op.12?). 17th December, Beethoven's Wind Quintet. 1813 – February, Winter's Concerto. 13th April, his Symphonie Concertante op.3. 20th April, his concerto op.1. 10th September, an Adagio & Rondo by Du Puy. 11th November, Beethoven's Septet. 23rd December, his "Variations on a Swedish Drinking Song" (op.12?). 1814 – 19th March, concerto by Du Puy and the obligato to an aria by himself for Mme Casagli. 26th March, trio by himself. 3rd April, his Symphonie Concertante op.3. September, Du Puy's Adagio & Rondo. 26th November, Beethoven's Septet. 1815 – March, concerto by himself and obligato to an aria by himself for Mme Casagli. 8th April, his own Adagio & Polacca (op.11?). April, Paer's "una voce al cor mi parla" for Mlle Wäselia. 6th May, a concerto by himself. 20th May, a double concerto by Krommer. November, his own Adagio & Rondo (op.1). 1816 – 9th November, a potpourri by Danzi. 1817 – 22nd November, Mozart's "Parto!" for Mlle Wäselia. December, a concerto by himself. 1818 –

January, Berwald's Septet. 29th May, Winter's Concerto. 15th November, Beethoven's Septet. 1819 – 11th February, a potpourri by Danzi. 13th & 20th March, Mozart's "Parto!" for Mlle Wäselia. 4th April, a concerto by himself. 7th December, Berwald's Septet. 14th December for Schatt's Benefit, a concerto by Krommer and Winter's Concertante for 2 violins, clarinet, horn, bassoon & cello.

Works: Concerto op.1 in E flat, dedicated to Count Gustave de Trolle-Bonde (1803. Kühnel 1811 – SKB, SKMA, ZAM. Peters – BoLM, MBS. Gambaro. Richault). Grand Concerto op.5 in F minor, dedicated to Alexander I, Emperor of Russia & King of Poland (Peters 1816 – BoLM, LRAM, MarPKS, SKB, ZAM). Concerto op.11 in B flat, dedicated to Prince Oscar of Sweden & Norway (Peters 1828 – BoLM, SKB, SKMA, VGM, ZAM). Introduction & Swedish Air Varié op.12 in B flat (see concert lists for permutations of this title) (Peters 1829 – BDS, SBS, SKB, ZAM. Richault – PBN). A concertante for 2 clarinets & wind orchestra listed by Nisser and by Spicknall is not an original work, although the hand-written copy in SKMA attributes it to Crusell; it is an arrangement of Krommer's double concerto op.35. Concertante op.3 in B flat for clarinet, horn & bassoon, dedicated to Baron Gustave d'Akerhjelm (Peters 1816 – OSB, SKB, SKMA, SKTB, VGM). 3 Progressive Duets op.6 in F, D minor & C (Part Ms. in BDS. Gambaro c.1818 – SKMA. Peters 1820/21 – SKB, SKMA. Richault). Grand Duets for Advanced Clarinettists in C, F, C, G & C (Seeling – BDS). Concert Trio in F for clarinet, horn & bassoon (Hand-written copies in SKMA). Quartet op.2 in E flat (Kühnel 1812 – AaS, SKMA, WLC, ZAM. Costallat. Richault). Quartet op.4 in C minor, dedicated to M. Genséric Brandel (Peters 1816 – SKB, SKMA, WLC. Gambaro. Richault). Quartet op.7 in D, dedicated to Count Gustave de Loewenhielm (Peters 1823 – AaS, BoLM, SKB, SKMA). (The flute quartet op.8 in D is identical to op.7). Air for soprano & clarinet (unpublished).

Bibliography:

RAU, Ulrich – "Bernhard Henrik Crusell." MGG Supplement, 1972.
SPICKNALL, John – *The Solo Clarinet Works of Bernhard Henrik Crusell.* (Unpublished Dissertation). University Microfilms, 1974.
WESTON, Pamela – "Finnish Virtuoso." MM, October 1975.

CUBONI, Raimund. Sardinian. He was first clarinet in the court orchestra at Modena in 1825. He played other instruments as well as the clarinet.

CURTH. German. He was a clarinettist in the court

orchestra at Kassel. In 1838 he played Iwan Müller's double concerto with Bättenhausen. In 1841 he took part in the Symphonie Concertante for 4 clarinets by Schindelmeisser with Bättenhausen, Kollman and Wenderoth.

CZERMACK (CZERMAK), Abundius. Schlan, 1768-? Czech. He also played the violin, flute and oboe. He entered the Order of Charitable Brothers at Prague in 1791, but left it the following year. He married Mlle Nuth, a Prague singer, and they settled at Königsberg about 1809. On 7th April 1810 he played Cartellieri's Concerto, and Mozart's "Parto!" for Wilhelmine Müller. He performed again on April 18th, but had eventually to give up playing wind instruments owing to a physical weakness. In 1815 he was engaged as scene painter at the opera theatre.

(B–H). **CZERNY, Kaspar.** Born at Horzig. Czech. Dlabacz says he learnt the basset-horn at Prague University, then left his fatherland and spent some time in St Petersburg. When he came back from Russia he was employed with Matauschek and Oliva by Princess Poniatowsky, who sent them to Linz to perfect themselves on the basset-horn, probably with Glöggl. In 1781 the three toured Germany and Russia, playing trios for clarinet and basset-horn. In 1786 Czerny was employed as third basset-horn and bassoon at the Court of Princess Elizabeth of Baden-Baden at Freiburg in Breisgau, in company with Kirstein (first basset-horn & clarinet), Matauschek (second basset-horn & bassoon) and Tirry (clarinet).

DACOSTA, (Isaac) Franco. Bordeaux, 17 Jan 1778-1866 July 12, Bordeaux. He also played the bass clarinet. His father was Jewish, probably of Spanish origin, and earned a living as a merchant in Bordeaux. He was a good amateur violinist and taught Franco the rudiments of music, also to play the flageolet. Dacosta then took up the clarinet, which he taught himself. On this he made rapid progress and at fourteen was playing in the band for the local garrison. After the success of a concert he gave in 1796 in the town theatre he determined to go to Paris and set off the following year with a pianist friend. They took three months over their journey, paying their way by giving concerts in the towns and villages en route. Dacosta entered as a pupil at the Paris Conservatoire under Lefèvre and gained a First Prize in 1798. He was then conscripted into the Directoire Guards, which the following year became Consular Guards. Pierre Rode, the Consul's solo violinist, recognized Dacosta's talent and in 1802 was instrumental in getting him made solo clarinet. Dacosta remained in this post when the regiment became Imperial Guards in 1804. Many years later, in the reign of Charles X, he became assistant director of the band.

Besides his military appointments, Dacosta played a big part in the general musical life of the city. From 1798 to 1802 he played at the Théâtre Moliére, 1802 to 1807 at the Théâtre Feydau (Opera Comique) and from 1807 to 1817 was first clarinet at the Théâtre Italien. He then shared first clarinet at the Opéra with Louis Lefèvre and in 1825 became principal clarinet on his own. In 1833 he stepped down to second and remained in this position until 1842, when he retired on a pension. Dacosta also played first clarinet for the Société des Concerts from their inauguration in 1828. As if this was not enough, he became a member of Napoleon's orchestra in 1805 and remained in the court orchestra under the Restoration in 1815, when he was also made assistant director of the bodyguard for the tragic Duchess d'Angoulême. Dacosta married a daughter of Abraham Fleury, the great French comedian. They had several children, but it was not a happy marriage and they eventually separated. On his retirement Dacosta went back to live at Bordeaux, his birthplace. At the age of eighty five he lost his sight, but does not appear to have suffered for want of companionship, and at the funeral service, which was conducted by the Chief Rabbi, there was a large number of devoted friends. Dacosta lived at the following addresses: 1821 – no.8 faubourg Poissonnière; 1822 – no.33 rue de Grenelle St Honoré; 1825 – no.5 rue Froidmanteau; from c.1830 – no.70 rue Montmartre.

Opinions about Dacosta's playing are varied. In 1805, when he performed his own compositions at the Ridotto Room in the rue de Grenelle, they said he had a fine tone and considerable dexterity. They found his compositions commonplace. When he shared a concert with the flautist Tulou and horn-player Puzzi in 1817 the reviewer said the tone of all three players was dead. Although none of them had reached the age of forty, he further remarked that they were not in a condition to put life into their playing. Sievers, on the other hand, after a performance by Dacosta of Heinrich Baermann's Variations in E flat in June 1818, found Dacosta's power of flying up and down the instrument exceeded that of Baermann himself, whom Paris had heard earlier in the year. Mendelssohn, writing to his dear friend Baermann on 16th April 1832, after attending the Société des Concerts, gives the following anecdote of Dacosta: "There are two clarinets, neither of them fit to dust your coat, if tone, execution, mode of playing and ordinary fairness still go for anything in this world. The first one recently, in the minuet of the Pastoral Symphony, began his solo a bar too soon, but went on puffing away as merrily as possible, never observing that it sounded quite infamous, and that some of the audience, and among them the undersigned, were making dreadful wry faces, and that the director had got stomach-ache; the horn ought then to have come in, but took fright and did not come in, on which the violins took fright also and played softer and softer, on which the thing every moment became more like a Dutch concert, for they were all out, and only a movement in three-four time being close at hand saved them from the disgrace of stopping short, or beginning all over again . . . . . This fellow is a Professor in the Conservatoire, and, I understand, the best here. I believe his name is Dacosta." Another friend of Baermann's, the composer Meyerbeer, probably had a higher opinion of Dacosta and in the years 1836 to 1838 was much in his company.

When Dumas' 13-keyed bass clarinet was recommended to the Imperial Guard in 1810 the bandsmen, used to instruments of six keys, rejected it. There seems little doubt that Dacosta, in his position as solo clarinettist to the band, was a major influence in this decision. Another example of opposition to the idea of instruments with more than twice the normal number of keys came two years later when the Conservatoire rejected Müller's clarinet out of hand. Dacosta could be accused of an ulterior motive, for by 1814 he had himself made some improvements to the bass clarinet. By 1822 he was actually using a 12-keyed soprano instrument. Dumas apparently bore him no grudge and on his deathbed in 1832 presented his beloved bass clarinet to Dacosta. Dacosta lost no time in benefitting from the gift and in collaboration with Louis-Auguste Buffet produced an instrument of similar design. This model, with a straight body and curved crook to carry the mouthpiece, he introduced to the public in a recital at the Salle Saint-Jean de l'Hôtel-de-Ville. Fétis says that he played with such ease and rapidity that it might have been a soprano clarinet, and that his tone was strong yet mellow. It was announced in the press during 1839 that Dacosta was going to travel abroad to demonstrate the new bass clarinet. This provoked Sax, who had just produced a greatly improved instrument, to journey to Paris to see Dacosta. He went straight to Dacosta's house and insisted on demonstrating the solo from Meyerbeer's *Les Huguenots.* Mme Dacosta is said to have exclaimed to her husband: "When M. Sax plays, *your* instrument sounds like a kazoo!" Dacosta was bound to admit the advantages of Sax's instrument and complimented the young virtuoso on his skill both as a performer and inventor. He gave up the projected tour and was not long in acquiring a Sax instrument for himself.

Works: Concerto op.1 no.1 in B flat (Chapelle c.1802/4 – PBN. Janet). Concerto no.2 in C (Jouve c.1818. Hentz). Concerto no.3 in E flat (Sieber). Concerto no.4. Concertino, dedicated to Berr. Souvenir, fantaisie (Costallat). Air de Garat, with string quartet (Gaveaux). Air de Mozart varié, with string quartet (Dufaut & Dubois). Étude pour les cadences de la clarinette à douze clefs (Dacosta c.1822 – PBN).

Bibliography:
Obituary – SM. 30 July 1866.

DAHLINGER. In 1785 he was engaged for the court orchestra at Carlsruhe.

DAMSE, Józef. Sokotow, 23 Jan 1788-1852 Dec 15, Rudno. Polish. He also played the trombone, composed and acted. He was first a bandsman, then a regimental music director and in 1814 settled in Warsaw as director of the theatre. In January 1815 he performed a Lefèvre concerto "dexterously". He composed religious works and some forty operatic pasticcios, but nothing for the clarinet. He died at the country home of his daughter Therese, who was a well known actress.

DANAÏS. He was second clarinet at the Théâtre du Vaudeville in Paris in 1829.

(B–H). **DAVID, Anton.** Offenbourg (near Strasbourg), 1730-1796, Löwenburg. German. See OV. He was one of the first virtuosi on both clarinet and basset-horn. He learnt the clarinet at Strasbourg and in 1750 travelled to Italy where he spent the next ten years employed at various courts. In 1760 he moved to Hungary where he was employed by Prince Breschinski. Later he moved on to St Petersburg but the climate affected his chest and he came back to Hungary. Here in the 1770s he learnt to play the basset-horn, for he felt this might be less fatiguing than the clarinet. The instrument he used was pitched in G and had 7 keys with a diatonic extension. He played the basset-horn to the Berlin Court in 1780. The following year he travelled back to St Petersburg in company with Vincent Springer, to whom it is said he taught the clarinet. They left St Petersburg in the early part of 1782 and later that year played at Berlin and Lübeck. David's health had apparently improved, for he played the clarinet again at Hamburg in November. In 1783 he travelled with Springer and Dworschak in Germany, and then parted company with his friends, leading a dissolute life and scraping a living by playing in the streets and taverns.

He is next heard of with Springer in October 1785 at Vienna. They had failed to find employment in the town and did not have enough money to get themselves elsewhere. The freemasons of Vienna came to their rescue and the "Three Eagles" and "Palmtree" lodges put on a concert to raise funds for them, at which Brothers Mozart and Stadler performed. A second assembly was held for their benefit on 15th December, when the "Crowned Hope" was host, and on this occasion the visitors contributed a concerto for 2 basset-horns.

The following year Baron Hochberg of Plogwitz in Silesia rescued them both from poverty, housed them and gave them employment. They visited Leipzig in 1787 and on 17th December performed a work for 2 basset-horns and cello with Carl Wilhelm Möller. David remained at Plogwitz until the Baron died in 1789 and during this time taught clarinet and basset-horn to the Krause brothers. In the summer of 1789 he travelled to London with Springer and Dworschak and played in the concerts at the Vauxhall Gardens. The trio toured again in the summer of 1790, playing in Germany, northern Italy and Holland. They were back in London again for the Vauxhall Garden season of 1791, playing a wide variety of solo and concerted items for clarinet and basset-horn. From 1790 to 1792 David joined Springer with an appointment at the Court of Bentheim-Steinfürt. After this he once more became a vagabond and died at Löwenburg in a state of acute distress.

Works: 6 Trios for 3 basset-horns.

DAZZI. Italian. He played the clarinet at a concert in Marseilles in 1833 with the flautist Bertini and trumpet-player Liugin.

DEICHERT. In 1829 he joined the court orchestra at Kassel as bass clarinet player and violinist. At the Kassel Subscription Concerts on 14th January 1830 he performed an Adagio & Variations for bass clarinet, and an arrangement of a folk song for bass and contrabass clarinets, the contrabass being played by Conrad Bänder. In 1846 Deichert moved to Marburg University as director of music. He composed dance music, but nothing for the clarinet.

DELAMOTTE (DELAMOTHE, LA MOTHE), Gabriel Eugène. Paris, 19 May 1796-? French. He won Second Prize at the Paris Conservatoire in 1822 and in the same year obtained a post as clarinettist at the Panorama Dramatique. During 1824 and 1825 he played at the Ambigu Comique and in 1826 became second clarinet at the Théâtre des Nouveautés, moving up to first clarinet in 1829. He lived at no.37 rue du Bac.

DEMAJO, Babini. Italian. He was teaching at the Conservatoire in Bologna about 1800.

DEMNITZ, Friedrich. Wünschendorf, 12 Jan 1845-1890 Apr 2, Dresden. German. He studied at the Dresden Conservatoire and in 1868 obtained his first post, at the Court of Mecklenburg-Schwerin. In 1875 he came back to Dresden to be first clarinet in the court orchestra. From the same year he became clarinet teacher at the Conservatoire. He formed many fine pupils who included Marhefka, with whom he kept in close touch in after years. Demnitz married Julie Otto, a member of a well-known musical family in Dresden.

Work: Clarinetten Schule (Breitkopf & Härtel. Peters).

DENIS. During the 1786/7 season he was a member of the orchestra for the Société du Concert at Neuchâtel and also played in the royal cavalry band.

DERLIEN, Gotthard Heinrich Andreas. 13 May 1820-1867 Oct 25. He spent most of his life in Lübeck, where he first performed as a clarinet soloist in 1840. In 1859 he performed one of Weber's concertos and in the same year became town musician.

DESVIGNES, Hippolyté. French. He trained at the Paris Conservatoire, gaining a First Prize in 1829. From 1828 to 1830 he was second clarinet at the Théâtre des Variétés.

DETTMANN, Friedrich Elias. Grimmen, 17 Mar 1822-? German. In 1844 he was solo clarinet in the band of the Alexander regiment. In 1860 he was made a Chamber Musician at the Berlin Court.

DICKERHOF, Eduard. ?-1805, Darmstadt. From 1795 until his death he was a court musician at Darmstadt. He also played the violin.

DIETRICH. As a young man, in 1821, he appeared as a clarinet soloist at Pressburg, where he was already a member of the theatre orchestra.

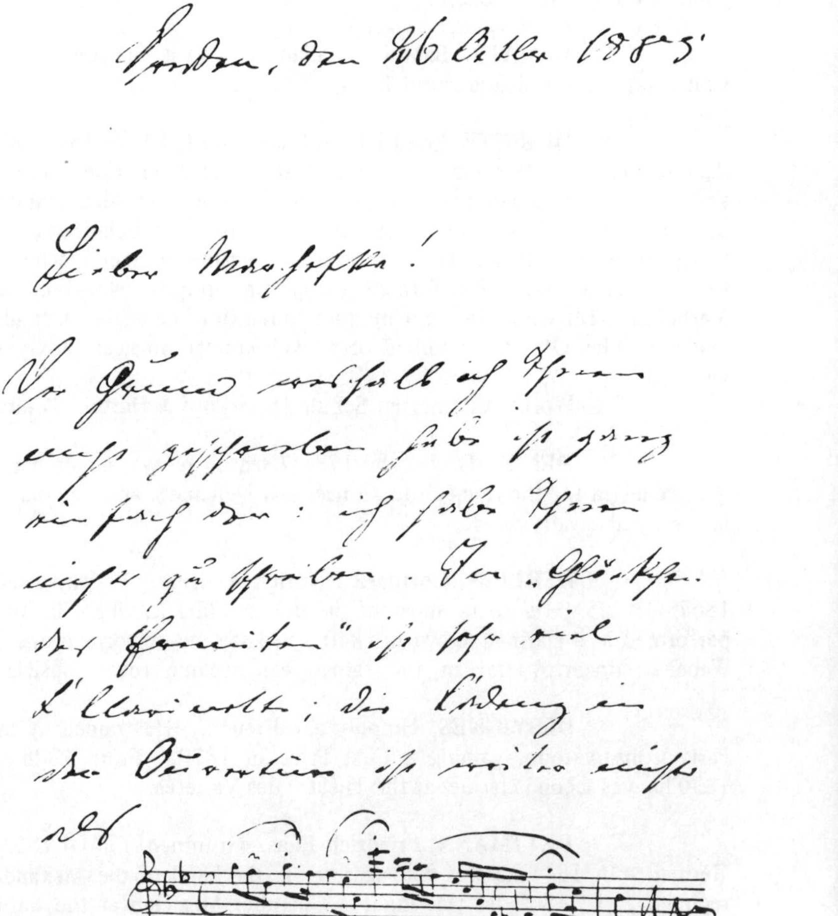

Dresden, den 26 Oktbr 1885

Lieber [illegible]!

Der Grund weshalb ich Ihnen nicht geschrieben habe ist ganz einfach der: ich habe Ihnen nichts zu schreiben. Das „Glöckchen des Eremiten" ist sehr viel Clarinette; die Cadenz in der Ouvertüre ist weiter nichts als

Ich wünsche Ihnen viel Glück damit! Wir sind mitten in den Singspielproben; zum Reformationsfest

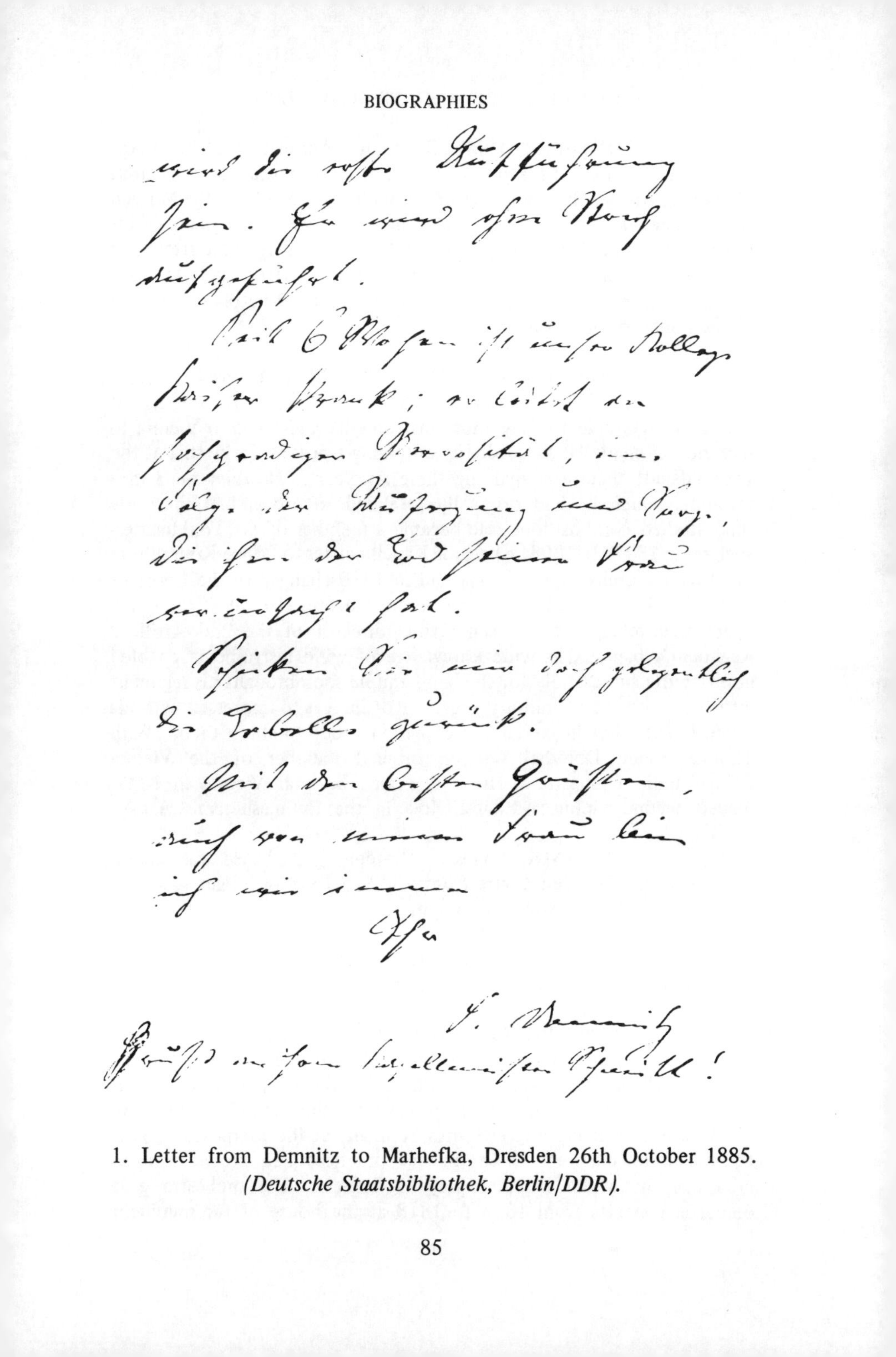

1. Letter from Demnitz to Marhefka, Dresden 26th October 1885. *(Deutsche Staatsbibliothek, Berlin/DDR).*

DIMMLER (DIMLER), Franz (Anton). Munich, 24 Apr 1783-? He also played the guitar. He received his musical training from his father, Anton, the composer and double bass player in the Munich court orchestra. His first appearance in public was at a concert of his father's works on 14th May 1795. In 1796, at the age of thirteen, he was taken on as a clarinettist in the court orchestra and was still occupying this post in 1806. From 1811 to 1829 he played for the Munich Subscription Concerts.

DOBYHAL (DOBIHAL, DOBYHALL), Josef. Krasowitz, 13 June 1779-1864 Sept 16, Vienna. Czech. By the age of fifteen he was able to play most instruments and went to Vienna to seek employment. He succeeded in obtaining a post as clarinettist at the Leopoldstadt theatre, remaining there six years. He then went into teaching, which he had originally intended to do, and at the same time studied composition. He became a member of the Tonkünstlersocietät in 1807. In 1808 he became Kapellmeister to Prince Kourakin at the Russian Embassy in Vienna and in 1810 changed to the Court of Prince Lobkowitz. After this he became second clarinet at the court opera theatre and at the same time director of the 2nd Artillery Regiment's band. His wide knowledge of wind instruments enabled him to write successfully for the band and he soon brought his regiment into the forefront of military music. Rossini was so impressed with his arrangements that he asked for copies in order to study them. With Thomas Klein, Dobyhal was an original member of the Vienna Philharmonic Orchestra. His son Franz, born at Vienna in 1817, played second violin and later viola in the Hellmesberger Quartet.

DOMINIK, August. Dresden, 1821-? He was second clarinet at the Dresden Court from 1840 to 1849 or longer. He also played the violin and piano, and composed.

DONAT. Czech. He was employed at the Court of King Stanislas II at Warsaw about 1780.

DOPPLER, Josef. German. He was an amatuer clarinet, bassoon and viola player in Vienna. He became manager for the publisher Diabelli and was still working for the firm in 1867 after it became C.A. Spina. Doppler was present at Schubert's christening. In 1814 he played string quartets with Schubert at the composer's home. By the following year these quartet practices had grown into an orchestra, in which Doppler played clarinet. The orchestra gave domestic concerts from 1815 to 1818 at the house of the merchant

Franz Frischner. In 1816 Schubert wrote his First Offertorium, *Totus in corde,* which he dedicated to the tenor Ludwig Tietze. Page one of the manuscript bears the inscription: "Allegretto. Aria mit Clarinett-Solo . . . . . für Hr (Josef) Doppler." Pohl, writing in the first edition of Grove's *Dictionary of Music & Musicians,* says: "Troyer is stated, on the authority of Doppler (manager for Diabelli & Co.) to have given Schubert the commission for his well-known Octet."

DORN. German. He was second clarinet in the court orchestra at Rudolstadt in 1811 and also played in the wind music.

DOSSENBACH. German. He was a member of the Duke of Brunswick's orchestra. He gave a private concert on 4th April 1771 at Hamburg.

DOUGLAS, F. English. He was fourth clarinet in the Hallé Orchestra at Manchester in 1900. The following year, until 1906, he was third clarinet.

DRAPER, Charles. Odcombe, 23 Oct 1869-1952 Oct 21, Surbiton. English. See OV. His father was the village carpenter and an amateur flute and cello player. On 9th October 1893 Charles took part in a concert given by Coleridge-Taylor, who like him was then a student at the Royal College of Music, at Croydon's Small Public Hall. The programme included Mozart's Quintet and one movement from a Sonata in F minor by Coleridge-Taylor, who played the piano part. The Sonata, probably never completed, is now lost. On 31st March 1906, again at Croydon's Public Hall, Draper performed Coleridge-Taylor's Quintet, with a quartet led by his friend John Saunders. Draper played first clarinet in the London Symphony Orchestra on occasion, but not on a regular basis. From 1915 to 1937 he taught at Trinity College of Music.

In 1895, when a pupil of Egerton, Draper decided to change to Boehm system clarinets, a move inspired by Manuel Gomez. He chose wide-bored instruments by Martel. These instruments undoubtedly contributed to the extraordinary breadth of his tone. The other important factor was of course his embouchure. There have been conflicting opinions on the latter and the author is indebted to Charles' son, the late William Draper, for putting the matter straight by declaring that his father used double lip. The opinion that he tongued from the roots of his top teeth appears also unfounded, for he certainly taught that it should be done from the reed. Draper tuned instruments for Hawkes & Co. for many years and it was probably due to his influence that the firm imported Boehm clarinets made by Martel during the years 1900 to 1915. In 1923 Draper started his own firm, The Louis Musical Instrument Co. Ltd., at no.2 Burnsall Street, Chelsea. They made clarinets modelled on Martels, as well as other wind instruments, including tabor pipes for the new folk-song movement. The firm was later bought up by Rudall Carte & Co. Ltd., and the premises were vacated.

The following pieces, of a predominantly light character were dedicated to Draper: Lorito Caprice by Francisco Gomez (1896), Andante & Presto by Joseph Holbrooke, Souvenir d'Ispahan by Alfred Pratt, Three Light Pieces by Harold Samuel. Draper made more recordings than any other clarinettist in the pre-electric era. After the advent of electrical methods he made the following memorable discs with the Lener Quartet: Schubert Octet (1927), Brahms Quintet (1928), Mozart Quintet (1929), Beethoven Septet (1930).

Recordings made by Draper not listed in OV:

Brahms – Trio op.114. Columbia 19. With W.H. Squire and Sir H. Harty.

Ravel – Introduction & Allegro. H.M.V. (1927).

Schubert – "The Shepherd on the Rock." Columbia 9613. With "Bella" Baillie.

Weber – Concertino. Gramophone Monarch 06000.

Writing:

"The Clarinet." MY. September 1926.

Bibliography:

WESTON, Pamela – "Charles Draper: the Grandfather of English Clarinettists." MTe. October 1969.

DRAPER, Haydn (Paul). Penarth, 21 Jan 1889-1934 Nov 1, London. English. He was the nephew of Charles Draper and brother of Mendelssohn Draper. He began his training at the age of six, from his father Paul Draper, and at twelve was playing solo clarinet in several bands that his father conducted in the Cardiff area. By thirteen he was in London and playing first clarinet for the Savoy Opera Company. His exceptional talent won him several prizes and then in 1908 a scholarship to the Royal College of Music. Here he learnt first with Julian Egerton and then with his uncle Charles Draper. During his first year at the College he was made a member of the New Symphony Orchestra. In 1911 he toured Germany with the Russian Ballet under Beecham. He played at Covent Garden also under Beecham and at the Leeds Festival. He was principal of the Queen's Hall Orchestra from 1915 to 1930, and from 1927 until his death he led the BBC Military Band. In the 1920s he played with the London Wind

Quintet and he also toured with the Lener String Quartet. He was a remarkably fine soloist, one of his most important concerts being the first British performance of Busoni's Concertino on 6th May 1921 at the Aeolian Hall. From 1923 Haydn taught at the Royal Academy of Music. He used plain Boehm clarinets with no additions and for some time was principal tester in this country for the firm of Albert.

Recordings:

Mozart – Concerto K622. Columbia DB834 (c.1931).
Mozart – Concerto K622. Brunswick 20076/7/8.
Pfyffer – Serenade. Columbia 3288 (c.1920/24).) With Robert
Saint-Saens – Tarantelle. Columbia 3288 (c.1920/24) Murchie
Weber – Grand Duo. (First movement only, abridged).
Pathe (1912). With Lillian Bryant.

DRAPER, Mendelssohn. Penarth, c.1891-1970, London. English. He was the nephew of Charles Draper and brother of Haydn Draper. He played bass clarinet for the London Symphony Orchestra from 1919 to 1923 and 1930 to 1948, and was a member of the clarinet section in the Queen's Hall and Covent Garden orchestras for a considerable time. He was also a professor at the Royal Academy of Music.

DREIKLUFTS (DRYKLOFF). Dutch. He acquired an excellent reputation as a clarinet teacher at Amsterdam. His most famous pupils were J.C. Kleine and Rooms, who both studied with him about 1805.

(B–H). **DRESCHER.** On 27th April 1863 he performed a Phantasie of his own composition for basset-horn and some clarinet solos at Regensburg. He was hailed as from Lima, Peru, and they said his playing was beautifully soft and expressive.

Work: Phantasie for basset-horn.

DREWES, F. He was first clarinet in the New York Philharmonic Orchestra in 1892.

DROBISCH, Johann Gottfried Traugott. Oberspar, 24 May 1784-1848 Feb 21. German. He was a member of the Gewandhaus Orchestra in Leipzig, playing second oboe from 1818 to 1829 and then second clarinet from 1829 to 1837.

DUBOIS, William. French. He also played the lute, sang and composed. He landed in America early in 1795, probably in

South Carolina, where in the same year he performed a concerto of his own composition. He then settled in Philadelphia where there are reports of him playing his own concertos on 26th March 1795, 12th March and 25th April 1798. On 24th April 1798 he had a Benefit concert when he and Beranger performed Pleyel's Symphonie Concertante. Later the same year Dubois played a concerto by Yost. At Baltimore on 26th April 1799 he shared a Benefit with Wolfe and played lute in a "Medley Trio for clarinet, violin and lute." Further performances that year included a duet for clarinet and violin by "Michel" (Yost) and Pleyel's Symphonie Concertante for 2 clarinets. He may be the "W. Dubois" who had a publishing business plus piano and music store at no.126 Broadway, New York, from 1818 to 1826, and who issued about 1818 a "Complete Preceptor for the Clarinet, Containing the most approved Instructions relative to that Instrument, Explained in the most simple and comprehensive manner, including a progressive series of Popular Airs." There is another tutor, also in the Library of Congress, which has an identical title and was published anonymously about 1823 by Frederick Land of Boston.

Works: Concerto(s). Complete Preceptor (Dubois c.1818 – WLC).

DUFOUR. French. He fled from France during the Revolution and lived in Hamburg until 1807 or later, with a post as first clarinet at the theatre. On 8th November 1801 he gave his own concert at the theatre. It may be him or a son who appears in Parisian orchestral lists later as follows: 1821 – first clarinet at the Odéon; 1824/5 – second clarinet at the Odéon; 1827/8 – first clarinet at the Théâtre des Nouveautés; 1831/3 – Théâtre des Folies Dramatiques. His address in 1824 and 1825 was no.276 rue Neuve St Martin.

DUMAS. Sommières, ?-1832, Versailles. French. He was chief goldsmith to Napoleon and also an instrument maker, as well as being a clarinettist. In 1807 he presented a bass clarinet of 13 keys to the Paris Conservatoire for their examination. It was warmly praised by Méhul, Cherubini, Catel and others. Encouraged by this he produced a contrabass the following year, but this was not successful. In 1810 his bass clarinet was recommended to the Imperial Guard but the musicians turned it down because of the increased number of keys. In 1814 he resumed work on the instrument, but became disillusioned and kept it to himself. The events of the following year, with the break-up of the Empire, ruined him. In 1822 he was living in a first floor flat at no.27 rue des Marmousets, but his last days were spent in hospital at Versailles. Before he died he sent for his friend Dacosta and bequeathed to him the precious bass clarinet.

DUPORT, Charles. French. He was clarinettist to Louis François, Prince of Conti, in the 1760s. The cellist, Jean-Pierre Duport, who was employed by the Prince at the same period, was probably his brother.

DUPREZ, E. French. He was a noted bass clarinet player and the brother of the famous singer Gilbert Duprez. He adopted an instrument of Sax's design (preserved in the Museum of the Paris Conservatoire) and brought this to the public's notice in performances of Meyerbeer's *Les Huguenots* and *Le Prophète.* On 3rd February 1844 he took part in the one and only performance at the Salle Herz of Berlioz' "Chant Sacré," which had been written for six of Sax's instruments.

DUQUES, Augustin. Toulouse, 3 Mar 1899-1972 Aug 14, New York. French. Soon after winning the Paris Conservatoire's First Prize in 1919 he went to the United States and became first clarinet in the New York Symphony Orchestra, a post he held for ten years. Later he was principal in the N.B.C. Symphony Orchestra for seventeen years. From 1923 to 1963 Duques taught at the Juilliard School of Music.

Recording:

Mozart – Quintet K452. Stradivari 601.

DUVERNOY, (Jacques Georges) Charles (François). Montbéliard, 1766-1845 Feb 28, Paris. French. He was taught the clarinet by the director of the garrison band at Strasbourg. He then spent several years in a military band and came to Paris in 1790, to be a musician of the first class in the National Guard. In the same year he was made first clarinet at the Théâtre de Monsieur, a post which he held with honour through the company's many changes of name, until he retired in 1824. In 1804 Duvernoy became a member of Napoleon's private orchestra, becoming principal in this in 1806. Fétis says he produced a beautiful tone and executed rapid passages with great clarity, but that his style lacked elegance. As a member of the National Guard he had taught at its École Gratuite de Musique which became the Institut National de Musique. When the latter was merged with the École Royale de Chant in August 1795 to form the Conservatoire, Duvernoy was taken on as a professor of the second class, but he left in November. In 1800 he was re-engaged as a second class professor and almost immediately promoted to first class. He became highly thought of as a teacher and his pupils included Petit (Müller's financier) and Buteux. He was on the committees appointed to discuss Lefèvre's tutor in 1801 and Müller's clarinet in 1812. In 1816 he retired from the Conservatoire with a pension. He lived at the following addresses: 1821 – no.4 rue Papillon; 1822 – no.102 faubourg Poissonière; 1823 – no.103 faubourg Poissonière. Three of his sons became well-known in the musical world: Charles (1796-1872), a tenor at the Opéra Comique and professor at the Conservatoire; Antoine, a horn player at the Opéra; Henri (born 1820), a solfeggio teacher at the Conservatoire.

Works: Concerto no.1 in B flat (Ms. score only – PBN, Sieber). Concerto no.2 op.3 in E flat (Haslinger). Concerto no.3 in C (Jouve c.1818 – VGM). 3 Sonatas op.1 (Gaveaux). 3 Sonatas op.5 dedicated to Alex. Girardin (Gaveaux – PBN. Petit). 6 Airs variés op.2 (Porthaux – PBN. Gaveaux). Thême varié op.15 (Janet). Airs d'Opéra Comique for 2 clarinets (Sieber). 6 Duos op.4 (Sieber). 3 Nouveaux thêmes variés for 2 clarinets & piano (Petit). 3 Thêmes variés for 2 clarinets & piano (Petit. Breitkopf & Härtel – VGM). 3 Trios for clarinet, horn & bassoon (Schlesinger). 3 Quartets, dedicated to "son élève et son ami Mr de Chatenet" (Hentz. Jouve c.1806 to 1814 – BarBM, VGM).

(B–H). **DWORSCHACK (DVORAK), K. Franz.** Prague, ?-1800 or later. Czech. He also played the bassoon. He studied under Beer at St Petersburg and in 1781 travelled with his master to Warsaw. In 1783 he joined David and Springer for a tour of Germany, playing bassoon. He was with them again in 1789 for the Vauxhall Garden season at London, but playing clarinet and basset-horn. In 1790 all three toured through Germany, northern Italy and Holland. In 1791 they were back in London and on 1st April Dworschack and Springer played a concertante for 2 basset-horns in a Haydn-Salomon concert at the Hanover Square Rooms. In the Vauxhall Garden season from May to August of that year Dworschack played at more than forty concerts. He performed a basset-horn concerto 16 times, a clarinet concerto 4 times, a concertante for clarinet and bassoon (with Parkinson) 6 times, as well as many duets and trios with David and Springer.

Bibliography:
CUDWORTH, Charles – "The Vauxhall 'lists'." GSJ. March, 1967.

EBERT, Carl. German. He lived at Berlin, where he learnt the clarinet from F.A. Bliesener. When he was quite young his father went blind and he had to support him by his playing. His

2. Excerpt from Concerto no. 1 in B flat by Duvernoy. *(Bibliothèque Nationale, Paris).*

concerts included the following: 1822 – 13th May, Introduction & Variations by Heinrich Baermann, concerto by Iwan Müller. 1825 – 2nd December, concerto by Crusell, Beethoven's Wind Quintet.

EDLING (EDELING), Johann. Falken, 1764-1786, Weimar. German. When very young he was appointed to the Duke of Saxe-Weimar's orchestra. He showed great promise and his early death was a tragedy.

Works: Several concertos (Ms.)

EECKHOUND (EECKHOUD, EECKHOUNDT), Pierre Joseph van. Antwerp, 1756-1812 Dec 27, Antwerp. Belgian. He had a reputation for clear tone and beautiful phrasing. From 1773 until about 1780 he played in the orchestra for Antwerp cathedral and then played for the Théâtre de la Monnaie at Brussels.

EGERTON, Julian (I). London, 24 Aug 1848-1945 Jan 22, Bilsington. English. See OV. His father was William Egerton. Sir Percy Buck paid this tribute to Julian: "I do not think I have ever heard such beautiful tone got out of a clarinet by anybody as Egerton used to produce . . . . . (He) made the most perfect sounds I ever heard." He was the father of Julian (II) and Percy.

His solo performances included: 1879 – 2nd October at Covent Garden, Valentin Bender's Concertino no.2. 1880 – 14th February & 22nd November at St James's Hall, Mozart's Serenade K388 with Lazarus. 1884 – 5th April at St James's Hall, Spohr's "The Bird and the Maiden" for Carlotta Elliot. 1891 – 9th February at St James's Hall, Beethoven's Septet. 1892 – 8th February, ditto. 24th March at Nottingham, ditto. 1898 – 1st June at Queen's Hall, Brahms' Quintet. 1900 – 6th May, Brahms' Sonata in F minor, Carl Baermann's "Melancholie" with Richard Walthew.

EGERTON, Julian (II). London, 1887-1932. English. He was the son of Julian Egerton (I). He was a member of the Philharmonic Orchestra and played for the Royal Horse Guards band from 1905 to 1925.

EGERTON, Percy. London, 1873-1905, Davos. English. He learnt the clarinet from Lazarus at the Royal Academy of Music. He then joined the band of the Coldstream Guards and was a member of Queen Victoria's private orchestra. He played for the Philharmonic Orchestra from 1899 to 1902 and was with the London Symphony Orchestra for their first concert in June 1904, but had to give up playing shortly after and died from tuberculosis of the throat.

EGERTON, William. Chelsea, 28 Oct 1798-1873. English. In 1815 Egerton enlisted in the Coldstream Guards and played alongside first Willman and then Lazarus. At the Adelphi Theatre in 1822 he played a concerto and the obligato to Guglielmi's "Gratias agimus." In 1835 he discharged himself from the army. When Queen Victoria ascended the throne in 1837 Egerton became one of the original nine members of her private band, remaining in this until 1869. In 1838 he was first clarinet at the Theatre Royal, Covent Garden, and in 1846 was playing in Jullien's orchestra. His address in 1838, the year he joined the Royal Society of Musicians, was no.5 Cary Street, off Vincent Square, Westminster. Three of his sons became professional musicians: Gustavus Robert, William and Julian (I) (q.v.)

EGGER. He was second clarinet at the Théâtre des Nouveautés in 1829.

EGLING. German. In 1823, for Kassel's Euterpe Society, he played a double concerto by Krommer with Conrad Bänder.

EHLEN, Johann Georg. German. In the late eighteenth century he was a member of the Elector of Trevès orchestra at at Ehrenbreitstein, Coblenz.

EHRENREICH, Carl. 1799-1866 Feb 5, Stockholm. German. He came to Sweden in 1822 and became a military bandsman, later a bandmaster, in various regiments of guards. It is thought that he had some lessons from Crusell. From 1853 until his death he was a member of the court orchestra at Stockholm and from 1858 to 1864 was professor of wind instruments at the Conservatoire. He was held in high regard as a military bandmaster and also as an active committee member of the Conservatoire.

EHRLICH, Max. German. He was first clarinet in the court orchestra at Detmold in 1871 and 1872.

EICHHORN. German. He was first clarinet in the court orchestra at Mannheim in 1824. He performed a Potpourri by Danzi there in 1831.

EICHHORST, Karl. Berlin, 1808-? German. He was a pupil of F.W. Tausch, from whom he inherited a beautiful tone. In April 1827 he performed a double concerto at Berlin with his master. In 1830 he was made a Chamber Musician in the Mecklenburg-Schwerin court orchestra.

Work: Variations op.1 on an Original Theme (Wagenführ 1830).

EIGLER, Melchior. ?-1794. German. He was playing clarinet, flute and violin in the court orchestra at Carlsruhe in 1775.

EISERT. German. He went to Spain as a clarinettist in a French military band and took part in battles against the British at the beginning of the nineteenth century. He was captured and brought to England where his brilliant playing earned him the position of first clarinet in the Prince of Wales' band. When Queen Victoria came to the throne in 1837 he was demoted to second clarinet in her private band.

ELEY (ELY), Christopher (Friedrich). Hanover, July 1756-c.1832. German. He also played flute, violin and cello. He came to England in 1785 as one of a group of twelve musicians recruited at the behest of George III to enlarge and improve the band of the Coldstream Guards. Pohl mentions that he performed the clarinet at a London concert in 1786. When the Haydn-Salomon concerts were inaugurated in February 1791 Eley was made first clarinet. He became bandmaster of the East India Co.'s Volunteer Band and in this capacity taught Willman in the late 1790s. He then became bandmaster of the Coldstream Guards until he retired in 1816, when Willman succeeded him. Eley was much sought after as a teacher and Sir George Smart records having a series of thirteen lessons on the scales of wind instruments from him in 1811 at 7 shillings a time. He joined the Royal Society of Musicians in 1793.

ENGEL, Engelhard. German. He was second clarinet in the Thurn & Taxis court orchestra at Regensburg from 1755 until about 1781.

ERHARDT, Jakob. German. He was in the court orchestra at Carlsruhe in 1793.

ERMEL. Originally from Dresden, he became a member of the court orchestra at Dessau in 1798.

Georges Bachmann. *(Royal Conservatoire of Music, Brussels).*

Heinrich Backofen. Self-portrait. Engraved by I. C. Bock. *(Deutsche Staatsbibliothek, Berlin/ DDR).*

PLATE 2

Franz Bartolomey. In court uniform. *(Family possession).*

Aloysius Beerhalter. Lithograph by C. Glocker, Augsburg, 1836. *(Deutsche Staatsbibliothek, Berlin/DDR).*

The Bellison Clarinet Ensemble, 1936. Kalman Bloch leading, with David Weber on his left, Leon Russianoff behind Weber. *(Kalman Bloch, Los Angeles).*

Simeon Bellison. Inscribed 1938 to Kalman Bloch. *(Kalman Bloch, Los Angeles).*

Valentin Bender. Drawing by Banquit, 1841. *(Deutsche Staatsbibliothek, Berlin/DDR).*

Berr in group of famous contemporary musicians. Left to right, from top: Friedrich Kalkbrenner (piano), Gustav Vogt (oboe), Jean Louis Tulou (flute), Nicolo Paganini (violin), Frédéric Berr (clarinet), Jacques François Gallay (horn), Pierre Baillot (violin), Heinrich Herz (piano). *(Civica Raccolta delle Stampe A. Bertarelli, Milan).*

PLATE 6

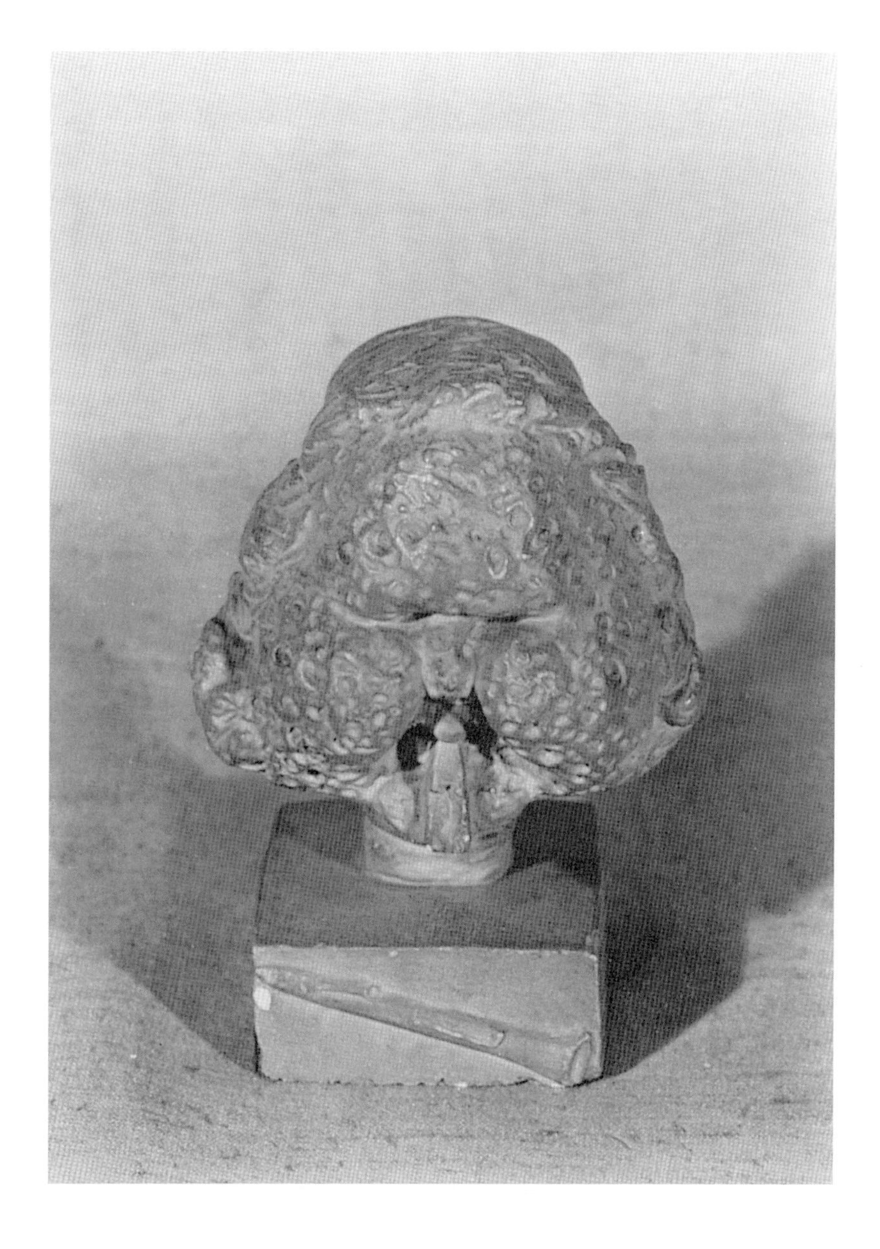

Frédéric Berr. Caricature by Jean Pierre Dantan. (Originally thought to depict Joseph Beer). *(Musée Carnavalet, Paris.* Photographie Lauros-Giraudon*)*.

Joseph Blaes. Caricature by Jean Pierre Dantan. *(Musée Carnavalet, Paris. Photographie Lauros-Giraudon).*

PLATE 8

Frédéric Blasius. Engraving by Lambert. *(Deutsche Staatsbibliothek, Berlin/DDR).*

Ferdinando Busoni. Photograph by M. Zanutto, 1897. From *Ferruccio Busoni* by Edward Dent.

Louis Cahuzac. *(Yona Ettlinger, Tel Aviv).*

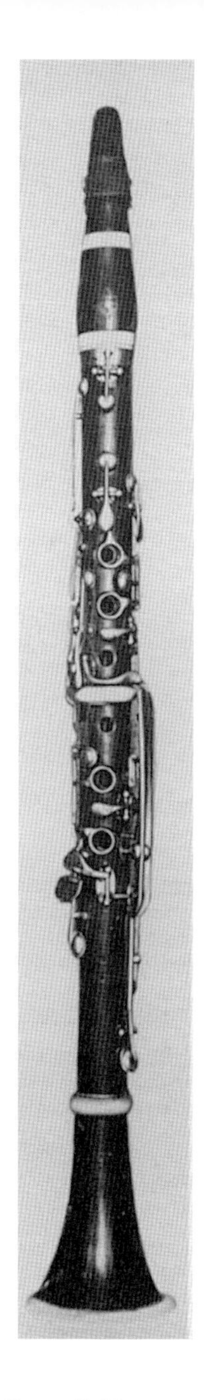

Busoni's Vinatieri clarinet. *(Sammlung der Staatlichen Hochschule, Berlin).*

PLATE 10

Ernesto Cavallini as a young man. Lithograph by Guillet. *(Museo del Conservatorio di Musica 'Giuseppe Verdi', Milan).*

Ernesto Cavallini

Ernesto Cavallini in later years. *(Civica Raccolta delle Stampe A. Bertarelli, Milan).*

Haydn and Mendelssohn Draper with members of the London Wind Quintet and the composer after a performance of Janaček's *Mládi* in London, 1926. Left to right, standing: Aubrey Brain (horn), Mendelssohn Draper (bass clarinet), Fred Wood (bassoon), Leon Goossens (oboe). Seated: Haydn Draper (clarinet), Janaček, Robert Murchie (flute).

Charles Duvernoy. *(Bibliothèque Nationale, Paris).*

PLATE 12

William Egerton. *(Royal Society of Musicians, London).*

Carl Ehrenreich. From *Kungl. Hovkapellets historia* by Tobias Norlind. *(British Library, London).*

Joseph Faubel. From a photograph c. 1860. *(Deutsche Staatsbibliothek, Berlin/ DDR).*

Anton Friedlowsky. Photograph. *(Gesellschaft der Musikfreunde, Vienna).*

Maximilian Gabler. From programme collection of 1915/16. *(Sächsische Landesbibliothek, Dresden).*

Karl Goepfert. *(Gesellschaft der Musikfreunde, Vienna).*

Gustav Heinze. Drawing lithographed by S. Lankhout of the Hague. *(Deutsche Staatsbibliothek, Berlin/ DDR).*

Gustaf Hessler. From *Kungl. Hovkapellets historia* by Tobias Norlind. *(British Library, London).*

Johan Kjellberg. From *Kungl. Hovkapellets historia* by Tobias Norlind. *(British Library, London).*

Thomas Klein. *(Gesellschaft der Musikfreunde, Vienna).*

Jacob Kleine. Print by Th. Brüggemann. *(Collection Haags Gemeentemuseum, The Hague).*

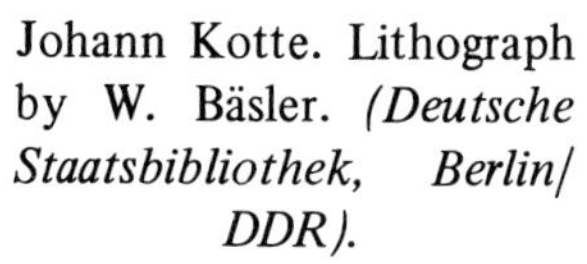

Johann Kotte. Lithograph by W. Bäsler. *(Deutsche Staatsbibliothek, Berlin/ DDR).*

Lazarus in group of Kneller Hall professors, 1859. From left, back row: Albert Hartmann (flute), Carl Zeiss (cornet and trumpet), Snelling (bassoon), Carl Mandel (director of music), Martin (clarinet), T. E. Mann (horn). Front row: Samuel Hughes (ophicleide), Alfred James Phasey (euphonium), Henry Lazarus (clarinet), Apollon Barret (oboe), Thomas Sullivan (bombardon), Cole (school master). *(Kneller Hall, Twickenham).*

Henry Lazarus. Carte de visite photograph by Clarkington, London. *(Royal Academy of Music, London).*

Henry Lazarus. Carte de visite photograph by Tradelle & Marshall, London. *(Royal College of Music, London).*

PLATE 20

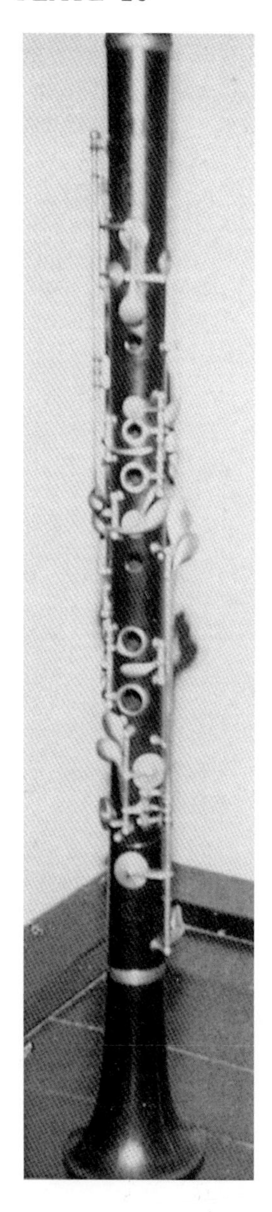
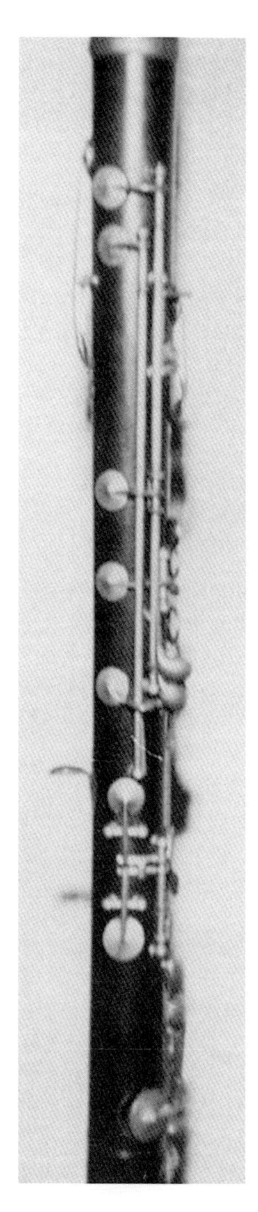
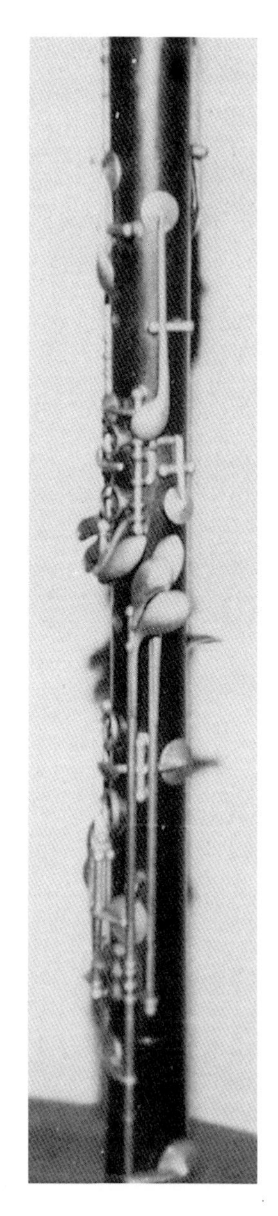

Lazarus' Fieldhouse clarinet. *(Rendall Collection, Edinburgh).*

Adolphe Leroy. Photograph. *(Musée de l'Opéra, Paris).*

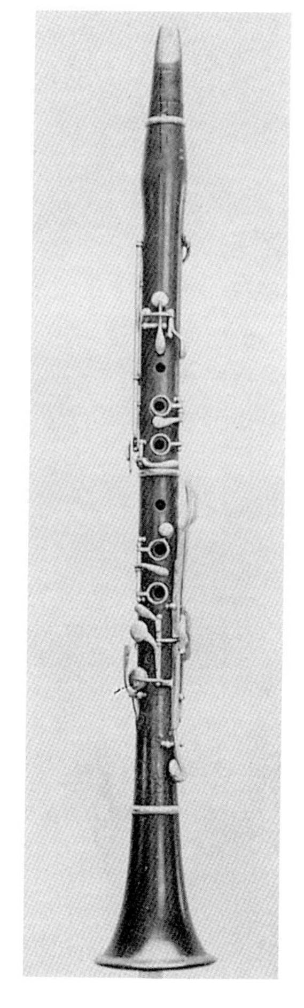

Iwan Müller's Schuster clarinet. *(Sammlung der Staatlichen Hochschule, Berlin).*

PLATE 22

John Maycock. *(Royal Society of Musicians, London).*

Ralph McLane. *(Richard Gilbert, New York).*

Prospèr Mimart. Stereotype by Nadar. *(Archives Photographiques de la Bibliothèque Nationale, Paris).*

Franz Otter. *(Gesellschaft der Musikfreunde, Vienna).*

Henri Paradis. Picture postcard, 1916. *(Royal College of Music, London).*

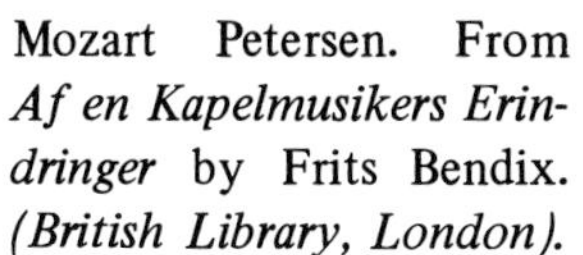

Mozart Petersen. From *Af en Kapelmusikers Erindringer* by Frits Bendix. *(British Library, London).*

PLATE 26

Joseph Proksch. From *Joseph Proksch* by Rudolf Müller. *(British Library, London).*

Antonio Romero. Lithograph by S. Gonzalez after Casado. From his *Método completo de clarinete.* *(British Library, London).*

Antonio Romero

Cyrille Rose. Stereotype by Nadar. *(Archives Photographiques de la Bibliothèque Nationale, Paris).*

Adolphe Sax. From "Die Musik", Berlin 1904. *(British Library, London).*

Louis Schindelmeisser. From "Die Musik", Berlin 1903. *(British Library, London).*

Oskar Schubert. From *Das Goldene Buch der Musik* by W. Spemann, Berlin & Stuttgart 1900.

Henri and Alexandre Selmer testing clarinets in the Selmer factory. *(Author's collection).*

Robert Stark. Photograph by F. Jäger, Würzburg. *(Deutsche Staatsbibliothek, Berlin/DDR).*

Friedrich Wilhelm Tausch. Lithograph by Heinrich von Wintter, 1817. *(Deutsche Staatsbibliothek, Berlin/DDR).*

Cadwallader Thomas. *(Royal Society of Musicians, London).*

George Tyler. *(Royal Society of Musicians, London).*

Leopold Wlach. Photograph. *(Family possession).*

Miguel Yuste. Pen and ink reproduction from "Musica", January 1917. *(Señora Laueiro, Madrid).*

ERNEST (ERNST). He was engaged with Scharf on a regular full-time basis at the Paris Opéra from 1773. Both remained there until they died. Ernest was also first clarinet at the Concert Spirituel from 1785 to 1790, and taught the instrument.

Work: Pieces for 2 clarinets, 2 horns & 2 bassoons (1792).

ERNST. In June 1836 he played Iwan Müller's double concerto with Griesel at Kassel.

ESSBERGER, Carl. German. He was a Chamber Musician at the Berlin Court. On 13th January 1921 he performed Busoni's Concertino during a festival of the composer's works organised by *Der Anbruch* at Berlin. He wrote six volumes of orchestral studies which were published in 1912.

Recording:
Verdi/Bassi – Rigoletto Fantasia. Twin Zonophone T5152 (1906).

FARNARI. He was first clarinet for the Italian Opera orchestra at Moscow in 1824, and received special mention by AMZ for his "industry and knowledge."

(B–H). **FARNÍK, Wenzel.** Dobuzichowitz (near Beroun), 1765-1838 Nov 30, Prague. Czech. He was a distinguished and popular clarinet teacher and performer. Whilst a child he learnt to play the piano and violin, and also had a good voice. At twelve years old he became a choirboy at the St Franz Monastery in Prague and during his stay of five years here, he taught himself to play the clarinet and oboe. When he came out of the monastery he held various orchestral posts until 1799 he was appointed first clarinet to Count Johann Pachta, at whose mansion on the Zeltenergasse he was to lodge till the end of his days. The Count took a leading part in the foundation of Prague's Conservatoire and when the institution was opened in 1811 he secured the appointment of teacher for clarinet and basset-horn for Farník. Farník had to teach four pupils two hours a day, for which he earned 600 florins. He was a brilliant teacher and numbered amongst his pupils Blatt, Budinsky, his own son Gustav Farník, Pisařovic, Joseph Proksch (at Prague's Blind Institute), August and Franz Swoboda. His increasing skill as the years went by gained him no corresponding monetary reward and in 1832 when he had three hours teaching a day his salary was only 900 florins. He continued however to teach at the Conservatoire until his death.

Farník was first clarinet for Prague's National Theatre from 1807 until 1834 and then retired from playing. There is only one report of him away from home and this is at Vienna in 1805, when he performed a concerto at a morning concert in the Augarten. Like his pupil Blatt he seems to have shunned the limelight as a soloist and when he performed Cartellieri's Concerto in 1807, AMZ's Prague reporter said he was not as well known as he should be. They spoke out in his favour again in 1808 when Joseph Beer performed in the city. At a Mozart Commemoration Concert in May 1837 Farník, aged 72 and the only remaining contemporary of the composer, came out of retirement to play the Clarinet Concerto.

FASANO, Tommaso. Naples, c.1800-? Italian. He had commenced a successful career in Paris as a clarinettist when an attack of apoplexy sent him blind. Orchestral playing became out of the question and he turned to travelling as a virtuoso. In spite of his handicap he did well and managed to support a wife and family. He played always on a clarinet in C, with the reed on top. His concerts included the following: 1840 – 17th January at Milan. 1841 – Frankfurt a. M. and Weimar. 1842 – 3rd February at Dresden's Saale der Harmonie, a concerto of his own composition.

Work: Concerto.

FASCH. German. From 1767 he was first clarinet in the court orchestra of Frederick the Great at Berlin.

FAUBEL, (A?). German. He was the director of military music in Aschaffenburg from 1801 to 1816 or later. He taught his sons Joseph and Philipp, who both became distinguished clarinettists.

FAUBEL, Joseph. Aschaffenburg, 12 June 1801-1865 Munich. German. An outstanding clarinettist, he was well taught when a youngster by his father (see above) and in later years became a pupil of Heinrich Baermann's. When ten years old he played a solo to the Grand Duke of Frankfurt who was so impressed that he gave the boy a position in the court orchestra at Aschaffenburg. The orchestra was disbanded two years later, when Aschaffenburg was annexed to Bavaria, and Faubel was absorbed into a military band, probably one of those conducted by his father. Faubel took part in the French campaign of 1814 and when he returned from this he came out of the army. On 25th October 1816 he performed for the Frankfurt Museum Society and on 18th November gave a public concert which created a considerable stir. It was reported that his tone was very beautiful. Encouraged by this success he travelled to Munich where the opportunities were greater and after a series of concerts to show off his talents, succeeded in 1818 in obtaining an appointment at the Royal Opera House. He was an ardent admirer of Heinrich Baermann and from 1818 to 1824 studied with him. Carl Baermann thought very highly of Faubel. Faubel was Chamber Musician in the Munich court orchestra from 1824 to 1864. It was generally he who took over as first clarinet when the Baermanns were away from home. He also played at the Subscription Concerts from 1818 to 1865, and was on the board of directors for these from 1829. Hartmann Stunz, director of the Royal Opera at Munich, dedicated his Concerto no.1 in F minor to Faubel.

Like Heinrich Baermann, Faubel was given ample opportunity to travel. The following were his principal concerts: 1825 – an extensive tour in northern Germany with Thomas Täglichsbeck, a violinist at the Munich Court; this took in Frankfurt a. M., where on 4th February he played Reissiger's Concertino. 1827 – 27th November in Munich, a concerto by Weber. 1828 – 1st December at the Berlin Subscription Concerts, a concerto by Heinrich Baermann. 1829 – a tour which included a performance at the Stuttgart Court. 1830 – in Munich, his own Andante with Variations (6 Variations on a Theme in C?). 1831 – Vienna. 1832 – 22nd October in Munich, obligato to an aria by Pacini for Violanda Dulken. 3rd December at Munich in a concert given by Menter, a cellist in the court orchestra, Adagio by Reissiger. 1834 – 6th January at Neuchâtel, concert with Mlle Halbreiter; the critics went into ecstasies over him and called him "a great artist." Later in the year he was at Zurich where he performed some of his own compositions as well as works by Reissiger and Hartmann Stunz (probably the First Concerto). He also performed Iwan Müller's double concerto with Zurich's Kapellmeister-clarinettist, Ott-Imhoff. 1837 – 15th January for the Société des Concerts at Paris, Adagio & Rondo by "Strunz" (Stunz?). Faubel remained in Paris until April and was much in the company of Meyerbeer, who sent back with him to Munich a copy of the piano reduction of *Les Huguenots* for Heinrich Baermann. 1839 – concert for Munich's Museum Society. 1841 – Amsterdam, with Menter. 1842 – 5th September at Salzburg for the unveiling of the Mozart memorial, a wind octet by Mozart with Carl Baermann playing second to him.

Works: 24 Waltzes for solo clarinet (André). 6 Variations on a Theme in C (André). 6 Duos (Breitkopf & Härtel). Air de la Donna del Lago varié op.1 in E flat for 2 clarinets & piano (Falter).

FAUBEL (VAUBEL), (Johann) Philipp. Aschaffenburg, 14 July 1803-1856, Paramaribo (Dutch Guiana). German. He was the younger brother of Joseph Faubel and, like him, was taught by his father. His performance was said to have great nobility; he had no affectations and produced a beautiful tone. Towards the end of 1821 he was engaged for the court orchestra at Frankfurt a. M. with Bretschneider, to take the places of de Groot and F. Reinhard. In 1829 he moved to the Hague, where the following year he once more succeeded de Groot, who was relinquishing the post of first clarinet and Chamber Musician to the Dutch court. Faubel was also appointed to the Hague's Royal Music School, where he trained some fine pupils who included Becht. Later he played for the French opera. In 1854 he went on an extended concert tour to America and died in Dutch Guiana. His son August, who was born at the Hague in 1835, became a good pianist.

He performed at the following court concerts in Frankfurt: 1825 – August, a double concerto by Krommer with Bretschneider. 1826 – Variations (probably op.20) by Heinrich Baermann. And at the following concerts for Frankfurt's Museum Society: 1821 – 2nd November, J.B. Cramer's Concerto. 1822 – 17th January, Mozart's Quintet K581. 1825 – 14th January, a double concerto by Tausch with Bretschneider. 18th November, an unspecified quartet. 1828 – 9th November, Trio for harp, clarinet & horn by C.R.N. Bochsa. 1829 – 16th January, a concerto by Weber. 27th March, Mozart's Quintet K581.

FAUELHABER, Emmanuel (Jan). Prague, 1772-1835. Czech. In 1792 he was a school teacher and choir conductor at Laun. Some years later he gave up his appointments to travel as a clarinet virtuoso throughout Bohemia. His concerts were well received and particularly at Dresden, where he was heard at Court. In Dresden he learnt to make instruments and then returned to Laun where he manufactured fine clarinets and pianos.

Works: Several concertos.

FAWCETT, Charlesworth. English. He was a member of the well-known north-of-England musical family and a cousin of Mendelssohn Fawcett. Until about 1910 he was first clarinet in the Queen's Hall Orchestra. Sir Henry Wood wrote a cadenza for him in his Fantasia on British Sea Songs, later writing a different one for Haydn Draper.

FAWCETT, Mendelssohn. English. He was a cousin of Charlesworth Fawcett and well-known as a clarinettist at the beginning of the twentieth century.

FELDT. German. He had a very sweet tone and his delivery was likened to that of Hermstedt's. He was solo clarinet in a military band at Magdeburg when in 1824 he came suddenly into the limelight with a series of very successful concerts in the town. A brilliant future was predicted for him and it was expected that he would move to a court post somewhere. He stayed in Magdeburg, probably as a member of the theatre orchestra, until 1828 when he moved to Aachen. He travelled again in 1835, going via Amsterdam and Königsberg to St Petersburg, where he remained about a year. His performances were variable and this was probably why he did not fulfill his early promise. On one occasion Magdeburg called his playing of Mozart's Concerto and Quintet "an aural feast," but on another they said he played "not as well as usual." In 1836 Neuchâtel was moved to say: "Mr Feldt used to be a fine clarinettist, his tone is pleasant in the middle register, but high up it is insecure and his delivery is tasteless. The unpleasant continuous tremolo which he has shows either a faulty method or that there is something wrong with his teeth. Artists of this kind should stay at home these days." This harsh criticism may have done him good, for Rostock the following year were delighted with his beautiful tone and delicate delivery. Feldt married a singer.

His concerts, at Magdeburg unless otherwise indicated, included the following: 1824 – for the Harmonie Concerts, both Weber concertos, a Potpourri by Gaspard Kummer, a Concertante for flute & clarinet by Danzi with Buschinsky, Spohr's First Concerto, Mozart's Concerto and Quintet. For the Lodge Subscription Concerts, both Weber concertos again, Eberwein's Concertino, a concertino (probably op.19) by Lindpaintner and a Polacca by Pechatzeck. 16th October, his own concert when he played Weber's "newest" concerto and Georg's Potpourri on themes from *Der Freischütz*. 1825 – for the Harmonie Concerts, a double concerto by Krommer with Kühne. For the Friendship Society, Weber's Concertino and Danzi's Concertante again with Buschinsky. For the Lodge Concerts, Spohr's First Concerto, Georg's Potpourri, a concertino by Heinrich Baermann. 1826 – for the Harmonie Concerts, a concertino for clarinet & bassoon by Danzi with Krause. 1828 – for the Lodge Concerts, Lindpaintner's Concerto. 1835 – at Königsberg, he gave a concert in the theatre. 1836 – end of the year at Neuchâtel, he gave a concert with Franz and Mme Siebert. 1837 – at Rostock for the Lodge Concerts, Weber's Concertino.

FELIX. He was first clarinet in the orchestra for the Panorama Dramatique at Paris in 1821.

FELLER, Immanuel. Ronneburg, 17 Sept 1830-1891

Apr 26, Hanover. German. He played in a regiment of Guards until 1853, when he became second clarinet in the court orchestra at Hanover. In 1870 he was made a Royal Chamber Musician. He retired in 1884.

FERRÁN, Louis. During the first half of the nineteenth century he was employed as a clarinettist at the Casa de Comedias in Montevideo. He was also director of the Musica del Estado.

FETTER, Giuseppe. From 1794 to 1801 he taught at the Conservatorio della Pietà de' Turchini in Naples.

FISCHER, Enrique. He followed Rodriguez as clarinet professor at the Madrid Conservatoire, until González was given the post in 1883.

FISCHER, Konrad. He performed at the Munich Subscription Concerts from 1882 to 1911 or later.

FISCHER, Michael. German. He played in the court orchestra at Meiningen from 1817 until about 1854. He performed as a soloist with the orchestra for the first time on 26th February 1824.

FLATH. German. Two brothers of this name, with their two sisters who were horn players, were engaged for the autumn season at Neuchâtel every year from 1779 to 1789. They were very popular performers. Between seasons they returned to their home town, which was first Heilbronn and later Mannheim.

FLIEGER, Simon. He and Gaspard Procksch were the clarinettists in the private orchestra of Jean le Riche de la Pouplinière in Paris from about 1750. Rameau was then the orchestra's director and in 1753 they took part under him in a performance of *Acanthe et Céphise.* When the work was played at the Opéra the same year, Flieger and Procksch were engaged for a fee of 6 livres each per performance. In 1755 both of them played in the orchestra for the Concert Spirituel, directed by Johann Stamitz. In 1763 Flieger became "professeur de clarinette" for Jean François de Bourbon, Prince of Conti. He visited England in 1791.

FLITTNER. German. He studied clarinet in Dresden with Traugott Roth, and also learnt the viola. In 1811 he was first clarinet in the court orchestra at Rudolstadt and also second clarinet in the wind band in which F. Müller, another of Roth's pupils, played first.

FÖRSTER, Karl. German. He was a pupil of Kotte and became bass clarinettist in the Dresden court orchestra.

FÖRSTER, Wilhelm. German. He was first clarinet in the town theatre orchestra at Riga in 1885.

FORCKERT, Johann Gotthelf. ?-1874, Dresden. German. He was a pupil of Kotte. From 1833 to 1874 he played in the Dresden court orchestra. He also played bass clarinet in the theatre orchestra and taught it at the Conservatoire. He did much to help Wohllebe, one of his pupils at the Royal Blind Institute, and gave the following concerts with him: 1833 – 28th November at the Leipzig Subscription Concerts, Iwan Müller's double concerto; 1837 – 20th February with the Dresden court orchestra, a double concerto (in Ms.) by Dagobert Fischer (the Institute's blind singing teacher) and, by himself, Lindpaintner's "Grand Rondo" (probably the Rondo brillant op.45). A report on the first concert says that they played well together with beautiful tone and dexterity, but suggests that Forckert takes the poor blind man by the hand and gets him a better instrument.

FOUCARD. French. In 1787 he was employed at Santo Domingo, where his name appears on many programmes. By 1793 he had settled in America and from 1796 to 1799 was a member of the theatre orchestra at Charleston. His concerts included the following: 1793 – Boston. 17th December at Philadelphia, a concerto of his own composition. Charleston. 1796 – 21st March at Charleston, a concerto by Yost. 1799 – 5th March, Pleyel's Concerto.

Work: Concerto.

FOURNIER. He was engaged by Dittersdorf about 1764 for the theatre orchestra at Pressburg.

FRANCK, Frédéric. Brussels, 1811-? Belgian. He won a First Prize at the Brussels Conservatoire in 1839 and became first clarinet in a regiment of Guides. From 1840 to 1843 he was first clarinet at the Grand Theatre in Ghent. He then travelled considerably in Holland and France and settled in Paris with an appointment at the Théâtre Ventadour.

FRANÇOIS. French. He was second clarinet at the

Théâtre des Variétés in Paris from 1831 to 1833.

FRANKE, Sylvain F. German. As a young man, in 1823, he performed a concerto at an entr'acte concert at Weimar. From 1823 until 1833 he held an appointment in the Weimar court orchestra.

Work: Variations & Rondo on a Theme from Auber's *La Muette de Portici* (Breitkopf & Härtel).

FREUDENFELD, August(e). He and Rosenburg are the earliest clarinettists to be mentioned by name, preceding "Mr Charles" by nearly ten years. They held joint Benefit concerts at Hickford's Great Room, London, on 25th March 1726 and 15th March 1727.

FRICKLER. He and Heinnitz were the clarinettists in "Choice pieces on the Clarinets and French Horns" which were played at the Marylebone Gardens, London, in 1766.

FRIEDLOWSKY, Anton. Vienna, 2 Aug 1804-1875 Vienna. Austrian, of Czech descent. He was the son of Joseph Friedlowsky. When his father died in 1859 he succeeded him in the Vienna court orchestra, retiring in 1867. Before this appointment he was first clarinet at the Burg Theatre. He became a member of the Tonkünstlersocietät in 1838 and served on its committee from 1862. He was a fine teacher, working at the Conservatoire from 1835 until his death.

His concerts included the following: 1821 – 2nd December, a double concerto by Krommer and a Potpourri (Späth's?) with his father. 1835 – a duo concertante for flute and clarinet with Alois Khayll, who probably composed the work. 1836 – Spring, a concerto by Spohr. 1837 – Mozart's Concerto. Autumn, another concert with Khayll.

(B–H). **FRIEDLOWSKY, Joseph.** St Margareth, 11 June 1777-1859 Jan 14, Vienna. Czech. See OV. He was a member of the Tonkünstlersocietät from 1808 to 1839 and also of the Vienna Philharmonic. He had a strong loyalty to composers connected with Vienna and this will be noticed in the following list of his concerts: 1813 – 24th April, unspecified solo. 1814 – Spohr's Octet. 1816 – 25th May, first movement of Mozart's Quintet "with indescribable tenderness." 3rd November, Weber Potpourri (probably Georg's Potpourri on themes from *Der Freischütz*) and an unspecified concerto. 1817 – 14th December, Riotte's Third Concerto, Weber Potpourri in

E flat (Georg's?). 1818 – 5th February, Variations for clarinet & piano by Anton Halm, with the composer at the piano. 17th May, Paer's "Una voce al cor mi parla" for Mme Heurteur. 22nd November, Rondo (from op.1 or op.5) by Crusell, Variations by Riotte, Guglielmi's "Gratias agimus" for one of his daughters. 1819 – 6th April in a concert of works by von Seyfried, Concertante for wind, obligato to an aria for Lisette Vio. On this occasion AMZ reported that Friedlowsky "had never sung more beautifully on his instrument." 1821 – 25th March, "Allegro di bravura." 2nd December, double concerto by Krommer and Potpourri (Späth's?) with his son. 1825 – December, Mozart's "Parto!" for one of his daughters. 24th December, Beethoven's Septet. 1827 – January in a Schuppenzigh Subscription Concert, Mozart's Quintet.

FRIEDRICH, Joseph F. German. He was principal clarinet of the Bolshoi Theatre Orchestra in Moscow at the end of the nineteenth and beginning of the twentieth centuries. He was one of the leading teachers of the time, succeeding Zimmermann at the Conservatoire in the 1890s and numbering Simeon Bellison and Zuckerman amongst his pupils.

FRION. French. In 1828 he played for the Société des Concerts in Paris and was also first clarinet at the Théâtre de l'Ambigu Comique. From 1831 to 1833 he was sub-principal at the Opéra Comique. C.L. Frion, who was a First Prize winner at the Conservatoire in 1829, was probably a son.

FRISCH, (Johann) Joseph. He was employed at the Russian Imperial Court. During an extended tour in 1814 he played at Leipzig on 9th October and Warsaw in December. Warsaw gave him considerable applause for his performance of Winter's Concerto in an entr'acte concert at the theatre.

FUCHS, Georg (Friedrich). Mainz, 3 Dec 1752-1821 Oct 9, Paris. German. He learnt the clarinet, bassoon and horn when young. As he studied composition from Cannabich at Mannheim it is probable that his clarinet teacher was either Quallenberg or Hampel. He then became a clarinettist in a military band at Zweibrücken, later becoming their director and travelling with them to Paris in 1784. In 1793 he joined the National Guard as a musician of the first class and also taught at their Institut National de Musique. When the Conservatoire was opened in 1795 he was made a clarinet professor of the second class, but was dismissed in 1800. He spent the rest of his life composing and making arrangements for various publishing houses in Paris.

Works: First Concerto op.14 in B flat (Ms. – PBN. André 1797 – VGM. Naderman 1797). Symphonie Concertante for clarinet & horn (Janet). Airs for 2 clarinets (Leduc). Airs & Waltzes from *The Magic Flute* for 2 clarinets (Sieber c.1798). Airs des Visitandines et autres for 2 clarinets (Sieber). Walses for 2 clarinets (Naderman). 6 Duos (Gaveaux). Duos op.4 (Sieber 1798). 3 Duos op.7 (Sieber 1798). 3 Duos op.10 (Sieber). 6 Duos op.22 (Imbault 1798). 12 Duos op.28 (Janet). Duos mêlés de Danses op.29 (Janet). 3 Duos op.55 (Sieber). 3 Duos op.19 for flute & clarinet (André 1797. Ozi 1802. PBN). Duos op.20 for flute & clarinet (Ozi 1802. PBN). 6 Duos op.4 for clarinet & bassoon (Sieber 1793 – BrBC). 6 Duos op.6 for clarinet & bassoon (Naderman – BrBC). Duos for clarinet & horn (Lemoine). 6 Duos for clarinet & horn (Sieber). Duos op.36 for clarinet & horn (Janet). 6 Duos en 24 Morceaux op.37 for clarinet & horn (Sieber). 6 Duos for clarinet & violin (Janet). 3 Duos op.1 for clarinet & violin (Imbault 1792. PBN). 6 Duos op.13 for clarinet & violin (Sieber). 3 Duos op.14 for clarinet & violin (André 1797. Ozi 1802. Schlesinger. PBN). 3 Duos op.15 for clarinet & violin (André. Ozi 1802. Schlesinger. PBN). Duos op.18 for clarinet & violin (Sieber c.1798). 3 Duos op.38 for clarinet & viola (Sieber). Trios, 2 books (Sieber c.1800 to 1810 – LRAM). 3 Trios op.1 for flute, clarinet & bassoon (Gaveaux). Trios for clarinet, bassoon & horn (1802). Trios for clarinet, bassoon & horn, 2 books (Decombe c.1805 – LBL). 3 Trios for clarinet, violin & cello op.64 (Lemoine – VGM). Trio for clarinet, viola & cello (Ms. copy – VGM). 3 Trios for 2 clarinets & bassoon (Sieber). 3 Trios for 2 clarinets & horn (Jouve – VGM. Hentz – VGM). Trio for 2 clarinets & violin (Jouve. Hentz). 3 Quartets ops.5 & 6 (Imbault – VGM). 3 Quartets op.7 (Gaveaux – VGM). Quartets op.13 (Imbault). 2 Quartets for clarinet, bassoon, horn & cello (Ozi). 3 Quartets for clarinet, bassoon, horn & cello (PBN). 6 Quartets for clarinet, bassoon, horn & bass (1798). 6 Quartets for clarinet, bassoon & 2 horns (clarinet part only – PBN). 6 Quartets ops.5 & 6 for 2 clarinets, viola & bass (Naderman 1793). 3 Quartets for 2 clarinets, viola & bass (Gaveaux). Quartet for 2 clarinets & 2 horns (Lemoine). Quintet for flute, clarinet & strings (Ms. copy – VGM). Sextet op.34 for clarinet, bassoon, horn, violin, viola & bass (Imbault).

Bibliography:

RAUGEL, Felíx – "Georg Fuchs." MGG.

FÜRST, Michael. In 1778 he was employed at the Court

of Öttingen-Wallerstein.

FÜSSEL, Carl Gottlob. He was in the court orchestra at Copenhagen in 1806.

FUNK. German. He was probably a member of the theatre orchestra at Frankfurt a. M. He performed for the following Frankfurt Museum Concerts: 1832 – 23rd March, Mozart's Concerto. 1835 – 13th April, Concertante for oboe & clarinet (composer unknown) with Scheelith.

GABLER, Egon. Dresden, 9 Sept 1876-1959 Apr 30, Lehrte. German. He played in the 107th Infantry Regiment at Leipzig until 1901 when he became first clarinet in the court orchestra at Hanover. He was made a Royal Chamber Musician the following year and retired in 1944.

Works: Concerto no.1 in F (Oertel). Concerto no.2 in E flat (Oertel).

GABLER, Maximilian. Born Wunschendorf. German. He was probably related to Egon Gabler. He trained at the Dresden Conservatoire. From 1881 until about 1906 he played in the Dresden court orchestra.

Work: Theoretisch-praktische Klarinettenschule (Breitkopf & Härtel 1906).

GÄBLER, (Joseph) Christoph. German. He was in the court orchestra at Dresden from 1813 to 1823.

GALILEI. Florence, ?-? Italian. In 1824 he performed Weber's Second Concerto at Magdeburg.

GALLET. French. He was second clarinet at the Théâtre des Variétés in Paris from 1821 to 1827. His address was no.2 rue Cadet.

GAMBARO, Giovanni (Battista). Genoa, 1785-1828, Paris. Italian. See OV. He made a name for himself as a brilliant principal clarinet at the Théâtre Italien in Paris. He championed the cause of Müller, using his clarinets at a time when others were still refusing to see their merits, and was the first to publish Müller's tutor for the new instrument. Gambaro originally served as a clarinettist and then bandmaster to an Italian regiment in the service of the French. By

March 1814 he was established in Paris with a music business which included publishing and the selling of music and wind instruments for the army. In 1816 he became second clarinet to Dacosta at the Théâtre Italien. The following year Dacosta moved to the Opéra and Gambaro became first. Fétis says of Gambaro's playing that he produced a beautiful sound and sang on his instrument in a noble and expressive manner. Gambaro influenced Berr, who joined the orchestra in 1825, to use Müller clarinets, and they made such a brilliant pair that Rossini introduced a special item for them at Charles X's coronation festivities on 19th June 1825. This was an Air & Variations (written originally in 1819 as part of a cantata in celebration of the King of Naples' recovery from illness) which he inserted during the ballet for his stage cantata *Il viaggio a Reims.* From 1825 Gambaro's health began to decline. The chest ailment from which he suffered grew progressively worse and he died in the summer of 1828.

A considerable amount of music for clarinet was published under the name of Gambaro by the family firm and by other publishers. How much of this is by Giovanni Battista (known in France as Jean Baptiste) or how much is by Vincenzo (known as Vincent, and probably Giovanni's brother) is open to doubt. There is much conflicting evidence on the printed page, the worst being Schott's publication of the 10 Caprices op.9 where "J.B. Gambaro" appears on the title page and "V. Gambaro" on the verso. The fact that there is no duplication of opus numbers in the compositions suggests that all came from the same pen, be it Giovanni's or Vincenzo's.

Gardeton, a reliable and contemporary authority, gives the following information in his *Bibliographie Musicale* of 1822: "Gambaro (V.), éditeur marchand de musique, clarinette au théâtre Italien, rue Croix-des-Petits-Champs, no.44, au second étage." He further says that V. Gambaro is the composer and publisher of "Caprices ou études pour clarinette op.9." This evidence cannot be discounted, although all other authorities state that it was J.B. Gambaro who played at the Théâtre Italien and owned the commercial business. Fétis attributes the following works to J.B.: 3 quatours concertants for flute, clarinet, horn & bassoon op.4, first & second concertos, 3 duos op.3, 3 duos op.6, 12 caprices op.18.

Hopkinson gives the following addresses for Gambaro's publishing firm: 1) Under "Gambaro"; March 1814, 1816 – no.42 rue Croix des Petits Champs. April 1817 – no.22 ditto. July 1818, 1825 – no.44 ditto. October 1830, 1832 – no.23 ditto. March 1835 – no.18 rue des Vieux Augustins. 2) Under "Gambaro ainé"; 1847 – no.16 rue St Anne. 3) Under "Gambaro ainé Vve"; 1859 to 1861 – no.33 rue Caumartin. The *Almanach des Spectacles* gives the following address for the period 1821 to 1827 of "Gambaro," clarinettist at the Théâtre Italien: no.44 rue Croix des Petits Champs.

About 1833 the firm was taken over by one of Giovanni's sons, known to the profession as "Gambaro ainé." A branch was opened in Brussels at no.22 rue de la Madeleine and this was run by Auguste Gambaro, probably a younger son. "Gambaro ainé" was well-known in military circles and in 1832 published a *Journal royal de musique.* In the 1840s, as a committee member for the Association of Instrument Makers, he became involved with Sax and showed himself actively hostile to the latter's inventions. He died in August or early September 1852 and the family business was then carried on by his widow until 1861, when it ceased to exist.

Works: A) without opus numbers –

1) First Concerto by J.B. Gambaro (Gambaro. Breitkopf & Härtel).
2) Second Concerto by J.B. Gambaro (Gambaro. Breitkopf & Härtel). (The solo part of a "Grand Concerto in D minor" by Gambaro in the possession of Ricordi of New York was printed from plates owned by "Lafleur ainé," an instrument maker. No indication as to whether this is the first or second concerto can be gained from the part).
3) Sonate pour le Pianoforte et Clarinette obligée, comp. par Boieldieu et Gambaro (Schlesinger 1818).
4) Thême de Boieldieu varié for clarinet & piano by Gambaro (Janet c.1828).
   Thême de Boieldieu varié for clarinet with accompaniment for piano by V. Gambaro (Boieldieu jeune).
5) Divertissemens faciles for 2 clarinets by Gambaro (Gambaro c.1828).
6) 3 Duos concertans for 2 clarinets by J.B. Gambaro (Gambaro c.1832 to 1847 – LRAM).
7) 24 Very easy duets by J.B. Gambaro (Gambaro c.1832 to 1847 – LRAM).
8) Méthode facile de Clarinette à six Clefs, dedicated to the Royal Conservatoire of Music, by "GAMBARO/MV" (Gambaro c.1825 to 1830 – PBN).

Works: B) with opus numbers, in order of opus –

9) Divertissement pour deux clarinettes, Sérénades, Marches et Suite op.1 by Gambaro (Gambaro c.1822).
10) 3 Duos concertans op.3 for 2 clarinets by Gambaro (Gambaro, Ricordi, Simrock c.1828).
11) 3 Quatours concertants for flute, clarinet, horn & bassoon op.4 (Gambaro – BrBC).
    3 Quatours concertans for flute, clarinet, horn & bassoon from

works of Beethoven by Vt. Gambaro (André c.1825 – LBL).
3 Quatours concertans for flute, clarinet, horn & bassoon op.4 by Vincenzo Gambaro (Breitkopf & Härtel – BoLM, VGM).

12) 3 Quatours concertans op.5, 2nd book of quartets, for flute, clarinet, horn & bassoon, dedicated to "son ami Xavier Lefèvre" by Vnt. Gambaro (Gambaro c.1815).
13) 3 Duos concertans op.6 for clarinet & violin by Vnt. Gambaro (Gambaro c.1816 – LBL, WLC).
14) 3 Duos concertans op.7 for 2 clarinets, dedicated to "son ami Dacosta" by Vt. Gambaro (Gambaro c.1818 – LBL).
15) 6 Airs variés op.8 by Gambaro (Gambaro c.1820 to 1828).
3rd Air varié de Concert, dedicated to "Mr Mohr jeune" by J.B. Gambaro (Gambaro c.1832 to 1847 – LBL).
4th Air varié for orchestra, wind band or piano, dedicated to Klosé by J.B. Gambaro (Gambaro c.1841 to 1847 – LBL).
16) 10 Caprices op.9 by J.B. Gambaro/V. Gambaro (Schott c.1821 – LRAM).
Caprices op.9 (Schott – VGM).
Caprices ou études op.9 by V.Gambaro (Gambaro c.1822).
6 Caprices ou études op.9, book 1, by Gambaro (Gambaro. Schott c.1828).
6 Caprices ou études op.9, book 2, by Gambaro (Gambaro c.1828).
17) 3 Duos concertans op.10, 4th book of duos, for 2 clarinets, dedicated to "Mr de Champmartin, Amateur à Autun" by Vt. Gambaro (Gambaro c.1818; noteworthy in being an early publication to use metronome speeds. Hofmeister).
18) 12 Caprices by G.B. Gambaro (Bertuzzi c.1813).
12 Caprices op.18, 1st suite, by J.B. Gambaro (Schott 1829).

GAREIS, (Gottlieb Wilhelm) Albert. Berlin, c.1811-1860 Jan 3, Berlin. German. He and his brother Gustav made several concert tours together. Their partnership in double concertos was outstanding and they were considered two of the best players of their day. They were said to have a full round tone and a beautiful portamento. Albert learnt the clarinet from his father and in his turn taught his brother Gustav. In 1834 he became a Royal Chamber Musician at the Berlin Court. He fell ill and died only a short time after celebrations to mark his twenty five years of court service.

His principal concerts, at Berlin unless otherwise stated, were as follows: 1837 – December, Ludwig Maurer's Concertino. 1841 – February in a concert of works by Wenzel Gährich at the Academy of Singing, Gährich's Concertante for 2 clarinets with his brother. (The work was probably written for them, as they played it often). Summer at the theatre in Potsdam, Rondo & Variations by Gährich with his brother. 1842 – 27th January at the Leipzig Gewandhaus, Gährich's Concertino for solo clarinet and, with his brother, Gährich's Concertante. 1843 – early November at Berlin's Academy of Singing, Lindpaintner's Concertino, Gährich's Concertante with his brother, obligato to "Die Loreley" for tenor and bass by Joseph Netzer. (This concert, in which they were supported by the court orchestra, was given for the benefit of the Gareis' sister, Mme Schlegel, whose husband had been brutally murdered in his sleep by an apprentice). 30th November at the Leipzig Gewandhaus, Gährich's Concertante with his brother. 1844 – June, an unspecified double concerto with his brother.

GAREIS, (Johann) Gustav. Berlin, 14 Nov 1822-1846 May 8, Berlin. German. He learnt the clarinet from the age of nine with his brother Albert (q.v.), and with him formed an outstanding partnership for double concertos. In 1839 he made a concert tour to Copenhagen and soon after became a Royal Chamber Musician at the Berlin Court. Whilst preparing for a further tour to Paris in 1846 he caught cold and died.

For duo performances with his brother, see under Albert Gareis. Gustav's solo performances included the following: 1833 – October, unspecified solo. 1839 – October, unspecified Adagio & Rondo (probably from Weber's First Concerto), Mozart's "Parto!" for Hedwig Schultze. 1843 – November (see Albert Gareis), variations ("new and too long") by Carl Baermann. 1845 – April, Weber's Grand Duo with Brissler.

GARNER, Horatio. He played a prominent part in the general musical life of Portsmouth, U.S.A., and on 14th December 1791 performed a concerto of his own composition.

Work: Concerto.

GASSEAU. French. He played in the band of the Royal Swiss Guard at Versailles. He also played the flute.

Work: 20 Airs Italiens for 2 clarinets (Gaveaux c.1793 to 1797).

GASSNER. German. He was second clarinet in the court orchestra at Mannheim in 1824. In 1830 he played both the Weber concertos and was reported to be a very fine player. In 1831 he performed a solo by Frey, Mannheim's Kapellmeister, and a Potpourri by Späth.

GAUTIER (GAULTIER). French. He emigrated to America and settled in Philadelphia. Here he had a Benefit on 1st December 1795, when he played a concerto by Lefèvre and one by himself. He also had a Benefit in 1796 and played concertos by Lefèvre and himself. On 23rd March 1802 he performed his own concerto at Broadway, New York.

Work: Concerto.

GAVEAUX, Guillaume. French. He may have been the Gaveaux employed as second clarinet and bassoon for the court orchestra at Neuchâtel from 1790 to 1792. By 1796 or earlier he was in Paris and in 1798 is listed as first clarinet in the orchestra at the Théâtre Lyrique. With his brother Simon he had a music business. Another brother was the composer Pierre, who wrote clarinet obligatos in his operas "Le Trompeur trompé" and "Monsieur Deschalumeaux." Guillaume's compositions for flute and flageolet were popular in Paris and Schilling considered his tutor for flageolet second only to that by Collinet.

Works: Petits Airs (Gaveaux). Airs de Sophie et Moncars for 2 clarinets (Gaveaux). Contredanses et Walses for 2 clarinets (Gaveaux). Operatic works for 2 clarinets (Gaveaux. Petit).

GELHAAR, Carl Sigismund. Dresden, 1767-1814 Mar 11, Stockholm. In 1785 he became the first clarinettist to be engaged for the court orchestra at Stockholm. The following year Thielemann joined him and he then occasionally doubled on timpani. When Crusell became first clarinet in 1793 Gelhaar left the section and was official timpanist until his death.

GENSLER, Vladimir Ivanovich. 1906-1966? Russian. He studied with Brekker and then with Berezin in Leningrad, completing his studies in 1929. In 1935 he won first prize at the All-Union Musicians' Contest in Leningrad. He became principal clarinet in the Leningrad Philharmonic and was a professor at the Conservatoire from 1937. In 1940 he was made a Doctor, 1950 Professor and 1956 Honoured Artist of the RSFSR.

GENTZSCH, Traugott. Rehmsdorf (near Zeitz) 14 Aug 1838-1902 May 19. German. He was second clarinet in the Leipzig Gewandhaus Orchestra from 1863 to 1881, and then became principal in place of Landgraf, retiring in 1885. His first solo performance with the orchestra was on 18th March 1880. He taught at the Conservatoire.

GEORGE, Lorenz. ?-c.1783, Berlin. He was a good clarinet player, one of the earliest, and an exceptional double bass player. From 1739 he was the town musician of Berlin, employed at St George's Church and in the royal orchestra.

GEORGES. French. He was second clarinet at the Théâtre de la Gaité in Paris in 1825, and at the Théâtre de S.A.R. Madame from 1827 to 1829. From 1831 to 1833 he was the only clarinettist at the Théâtre du Palais Royal. He lived at the following addresses: 1825 – no.4 rue des Fosses du Temple. 1827 – no.28 rue de Lancry, which was the same house that Clermont had lived in during 1822. (Bazin was at no.23 in 1824).

GIAMPIERI, Alamiro. S. Giovanni Valdarno, 3 June, 1893-? Italian. He studied at the Royal Music Institute in Florence, where he won the Gold Medal, also diplomas in clarinet and band arrangement. From January 1922 he taught clarinet at the Paganini Institute in Genoa and later moved to the Milan Conservatoire. He published several excellent books of studies and revised the Lefèvre and Klosé tutors.

Works: Carnival of Venice (Ricordi). Fantasia (Ricordi).

GILLER, Josef. ?-1903 July 14, Vienna. Austrian. He was a pupil at the Vienna Conservatoire, finishing his training in 1858. He became a member of the court opera orchestra and then of the Vienna Philharmonic Orchestra from 1863 until 1884, when he was pensioned.

GLADNEY, J. English. He played second clarinet and bass clarinet in the Hallé Orchestra at Manchester from 1862 to 1892.

(B–H). **GLÖGGL, Joseph.** Austrian. He was one of the earliest known basset-horn players. By profession he was the town gymnastics master at Linz. Almost certainly it was to him that Princess Poniatowsky sent Czerny, Matauschek and Oliva in the 1770s for instruction on the basset-horn.

GODECHARLE. Belgian. He played in the court orchestra at Brussels in the eighteenth century.

GOELLER. In 1842 he was second clarinet in the New York Philharmonic Orchestra.

GOEPFERT (GOEPFART), Karl (Andreas). Rimpar (near Würzburg), 16 Jan 1768-1818 Apr 11, Meiningen. German. His father was the official surgeon at Würzburg. Karl Andreas first learnt piano, organ and singing. At the age of twelve he took up the clarinet and went for lessons to the famous teacher Meissner, who was a chamber musician at Würzburg. Meissner dedicated his Deux duos concertants op.4 to Goepfert and Goepfert returned the compliment with his Third Concerto and the 2 Duos concertants op.19. Goepfert made such rapid progress under Meissner that after four years he gave up the lessons and continued to work on his own, applying himself at the same time to composition. He then went to Vienna and studied for a year and a half with Mozart, during which time Mozart set him the task of arranging his operas for wind ensemble. In 1793 Goepfert was made first clarinet in the court orchestra at Meiningen and not long after this, director of the court military music. In 1798 he went again to Vienna, hoping to make a name for himself as a soloist, but his leave was rescinded and he was enticed back with a promise of becoming music director at Meiningen. The preferment never materialised and Goepfert remained at Meiningen for the rest of his days, a sadly disillusioned man. As a clarinettist he was considered amongst the greatest of his time, although he did not travel. As a composer he was also successful and the performance of his Military Fantasia op.33 on 18th October 1815 at a festival in Berlin brought a gold medal and a gracious hand-written note from King Friedrich Wilhelm III. Goepfert died from angina.

Works: Concerto op.1 in B flat (Simrock c.1798). Concerto op.14 in E flat (André c.1806/8 – ZAM). Concerto op.20 in B flat, dedicated to Meissner (André. Zimmermann). Concerto op.27 in B flat (André). Concerto op.35 in E flat (André. Hofmeister). Concertino. Concertante for clarinet & bassoon on the opera *Die Schweizerfamilie* (LüMS). Symphonie concertante for clarinet & bassoon (André). Drei Stücke op.29 (Merseberger – LRAM, LRCM). Potpourri op.32 in B flat (André. Hofmeister). Potpourri op.38 in F (André). 16 Anglois, Ecossaises et Walses (Breitkopf & Härtel). 8 Walzes avec code (Breitkopf & Härtel). 3 Duos concertantes op.22 in C & F for 2 clarinets or clarinet & bassoon (André 1821). 6 Duos faciles op.30 for 2 clarinets or clarinet & bassoon (Hofmeister). 2 Duos concertants op.19 in C major & A minor for clarinet & bassoon, dedicated to Meissner (André 1813). Concertante for clarinet & bassoon (unpublished). Andante religioso for clarinet & violin (Zimmermann). Quartet op.2 (André). Quartets op.16 in C minor & B flat major (André). Quartets op.36 in F, B flat & E flat (André). Quartet for flute, oboe, clarinet & bassoon. 12 Pièces op.26 for 2 clarinets, 2 bassoon & 2 horns (André). 6 Lieder with accompaniment for clarinet or guitar (Breitkopf & Härtel 1810). Terzetto for voice, clarinet or flute & guitar (Ms. – PBN). 6 Marches of Mozart arr. for wind band (PBN).

Bibliography:

Obituary – AMZ. 1818, ps.505/6/7

BECKER, Heinz – "Carl Andreas Goepfert." MGG.

GÖTZSCHER, Anton. German. In 1785 he was a clarinettist in the court orchestra at Cologne. Later he became orchestral conductor.

GOMEZ, Aurelio Fernández. Spanish. He was no relation to Francisco and Manuel Gomez. He played in the Royal Corps of Halberdiers and in the Madrid Philharmonic Orchestra. From 1943 until 1950 he was clarinet professor at the Madrid Conservatoire. He was also proprietor of a music magazine.

(B–H). **GOMEZ, Francisco.** Seville, 6 June 1866-1938 Jan 5, Belfast. Spanish. See OV. He was the brother of Manuel Gomez. He also played the bass clarinet, acquiring a particularly fine reputation on "the Goose", as he called it.

Work: Lorito Caprice, dedicated to Charles Draper (Hawkes c.1896 – TwKHL).

GOMEZ, Manuel. Seville, 30 Aug 1859-1922 Jan 8, London. Spanish. See OV. He was the brother of Francisco Gomez. From 1904 to 1915 he was first clarinet in the London Symphony Orchestra. He also played in the London Symphony Orchestra's Wind Quintet with Daniel Wood (flute), William Malsch (oboe), E.F. James (bassoon) and A.E. Borsdorf (horn). His original cocus wood full-Boehm clarinet is in the Boosey & Hawkes Collection at Edgware. His final instrument, of which the glass mouthpiece is unfortunately broken, is in the possession of his grandson in Canada.

GONZÁLEZ y Val, Manuel. Madrid, 20 Nov 1835-1909 Dec 7, Madrid. Spanish. He was a pupil at the Madrid Conservatoire under Romero, gaining a First Prize in 1857. He became a military bandmaster and in 1865 was playing first clarinet at the Variety Theatre in Madrid. From there he went to first clarinet at the Theatre Royal and for the Society of Concerts, and later became a member of the court orchestra. In 1883 he was made professor at the Madrid Conservatoire, where he trained many fine pupils who included Miguel

Yuste and Enrique Calvist. On his death Yuste succeeded him in the professorship. González won a first class medal in the Third Carlist War and was made a Knight of the Red Cross. He lived first at no.9 Calle Arrieta and then nos.12 and 14 Calle Leganitos.

GOUDSWAARD (GOULDSWARRD), David. Rotterdam, 13 May 1808-? Dutch. He was a popular soloist both in his own country and abroad. He was said to have a wonderfully sweet tone and good intonation, and played in a light brilliant style. Berlin first heard him on 18th December 1840 and London on 4th April 1842, when he performed a Fantasia by Reissiger for the Philharmonic Society. He was made an honorary member of the Music Society of the Netherlands in 1849 and of the Artistic Circle of Antwerp in 1860.

GRACHT, Arthur Joseph van der. Diest, 5 Apr 1853-? Belgian. In 1867, whilst an apprentice musician in a military band, he became a pupil under Blaes at the Brussels Conservatoire, where he gained a First Prize in 1871. In 1876 he left the army and played solo clarinet in the orchestra at Spa. Following the death of Henri Weber in June of that year, Ghent Conservatoire held a contest to fill the vacant post. Gracht entered and was unanimously elected professor of both clarinet and saxophone. He was active as a conductor of wind orchestras and in 1895 received a Civic Medal of the First Class in recognition of his services to music.

GRANGER, Frederick. 1770-1830. He is probably a brother of Thomas Granger, and performed at Boston from about 1793. On 19th May 1801 he performed his own concerto at Boston Conservatory Hall. He was still at Boston in 1820, though aged and infirm.

Works: Concerto. 25 Duets (1811).

GRANGER, Thomas. He is probably a brother of Frederick Granger. With the oboist Gottlieb Graupner he founded the Boston Philharmonic Society in 1810. He and Louis Schaffer were the original clarinettists in the orchestra.

GRAZIOSI. He performed a concerto by Yost at the Concert Spirituel in Paris on 15th August 1786.

GREDING. In 1827 he was playing second clarinet to Iwan Müller in the Saxe-Coburg court orchestra.

(B–H). **GRIESBACHER (GRIESSBACHER, GRISBACHER), Raymund (Reimund).** Vienna, 1752-1818, Vienna. Austrian. He also played the baryton and the bassoon. From 1776 to 1778 he was employed as a clarinettist in the Esterházy orchestra. Then until 1781, he was basset-horn player to Count Pálffy. By 1795 he had become extra clarinettist and instrument maker to the Court at Vienna. About 1796 he was clarinettist and music director to Prince Grassalkovics. Langwill records the following instruments made by him: 5-key clarinet (Lek-MU); 12-key basset-horn of c.1800 (LRCM).

Work: Allegro & Romance for 2 clarinets, 2 bassoons & 2 horns (Ms. in ScML).

GRIESEL. He played in the court orchestra at Kassel. In June 1836 he performed Iwan Müller's double concerto with Ernst. In June 1839 he played Späth's Potpourri with "Bader" (probably a misprint for Bänder – i.e. F. Bänder).

GRIMM, Joseph. ?-1831, St Petersburg. Czech. He received his training in Prague and then went into the service of Count Hartig. From 1779 he was an Imperial Musician at the Court of St Petersburg. By 1784 he had risen to become first clarinet of the first orchestra and was receiving a salary of 500 roubles with a lodging allowance of 120 roubles. In 1789 he gave a farewell concert and departed on six months leave to visit his homeland. He came back and resumed his post, and by 1801 was receiving a salary of 1,000 roubles. He taught at the theatrical school from about 1787.

GRISEZ, A. Léon. French. He was a pupil of Klosé at the Paris Conservatoire, gaining First Prize in 1857. He played at the Opéra Comique and for the Société des Concerts, also for the Société des Instruments à Vent from its inception in 1879. The following music was dedicated to him: Deux Pièces by C. de Granval; Trois Pièces op.20 by René de Boisdeffre. Leduc published an edition by Grisez of Klosé's tutor (BrBC).

GROENEVELT, T.W. He was first clarinet in the New York Philharmonic Orchestra in 1842.

GROOT, David (Eduard) de. Amsterdam, 8 Apr 1795-1874 Mar 29, Paris. Dutch. He was a much-loved Jewish artist, whose playing was characterised by a gentle tone, great dexterity and, on occasion, "lively capers." Spohr was much impressed with his ability and secured him for his orchestras at Frankfurt and Kassel.

David de Groot received his early training from his father, Henri de Groot, and then became a member of a military band. When the band was dissolved he obtained the post of first clarinet in the French Theatre at the Hague. It was here in 1817 that Spohr first met him. The following year Spohr was appointed conductor of the orchestra at Frankfurt and invited de Groot to be his first clarinet. De Groot remained at Frankfurt three years and during this time formed an exceptionally good partnership with the other clarinettist, Georg Reinhard. Together they gave many performances of the Krommer and other double concertos. De Groot performed a solo concerto by Krommer in 1820 and some variations by Maurer in 1821. In recognition of his talents he was given honorary membership of Frankfurt's Museum Society. The violinist Hofmann, his colleague in the orchestra, was the only other musician to be a member at the same time, the rest being drawn from literature and painting.

In the autumn of 1821 de Groot left Frankfurt – Spohr had already gone – and travelled throughout Germany, before returning to his homeland, where he resumed his original appointment as first clarinet in the French Theatre at the Hague. From here he visited other towns, playing at Amsterdam in May 1822 and Rotterdam in 1823. In 1822, after a successful appearance at Court with Henriette Sontag, the Prince of Orange gave him a testimonial for a proposed tour to Italy. The tour however did not materialise, for Spohr wrote begging him to come and play in the orchestra at Kassel, of which he was now conductor. De Groot went to Kassel in 1823 and remained four years, sometimes deputising for Spohr as conductor. From here he visited several German courts and gave recitals with both Moscheles and Hummel. He began to compose a good deal at this time. At Kassel in March 1824 de Groot performed a concerto by Avelino Canongia, which was said to be very difficult, but he delivered it with ease. In 1825 he gave them a concertino by Lindpaintner, and the following year he returned to his original post at the Hague. He was now appointed solo clarinet to William I, King of the Netherlands, and clarinet professor at the newly opened Royal Conservatoire of Music.

In the early part of 1830 de Groot played at Rotterdam. Towards the end of the year revolution put an end to all his appointments and he once more left the Hague. He journeyed to Paris and was invited to play at the Opéra Comique, but turned this offer down. He next went to Strasbourg and settled here for two years as a member of the theatre orchestra and conductor of the 59th regiment of the line. He performed as a soloist in 1831 and, in March and April 1832, the obligato parts to the aria and duet from Paer's *Sargino*. Shortly after this he was on the move again, for the opportunities offered an artist of his calibre in Strasbourg were negligible. By 1837 he was back at the Hague with a post as conductor of the orchestra at the Grand Theatre. He gave first performances at the theatre of Spohr's *Faust* and Meyerbeer's *Les Huguenots.*

De Groot was in Paris again in 1838 and playing at a concert given for the benefit of Paganini, who was dying. For his playing on this occasion he earned much praise, even from the great violinist himself. When Berr died suddenly in September the same year de Groot was asked to write the final operatic fantasia in a series of twenty nine which Berr had left uncompleted. De Groot played for two years at the Théâtre de la Renaissance and then was invited by his friend Clerisseau to direct the theatre orchestras at Marseilles and Nice. In 1847 he made a tour through Switzerland and Italy, and finally established himself at Chambéry as teacher of clarinet at the Conservatoire and at the Philharmonic Society's Music School. He gave these appointments up in 1854 and retired to Paris to live his life out in seclusion. He had three sons who all became well-known musicians: Henri, a horn player; Adolphe, composer and orchestral leader at the Imperial Theatre in Chatelet; Jules, composer and pianist, who married a sister of the French pianist, Emile Prudent.

Works: Fantasy on *Le Brasseur de Preston*, with Fessy – no.29 in the series started by Berr (Schott – LRAM). Grand Fantasia on *Der Freischütz*. Grand Fantasia on Russian Themes, dedicated to Cavallini. Introduction & Rondo. Potpourri on *La Dame Blanche*. Duo for 2 clarinets, dedicated to Iwan Müller.

GROSS. In 1807 he was playing second clarinet in the orchestra at Hamburg.

GROSSE, Friedrich Wilhelm. Halle, 1824-1886, Manchester. German. He showed remarkable talent as a youth in a Prussian army band and at the age of fourteen was engaged by the orchestra at Halle. In 1840 and 1843 he appeared as soloist with the orchestra and in 1848 secured an engagement in a German opera company which came to London for a season at Drury Lane Theatre. Grosse remained in London for three years, playing for the Italian opera season at Her Majesty's, at Covent Garden and Drury Lane, and also as soloist in Jullien's band. He was a popular man and made many friends who included the composer Balfe. In the winter of 1851 Grosse was engaged as clarinettist for the Gentlemen's Concerts in Manchester. Charles Hallé was the pianist and conductor for this body and became a great admirer of Grosse's playing; he wrote in his diary of 19th

December 1855: "A clarinet concerto in A by Mozart was capitally played by our excellent clarinettist, Grosse. The composition, although by Mozart, is such a grandfatherly production and so lengthy that the finale had to be left out, not to try the patience of the public beyond endurance." When Hallé formed his famous orchestra in 1858 Grosse was engaged as principal clarinet and remained in this position until his death. Grosse also became bandmaster to the 3rd Manchester Volunteers. He gave the following solo performances with the Hallé Orchestra: 1858 – 3rd November, Grand Fantasia (op.146?) by Reissiger. 1860 – 25th January, Introduction & Variations on Schubert's *Sehnsuchtswaltzer* by David. 1868 – 13th February, Weber's Grand Duo with Hallé. 1872 – 4th January, Reissiger's Fantasie op.146.

Bibliography:

Obituary – *Manchester Evening News.* 9 Dec, 1886.

GRÜNDLINGER. German. From 1802 to 1812 he played in the court orchestra at Kremsmünster.

GRÜTZMACHER. 1804-1862 Mar 1, Dessau. German. He was a member of the court orchestra at Dessau from about 1832 until his death and appeared as soloist in the Subscription Concerts of 1841. He had two sons, Friedrich (born 1832) and Leopold (born 1835) who both achieved fame as cellists.

GRUNER, F. German. He played in the Brunswick court orchestra from 1840 to 1855.

GUGEL. German. He was a Chamber Musician at Hildburghausen. On 3rd and 12th October 1802 he was a soloist at the Leipzig Gewandhaus.

GUMPELSHAMER, Sigismund Anton. German. From 1769 to 1772 he played in the Elector of Trevès' orchestra at Ehrenbreitstein, Coblenz.

GUYOT (GIOT, GUIL, GUILLOUD). French. He held the following posts in Parisian theatres as second clarinet: 1824 – Vaudeville; 1827 – Gaité; 1828 – Ambigu Comique. In 1829 and 1830 he was one of the eleven clarinets in the wind orchestra at the Odéon. He lived at no.16 rue St Avoye in 1824 and by 1827 was at no.26 rue du faubourg du Temple, near Buteux, who lived at no.24.

GUYOT, Jean François. Lyons, 4 Sept 1875-? French. He trained at the Paris Conservatoire, gaining First Prize in 1896. He was the clarinettist for the Société Moderne d'Instruments à Vent. On 14th May 1913 they performed Rimsky-Korsakov's Quintet for the Concerts Dandelot in Paris.

HABERLAND, Johann Christian Friedrich. 1745-1810 May 7. German. He played second clarinet in the Leipzig Gewandhaus Orchestra from 1784 to 1806.

HABERMEHL, Georg Martin. Darmstadt, 5 Feb 1768-1807. German. He was first clarinet in the court orchestra of the Grand Duke of Hesse-Darmstadt from 1790 until his death. He played the violin and viola as well and learnt composition from Johann Theophil Portmann.

Works: Several concertos (Ms. of one in C, written c.1800, was in the Royal House Library, Berlin, but this was destroyed in World War II).

HABERT, J.M. German. In 1763 he and Jakob Mayer found employment with Duke Christian IV of Nassau at Zweibrücken, at a salary of 384 gulden, food and lodgings provided. When the Duke died in 1785 the orchestra was dissolved, but they were kept on for house music. The Court was in dire straights at this time and their agreed salary was not paid, so that they ran heavily into debt over lodging expenses. Their plight was alleviated in 1789 when Duke Friedrich Wilhelm took them into his orchestra at Weilburg. This orchestra was dissolved in 1792 and they then moved to the court orchestra at Mannheim.

HABGOOD, Thomas. English. He and Pearson played at the King's Theatre in the Haymarket on 13th March 1758.

HÄRTEL. German. In 1811 he was solo clarinettist, playing oboe when required, in the court orchestra at Meiningen.

HALLER, Max. ?-1858. German. He was clarinettist and music director at the Darmstadt Court from 1810, receiving a decoration in 1850. He also played the oboe, bassoon and violin.

HAMBURGER (HOMBURGER). German. In 1834 he was playing in the military band at Fulda. On 11th January 1835 he performed Späth's Concertino with the Fulda court orchestra and was probably one of the players who, later the same year, performed Schindelmeisser's Symphonie Concertante for 4 clarinets. In 1845 he performed Weber's Concertino. By 1850 he had moved to Kassel and became fourth clarinet in the court orchestra there.

HAMELIN, (Emile) Gaston. Saint-Georges, 27 May 1884-1951 Sept 8, Paris. French. He studied under Turban at the Paris Conservatoire, gaining a First Prize in 1904, the same day as Périer. He became a fine teacher, numbering Ralph McLane amongst his pupils. In 1926 he went to America to be principal of the Boston Symphony Orchestra. By 1932 he had returned to Paris and when the Orchestre National was formed in February 1934, he became its first clarinet, remaining in this position until his death.

Recording:
Debussy – Rhapsody. Victor 11433.

HAMMERL, (Paul) Cornelius. Munich 13 Oct 1769-1839 Apr 27. He was first employed by the Duke of Bretzenheim at Mainz. About 1795 he became first clarinet in the court orchestra and in the wind band belonging to the Duke of Mecklenburg-Schwerin at Ludwigslust. In 1806 he performed a concerto for clarinet & bassoon by G.A. Schneider with Haidner at Doberan. He remained at the Schwerin Court until about 1825. His death came from typhus. He composed for wind band.

HAMPEL, Johannes M. ?-1792 Apr 5. Czech. He also played the viola. He was first employed as a clarinettist, with Quallenberg, at the Court of Thurn & Taxis at Regensburg. In 1758 or 1759 they became the first clarinettists appointed to the Mannheim Court, and received a joint remuneration of 576 gulden. They moved with the Elector Palatin and his Court to Munich in 1778. Hampel was of disreputable character, cheating on his salary in 1776 and finally being sentenced to death.

HANNON, David. 1865-1906. Belgian. He was a pupil at the Brussels Conservatoire under Poncelet. In 1901 he succeeded Poncelet as clarinet professor and held the post until his death.

HARBURGER, Johann. German. He was employed as a clarinettist at the Court of Mainz from 1774 to 1803.

HART. In August 1820 he played a concerto by Francis Schaffer (q.v.) at the Boylston Hall in Boston, Massachusetts.

The concert was a Benefit for Schaffer.

HARTIG. German. In 1819 he was the town musician at Schwerin, playing clarinet and violin. He performed on the clarinet at Lübeck in 1847.

HARTIG, Count Ludwig. ?-1813 Oct 20, Prague. Czech. He was probably the son of Grimm's patron. Himself a patron, he was also a good clarinettist and played at concerts in France and Holland, as well as Vienna and Prague.

(B–H). **HARTMANN, Carl.** German. He also played the oboe. In the 1780s he settled in England for a time. He played at the following Salomon Concerts given at the Hanover Square Rooms: 2nd March 1792 (clarinet quartet by Yost), 24th March and 7th April 1794. Not long after this he removed to Hamburg and secured an appointment at the French Theatre as principal clarinet, doubling on oboe when required. He gained loud applause at a public concert which he gave on 26th April 1801 and AMZ's critic reported that he would be one of the foremost players if he had chosen to live where there was more money available for the arts than at Hamburg. Hartmann however remained at Hamburg and acquired a particular reputation for obligato playing. In 1818 he is mentioned as first basset-horn player, with Jodry as second, in a performance of Mozart's *Requiem.* On 24th February 1825 he performed some basset-horn variations, composer unspecified, at a concert given by Moscheles at Hamburg's Apollo Hall. Hartmann probably taught his nephew Johann Friedrich Schwenke, who besides the clarinet played other instruments and later became well known in the town as an organist and composer. The boy's father was C.F.G. Schwenke, town cantor at Hamburg.

Work: 3 Duetts Concertante (Milhouse).

HARTMANN, Ferdinand. Austrian. He worked first at Mannheim where in 1858 he performed a concerto by Hartmann Stunz. He was a soloist again the following year. Later he moved to Munich where he was a performing member of the Akademie from 1869 to 1899, and also a member of the court orchestra.

HASENIER, Georges. 1845-1905. Belgian. He was clarinet professor at the Royal Conservatoire in Liège.

HASTIE. He was a member of the orchestra at Santo Domingo in 1798.

HAUSHÄLTER, Karl Wilhelm E. ?-1867. German. He played a concerto by Crusell at Weimar at an entr'acte concert in June 1826. From 1827 until about 1863 he played as a clarinettist and in the second violins in the court orchestra at Meiningen. He performed as a clarinet soloist there many times, the first occasion being on 18th January 1827.

HAUTE, Isidore François van den. Oudenarde, 15 Feb 1813-1870 July 12, Ghent. Belgian. He was principal clarinet at Ghent's Grand Theatre from 1844 and from 1847 until he died taught at the Conservatoire. He was also Kapellmeister of the second legion of the town guard from 1853. Charles Hanssens dedicated a concerto to him and Haute premièred it at the Casino Concerts for which he was first clarinet.

HAYENSCHINCK (HAYENDSCHINK, EICHENSCHENCK, EIGENSCHENK). He was a member of Louis XVI's court orchestra, with Solère. He played second to Solère in performances of Devienne's Symphonie Concertante on 24th December 1787 and 17th March 1788, also in that by Jadin on 20th March 1788, all for the Concert Spirituel. He had a younger brother who was a violinist in the court orchestra.

HEBESTREIT. German. He was a protégé of Jacobi, the town musician at Göttingen. He played second clarinet in Jacobi's orchestra, appearing as soloist with them in 1828.

HEFELE, Joseph. He played at the Munich Subscription Concerts in 1881 and 1882.

HEINNITZ (HENNIZ), John. ?-c.1803. He and Frickler were the clarinettists in "Choice pieces on the Clarinets and French Horns" which were played at the Marylebone Gardens in London in 1766. The horn players were Peter Seipst (Seipts) and Adam Rathgen (Rathyen). Heinnitz joined the Royal Society of Musicians in 1768 (Seipst and Rathgen became members in 1765). He is reported as playing the oboe about 1789.

HEINRICI, Georg Friedrich. German. He played second clarinet to Hermstedt in the wind band at Sondershausen in 1805. His younger brother Wilhelm played trombone in the band.

HEINZE, (Friedrich August) Ferdinand. Leipzig, 7 June 1793-1850 July 12, Leipzig. German. He was a pupil of Wilhelm Barth. After some early concerts which were badly criticised he became very popular as a soloist. He was a member of the Leipzig Gewandhaus Orchestra from 1811 to 1850 (1829 to 1842 as first clarinet). He taught his son Gustav Heinze, who also became a member of the Orchestra. The article by Fétis on Ferdinand Heinze is misleading and there is much wrong information on him in other biographical dictionaries.

Ferdinand Heinze's solo performances at Leipzig were as follows: 1815 – 9th February, Krommer's double concerto op.91 with Wilhelm Barth. 14th December, a concerto by Abraham Schneider. 1818 – 8th January, Friedrich Müller's Concerto op.10 in E flat. 3rd December, concerto by Abraham Schneider. 1819 – 4th November, Crusell's "new concerto in F minor" (op.5) – he received much applause and the review said that although his fast movements were rather dull his Adagios were excellent and similar to those of Baermann. 1821 – 25th October, Weber's Concertino and a concerto by Crusell. 1822 – 28th November, he performed a concerto, when they said he handled his instrument well but that his tone was not good. 1823 – 12th October, Crusell's First Concerto and one of Weber's concertos. 1824 – 2nd December, concerto by Abraham Schneider – he was taken to task for having an unsuitable reed. 1825 – 25th September, Weber's First Concerto. 1826 – 8th October, Crusell's Second Concerto – his failings were forgiven for some beautiful tone. 1828 – 21st January, Lindpaintner's Concertante for wind. 30th October, Crusell's First Concerto. 1829 – Weber's Concertino. 1830 – 21st January, an Adagio & Rondo (from op.1) by Crusell. May, Adagio & Rondo (from the First Concerto) by Weber. 1831 – 27th October, Potpourri op.3 for wind quintet by Nohr – this was played from the manuscript. 1832 – a "new" concertino by Reissiger – he was given loud applause and they said he played with great dexterity and beautiful tone. 13th December, a Rondo Brillaint for 2 clarinets by Nohr, with his colleague Rosenkranz. 1834 – Weber's Concertino, an Adagio by Spohr, Nohr's Potpourri (13th February), Mozart's "Parto!" for Elisabeth Fürst, and Concertino for 2 clarinets by Friedrich Müller with Rosenkranz (30th October). 1835 – 17th December, Weber's Concertino. 1836 – February, Adagio & Rondo by Weber. 12th December, Weber's Concertino. 1837 – Weber's Adagio & Rondo again, with long applause. Beginning of April, a concert with his son for the Euterpe Society. 23rd April, Beethoven's Septet. 1838 – 22nd March, Potpourri by Gerke on themes from Spohr's *Jessonda* and *Zemira.* His final appearance as soloist was on 14th March 1839.

HEINZE, Gustav (Adolph). Leipzig, 1 Oct 1820-1904 Feb 20, Muiderberg (near Amsterdam). German. He was a brilliant clarinettist, like his father Ferdinand, but at the age of twenty-four forsook playing for conducting and composition. He learnt the clarinet first from his father and by the age of seventeen was playing beside him as a member of the Leipzig Gewandhaus Orchestra. Mendelssohn, the orchestra's conductor, gave Gustav lessons in composition, and also proved an invaluable friend. In November 1837 Kotte gave several concerts at Leipzig and it was no doubt the considerable success of these which prompted Mendelssohn to give Gustav leave of absence the following year to go to Dresden and study with Kotte. Whilst there Heinze had composition lessons with Reissiger. Before returning home he made a short concert tour to Hanover, Kassel and Hamburg, during which he made friends with Marschner and Spohr. Many dictionaries give the year of the Dresden visit as 1840, but AMZ's report of Heinze's performances on 20th December 1838 in Leipzig states that he had then just returned from studying with Kotte. In December 1842 Heinze took over the post of first clarinet in the Gewandhaus Orchestra from his father. In 1844 he was offered the post of second Kapellmeister at Breslau and left Leipzig abruptly, never to play his clarinet again. He had great success at Breslau with two of his operas, the librettos of which were written by his wife. In 1850 he moved to Amsterdam as conductor of the German Opera.

Gustav Heinze's solo performances at Leipzig were as follows: 1837 – April, with his father for the Euterpe Society. 1838 – 22nd January, Introduction & Variations on Schubert's *Sehnsuchtswaltzer* by Ferdinand David, who was leader of the Gewandhaus Orchestra. 20th December, Weber's First Concerto, for the Subscription Concerts. 1839 – March, obligatos to Spohr's "Im Fliederbusch ein Vöglein sass" and Eberwein's "Wie die Nacht mit heiligem Beben" for Henrietta Bünau, with Mendelssohn accompanying. 14th November, Reissiger's Concertino. 1840 – February, solos. 22nd April, David's Introduction & Variations, with the composer conducting the orchestra. 2nd November, Andante Pastorale (from op.5) by Crusell, with Mendelssohn conducting. 26th November, a "new" Fantasia (op.180) by Reissiger. 1841 – 9th January, Mozart's Quintet with David leading, for a chamber music concert at the Gewandhaus – his rendering of the slow movement was especially commended. 3rd October, Weber's Concertino in a concert shared with Elisa Meerti – they said he was a very popular player. 1842 – 1st December, Adagio from a concerto by himself, with piano. 1843 – 9th February, Adagio (from op.1) by Crusell. 1844 – 8th February, a "new" Introduction & Variations by Kalliwoda, which earned "lively" applause.

Works: Concerto. Variations op.28 (Bachmann). Variations Concertantes for flute, clarinet & orchestra (Gombart).

HEISTERHAGEN. German. He was in the court orchestra at Kassel. On 27th March 1835 he played a double concerto by Krommer with Vauth. On 15th November 1839 he took part in Schindelmeisser's Symphonie Concertante for 4 clarinets with Lesser, Schultheis and Vauth. He was also an accomplished violinist and performed a Spohr concerto, also works by Lafont and Czerny.

HELD, Karl. He played in the court orchestra at Munich from 1824 to 1864, performing as a soloist there for the first time in 1827. He was a performing member of the Munich Akademie from 1818 to 1874. It was probably his son who became a violinist in the court orchestra.

HELFRICH. He played clarinet and oboe in the orchestra at Bremen and in 1821, on the death of Klingenberg, became director of the Hanseatic Music Corps. In December 1822 he performed on the clarinet, which was his principal instrument, in a concert shared with the clarinettist Rakemann senior and the latter's flautist son. The following year he gave several successful performances at the Trade Hall, playing works by Crusell, Iwan Müller, Späth and Spohr. In 1824 he gave a recital at the Trade Hall with the young pianist C.F. Schröter. He conducted the Hanseatic Band in public concerts during 1825, and in 1826 appeared again as soloist. In 1828 he performed a concerto by Crusell and was soloist again in 1830. He played the oboe in trios for flute, oboe and clarinet with Rakemann's two sons in 1834.

HELLENDAEL, Peter. Dutch. He was the son of the violinist Peter Hellendael, and was active as a clarinettist at Cambridge in 1789.

HELLER, Anton. 1743-1791 May, Prague. Czech. With his brother Eustach he was employed by Prince Carl Alois (Dlabacz says Carl Egon, but the latter was not born until 1796) Fürstenberg at Donaueschingen and then by the Archbishop of Prague, Anton Peter Pržichowský. When the latter's musical establishment was dissolved Heller was kept on as financial administrator.

Works: Concertos & solos (Ms.).

HELLER, Eustach. Czech. With his brother Anton he

was employed by the same two patrons and then went to Salzburg where in 1799 he is reported to be playing for another prince.

HELLWIG. ?-1829 June 27, Hanover. German. He was second clarinet in the court orchestra at Hanover from 1825 until his death. He also played violin.

HENGEL, Jacob. German. He played clarinet and horn in the Durlach court orchestra in the 1760s.

HENRI. He was employed at the Théâtre du Cap at at Santo Domingo. In 1782 he was also reported as a military musician.

HENRY (HENRI?) French. Fetís thinks he may be the son of the violinist Bonaventure Henry. He may be the "Mr Henri" who played his own concerto at Philadelphia on 4th April 1794 and who played in the Old American Company's orchestra at New York in 1798/9. In 1815 he was active in Paris.

Works: Concerto? Etudes ou caprices op.2 (Sieber). 6 Duos op.1 (Sieber). 3 Duos op.3 (Sieber). 3 Duos op.6 (Omont). 3 Duos (Dufaut & Dubois).

HENTSCHEL (HENTZSCHEL), Johann F. German. He was blind and learnt the clarinet from Kotte at the Blind Institute in Dresden. He then found employment at Carlsruhe. In 1848 he gave a concert in Kassel at which he performed a concerto by Weber, Beethoven's "Adelaide" (probably Iwan Müller's arrangement) and the obligato to two of Spohr's op.103 for Mlle Molendo. The report on his playing was very good. In 1852 he gave a concert at Lübeck.

HERMANN. He was a pupil of Heinrich Baermann and played a concerto by his teacher at Munich on 4th December 1833, when still a young man.

HERMBERG. He was employed as a clarinettist by the corporation of Lübeck about 1800. He had a brother who was a horn player.

HERMSTEDT, (Johann) Simon. Langensalza, 29 Dec 1778-1846 Aug 10, Sondershausen. German. See OV. The earliest performance by Hermstedt of Spohr's *Alruna* Variations was not in the autumn of 1810 at Leipzig, but on 15th January 1810 at Weimar. Hermstedt made an arrangement of these variations for clarinet and string quartet, which was published by Peters some time prior to 1828. Hermstedt performed Weber's Second Concerto at both his Prague concerts of 10th and 17th February 1815. Weber accompanied him at the second concert. Hermstedt taught Kellermann and C. Mahr.

Bibliography:

BECKER, Heinz – "Johann Simon Hermstedt." MGG.

HERRIG (HERIG). German. He played in the Brunswick court orchestra from 1826 to 1848.

HERZOG, August (Alois). Hamburg, c.1815-? German. He was a student at the Vienna Conservatoire, finishing his training in 1829. He performed Weber's Concertino at the public examinations in 1825. He then returned to Hamburg and earned a good reputation as a clarinettist. He also directed and composed dance music which had a considerable vogue. He appeared as a clarinet soloist in 1841 and 1845.

HESSE. German. He played at the National Theatre in Lübeck. In 1814 he shared a concert at Königsberg with Mlle Jülich, a singer whom he subsequently married, and her brother, an oboist. The programme included Paer's "Una voce al cor mi parla." Hesse later became a well-known theatrical designer and painter, his wife continuing her singing career.

HESSE, (Johann) Wilhelm. Nordhausen, 1760-1795. Brunswick. German. In 1783 he was first clarinet at the Court of Bentheim-Steinfürt. He then made an extensive concert tour and in 1784 secured an appointment to the Brunswick Court, where he remained until his death. He was also an instrument maker and in the Stearns Collection, Ann Arbor, is an 8-keyed basset-horn with his stamp, dated 1789. In 1786 he put a clarinet mouthpiece on a bassoon of his own manufacture, because he considered this gave the instrument a steadier sound. The Duke of Brunswick was particularly pleased with the invention and gave Hesse a gratuity of 100 thaler per annum. The only person to adopt this instrument however was Hesse's younger brother, Johann Georg Christian, who was bassoonist to the Prince of Bernburg.

HESSLER, Gustaf (Emil). Stockholm, 23 Feb 1873-? Swedish. He began life as a recruit in the Swedish Life Guards in 1886 and from 1888 to 1897 was a student at the Stockholm Conservatoire. In 1894 he was made solo clarinettist to the Court and remained in this position until 1905, when he was pensioned. In 1904 he was made professor of clarinet and in 1907 of ensemble playing at the Conservatoire. In 1921 he was elected a member of the Royal Academy of Music. He conducted the band of the 1st battalion Swedish Life Guards from 1904 and was given the rank of Captain in 1922. He composed 15 military marches.

HESSLER, Martin. ?-1807 Dec 22, Würzburg. German. He played at the Court of Würzburg from 1760 until his death. He was a good teacher, his most famous pupil being Meissner.

HEYNECK, Edmund. German. He played in the Leipzig Gewandhaus Orchestra, retiring in 1902.

HIEBETSCH (HIBISCH, HIEBESCH), Carl Ernst. Birkhausen, 14 Nov 1777-? He was second clarinet in the Öttingen-Wallerstein court orchestra about 1810.

HINZE. In 1909 he was playing in the Weimar court orchestra.

HOFFMAN(N). He appeared as a soloist at Philadelphia on 16th November 1769.

HOFFMANN, A. German. He was first clarinet in the Hallé Orchestra at Manchester from 1887 to 1897.

HOFFMANN (HOFMANN), Johann Georg Gottfried. Lübeck, 1781-1814 Jan, Frankfurt a. M. German. He was engaged in 1804 for the theatre orchestra at Frankfurt. In April 1806 it was announced that he would be leaving for the Munich Court in a few months, but whilst there is no record of him at the Bavarian capital, concert reports cease until he appears back at Frankfurt in 1812. Two years later he caught typhus and died, leaving a widow and four children. He was said to have played with "indescribable charm" and a "speechlessly beautiful tone," but without much expression. There is no doubt he created a sensation, for audiences often interrupted his playing with spontaneous applause. Some of the appeal may have been due to the unusual compositions he chose for his programmes.

Hoffmann's concerts at Frankfurt were as follows: 1804 – 14th March, a concerto by Riotte. 25th December, a concerto by Krommer and the obligato to a duet by Florio (Italian flautist, the protégé of Mme. Mara). The accompaniment was for clarinet with 2 guitars and the singers were Catherine Buchwieser and Aloysia Lange, Mozart's sister-in-law. 1805 – 20th February, concerto by Witt and an obligato for Mlle Buchwieser . The concert was shared by two of his brothers who played the piano and violin. 1st March, a double concerto by Tausch with Baumgártner. 1812 – 28th March, a concerto by Duvernoy and Variations by Ahl. 1813 – 19th February, Witt's Concerto again and a Symphonie Concertante for 7 clarinets with wind orchestra & Turkish music by Düring, the bassoon part being taken by the composer.

HOFMANN, Richard. Spergau, 7 Jan 1859-1924 Nov 9, Hanover. German. He played at the town theatre in Hamburg until 1889 when he became second clarinet in the court orchestra at Hanover. He was made a Royal Chamber Musician in 1890 and retired in 1922.

HOLLENSTEIN, Michael. German. He was in the court orchestra at Stuttgart in 1823.

HOLLNSTEINER. German. He was a member of the court orchestra at Kremsmünster about 1814.

HOLMANN, U. German. In 1783 he was playing clarinet in the court orchestra at Bentheim-Steinfürt.

HOLMÈS, Augusta. Paris, 16 Dec 1847-1903 Jan 28, Paris. French, of Irish parentage. She became a well-known composer, but in her youth achieved some virtuosity on the clarinet. She had private lessons in both clarinet and orchestration from Klosé.

Work: Fantasie, written in 1900 for the Conservatoire contests and dedicated to Cyrille Rose (Leduc).

HOLZAPFEL. German. He was a member of the court orchestra at Kassel. On 6th December 1843 he performed a Reissiger Fantasie at the Subscription Concerts. In 1847 he played Reissiger's Concerto and in 1848 a Rondo Brilliant by Lindpaintner.

HOPKINS, Edward (Samuel George). London, 25 Feb 1779-1860. English. He played the violin as well as clarinet and was the son of the horn player Edward Hopkins. His brother George was also a clarinettist. As with John and William Mahon, the activities of the Hopkins brothers are difficult to disentangle, for generally no forname is given in concert reports. Edward was a member of the band of the Scots Guards from 1797 and in 1815, after the return of the regiment from the Waterloo campaign, he was made bandmaster. Later he became music director at the Vauxhall Gardens. He was principal clarinet at Covent Garden from 1812 until January 1829 when Willman came in as first and Hopkins moved down to second. In 1838 he was pensioned from the army. Hopkins was popular as an obligato player, the following being some of his performances: 1820 – Bishop's "The Ray of Hope can cheer the Heart" for Miss Stephens. 1827 – 30th January, (C.L.J?) André's "Benedictus" with obligati for clarinet, horn, violin and cello. 28th March, Guglielmi's "Gratias agimus."

HOPKINS, George. ?-1869. English. He was the son of the horn player Edward Hopkins and brother of Edward, the clarinettist. He was in the orchestra at Covent Garden from about 1812, probably until 1829 when Willman came in. With his brother he took part in the 1826 production of *Oberon* conducted by Weber.

HORN. He played as a clarinet soloist at Riga in 1847.

HORNÍK. Czech. He was a Chamber Musician to Prince Esterházy in Vienna. After he was pensioned by the Prince he appeared as a soloist on 28th March 1817 to support his two daughters, Caroline and Johanna, both of whom were well-known singers. He played Cartellieri's Concerto, and the obligato to an aria by Hummel for Caroline. On 19th April 1818 he gave another concert with his daughters. Both concerts received good reviews.

HOSTIÉ (HOSTIER), J.(M). ?-1834, Berlin. French. He also played the violin. He first earned a name for himself as a clarinet soloist in Paris, where he played the following solos at the Concert Spirituel: 1787 – 2nd April, concerto by Yost. 5th April, ditto. 15th August, a "new" concerto by himself. 1788 – 22nd March, an unspecified concerto. In 1788 he was appointed clarinettist to the Duke of Montmorency. He was in the National Guard until 1794 and later travelled, settling in Königsberg in 1812 as a member of the of the town's theatre orchestra. Here he was very popular as a soloist, playing in the following concerts: 1812 – autumn, a concerto by Crusell. 1817 – unspecified works. 1819 – 24th February, concerto for flute & clarinet by Friedrich Westenholz with Mme George, a flautist from the Court of Mecklenburg-Schwerin. In the summer of this year Mozart's aria "Parto!" was sung by Auguste Knorre, accompanied by Mozart's son, Franz; there is little doubt that Hostié would have been the clarinettist. 1820 – unspecified works. 1822 – 8th January a concertino for clarinet by Wilhelm Braun and a concerto for 2 violins by Spohr with Edward Maurer. 1823 – 28th September, Adagio & Rondo (from the concerto?) by Crémont. 1824 – 16th March, his farewell concert in which he played a concertino in E flat (probably op.19) by Lindpaintner, the obligato to an aria from Spohr's *Der Zweikampf mit der Geliebten* for Emilia Cartellieri, and Lindpaintner's Concertante for wind.

Hostié moved to Berlin in 1824 with an appointment as violinist in the orchestra at the Königsberg Theatre. He did no more solo performing but was a clarinet teacher at the High School for Music. He taught Schindelmeisser at the High School and possibly also earlier in Königsberg. Schindelmeisser dedicated his Concertino in E flat to Hostié.

Works: Concerto no.1 (Naderman 1788). 6 Duos op.1 (Naderman). 6 Duos op.4 (Naderman – PBN).

(B–H). **HÜBLER Carl Friedrich.** ?-1792 Apr 10 or 11, Leipzig. German. He also played the flute and oboe. He was mainly employed as a clarinettist and basset-horn player in the Leipzig Gewandhaus Orchestra from 1784 until his death. On 16th March 1789 he took part in an obligato for clarinet & bassoon (the latter taken by Schwartz the elder) to an aria by Paisiello for Mme Schicht. He was a basset-horn soloist in 1790 and 1791.

HUGOT, Adolphe. 1799-? French. He was a brother of Pierre Hugot. They were probably sons of the flautist A. Hugot. Adolphe was, like Pierre, a pupil of Lefèvre at the Conservatoire. He gained a First Prize in 1822 and in the same year became second clarinet at the Théâtre de la Gaité. He did well and after a second season at the Gaité moved in 1824 to the Opéra Comique as sub-principal. Here he remained until 1833 or later, becoming principal clarinet in 1831. His various addresses were as follows: 1824 – no.22 rue des Deux Portes St Sauveur; 1825 – no.10 rue Chantereine; 1827 – no.18 rue Montholon; 1831 – no.13 rue Cadet.

HUGOT, Pierre. 1804-? French. (See Adolphe Hugot). He was a pupil of Lefèvre and gained a First Prize in 1825. Before his graduation he had already been playing second clarinet at the Théâtre de la Porte St Martin since 1823. In 1823 and 1824 he was living at no.23 rue St Sauveur, but had moved to no.3 rue Chauchat by 1825.

Works: 5th Air varié for clarinet & strings (Hofmeister). Variations on "Chant d'Avenel et Air eccosais (sic)" from Boieldieu's

La Dame Blanche (Janet).

HUGRAY (HUGRAIS). French. In 1818, when Vanderhagen moved down to second and Péchignier changed to the Opéra orchestra, Hugray became first clarinet at the Théâtre Français (Comédie Française), remaining in the post up to 1830. He lived at no.32 rue St Benoît.

HUMMEL, Friedrich. Memmingen (near Augsburg), 18 Sept 1800-1883 or later. Austrian. He also played the flute and received his initial training from a musician in the village where he was born. In 1819 he went to Munich to join the band of the 1st King's regiment. His brother Tobias Hummel played bassoon in the same band and then became a member of the Munich court orchestra. Friedrich had clarinet lessons from Heinrich Baermann, who was much struck by his ability and made him into a fine player. In 1833 he gave concerts in the southern Tyrol and in 1836 played at Salzburg, Prague, Zittau, Leipzig (28th January), Altenburg, Weimar and Meiningen (12th February).

HUNGER, Johann Heinrich. German. He played first clarinet and second oboe in the Leipzig Gewandhaus Orchestra from 1788 to 1800.

HUTH. In 1886 he was in the Berlin court orchestra.

ITJEN. He was clarinet soloist for Jullien at the English Opera House in 1842.

JÄGER, Christian. Anspach, ?-1827 Oct 24, Berlin. German. He played in the Berlin court opera orchestra from 1810 to 1823 or later. On 15th December 1820 he played the obligato to Mozart's "Parto!" for Mme Arnold. He composed, but nothing for clarinet.

JANDOT. French. He was first clarinet in the theatre at Bordeaux in 1822. Not long afterwards he emigrated to the U.S.A. and settled in New Orleans.

JANSSEN (JANSSENS, JANSSON, JENSSENS), César. Paris, 11 Apr 1781-1835. French. He is best known as the inventor of rollers for the clarinet, which were applied also to the flute and bassoon. Although not an instrument maker himself, a clarinet with rollers of his design was shown at the Louvre Industrial Exhibition of 1823. When he was fourteen years old, in 1795, he entered the newly opened Paris Conservatoire to study under Lefèvre. He left the following October so was not a prize winner and never became more than a second-rate player. For a time he picked a living in the fringe theatres and was finally second clarinet at the Opéra Comique from 1814 until he retired in 1835. In 1821 and 1822 he was living at no.14 rue Lévêque.

JARDIN, Magin. Cervera, 30 Dec 1782-1869 Feb 17, Madrid. Spanish. He was first clarinet in the Madrid court orchestra until 1858. From 1829 until 1857 he taught clarinet and also flute at the Madrid Conservatoire. His best known clarinet pupils were Pedro Arias and Pedro Sarmiento. He also taught his nephews Manuel and Jerónimo Jardin. A niece of his, Josephine Jardin, became a harp virtuoso.

JARDIN, Manuel. Spanish. He was taught by his uncle Magin Jardin at the Madrid Conservatoire, winning medals at the contests in 1832 and 1833. For his First Prize he played a Thême varié by Gambaro.

JEANJEAN, Paul. 1874-1928. French. He was a pupil of Cyrille Rose at the Paris Conservatoire, gaining a First Prize in 1894. He became solo clarinet of the Garde Républicaine and was also first clarinet of the Classical Concerts at Monte Carlo. He wrote some splendid books of studies which were published by Leduc.

Works, all published by Andrieu: Arabesques. Clair Matin. Deuxième Andantino. Heureux Temps. Rêverie de Printemps. Variations sur "Au clair de la lune."

(B–H). **JODRY.** He played in the orchestra for the French Theatre at Hamburg in 1818. Also during 1818 he played second basset-horn in Mozart's *Requiem*, with Carl Hartmann playing first.

JULIÁ, Manuel. Spanish. In 1806 he was playing first clarinet at the Teatro del Principe in Madrid.

JUNDT. German. He was a clarinettist at Strasbourg. In 1822 he performed a double concerto by Tausch with Kern, a concerto by Cramer (J.B.?) and variations by Danzi and by Präger. He is probably related to Mlle A. Jundt, who was a solo pianist at Strasbourg in 1822 and 1824.

KAISER. German. He played in the orchestra of the French Theatre at Hamburg in 1818, with Jodry.

KAISER, Julius. German. He played in the court orchestra at Dresden about 1875 to 1885. He taught Marhefka and on the death of the latter's father, became his guardian.

KANIA (KANNYA), Johann. ?-1849 Mar 14, Vienna. He came from Rostock to Vienna in 1836 and gave a concert at the Kärntnerthortheater with the flautist Prosper Amtmann and the violinist Joseph Scaramelli. It was reported that Kania, leader of the "clover leaf," took the prize. The flautist was described as "one fallen from the clouds." Kania became a member of the Vienna Philharmonic Orchestra until his death.

KASTUS, Anthoine Joseph. Swiss. In 1789 he moved from Porrentruy at La Chaux de Fonds to live at Neuchâtel. From 1790 to 1801 he was first clarinet for the Société du Concert; the following year he moved to second.

KASZUBA, Pawel. Polish. He was a well-known clarinettist of the eighteenth century.

KAUER, Ferdinand. Czech. He also played the flute. He was first employed as a court musician at Rumburg and, after some years in Vienna, settled in Prague about 1808.

Work: Neue Clarinettschule (Bermann).

KELLERMANN, Thilo. Sondershausen 1811-? German. He learnt the clarinet from Hermstedt. On 5th March 1846 he gave a performance of a concerto by Spohr at Leipzig which was very highly commended. He became first clarinet of the Loh Orchestra at Sondershausen.

KELLNER, Joseph. Gmunden, ?-? Austrian. He played in the town theatre at Riga until 1884, when he moved to Hanover to become first clarinet in the court orchestra there. In 1886 he was dismissed from his post at Hanover.

KERMAZIN, Franc de. German. He was a bassoonist at the Concert Spirituel who, according to Constant Pierre, performed a clarinet concerto for the Society on 25th March 1750. *Mercure de France* announced the work as being for the "clarine."

KERN, A. German. He was a member of the orchestra at Strasbourg. In 1822 he played a double concerto by Tausch with Jundt. It was probably he who, at a later date, was choral director and court secretary at Strasbourg.

KIESELER. German. He played in the garrison band at Strasbourg. He was reported to have a good tone and plenty of expression when he performed variations by Berr in 1830.

KIRCHEIS. ?-1856. German. He was first a general music teacher and then fought in the wars. From 1819 to 1823 or later he became a member of the court orchestra at Darmstadt, playing violin and bass drum as well when required.

(B–H). **KIRSTEIN (KIRRSTEIN, KIRSTEN).** He played clarinet and first basset-horn at the Court of Princess Elizabeth of Freiburg in the late 1780s. At Leipzig he performed a basset-horn solo on 19th February 1795 and was a soloist on the clarinet there in 1792, 1793 and 1795.

KJELLBERG, Johan (Gustaf). Gillberga, 13 Aug 1846-1904 Oct 2, Stockholm. Swedish. He was the foremost clarinet player and teacher of his time in Sweden. From 1868 to 1872 he was a pupil at the Stockholm Conservatoire. During this time he made copies, preserved in the library of Stockholm's Royal Academy of Music, of Crusell's concertos op.5 and op.11 and of the Concert Trio. This is interesting evidence that although at that time Crusell's works had been largely forgotten by the rest of the world, their value was still appreciated in his adoptive country. Kjellberg was in the court orchestra at Stockholm from 1871 to 1890. In 1876 he became music director of the Dal regiment and in 1882 was in the Swedish Life Guards. He taught at the Conservatoire from 1886 until his death.

KLEE, Johann. He was first clarinet in the court orchestra belonging to the Elector of Trevès at Coblenz-Ehrenbreitstein from 1773 to 1794. He was frequently heard as a soloist.

KLEIN (KLEYN, KLIN, KLYN). He performed for the Concert Spirituel in 1773 and on 25th March 1775 played with Reiffer in a work for 2 clarinets, 2 horns & 2 bassoons. He was still living in Paris as a clarinet teacher in 1788.

KLEIN, Georg. 1753-1832 July 29, Vienna. Austrian.

He was not related to Thomas Klein. In 1796 he succeeded Anton Stadler as second clarinet in the court orchestra at Vienna. When Johann Stadler left the orchestra in 1804 Klein moved up to first and retained this post until his death. He took part, aged seventy-four, in the first public performance of Schubert's Octet on 16th April 1827, at the "Red Hedgehog."

KLEIN, Johann Heinrich. German. He played clarinet in the cathedral orchestra at Cologne in 1785.

KLEIN, Thomas. Nuremberg, 10 Aug 1802-1888 Jan 18, Vienna? German. He was not related to Georg Klein. According to Mendel he learnt the clarinet from Kapellmeister Alois Maurer. By 1826 he was a Royal Bavarian court musician. In the autumn of that year he was given a splendid reception when he went back to Nuremberg to perform as a soloist. In 1828 he became first clarinet of the court opera orchestra at Vienna. He was in the court orchestra proper from 1838 to 1867; in this he played only second clarinet and his undoubted talent was not allowed to shine, for he was overshadowed first by Joseph and then by Anton Friedlowsky. The situation was different in the Vienna Philharmonic Orchestra; here he was the original first clarinet and reigned supreme from 1828 until he was pensioned in 1881. From 1851 to 1881 he taught at the Conservatoire. He joined the Tonkünstlersocietät in 1839.

His solo performances were as follows: 1826 – autumn, at Nuremberg. 1827 – February at Stuttgart, Molique's Concerto. 1829 – 20th February at Vienna's Large Ridotto Room, his own Divertissement op.2. 28th February at the Kärntnerthortheater, "Variations" (probably his own Air varié op.1). 1832 – unspecified solos. 1833 – Weber's Concertino, Adagio & Rondo by Franz Grutsch, the assistant director at the theatre, and Lindpaintner's Concertante for wind. 1835 – Potpourri by Grutsch and wind quintet by Wilhelm Reuling, the director of the court orchestra. 1841 – Molique's Concertino, from the manuscript. 1843 – 19th November, Mozart's "Parto!" for Maria Stöckl-Heinefetter with the Philharmonic Orchestra.

Works: Air varié op.1 (Richault). Divertissement op.2 (Richault). Fantasie? (See F. Tretbar article).

KLEINE, (Jacob) Christoph. The Hague, 6 Mar 1785-1832 Apr 24, Amsterdam. Dutch. He was the second son of a wind player, Wilhelm Georg Kleine, who came to the Netherlands from Austria in the second half of the eighteenth century. He learnt the clarinet from Dreiklufts in Amsterdam at the beginning of the nineteenth century and became one of Holland's finest players. He had a good, full tone and great speed, but his style was said to be rather lacking in taste. He first played at the French Theatre in The Hague. Then he moved to Amsterdam, where he was first clarinet for the opera orchestra and for the Felix Meritis Society. Of particular interest in his career were his collaborations with Hermstedt and Christiani. His son, J.W. Kleine, became an excellent clarinettist.

His solo performances at Amsterdam included the following: 1808 – three concerto concerts. 1812 – Witt's Concerto. 1814 – one solo date. 1815 – Concerto by Schneider (probably G.A.), a double concerto by Krommer with Planke junior. On 19th December, a Benefit at which eleven items were played, including Schneider's Concerto again and a Rondo by F. Müller, a cellist at Amsterdam. 1817 – Concertos by Schneider, Wilms, Stumf and F. Müller (Friedrich Müller, the clarinettist). 1819 – 9th, 12th & 14th November double concertos by Krommer with Hermstedt. Danzi's Concertino. 1823 – April, a double concerto by Krommer with Christiani. 1825 – June, Military Concerto by Bernard Koch, a violinist and conductor in Amsterdam.

KLEINE, Dietrich Wilhelm. The Hague, 1778-1837, Carlsruhe. Dutch. He was the son of Heinrich Kleine, from whom he learnt, and a cousin of Christoph Kleine. First he was Kapellmeister to a regiment of huntsmen and in 1815 went to Carlsruhe to be first clarinet in the court orchestra, remaining there until his death. Danzi, Carlsruhe's Kapellmeister, dedicated his Second Potpourri to Kleine.

Works: Concertino in E flat (Simrock c.1825 – LBL. Hofmeister 1844). Adagio & Polacca (Simrock). Introduction & Variations (Simrock).

KLEINE, Heinrich. The Hague, ?-1798, Amsterdam. Dutch. He was the second son of Johann Wilhelm Kleine, a wind player and regimental Kapellmeister, and was the father of the clarinettist Dietrich Kleine. He played at the French Theatre in The Hague and at the court of Prince William V of Orange. Later he moved to Amsterdam and played in the orchestra for the German Theatre. He had four other musical sons.

KLEINE, Jacob (Willem). Amsterdam, 1815-1898 Oct 20, Amsterdam. Dutch. He learnt the clarinet from his father, Christoph Kleine, and developed great beauty and softness of tone. At some time before the revolution of 1830, while still a youth, he performed with his father at a court concert for William I. His father died in 1832 and he then took over the post of second clarinet in the Felix Meritis Society. Later he came to England with the Boer Orchestra. He was much fêted by the English and remained some years, playing for the Drury Lane theatre orchestra and for Jullien at the Surrey Gardens. In spite of this success he returned to Amsterdam in 1847 and played for the Cecilia Concerts and for the Park Orchestra. In 1860 he was a member of a wind quintet. After the dissolution of the Park Orchestra he played a few more years for Amsterdam's orchestral society before retiring in 1887.

KLEINHAUS. German. He learnt from Meissner and became a well-known clarinettist.

KLETT (KLET, KLEET, KLEIT). He was second clarinet at the Gymnase Dramatique in Paris from 1821 to 1825. His various addresses were: 1821 – no.40 rue de l'Université; 1822 – café de Beaune in the rue de Beaune; 1823/4 – 140 faubourg St Antoine; 1825 – the "Gros Caillou" at no.6 rue de Grenelle.

KLINGENBERG. ?-1821 June, Bremen. German. He was a director of the Hanseatic Military Band in Bremen. On 23rd June 1819 in Bremen cathedral he played the clarinet obligato in Guglielmi's "Gratias agimus" for Catalani. His strong full tone, said also to be throaty and metallic, filled the building and the performance was very brilliant. Klingenburg died two years later, still only a young man.

KLIPFELE, Georg. German. He played clarinet and oboe in the court orchestra at Carlsruhe from 1772 to 1775.

KLOSÉ, Hyacinthe Eléonore. Corfu, 11 Oct 1808-1880 Aug 29, Paris. French. See OV. He conducted the 9th Light Infantry regiment from 1831 to 1835 and the 11th Artillery regiment from 1836. During this time he played first clarinet for the orchestra at the Gymnase Musical. Berlioz heard him in this environment and wrote the following panegyric in *Le Rénovateur* of 17th May 1835; "La facilité avec laquelle il se joue des plus scabreuses difficultés de l'instrument n'est pas à nos yeux son principal mérite, il en possède un autre d'autant plus précieux que le travail le plus opiniâtre ne saurait le donner, je veux perler de l'embouchure et de la qualité de son. Bien que le timbre de la clarinette jouée par M. Klosé offre beaucoup de rapport avec celui que sait en tirer son habile maitre, il y a pourtant en lui un caractère particulier qui lui donne une physionomie originale, une douceur et une expression avec laquelle lutterait en vain tout autre instrument à vent. La voix humaine, a mon gré, s'approche même pas du velouté et de la tendresse mélancolique de ces sons de clarinette . . ."

He played at the Théâtre Italien from 1836, first as second clarinet to Berr and after the latter's death in 1838 to Iwan Müller, finally becoming solo clarinet when Müller left in 1841. He performed for the Société des Concerts as follows: 1837 – 5th March, Berr's 10th Air varié. 1844 – 10th March, one of his own compositions. 1848 – 20th February, ditto. The *Süddeutsche Musikzeitung* of 26th September 1864 announced the awarding of Klosé's Legion of Honour, the same day as his pupil Paulus. This refutes the oft repeated date of 1869.

Klosé's many notable pupils included Boutruy, Grisez, Augusta Holmès, Leroy, Mayeur (to whom he also taught the saxophone in the early 1850s), Paulus, Rose, Frédéric Selmer and Turban. He composed all the test pieces for the Conservatoire contests during his lengthy term of office. After his retirement in 1868 the tradition that these had to be the composition of the professor concerned was dropped and a commission to write the test piece generally given to one of the composition professors. Klosé's compositions however proved so suitable that they were frequently set again in later years.

Works: Concerto. Concertino (Leduc). 8 Airs variés – no.6 dedicated to Turban (Leduc – copies, except for no.5, in LBL). Dernière pensée de Weber (Leduc 1880). Fantasias on *Barber of Seville, Der Verführung, Der Freischütz, La Fille de la Vallée, Le Bijou Perdu, L'Invitation à la Valse, Norma, Oberon* (Rivière & Hawkes – LBL). Les Lilas, Fantaisie Concertante (Leduc 1874 – LBL). Moïse de Rossini (Leduc 1880). Polonaise. Solo Bolero. 12 Solos. Trois pensées musicales (Leduc 1882 – LBL). 8 Duos concertants op.8. Solo for alto saxophone & piano, dedicated to Adolphe Sax (1860s). Méthode pour servir à l'enseignement de la clarinette à anneaux mobiles, dedicated to Carafa (Meissonnier 1843 – LBL). Méthode complète de Saxophone-Baryton Mi bémol (Leduc 1880 – LBL).

KLOTZSCH. In 1885 he was first clarinet in the court orchestra at Kassel.

KNIRSCH, Emil. He played at the Munich Subscription Concerts from 1894 until 1911 or later.

KNITTEL, Mme. German. She played a clarinet quartet at a Subscription Concert at Kassel in 1816. AMZ said: "Her delivery is cold, her skill trifling, but she received some applause for the unusualness of seeing the instrument played by a lady."

KNOCH. German. He was highly spoken of when he appeared as clarinet soloist at Erfurt in 1843.

KÖBEL, Carl J.P. Aken, 7 Sept 1806-1871 Jan 16, Stockholm. German. He was a pupil of Crusell and joined the court orchestra at Stockholm in 1834. On Crusell's death in 1838 he took over his regimental post. There are hand-written copies by Köbel of Crusell's Concerto op.1 and Progessive Duets op.6 in the library of Stockholm's Royal Academy of Music. Spicknall records a performance by Köbel of Crusell's Concert Trio with a doubtful date of March 1828.

KOEHN. German. He was a Chamber Musician to the Grand Duke of Oldenburg. In 1845 at a court concert of Spohr's compositions he performed the First Concerto. Spohr, who was in the audience, recorded his pleasure in the performance.

KÖTTLITZ. German. He was a clarinettist and timpanist in the orchestra at Königsberg. He was first employed as timpanist. When the post of first clarinet became vacant in 1840 AMZ reported that Köttlitz was abandoning his "frequent musings and unproductive leisure as a drummer to get employment as first clarinet, for on this he has dexterity and a beautiful tone."

(B–H). **KÖTZSCHAU (KÖTZSCHKE), Hermann.** German. He studied soprano clarinet with Kotte and bass clarinet with Forckert. From 1857 to 1890 he was a Chamber Musician at the Dresden Court, and he also taught the basset-horn at the Dresden Conservatoire.

KOHLSCHMIDT, Leopold. German. He played in the court orchestra at Weimar in 1855.

KOLBE. German. In 1814 he was second clarinet in the court orchestra at Kremsmünster.

KOLLMANN. German. In 1841 he took part in a performance of Schindelmeisser's Symphonie Concertante for 4 clarinets at Kassel with Bättenhausen, Curth and Wenderoth.

KOPP, Franz Joseph. German. In 1792 he played in the court orchestra at Donaueschingen. He also played the violin.

KOTTE, Johann (Gottlieb). Rathmansdorf (near Schandau) 29 Sept 1797-1857 Feb 3, Dresden. German. He was a very fine clarinettist at the Saxon Court and deserves to be better known than he is. Dresden itself called him Germany's premier clarinettist, saying he was of the "old school" who kept the instrument's true character with a full, tender and rounded tone. Other reports mention great sensitivity and the ability to produce the faintest pianissimo. Most of his success was due to talent and determination, but some also to the patronage of Weber who, as Moritz Fürstenau said, "helped him in in word and deed." Both Rendall (in his private notes) and Profeta state that Weber wrote the Grand Duo for Kotte, but this is incorrect, for the work was completed in 1816, before Kotte came into contact with the composer. Kotte did however give the first known complete performance of it, at Dresden in the Spring of 1824. Kotte certainly inspired composers and the following works were dedicated to him: Karl Boehmer's Concertino op.9 and Reissiger's Second Fantaisie op.180. It is also probable that some of Kummer's works, which Kotte played so often, were written for him.

Kotte's origins were humble. His parents, who were serving folk, sent him away from home at sixteen, as an apprentice to Böhme, the town musician at Stolpen. He lived for four unhappy and unproductive years with this man and during this time walked on several occasions the ten to twelve miles into Dresden in order to have lessons from the elder Lauterbach. Finally, at Easter 1817, he absconded and apprenticed himself to Krebs, the town musician at Dresden. By the autumn of that same year his talents had won him the post of second clarinet in the court opera orchestra. His success was immediate and not long after, he took over Lauterbach's place as first clarinet. In 1823 he was made a Royal Chamber Musician and was still playing in the orchestra in 1849. He thus provided not only Weber but Wagner with a superb principal clarinet. He was friendly with both the Baermanns, especially Carl, whose compositions he was particularly fond of playing. A letter in the Deutsche Staatsbibliothek from Kotte to Carl Baermann shows him to have been an interesting and good correspondent, and a warm-hearted man. He was a very fine teacher and was professor at the Dresden Conservatoire up to the time of his death. His many notable pupils included Karl Förster, J.G. Forckert, Gustav Heinze, Hentschel, Kötzschau and Eduard Meyer.

His solo concerts, at Dresden unless otherwise stated, were as follows: 1823 – 23rd December at his own concert, Variations (probably op.20) by Heinrich Baermann and "a new concerto for clarinet" (probably the Second Concerto) by Weber. 1824 – Spring, in the Public Quartet Concerts, a "concertante" by Weber, with Julius

3. Final page of letter from Kotte to Kranklin, Dresden 10th October 1852. *(Deutsche Staatsbibliothek, Berlin/DDR).*

Benedikt playing the piano; this is the first known complete performance of the Grand Duo. 30th December, a concerto by Riotte and a wind quintet by Reicha. 1832 – 7th December in the Poland Hotel, Mozart's "Parto!" for Wilhelmine Schröder-Devrient; this must have been a superb partnership. 1834 – 7th February at his own concert in the Harmonie Hall, a concerto by Kummer (cellist at the Dresden Court, who also played the clarinet and horn) and Schweizer Variations by Wieprecht. The latter work involved a good deal of "klap-trap" with trumpets, drums and 3 "droning" trombones. "Que de bruit pour une omelette!" remarks the critic, but Kotte played "beautifully." Near the end of the year Kotte performed with great success in a concert at Berlin's Royal Opera House. 1835 – 9th February at his own concert in Dresden, Concertino and Variations op.33 by Weber, "Slumber Song of the Mute" for clarinet & harmonichord by Friedrich Kaufmann. Kaufmann himself played the harmonichord, which he had invented. 13th February, Beethoven's Septet. 7th November, Adagio & Polacca by Kummer. Nocturne for clarinet, violin and harp by C.R.N. Bochsa with Louis Haase and Mme Friedrichs. 1837 – 17th October, Weber's Grand Duo with Johann Eisert. 2nd November at a concert he shared with Kummer in Leipzig, a Fantasy on themes from Bellini's *Capulets and Montagues* by Kummer; AMZ's critic liked his tone, but said the extreme register lacked quality. 6th November at the Leipzig Gewandhaus in a concert conducted by Mendelssohn, a 'new' concertino by Kummer and Iwan Müller's arrangement of Beethoven's "Adelaide." 13th November, also at Leipzig, Weber's Grand Duo with Charlotte Fink, who had played it with Heinrich Baermann the year before.

1838 – 19th February in Dresden, unspecified solo works. 28th February, a double concerto by Kummer with F.W. Lauterbach. 30th April in a concert given by Louis Lacombe, Adagio & Rondo by Lacombe. 1839 – again Lacombe's Adagio & Rondo, which earned loud applause. Towards the end of the year he appeared in Vienna with great success, and then Prague, where they raved over him. The Prague performances consisted of two entr'acte concerts in which he played a Fantasie (probably the Second) by Reissiger, Kummer's *Capulets and Montagues* Variations, Wieprecht's Schweitzer Variations and Müller's "Adelaide." 1841 – 4th February in Dresden, a Fantasie (Rummel's) on Beethoven's "Ah perfido," in which he was accompanied by Joseph Netzer. AMZ took him to task over these compositions by saying "he charms his audience not only with his talent, but by choosing simple things that appeal to the young. Why does he not let them hear Weber or Spohr? When the concert-giver has only his own interests at heart he should not be thanked, for it is gold he is after. Light pieces should be played in the salons, but with a fine orchestra major works should be performed." 1842 – 20th January in his own concert, Iwan Müller's Concertino Capriccioso, Adagio from Mozart's Concerto, Beethoven's Septet, Reissiger's Introduction & Variations. "The choice of works was happy" – they were mollified! 1843 – 11th December, a Fantasie (probably the Second) by Reissiger and Phantasiegebilde by Carl Baermann. 1846 – 20th March in his own concert, Weber's Concertino, Adagio from Mozart's Concerto and Anton Fürstenau's "Reminiscences of Euryanthe." There was a large audience and he received much applause. Later in the year at Charles Mayer's concert, an Adagio by Weber. 1847 – Beethoven's Septet.

KRAG. He was in the court orchestra at Copenhagen in 1806.

KRAMER (CRAMER), Christian (Carl Christopher). Hanover, 1767-1834 Feb, London. German. See OV. He and Willman were appointed to teach the clarinet at the Royal Academy of Music, London, when it was opened in 1823. Kramer resigned in 1825.

Bibliography:

Obituary – *(The Athenaeum).* 1st March 1834, p.170.

KRAUSE. German. He played in the court orchestra at Schleiz in 1849.

KRAUSE. German. He trained at the Dresden Conservatoire and by 1885 was a member of the orchestra at Danzig.

(B–H). **KRAUSE, Johann Gottlieb.** Guben, 31 July 1777-? German. He was the younger brother of Karl Joseph Krause. He was principally a clarinettist but learnt also to play the violin, oboe, bassoon and horn. It was probably this lack of specialisation and the fact that he was employed at a number of the smaller courts where opportunities were small that caused him finally to turn to non-musical employment. His father was a horn and bassoon player who in 1780 obtained a position at the Court of Baron Hochburg at Plogwitz near Löwenburg, Silesia. Johann first learnt to play the horn and violin, but when David and Springer arrived to join the Court in 1786 he learnt clarinet and basset-horn from them. The Court was disbanded when the Baron died in 1789 and the father then moved to nearby Holstein where he was employed by Count Röder. Here Johann completed his clarinet studies, though with whom is not known, and learnt the oboe under Blaha. In 1794 the Holstein orchestra was also disbanded and Johann found employment with his brother at the Court of Count Hoym in Breslau. Although the clarinet remained his principal instrument he now had lessons on the bassoon. He gave two performances of double concertos by Krommer with his brother in 1804 at Breslau which caused a furore. Johann's tone was said to be cutting, though at the same time not coarse. His brother's tone was gentle, as was his character, and his rubato was exceptionally telling. Their ensemble was said to be very fine. In 1805 Johann ceased musical employment and went into civil adminsitration at nearby Oels. He played his clarinet again at Breslau in 1809, but this time as an amateur. He was still living at Oels in 1830.

Work: 3 Duos (Dufaut & Dubois).

(B–H). **KRAUSE, Karl Joseph.** Forsta, 15 July 1775-1838 or later. German. He was the elder brother of Johann Gottlieb Krause. He fared better than his brother and although forced into many moves from early childhood and having to undertake a certain amount of civil duties (common practice in any case at that period) he rose above these hindrances to become an excellent clarinettist. From 1780 the family lived at the Court of Baron Hochburg at Plogwitz. Karl learnt to play the clarinet and horn first from his father, who was a bassoon and horn player to the Baron, and in 1783 he performed on both instruments in public. In 1786, when David and Springer joined the Court, Karl learnt clarinet and basset-horn from them. In 1787 he was adopted by Herr von Hartmann and went to live at Graz near Glogau as a son of the house. His patron provided him with further musical training and instruction in the sciences and reading. When the Court at Plogwitz was dispersed in 1789 the Krause family moved to Holstein and here Karl joined them, becoming court clarinettist to Count Röder. This Court too was disbanded in 1794 and Karl and his younger brother then found employment as clarinettists to Count Hoym at Breslau. Karl may have been the Krause recorded as first clarinet of the Hamburg orchestra in 1795. After some time in Vienna in 1811 he went to Potsdam and here, through the auspices of General Persch, was made conductor of the 1st regiment of the Prussian Guard. With this regiment he took part in the French Campaign of 1814. He remained at Potsdam and was still living there in 1838. He arranged music for military band and composed small solos for various instruments.

His concerts included the following: 1804 – at Breslau, a double concerto by Krommer with his brother. Ditto at their joint Benefit, when he also played the obligato to Mozart's "Parto!"; it was said that "he gave full measure to the notes without displacing the bars." 1810 – soloist at Breslau, unspecified works. 1811 – 25th March at Vienna, a concerto by Beer and variations by Joseph Schnabel; he played on a clarinet of his own invention, but no details of this are given. 26th May in the Small Ridotto Room, a concerto and variations (probably the same as on 25th March); he was accompanied on the piano by the fourteen-year-old Franz Schoberlechner.

KREUTZER, Conradin. Messkirch (Baden) 22 Nov 1780-1849 Dec 14, Riga. German. He is known mainly as a clavier performer, conductor and composer, but he also played the clarinet in his youth and composed for the instrument. His father was a miller and, although Conradin had music lessons at an early age and showed talent, was against his taking music up as a career. Conradin began to study law at the University of Freiburg i. B., but on his father's death in 1800, abandoned this for music. For the next few years he lived at Constance and then Zurich, giving performances on the clarinet and clavier. In 1807 he went to Vienna, where he made an impression as a clarinettist. He travelled as a virtuoso again in 1811 and after this held various posts as Kapellmeister, one of the most important being at the Kärntnerthortheater in Vienna. He died from a brain-storm, while at Riga accompanying his daughter, the singer Marie Kreutzer.

Works: Divertissement. Fantasie et Variations sur un air suisse op.66 for clavier with accompaniment for clarinet or violin (Hofmeister – ScML, VGM) Masurka varié op.76 no.5 for piano & obligato clarinet (Peters 1830 – MBS, VGM). Variations op.35 (Gombart). Variations op.36 (Gombart – DoFB). Duets. 6 Pièces faciles for clarinet & violin. Trio op.43 in E flat for clarinet, bassoon & piano (Peters – VGM). Fantaisie sur un thême suisse op.55 for clarinet, viola, cello & clavier (Pennauer – VGM). Quintet in A for flute, clarinet, violin, cello & piano (Ms. – VGM). Grand Septet op.62, dedicated to "son ami I. Schuppenzigh" (Pennauer c.1830 – LBL). "In Yonder Valley, or the Mill-Wheel" for voice, clarinet & piano (Wessel 1857 – LBL).

Bibliography:

REHM, Wolfgang – "Conradin Kreutzer." MGG.

KRÖPSCH, Fritz. Austrian. He was a clarinet pupil at the Vienna Conservatoire from 1824 to 1826. On 7th September in his final year he performed variations by Riotte at the public examinations. He is well known for his excellent 416 Etuden für Klarinette (Schmidt/Heilbronn).

Works: Burlesque for half a clarinet (Oertel). Fantasie concertante op.2 (Schmidt). Fantasie & Variations on the drinking song "Im Tiefen Keller" (Schmidt). 5 Duets (Schmidt).

KROLL, François. He was a student at the Paris Conservatoire, gaining a First Prize in 1830. While still a student, in 1829 and 1830, he played in the wind orchestra at the Odéon.

KRZYZANOWSKI. Polish. He played in the orchestra at Cracow in 1821.

(B–H). **KÜFFNER, Josef.** Würzburg, 31 Mar 1776-1856 Sept 9, Würzburg. German. He first studied law and then took up music, becoming a Chamber Musician at the Würzburg Court on violin and basset-horn in 1797. He lost this post in 1802 when Würzburg was annexed to Bavaria and the bishopric secularised. He then became a military bandmaster and composed a considerable amount for the medium. In 1805 Würzburg became a grand-duchy under Ferdinand of Tuscany and Küffner was re-employed as a Chamber Musician. When the town was handed over to Bavaria once more in 1815 Küffner was pensioned. He made a considerable income from his compositions.

Works: Introduction et Thême varié. (This has been erroneously published as written by Weber in 1815 for Heinrich Baermann). Potpourri sur un Thême suisse op.190, dedicated to Baron Adelsheim (Schott c.1830 – BoLM, LBL). Sérénade op.21 (Schott c.1814 – LBL). 50 Leçons méthodiques en Duos op.80 (André. Richault). 3 Duos dialogués et progressifs op.81 (André 1820/1). 3 Duos concertans op.105 (André). 32 Easy duets op.328 (Seeling). Quintet op.32 (Schott. Richault). Quintet op.33 (Schott c.1815 – LRAM). Pièce d'Harmonie op.40 for flute, 2 clarinets & basset-horn (Schott). Potpourri op.198 for basset-horn, piano & guitar (Schott). Method op.80 (André). Principes elementaries de la musique et gamme de clarinette op.200 (Schott c.1820).

KÜHN, Friedrich Wilhelm. German. He and Kuntz were the first clarinettists to be appointed to the Berlin court opera, their employment dates being 1787 to 1799. Both were made Chamber Musicians.

Work: 25 Ländlertänze (Böhm).

KÜHNE. German. He played in the theatre orchestra at Magdeburg. In the early part of 1824 he performed a Potpourri by Danzi, and in 1825 at the Harmonie Concerts a double concerto by Krommer with Feldt.

(B–H). **KUHLAN.** In 1828 Kuhlan, "from Madras," performed a basset-horn concerto in Calcutta.

KUKRO. In 1829 he played a concertante for 2 clarinets by Maurer with Weismüller at Fulda, where he was probably a member of the court orchestra.

KUNTZ. German. He and Kühn were the first clarinettists to be appointed to the Berlin court opera orchestra. They were employed from 1787 to 1799. Both were made Chamber Musicians.

KUNZE, K. German. He was a clarinettist at Leipzig in 1832 and 1833. On 15th February 1833 he performed Iwan Müller's double concerto at Merseburg with Amme. In November of that year he took part in Lindpaintner's Concertante for wind, for the Euterpe Society in Leipzig. By 1848 he had removed to Dresden as director of military music.

KUSTNER, Ludwig. German. He played clarinet and oboe in the Carlsruhe court orchestra from 1772 to 1775.

LABANCHI, Gaetano. Palermo 1829-1908. Italian. He learnt first from his father and then from Cavallini. He taught at the Naples Conservatoire and formed many fine pupils. Verdi and other composers were inspired by him. He wrote a method and numerous compositions.

LABATUT. At Charleston, South Carolina, he played a concerto by Vanderhagen on 14th December 1799.

LACHER, Joseph. Haustetten (near Augsburg), 5 Nov 1739-c.1805. German. He was the son of an impecunious village musician who could not read music, but who was a good performer on the clarinet, oboe and violin. Joseph learnt all these from his father from the age of seven and later the bassoon and cor anglais. He held a variety of appointments on one or other of his instruments, finishing as Kapellmeister to a convent at Kempten.

Work: Concerto.

LADUNKE, Theodor. He belonged to a German family which settled in Russia. In 1764 he was appointed first clarinet in the second orchestra at the St Petersburg Court. He was also a good singer and the same year took the part of Pluton in a court performance of Raupach's *Alceste*. His salary in 1800 was 650 roubles, lodgings and firewood being provided.

LAMBELÉE, Gabriel. Brussels, 1811-? Belgian. His studies at the Brussels Conservatoire were interrupted by the 1830 revolution and he then became a solo clarinet in a regimental band. In 1834 he resumed his studies and gained a First Prize that year. He became a well-known soloist, played in the orchestra at La Monnaie and conducted several wind societies. From 1842 to 1872 he taught at the Brussels Conservatoire. His daughter Aline Lambelée-Alhaiza was a well-known singer.

Works: Caprices. Duets.

LAMOUR (AMOUR), Charles Gautier. Metz, 6 Jan, 1808-1874 Aug 27, Paris. French. He gained a First Prize at the Paris Conservatoire in 1834. From 1835 to 1840 he was an assistant professor at the Conservatoire. In 1850 he was Berlioz' first clarinet for the Société Philharmonique. He was living at that time at no.1 rue de Douai.

(B–H). **LANDGRAF, (Johann Friedrich) Bernhard (Wilhelm).** Dielsdorf, 25 June 1816-1885 Jan 25, Leipzig. German. He had a long and successful career as a clarinettist at the Leipzig Gewandhaus. He possessed a splendid technique, his tone was beautiful and he played with great style. When he was fourteen he took lessons on several instruments from the town musician at Jena. From 1837 to 1840 he was solo clarinet in the 32nd regiment of Prussian Infantry which was stationed at Erfurt. He then moved to Leipzig and became second clarinet in the Gewandhaus Orchestra. When Gustav Heinze left the orchestra in 1844 Landgraf took over first clarinet, a post which he retained until 1881. In 1874 a celebration was given for his thirty years service as first clarinet. The orchestra presented him with a valuable ring, Reinecke the Kapellmeister gave him portraits of Mozart and Beethoven, and he was also awarded the Albrecht Order for Art and Knowledge. He retired from the orchestra in 1884.

His principal solo performances were as follows: 1841 – early in the year, a concertino by Lindpaintner. 1844 – 6th October, Rondo (from the First Concerto) by Weber. 24th October, Weber's Concertino. 1846 – 29th October, one of Reissiger's Fantasias, also his Adagio & Variations. 1848 – 13th January, Adagio & Rondo (from the First Concerto) by Weber. 8th October, Weber's Concertino. 1849 – 1st November, Fantasie by Gerke. 1853 – 20th October, Mozart's Concerto. 1855 – 20th December, concerto by Ferdinand David. 1857 – 29th October, David's Concerto again. 1864 – 24th November, solo on the basset-horn. 1869 – 11th & 15th March, Schubert's "Der Hirt auf dem Felsen" for Anna Straus. 1870 – 24th February, Adagio from Mozart's

Concerto. He appeared on very many other occasions of which no details are available.

LANG. c.1760-? Czech. He was described by Fétis as an "excellent clarinettist," but seems to have been of rather doubtful character. Early in his career he was music director for the 1st Imperial Artillery regiment, which was stationed at Prague. In 1786 he gave a solo performance in Prague's National Theatre. In 1802, for reasons unknown, he renounced his directorship and served as a corporal. He then tried to stage a come-back and gave a concert on 11th July 1807 at Karlsbad in which he announced that he was still Kapellmeister of the same regiment. AMZ threw doubts on the statement and advised him to be satisfied with being a good orchestral musician, as he showed too many difficulties in performance to succeed as a soloist. The following year he was sacked from the regiment, but in 1809 succeeded in landing an excellent post as music director to Count Metrowsky's regiment in Moravia, which carried a considerable salary and exemption from ordinary military duties. He still held this appointment in 1816. He composed concertos and sonatas for clarinet, also suites for wind band, but none were published.

LANGE, Hermann. Born Grosschönau. German. He studied at the Dresden Conservatoire and from 1890 until 1925 or later was a Chamber Musician at the Dresden Court.

Work: Method (1911).

LANGENBECK, Johann Georg. German. In 1769 he was a member of the Elector of Trevès' orchestra at Ehrenbreitstein, Coblenz.

LANGENUS, Gustave. Malines, 6 Aug 1883-1957 Jan 30, Long Island, New York. Belgian. He studied under Poncelet at the Brussels Conservatoire and graduated from there in 1900. He was a very artistic player, with a light delicate tone. In 1903 he came to England and for two years was in the 8th Duke of Devonshire's private band before becoming a member of the Queen's Hall Orchestra. In 1910 Walter Damrosch, on a visit to England, invited him to become first clarinet of the New York Symphony Orchestra. Langenus founded the New York Chamber Music Society with Caroline Beebe Whitehouse in 1916. In 1923 he resigned his orchestral post to devote himself to chamber music and teaching. He also entered into various commercial projects which included running a music publishing business, founding the Celesta Record Company, editing *Woodwind News* in 1926 and

The Ensemble News in 1927. As well as writing his own tutor he also edited the Baermann method.

Works, all published by Carl Fischer: Chrysalis. Donkey-Ride. Examinations. Indian Mother Song. In Cowboy Land. In the Forest. Irish Serenade. Lullaby. Mount Vernon Menuet. Old New Orleans. Scale Waltz. The Commuters' Express. Complete Method for the Boehm Clarinet (1913). Clarinet Cadenzas. Modern Clarinet Playing. Monograph on the Clarinet. Practical Transposition. Six Articles for Woodwind Players.

Writings:

"Heinrich Baermann." WN. Spring 1926 & Summer 1926.
"Joseph Schreurs." WN. Winter 1926.

Recording:

Guilhaud – Concertino. Celesta 101A–B (1926).

(B–H). **LANGER, Dominik.** Czech. He played in the court orchestra at Breslau in 1819 with Schnabel. He was also a violinist, conductor and composer. He was still living in 1835, but was then very old.

LANGLOTZ, Karl August. ?-1884. German. He was a clarinet and violin player in the court orchestra at Meiningen from 1827 until about 1866, performing as clarinet soloist first on 15th February 1827. In 1831 he visited Weimar to play at an entr'atce concert, performing a Potpourri by Nohr (the Kapellmeister at Meiningen) and a Concertino by Dotzauer.

LANKAMMER (LANGHAMMER), Christoph Benjamin. ?-1791. German. He was one of the earliest known German clarinettists. A memorandum of 1759 in the court archives at St Petersburg proposed the engagement of Lankammer and Compagnon, "two clever clarinettists." There is no evidence that the proposal was carried out at the time, but Lankammer was on the pay roll of 1763, as oboist to the concert orchestra with a salary of 600 roubles. Doubtless he doubled on clarinet when required. In 1764 he performed clarinet duets with Count Michael Ogínski. He was appointed to teach at the Theatre School in 1786 but retired the following year with a pension of 200 roubles. This was still being paid to him in 1791.

LAPPE. W. Philipp. Danzig, 7 Oct 1802-1871 Jan 2, Schwerin. German. He was employed at the Mecklenburg-Schwerin Court. At the Hamburg Festival of 1841 he played the obligato to

Mozart's "Parto!" for Mme Schröder-Devrient. In 1847 he performed at Lübeck. He composed, but nothing for clarinet

LAUEL. French. In 1827 he was second clarinet at the Théâtre de la Porte St Martin in Paris. He was living at no.25 rue Popincourt.

LAURENT. French. In 1826 he was second clarinet at the Théâtre de S.A.R. Madame in Paris.

LAUTERBACH, Friedrich (Wilhelm). Dresden, 1805-1875 Jan 1, Dresden. German. He was the son of Johann Gottlieb Lauterbach. Like his father he was a member of the court orchestra at Dresden, his dates of employment being approximately 1824 to 1849. He first appeared as a soloist with his father on 3rd December 1824 in a Potpourri for 2 clarinets by Späth. On 28th February 1838 he played second clarinet to Kotte in Kummer's double concerto. He taught at the Dresden Conservatoire from 1857 to 1875, Stark being his most famous pupil.

LAUTERBACH, Johann Gottlieb. Klein-Borthen (near Lockwitz), 20 Feb 1780-? German. He was the father of Friedrich Lauterbach whom he probably taught. He had a big reputation as a teacher and in 1815 and 1816 Kotte tramped miles from a country district to have lessons from him. From 1817 to 1824 or later Lauterbach played in the Dresden opera orchestra. On 19th October 1809 he performed a concerto by Johann Brendler at the Leipzig Gewandhaus. On 3rd December 1824 he performed one of Weber's concertos and, with his son, Späth's Potpourri for 2 clarinets, at Dresden.

LAYER, Antoine. ?-1800 Nov 14, Paris. French. He also played the bassoon. In 1793 he was a member, second class, of the National Guard, and taught at the Institut National de Musique in Paris. In 1794 he played clarinet at the Théâtre Italien and the following year, bassoon at the Opéra. From 1795 until his death he was a clarinet professor of the second class at the Conservatoire.

(B–H). **LAZARUS, Henry.** London, 1 Jan 1815-1895 Mar 6, London. English. See OV. He also played the saxophone. He was clarinet soloist for Jullien from 1841 to 1855. When Jullien gave the flautist Joseph Richardson a Benefit on 29th November 1843 Lazarus played the voice part in Bishop's "Lo, here the gentle Lark" with Richardson playing the obligato. Lazarus and Richardson played the work again on 23rd November 1844. Jullien introduced an "English Quadrille" as a novelty for his 1853 season in which Lazarus, with his friends Barret and Baumann, Jullien himself and six others, played English fifes. When the New Philharmonic Orchestra was formed in 1852 to play the works of Berlioz, Lazarus was appointed first clarinet. Lazarus is also said to have been a member of the Hallé Orchestra for their 1861/2 season, and from 1875 to 1877 he played under Arditi at the Covent Garden Promenade Concerts. His sight began to go, as he got older, and in 1891 he underwent an operation for cataract. This was unsuccessful and he lost the sight of one eye, so that he retired from the concert platform in the same year. He had taught at Trinity College of Music from 1881 and retired from this appointment in 1892. In 1894 he retired from the Royal Academy of Music, Royal College of Music and Kneller Hall. He died at no.2A Neville Terrace in South Kensington, which had been his home since 1878.

The following works were dedicated to Lazarus: Andante & Polacca (1877) by Arthur Clappé; Original Fantasia by Hamilton Clarke (known as an organist and conductor, he was also a good clarinettist); Sonata (1879) by Charles Swinnerton Heap; Six Nocturnes by Charles Oberthür; First Grand Duet Concertante for 2 clarinets by James Waterson.

William Husk wrote about Lazarus in the 1st edition of Grove's *Dictionary of Music & Musicians* that "the beauty and richness of his excellent phrasing, and his neat and expressive execution, are alike admired." These sentiments were universally voiced, in particular the superb quality of his tone. The secret of his tone would seem to lie in a completely natural embouchure and one which was highly adaptable, for he possessed and used more mouthpieces and instruments than any other player has dared to do. Jack Brymer tells a story of one of Lazarus' pupils who said his master's drawing room table groaned "under the weight of not less than fifty mouthpieces, all complete with reeds, which the great man used in turn as he felt necessary."

Besides this quantity of mouthpieces Lazarus also had a considerable number of instruments. He did not dispose of them when no longer required, but built up a collection which gives to the historian of musical instruments a remarkable picture of mechanical advancements on the clarinet during a greater part of the nineteenth century, as they were accepted by the profession. The list of his instruments which follows has been arranged in their probable order of acquisition. He lent nos. 4 & 6 to the Royal Military Exhibition of 1890. With the exception of these and no.5, all his instruments were sold by his executors on 19th June 1895 at the auction rooms of Puttick & Simpson. Data from the sale catalogue is given in italics.

1) *A very old Bassoon, by Key. + This instrument was presented to Mr. Lazarus by the celebrated Bassoon player Mr Baumann.* This may possibly be the alto fagotto which Lazarus played in the Coldstream Guards.

2) *A Clarionet in B flat, by Key, boxwood, ivory mounts, brass Keys. + Mr. Lazarus's earliest Instrument, presented to him when a boy by the Bandmaster of the Coldstream Guards.* 1825. 12 flat rounded keys (some are later additions), including 3 on saddles. An early form of rollers. Given by John Blizzard to Lazarus, who used it from 1838 to 1855. (EdBHC).

3) *A Clarionet in A, by Key, stained boxwood, ivory mounts, brass keys.* c.1820. 13 slightly domed keys, including one for covered f/c'', on blocks and saddles. R.H. ring key added by Lazarus. Bore enlarged. Bought second-hand by Lazarus. (EdBHC).

4) Basset-horn in F by Key. c.1825, a rare example of early English workmanship. Dark stained boxwood. Brass and ivory mounts, 16 flat rounded keys mounted on knobs. Short curved brass crook and big straight wooden bell. Entirely straight 3-piece tube, with d & c basset keys located at the back. R.H. ring key added by Lazarus. Length 96.5 cms.. Bore 1.52 cms.. (ERC).

5) Clarinet in B flat by Fieldhouse. 1855. Cocus-wood. Nickel-silver mounts, 16 keys, 4 rings. Tube in one piece, enabling the holes to be well placed acoustically. Dispensing with rollers, the instrument incorporates Boehm-type improvements for the little fingers as follows: L.H. keys for e, f and f sharp, all working independently through ingenious linking with R.f key; R.H. keys for g sharp and duplicate f. No e'flat/b''' flat side key, but one for semitone trills on a long rod and lever for use by R. middle finger. The rings, 2 for each hand, are attached to elaborate mechanism for cross fingerings, those for L.H. being for middle and ring fingers. (ERC).

6) Clarinet in A by Fieldhouse. 1855. Similar to instrument 5). Length 59.7 cms.. Bore 1.50 cms.. Speaker hole has been moved from front to back and further down the body. Position of holes opened by a key also altered. Lazarus enlarged the bore and described it's dimensions to Day as "between that of the old English clarinets and that of the more modern Belgian instruments." He used the Fieldhouse pair from 1855 to 1865. (ERC).

7) *A Corno di Bassetto, by Pask, cocus wood, Boehm fingering, in case.* Pre 1859. In F. Nickel-silver mounts. 21 saltspoon keys, 5 rings. Curved metal crook and metal bell half turned forwards. Two straight tube-pieces with metal U-bend taking a 3rd up-turned joint

for 4 basset-keys. This 3rd joint is pinned to the main tube, slightly to the rear on L. side. Stamped "Pask, 8 Lowther Arcade, Strand, London." Length 109.8 cms.. Bore 1.59 cms.. The fingering is pure Boehm and its appearnace at a time when the system was virtually unknown in England is explained by Rendall's suggestion that it is of French workmanship. Lazarus probably bought it at much the same time as the Fieldhouse pair, though certainly no later than 1859 when Pask moved to no.7 Lowther Arcade. (EdBHC).

8) *An E flat Saxophone.*

9) *An E flat Saxophone, by Sax, of Paris.* Instruments 8) & 9) were probably bought some time after 1850, when the saxophone was first introduced to England. Lazarus would almost certainly have played one of them at Covent Garden in 1869 when Ambroise Thomas' *Hamlet*, which requires 3 saxophones, was staged.

10) *A Bass Clarionet, in case.* There is unfortunately no information to hand on this instrument.

11) *A Clarionet in B flat, by Albert, 13 keys.* Pre 1860?

12) *A ditto in A, ebony.* If it can be assumed that instruments 11) & 12) were identical, then Lazarus owned no less than eight clarinets by Albert: the above pair, the "presentation set" (nos.13, 14 & 15) and the "favourite set" (nos.16, 17 & 18). This suggests that he found in this brand his ideal. The large bore of the Albert clarinets would give the richness of tone he so desired and that he had already attempted to achieve by enlarging the bores of his Key and Fieldhouse clarinets. Albert's 13-key system was introduced to England in the 1850s so that Lazarus probably bought nos.11 & 12 shortly before 1860, at which date he received the 16-key "presentation set." As far as is known he did not use the 13-key model professionally. This may have been because he found ebony lacking in response compared with other woods.

13) *A Clarionet in A, by Albert, cocus-wood.* Presented to Lazarus by Eugène Albert in 1860. No serial no.. Silver mounts, 16 keys, 2 rings, rollers on all cross and little finger keys. This is basic Albert 14-key system, but with an extra side key for e' flat/b'' flat and trill a'-b' flat. Stamped "A. Chappell, 45 New Bond Street, London." Length 61.5 cms.. Bore 1.51 cms.. (Author's collection).

14) *A Clarionet in B flat, silver-keyed.* (Probably identical with 13).

15) *A Clarionet in C, by S.A. Chappell. + The last three Instruments formed the 2nd set of the late Mr. Lazarus.* Lazarus is said to have treasured this "presentation set" greatly and not used them much, but he must at least have used no.15 until 1879 when he purchased the C clarinet of the "favourite set."

16) *A Clarionet in A, by Eugène Albert, of Brussels, cocus-wood,*

silver-keyed. Between 1866 and 1871. Serial no.2470. Albert system, with extra keys as in no.13. Silver mounts, 16 keys, 2 rings, rollers on all cross and little finger keys. Body stamped "A. Chappell, 45 New Bond Street, London". Bell stamped "Approved by Mr. Lazarus". Length 61.7 cms.. Bore 1.51 cms.. Wood mouthpiece, stamped "E. Albert. S.A. Chappell. 2". Lay 16 mms.. (ERC).

17) *A Clarionet in B flat.* Between 1866 and 1871. Similar to no. 16. (OBC).

18) *A Clarionet in C. + These three Instruments were the favorite set of the late Mr. Lazarus.* 1879. Cocus-wood. 14 nickel-silver keys, no rollers. Stamping: upper joint in front "Sole agents S.A. Chappell 52 New Bond St. London", on back "1879 RAB 4109"; lower joint "Approved by Mr. Lazarus"; side of bell "RAB 1879". (OBC).

19) *A Clarionet in A, by Buffet, of Paris, Boehm fingering.* 1870. Buffet-Crampon. Cocus-wood. Speaker key hole in front. Stamped "Approved by J. Pask" and "Lazarus." Lazarus probably bought this between the early 1860s when James Conroy demonstrated a pair of boxwood Boehms by Buffet to him and 1872 when John Pask went out of business. It was his only excursion into a clarinet with true Boehm fingering. (EdBHC).

20) *A Clarionet in A, by Buffet, flat pitch, ivory mounts, 13 brass keys.* 1879? It is more than probable that Lazarus had a B flat instrument to match this one. The purchase of nos.20, 21 & 22 was forced on him as the result of a dramatic incident at Covent Garden. In 1879 the diva Adelina Patti refused to sing again at the house unless the pitch of the orchestra, which had been steadily rising over the years to reach A455, was lowered. After much heated argument her demands were met and the orchestra had perforce to buy new instruments at French standard of pitch A435. Instrument 20) and its companion were probably a make-shift until Lazarus found the models he liked – nos.21 & 22.

21) *A Clarionet in A by Buffet, of Paris, flat pitch.*

22) *A Clarionet in B flat. + These two instruments used by Mr. Lazarus when playing at the Opera, where the flat pitch is necessary.* For other engagements Lazarus was still able to use his beloved Alberts, as it was some time before the lower pitch was enforced elsewhere.

For most of his long professional life Lazarus had had to contend with varieties of pitch – much more than is normally met with today – and to cope with this contingency he carried around with him a set of three tuning forks of different frequencies. These forks he bequeathed to one of his favourite pupils, George Anderson.

Lazarus played in the following concerts not listed in the original volume: 1853 – 18th April, second clarinet to Williams in Mozart's Serenade K388, for the Philharmonic Society. 1858 – 13th December at Exeter Hall, obligato to Guglielmi's "Gratias agimus" for Anna Bishop. 1861 – 4th October at the Royal Italian Opera, basset-horn obligato to Mozart's "Non più di fiori." 7th November with the Hallé Orchestra, his own Fantasia on *I Puritani.* 1868 – 24th June at St James' Hall, Mendelssohn Concertstück. The name of the basset-horn player is not mentioned, but it is likely to have been Maycock. The report says: "A Ms. Concertstück by Mendelssohn . . . . . will be performed for the first time." One is tempted to connect this performance with the picture received by Lazarus from Carl Baermann, signed "Munich, 18th May 1868." (See OV, page 257). Did Lazarus go to Munich to collect the work from Carl Baermann? Was the original Ms. used or Carl Baermann's? (See OV, page 147). 1881 – 12th December at St James' Hall, Schubert's Octet.

Works: Cavatina from Verdi's *Ernani* (Lafleur – LBL). Fantasia on a Favorite French Air (Lafleur – LBL). Fantasia on Favorite Scotch Melodies (Lafleur – LBL). Fantasia on *I Puritani* (Lafleur – LBL, LRCM). Obligato to Arne's "When Daisies Pied" (Chappell 1888 – LBL). New and Modern Method for the Albert and Boehm system (Lafleur 1881 – LBL).

Bibliography:

BRYMER, Jack – "Henry Lazarus." TC. Summer 1950 & autumn 1956.

(*Illustrated London News*). 25th November 1843.

(*The Orchestral Times &Bandsman*). October 1891.

WESTON, Pamela – "Lazarus' Instrument Collection." NACWPI November 1974.

LECERF. In 1829 and 1830 he played in the wind orchestra at the Odéon in Paris. He was a friend of Fessy, who dedicated to him a Fantasia on Schubert's *Ave Maria* & *Serenade.* E.F. Lecerf who won Conservatoire prizes in 1834 and 1836, and B.A.A. Lecerf who won one in 1845, were probably his sons.

LEFÈBVRE, (Pierre) Henri (Casimir). Lillers, 20 Oct 1898-1925, Paris. French. His father was a postmaster. Lefèbvre took up the clarinet at an early age and became a pupil of Rose at the Paris Conservatoire, gaining First Prize at the age of eighteen. Rose was devoted to his pupil and bequeathed him his Buffet instruments (which subsequently went to Daniel Bonade) and music. Lefèbvre was a splendid teacher himself and although he never became a professor at the Conservatoire, thirty five First Prizes were gained at that institution by his pupils, amongst whom was his nephew Pierre Lefèbvre. Henri Lefèbvre played for a short time in the Garde Républicaine. He was solo clarinet in the Colonne Concerts, the Lamoureux Orchestra and the Opéra orchestra until near his death. He was one of the founders of the Société du Double Quintette, an ensemble of French woodwind players who toured Europe with great success.

LEFÈVRE, Louis (François). Salins, 18 Apr 1773-1833 French. He was definitely a younger brother of Xavier Lefèvre. He had a distinguished career in the following bands: 1784-1789 French Guard; 1789-1795 National Guard; 1797-1798 Grenadiers of the National Assembly; 1799-1802 Huntsmen of the Consular Guard; 1802-1814 134th regiment of the line; 1814-1827 and 1830-1831 National Guard. He taught at the Institut National de Musique from 1789 and in 1795 was appointed a professor of the second class at the Conservatoire. In 1801 he was on the committee appointed to discuss the official tutor Xavier had been commissioned to write. When the number of professors was cut in 1802 Louis Lefèvre lost his post, but he was recalled at Xavier's retirement in 1824 and served until he was pensioned in 1832. He was a member of the Opéra orchestra from about 1818, playing first clarinet from 1821 to 1824. He lived in the faubourg Monmartre, at no. 8 in 1821 and either no.17 or 18 from 1825.

LEFÈVRE, (Jean) Xavier. Lausanne (Cressis), 6 Mar 1763-1829 Nov 9, Paris (Neuilly). Swiss. See OV. In 1778 he became a member of the French Guards band. When the National Guard was formed in the year of the Revolution he played in this and from 1790 was it's deputy conductor. In 1814 he was made a Chevalier de la Légion d'honneur. He had many famous pupils at the Paris Conservatoire who included Janssen 1795/6, Péchignier 1797, Boufil 1801 to 1806, Crusell 1803, Buteux 1814 to 1819, Crépin 1816 to 1821, Adolphe Hugot 1817 to 1822 and Pierre Hugot 1820 to 1824. He may also have taught Dacosta in 1797 and 1798, but some authorities say Duvernoy did. Very many of Lefèvre's pupils gained First Prizes. Up to the year 1817 a First Prize carried with it the award of a pair of French-made clarinets in B flat and C. From 1818 to 1892 the Prize was of music worth 100 francs. During Lefèvre's term of office the contest piece had always to be the composition of the professor and Sainsbury mentions that in 1799 Lefèvre set his Concerto no.5. Early Conservatoire records are unfortunately incomplete and the only year listed in these is 1824, Lefèvre's last year as professor, when he set his Concerto no.3.

Lefèvre's appearances at the Concert Spirituel were as follows: 1783 – 1st November, concerto by Vogel (Yost/Vogel). 1784 – 1st November, ditto. 24th December, unspecified concerto. 1785 – 18th March, ditto. 23rd & 26th March, "new" concerto by Vogel (Yost/ Vogel). 1787 – 1st November, Symphonie Concertante for clarinet & bassoon by Devienne. 25th December, "new" concerto by himself. 1788 – 2nd February, repeat of the latter. 16th March, concerto by Yost. 21st March, Symphonie Concertante for clarinet & bassoon by Devienne. 23rd March, concerto by himself. 28th March, "new" concerto by Yost. 1789 – 5th April, concerto by himself. 9th April, Symphonie Concertante for clarinet, bassoon & horn by Wolf. 17th April, concerto by himself. 24th December, Symphonie Concertante for clarinet & bassoon (probably Devienne's). 25th December, Symphonie Concertante for flute, clarinet & bassoon by Devienne, with Hugot (flute) and Devienne (bassoon). 1790 – 2nd April, "Airs variés" with the group of musicians with whom he went to England this year (See OV), namely: Antoine Buch (horn), Frédéric Duvernoy (horn) and Perret (bassoon). 4th April, concerto by himself. 5th April, Symphonie Concertante for clarinet & bassoon by himself. The Concert Spirituel came to an end in 1791 and Lefèvre then became a member of the Opéra orchestra. It was the custom at this time to insert wind instrument concertos during opera performances and Lefèvre was frequently given this opportunity. He performed a "new" Symphonie Concertante for clarinet & bassoon by himself, for the Concert de la Loge Olympique on 15th May 1805.

Works: Concerto (Ms. – VNB). Concerto no.1 in E flat (Hummel c.1791 – copy minus solo part in LRCM). Concerto no.2 in B flat (Sieber). Concerto no.3 in F (Naderman). Concerto no.4 in B flat, dedicated to Mr A. Bronice (1796. Conservatoire –PBN. Breitkopf & Härtel – BDS). Concerto no.5 in B flat (1798. Magasin de Musique – solo part only in AKVM, parts minus solo in PBN. Ozi c.1799). Concerto no.6 in B flat, dedicated to "Monsieur Deprez, Banquier du Trésor Imperial" (Jouve c.1805 – LBL, PBN, VGM. Hentz. Breitkopf & Härtel – BDS, VGM). Fétis says his concertos were also published by Troupenas. 2 Symphonie concertantes for 2 clarinets (Janet 1802?). 2 Symphonie concertantes for clarinet & bassoon (Sieber). Symphonie concertante no.3 for oboe, clarinet & bassoon (Janet 1802?). Trois Grandes Sonatas op.12, dedicated to "Mr Simonet" – this is probably François Simonet, the horn player (Ozi 1802. Janet 1803/4 – PBN). Sonates pour commençans (Ozi 1802). 3 Airs variés for clarinet solo (PBN). 40 Airs et duos (Simrock). 6 Duos concertans ops.9 & 10 – op.9

dedicated to "mon ami Rodolphe", the horn player (Naderman c.1810 – LBL). 6 Duos op.1, dedicated to Michel (Jouve c.1818 – PBN. Sieber – PBN). 6 Duos op.2, dedicated to Cramayel (Naderman – PBN). 6 Duos op.3 (Jouve c.1818. Sieber – PBN). 6 Duos op.4 (Jouve c.1818, Sieber – PBN). 6 Duos op.8 (Jouve – PBN. Leduc). 6 Duos op.9 (Naderman – PBN). 6 Duos op.10 (Naderman – PBN). 6 Duos op.11, dedicated to Simonet (Janet c.1810 – LBL, PBN). 6 Duos op.13 (Jouve c.1818 – PBN). 6 Duos faciles (Janet). 3 Duos for clarinet & bassoon, ops.A & B (Conservatoire – BrBC, PBN.). 3 Duos for clarinet & bassoon (Schlesinger). 3 Trios for 2 clarinets & bass. 6 Trios op.5 for 2 clarinets & bassoon (Sieber c.1798). 3 Quartets op.2, dedicated to "Mr Balthaz Moutton, Négociant à Brignolles" (Jouve c.1818 – BarBM, LBL). 3 Quartets vol.3 (Sieber – VNB, WLC). Quartets, with François Simonet (Naderman). Méthode de clarinette (Conservatoire 1802 – PBN. André 1805 – LBL).

Bibliography:

YOUNGS, Lowell – *Jean Xavier Lefèvre. His Contributions to the Clarinet and Clarinet Playing.* (Unpublished Dissertation). University Microfilms, 1970.

(B–H). **LEFFLER.** In 1801 he played basset-horn with Munro at Covent Garden in a performance of Mozart's *Requiem.*

LEGENDRE, August Amand (Arnault). Toulouse, 30 May 1760(9?)-1843 Apr 2, Paris. French. He was a member of the National Guard and a teacher at the Institut National from 1793 and became a solfège professor of the third class when the Paris Conservatoire opened in 1795. In 1800 he was made a clarinet professor of the second class and served on the committee of 1801 which met to discuss the official tutor Xavier Lefèvre had been commissioned to write. In 1821 and 1822 he was first clarinet at the Vaudeville. From 1826 until his death he was director of the Conservatoire boarding school. His wife also helped in the administration of this.

LELLMANN, Georg (Franz). Bückeburg, 8 Apr 1798-? German. He had a chequered career in which his intellectual ability was at variance with his desire to be a musician. As he was destined for a science career he was not allowed to learn music until he was thirteen. He then had lessons on the clarinet from a musician at the Bückeburg Court named Wagner. In 1814 a Swedish regiment visited the town and the colonel was so impressed with his playing that he offered him the post of first clarinet in the band. Lellmann took this opportunity to follow his bent and went with them to the wars in

Belgium, but they had no sooner arrived than peace was signed with France and the regiment returned to Bückeburg where he started to study the violin. In 1819 he was back in military service as solo clarinet to a Belgian regiment stationed at Ypres. This engagement ceased in 1821 when he accepted the post of conductor to the Philharmonic Society of Turcoing. From here, during the next few years, he made several excursions to Paris to perform at concerts, to have clarinet lessons from Iwan Müller and composition lessons from Reicha. He hoped to find an appointment in Paris but did not succeed and in 1830 abandoned music for a scholastic career. He returned to Germany and taught languages first at a private school in Hanover and then in 1833 at the High School in Zerbst. In 1834 he went to Vienna and subsequently received a doctor's degree in philosophy and the arts at Jena University.

Works: Air varié (Simrock). Introduction & Rondo in E flat (Simrock 1828 – ZAM). Variations on a Romance of Weber (Zetter. Breitkopf & Härtel). Air varié for 2 clarinets (Simrock).

LENGERKE, Karl von. ?-1885 Nov 1, Vienna. Austrian. He was a pupil at the Vienna Conservatoire, finishing his training in 1868. He became a member of the Vienna court orchestra and, from 1870 until his death, played in the Vienna Philharmonic.

LERICHE, Mathias. French. From 1795 to 1800 he was a professor of the third class at the Paris Conservatoire. He was second clarinet at the Vaudeville theatre in 1821 and 1822.

LEROY, Adolphe (Marthe). St-Germain-en-Laye, 16 Aug 1827-1880 Sept 1, Argenteuil. French. He was a distinguished pupil at the Paris Conservatoire under Klosé, whom he succeeded in the professorship in 1868. He became first clarinet in the court orchestra and at the Opéra, and conducted the Imperial Guard. Berlioz sent for him early in 1857 to try out the famous solo in *Les Troyens* and found Leroy "a virtuoso of the first order, but cold." From 1859 to 1865 Leroy was a director of the Buffet-Crampon instrument company. In 1876 he was given indefinite sick-leave from the Conservatoire and died four years later, just three days after Klosé. During his short term as teacher he formed some fine pupils, including Henri Selmer. Saint-Saëns dedicated his Tarantelle op.6 (1851) to Leroy and the flautist Dorus. Eugène Walckiers, the flautist-composer, dedicated his First Clarinet Sonata op.91 to Leroy and Leroy's father, Léon.

Leroy was first clarinet for the Société des Concerts from 1849 to about 1859 and gave the following solo performances for them: 1849

– 18th March, "concertino de Beer" (probably one of Berr's concertos). 1853 – 6th February, solo by Berr. 1855 – 14th Janaury, ditto. 1856 – 13th April, movements from a Reicha quintet. 1857 – 8th March, ditto.

LESSER. German. He played in the court orchestra at Kassel. On 7th March 1838 he performed a concertino by Heinrich Baermann at a Subscription Concert. On 15th November 1839 he took part in Schindelmeisser's Symphonie Concertante for 4 clarinets with Heisterhagen, Schultheis and Vauth.

LIMMER, J. Franz. 1806-? Austrian. He was a pupil at the Vienna Conservatoire from 1824 to 1828, shining not only as a clarinettist but as a composer. He performed at the following Conservatoire test concerts: 1824 – September, a double concerto with Kröpsch. 1827 – 21st August, a Rondo of his own composition. 1828 – 7th November, a Polonaise of his own composition and the obligato ("wondrous beautifully") to Mozart's "Parto!" for Mlle Jeckl. After leaving the Conservatoire he became Kapellmeister at Temesvár in Hungary.

Works: Polonaise. Rondo.

LINDNER, Friedrich. Dessau, 5 July 1798-1846 Aug 1, Dessau. German. He also played the violin and composed. His father was a veterinary surgeon. Lindner studied music in Berlin and from 1814 to 1817 was a clarinettist in the Berlin court opera orchestra. He then returned to Dessau to take up a similar post there. He rose to become Chamber Musician and in 1827 was made Orchestral Director. On 29th September 1827 he performed a concerto at the Leipzig Gewandhaus. His son Roderich August (born Dessau 1820) was a cellist and composer.

LINK, Joseph Albanus. Wallerstein, 19 June 1793-1856 July 3, Wallerstein. German.. He was the son of Xaver Link and learnt the clarinet from Heinrich Baermann. He spent all his professional life as a clarinettist and violinist at the Wallerstein Court.

LINK, (Franz) Xaver. Wallerstein, 27 Feb 1759-1825 June 4, Wallerstein. German. His family were closely connected with the Wallerstein Court for several generations. He was taught by his father, Sebastian Link. From about 1780 until his death he played second clarinet and violin in the court orchestra, and was a member of the wind ensemble. His son, Joseph Albanus Link, was a clarinettist.

LIVERANI, Domenico. Castelbolognese, 1805-1877 May 20, Bologna. Italian. He introduced the Boehm clarinet to Italy and, on Rossini's suggestion, the saxophone. He taught both instruments at the Rossini Liceo in Bologna. Magnani was one of his most distinguished pupils. Liverani visited England in 1836.

Works: Concerto in C minor, dedicated to Rossini (Magnificently bound Ms. – BoLM). 2 Chants religieux from Rossini's *Stabat Mater* (Ricordi). Melody from Bellini's *I Puritani* (Ricordi). 6 Morceaux (Troupenas – LRAM). Trio on Verdi's *Il Trovatore* for clarinet, cello & piano. Método (RBC).

LOHMANN. German. He was first clarinet in the court orchestra at Kassel in 1905.

LOPITZSCH. He played the clarinet for the Leipzig Euterpe Society and was also director of a military band. In 1833 he performed a concerto by Spohr, and on 13th March 1834 a concertino by Iwan Müller. He was still living at Leipzig in 1847.

LORENZ. German. He played the clarinet from about 1823 to 1849 in the court orchestra at Dessau, where an elder brother played the oboe and a younger brother the bassoon. In the summer of 1823 he performed concertos by Crusell and Spohr. He was a soloist again at the Subscription Concerts in 1841.

(B–H). **LOTZ, Theodor.** 1748-1792, Vienna. Czech. He also played the viola and contra-bassoon. In 1772 he played clarinet solos at a concert for Vienna's Tonkünstlersocietät. At that time he was employed by the notorious Cardinal-Prince de Rohan, with whom Meissner had travelled from Strasbourg to Paris at an earlier date and who lived at Vienna from 1772 to 1774. It was probably about 1774 that Lotz became a member of Count (Johann?) Esterházy's orchestra in Vienna. From 1781 to 1783 he was living at Pressburg as principal clarinet, and viola when required, for Prince Joseph Bathyány. In 1784 he moved back to Vienna. On 15th December 1785 he took part in the concert given by the "Crowned Hope" Lodge for David and Springer, playing contra-bassoon in some Partitas for wind instruments by Stadler. Lotz was also an instrument-maker, first at Pressburg during the time he was employed by Prince Bathyány and then at Vienna, where he supplied the Court from 1784 until the year of his death. Mendel says that he improved the basset-horn as early as 1772, though other authorities give 1782. About 1786 Lotz embarked on making Stadler's basset-clarinet. There is a 5-keyed clarinet by him in the Ernst Collection at Geneva and a basset-horn in the Staatliches Hochschule für Musik at Berlin.

LOUDELLE (LANDELLE). French. He was first clarinet at the Théâtre de S.A.R. Madame at Paris in 1826. When Gambaro died in 1828 Loudelle took his place as first clarinet at the Théâtre Italien. Berr moved up from second desk to replace Loudelle in 1830.

LOUIS. In the 1780s he was playing in the Comédie theatre orchestra at Port-au-Prince and was also engaged as a military musician.

LUBERTI, Carlo. Cineto Romano (Rome), 27 Jan 1885-? Italian. He studied with Magnani at the St Cecilia Academy in Rome. In 1913 he was made an assistant professor at the Academy and on Magnani's death in 1921 became principal clarinet professor. From 1913 to 1919 he played in the orchestra of the Augusteo and then became first clarinet at the Costanzi Theatre. He was well-known as a soloist.

LUCCHESI, Giuseppe. Italian. From 1818 to 1839 he played second clarinet in the court orchestra at Lucca.

LUDWIG, L. On 1st November 1786 he performed a Symphonie Concertante for clarinet & bassoon, with his brother playing the bassoon, at the Concert Spirituel in Paris. He may be the "Ludwig" who was playing at the National Theatre at Frankfurt a. M. from 1800 to 1804 and also appeared as soloist.

Works: 3 Concertos (Boyer 1788). Concerto no.4 in B flat (André 1800).

LULLIER. Probably French. On 3rd March 1793 he performed a symphonie concertante for 2 clarinets in Philadelphia with Beranger.

LUTZ, Eduard. He first found employment in Munich and from there visited Darmstadt in 1827 to perform Weber's First Concerto. By 1837 he had settled in Basle and become their director of military music. In 1841 he performed Weber's First Concerto and in 1848 a concertino by Heinrich Baermann.

MACCAGNANI. Italian. He played in the orchestra for the Rome Operatic Society. In the autumn of 1839 he was specially selected, with a cellist and four singers from the Society, to go on a concert tour to Cuba – an exceptional venture for those days.

MACCAGNI, Clemente. c.1850-1915. Italian. He was a pupil at the Bologna Conservatorio under Bianchini, whom he succeeded as professor.

MAGNANI, Aurelio. Longiano (Romagna), 26 Feb 1856-1921 Jan 25, Rome. Italian. He did much to raise the general standard of playing in Italy and to foster ideals of tone. He studied clarinet with Liverani and then with Bianchini, also composition with Alessandro Busi, at the Bologna Conservatorio, and gained diplomas in both subjects. He then taught for some years at the Benedetto Marcello Liceo at Venice and in 1888 moved to Rome where he was professor at the St Cecilia Academy until his death. Blonck-Steiner and Luberti were both his pupils at the Academy. Magnani played in a group of five instrumentalists at the Court of Queen Margherita and appeared as soloist with many European and American orchestras. His method for the Boehm clarinet received the Spanish International Gold Medal in 1900. It was translated into English, French and Spanish, and adopted by many of the principal training schools.

Works: 3 Sonatas for unaccompanied clarinet (Evette & Schaeffer). 10 Etudes – Caprices for clarinet solo (Evette & Schaeffer 1897 – PBN). Elegie (Evette & Schaeffer 1910 – PBN). Mazurka-Caprice (Leduc). Mélodie Originale Romantique (Evette & Schaeffer 1907 – PBN). Solo de Concert (Leduc). 6 Duos Concertants (Cundy-Bettoney). Romantic Melody for oboe, clarinet & violin. 1st Divertissement for clarinet, bassoon & piano (Evette & Schaeffer 1904 – PBN). 2nd Divertissement. Méthode Complète (Evette & & Schaeffer c.1900).

(B–H). **MAHON, John.** Oxford, 1746-1834, Dublin. English. See OV. He was the brother of William Mahon. He also played the violin and viola. He performed at the following concerts not listed in the original volume: 1783 – the Salisbury Festival with his brother William and a sister, probably Sarah. 1791 – July, the Oxford Commemoration Concerts on the occasion of Haydn receiving his doctorate. 1797 – 7th March at the Theatre Royal, Covent Garden, unspecified concerto, probably his own.

Works: Concerto no.1 (Bland 1785). Concerto no.2 in F (Bland c.1790 – ManPL, VNB). Variations on "The Wanton God" from Arne's *Comus*. 4 Duets (Clementi 1803). 6 Easy duets op.41. "Hope, thou cheerful Ray of Light" for soprano & clarinet (Longman

& Broderip 1796 – LBL). A new and complete Preceptor for the Clarinet (Goulding, Phipps & D'Almaine 1803 – ERC).

Bibliography:

CUDWORTH, Charles – "John Mahon." MGG.
HOGAN, Ita M. – *Anglo-Irish Music 1780-1830.* Cork 1966.
MEE, John H. – *The Oldest Music Room in Europe.* New York, 1911.

MAHON, William. Oxford 1753-1816 May 3, Salisbury. English. See OV. He was the brother of John Mahon. He also played the oboe, violin and viola. By 1777 he was living with his brother at no.135 Jermyn Street, London. When John married in 1792 William moved out and went to live at no.11 Margaret Street. During the brothers' many visits to the Salisbury and Winchester festivals they frequently stayed at the house of their youngest sister Catherine in Salisbury. Catherine (1769-1833) had a beautiful voice like her elder sisters and had been trained by Joseph Corfe, but did not sing professionally after marrying Joseph Tanner, a man of considerable means and importance in Salisbury. The Tanners' house at no.45 Castle Street, where Assemblies were often held in the fine music room, is still standing. On 12th February 1816 William should have performed at a concert with Mrs Salmon at the public Assembly Rooms in Salisbury, but was prevented by illness. He died on 3rd May at his sister's home and was buried in the Tanner vault at St Thomas' Church. An inscription in the centre aisle of the church records his death and that of his mother Catherine (Salisbury, 1720-1808 July 12, Salisbury).

Bibliography:

CUDWORTH, Charles – "John Mahon." MGG.
HOGAN, Ita M. – *Anglo-Irish Music 1780-1830*. Cork 1966.
MEE, John H. – *The Oldest Music Room in Europe.* New York, 1911.
Obituary – (*The Gentleman's Magazine*). June, 1816.

MAHR (MAYR), C. Born at Hilburghausen. German. He went to Sondershausen to learn from Hermstedt. In 1819 he returned to Hildburghausen and performed a concerto and the Symphonie Concertante for clarinet, horn & bassoon by Crusell. In 1821 he gave the only known performance of Spohr's Recitative & Adagio, written c.1804/5 for Tretbach.

(B–H). **MAINTZER (MEINTZER, MEINZER), Franz.** German. He was probably the father of Friedrich Mainzer. He was employed as a clarinettist, violinist and music director for the Mecklenburg-Schwerin Court at Schwerinsburg, near Anklam. He performed as a soloist at Danzig in 1781, at Königsberg on 17th January 1782 and at Lübeck in 1792.

MAINZER, Friedrich. c.1760-? German. Franz Maintzer was probably his father. Friedrich was employed at the following courts: Brandenburg-Schwedt, 1785-1792; Mecklenburg-Schwerin (at Ludwigslust), 1792-1795; Mecklenburg-Strelitz (at Neu-Strelitz), 1795-1807; Munich, 1807-1827. He also played the violin.
Works: 12 Quartets (Breitkopf & Härtel 1785/7).

MAIOROV, I.N. 1896-1955. Russian. He was a pupil of Rozanov at the Moscow Conservatoire. He became principal clarinet for the Bolshoi Theatre Orchestra and was professor at the Military Conductors' Institute.

MANGOLD, August Daniel. Darmstadt, 25 July 1775-1842, Darmstadt. German. He was a member of the well-known musical family at Darmstadt. His father was Johann Wilhelm Mangold who taught various orchestral instruments and led the Darmstadt orchestra. In 1798 August Daniel was employed by a wealthy merchant by the name of Bernhard at Offenbach, first as clarinettist in the private orchestra and then as orchestral director. After the turn of the century he took up the cello and became a member of the theatre orchestra at Frankfurt a. M. In 1814 he was living at Darmstadt again and playing in its court orchestra, of which he eventually became director.

MANNSTEIN, Karl. From about 1789 to 1794 he was teaching clarinet at the Theatrical School in St Petersburg, but was not a member of the court orchestra.

MARASCO, Giuseppe. Italian. He taught clarinet at the Liceo in Venice.

MARÉ (MARET), senior. French. He was first clarinet at the Gymnase Dramatique (Théâtre de S.A.R. Madame) in Paris from 1821 to 1825. One of his sons played first cello in the same orchestra, and Maré junior (see below) was probably a younger brother. Maré senior lived at the following addresses: 1822 – no.15 boulevard Bonne Nouvelle; 1824 – no.16 rue de la Lune; 1825 – no.1 rue Coquenard.

MARÉ (MARÈS, MALET), junior. French. He was related to the above. He played second clarinet at the Panorama Dramatique in 1821, the Comédie Française in 1822 and 1823, and the Théâtre Français (successor to the Comédie Française) from 1824 to 1829. He lived at the following addresses: 1822 – no.12 rue de la Lune; 1824 – no.16 rue de la Lune.

(B–H). **MARHEFKA, Franz (Joseph).** Dresden, 1862-1933, Schwerin. German. His father was against him making music his career, though he allowed him to have clarinet lessons from Julius Kaiser. In 1876 his father died and Kaiser became his guardian. Two years later Marhefka became a pupil at the Dresden Conservatoire and in 1880 entered Demnitz' special class there. Through the auspices of Demnitz he was engaged in 1883 for the opera orchestra at Schwerin, where he remained for the rest of his life, receiving a pension in 1924. In 1895 he accompanied Mme Schumann-Heink in Mozart's "Non più di fiori." In 1896 he toured to Dresden and other towns and was also engaged for the Bayreuth Festival. Being greatly impressed by the Boehm flute he had the courage, half way through his professional life, to change to Boehm clarinets, buying them from Buffet-Crampon. The Grand Duke Friedrich Franz IV of Mecklenburg-Schwerin awarded him the Silver Medal for Knowledge and Art.

MARTINEZ, Andréas. Spanish. He was the best teacher of his time in Madrid. Pedro Broca was his pupil in 1805.

MARTINEZ, Juan Antonio. Cartagena, 14 Sept 1798-? Spanish. He played in the court orchestra at Madrid.

MARX, Michael. He played at the Munich Subscription Concerts from 1886 to 1907.

MASSAERT, Jean Pierre. Liège, 1796-? Belgian. He was a good teacher as well as performer and lived at Liège all his life. At the age of twelve he played concertos by Blasius, Crémont and Pleyel on a 6-keyed clarinet for the Société d'Émulation. He later became solo clarinet at the town theatre. When the Liège Conservatoire was founded in 1827 he was made clarinet professor, a post he retained until 1862. Postula was his best known pupil.

Works: 2 Fantasias, dedicated to King Leopold I (Muraille). Trios for clarinet & 2 horns.

(B–H). **MATAUSCHEK (MATOUŠEK), Johann (Jan).** Czech. He also played oboe and bassoon. In the 1770s he was employed with Czerny and Oliva by Princess Poniatowsky who sent them to Linz to perfect themselves on the basset-horn. Their teacher is thought to have been Joseph Glöggl. In 1781 they toured Germany and Russia, performing clarinet and basset-horn trios. In the late 1780s Matauschek was employed as second basset-horn and bassoon in the Hauskapelle of Princess Elizabeth of Freiburg. At Vienna in 1797 and 1798 he played bassoon in Beethoven's Wind Quintet, with Bähr playing clarinet and and Beethoven the piano.

(B–H). **MAURER, Gottlob (Anton Friedrich).** 1763-1813 Sept 24, Leipzig. German. He was celebrated as a town musician at Leipzig and played a prominent part in the city's musical life. He also played clarinet, basset-horn, and sometimes oboe, for the Leipzig Gewandhaus Orchestra from 1792 until his death. With them he appeared 12 times as clarinet soloist and 3 times as basset-horn soloist; the only details available are of a concert on 23rd December 1804, when he played Krommer's Concerto op.35 with Wilhelm Barth, who later succeeded him as town musician. The same year Maurer was commended for an oboe obligato in an opera performance. His son Edward became a well-known violinist and on one occasion performed a concerto for 2 violins with Hostié (q.v.) at Königsberg.

MAURER, J.M. He was a clarinettist and music director at Strasbourg from 1821 to 1836. His wife was a singer. In 1821 he performed the obligato to Mozart's "Parto!" and in 1829 the two obligatos from Paer's *Sargino.* He composed operas, but nothing for the clarinet.

(B–H). **MAYCOCK, John (Henry).** 1 May 1817-1907. English. He also played the bass clarinet. He received his musical training in the Coldstream Guards and later became a well-known soloist in the concert world, second only to Lazarus in popular esteem. In 1842 he joined the Royal Society of Musicians and was then living at no.3 Howick Terrace, Vauxhall Bridge Road. He was already first clarinet for the Royal Italian Opera at the Haymarket and had played at St James' Theatre. Jullien engaged him in 1849 to take part in an unusual trio, composer unknown, for oboe, basset-horn and ophicleide. From 1857 to 1892 Maycock was first clarinet at Drury Lane. Balfe was much taken with his talent and wrote the bass clarinet solo in *The Daughter of St Mark* for him and also the basset-horn obligato to "The Heart bowed down." Maycock may have been the basset-hornist who played with Lazarus in a Mendelssohn Concertstück at St James' Hall on 24th June 1868.

MAYER (MEYER). Born at Frankfurt a. M. German.

He played in Frankfurt's theatre orchestra for nine years before joining a French regiment and going with them to France. In Paris he married a singer called Mlle Lévêque. The Mayers escaped from France at the time of the Terror and 1799 finds them in Königsberg. On 5th February Mme Mayer accompanied her husband at a concert and on 21st March she gave birth to a son Charles, who was to become a famous pianist. The Mayers next lived in St Petersburg for some years, before removing to Moscow in 1803. When Moscow was sacked in 1812 they fled back to St Petersburg. In 1814 Mayer and his son undertook a concert tour together. Charles had a great success in Paris and the following year father and son performed at Frankfurt. There are no further reports of concerts from the father. In 1819 he returned to live at St Petersburg and remained there until his death.

MAYER (MAIER), Jakob. German. He came from Kirn to Weilburg in 1789 and was given a post in Duke Friedrich Wilhelm of Nassau's orchestra. When this was dissolved in 1793 he removed to Mannheim and the following year secured the post of first clarinet in the court orchestra there.

MAYEUR, Louis A. 1837-1894. French. He played the saxophone as well as clarinet and studied both under Klosé at the Paris Conservatoire. In 1860 he gained a First Prize for clarinet. He also conducted the Spring Concerts in the Jardin d'acclimation. He was the best saxophonist of his time.

Works: Fantaisie originale (Lafleur – LBL). Tutor.

MAZZOLENI, Pietro. Spanish. In 1834 he played with a wind quartet at Cadiz.

McLANE, Ralph. Lynn, Massachusetts, 19 Dec 1907-1951 Feb 18. American. He began to learn the clarinet at the age of nine, first from Elzier Therrien who had been a pupil of Rose, Porteau and Selmer. He then had lessons from Vannini and won a scholarship to the New England Conservatory at Boston. Here he learnt from Hamelin, then principal clarinet of the Boston Symphony Orchestra, and when Hamelin returned to Paris in 1930 he went with him for a further two years of study. McLane came back to America and played with the C.B.S. and W.O.R. Radio Symphony Orchestras before becoming first clarinet of the Philadelphia Orchestra in 1943. With the latter orchestra he gave the first performance in New York of Copland's Concerto, on 24th November 1950. He performed with the Budapest, Busch, Stradivarius, Stuyvesant and Kolisch Quartets.

He also taught at the Curtis Institute in Philadelphia. McLane produced a wonderfully centred, firm and beautiful tone. He used a double-lip embouchure inherited from Hamelin and in later years introduced a certain amount of vibrato to his playing. He always sat to perform and held his clarinet well up, at an angle of 45°. His instruments were old and had many imperfections, but he had the ability to adjust to these and make them sound superb.

Recordings:

Brahms – Trio op.114. With Sterling Hawkins & Milton Kaye. Musicraft 15.

Ravel – Introduction & Allegro. Columbia X167.

MEDER, Konrad. German. He was probably related to Valentin Meder. In 1759 he was a member of the Elector of Treves' court orchestra at Ehrenbreitstein, Coblenz.

MEDER, Valentin. 22 Oct 1733-1797 Mar 26. German. He was probably related to Konrad Meder. During the latter half of the eighteenth century he, like Konrad, played in the Elector of Treves' orchestra at Ehrenbreitstein, Coblenz. He also played the violin and cello.

MEHNER (MEHNERT), F. German. The early part of his life was spent at Leipzig where he became popular as a soloist. Leipzig attracted many very good players and he failed to secure a regular engagement with the orchestra. He therefore moved to Frankfurt a. M. where he was first clarinet in the theatre orchestra from 1836 to 1861 or later.

He gave the following concerts whilst he was at Leipzig: 1830 – 18th November, concerto by Iwan Müller. 1831 – 5th August, visited Erfurt, where he gave a concert in the theatre. 1832 – 12th January, Georg Müller's Concertino. 29th March, Schindelmeisser's Symphonie Concertante for 4 clarinets with "Mey" (Eduard Meyer?), Rosenkranz and Schindelmeisser. 1835 – 15th January at the Gewandhaus, Adagio & Variations by "Berr" (Beer).

He gave the following concerts for the Frankfurt Museum Society: 1836 – 18th November, unspecified concertino. 1837 – 17th November, "Der Friede" for vocal quartet with obligato clarinet by Schnyder von Wartensee. 1839 – Mozart's Wind Quintet, also Spohr's "Six German Songs" for Mlle Kratkh. 1840 – 27th March, Potpourri on themes from Meyerbeer's *Robert le Diable* by Rummel. 1841 – 5th March, unspecified concertino. 1844 – 8th March, Beethoven's Wind Quintet. 1847 – concerto by the clarinettist Röhrig. 1848 – 7th

January, Schubert's "Der Hirt auf dem Felsen" for Caspari. 3rd November, Röhrig's Concertino. 1850 – 1st March, Cherubini's "Ave Maria" for Elise Anschütz-Capitain. 1851 – 14th February, Beethoven's Wind Quintet. 1854 – 17th February, solo by Reissiger. 1856 – 15th February, Weber's Concertino.

On 12th March 1861 he performed Mozart's Quintet and Weber's Grand Duo in a concert given to celebrate his twenty five years service as solo clarinet in the theatre orchestra.

MEIER, Wilhelm. Hanover, 1820-1900 Jan 28. German. He was trained at Göttingen by the town musician Jacobi and then secured a place in a Royal Hanoverian Life Regiment. In 1846 he was in Detmold as a clarinettist in the Leopold-Corps and as violinist in the court orchestra. He became first clarinet in the orchestra in 1849 when Steffens died. Because of asthma he had to give up playing the clarinet in 1871 and thereafter, until he retired in 1876, played in the second violins. He gave the following solo performances at Detmold: 1849 – Wieprecht's Fantasia. 1850 – solo by Heinrich Neumann, formerly clarinettist at Detmold. 1851 – a composition by Weber.

MEINBERG (MEYENBERG), Johann Georg. Mühlhausen, 21 Oct 1807-? German. He was the son of the town musician at Mühlhausen. When old enough he was sent to Göttingen to be apprenticed to their famous town musician, Jacobi. As Göttingen had no Court, Jacobi provided the town with an orchestra enlisted from his students, and Meinberg was given a chance to perform solos with it on several occasions. Meinberg went into a military band at Erfurt and from thence in 1823 to the Royal Guard at Potsdam. He returned as guest artist to Göttingen on 7th January 1837 and performed two compositions by Wieprecht, the Royal Guard's music director. Dr Heinroth, professor of music for Göttingen University, wrote a rave review of the concert for AMZ in which he said that they had not heard such dazzling playing since Hermstedt had visited the town. Potsdam affectionately dubbed the clarinettist "our Meinberg" when he performed a composition of Iwan Müller's for their Philharmonic Society in 1839. In 1841 Meinberg played again for the Potsdam Philharmonic Society and also at Sondershausen. In the summer of 1844 he conducted concerts in the Möser Flower Garden, Berlin. From 1849 he became a teacher at the Potsdam Royal Music School.

MEISSNER, Philipp. Burgebrach (near Bamburg), 14 Sept 1748-1816 July 6, Würzburg. German. He was the first great clarinet teacher and can be given credit for the development of a stylized German school of playing. His pupils included Bähr, Goepfert, Kleinhaus, Georg Reinhardt and the Viersnickel brothers. Meissner began to play on an old clarinet at seven years old and by the age of twelve was showing such aptitude for it that his father bought him a good instrument and sent him for lessons to Martin Hessler, clarinettist in the Würzburg court orchestra. When he was sixteen Meissner performed to Adam Friedrich, the Prince-Bishop of Würzburg, who offered him a sum of money to enable him to travel. In May 1766 he set off, playing at the courts of Höchst, Mainz, Mannheim, Schwetzingen and Bruchsal. Arriving at Strasbourg, he entered service with the Cardinal Prince of Rohan, well known for his connection with "The Affair of the Diamond Necklace." The Prince departed for Paris shortly afterwards and took Meissner with him. Meissner became immediately popular as a soloist in Paris for, although the clarinet was now familiar to them, this was the first time Parisians had had a chance to hear a true specialist on the instrument. He was probably one of the Cardinal's two clarinettists who performed at the Concert Spirituel in March and again at Passiontide in 1769. At some time during 1769 Meissner entered the service of the Marquis of Brancas and through the auspices of the latter joined the band of the Life Guards. He also played in the orchestra at the Opéra. In 1774 he performed as a soloist at the Concert Spirituel under his christian name, as had Michel Yost many times.

Meissner was by now so well known that in 1776 Prince Vincenz Potocki offered him a substantial bribe to join his own household and return with him to Poland. On the long journey across Europe the Prince made a protracted stop at Frankfurt and Meissner asked leave to visit his family again at Würzburg. His former patron the Prince-Bishop, being advised of his visit, sent for him to play at his private residence at Weitshoecheim. As a result, Meissner was pressed back into the Bishop's service and abandoned his journey to Poland. He remained at Würzburg for the rest of his life, except to undertake the following concert tours: 1780 – Frankfurt, when he played a concerto by Sterckel on 9th April; 1784 – Carlsruhe; 1787 – Wallerstein, Dillingen and Augsburg with the bassoonist Moritz Braun; and later – Munich, Dresden and Switzerland. He retired from court service in 1806 but continued to teach until his death. Goepfert dedicated his Third Concerto and 2 Duos Concertants op.19 to Meissner.

Works: Several concertos. Duos op.3 (Schott). 2 Duos concertants op.4, dedicated to his pupil Goepfert (Schott 1815). 4 Progressive Duos (Plattner). 2 Quartets ops.1 & 2 (Schott). Harmonie Musik, 2 books (Breitkopf & Härtel).

MEJO (MAJO), (August) Wilhelm. Nossen, 1793-? Silesian. He studied music first at Oederan, near Chemnitz, and later at Leipzig. From 1814 to 1821 he was employed in the Leipzig Gewandhaus Orchestra. His solo dates with them were as follows: 1817 – 18th December, unspecified works. 1819 – 16th December, Variations (probably op.20) by Heinrich Baermann. 1820 – Concertino by himself. He was not however a popular soloist. From 1821 to 1832 he was music director for a small court at Domanzi in Silesia, and from 1832 until 1846 or later he was music director at Chemnitz. Here he did good work with an orchestra of twenty four players, raising the standard sufficiently to be able to perform Beethoven symphonies at the winter subscription concerts. His opera *Der Gang nach dem Eisenhammer* was presented with success at Brunswick in 1840.

Works: Concertino. Variations on *Gaudeamus igitur* for 3 clarinets & wind band, dedicated to Wilhelm Barth (Breitkopf & Härtel c.1824 – LBL).

MENZ, Robert. Kaimberg, 16 June 1859-1925 May 17, Hanover. German. He also played the bass clarinet. His first appointment was in the Bilse Orchestra at Berlin. In 1885 he moved to Hanover as second clarinet in the court orchestra and remained there for the rest of his life. In 1886 he was made a Royal Chamber Musician.

MERCADANTE, Giacinto. Altamura, 1778-c.1850. Italian. In 1799 he underwent trial for some unknown crime and was condemned to deportation. It seems that he later had musical instruction from his half-brother, the composer Saverio Mercadante, and became a clarinettist and guitarist.

MÉRIC, Jean. He was a clarinettist in the French Guard, which in 1789 became the National Guard. By 1793 he had risen to the rank of corporal. He taught at the Institut National from 1789 and when the Conservatoire was opened in 1795 he was made a professor of the second class. At the reconstitution in 1802, when many professors were dismissed, he was kept on as warden of the music stores. He was pensioned in 1816.

MERLATTI. Italian. He was playing in the theatre orchestra at Turin in 1816. By 1823 he had become a member of the Turin court orchestra.

METZLER. German. On 16th December 1826 he gave a public concert at Breslau, when he was probably already in the employ of the Prince-Bishop. By 1831 he had been made Kapellmeister. He was still employed in this capacity, and as a clarinettist, in 1833.

MEUSER (MEISER), Christian. On 9th April 1780 he performed at Frankfurt a. M. in a concert given by Karolina Steffani. From about 1783 to 1790 he was a member of the Elector of Bonn's court orchestra and of the wind octet that played at meal times. He had a reputation for being a good solo clarinettist, and for partiality to the bottle.

MEYER, Eduard. German. He learnt the clarinet from Kotte at Dresden. He was doubtless the "Mey" who took part in the performance of Schindelmeisser's Symphonie Concertante for 4 clarinets with the composer, Mehner and Rosenkranz on 29th March 1832 at Leipzig. He settled in Leipzig and appeared as soloist with the Symphony Orchestra in 1836. On 15th November 1838 he played Variations (probably op.20) by Heinrich Baermann for the Subscription Concerts. After this he set off on a grand tour to St Petersburg, playing in December at Berlin, where they commented on his beautiful tone, and later at Hamburg.

(B–H). **MEYER, Hermann.** Brunswick, 1814-? German. He was first clarinettist and music director in a regiment of Life Guards. After this he was second clarinet in the court orchestra at Hanover from 1844 to 1851. He then spent some years at the Court in Stuttgart where he appeared as soloist at the following concerts: 1864 – 28th March, Duo for clarinet & piano by Zahlberg, Mozart's Quintet K581, Schubert's Octet. 1865 – towards the end of the year, Phantasiestück by Lindner (possibly Friedrich Lindner, the Dessau clarinettist.) In 1866 he moved to Munich and took over Schülein's post in the court orchestra.

MIEDZNY, Stefan. Polish. He was a well-known clarinettist in the eighteenth century.

MIKESCH. German. He was active at Kremsmünster between 1811 and 1819. In 1814 he is recorded as a member of the court orchestra, playing both first clarinet and first oboe.

MILLS, Edward. 31 May 1865-1944 Feb. English. He studied the clarinet and saxophone with Poncelet at Brussels. He then came back to England and was appointed first clarinet and saxophonist to the Hallé Orchestra at Manchester, a post which he held from 1897 to 1919. He played soprano clarinet and bass clarinet for the Leeds festivals of 1913 and 1922 respectively. He joined the Royal Society of Musicians in 1899.

MILLS, O. English. He played in the London Symphony Orchestra from 1905 to 1913.

MIMART, Prospèr. ?-1928. French. He was probably the son of P.A. Mimart, who was highly commended at the Paris Conservatoire contests in 1847, the year Rose won the First Prize, and who won First Prize himself in 1850. Prospèr learnt from Rose and gained First Prize in 1878. He played in the Pasdeloup and Lamoureux orchestras, for the Opéra Comique and, from 1892 to 1897, for the Société des Concerts. He was a distinguished soloist, and from 1905 to 1923 was clarinet professor at the Conservatoire. During his professorship the following music set for the contests was dedicated to him: 1910 – Debussy's Première Rhapsodie (he gave the first performance on 16th January 1911); 1911 – Gaubert's Fantaisie; 1923 – Grovlez' Lamento et Tarantelle. Mimart edited Berr's tutor and this was published in 1909.

Work: Méthode nouvelle de clarinette (Enoch 1911).

Recording:

Schubert – "The Shepherd on the Rock." Technicord 1129.

MOCKER (father). He was first clarinet in the Grand Theatre at Lyons from 1790 to 1822 or later and was also a teacher. Several of his descendants became well-known as pianists in Lyons. It was probably one of his sons who held various positions as principal clarinet in the Parisian theatres during the 1820s (see article below).

Works: Fantaisie concertante op.4 (Arnaud). Duos op.1 (Arnaud c.1790).

MOCKER (son?) French. (See above). From 1824 until 1827 he was first clarinet at the Odéon in Paris. In 1829 he was the only clarinet employed at the Spectacles de Curiosités. His address in 1824 was no.33 rue M. le Prince. In 1825 he could be found "au Théâtre ou rue Monsieur-le-Prince, café Racine." In 1827 he lived at no.41 M. le Prince and by 1829 in the rue Croix-des-Petits-Champs, the road where Gambaro's printing press was.

MÖHRENSCHLAGER. He was employed as a clarinettist at Erlangen. He appeared as soloist at Frankfurt a. M. in 1847.

MOHR (MOHRE), J. In 1823 he was playing clarinet and double-bass at the Ambigu Comique in Paris. In 1827 he was sub-principal clarinet at the Odéon, and living at no.125 rue du Bac, the same road as Delamotte. By 1828 he was principal clarinet at the Odéon and had moved to no.6 rue Rousselet. From about 1843 to 1848 he was principal clarinet at the Académie Royale de Musique (Opéra). Gambaro dedicated his 3rd Air varié to Mohr.

Works: Air varié no.3 (Wessel – LRAM). Air varié no.4 (Hawkes 1877 – LBL). 3 Duos concertants op.2 (Hofmeister). Morceaux for 2 clarinets (Meissonnier – LRCM).

MOOCK. In 1783 he was second clarinet in the house quintet of Count Belderbusch at Bonn, with Pachmeier playing first.

MORELLI. Portuguese. He played as a clarinet soloist at Lisbon in 1816.

MORTIMER, Harry. English. In 1917 he became third clarinet in the Hallé Orchestra at Manchester and from 1919 to 1936 was an exceptionally fine first clarinet. In spite of tempting offers elsewhere he remained with the orchestra through its many vicissitudes and in 1933 was made orchestral secretary. In 1936 he stepped down in favour of Pat Ryan.

MOYSARD, Michel. Orleans, 1777-1824 June 14, Antwerp. He played in the opera orchestra at Antwerp, during the early nineteenth century. He lost his reason following a duel in which he mortally wounded the French oboist Laurent, and was committed to an asylum in 1820.

Work: Concerto in B flat (Ms. score in AKVM).

MRAZ, Josef Franz. Nikovic, 1843-1910 Mar 23, Göteborg. Czech. He was a student at Prague Conservatoire, playing Reissiger's Fantasie "L'Attente et l'Arrivée" at their public concerts on 10th April 1862. He was said to have a sweet soft tone. During the wars of 1864 and 1866 he served as a serjeant major. In 1874 he settled in Göteborg as solo clarinet to the Music Society and as a piano teacher. From 1880 to 1900 he played in the band of the Västgöta Dals regiment. During the last years of his life he organised a successful series of chamber music concerts.

MÜHLFELD, Richard. Salzungen, 28 Feb 1856-1907 June 1, Meiningen. German. See OV. Additional concert information: 1892 – 11th March at Meiningen, Princess Marie's Romanza with Steinbach; 15th December at Manchester, Weber's Concertino with the Hallé Orchestra and Weber's Grand Duo with Charles Hallé. 1901 – 30th October at Carlsruhe, Stephen Krehl's Quintet op.19. 1905 – 15th October at Berlin, Robert Kahn's Trio with Kahn and Hausmann. A further work to be dedicated to Mühlfeld was Theodor Verhey's Concerto op.47, written in 1900.

MÜLLER. German. In 1828 he was first clarinet in Jacobi's orchestra at Göttingen.

MÜLLER, Carl? German. At Osnabrück on 28th November 1799 he played the clarinet d'amour in variations for basset-horn (played by Rehm) and clarinet d'amour. He gave performances of unspecified clarinet concertos on 2nd November 1799, 21st and 23rd January and 20th February 1802. He may be identified with Carl Müller from Zweibrücken, who was appointed violinist at Osnabrück in 1797.

MÜLLER, Friedrich. Orlamünda (near Rudolstadt), 10 Dec 1786-1871 Dec 12, Rudolstadt. German. He was taught several instruments by his father, who was town musician at Orlamünda. In 1803 he was appointed to the Schwarzburg-Rudolstadt Court as clarinettist and cellist, playing violin when required. The Prince of Schwarzburg-Rudolstadt sent him and Flittner, the other court clarinettist, to Dresden to have lessons from the elder Roth. Müller had composition lessons from Heinrich Koch at Rudolstadt. In 1811 he was promoted to first clarinet in the Rudolstadt wind band and in 1816 was given charge of the military music, for which services he was made Chamber Musician. On 29th February 1824 he played a concertino of his own composition at Berlin. For the Halberstadt Festival of 1827 he performed Mozart's Trio K498 with two of his greatest friends, Spohr (in an unusual rôle as viola player) and Friedrich Schneider. Müller became music director at Rudolstadt in 1831, on the death of Eberwein. In 1853 he was given the title of Ducal Councillor, in recognition of his fifty years service. He retired in 1854.

Works: Concerto op.10 in E flat (Breitkopf & Härtel 1816). Concerto op.11 in B flat (Breitkopf & Härtel). Concertino op.20 in B flat (Breitkopf & Härtel). Concertante op.44 for 2 clarinets (Hofmeister). Concertino op.27 in F for 2 clarinets (Breitkopf & Härtel). Concertino op.51 for clarinet & bassoon (Müller 1841). 2

Symphonies concertants ops.? & 31 for clarinet & horn (Breitkopf & Härtel). Divertissement op.32 (Müller). Fantasie sur un Chant pastoral suisse (Breitkopf & Härtel. Richault – PBN). Potpourri op.21 (Breitkopf & Härtel). Romance variée op.9 (Brietkopf & Härtel). Introduction & Thême varié for 2 clarinets (Breitkopf & Härtel). Quartet op.80 (Hofmeister). Introduction & Thême varié for clarinet & string quartet (Breitkopf & Härtel – LRCM).

(B–H). **MÜLLER, Iwan.** Reval (Talinn), 3 Dec 1786-1854 Feb 4, Bückeburg. German. See OV. He also played the bass clarinet and bassoon. Between Mannheim and Strasbourg in 1817 Müller stopped at Frankfurt and on 12th September played a Fantasie of his own composition for the Museum Concerts. He was accompanied by Mme Müller-Bender, a popular Frankfurt artiste who was also the composer of some variations for clarinet. Mme Müller-Bender was not related to the clarinettist. After his visit to Kassel in 1824 Müller played at Lübeck and then at Hamburg, where he remained into 1825. On 17th October 1825 he gave a concert of his own compositions at the Leipzig Gewandhaus, when he played the Sixth Concerto, Variations on a New Theme and Fantasie on an Air of Rossini. At Magdeburg in January 1826 he played his own Second Concertino and Siciliano. For a short spell in 1827 he played first clarinet at the Coburg Court with Greding as his second. Many years later he was to come back to this Court, after it had been annexed to Gotha. In April 1827 Müller was in Rome, in second floor lodgings at no.7 Via S. Bastianello, from where he announced a public concert. He returned to this pied-à-terre after his triumph at Bologna in the Spring of 1829, and gave his own concert on 2nd May at the Argentine Theatre. He performed his newly written Seventh Concerto, which was dedicated to the Bologna Philharmonic Society, who had just made him an honorary member. And also his own Pacini Fantasie op.58 and arrangement of Beethoven's "Adelaide." At this time he was styling himself "Royal Chamber Musician." By 1835 he was once more domiciled in Paris and on 24th April gave one of a series of concerts at the Laffitte Hall.

Glinka heard Müller play his "new" clarinet at Milan, probably in 1832. He disliked it intensely and in his memoires criticized it's "harsh tones, like the screech of a goose; yet the inventor was proud of his invention. Fortunately for lovers of good music, this clarinet was not introduced into the orchestra." There was certainly a lack of refinement in Müller's playing and this evidently told against the invention itself. Müller's life contained many triumphs and some cruel failures. He did not reap the financial rewards that his invention and the concerts he staged to promote it deserved. In later years he became disillusioned and excessively sensitive to criticism. His final years at Bückeburg were spent in poverty, separated from his wife and child. He was still totally absorbed in his clarinet and so withdrawn that he scarcely communicated with his fellow men. Neither the interest of his patron, Prince Georg Wilhelm of Schaumberg-Lippe, nor the devoted friendship of his fellow clarinettist Bargheer could dispel the bitterness and he died with words of anger on his lips.

Gardeton's *Bibliographie musicale* of 1822 records the publication by V. Gambaro of Müller's tutor. This is an earlier date than had previously been thought. Carse is incorrect in saying that Conrad Bänder was Müller's only pupil, for Fétis states that Lellmann went to Paris for lessons from him – this would have been c.1821-1824. It seems more than probable that Müller also taught Conrad Bänder's brother Ludwig, both of them in St Petersburg at some time prior to 1807. A further work to be dedicated to Müller was de Groot's Duo for 2 clarinets.

Works: Concerto no.1 in D minor, dedicated to Nikolaus Simrock (Simrock c.1810 – solo part only in AKVM). Concerto no.2 in E flat (Jouve). Concerto no.3 in B flat (André 1821). Concerto no.4 in F minor (Ms. score in PhFL. Dufaut & Dubois. Simrock – solo part only in AKVM. Lemoine). Concerto no.5 in E flat (Dufaut & Dubois. Simrock. Lemoine). Concerto no.6 in G minor (Dufaut & Dubois. Simrock 1824 – LBL). Concerto no.7, dedicated to the Bologna Philharmonic Society (1829?). Concertino no.1 (1825?) Concertino no.2 (1826). Concertino capriccioso. Symphonie concertante op.23 in E flat for 2 clarinets, dedicated to "Monsieur Doizi, amateur clarinette à Amiens" (Hofmeister 1825 – LRAM, SKMA, ZAM. Ricordi – BoLM. Richault – PBN).

Adagio & Polonaise op.30, dedicated to F.C. Hagen (Richault – PBN. Hofmeister). Adagio & Polonaise op.54 (Richault – PBN. Diabelli – LRAM). Air italien varié (Gambaro). Beethoven's "Adelaide" (1827). Cavatina "Una voce poco fà" from Rossini's *Barber of Seville* (Spehr c.1825. Ms. copy in LRCM). Divertissement (Dufuat & Dubois). Don d'Amitié, air varié op.25 (Hofmeister. Ricordi). Duo op.13 (Bachmann). Fantaisie op.58 on a Grand scene from Pacini's *l'Ultimo Giorno di Pompei,* dedicated to "Monsieur C. van Rinsum jr., amateur très distingué de Clarinette à Amsterdam" (Nagel 1853 – LBL, LRAM). Fantaisie on a Cavatine by Pacini (Leidesdorf). Fantaisie on a Minuet of Mozart (Steup. Simrock 1821). Fantaisie on an air from Bellini's *Il pirate* op.70 (Schott). Fantaisie on a Venetian Air (Spehr – LBL. Ms. copy in LRCM). Fantaisie on a Theme of Rossini. Grand Polonaise, *le château de Madrid* op.79 (Schott). Grand Solo in C minor (Dufaut & Dubois). Introduction &

Conoscendo il gusto elevato, che possiede l'
Eccellenza Vostra per le belle arti, mi faccio un dovere di
avvertirla, che mi sono [illegible] di dare un' accademia
di musica vocale ed istrumentale in questa capitale
e nella speranza, ch'Ella si degnerà onorarmi di
sua presenza, ardisco trasmetterle il foglio d'
associazione, pregandola di restituirlo all'latore.
Con sensi di profondo ossequio, ho l'onore di
essere

Dell'Eccellenza Vostra

27. Aprile 1827

Umo ed Obbmo Servitore
Iwan Müller

S. Bartianello N° 3

4. Concert invitation from Iwan Müller, Rome 27th April 1827.
(Deutsche Staatsbibliothek, Berlin/DDR).

Rondo amabile op.112, dedicated to H. Tinholt, first clarinet of Amsterdam's Grand Wind Society (Hofmeister c.1851 – LRAM). Le Rêve, episode romantique op.73 (Schott 1844/5 – LRAM). Romance de Blangini, Fantaisie (Steup. Simrock 1821). Rondo from Rossini's *Barber of Seville*. Scène romantique op.96, dedicated to V. Bender (Schott 1844/5 – LRAM). Serenade from Rossini's *Barber of Seville* (Schott c.1825 – WLC. Ms. copy in LRCM). Siciliano et Rondeau in E minor (André 1821). Six easy pieces op.26 (Spehr. Hofmeister. Ricordi. Petit). Souvenir de Rome op.92 (Nagel – LRAM). Variations brillantes on Carafa's "O cara memoria" op.69 (1827. Schott). Variations on a Russian Folk Song (c.1809). Variations on Mozart's "O dolce concento!" (Laffilé).

Duo from Rossini's *Armide* for clarinet & bassoon (Dufaut & Dubois. Ricordi – ZAM). Serenade for clarinet & guitar (Schott). Souvenir de Dobberan op.28, duo concertante for clarinet or horn & piano (Richault – PBN. Hofmeister c.1826 – BaU, LRAM). Air de Baillot op.29 for clarinet, violin & piano (Hofmeister. Ricordi – ZAM). Trio in G minor for 3 clarinets (Cundy-Bettoney). Quartet no.1 in B flat, dedicated to "Monsieur Boscavy à Paris," commissioned by the Philharmonic Society of London (1816. André 1821 – LRAM). Quartet no.2 in E minor, dedicated to Hermstedt (Ms. parts – BoLM. André 1821. Ricordi). Quartet no.3 (Gambaro). Variations on Mozart's "O dolce concento!" for clarinet, harp, viola & bassoon (Petit. Ricordi). Quintet. Septet. Solos for basset-horn.

Méthode pour la nouvelle clarinette et clarinette-alto (Gambaro 1822 – LBL, NYPL, PBN, WLC. Ricordi 1825 – PBN). Anweisung zur der neuen Clarinette und der Clarinett-Alto (Hofmeister, early 1826 – LBL); this is a revised edition of the Gambaro publication.

Bibliography:

HANSING, Siegfried – "Das Grab Iwan Müllers." ZI. 11/1897.
SMIGELSKI, Werner – "Ivan Müller". MGG.
TENNEY, Wallace – "Iwan Mueller and His New Clarinet". WM. February 1951.

MÜLLER, Johann Gustaf Gottfried. He was a clarinettist and double bass player at the theatre in Stockholm. He may have been a pupil of Crusell's because there is a copy in his hand of the latter's Concerto no.1, dated 1822, in the SKMA.

(B–H). **MUNRO.** He played basset-horn with Leffler in a performance of Mozart's *Requiem* at Covent Garden in 1801.

(B–H). **NAGEL, Heinrich.** German. He was appointed to the

Bentheim-Steinfürt Court in 1793 as clarinet, basset-horn and viola player. On 30th March 1794 he performed a basset-horn concerto at Osnabrück. Later he became an organist at Osnabrük.

NASON, Georg. He was unique as an eighteenth century clarinettist in being able to play two notes together. In the 1790s he travelled extensively in Germany and Italy demonstrating this technique. Paul records one such demonstration of 1797 at Gotha.

NEFF, A. German. In the 1830s he became a member of the court orchestra at Kassel and remained there for the rest of his professional life. He is reported to have played with Hermstedt under the direction of Spohr. The first mention of a solo performance by him comes in January 1845, when he played Rummel's Concertino. They liked his playing but said his legato was not good enough. On 2nd April he played a Concertstück by Späth at a Subscription Concert and later in the year a Divertissement by Baermann (Carl) at a court concert. On both these occasions he had a good reception, On 25th February 1846 he played in Spohr's Octet; this was led by Deichert (q.v.), who was also a bass clarinet player. In 1848 Neff played Weber's First Concerto. He was still only third clarinet in the orchestra in 1850 but by 1866 had risen to first. He was an authority on instrument design and Oehler came to Kassel to consult with him on this towards the end of the century.

NEHRLICH, Wilhelm. ?-1883 July 18, Stolpmünde. German. He had an extremely beautiful tone, though small and therefore inclined to be monotonous. He learnt the clarinet from Agthe at Weimar and then joined a military band at Berlin. It was probably in these early years that he made a copy of Crusell's Concertante op.3 which is preserved in the BSPK. In December 1826 he revisited Weimar as a soloist. In 1827 he was made a Chamber Musician in the Berlin court opera orchestra. His concerts, all at Berlin except for 1839, were as follows: 1833 – 16th March, Schubert's "Der Hirt auf dem Felsen" for Francisca Ganz with Wilhelm Taubert. 1835 – Beethoven's Wind Quintet; Variations by Karl Böhmer, a viola player at the Berlin Court. 1839 – 12th December at the Leipzig Gewandhaus, Variations by David, Adagio & Rondo by Weber. 1844 – with the pianist Löschorn, an "Adagio and Rondo from a Sonata for piano and clarinet by Weber (written for the composer and his friend Baermann, the father)." This is undoubtedly the Grand Duo op.48. He also performed at a concert given by Professor Karl Kloss. 1845 – April, in a concert given by Jenny Lind, Iwan Müller's double concerto with his pupil

K.F.W. Becker, also solos. June 15th, solos.

(B–H). **NEJEBSE.** Czech. He was principal clarinet in the theatre orchestra at Prague. He taught Joseph Friedlowsky to play both the clarinet and basset-horn about 1793.

NEUMANN, Heinrich. Heiligenstadt, 1792-1861 Apr 4, Heiligenstadt. German. He was a clarinettist and general music teacher at Frankfurt a. M. before going to Paderborn, where he was conductor of a wind band. In 1823 he moved to Detmold to become principal clarinet in the court orchestra and for the Leopold Corps. His younger brother Philipp played the clarinet and flute in the same band. Heinrich was made director of the band in 1824 and then ceased to play in the orchestra. He wrote a large number of compositions and arrangements for the band which are preserved in the Detmold Landesbibliothek. He left Detmold in 1829 and became conductor of a military band at Cologne. Later he conducted the Royal Wind Society at Antwerp, probably in succession to Jacob Bender who retired in 1843. Fétis says that in 1855 he won a competition at Mannheim for the composition of a symphony.

Works: Concertino op.19 en Forme de scène chantante (André). Concertino op.48 (Mompour). Etudes or Caprices op.23 for solo clarinet (André). Amusement op.43 (Schott). Duets op.24 (André). 3 Duets op.20, dedicated to "Herr Stadtdirector Brandis in Paderborn" (André 1823). Serenade op.2 for clarinet & guitar (André). Trio op.40 for clarinet, horn & bassoon (Haslinger). Serenades ops.5 & 16 for basset-horn & guitar (André). Variations op.9 in F for basset-horn & strings (André).

NEUPARTH, Eduard. Poelwitz, 6 Jan 1784-1871 June 23, Lisbon. German. He learnt the clarinet and violin at an early age and by fifteen was playing regularly in a group of local musicians. In 1804 the Prince of Löwenstein appointed him first clarinet to his Court, but when Napoleon's forces devastated the Prince's lands in 1806 the musicians were dismissed. Neuparth next found employment for a short time at the Court of Amorbach and then went to Freiburg to become director of a regimental band. From 1808 he played in several French bands and when peace was signed joined a Portuguese regiment, going with them to Lisbon. Here he became a member of the orchestra for the San Carlos theatre. In 1817 he was made director of the band selected to accompany the Princess Leopoldina to Rio de Janeiro (see Campos). He remained in Brazil until 1821, playing in the theatre and church orchestras and conducting various bands, and then returned to Lisbon, where he opened a music shop.

NEVUE. French. He was first clarinet at the Théâtre de la Gaité in Paris from 1827 to 1829. He lived in Vincennes, at no. 18 rue du Midi. It was probably his son Maurice who won the Conservatoire's First Prize in 1830.

NIDMAN, Karl (Christianovich). 1823-1901. He studied clarinet, violin and cello at Brunswick. From 1868 until he died he taught clarinet and wind ensemble at the St Petersburg Conservatoire.

NIEBERGALL, Georg. ?-1826, Darmstadt. German. He was a Chamber Musician at the Darmstadt Court from 1795 until his death. The instruments he used were made by Backofen. He also played the oboe, bassoon, violin and cello.

NIKOLAEVSKY, F.O. 1880-1951. Russian. He learnt the clarinet from Friedrich at the Moscow Conservatoire. He became first clarinet in the Bolshoi Theatre Orchestra and also conducted a military orchestra.

NIZINSKI, André. ?-1820. Polish. He was principal clarinet in the orchestra at Warsaw. In 1819 he played the piccolo in a concert at the Institute for the Poor.

NOCENTINI, Domenico. Florence, 1848-1924. Italian. He taught the clarinet at the Conservatoire in Florence.

Works: Fantasia *Ricordi di Venezia* (Bratti). 40 Duets.

NÖTHLICH, Wilhelm. German. He played in the Dresden court orchestra from late in the nineteenth century to about 1925.

NOLTE (NOLDE). German. He is first heard of as a clarinettist and oboist with excellent phrasing at Halberstadt about 1805. He then became second clarinet in the court orchestra at Kassel from 1809 to 1812. He also composed.

NORTON, F. English. He played second clarinet and bass clarinet in the Hallé Orchestra at Manchester from 1893 to 1900.

NORTON, Haydn (Harry). English. He played in the

Hallé Orchestra at Manchester in 1899 and 1900.

NUDER. Polish. About 1820 he was first clarinet in the orchestra at Romano castle in St Petersburg.

ODALDE, Thiago de Deos. Catalonian. He settled in Lisbon as a young man and became popular as a clarinet soloist. In 1822 he performed Iwan Müller's Third Concerto. At the Lisbon Subscription Concerts of 1824 he played a concertino by Krommer, a concertante (concerto?) by Witt and Variations in G after Rode by Canongia. He used a 5-keyed clarinet.

OEHLER, Oskar. Annaberg, 5 Feb 1858-1936 Oct 1, Berlin. German. He is famous as the designer of a clarinet system bearing his name. Before putting his constructional ideas into practice he had a distinguished career as an orchestral clarinettist. He first played in orchestras at Weide and Halle. Müller-Berghaus then invited him to Nice and in 1881 he returned to Germany to play in the Laube Orchestra at Hamburg. In 1882 he went to London to take part in a performance of Wagner's *Ring of the Nibbelungs* under Anton Seidl. The same year he was a co-founder of the Berlin Philharmonic Orchestra, with whom he played until 1888.

Oehler's interest in the mechanics of wind instruments began when at the age of fifteen he was apprenticed to an organ builder. Whilst travelling as a performer he took pains to discover the thoughts and experiences of well-known players, who included Carl Baermann of Munich and Neff of Kassel. In 1887 he opened a workshop in the Alvenslebenstrasse at Berlin and this was moved in 1890 to no.8 Katzlerstrasse. The Oehler clarinet is basically an improved Baermann system, having a lighter mechanism, with 22 keys, 5 rings and a finger-plate. It is the system most commonly used in Germany and Austria today. Oehler also designed a mouthpiece with a curved lay. He was opposed to the use of a metal ligature, preferring the old method of tying the reed on, for greater elasticity.

OGÍNSKI, Count Michael (Casimir). Warsaw, 1731-1803, Warsaw. Polish. See OV. In 1763 and 1764 he was playing in an orchestra of dilettantes in Moscow and "showed an astonishing virtuosity." Procksch dedicated his 6 Sonatas op.5 to Ogínski.

(B–H). **OLIVA, František (Franz).** Naustupow, 1754-? Czech. He was schooled in Seelau and Mühlhausen as a child singer and then went to Prague to study philosophy. In the late 1770s he was employed by Princess Poniatowsky at Vienna with Czerny and Matauschek. The Princess sent them to Linz to perfect themselves on the basset-horn, probably with Glöggl. In 1781 they toured Germany and Russia, playing trios for clarinets and basset-horns. From about 1787 to 1789 Oliva was at the Court of Prince Schwarzenberg in Vienna. He then went back to Russia and was still there in 1796. At some time he was active in Vídni.

OLIVER, James Aldwell. 1758-c.1818. He was probably the brother of Richard Oliver. He also played oboe, violin and viola. He was music director for the 2nd Scottish Infantry regiment towards the end of the eighteenth century, and had "40 military divertissesments" for 2 clarinets, 2 horns & 2 bassoons engraved in London in 1792. On 6th June 1810 he played with John Mahon in a Concertante for 9 wind instruments by Mayer at a concert given in London by Mrs Billington. He was a member of the Royal Society of Musicians from 1782 and of the Philharmonic Society during it's early years.

OLIVER, Richard. 1761-? He was probably a brother of James Oliver, and like him was a member of the Royal Society of Musicians, joining it in 1786. He also played bassoon, violin and cello. He died young, before the end of the century.

ORSI, Romeo. Como, 18 Oct 1842-1918 June 11, Milan. Italian. He had a distinguished career as clarinet soloist but is best known for the musical instrument factory which he established at Milan in 1880. Besides producing standard models of woodwind, brass and percussion instruments the firm made rareties such as clarinets in G with 16 keys, bass clarinets in A (made especially for Verdi's *Otello*) and bass flutes. In 1881 Orsi patented a clarinet *à doppia tonalita.* He translated and edited Lefèvre's clarinet tutor, and wrote a method for the saxophone.

Orsi studied the clarinet with Carulli at the Milan Conservatoire from 1856 to 1864, and in 1873 became a professor there himself. When he performed at Vienna in 1866 he was slated by the critic Eduard Hanslick, who advised him to go and join an orchestra, saying: "That is the place we like to see the players of clarinet, oboe and bassoon; the times are past when crowds of these artists came from everywhere to perform on their boring little pipes." Orsi was undeterred and went on to become well-known as a soloist in London, Paris, Baden-Baden, Monaco, Vichy, Biarritz and throughout Italy. He was principal clarinet at La Scala, Milan, and in 1878 founded the theatre's Orchestral

Society in collaboration with the publisher Giulio Ricordi. He was president and then vice-president of this society for eleven years.

Works: Método popolare for alto and bass clarinets (Ricordi). Método popolare for saxophone (Ricordi).

ORTEGA, Tiburcio. Buenos Aires, 1759-1839 Oct 28, Montevideo. Argentinian. About 1780 he settled in Montevideo and became one of their most popular musicians. He was a capable performer on the clarinet, violin and organ and also directed the music for church services and official functions. He was conductor of the orchestra at the Casa de Comedias until about 1822. His son, Hermenegildo Ortega, was a distinguished clarinettist.

OTTER, Franz. 15 Apr 1837-1898, Vienna? Austrian. He played in the Vienna Philharmonic Orchestra from 1862 until he was pensioned in 1892. From 1881 until his death he taught at the Conservatoire. He joined the Tonkünstlersocietät in 1869.

OTT-IMHOFF, C. Swiss. He was a member of the orchestra at Zurich and a well-known soloist in the 1820s. In the early 1830s "Mr Ott," as he was called, was made Kapellmeister of the Zurich Music Society. He was still playing clarinet solos at Zurich in 1852. Carl Eschmann dedicated his Fantasiestück op.9 to Off-Imhoff. Mr. Ott's concerts were as follows: 1820 – June, for the Basle Music Society, Adagio & Rondo (from op.1) by Crusell. 1822 – at Zurich, Variations by Gambaro and by "L. Kreutzer" (this is probably an error for Conradin Kreutzer). 1823 – solo at the Lausanne Festival. 1824 – 17th February at Zurich, Crusell's Symphonie Concertante. April, Weber's First Concerto. 1825 – at Zurich, Spohr's First Concerto. 1826 – at Zurich, Weber's First Concerto and Heinrich Baermann's Concerto in D minor. 1830 – soloist at Winterthur. 1834 – at Zurich, Maurer's Concertino, and Iwan Müller's double concerto with Joseph Faubel.

OWENS, Joseph. Irish. He taught clarinet as well as flute and oboe at Belfast in 1801. He lived at no.33 John Street.

OXENVAD, Aage. Danish. He was the clarinettist for whom Nielsen wrote his Concerto op.57 in 1928.

PACHMEIER (BACHMEIER, PACHMAYER), Joseph. He lived at Bonn and about 1783 was first clarinet in the house music of Count Belderbusch. This music consisted of 2 clarinets (Moock was second clarinet), 2 horns and bassoon. In 1789 and 1790 he was a member of the Elector of Bonn's orchestra.

PALATIN, Antonio. Spanish. He was a clarinet teacher in Seville. Manuel Gomez was his pupil about 1870.

PALMBLAD, Karl Johan. Östergötland, 4 Aug 1853-? Swedish. He was an outstanding pupil at the Stockholm Conservatoire from 1877 to 1882 and during this time, in 1879, was made a member of the court orchestra. From 1886 he was music director of the Bohuslän regiment.

PAPÉ, Carl. 1820-1874. German. By 1851 he was in the Kaiser Franz regiment at Berlin and performing as a soloist. He went to Leipzig to perform as clarinet soloist on 8th December 1853. Soon afterwards he came to England and from 1855 until his death was principal clarinet in the Crystal Palace Orchestra.

PARADIS, Henri. 1861-1940. French. He was a pupil at the Paris Conservatoire under Rose. From 1882 to 1909 he was solo clarinet in the Garde Républicaine. In 1891 he succeeded Rose at the Opéra and remained there intil 1934, aged seventy three. He also played in the Lamoureux Orchestra. He married a pianist who frequently accompanied him. In 1916 they were living at no.87 rue de Maubeuge.

Works: Fantasias on "Malbrouck" & *Le Pré aux Clercs.* Fascicule du clarinettiste.

PARÈS family. French. The following members won prizes for clarinet at the Paris Conservatoire: Eugène Parès, Second Prize (no First was awarded) in 1841; Philippe Parès, First Prize in 1848; C.I. Parès, First Prize in 1854. As there is no further record of them it is possible that they were all absorbed into military bands. One of them was probably the father of Gabriel Parès, the composer and arranger of music for saxophone and conductor of the Garde Républicaine.

PARRA, Leocadio. ?-1971, Madrid. Spanish. He was solo clarinet for the Madrid Philharmonic Orchestra and the National Orchestra (Society of Concerts). He also taught at the Conservatoire from 1950 until his death.

PAUER (PAUR), Franz. Born at Zerkwitz. Czech.

He was a student under Blatt at the Prague Conservatoire from 1816 to 1822. The following year he secured a post in the opera orchestra at Vienna. His performances at the Conservatoire public concerts were as follows: 1820 – 22nd February, Variations by Heinrich Baermann. 1821 – 16th March, Allegro (first movement) from the concerto by Wilms. 1822 – 15th March, Concertino by Heinrich Baermann.

PAULUS, I.G. French. He was a pupil of Klosé at the Paris Conservatoire, gaining First Prize in 1835. He became distinguished as the conductor of the Parisian Guards and was given the Legion of Honour in 1864, the same year as Klosé.

PEARSON, Hugh. ?-1782. English. He played the clarinet on the 13th March 1758 with Habgood at the Kings Theatre in London. In 1764 he joined the Royal Society of Musicians.

PÉCHIGNIER, (Claude) Gabriel. Paris, 16 Dec 1782-1853, Paris. French. He studied the clarinet with Xavier Lefèvre at the Paris Conservatoire from 1797 to 1802. He carried out the standard five-year course, gaining a Second Prize in 1801 and a First Prize in 1802. From 1815 to 1818 he was second clarinet at the Théâtre Français, with Vanderhagen on first. From 1818 to 1825 he was second clarinet at the Opéra, and then became sub-principal until he retired in 1840. In August 1818 he shared a concert with the seven-year-old violinist, Larsonneur. He was accused of being a poor imitation of Baermann, who had performed in the capital earlier the same year, but when he gave his own concert at the Hôtel des Fermes on 3rd March 1822 he was reported as one of France's best clarinettists. He lived at no.25 faubourg Monmartre, near Louis Lefèvre.

Work: Thême varié op.1 (Dufaut & Dubois).

PEDRIZZI. Italian. He played some variations for clarinet, possibly of his own composition, at Rimini in 1833.

PEDRO, Dom d'Alcantara. Lisbon, 12 Oct 1798-1834 Sept 24, Lisbon. Portuguese. Emperor of Brazil and King of Portugal. He was a great patron of music, clarinettist, singer and composer. The Portuguese royal family fled to Brazil in 1807. In 1810 Marcos Portugal came to Rio de Janeiro as their Kapellmeister and it was from him that Dom Pedro received his basic musical instruction. From 1816 the Chevalier Neukomm was Kapellmeister and he taught the Prince composition. No doubt Campos and Neuparth, who came over in 1817 with the band that accompanied Princess Leopoldina of Austria, Dom Pedro's betrothed, gave the Prince much help on the clarinet, and he became good enough to play first clarinet in the orchestra at Santa Cruz.

PEGER. German. He was employed as a clarinettist at Erfurt. He was first heard as a soloist at Jena in 1840 in Weber's Concertino. He played the work again at Erfurt in 1842 as well as the Rondo from the First Concerto. In 1843 he was a soloist again at Erfurt.

PEINTE (PEINTRE), Antoine. French. He trained at the Paris Conservatoire, gaining a Second Prize in 1826. In 1826 and the first part of 1827 he was the only clarinettist at the Ambigu Comique in Paris. From the second half of 1827 until 1829 he was first clarinet at the Théâtre de la Porte St Martin, and was living at no.9 rue Four St Honoré.

PELLEGRINI, Antonio. Italian. With his brother Donato he was a member of the court orchestra at Lucca in 1822 and 1823.

PELLEGRINI, Donato. Italian. See above.

PEREZ (called Tribourg). French. In 1850 he was second clarinet for the Société Philharmonique, founded and conducted that year by Berlioz. He lived at no. 33 rue de Sèvres.

PÉRIER, Auguste (Eléonore). Lunel, 22 Mar 1883-1947 Oct 26. French. He was a pupil at the Paris Conservatoire from 1900 to 1904 and gained a First Prize in the latter year, the same day as Hamelin. He had a remarkably fine technique and his playing was distinguished by a rapid throat vibrato. He was first clarinet at the Opéra Comique and on the staff at the Conservatoire from 1919 until his death. Saint-Saëns dedicated his Sonate op.167, written in 1921, to Périer. The following Conservatoire test pieces were also dedicated to him: 1924 – Henri Busser's Cantegril. 1927 – Raoul Laparra's Prelude, Valse et Irish Reel. 1928 – Armand Bournonville's Fantaisie-Impromptu. 1930 – J.M.L. Maugüé's Bucolique. 1931 – Paul Pierné's Andante-Scherzo. 1932 – Marcel Gennaro's Andante et Scherzo. 1933 – Stan Golestan's Eglogue. 1936 – Jules Mazellier's Fantaisie-Ballet. 1938 – André-Bloch's Denneriana. 1939 – J.Ed. Barat's Solo de Concours. 1943 – M. Dautremer's Récit et Impromptu.

1944 – Gaston Litaize's Récitatif et Thême varié. 1945 – Henri Martelli's Préambule et Scherzo op.60. 1946 – Raymond Gallois Montbrun's Concertstück.

Works: Premier Air varié (Costallat). Thême varié et Presto (Leduc). Enseignement complet de la clarinette, 5 vols. (Leduc 1931/2).

Périer recorded the following contest pieces:
Henri Busser – Cantegril. Columbia D 19125.
Stan Golestan – Eglogue. Columbia DF 1241.
Henri Rabaud – Solo de Concours (1901). Columbia D 11015 (Re-issue: Grenadilla GS 1006).

PETERSEN, (Christopher Knudsen) Mozart. Copenhagen, 4 May 1817-1874 Feb 26, Copenhagen. Danish. From 1832 he was clarinettist to the court at Copenhagen. The following works were dedicated to him: Fantasiestücke op.43 by Gade (1864); Drei Phantasiestücke by August Winding.

PETIT, Marie Pierre. Bordeaux, 5 Sept 1782-? French. He may have been the brother of Charles Petit, the horn player. He was a pupil at the Conservatoire possibly first under Leriche, but then with Duvernoy, from 1798 to 1802, gaining Second Prize in his final year. He became a stockbroker and when Müller came to Paris in 1810 with his new clarinet he was sufficiently impressed with the invention to finance the manufacturing of the instrument. Petit's generosity went for nought and after the Conservatoire turned down the invention in 1812 the factory had to close.

PETSCHACHER, Friedrich. 19 Feb 1817-? Austrian. He played in the court opera orchestra at Vienna and joined the Tonkünstlersocietät in 1860.

PETZ, Martin. He played second clarinet in the court orchestra at Modena in 1825, with Cuboni on first.

PEZZANA. Italian. He taught the clarinet at Venice. In 1816 Nicola Vaccai (Vaccaj) wrote a concerto for him.

PFAFF(E), August. Dessau, c.1796-1834 Feb 15, Berlin. German. He was a member of a very musical family and became, with two of his brothers who were horn players, a Royal Chamber Musician at the Berlin Court. He was first engaged for the court opera about 1817. His concerts, at Berlin unless otherwise stated, were as follows: 1818 – November, Adagio & Polonaise by Krommer with Tamm. 1820 – October, at the theatre in Stettin, Variations (probably op.20) by Heinrich Baermann. 1822 – 16th December, clarinet obligato in the Adagio movement of G.A. Schneider's bassoon concerto; C.G. Schwarz was the solo bassoon. 1824 – 8th March, Introduction & Variations by Heinrich Baermann. 1825 – 1st June, a double concerto by Krommer with Berendt. 1829 – September, at the Halle festival, a double concerto by A. Müller with F.W. Tausch (A. Müller cannot be identified and is probably a mistake for Friedrich Müller); the two performances earned much applause.

PFEFFEL, Konrad. 1770-? German. Established in Cologne from 1811, his name appears in cathedral orchestral lists of 1822, 1825 and 1830.

PFEILSTICKER (PFEILSTÜCKER), Nicolas (Franz?). German. He was a clarinettist and then conductor of the 7th Infantry Regiment stationed at Paris in 1802 and 1803. At some time he was a pupil of Franz Tausch and later became a teacher himself.

Works: Concerto no.1 in B flat (Pleyel 1802 – VGM). Waltzes for 2 clarinets (Pleyel).

PHILIPP, Joseph. He played for some time in the Vienna Philharmonic Orchestra and by 1851 was first clarinet at the theatre in Warsaw.

PINOT. French? He was active at Santo Domingo in the 1790s and in 1795 performed a concerto by Stamitz.

(B–H). **PISAŘOVIC, Julius.** Prague, c.1813-1881. Czech. He was a fine clarinettist, noted especially for his obligato playing. He studied the instrument under Farník at the Prague Conservatoire from 1825 to 1831. When Blatt was dismissed from the post of clarinet professor in 1834 Pisařovic took his place, teaching basset-horn as well. Pisařovic was a splendid teacher, his most famous pupils being Reinel, Reitmayer (II), Sobeck and Syrinek. He became first clarinet for Prague's National Theatre in 1834, when Farník retired, remaining in the orchestra until the year of his death. He took part in the following public concerts at the Conservatoire as a student: 1830 – 5th March, concertino by Heinrich Baermann. 1831 – 25th February, Divertimento on Weber's *Der Freischütz* by Kummer. 18th

March, Iwan Müller's Concertante with Budinsky. 1836 – 26th March, Variations (op.20?) by Heinrich Baermann. His professional concerts were as foilows: 1840 – Reissiger's Concertino, also the obligato to Spohr's "Das heimliche Lied" for the tenor Emminger. 1841 – Spohr's Wind Quintet. 1842 – Paer's "Una voce al cor mi parla" for Louise Jahnel. 1843 – Variations by Berr, also the obligato to Titl's "Der Sennin Heimweh" for Mlle Wander von Grünwald. 1844 – Onslow's Sextet. 1846 – in a performance of Flotow's *Alessandro Stradella* at the National Theatre he was specially commended for a clarinet obligato in the Serenade. 1878 – 17th April, Konzerstück in F (Idyllic Scene) for wind quintet & orchestra by Julius Rietz, with other professors, at a Conservatoire concert in memory of the composer.

Work: Method, based on Lefèvre's.

PLANKE (PLANQUE) junior. Dutch. He lived in Amsterdam and probably learnt the clarinet from his father (see below). Two performances for the Felix Meritis Society of Krommer double concertos in which he played the second clarinet are recorded: 1815 with J.C. Kleine playing first; 1817 with his father playing first.

PLANKE (PLANQUE) senior. Dutch. He and his son (see above) were well known clarinettists at Amsterdam. He taught Christiani and probably also his own son. In 1817 he performed a double concerto by Krommer with his son for the Felix Meritis Society.

PLATER. In 1821 he was second clarinet at the Odéon in Paris.

PLATT, E. English. He played with Spindler in the orchestra for the Theatre Royal, Edinburgh. They had a Benefit on 24th May 1827 at which they performed a Scottish Air with Variations for 2 clarinets.

POGGIALI, Gaetano. Italian. He lived in Florence, where he played second clarinet at the Teatro degli Intrepidi from 1793 to 1798, and first clarinet at the Cocomero Theatre from 1800.

POHL, Julius. German. In 1852 he was playing first clarinet for the Engel Orchestra at the Kroll Theatre in Berlin. From 1860 to 1886 he was a Chamber Musician in the Berlin court orchestra.

POLATSCHEK, Viktor. 29 Jan 1889-1948 July 27. Austrian. He was a pupil at the Vienna Conservatoire, completing his studies in 1907. From 1921 to 1930 he himself taught at the Conservatoire, his most famous pupil being Wlach. He played in the Vienna Philharmonic Orchestra and also belonged to the Konzertverein. In 1930 he went to America to play first clarinet in the Boston Symphony Orchestra.

POLLARD, William. 26 Dec 1833-1866 Apr 7, London. English. He was a corporal in the Coldstream Guards and living at no.3 Vincent Square, Westminster, when he joined the Royal Society of Musicians in 1859. The same year he married Charlotte Godfrey, the daughter of Charles Godfrey, the first of the famous bandmasters of that name. Pollard played at the Haymarket and was first clarinet in Jullien's orchestra. He also performed in the Hallé Orchestra's 1861/2 season. He went insane and hanged himself in the wash-house, aged thirty-two.

POLLASTRI. Italian. He was a well-known clarinettist at Arezzo. In 1835 he conducted the town's Philharmonic Society for the Carnival.

POLLMÄCHER. German. He was a clarinettist and then conductor of the 24th Regiment of the Line, which was garrisoned at Neu-Ruppin. He was reported to be still young when he performed Weber's Concertino in 1836. In 1839 he played solos and conducted a military choir. He composed a Festival March which was performed at Neu-Ruppin in 1841.

PONCELET, C. Gustav. 1844-1903. Belgian. He was well known as a soloist throughout Belgium and also played principal clarinet at La Monnaie. He was a pioneer in the realm of large clarinet ensembles and with a group of twenty-seven players, whose instruments included a contra-basset-horn and pedal clarinet, he toured with great success. Poncelet was a fine teacher of both clarinet and saxophone, and was professor at the Brussels Conservatoire from 1871. Amongst his many famous clarinet pupils were Bageard, Hannon, Hublard, Langenus, Edward Mills and Schreurs. Although he always played on a simple system clarinet he saw the value of the Boehm and taught this in his later years. He retired officially from the Conservatoire in 1901, but was kept on as saxophone teacher. When he died two years later the saxophone post remained unfilled for some time.

POSTULA, Hypolite. Liège, 1826-? Belgian. He was inspired in his youth by hearing Massaert play and became a pupil under him at the Liège Conservatoire, gaining First Prize in 1843. During his varied professional career he held the following appointments: at Liège, first clarinet at the spa, then the theatre, the wind orchestra and the cathedral, also teacher at the Athénée; at Oudenarde from 1847, first clarinet for the Société des Beaux-Arts and teacher at the Conservatoire; at Bordeaux from 1856, first clarinet at the theatre and, from 1861,teacher at the Conservatoire of St Cecilia.

POULAIN. French. In 1821 and 1822 he played second clarinet at the Ambigu Comique in Paris. His father led the second violins.

(B–H). **POWELL, Philip.** ?-1847, America. English. He played second clarinet to Willman for the Philharmonic Society of London and for other concert organisations. He is mentioned on the following occasions: 1826 – 16th June at Moorfields Chapel, Mozart's *Requiem* for Weber's Memorial Service. 1828 – 13th February at the Mansion House. 1830 – 19th April, Mozart's C minor Serenade K388 for the Philharmonic Society. 1831 – 7th March, ditto. Concert at Derby. 1836 – Concert at Manchester. Powell experimented with clarinet mechanism and his thumb extension key for e/b was used by Willman, who acknowledges the inventor in his tutor of 1826. In 1837 Powell went to America, and his place in the Philharmonic Society's orchestra was taken by Lazarus.

POWOLNY, Anton. He trained as a clarinettist at the Vienna Conservatoire until 1889 and then became a music director at Baden and Graz.

PRADA, Victor de la. He also played the flute, piccolo and bassoon. He studied in Paris after the Revolution and went out to the Argentine about 1800. In 1803 he was active as a clarinet player in Buenos Aires and in 1806 was playing in the cathedral orchestra at Córdoba. He was appointed to the Academy of Instrumental Music at Buenos Aires in 1810.

PREIS. German. His playing was praised when he performed at an entr'acte concert in Weimar in 1832. The works he played were the Potpourri on themes from Weber's *Der Freischütz* by Georg and Variations (probably op.20) by Heinrich Baermann.

PRELLER, Louis. German. He was a Chamber Musician at Meiningen from 1888.

PRENTANO, Baron. He was a patron of music and dilettante clarinettist, playing in the orchestra for St Michael's Church in Vienna. This "middle-aged man who wears spectacles" acted as guide to Sir George Smart during the latter's visit of 1825, taking him on a tour of the city's churches to hear their music. He appears on the subscription list for the private concert given by Caroline Schleicher and her husband at the Gesellschaft der Musikfreunde on 15th February 1833.

PRINTZ, Jean X. Schlettstadt (Alsace) 1762-1846, Berchem. Alsatian. He was a clarinettist in a French military band and then became conductor. He saw service in the German and Spanish campaigns. From 1809 he made his home at Antwerp and was first clarinet for many years at the theatre and for church concerts. In 1814 he founded the Antwerp Wind Society. The Society commissioned Van Bree to paint Printz's portrait in 1819. In 1835 Printz conducted the St Cecilia Concerts. The following year, aged seventy-four, he again became first clarinet at the theatre, taking the place of his son Jean, who had just died.

PROCKSCH (GASPROCKSCH), Gaspard (Kaspar). Born in Czech-Slovakia. German. He is first heard of in September 1750 when, in a state of distress, he applied to the Paris Opéra for assistance. The authorities gave him 150 livres to help him find work or return to his own country. He made good both as a clarinettist and as a composer in the land of his adoption and did not go back to Bohemia. Following a custom of the time, he, like his colleagues Meissner and Yost, let himself be known principally by his christian name, and the majority of reports of his activities and title pages on compositions bear the name "Gaspard." Either at the end of 1750 or the beginning of 1751 he and Flieger entered service with the tax-farmer, Jean le Rich de la Pouplinière. La Pouplinière sported the best private orchestra in Paris, directed at that time by Rameau. On Sundays and for religious festivals it gave an hour's morning concert and then played for the Mass which followed. Each day of Holy Week the populace was treated to music on clarinets alone. In 1753 performances of Rameau's *Acanthe et Céphise* were given in La Pouplinière's fine theatre at Passy and at the Opéra; an entr'acte between acts 2 and 3 required 4 clarinets which were taken by Procksch, Flieger, Schenker and Louis. (The last two were also horn players for La Pouplinière).

Each player received 6 livres for the first performance at the Opéra and 126 livres for all the repeats. Procksch and Flieger played in the orchestra for the Concert Spirituel when Stamitz conducted in 1755. La Pouplinière died in 1762 and for November and December of that year Procksch, Flieger, Schenker and Louis were each paid 333 livres. After this they all, except Louis, found employment with Louis François de Bourbon, Prince of Conti. Procksch was principal clarinet for the Prince, as he had been for La Pouplinière. He took part with others of the Prince's wind players in some Morceaux for 2 horns, 2 clarinets and 2 bassoons by Rameau which were performed at the Concert Spirituel on 29th May 1766. From 1771 to 1775 he was engaged as clarinet and double-bass player at the Opéra and was living at the time in the rue des Boucheries. During the next eight years he earned his living as a teacher of the clarinet. He was still alive in 1785.

Works: 6 Sonatas op.5 with accompaniment for cello, dedicated to Count Ogínski (1773). 8th Recueil concertant (PBN). 38 Airs et duos for 2 clarinets or horns op.11 (Bignon – PBN). Recueils d'airs for 2 clarinets or 2 horns (Girard 1773 – LBL). 6 Trios op.4 for clarinet, violin & cello (Bureau d'Abonnement 1773). 6 Quatuors concertantes op.1 for clarinet & strings (Sieber c.1770).

Bibliography:

CUCUEL, Georges – *Études sur un orchestre au XVIII siècle.* Paris 1913.

PROKSCH, Joseph. Reichenberg, 4 May 1794-1864 Dec 20, Prague. Czech. He was a remarkable blind clarinet player and pianist. By the age of eight he had lost the sight of his right eye and by seventeen was totally blind. From 1809 to 1816 he was a student at the Blind Institute in Prague, studying clarinet with Farník and piano with Kozeluch. Having learnt the system of notation before losing his sight he progressed quicker than the other students and did extremely well. In August 1817 he set off on a concert tour with the harpist Rieger. They travelled to Jung-Bunzlau, Pardubitz, Brünn and finally Olmütz, where the Archduke Rudolph commanded a private performance. The Archduke gave Proksch numerous introductions for the remainder of his tour, which he undertook without Rieger. He next played at Türnau, Pressburg, Raab, Komorn, Pesth, Erlau, Graz and then Vienna, where he performed a concerto and some variations of his own composition at the university. He stayed some time in Vienna and was befriended by Maria Theresia von Paradies, the blind pianist and composer. Through her influence a renowned surgeon made an attempt to restore Proksch's sight, but the operation was unsuccessful. In the summer of 1818, having recovered from the rigours of this experience, he started on his journey home. He played first at Teplitz, to King Friedrich Wilhelm III, and then went on to Dresden, where he met Weber. Then followed concerts at Görlitz, Zittau and Herrnhut. In the autumn of 1818 he arrived at Prague, richly rewarded. He now took stock of his situation and decided to give up the clarinet in favour of the piano. He was a man of great enterprise and took up the Logier piano education system with enthusiasm. He founded a school for teaching this, which was carried on by a son and daughter after his death.

Works: Concerto. Concertino. Adagio concertante. Rondino in C. Rondoletta – Polacca. Variations. Waltzes in E flat. "Freut euch des Lebens," Fantasie for 2 clarinets. Variations on Schubert's "Die Forelle" for 2 clarinets. Sonata for clarinet & violin. Concertino in D minor for 3 clarinets. Skalen-Sonata for 4 clarinets. Overture to Mozart's *Titus* for 8 clarinets.

Bibliography:

MÜLLER, Rudolf – *Joseph Proksch.* Reichenberg 1874.
QUOIKA, Rudolf – "Joseph Proksch." MGG.

PUREBEL (PUREBL), Josef. 1768-1838 Mar 5, Vienna. He was engaged as second clarinet in the court orchestra at Vienna on 1st February 1807. In time he became a Royal Chamber Musician. He gave a concert for the Tonkünstlersocietät in 1815.

Works: Variations in B flat (Haslinger). 12 Ländler for 2 clarinets (Haslinger). 12 Neue Ländler for 2 clarinets (Bermann).

QUALLENBERG (QUALENBERG), (Johann) Michael. Vienna ?-1793, Mannheim. Czech. He received his training in Vienna and then was employed, with Hampel, at the Court of Thurn and Taxis in Regensburg. About 1758 or 9 he and Hampel were engaged as the first clarinet players in the Mannheim orchestra, with a joint remuneration of 576 gulden. Saam says they both moved with the the Court to Munich in 1778 when the orchestras were amalgamated. Quallenberg was made a court counsellor by the Elector-Palatin. He taught Tirry from about 1772 to 1778.

RADZIWILL, Count Karol. Polish. See OV.

(B–H). **RAKEMANN (PACKEMANN, PACKMANN, RACKMANN).** German. He had a very gentle tone and this led sometimes to criticism for lack of dynamics. He is listed in the orchestra at Bremen in 1807 and was still there in 1823. He played both his instruments in December 1822 at a concert which he shared with his eldest son, who was a flautist, and Helfrich, a fellow clarinettist in the Bremen orchestra. In 1823 he gave another concert with the same son, and at Schalk's concert later in the year he played second basset-horn in Mozart's "Al desio, di chi t'adora." He had two younger sons, one of whom, C. Rakemann, became a clarinettist in the Bremen orchestra and the other, Louis, became a well-known pianist.

RAKEMANN (RACKEMANN, ROTTMANN), C. German. He played in the orchestra at Bremen, which his father (see above) also belonged to. In 1834 and 1835 he gave concerts with his elder brother who played the flute. In 1836 he gave a big concert in the Poland Hotel at Leipzig at which he performed Mozart's Concerto, the obligato to Paer's "Una voce al cor mi parla" for Mme Franchetti-Walzel, and Weber's Variations op.33 in which he was accompanied on the piano by his younger brother Louis. The applause was good and although they said he was not top rank, yet he was very fine. He was still in the Bremen orchestra in 1842.

RASCH. German. He played at the Brunswick Court from 1819 to 1827.

RATHÉ (RHATEL). German. He studied with Beer and Yost, and became popular with audiences at the Concert Spirituel. He first performed for this society in April 1777. On 14th May 1780 he played them his own concerto and this was requested again on 25th May. *Mercure de France* of the following June reported that he had a lively mind and a strong chest, that he ran with marvellous agility over the complete compass of the instrument. They said his tone was good in the high and medium registers, but that he forced the low notes, which became so ill-matched with the rest as to make them sound as if they "came from another instrument." He performed his own concerto again on 30th March and 9th May 1782.

Work: Concerto.

RAUCHSCHINDEL. German. He was a clarinettist at Dessau from about 1805 to 1849. On 7th March 1805 he played Westerhoff's Concerto op.7 at Leipzig. Again at Leipzig, in April 1805, he performed a concerto by Wilhelm Franz Westenholz.

(B–H). **RAUSCHER, Jacob.** Pirmasens, 1771-1834, Amsterdam? German. In 1793 he went to Maastricht in the Netherlands and joined a military band. In 1807 he became a member of the court orchestra and director of the royal band for King Louis Bonaparte at Amsterdam.

Work: Concerto for basset-horn.

REBEYROL, Pierre. Nantes, 1798-? French. He came to Paris to study with Lefèvre at the Conservatoire in 1818 and gained a First Prize in 1820. He learnt composition from Reicha. By 1822 he had returned home to Nantes and become well-known as a clarinet teacher.

Work: Concerto.

RECHTENBACH, Christian Tobias. ?-1865. German. He was a clarinettist and viola player in the court orchestra at Meiningen from 1831 to 1865. Before his appointment he performed there as a clarinet soloist on 14th February 1828.

REGNAULT. French. In 1821 he was the only clarinet player at the Cirque Olympique in Paris, and was living in the rue Boucherat.

REHAGE. He was a very good amateur clarinettist at Königsberg, by profession a merchant. He performed at the following concerts given by the theatre orchestra: winter season of 1828/9 – several obligatos. 1830 – 2nd May in a concert given by Heinrich Dorn, concerto by Adolph Fischel. 14th December in a concert given by Fischel, Gerke's Potpourri on Themes from Spohr's *Jessonda* and *Zemira*. 1831 – 26th January, solos.

(B–H). **REHM, Johann Georg.** Zeulenroda, ?-1836, Osnabrück. German. He became well-known as a soloist at Osnabrück. In 1814 he was appointed organist to St Mary's Church and the following year was given burgher's rights. His concerts included the following: 1799 – 14th & 16th November, basset-horn concerto by Hofmeister (Franz Anton?); 28th November, variations for basset-horn & clarinet d'amour with (Carl?) Müller. 1802 – 11th February, Symphonie Concertante for clarinet & bassoon by Devienne with Katzung; 20th March, Hofmeister's concerto for basset-horn; 23rd October, unspecified clarinet concerto. 1803 – 10th February, ditto.

REIBNITZ, Baron Ludwig Georg Christoph. 1775-1845. German. He was a dilettante clarinettist and Court Intendant at Gotha. He performed the obligato to Spohr's Six German Songs op.103 with one of the court singers.

REIF, Wilhelm. Schwallungen, 4 Feb 1832-1890 Jan 16, Meiningen. German. He was first clarinet and music director at the Saxe-Meiningen Court when Mühlfeld arrived there, and doubtless had an influence on the latter's playing. He first appeared as a soloist at Meiningen on 2nd July 1855 and was then engaged for the orchestra. Duke Bernhard sent him first to have lessons at Kassel, probably from Neff, and then to Carl Baermann at Munich. In 1868 Reif became music director at Meiningen and was responsible for the incidental music at the court theatre. In the summer months of 1872 to 1874 he played in the concerts at Bad Liebenstein, given by the joint orchestras of Meiningen, Gotha and Weimar. Periodical bouts of ill health finally decided Reif to surrender his position of principal clarinet to Mühlfeld in 1879, but he continued as music director until 1890. He wrote a concerto for Mühlfeld which the latter performed at Meiningen on 25th December 1885. The young Richard Strauss, who was Meiningen's Kapellmeister that winter, stood down on this occasion for Reif to conduct his concerto. Strauss wrote afterwards to Bülow that the work is "very pretentiously scored, is a decoction of every conceivable coronation opera, in formal respect a hair-raising nonsense. For that reason, and played with great virtuosity by Mühlfeld, it will not fail to impress the public." The concerto was never published.

Work: Concerto, dedicated to Mühlfeld.

REIFFER (REISSER, RAEFFER, RAIFFER, REYFFER), François. French. On 5th December 1749 he and Schiefer played in the first performance of Rameau's opera *Zoroastre* at the Paris Opéra. During 1751 and 1752 they were engaged for twenty eight performances of the work at a fee of 3 livres per performance. They both played under Stamitz in 1753 and 1755. Reiffer took part with Klein in a work for 2 clarinets, 2 horns & 2 bassoons which was played at the Concert Spirituel on 25th March 1775. Whether the Reisser employed 1763 to 1775 and the Raeffer employed (also as flautist) 1785 for the Concert Spirituel are the same person is uncertain.

REINECKE, R. In 1892 he was second clarinet in the New York Philharmonic Orchestra.

REINEL, Albin. 1831-? Czech. He studied under Pisařovic at the Prague Conservatoire and while there performed some variations by one of the Baermanns at a concert on 7th March 1847. He was a member of the Dresden court orchestra for a short time and from 1852 played at the Hungarian National Theatre in Budapest. He composed, but nothing for clarinet.

(B–H). **REINHARDT, F.** German. He played clarinet and basset-horn at the Stuttgart Court from about 1815 to 1823. He may have been the elder brother of Georg Reinhardt, who joined the orchestra in 1821. He received an excellent review of a public concert he gave in 1819 at which he played Weber's Concertino. At a second concert of that year he played the clarinet and basset-horn obligatos for the arias from Mozart's *Titus.*

(B–H). **REINHARDT, Georg.** Würzburg, 28 Sept 1789-? German. He was a remarkably fine player, Schilling considering him the equal of Baermann and Hermstedt. His father was a musician at the Court of Würzburg. Learning many instruments first, Georg finally settled on the clarinet and went to Meissner for lessons. Meissner gave him several opportunities to play with him and their partnership in double concertos caused considerable excitement. From 1804 to 1807 Reinhardt was in Berlin, where he had a further course of study with the great Tausch. While in Berlin he performed with Tausch and the latter's son, also with Bliesener, another pupil of Tausch. Next he undertook some short concert tours and then took an orchestral job at Wiesbaden. He played for a time in the court orchestra of the Grand Duke of Hesse at Darmstadt. In 1814 he moved to the theatre orchestra at Frankfurt, where in 1818 de Groot joined him. Together they formed a quite outstanding partnership. Reinhardt left Frankfurt in 1821, shortly after de Groot, and went to Stuttgart as first clarinet in the King of Würtemberg's orchestra, remaining in this post until 1838 or later. His second clarinet here was F. Reinhardt, to whom he was probably related. In 1829 he visited Vienna and played for the Emperor Franz at the court theatre. In his later years he used instruments made by Backofen.

Reinhardt's concerts included the following: a) at Berlin; 1804 – Krommer's double concerto op.35 with Bliesener. 1805 – 20th July a double concerto with F.W. Tausch. 1807 – 12th November at the Theatersaal, trios for 3 basset-horns by Franz Tausch with Tausch and his son. b) at Frankfurt; 1814 – 13th May for the Museum Society, unspecified concerto. 7th October for the Museum Society, Variations (possibly his own). 1815 – 25th December, a concerto by Weber. 1816 – 25th February, a concerto by Crusell and Variations by himself. 17th May for the Museum Society, unpsecified Rondo. 1818 – 2nd March, Variations (probably his own). 1819 – 7th April for the Museum Society, (Introduction, Adagio &) Variations by

Mme Müller-Bender with the composer playing the piano. May, a concertante (possibly the one by Schnyder von Wartensee) with de Groot. 1821 – 19th January for the Museum Society, "Der Friede" for vocal quartet, clarinet & piano by Schnyder von Wartensee. 2nd March, clarinet quintet (dedicated to the reigning Princess of Sondershausen) by Andreas Romberg. At a later concert, a double concerto by Krommer with de Groot. c) at Stuttgart; 1823 – Lindpaintner's Concerto. 1826 – Polonaise by Lindpaintner. 1829 – a concertino by Iwan Müller and a composition by Späth (possibly the Scène Chantante – see 1831). 1830 – a concerto by Riotte and Lindpaintner's Concertante for wind. 1831 – Scène Chantante sur deux airs suisses by Späth. 1832 – Maurer's Concertino. 1833 – Spohr's Octet, Lindpaintner's Concertante and basset-horn obligato to Cherubini's "Ave Marie" for Mme von Knoll. (Better known with clarinet obligato, this piece was originally set by Cherubini for cor anglais and it was performed in this version by Gustav Vogt at Paris in 1824). 1834 – concertos by Spohr and Weber.

Work: Variations.

REITHARDT, Heinrich August. Schleiz, 10 Aug 1793-? Berlin. German. Except for service in the Prussian Campaign of 1813-1815 he played in the court orchestra at Schleiz until 1816. He then moved to Berlin where he lived for the rest of his life, becoming court music director in 1839.

REITMAYER (REITMAIER), Franz (I). He played for the Munich Subscription Concerts from 1823 to 1881 and was a member of the court orchestra from 1839 to 1864.

REITMAYER, Franz (II). Born at Mireschau. Czech. He was a very distinguished student at the Prague Conservatoire under Pisařovic from 1867 to 1873. When Pisařovic died in 1881 he took his place as professor. On 8th December 1881 he performed Weber's First Concerto for the Conservatoire's Pension Fund. In a concert on 6th December 1891 to commemorate the centenary of Mozart's death he took part in the Symphonie Concertante with other members of the Conservatoire staff. One of his most distinguished pupils was Richard Schida.

REITZ, Adolf. German. He played in the Darmstadt court orchestra from 1820 to 1850 or later. In 1850 he was joined by another Reitz, probably his son. At a concert in 1837 he played in Spohr's Nonet, a wind quintet by Wilhelm Mangold, Darmstadt's

Kapellmeister, also a concertino for oboe & clarinet, composer unspecified. He is known to have used instruments made by Backofen.

RENARD, Charles. Belgian. He came to England early in the twentieth century and founded the Renard Clarinet Quartet which had great success both in concerts and in the early recording field. The other members of the Quartet were James Park, Alex and Robert Smith. Renard was also a conductor of military bands, for whom he composed a considerable amount.
Works: Trios & Quartets for clarinets.

RENARD, Jean Jacques Théodore. Amsterdam, 14 May 1869-? He learnt the violin first, before taking up the clarinet, which he learnt from H. Seeman. At the age of sixteen he was engaged as first clarinet at the Grand Theatre in Amsterdam. Later he became conductor at the Salon de Variétés and then assistant-conductor of the Concertgebouw Orchestra. He composed a little, but nothing for the clarinet.

REUSCH, Johann. ?-1787. German. He also played the flute and oboe. He came to the Durlach Court in 1730 from Bayreuth. In 1771 he left Durlach and played for a short time in the Baden orchestra. From 1772 to 1775 he was in the court orchestra at Carlsruhe. It is thought probable that Molter wrote his four concertos for Reusch, in the 1740s.

RICHTER, Arthur. German. He was a member of the Dresden court orchestra in 1925. He may also be the "Richter" who had been second clarinet in the court orchestra at Kassel in 1905.

RICHTER, Friedrich August. Lemgo, ?-1907 May 29. German. He was second clarinet in the court orchestra at Detmold from 1843 to 1876. In 1851 he performed David's Introduction and Variations, and also a solo by "George" (probably the Potpourri on Themes from Weber's *Der Freischütz* by Georg).

RICKSECKER, John. He was lauded for his playing as first clarinet in a performance of Haydn's *Creation* at Bethlehem, Pennsylvania in 1811.

RIHL. German. He and his brother, a bassoon player, were members of the court orchestra at Fulda in 1800.

RODRIGUEZ, Teodoro. Spanish. He succeeded Romero as clarinet professor at the Madrid Conservatoire.

RÖDER, Philipp Jakob. German. He was a member of the court orchestra at Coblenz in 1814.

RÖHRIG. German. On 17th January 1834 he performed Maurer's Concerto at the Frankfurt Museum Concerts and on 14th March a concertino, composer unspecified. Later that year he joined the orchestra at Mannheim. Here he performed Maurer's Concerto in 1835 and had a good reception, but they said he "risked too much here and there." By 1841 he was working in Wiesbaden, probably at the Court. When he played in Frankfurt a. M. that year AMZ's critic said he had good tone, taste and dexterity, but that the piece was so short that it had no sooner begun than ended.

Works: Concerto. Concertino.

(B–H). **ROESER, Valentin.** Born Monaco, died Paris. German. In 1763 he was a musician to the Prince of Monaco. By 1769 he had moved to Paris. He was no doubt the "M. Valentin" whom *Mercure de France* announced in April 1774 had just played "sur le corno-bassetto ou contra-clarinette" at the Concert Spirituel.

Works: Gamme pour la clarinette avec 6 duos (Boyer). 12 Petits airs pour deux clarinettes (Le Menu). 1st & 2nd Duos (Sieber c.1798). Divertissements militaires for 2 clarinets, 2 bassoons & bass (1770 & 1771). Essai d'instruction a l'usage de ceux qui Composent pour la clarinette et le cor (1763? Le Menu – BrBC).

ROMBERG, Gerhard (Heinrich). 8 Aug 1745-1819 Nov 14, Münster. German. He and his brother Anton, the bassoonist, were inseparable and even dressed alike, as was the case also with Gerhard's son Andreas and Anton's son Bernhard, both born in 1767. Gerhard was clarinettist and music director to the Bishop of Münster and lived with his family at the village of Vechta just outside Münster. In 1784 Gerhard and Anton, with Andreas and Bernhard, went on an extended tour to Paris where they had a great success. The Concert Spirituel heard them perform a Symphonie Concertante for clarinet, bassoon, violin and cello by Cambini on 2nd February, 15th March, 24th March and 1st April 1785. In 1792 Gerhard and Anton set up house together with their families at Bonn, where they held appointments. In 1799 they gave a joint concert in Hamburg. Two other children of Gerhard's made a name in the musical world: Balthasser (born 1775) as a cellist and Therese (born 1791) as a pianist.

ROMERO y ANDÍA, Antonio. Madrid, 11 May 1815-1885 Oct 7. Spanish. He is best known for the clarinet system which bears his name. He was responsible for introducing the Boehm clarinet to Spain but became increasingly dissatisfied with this system and produced his own invention in 1853. This was made the regulation instrument at Madrid's Conservatoire in 1866. It was manufactured by Paul Bié, F. Lefèvre's successor, and he took out patents for it in 1862 and 1867. It was exhibited at Paris in 1867, Aragon in 1868, Salamanca, Madrid and Vienna in 1873. Basically the instrument was still Boehm, but it had many improvements, the most important of which was the transferring of the movement of break keys to the right hand. It's mechanism was exceedingly complicated, requiring fifteen adjusting screws, and as it was unreliable it did not become popular. Even after Bié succeeded in making a simplified model in 1890, few clarinettists adopted the system. There is a Romero clarinet of Bié's workmanship in the ERC.

Romero learnt the clarinet when very young and at the age of fourteen gave concerts on a 6-key clarinet throughout Spain, which aroused considerable interest. As first clarinet in the Royal Guard he distinguished himself in the First Carlist War of 1833-1840. In 1841 he became music director of the Royal Guard. From 1844 to 1867 he played at Court and again from 1875, when the Royal House was restored. He was well known as a soloist and was professor of clarinet at the Madrid Conservatoire from 1849 to 1876. His most famous pupil was González. He did a great deal to improve clarinet teaching in Spain and wrote three tutors for the instrument. The first appeared in 1845 and was written for the 13-keyed clarinet; it contained material from Lefèvre, Buteux, Müller and Berr. This was followed by one for both simple and Boehm systems, and one for the Romero system. Romero founded a publishing firm in 1856 which became one of the most important in Spain. He was a member of the Spanish commission sent to the London Exhibition of 1862 and wrote the official report for it. In 1867 he was on the jury for the European concours of military music at Paris. The following distinctions and decorations were given to him: Grand Cross of the Order of Avile de Maria Victoria, given him by Amadeo of Savoy (King of Spain 1870-1873); Commander of the Order of Charles III and of Isabella the Catholic; Academician of the Royal Academy of Fine Arts of San Fernando.

Works: Método para clarinete de 13 claves (1845). Método completo de clarinete, for simple & Boehm systems (Romero

1845?, 1860 – LBL, MaCSM). Método para clarinete sistema Romero (Romero 1868).

ROOMS. Dutch. He learnt the clarinet from Dreiklufts at Amsterdam, and when he performed a concerto there in May 1808 the remark was made that he brought great honour to his teacher. He received much applause. Later he became first clarinet in the orchestra at Rotterdam and earned a fine reputation there as a soloist. In 1823 he performed works by Crusell, Iwan Müller and Danzi. In 1825 he played Variations (probably op.20) by Heinrich Baermann at the Subscription Concerts.

ROSE, (Chrysogone) Cyrille. Lestrem (Pas-de-Calais), 13 Feb 1830-1902(3?), Méaux? French. He studied under Klosé at the Paris Conservatoire, gaining First Prize in 1847. Although he is mainly known as a teacher he was also a fine performer, with a beautiful tone and artistic phrasing. The only concert tour he is known to have undertaken was in 1852, when he went to Germany with the horn player Mohr. He played in the Opéra orchestra from 1857 to 1891 and their clarinet parts retain the many slurs he added, for he had a sluggish tongue. Gounod and Massenet frequently consulted him on technical points. Rose also played for the Société des Concerts from 1857 to 1872. He was particularly fond of the Weber concertos and performed one of them for the Société in 1862. He made an excellent edition of Weber's compositions, supplying the concertos with cadenzas. He was professor at the Conservatoire from 1876 until he retired in 1900, when he went to teach at the Conservatoire in Méaux. Dandelot said he was a most devoted teacher, for whom each annual competition was an assured triumph. Rose schooled the following well-known players: Cahuzac, Manuel and Francisco Gomez, Jeanjean, Henri Lefèbvre, Paradis, Henri and Alexandre Selmer, E.H. Stiévenard and R. Verney. The following Conservatoire test pieces were dedicated to him: Introduction et Rondo by Charles Widor and Fantasie by Augusta Holmès. Rose collaborated with the Buffet instrument company in experiments with the width of bore, and the cones at the top and bottom of the instrument. He was awarded the Legion of Honour in 1900.

ROSENBERG, Francis. He and Freudenfeld are the earliest clarinet players to be mentioned by name. They had Benefits at Hickford's Great Room in London on 25th March 1726 and 15th March 1727. They preceded "Mr Charles" by nearly ten years.

ROSENKRANZ. German. He played in the following concerts for the Euterpe Society at Leipzig: 1832 – 29th March, Schindelmeisser's Symphonie Concertante for 4 clarinets with Mehner, "Mey" (Eduard Meyer?) and the composer. 18th December, Rondo brillant for 2 clarinets by Friedrich Nohr with Ferdinand Heinze. 1834 – Potpourri for wind quintet by Nohr with other members of the Euterpe Society. For the Leipzig Subscription Concerts on 30th October he played a concertino for 2 clarinets by Friedrich Müller with Ferdinand Heinze.

ROTH. German. In 1867 he was first clarinet in the court orchestra at Carlsruhe.

ROTH(E), (Karl) Gottlob. Zwickau, 12 Oct 1774-1828. German. He was the younger brother of Traugott Roth, and a close friend of Weber. He was probably first a member of the same regimental band as his brother. In 1794 he was appointed second clarinet in the Dresden court orchestra. His salary was 400 thalers (about £60) in 1813. When Weber became Kapellmeister at Dresden in 1817 the brothers, along with most of the orchestra, objected strongly to the strict discipline he imposed, but Weber's charm and tact won their friendship and by the following year both were frequent visitors to his country residence at Hosterwitz. Gottlob in particular became the composer's companion and on several occasions during country walks, was the participant in significant moments of creation. Gottlob was himself a composer and on 22nd November 1818 a Mass by him was conducted by Weber. He was ill, early in 1826, and this was a cause of deep concern to Weber who was by then mortally ill himself. Later in the year when the news of Weber's death in London came through, it was Gottlob who went with Mlle von Hanmann to break the news to the composer's widow. Gottlob was pensioned in 1828, shortly before he died.

Work: Concerto.

(B–H). **ROTH(E) (RODE), (Johann) Traugott.** Zwickau, 23 Feb 1768-1847 May 5, Dresden. German. His elder brother Carl Friedrich Roth was music director to the Saxon Grenadier Life Guards, his younger brother was the clarinettist Gottlob Roth. In 1780 Traugott began to learn several wind and stringed instruments under the instruction of his elder brother. By 1785 his aptitude for the clarinet had become apparent and he was installed as a clarinettist in his brother's band, which was stationed at Dresden. The following year Carl Friedrich became seriously ill with a chest ailment from which he eventually died and Traugott took over his post as director. Two concerts at Dresden in 1789 – a private one on 25th January and a public one at the Poland Hotel on 30th March – brought Traugott to the public's notice. On the first occasion he was singled out, and on the second "the brothers Rothe" were given special praise. On both occasions an arrangement (by Goepfert?) for wind octet of Mozart's *Don Giovanni* was performed. Traugott's gifts were so outstanding that the three Dresden Kapellmeisters, Johann Naumann, Joseph Schuster and Friedrich Seydelmann petitioned King Friedrich August to employ clarinets in the court orchestra. Dresden, who had sported chalumeaux in the 1730s when Hasse was writing for the instrument, now in 1794 employed clarinets for the first time. Traugott was made first clarinet and Gottlob second. They became influential members of the town's music and in 1804 when Spohr came to visit, they helped organise concerts for him.

Traugott Roth developed an "improved method of playing" and clarinettists from other courts, notably Flittner and Friedrich Müller from Rudolstadt, came to study with him. His salary in 1813 was 600 thalers, the equivalent of about £90. In 1825 he stepped down from the position of first clarinet, but remained a member of the orchestra until he was pensioned in 1833. Of his solo performances only the following information has come to light: 1800 – at Leipzig, concerto by his brother Gottlob. 1803 – 1st April, a concerto with the court orchestra. 1815 – clarinet & basset-horn obligatos, for which he was singled out, in a performance of Mozart's *La Clemenza di Tito.* 1818 – clarinet obligato to a tenor aria from *Paolo e Virginia* by Pietro Carlo Guglielmi. It was Pietro Carlo's father, Pietro Alessandro, who composed the well known "Gratias agimus."

Bibliography:

Obituary – *(Neue Nekrolog der Deutschen).* Weimar, 1847.

ROTTWEIL. He was third clarinet in the orchestra at Regensburg from about 1769 to 1787.

ROZANOV, Sergei Vasilievich. 1871-1937, Moscow? Russian. He was a pupil at the Moscow Conservatoire, completing his training in 1891. He then became first clarinet at the Bolshoi Theatre and from 1916 until his death he taught at the Conservatoire. He was much respected as a teacher and edited a considerable amount of Western as well as Russian music for clarinet. His tutor, completed in the last year of his life and published posthumously, has become very popular in Russia. He used a Müller-type clarinet, to which he added an extra key.

Work: Shkola dlya Klarneta (Gosmuziz 1940).

RUCH, Justus. ?-1840. German. He also played the violin. He was music director to a regimental band before becoming a clarinettist at the Darmstadt Court in 1819, a post he retained to the end of his life.

(B–H). **RÜTTINGER, Christof.** 28 July 1776-1830 Nov 21, Vienna. Austrian. About 1807, or possibly earlier, he became second clarinet and basset-horn player at the Burgtheater in Vienna. He joined the Tonkünstlersocietät in 1807. On 25th March 1817 he and his son Johann (q.v.) gave a concert in the Roman Emperor's Room. They played Mozart's Wind Quintet K452, with Johann taking the piano part; Christof also performed an Adagio & Variations for basset-horn (Gaspard Kummer's?)

Work: 6 Variations on a theme from *Alcina* (Haslinger).

RÜTTINGER, Johann. Vienna, 18 Aug 1803-1848 Aug 12, Vienna. He was also a good pianist and on 25th March 1817, aged fourteen, he performed the piano part in Mozart's Wind Quintet K452 and two piano solos in a concert with his father Christof (q.v.) at the Roman Emperor's Room. In 1823 he became a clarinettist in the orchestra for the Burgtheater and in 1837 joined the Tonkünstler-societät. On 10th April 1825 he gave his own concert at the Red Hedgehog and in April 1826 he performed on both clarinet and and piano for the Tonkünstlersocietät.

RUFF, Johann Conrad. German. He played second clarinet at the Court of Brandenburg-Ansbach from 1770 to 1779.

RULF. German. He was a clarinettist at the Saxe-Coburg-Gotha Court in 1841.

(B–H). **RUMMEL, Christian (Franz Ludwig Friedrich Alexander).** Brichsenstadt, 27 Nov 1787-1849 Feb 13, Wiesbaden. Austrian. He also played the violin. He is held indirectly responsible for the second movement of Heinrich Baermann's op.23 being published as an Adagio by Richard Wagner. This came about through the owner of a hand-written score declaring he had it from a friend who had it from Rummel, who had commissioned it from Wagner when the latter was living at Würzburg. Rummel received his musical training at Mannheim under the Kapellmeister Wagner and violinist Ritter. He also had help from Vogler. In 1806 he became bandmaster to the Duke of Nassau's 2nd Infantry Regiment and in 1808 fought with them in the Peninsular War for Joseph Bonaparte, King of Spain. He married in Spain during 1811 and a year or two later was taken prisoner. He was released at the end of the war, in 1814, and returned to Wiesbaden with his family. After fighting at Waterloo in 1815 he left the army. Duke Friedrich Wilhelm of Nassau then commissioned him to form and direct an orchestra for his Court. This he did with great success and it became one of the best in Germany. In 1841 the orchestra was dissolved and replaced by the Wiesbaden theatre orchestra. Rummel made concert tours in Belgium (1824), Switzerland, Austria and Germany. In later years he was often accompanied by his daughter Franziska, a singer. Franziska, born Wiesbaden 1821, married Peter Schott, manager of the publishing firm's branch at Brussels. Of Christian Rummel's numerous and gifted family, two others made names for themselves: Josephine (born Manzanarès 1812) as a pianist and Joseph (q.v.) as pianist and clarinettist.

Works: Concertino op.58 in B flat, dedicated to his friend Adam Schott (Schott 1829 – BoLM, LRAM). Air favori from Auber's *La Muette de Portici* (Schott). Fantaisie brillante on motifs from Weber's last works op.55 (Schott). Fantasie on Beethoven's "Ah Perfido" op.77 (Schott). Fantasia on the Cavatina from Rossini's *Tancredi* op.10 (Schott 1820). Introduction & Variations brillantes on a Theme from de Bériot op.67 (Schott). 2 Nocturnes on motifs from Meyerbeer's *Robert le Diable* op.85 (Schott). Variations on a March from *Aline* op.36 (Schott). Variations on a Swiss Waltz op.35 (Schott). Quintet op.41 for oboe, clarinet, basset-horn, horn & bassoon (Schott). Quintet op.42 drawn from the works of Mozart for flute, cor anglais, clarinet, basset-horn & bassoon (Schott). Andante varié for basset-horn (Schott 1819 – BDS, MBS). Fantaisie op.88 on motifs from Donizetti's *Lucia di Lammermoor* for basset-horn (Schott). Nocturne op.87 for basset-horn (Schott).

Bibliography:

SIETZ, Reinhold – "Christian Rummel." MGG.

RUMMEL, Joseph. Wiesbaden, 6 Oct 1818-1880 Mar 25, London. German. He was the son of Christian Rummel and learnt to play the clarinet from him. He was also a good pianist and became court pianist to the Duke of Nassau. Later he was Kapellmeister to the Prince of Oldenburg, who also lived at Wiesbaden. He then moved to Paris and London where he had great success as a piano teacher.

RUPP, Michele. He was well known as a clarinet player at Naples and from 1805 taught at the Conservatorio della Pietà de' Turchini. In 1807 he received a pension.

RUPPERT, Stephen. About 1800 he was a member of the Munich court orchestra.

RUPRECHT. German. He played in the court orchestra at Kassel in 1823.

SABON. Swiss. He was a well-known clarinettist in Geneva. On 15th July 1841 he played the first movement of a Spohr concerto for the Lucerne Music Society Festival. In August 1843 he played the obligato to Cherubini's "Ave Maria" for Mlle von Rupplin at the Freiburg Festival.

SACHSE, Ferdinand. Latdorf, 14 Oct 1824-1917 Feb 23, Hanover. German. His first appointment was as clarinettist in a regiment of Life Guards. In 1850 he became second clarinet in the court orchestra at Hanover. He was made a Royal Chamber Musician in 1870 and retired in 1888.

SÄNGER. German. He was second clarinet in the court orchestra at Regensburg until 1806, when the orchestra was dissolved.

(B–H). **SALIERI, Girolamo.** Born in Venice. Italian. He was the nephew of Anton Salieri, the composer. On 7th October 1832 he performed in the Small Ridotto Room at Vienna. The critics classed him with the best virtuosi, saying he handled his clarinet well and played the basset-horn with sweetness. He played both instruments again on 15th December 1834.

Works: Adagio (Andante) & Variations on a theme from Vaccai's *Bianca di Messina* (Ricordi – VGM, ZAM). Cavatina on Verdi's *Ernani* (Ricordi). Fantasie (Ricordi – VGM). Variations on Pacini's *Saffo* (Ricordi). Andante with Variations on a theme from Bellini's *I Capuletti* for 2 clarinets (Ricordi). Ditto for clarinet & strings (Ricordi). Adagio with Variations on a theme of Rossini's for clarinet & strings (Ricordi).

SAN MIGUEL, Mariano. Oñate, c.1880-1935 Nov, Vitoria. Spanish. He was principal clarinet in the Madrid Symphony Orchestra, a member of the court orchestra and soloist in the band of the Royal Corps of Halberdiers. In 1910 he founded a Wind Instrument Chamber Music Society. He also launched the *Harmonia* review.

SARTORIUS, Georg Kaspar. Born at Mannheim. About 1780 he was employed at Darmstadt as clarinettist, flautist and director of the court orchestra.

SAUD. German. He played in the Nuremberg orchestra in 1822.

SAUL, Ernst Carl Christoph. In 1855 he was a Chamber Musician in the court orchestra at Weimar.

SAX, Antoine Joseph (known as Adolphe). Dinant, 6 Nov 1814-1894 Feb 4, Paris. Belgian. He was an instrument designer of genius, his most important invention being the saxophone. He was also a gifted performer on the clarinet and his early experiments were directed towards the improvement of this instrument. His abilities, coupled with strong personal ambition, led to his gaining the monopoly of supply to French army bands. In spite of this and a large foreign clientele he was no businessman and failed to do well financially. The monopolies he acquired spelt ruin to many manufacturers and this caused intense jealousies. The authenticity of his inventions was continually questioned and resulted in endless lawsuits. There were attempts on his life and he twice threatened to kill himself.

The year after Adolphe was born the family moved from Dinant to Brussels where the father, Charles Joseph Sax, set up in business as an instrument-maker. Charles Joseph had taught himself the trade and did extremely well, becoming official instrument maker to the Court of the Netherlands. Adolphe spent his childhood in his father's workshop and at the age of twelve was capable of making a complete clarinet, having mastered all the processes involved. He had already learnt to play the flute under Lahou at the Royal School of Singing and now took up the clarinet, with Valentin Bender as his teacher. Bender considered him one of his best pupils and when Küffner, visiting Brussels in 1834, heard Sax play he paid tribute in the dedication to him of a set of clarinet duets. Sax had by this time begun experiments to improve the clarinet and in 1835 showed an instrument of 24 keys at the Brussels Exhibition. No details of this model are available, but it was probably similar to clarinets he patented in 1840 and 1842. These, which were basically Müller system, included the following inprovements of special interest: 1) extensions to low e flat and d; 2) an automatic open brille to replace the b/f'' sharp key; 3) a second speaker key. Although Sax's clarinet did not become popular his improvements marked a big step forward in instrument design. There is a B flat clarinet made by him c.1840 in LHM.

Sax next applied himself to the bass clarinet, producing a model with a downward-pointing bell in 1836. By giving the instrument a second speaker key, like his soprano instrument, the upper notes were made considerably easier to produce and when it was patented in 1838 it was an immediate success. Sax received permission to give the instrument a hearing in the Royal Wind Band but met opposition from their solo and bass clarinet player, Bachmann. Sax challenged Bachmann to a public contest at which the superiority of his instrument was proved and after this he was allowed to play all bass clarinet solos for the Royal Wind Band and the court orchestra. When Habeneck visited Brussels in 1839 and heard Sax play the instrument he was so struck with its advantages that on his return to Paris he tried to persuade Buteux, the Opéra's bass clarinet player, to adopt it. Buteux refused and stuck out against it again in 1843 when Donizetti wrote a special part for Sax's instrument in *Dom Sébastien.* Manufacturers in Paris were also actively hostile.

On hearing in 1839 that Dacosta was planning to exhibit his Dumas/ Buffet bass clarinet in different countries Sax set off immediately for Paris to intercept the plan. Seeking Dacosta out, he gave a splendid rendering of the solo from *Les Huguenots* to demonstrate his instrument. Mme Dacosta exclaimed: "When M. Sax plays, *your* instrument sounds like a kazoo!" Dacosta himself did not doubt which was the better instrument. He was gracious enough to compliment Sax's virtuosity and not long after, changed to an instrument of Sax's design. Another well-known player to adopt the isntrument and give it much publicity was Duprez. While in Paris Sax made numerous influential friends who included Berlioz, Halévy and Kastner and he performed on his bass clarinet to members of the Conservatoire staff who were greatly impressed. He then returned to Brussels and the following year made an attempt to improve the contrabass clarinet. This led to a notorious wrangle with Wieprecht (q.v.) who accused him of imitation.

It is not known what specific train of thought led Sax during the course of his multifarious experiments with the clarinet to produce his "brain child," the saxophone, but by 1840 he had a prototype. Full of the possibilities of his new instrument and encouraged by the success of his bass clarinet, Sax decided to set up business in Paris. He arrived there at the end of 1842 with boundless self-confidence, a mere 30 francs in his pocket. Berlioz wrote an article drawing the attention of the public to Sax's inventions and it was not long before financial backers came forward, enabling him to buy a small premises at no.50 rue Saint Georges. Berlioz assisted further by composing a "Chant Sacré" to be performed on six of Sax's instruments. He used a theme from "Hymne Sacré" with which he had won the Prix de Rome, and gave each player in turn an extended passage to show off his instrument. "Chant Sacré," now unfortunately lost, was performed at the Salle Herz on 3rd February 1844 with Sax himself playing the bass saxophone (see Scudo). The other players were Duverné (soprano saxhorn), Dufresne (trumpet), Arban (alto saxhorn) Leperd (clarinet) and Duprez (bass clarinet).

Sax showed woodwind and brass instruments at the French Exhibition of 1844 and delighted the jury by demonstrating them all himself. The following year he patented the saxhorn, which proved so useful that it was adopted by bands throughout the French army. 1845 also saw the patenting of his saxotromba and the publication of a *Méthode* for saxophone by Kastner. The saxophone itself was patented in 1846. With Sax's expanding trade, his business premises had to be enlarged considerably. He insisted on workmanship of the highest order and was the first instrument manufacturer to make all parts on the premises.

Sax was given the following honours: 1845 – Couronne de Chêne from the King of the Netherlands; 1846 – Ordre pour le Mérite from the King of Prussia; 1849 – France's Légion d'honneur. Amongst the medals he won were the following: 1849 – Gold Medal at the Paris Industrial Exhibition; 1851 – Council Medal at London's Great Exhibition, for a display of 85 instruments; 1855 – Gold Medal at the Paris Exhibition. In spite of all these successes his financial affairs were never less than chaotic and in 1852 he went bankrupt. He rallied, managed to settle his creditors and with the help of many admirers, including Napoleon III, started business once more. In 1854 he was made official instrument maker and 1858 director of music to the Emperor. In 1857 he suffered the humiliation of having his Légion d'honneur taken away from him, because his discharge from bankruptcy had not been recorded.

The Paris Conservatoire inaugurated a saxophone class in 1857 and Sax was appointed professor. He taught more than 150 pupils before the class was abolished for economic reasons in 1870. Klosé, the Conservatoire's clarinet professor, wrote a "Solo" for alto saxophone and piano which he dedicated to Sax. Sax did not write a tutor for the saxophone, but his *Méthode complète pour Saxhorn et Saxotromba* was published by Brandus & Dufour in 1864. There is a sopranino saxophone in E flat made by him c.1856 in LHM.

Besides financial problems Sax had another burden to bear, for in 1853 a black tumour appeared at the corner of his top lip and continued to grow until by 1856 it was causing him great pain and difficulty in eating. He consulted the foremost medical men in Paris who were unanimous in diagnosing melanosis. They pronounced an operation essential if the cancer were not to prove fatal. His friends were opposed to the risk of an operation and in 1858 Comettant persuaded him to see an Indian named Vriès who had a considerable reputation for affecting cures where others had failed. Vriès treated the tumour with a herb from his native land and although nothing happened during the first eight months of application, the tumour then began to dwindle. Finally it disappeared, leaving Sax with no traces of disfigurement. So much public interest was aroused in the cure that Vriès became famous, much to the discomfort of the medical men.

Sax's spirit was undimmed and for several more years he continued to invent new instruments and make improvements. The seal was set on his achievements in 1867 when he was awarded the Paris Exhibition's Grand Prix for specimens of all the instruments he had invented and improved. From this time his powers began to wane and his trade declined. In all his productive years he had been interested only in the inventions he was determined to give to the world and not in the business of making money. He could have made a fortune in 1859 when the standardisation of French pitch necessitated the making of quantities of new instruments. Instead he left it to the smaller manufacturers to reap rich rewards. When his business began to fail his patrons withdrew their support. He became bankrupt once more in 1873 and was forced to close the establishment in the rue Saint Georges. As a final blow, in 1877 he had to sell his collection of 467 instruments. Some of these went to the Paris Conservatoire, some to the Brussels Instrumental Museum and others to the private collection of César Snoeck.

Bibliography:

COMETTANT, Jean Pierre Oscar – *Histoire d'un inventeur au dix-neuviéme siècle.* Paris 1860.

GILSON, Paul – *Les Géniales Inventions d'Adolphe Sax.* Brussels 1839.

REMY, Albert – *La Vie tourmentée d'Adolphe Sax.* Brussels 1939.

SCHÄFER. German. He performed at St Petersburg in 1840, and was in the Imperial Court Orchestra at Moscow in 1845.

SCHAFFER (SCHEFFER, SHAFFER) Francis C. He is possibly the brother of Louis Schaffer and, like him, settled at Boston, Massachusetts. In 1796 and again on 2nd April 1798 he performed a concerto of his own composition. A Benefit for him was given in August 1820 at the Boylston Hall, when Hart performed his concerto. Schaffer was described as "an infirm, aged, and decayed musician." Schaffer claimed to have invented "spiccato" for the clarinet. This probably meant he had discovered the advantages of playing with the reed against the lower lip – a Norwegian tutor of 1782 had already advocated this method – and was thus able to perform a true bouncing staccato.

Work: Concerto.

SCHAFFER, Louis. He is possibly the brother of Francis Schaffer. When the Philharmonic Society of Boston, Massachusetts, was founded in 1810 he and Thomas Granger were appointed clarinet players to the orchestra.

(B–H). **SCHALK, Franz.** German. He was undoubtedly a crank and as such a disgrace to the breed of basset-horn players. But one enjoys the impudence with which he bounced around the greater part of Europe and to Russia during a full seventeen years of concert-giving, his faith in himself never shaken although his bluff was called on several occasions. In many cities he succeeded by dint of bold publicity in duping the credulous. In others his performance, which must have been worthy of a music-hall act, unleashed streams of satire from the newspaper reporters who hadn't enjoyed themselves so much since they could remember. His very name was doubtless part of his act, for translated Schalk means "wag" or "rogue."

Schalk's principal concerts were as follows: 1818 – April and May at Aachen, billed as "from Prague." 1821 – 6th June at Berlin, Polonaise by Meyerbeer (probably an arrangement by Schalk) and his own Variations on a Theme from Rossini's *Cenerentola.* 1823 – March at Bremen, a mammoth concert in which he played a concerto by G.A. Schneider, Variations by himself, a Polonaise by Beethoven (again probably arranged by Schalk) and "Reminiscence of Switzerland or Swiss Round-Dance" with "Echo." He also played Mozart's "Non più di fiori" and, with Rakemann senior on second basset-horn, "Al desio, di chi t'adora." A further concert at Lübeck. 1824 – March at Milan, a concert with the singer Mariana Kainz. In April he was with Mariana again at Zurich. On 2nd October he played his own variations in an entr'acte at Vienna's Kärntnerthortheater. 1825 – 23rd August in the Theatre Hall at Leipzig, Swiss Round-Dance. On 4th November at Kassel he gave them most of his repertoire – Potpourri, Variations, Round-Dance and Polonaise – and then went on to Frankfurt. 29th November at Cologne, variations on a theme of Carafa. 1828 – 13th February, soloist at Bologna. 1829 – 7th November in an entr'acte at Munich, his Rossini Variations. 1830 – October, concerts in the theatre at Berlin, on his way to St Petersburg:

on 2nd and 8th, with the pianist Hamann; on 17th, with Kapellmeister Pott (August?). 1831 – a concert at Magdeburg and then one at Weimar where he played his own Variations, Round-Dance and Potpourri. 1832 – concert at Lausanne. 22nd October at the Frankfurt Museum Concerts, Variations (probably his own). 1834 – in Berlin's theatre, his own Variations. Also an evening concert at the Russian Hotel. In June at Königsberg, the Swiss Round-Dance.

His publicity and the way the critics took him were as follows: Berlin in 1821 – Publicity: "Concert master Schalk from Prague." This information, although suspect, seems to have been accepted. Königsberg in 1822 – Critics: "The deep notes are lovely, but the instrument is uneven." So far not so bad. Bremen in 1823 – Critics: "He has come via Petersburg, Stockholm and Hamburg, and a great reputation went before him; the great expectation however was not satisfied." Watch out, the wool is off! Zurich in 1824 – Critics: "He tore through his passages in a manner not at all to the public taste." Much worse is to come. Vienna the same year – Publicity: "Musician from Prague and honorary member of the Ducal Academy at Parma." Too close to suggest a concert master this time and one appearance at a ducal gathering is enough for the rest. Critics: "Risum teneatis amici! (Forbear from laughing, friends!) This was a veritable Schalks- or Eulenspiegel-prank to thoroughly tax our credulity and sell us frivolous bungling in place of the proper thing. Such a slanderer of art deserves to be flung from Parnassus!"

Sir George Smart went to Schalk's concert at Kassel in 1825 and has this to say: "It began soon after six o'clock, as soon as the Electress entered, she came with her daughter . . . . . About two hundred persons were present, who paid at the most sixteen groschen a ticket, which is about two shillings English. There were many free tickets, mine among the rest, but supposing all paid the profit would have been about twenty pounds . . . . . Many of the best of the band were engaged at a ball given by the favourite Countess of the Elector. However, the band was good enough for the music played . . . . . the second (piece), poor music, was a pot-pourri for the basset horn. His tone is not bad but he played out of tune . . . . . The fourth piece consisted of variations for the basset horn. It was as bad as number two. Then came about a quarter of an hour's stop but no refreshments. The company indeed seemed to want their dresses refreshed. They were a dirty set, the men in boots, great coats and cloaks, the ladies in bonnets. The Electress was tolerably dressed and there were about eight or nine officers present in blue uniform . . . . . Spohr said that these overtures . . . . . were chosen on purpose, the band being weak and having had no rehearsal. He disapproved altogether of the concert, Schalk, he said, being a quack . . . . . The third and fourth pieces in the second part were blended together. They consisted of the Schweizer *Ranz des Vaches* with echo, dreadful stuff, as was also the Polonaise. The concert was over at twenty minutes to eight . . . . . I rather think Marco Berra laughed at this man's pretensions when I was in Prague. Spohr does not seem to fancy him."

Munich was taken in, in 1829 – Publicity: "Chamber virtuoso in the employment of the Duke of Parma." Critics: "His performance deserves honourable mention, for there was a pleasant effect in the appropriately melting sound of the instrument." Berlin too, in 1830 – the critics said his tone was beautiful and he handled the instrument delicately in the soft passages. Magdeburg in 1831 – Publicity: "Basset-hornist to the Duke of Parma." Critics: "The announcement-maker shows such confidence in himself as to intimate he is a second Paganini. This intimation was nevertheless a joke, for Herr Schalk showed himself only a moderately good musician in every respect." Weimar in the same year found his tone beautiful and remarked that he had exceptional dexterity. Lausanne in 1832 – Publicity: "Member of the court of Her Exalted Highness the Archduchess of Parma and Plaisance." Critics: "This (rogish publicity) will furnish him no listeners, while the delicate tone of his instrument does not go well with a moustache. He did not please in any case." Berlin in 1834 – they found his tone soft, but to play with the orchestra it needed more fullness and depth. Königsberg the same year – Publicity: "Employed by the Grand Duchess of Parma." Critics: "His Swiss Kuhreigen (Round-Dance) pleased with a good echo and ppp."

Works for basset-horn: Polonaise by Beethoven. Polonaise by Meyerbeer. Potpourri. Reminiscences of Switzerland or Swiss Round-Dance. Variations on a Theme from Rossini's *Cenerentola.*

SCHALL, Christian. German. He played in the Carlsruhe court orchestra in 1793, doubling on violin when needed.

SCHARF. He and Ernst were engaged at the Paris Opéra on a full-time basis from 1773 until their deaths.

SCHATT(E), Johann Christian. He was a member of the court orchestra at Stockholm from 1802 to 1820. He performed a Krommer double concerto with Crusell on 20th January 1805. In 1819 a Benefit was given for him at which Crusell played.

SCHATZ, Johann Friedrich. German. From 1763

to 1785 he played first clarinet and cello at the Brandenburg-Ansbach Court.

SCHAUB. German. In 1866 he was third clarinet in the court orchestra at Kassel.

SCHECKER. German. On 1st April 1814 he performed a double concerto by Tausch with Baumgärtner at Frankfurt a. M. He was reported to be still young and may have been a pupil of Baumgärtner's.

SCHEFFAUER. ?-1828, Stuttgart. German. He was second clarinet in the Royal Würtemberg court orchestra at Stuttgart from 1815 until his death.

SCHERZER, Georg. ?-1834. German. He was a Chamber Musician at the Darmstadt Court from 1812. He also played the violin.

Work: Concerto (Ms. lost from DHLM during World War II).

SCHICK, Friedrich. Berlin, 6 Nov 1794-1860 Nov 28, Bernsdorf. German. He had a distinguished career both at the Berlin Court and in military music. He came from a well-known musical family, his father being the violinist Ernst Schick, his mother Margarete and sister Julie both being opera singers. His parents performed with Beer and Tausch in 1802 and it is probable that Friedrich became a pupil of the latter. Reports on Schick's playing say that he had a beautiful tone, deep feeling and a light attack. He had a very successful first public concert in 1812. On 21st January 1816 he played "with obvious talent and beautiful tone" a Phantasie (from the Quintet op.34) by Weber at the Saale der Stadt Paris. Later the same year he gave a farewell concert before going to Stralsund to join the band of the 33rd Infantry Regiment, and played a "concerto in C minor" (Spohr's First Concerto?). In 1818 he became first clarinet in the court theatre orchestra at Berlin with the title of Chamber Musician. In July of the same year he performed a Phantasie (Weber's?) and Variations (Weber's op.33). On 11th November 1819 he performed Lindpaintner's Concerto at an entr'acte concert in Königsberg. Again in Königsberg on the following 12th January he gave a public concert. When he played a Weber concerto at Berlin on 21st October 1825 it was announced that he was now Kapellmeister of his regiment at Stralsund. In 1828 he played an unspecified concertino. In 1832 he changed from the 33rd Infantry Regiment to that of the Emperor Alexander, which was garrisoned at Berlin; he became their director in 1842. In 1848 he was decorated with the order of the Red Eagle and in 1859 retired with a pension. He wrote a great deal of military music.

SCHIDA, Richard. He was a pupil at the Prague Conservatoire under Reitmayer (II) from 1885 to 1891. In 1907 he became a member of the Vienna Philharmonic Orchestra.

SCHIEFER (SCHIEFFER), Jean. In 1749 he played with Reiffer in Rameau's opera *Zoroastre* at the Paris Opéra. For twenty eight performances of the same work in 1751 and 1752 they were given a fee of 3 livres per performance. In 1753 and 1755 both played under Stamitz.

SCHIERLL (SCHULZ), Joseph (I). German. He was second clarinet in the Thurn and Taxis court orchestra at Regensburg from 1769 or earlier until about 1786. He taught his son (see below) and Wolfgang Wack.

SCHIERLL (SCHIEL, SCHIERL, SCHIRL), Joseph (II). Regensburg, 1757-1797, Regensburg. German. His father (see above) taught him to play the clarinet. He produced a gentle tone which bewitched his listeners. He was first clarinet to Prince Nicolaus Esterházy at Esterház in 1783, with Wolfgang Wack as second. In 1784 they both moved to Regensburg to hold similar positions in the Thurn and Taxis court orchestra.

Works: Concerto no.1 in B flat (Ms. – RTTH). Concerto no.2 in E flat (Ms. – RTTH).

SCHILLER, Christoph. German. He played in the second court orchestra at St Petersburg from 1776 until 1787, when he received a pension.

SCHINDELMEISSER, Louis (Alexander Balthasar). Königsberg, 8 Dec 1811-1864 Mar 30, Darmstadt. German. His mother Fanny was a pianist. She first married Dorn, a merchant at Königsberg, and had a son Heinrich who became famous as a conductor. Dorn died not many years later and she then married Schindelmeisser, a gentleman of independent means by whom she had another son, Louis, and a daughter. She was widowed a second time in 1817 and in 1824 moved with her family to Berlin, where she established a music school. Louis became a pupil at the Berlin High School, learning clarinet from Hostié and composition from Gährich. It is possible that he had already made the acquaintance of Hostié, for Hostié had previously lived in Königsberg and in fact moved to Berlin the same year as the Schindelmeissers.

Schindelmeisser became a Chamber Musician at the Berlin Court, performing for the first time as a soloist on 13th October 1830 at the Royal Theatre. He spent some time during the winter of 1831/2 at Leipzig where his step-brother Heinrich Dorn was music director at the theatre. On 10th November he performed a concerto by Weber and on 29th March 1832 he took part with Mehner, "Mey" (Eduard Meyer?) and Rosenkranz in a performance of his own Symphonie Concertante for 4 clarinets. The work was performed again on 15th December under G.A. Schneider at Berlin. It was well received and became popular wherever four good clarinettists could be assembled. At Prague in 1833 he gave a public concert in the National Theatre and performed a Phantasie (from the Quintet op.34) by Weber and a solo concerto of his own composition. The critics said it was a pity that someone writing for his own instrument should so overload the work with difficulties that the melodic line was obscured. On 13th February 1835 he took part in his own Symphonie Concertante at Fulda. The other soloists are not recorded but were probably André, Hamburger and Vilmar, all of whom were employed at Fulda around that time.

Schindelmeisser ceased his employment at the Berlin Court in 1833 and accepted a series of conducting appointments, at Salzburg, Innsbruck and Graz. At the same time he continued to perform as a clarinet soloist. In 1837 he returned to Berlin for one year as conductor at the Royal Theatre. Then followed conductorships at Pest in 1838, Buda in 1846, Hamburg in 1847, Frankfurt a. M. in 1848, Wiesbaden theatre orchestra in 1851 and finally Darmstadt in 1853. He remained at the latter for the rest of his life and was given several honours, including the Golden Employment Medal. It is interesting to note that the step-brothers were at variance over Wagner; Louis Schindelmeisser was the composer's friend and championed his works, whereas Heinrich Dorn was strongly opposed to everything that Wagner stood for.

Works: Concerto op.1 in C minor (Breitkopf & Härtel 1833). Concertino in E flat, dedicated to Hostié (Breitkopf & Härtel 1832 – LRCM). Concertino for 2 clarinets (Breitkopf & Härtel). Symphonie Concertante (Concertstück) op.2 for 4 clarinets, dedicated to Karl Möser (Breitkopf & Härtel 1833 – ZAM).

Bibliography:
RÖNNAU, Klaus: "Louis Alexander Balthasar Schindelmeisser." MGG.

SCHINDTLER y GOMEZ, Francisco. Madrid, 14 July 1772-1823 July 28. Spanish. He was a Chamber Musician and first clarinet in the court orchestra at Madrid.

SCHLEICHER, Caroline. Stockach, 17 Dec 1794-c.1850, Vienna. Swiss. See OV. Caroline, her sister Sophie and father Franz Joseph, left Baden in October 1812 and on 27th of that month gave a concert at Biberach. Biberach's music director, Justin Knecht, gave them an excellent testimonial the next day, to help them at their next place of call. This and several other testimonials written on behalf of Caroline are in the Deutsche Staatsbibliothek at Berlin. The testimonials all speak highly of her skill, more particularly on the clarinet than the violin, and present her as of high moral character. On her journey to Vienna with her young nephew, Caroline performed again at Biberach in November 1821, and on 7th December played a Potpourri for clarinet (Danzi's?) at the Frankfurt Museum Concerts. After her very successful court concert at Vienna on 25th March 1822 Caroline played again at Darmstadt and then at a public concert on 25th April at Stuttgart. She settled her affairs at Carlsruhe and gave a final concert in the court theatre on 17th June before making her return journey to to Vienna to marry Ernst Krähmer.

At the Krähmer's first concert together in Vienna on 27th October 1822 they performed Ernst's concerto for oboe and clarinet. Caroline played an Adagio (Andante) & Polonaise by Tausch on the clarinet and a concerto by Rode on the violin. Their concert at Kiev on 23rd January 1823 was reported incorrectly by AMZ, for it was Krähmer's concerto for oboe & clarinet that they played, not an arrangement of a Krommer double concerto. Caroline performed Variations for clarinet by her husband on this occasion and a Potpourri for violin by Danzi. On 15th February 1833 they gave a private concert in the hall of the Gesellschaft der Musikfreunde. This concert had no public announcement, being given by private subscription. The subscription list, in the possession of the Deutsche Staatsbibliothek, has nearly a hundred names and these include the Empress, the Grand Dukes Anton & Franz, Grand Duchess Sophie, the King & Queen of Hungary, Baron Prentano, Baron Rothschild, her friend Danzi and publisher Haslinger. The programme included Ernst's "concertino" for oboe & clarinet, and Caroline played Beethoven's "Adelaide" (Iwan Müller's arrangement) for clarinet, accompanied by Joseph

Privat=Concert,

welches die Unterzeichneten
Freytag den 15. Februar 1833,
im

Saale der Gesellschaft der Musikfreunde,

unter den Tuchlauben
um 7 Uhr Abends,
zu geben die Ehre haben werden.

Vorkommende Stücke:

1. **Ouverture** von Mozart.
2. **Doppel-Concertino** für Oboe und Clarinette, componirt von Ernst Krähmer, vorgetragen von Ernst und Caroline Krähmer.
3. **Solo** für das Pianoforte, componirt und vorgetragen von Herrn Sigismund Thalberg.
4. Adagio und Rondo für die Violine, componirt von R. Kreutzer, gespielt von Caroline Krähmer.
5. **Die Schneeflöckchen am Kirchhofe**, Gedicht von A. Schmid, mit Musik von Herrn B. Randhartinger, Mitglied der k. k. Hofcapelle, vorgetragen von demselben, und am Piano-Forte begleitet von Herrn J. Fischhof. (Dieses Gedicht wird bey den Eingängen vertheilt werden).
6. **Declamation,** gesprochen von einer Kunstfreundin.
7. **Adelaide** von Beethoven, auf der Clarinette gespielt von Caroline Krähmer, und am Piano-Forte begleitet von Herrn J. Fischhof.
8. (Auf vieles Verlangen) **Bravour-Variationen,** für den Czakan (Flûte douce) über ein Thema aus J. Haydns Schöpfung, componirt und vorgetragen von Ernst Krähmer.

Ernst Krähmer,
k. k. Hof- und Kammer-Musiker.
Caroline Krähmer, geb. Schleicher.

5. Private Concert given by Caroline Schleicher and her husband, Ernst Krähmer, in Vienna, 15th February 1833.

Fischhof. Thalberg played a piano solo.

On 8th December 1834 the Krähmers gave a concert in the theatre at Pforzheim, which included Ernst's "duo concertant" for oboe & clarinet, and the first movement of Jansa's clarinet concerto. The announcement said: "For greater convenience tickets can be had 8 hours beforehand (the concert was at 7pm.) at the concert-givers dwelling, in the Guesthouse of the Knights . . . . . The theatre will be suitably heated." On 23rd of the same month they were at Carlsruhe and took part in a miscellany at the Grand Ducal Theatre. Between items from the Madrid court dancers they played Ernst's "duet" for oboe & clarinet and Caroline gave them Jansa's clarinet concerto. The Augsburg concert of 1840, mentioned in the original volume, took place on 19th October at the town's first Subscription Concert. As well as the concerto for clarinet & cello by Jansa which Caroline played with her son Ernst (born 1826) she also performed a Divertissement by Conradin Kreutzer.

Works: Sonatine (Sauer & Leidesdorf 1825 – VGM). Variations.

Writing:
Autobiography, auctioned at Berlin in 1922.

(B–H). **SCHLÖMILCH.** German. He played first clarinet and basset-horn in the Duke of Weimar's court orchestra. On 8th May 1803 he performed a clarinet concerto and variations for basset-horn, both by Franz Destouches, a colleague in the Weimar orchestra, at the Leipzig Gewandhaus. He was well received and they found his tone on both instruments soft and pleasing. In August 1823 at Weimar he took part in a performance of Crusell's Symphonie Concertante.

SCHLOSSER father and son. They performed together in 1838 at St Petersburg, where in 1840 one of them also played Vollweiler's Concertino.

SCHMIDL, Alois. He was a pupil at the Vienna Conservatoire, finishing his training in 1882. He became a member of the Vienna court orchestra and was engaged for the Philharmonic Orchestra from 1885 to 1910 or later.

SCHMIDT. German. In 1885 he was a member of the Berlin court orchestra.

SCHMIDT, R. (N?). German. He appeared as a soloist

at Paris in 1802.

Works: Duo (Sieber c.1789). Quartet (Sieber c.1789). 3 Quartets (Leduc).

SCHMIDT, Roy O. c.1903-1932. American. He was second clarinet in the Minneapolis Symphony Orchestra and first clarinet in the Sousa and Conway bands. In 1928 he made a recording of an extract from Bassi's *Rigoletto* Fantasia, using a silver clarinet.

SCHMIDT, Th. German. In 1815 he was engaged for the Duke of Wiesbaden's orchestra. In 1847 he was made Kapellmeister and in 1865 celebrated his fifty years of court employment. He was highly thought of as a clarinettist and used instruments made by Backofen. He was also a good teacher, his best known pupil being Staps. He performed at Mannheim in 1827 and again on 21st March 1859, when his programme was as follows: Oberthür's "Lieder ohne Wörte," a Phantasie trio on themes from *Oberon* for oboe, clarinet & piano, and Spohr's Nonet.

SCHMITTBAUER, August. German. He was playing in the Carlsruhe court orchestra in 1793.

SCHNABEL, Michael. Naumburg, 23 Sept 1775-1842 Nov 6, Breslau. German. His father was cantor at Naumburg. His brothers were Joseph Schnabel, the Kapellmeister at Breslau cathedral and composer of a concerto and variations for clarinet, and A. Schnabel, a violinist. Michael Schnabel was trained on several instruments, first from his father and then from his brother Joseph. Joseph was instrumental in obtaining for him an appointment in the Prince-Bishop's Court as clarinettist and singer. In 1814 Michael founded a piano manufactory and when players like Liszt and Hummel played in the town they always used his instruments. He continued to play in the court orchestra up to 1819 or later. After his death the piano workshops were carried on by his sons Karl and Julius.

SCHNEIDER. ?-1860 July, Stuttgart. German. He was first clarinet in the Stuttgart court orchestra and died in this post while still quite young.

SCHNEIDER, Gustav. German. From 1890 he was a Chamber Musician at the Dresden Court.

SCHNITTSPAHN, J. ?-1852. German. As a military bandsman, he arrived at Darmstadt in 1816. He was employed at the Court, eventually becoming a Chamber Musician, until his death. He also played the violin and viola.

SCHNURBUSCH. German. In 1905 he was third clarinet in the court orchestra at Kassel.

SCHÖFMANN, Karl. He was a pupil at the Vienna Conservatoire, finishing his training in 1875. He became a member of the Vienna court orchestra and was engaged for the Philharmonic Orchestra from 1885 until 1910 or later.

SCHÖNBERGER, Isidor. He was blind and an assistant teacher at the Blind Institute in Prague. On 3rd April 1824 he performed Weber's Concertino and had a very good reception. The same year, on 11th April, he played Crusell's Concerto op.5.

SCHÖNCHE (SCHÖNGE), Wilhelm. He was a pupil of Joseph Tausch. From 1811 to 1845 he played in the court orchestra at Munich and from 1811 to 1849 for the Subscription Concerts. In April 1814 he performed a concerto by Krommer for the latter society. Two Munich horn players of the same name were probably his brothers.

SCHOLLMEYER. German. He was a town musician at Mühlhausen. On 12th October 1833 he performed the obligato to Mozart's "Parto!" for Mme Schmidt in the Jacobite Church.

SCHOTT, Adam (Joseph). Mainz, 1794-1864 Aug 6, Bombay. German. He was the son of Bernhard Schott (q.v.), the founder of the Mainz publishing firm. His restless character unsuited him to his father's business, although he did play an important part in the opening of the firm's branches at Antwerp, Paris and London. He was an excellent clarinet player and had a distinguished career as a director of military bands in America, England and the British colonies. The family firm published a considerable amount of music which he had arranged for military band. Adam Schott was the dedicatee of the Concertino op.58 (Schott 1829) by Christian Rummel, whose daughter Franzisca later married Peter Schott, Adam's nephew.

On the recommendation of Josef Küffner, Schott was a pupil from 1812 to 1814 at Josef Fröhlich's Music Institute (Royal

Music School) at Würzburg. Küffner probably taught him himself; he dedicated his Serenade op.21 to Schott. Schott's instrument, bought for him in 1811, was made by Bühner & Keller of Strasbourg. His first solo appearance was at Frankfurt in 1816. In 1817 he travelled and spent some time studying in Brussels. February and March of 1818 finds him in Paris and by October of that year he was in Munich, where he became a pupil of Heinrich Baermann. From 1819 to 1824 or later he played in the Munich court orchestra. The "Adolf" Schott whom Bihrle lists as playing for the Munich Subscription Concerts from 1821 to 1829 most probably refers to Adam, for members of this society were always drawn from the court orchestra.

Family business took Adam to Antwerp on 1st October 1823 to open a branch of the firm, and on 1st August 1827 he was made manager of their newly opened shop at Paris. Before the latter occasion he had been performing in Belgium and in the French provinces. His playing had reached such a high standard that after a performance at the Théâtre Italien, the *Revue Musicale* of 8th November reported that he won the honours of the evening as an instrumentalist. They further said: "Jeunes gens qui vous livrez à l'étude de cet instrument, allez entendre souvent M. Schott, lorsque vous en trouverez l'occasion, car il a la véritable école, l'école allemande, l'école de Behr (Beer) et de Baermann. Dans cette école, on cherche moins un son volumineux qu'un son agréable, velouté, égal dans toute l'étendue de l'instrument, et une exécution nuancée."

On 15th April 1828 Schott embarked at Le Havre for America. Here he spent four weeks at a theatre in Providence and then moved on to Boston, where he played clarinet and violin at the Freement Theatre, and taught both these and guitar. On 15th September 1829 in Quabec he married Therese Ziegler, daughter of the music director of a British regiment. Schott spent the next eighteen months as music director of the 79th regiment at a fort on Lake Ontario and at some time after this came over to England. It is thought that he founded the London branch of B. Schott-Söhne in 1835, and for a short space of time in 1850 was the shop's manager. In 1840 he visited Manchester, Glasgow and Edinburgh. From 1844 to 1856 he was bandmaster of the Grenadier Guards and then, having a predilection for India, he returned to live there until his death.

His solo performances included the following: 1816 – Frankfurt a. M., concerto by Weber. 1822 – 15th November for the Frankfurt Museum Concerts, unspecified concerto. 1823 – April for the Felix Meritis Society, Amsterdam. 1827 – November at Théâtre Italien in Paris, Air varié by Heinrich Baermann. 1830 – 10th May in New York's City Hall, unspecified concerto. 1840 – 30th January & 28th May in Manchester. 1847 – concert given by Oberthür in the Hanover Square Rooms, London, a piece by Baermann.

Bibliography:

Obituary – SM. 26 Dec 1864.

SCHOTT, Bernhard. Eltville, 9 Aug 1748-1809 Aug 26, Heidesheim. German. He was the son of a master baker and became famous as the founder of the music publishing firm in Mainz. He received a good musical education at Mannheim and then matriculated in arts at Mainz University. From 1771 to 1773 he was a clarinettist in a military band at Strasbourg, whilst at the same time studying the art of engraving. He then spent several months in Paris, where he had lessons from Beer and played at concerts. After this he returned to Mainz and founded the publishing firm, becoming court music engraver in 1870. His son Adam was a well-known clarinet player (q.v.).

SCHRAMM, C.W. German. From about 1841 to 1846 he performed as soloist at the Hamburg Festival.

SCHRAMM, Johann Christian. Dresden, 1711-1796. German. He was the son of an organ builder. In 1767 he was playing second clarinet in the court orchestra of Frederick the Great at Berlin.

SCHRENK. He was clarinettist to Prince Karl Egon of Fürstenberg at Donaueschingen. In the winter of 1850/1851 he performed as a soloist at Zurich.

SCHREURS, Joseph. Brussels, 20 Apr 1863-1921 July 15, Chicago. Belgian. When very young his father gave him his first lessons and at the age of six he entered the Brussels Conservatoire as a pupil under Poncelet. He received the Conservatoire's First Prize at the age of ten from the hands of King Leopold, and then went on a tour of Europe as a prodigy, in company with Poncelet. At the age of eighteen he went to America and in New York secured an engagement to tour Mexico with Grau's Opera Company. The company foundered and he had to work his way back to New York. In 1883 he was engaged for the Theodore Thomas Orchestra. When Thomas was invited to conduct the Chicago Orchestra, in 1891, Schreurs went too to become his solo clarinet, and remained in this post until his death. So popular a player was he that for a year after his death his seat was left vacant and from time to time an admirer would place flowers or a wreath on it. Schreurs played Albert clarinets all his life as he found their tonal quality superior, and carrying power greater, than Boehm instruments.

Bibliography:

LANGENUS, Gustave – "Joseph Schreurs." WN, Winter 1926.

SCHRÖDER, Bonaventura. ?-1782 Jan 4, Brussels. He was clarinettist to Prince Albert at Pressburg and in 1772 became a member of the Tonkünstlersocietät in Vienna.

SCHUBERT, August. Berlin, 18 June 1811-? German. He was a pupil of F.W. Tausch. In 1829 he played in the band of the 2nd regiment of Guards, of which he became assistant director in 1844. In 1830 he joined the Berlin court orchestra and in 1845 was made a Royal Chamber Musician. Oskar Schubert was no blood-relation, but his pupil and son-in-law.

August Schubert's concerts included the following: 1839 – March, at one of Karl Möser's *Soirées*, Beethoven's Septet and wind quintets by Beethoven, Mozart and Spohr. 20th September in the Potsdam theatre, an unspecified concerto. At Dresden, Weber's Grand Duo and the Variations op.33. 1840 – late Spring at Weimar in an entr'acte concert. 1841 – Spring at Potsdam, solo by Rummel. Summer, at Berlin's opera house, an unspecified solo. December, concerts in Berlin and Potsdam. 1842 – 27th January, obligato to Mozart's "Parto!" for Mlle Tuczech. 1843 – Weber's Variations op.33 with Adolph Schulz.

SCHUBERT, Oskar. Berlin, 11 Oct 1849-1933 Sept 25, Berlin. German. He was a pupil at the Kullak Conservatoire and also studied privately with August Schubert, whose daughter he married. He fought with the Kaiser Franz regiment in the war of 1870/1871 and in the winter of the latter year played often at musical evenings in the home of Bismarck. He then came out of the army and after playing for a short time in the Berlin Symphony Orchestra, went to America. During 1872 he played both in Boston and New York. From 1873 to 1875 he lived in St Petersburg and then returned to Berlin to play in the Bilse Orchestra. In 1878 he joined the orchestra at the royal opera house. In 1892 he was made a Royal Chamber Musician and in the same year became a teacher at the High School of Music. As an orchestral soloist he had great success in tours throughout Germany, Austria, Italy, Russia and France and was conducted amongst others by Brahms, Reger and Wagner. He also performed with the Bohemian, Halir, Joachim and Rosé Quartets. He made editions of the Baermann tutor and of many of the principal works in the clarinet repertoire. The latter are reprehensible for liberties he takes with the original phrasing.

SCHUBERTH, Gottlob. Carsdorf, 11 Aug 1778-1846 Feb 18, Hamburg. German. He studied music at Jena and from 1804 was employed as a clarinet and oboe player at Magdeburg. In 1833 he moved to Hamburg and remained there until his death. Four of his sons became well-known in the musical world: Julius (publisher, 1804-1875); Ludwig (conductor and composer, 1806-1850); Carl (cellist, 1811-1863); Friedrich (publisher, 1817-?).

SCHÜLEIN, Ludwig. German. He was in the Munich court orchestra from 1812 to 1866 and in 1862 was given the Golden Employment Medal for fifty years service. He played also for the Subscription Concerts from 1821 to 1863 and appeared as soloist for them. On 18th December 1818 he performed Variations by J.B. Cramer for the Frankfurt Museum Concerts. In April 1819 he performed at Cologne.

SCHÜLER, G. ?-1814. German. He was a Chamber Musician in the court orchestra at Darmstadt from 1780 until his death. He also played various stringed instruments and composed. He may be related to Johann Peter Schüler, who played in the royal regiment at Darmstadt in the 1760s.

SCHULTHEIS. German. He played in the court orchestra at Kassel. On 21st December 1838 he performed a concerto by Crusell and on 15th November 1839 took part in Schindelmeisser's Symphonie Concertante for 4 clarinets with Heisterhagen, Lesser and Vauth.

SCHULZE, Michael Christoph. Ückermünde, 1756-? German. In 1790 he gave a concert as clarinettist at Lübeck and settled there as town musician until 1797 or later. He may be the "Schulze" ("Schultz") who gave the following performances at Stockholm in 1815: February, Weber's Concertino; April for the Music Society, an unspecified concerto.

SCHWÄRZER, (Abraham) Georg Peter. German. He was engaged as principal clarinettist at the Court of Brandenburg-Ansbach from 1786 to 1796 or later.

(B–H). **SCHWARTZ, Andreas Gottlob.** Leipzig, 1743-1804 Dec 26, Berlin. German. He was the father of Christoph Gottlob Schwartz. He played basset-horn, oboe and bassoon, the latter being his principal instrument. He spent his youth at Stuttgart and went to Carlsruhe for his musical training. He was an oboist in the Seven Years War and in 1770 became a court musician at Stuttgart. In 1776 he was appointed to the Court of Ansbach from where he was given ample opportunity to travel, and visited Poland, Vienna, Berlin, Frankfurt (1777) and the Netherlands. At some time during this period he learnt to play the basset-horn. In 1783 he travelled in France and then continued to England where in 1784 he and his son played basset-horns at the Hanover Square Great Concerts. During the same year they were both members of the Prince of Wales' band as bassoonists, doubtless playing basset-horns when required. Andreas returned to his appointment at Ansbach and in 1786 was made a Chamber Musician. He was still at the Court in 1796.

(B–H). **SCHWARTZ, Christoph Gottlob.** Ludwigsburg, 12 Sept 1768-1829, Berlin. German. He was the eldest son of Andreas Gottlob Schwartz, from whom he learnt to play the bassoon. He probably learnt the basset-horn at the same time as his father, during their travels of the late 1770s and early 1780s. He came with his father to London in 1784 and with him played basset-horn at the Hanover Square Great Concerts. During the same year they were both made members of the Prince of Wales' band as bassoonists, but doubtless played basset-horn when required. In 1787 Christoph entered the court orchestra of the Prussian Queen and in 1826 received a pension from this employment.

SCHWARZE, Gottlob. German. He was a clarinettist and Chamber Musician in the Meiningen court orchestra from 1867 to 1888.

SCHWEGLER. c.1760-? German. In 1806 he was first clarinet, doubling on oboe when required, in the Royal Würtemberg orchestra at Stuttgart. His elder brother Johann David Schwegler (born 1759) played the oboe and his younger brother the horn in the same orchestra.

SCHWEMER. German. He was playing in the Mecklenburg-Schwerin court orchestra in 1883.

SCHWENKE, Johann Friedrich. Hamburg, 30 Apr 1792-1852 Sept 28, Hamburg. German. He was the son of C.F.G. Schwenke and nephew of the clarinettist Carl Hartmann. He learnt the clarinet, probably from his uncle, but had to give it up because of tuberculosis. Instead he became an organist and in 1829 was appointed to St Nicholas Church at Hamburg. He also played the cello and composed.

SCRIBANEK, Johann. About 1791 he was a member of the court orchestra at Mainz.

SCRUDER (SCHRUDR). He played second clarinet at the Théâtre de Vaudeville at Paris in 1827 and 1828.

SCUDO, Pietro. He played at the Théâtre Français. He was also critic of the *Revue des deux mondes* and after Sax's famous Salle Herz concert in 1844, gave the following report: "The saxophones sound hollow and wrong – they are noisy and blaring!"

SEBASTIANI, Ferdinando. Naples, 1803-1860. Italian. He was the founder of the Neapolitan school of clarinettists. He was a pupil at the Naples Conservatoire, where he later became a professor. He was solo clarinet to the King of Naples and first clarinet in the orchestra of the San Carlo Theatre. In 1828 he went on a concert tour, visiting Paris first. At Vienna on 11th December he performed a concerto and some Variations on a Theme of Rossini, both of his own composition. The works were reported to show the instrument off well and his tone was said to be full, sweet and round. He was the friend of Rossini, Fioravanti and Mercadante, the latter writing some special solos for him.

Works: Concerto. Cavatina on a Theme from Bellini's *Norma* (Ricordi). 2 Fantasias on operatic themes (Pacini). Variations on a Theme of Rossini. Método (Cottrau – NCM).

SEDELMAYER, Ferdinando. From 1801 to 1805 he taught at the Conservatorio della Pietà de' Turchini in Naples.

SEDLAK, Wenzel. 1776-? Czech. He was clarinettist to Count Liechtenstein at Vienna, probably at the same time as Josef Bähr. On 1st May 1818 he gave a morning concert at the Summer Palace in the Rossau suburb at which he played the obligatos to arias by Niccolini (sung by Mme Brandsteller, soprano) and Simon

Mayr (sung by Josef Barth, tenor). Sedlak's ten-year-old daughter Anna also played some piano solos. On 1st May 1819 he gave another concert with his daughter at the Summer Palace and performed a concerto by Krommer. The same year he was made Kapellmeister at the Liechtenstein Court. He sang in a male voice quartet with three fellow instrumentalists, Johann Sedlatzek, Ernst Krähmer and August Mittag. They gave a performance of Schubert's "The Little Village" at a subscription concert in the County Hall on 4th April 1821.

Works: 12 Original waltzes (Haslinger). Variations for 2 clarinets (Artaria).

SEEL (SÖHL), Johann Hieronymus. German. He played clarinet and viola in the court orchestra at Brandenburg-Ansbach from 1770 to 1786.

SEEMAN, Adolf. Hanover, 24 Feb 1820-1890 Jan 2, Hanover. German. He was the son of Gottfried Wilhelm Seeman. From 1841 he was employed as an extra clarinettist in the court orchestra at Hanover, but in 1850 resigned in order to become a pianist. From 1863 to 1890 he was music director at Hanover.

SEEMAN (SÄMANN, SEEMANN), Gottfried Wilhelm. Herringen (near Nordhausen), 8 Feb 1793-1859, Hanover. German. He was a very distinguished clarinettist at the Hanoverian Court. Berlioz had a high regard for him, commenting in 1841 on his "excellent sound", and in 1843 on his "delicious tone". Seeman first played in a regiment of guards of which he later became music director. In 1818 he was made first clarinet in the court orchestra at Hanover, retaining this post until 1850. His son Adolf was also in the orchestra as a clarinettist from 1841 to 1850.

There is no record of Seeman's solo performances in Hanover itself, but his concerts abroad include the following: 1829 – 17th January in Hamburg's Apollo Hall for the Philharmonic Society, Maurer's Concertino and Variations by Iwan Müller. 1831 – Hamburg's Philharmonic Society again. 1832 – Ditto. 1833 – 24th October for the Leipzig Subscription Concerts, Maurer's Concertino and Iwan Müller's Fantasie on a Theme of Rossini; he received a great ovation. 9th November at Berlin's royal theatre, Maurer's Concertino. 1834 – Magdeburg's Festival, concerts in Lübeck and Neustrelitz. 1837 – a private concert to the Court at Weimar. 1838 – 9th June at a concert given by de Bériot and Pauline Garcia in Berlin's royal theatre. A private performance for Spohr, in a house at Karlsbad, of his Six German Songs op.103 with Ottilie Schubert and Marianne Spohr.

SELIKE. German. He was first clarinet and director of the Life Guards band for the Duke of Mecklenburg-Schwerin at Ludwigslust from about 1812 to 1819.

SELMER, Alexandre. 1864-1953, Chatou. French. He was the thirteenth child of the clarinettist Frédéric Selmer and the brother of Henri Selmer who founded the Henri Selmer Instrument Company. Alexandre Selmer was taught first by his father and then became a pupil under Rose at the Paris Conservatoire, where he gained a First Prize. He then played at the Opéra Comique and with the Lamoureux Orchestra. Before the turn of the century he had gone to America to become first clarinet in the Boston Symphony Orchestra. He played later in the Cincinnati Symphony and New York Philharmonic Orchestras, and also became a fine teacher. Receiving so many orders for instruments made by his brother, similar to those on which he himself was playing, he opened a retail shop in New York in 1904. In 1913 he left the American branch of Selmer in the hands of George Bundy and returned home to France.

Bibliography:

BUNDY, George M. – "Alexandre Selmer as I knew him." M. May 1932.

SELMER, Frédéric. Arras, 1819-1878, Paris. French. His father, Jean Jacques Selmer, was a clarinettist in the 2nd regiment of the Royal Engineers. His godfather was the famous clarinet teacher Frédéric Berr, whose forname he was given. Frédéric Selmer became a pupil at the Paris Conservatoire under Klosé and did so well that in his final year, 1852, a special "Prize of Honour" was created for him. He played for the Algiers Opera and then became bandmaster of the National Guard at Laon until he retired in 1869. Only five of his sixteen children reached adulthood, one girl and four boys. All four boys did well in the musical field: Alexandre and Henri as clarinettists (q.v.), Emil (1857-1920) as a trumpeter, and Charles (1860-1915) as a flautist at the Opéra Comique.

SELMER, Henri (Chery). Mézières, 1858-1941 July, Paris. French. He was the tenth child of Frédéric Selmer and brother of Alexandre Selmer, and is famous as the founder of the Henri Selmer Instrument Company. Henri Selmer learnt first from his father and then in 1876 entered Leroy's class at the Paris Conservatoire.

Leroy was a sick man and Selmer was soon transferred to Rose, under whom he won a First Prize. Selmer joined the Garde Républicaine and showed such promise that the bandmaster, Celinicke, ordered him to play solo clarinet. To stand out in front of the band was more than someone of such a nervous and retiring disposition could face and as Celinicke would brook no refusal, Selmer was forced to resign. He then joined the Opéra Comique orchestra and the Lamoureux Orchestra, touring with the latter. In 1883 Selmer married and, having to support a family, began to consider the possibility of carrying out his father's plans for manufacturing the "ideal clarinet," along lines which Klosé himself had talked about. He started business in 1885 by manufacturing reeds, using just a single machine. Francisco Gomez, a personal friend, became his agent for these in London, and later commissioned a basset-horn. From reeds Selmer progressed to mouthpieces and these went so well that he was able to afford an assistant. This assistant was experienced in woodwind mechanics and together they made a set of clarinets for Selmer's personal use. The success of these amongst the profession was immediate and in 1890 Selmer acquired the original Adolphe Sax establishment and founded the business of Henri Selmer & Cie.

SEMENOV, A.G. 1907-1958. Russian. He was a pupil of Rozanov at the Moscow Conservatoire. While still a student he was given the task of making a selection of studies and arranging them according to difficulty for use in the school. Later he became a professor himself and was made responsible for bringing out the second, third and fourth editions of Rozanov's tutor. Semenov played for the Shatsky Opera Studio.

SENFT, Luigi. Italian. In 1778 he played at the church of Santa Croce in Florence. By 1795 he was in the orchestra at the Royal Theatre.

SHAW, Oliver. Middleboro, Massachusetts, 13 Mar 1779-1848. American. He went to sea first but on going blind at twenty-one had to give this up and turned instead to music. He went to Boston to study the clarinet with Thomas Granger, and also learnt organ and theory. In 1807 he settled at Providence and earned a living by teaching and composing sacred music. He wrote "For the Gentlemen, a favourite selection of instrumental music . . . . (for) two clarionetts, flute and basson." (H. Mann of Dedham, Massachusetts 1807 – ChiNL, NYPL, ProPL).

SHTARK, A.L. 1910-1963. He was a pupil of Rozanov at the Moscow Conservatoire. In 1935 he won Second Prize at the All-Union Musical Competition in Leningrad. He was principal clarinet in the USSR State Symphony Orchestra and lecturer at the Gnesinykh Music-Teachers Institute. He wrote three books of studies and arranged much music for clarinet.

SILVA. From about 1807 to 1824 he was first clarinet at the Italian Theatre in Rio de Janeiro and also a member of the court orchestra. He was considered the best clarinettist of his time in Brazil.

SJÖBERG, (Johan) Frans (Leopold). Göteborg, 2 July 1824-1885 Dec 7, Stockholm. Swedish. He ranks with Kjellberg amongst his country's finest clarinet players. In 1848 he had a theatre position and then became music director of the 2nd regiment of Life Guards. From 1851 he played in Stockholm's court orchestra and from 1867 taught at the Conservatoire.

SLADE, G. English. He was fourth clarinet in the Hallé Orchestra at Manchester from 1906 to 1915 and then third clarinet for one year. After serving in the First World War he came back to the Hallé in 1919 and remained as third clarinet until 1937.

SOBECK, Jan. Krippau, 30 Apr 1831-1914 June 9, Hanover. Czech. He was a pupil under Pisařovic at the Prague Conservatoire from 1843 to 1849. He appeared at the following Conservatoire concerts: 1848 – 9th April, Variations (op.8?) by Carl Baermann. 1849 – 8th April, Fantasie by Reissiger. For the next two years he played in the theatre orchestra at Baden-Baden and gave concerts with Teresa Milanollo and Jenny Lind. In the Spring of 1851 he came to London in an orchestra made up mostly of Prague Conservatoire students. This did not meet with success and in August of that year he was offered and accepted the post of first clarinet in the court orchestra at Hanover. From here he travelled all over Germany as a soloist. He also built a reputation as a good teacher. On 7th July 1858 he was invited back to the Prague Conservatoire as guest artist and performed his own concerto. He was made a Chamber Musician in 1855 and retired from court service in 1901 after 50 years service. The following honours were given him: Corresponding Member of Boulogne's Beethoven Circle; Employment Medal for Art & Knowledge, from Duke Ernst II of Saxe-Coburg-Gotha; Order of the Crown, 4th Class (1892) from

Kaiser Wilhelm II.

Works: Jubel-Konzert op.16, dedicated to Kaiser Wilhelm II (Lehne). Concertino op.22 (Oertel). Konzertstück op.17 (Lehne). Konzertstück op.25. Nordische Romanze op.7 for clarinet solo. Concert Aria op.10 (Oertel). Duo concertant op.5 on themes from Mozart's *Don Juan* (Bote & Bock). Elegie op.2 (Nagel). Fantasia op.6 on motifs from Spohr's *Jessonda* (Schmidt). "Faust" Fantasie op.13 (Bote & Bock). Four Characteristic Pieces op.8 (Schmidt). Grand Fantasie op.12 on Boieldieu's *Dame Blanche* (Oertel 1886 – LBL). Lucia Fantasie op.3 (Oertel). Morceau de Salon op.1 (Bachmann). Duo concertant op.19 for 2 clarinets (Lehne 1894). Grand Trio op.20 for 2 clarinets & bassoon (Lehne 1898). Wind quintet op.9 in F, dedicated to Duke Ernst II of Saxe-Coburg-Gotha (Bote & Bock 1879 – LBL). Wind quintet op.11 in E flat (Bosworth 1891 – LBL). Wind quintet op.14 in G minor (Bosworth). Wind quintet op.23 (Lehne 1897 – LBL). "Meine Heimat" op.18 for soprano or tenor & clarinet (Lehne).

Bibliography:

Article on his retirement. DMDZ. July 1901.

"J. Sobeck." LZ. 29th April 1911.

SOBOLEWSKI, Michal. Polish. From 1865 to 1903 he took the clarinet class at the Warsaw Conservatoire.

SOLÈRE (SOLER, SOLLER), Étienne. Mont-Louis 4 Apr 1753-1817, Paris. French. At the age of fourteen he became a bandsman in an infantry regiment at Champagne. Later he came to Paris with the regiment and here took the opportunity to have lessons from Beer. In 1778 he came out of the army and took Beer's place as first clarinet in the wind music for the Duke of Orleans. At this time he had lessons from Yost, although the latter was a year younger than him. The Duke of Orleans died in 1785 and Solère then obtained the post of first clarinet to Louis XVI. At the Revolution he became a member of the National Guard and in 1793 became a teacher at the Institut National. When the Conservatoire was opened in 1795 he was made a professor (Lassabathie says of the second class, Pierre of the third). He was a member of the committee set up in 1801 to discuss the tutor Lefèvre had been commissioned to write. When the Conservatoire was reorganised in 1802 Solère was not taken on again. From 1790 he played at the Opéra Comique. When Chelard died in 1802 Solère took his place as second clarinet to Lefèvre at the Opéra, and remained in this post until 1816. In 1804 Solère was enlisted by Lesueur for Napoleon's orchestra. He lived at no.16 rue Vivienne, a few doors away from Bochsa at no.19.

Solère rose to fame largely through the success of his performances for the Concert Spirituel. The following are details of the concerts he gave for the society: 1782 – 25th March, concerto by the Chevalier de Saint-Georges. (Saint-Georges, a mulatto violinist, was closely associated with the Duke of Orleans and was riding master to the Duke's secret wife). 26th March, repeat performance. 24th December, "new concerto." 1783 – 2nd February, concerto by Saint-Georges. 6th April, concerto by himself and one by Deshayes. 15th April, concerto by Saint-Georges. 17th April, unspecified concerto. 19th April, ditto. 22nd April, appearance with Yost. 26th April, unspecified concerto. 1785 – 13th March, ditto. 21st March, ditto. 28th March, his own concerto. 3rd April, unspecified concerto. 5th May, his own concerto. 24th December, ditto. 1786 – 2nd February, Symphonie Concertante for clarinet, bassoon, horn & piano by Amélie Julie Candeille, with the nineteen-year-old composer herself playing the piano. 25th March, Symphonie Concertante for clarinet & bassoon by Ozi, with the composer playing the bassoon. 1787 – 8th December, "new concerto" by himself. 24th December, Symphonie Concertante for 2 clarinets by Devienne, with Hayenschinck. 1788 – 17th March, ditto. 20th March, Symphonie Concertante for 2 clarinets by Jadin, with Hayenschinck. 1790 – 28th March, his own Symphonie Concertante for 2 clarinets with Wachter.

Works: Concertos nos.1 in E flat, 2 in B flat, 3 in B flat, 4 in E flat (Sieber c.1798). Concerto no.5 in F (Imbault 1787. Sieber. Janet). Concerto no.6 in B flat (Imbault 1792. Janet). Concerto no.7. 2 Symphonies Concertantes for 2 clarinets; no.1 in F, no.2 in C (Imbault 1790 – PBN). Airs variés, 5 books (Sieber c.1798). 3 Fantasias (Hentz. Jouve). Duos ops.1 & 2 (Ozi c.1802. Janet c.1802). Fantaisies for 2 clarinets (Hentz). Variations for 2 clarinets (Hentz). Airs variés for clarinet & violin (Sieber). 6 Airs variés for clarinet & viola (André 1798. Sieber). 3 Trios d'Airs variés for 2 clarinets & viola (Sieber. c.1798). 75 Suites for wind orchestra (Boyer. Imbault. Leduc).

SONDERSHAUSEN, Duke (Friedrich Karl) Gunther I. Sondershausen, 5 Dec 1760-1837 Apr 22, Sondershausen. German. See OV.

SONNENBERG. German. He was principal clarinet for Jullien's winter seasons at Covent Garden, London, in 1844 and 1845. On 30th April 1847 at Winterton House he played in a trio for flute, clarinet & horn by Anton Wittek, with the composer playing the horn and Wustemann flute. In 1849 he toured with Jullien and did a series of concerts with him at Brighton in October 1850. He stepped down to second clarinet when Wuille came in as first, for Jullien's summer season at the Surrey Gardens in 1852 and his American tour in 1853.

SPADINA, Antonio. Como, 1822-? Italian. On 12th May 1833, aged only eleven, he performed in public at Como.

Work: Fantasia on Verdi's *La Traviata* (Ricordi).

SPÄTH, Andreas. Rossach (near Coburg), 9 Oct 1790-1876 Apr 26, Gotha. German. He had his early musical instruction from J. Georg Walter at Rossach. In 1810 he became a member of the court wind band at Coburg, and went with them to the wars of 1814/1815. From 1814 he began to compose a considerable amount, particularly for wind band, although he had had no formal instruction. In 1816 he was taken to Vienna by the Prince of Coburg and here had some lessons in composition from Riotte. He left his employment at Coburg in 1821 and went to Morges in Switzerland as an organist. From this period date most of his compositions for clarinet, a number of which he performed during the winter of 1831/2 at Lausanne. In 1833 he moved to Neuchâtel as music director and in 1838 returned to Coburg as concert master.

Works: Concerto. Concertino. Concertstück. Symphonie Concertante op.103 for 2 clarinets or oboe & clarinet (Schott 1828 – BoLM, ZAM). Divertissement op.91 sur une Romance française (André). Elégie op.178 (Schott c.1840 – LRAM). Fantaisie on an Air of Mozart op.119. Introduction & Variations op.104 on a Theme of Mozart (Schott). Introduction & Variations op.133 on a favorite Romance from Weber's *Preciosa* (André 1830 – ZAM). 2nd Potpourri op.77 (André c.1835 – LRAM). 3rd Potpourri op.105 on themes from Boieldieu & Nicolo (Schott). Scène chantante sur deux airs suisses op.113 (Schott 1831). Trois mélodies op.196 (André c.1849 – LRAM). Trois nocturnes op.175 (Schott – BaU). Potpourris ops.39 & 98 for 2 clarinets (André 1827 – ZAM). Variations ops.69 & 75 for clarinet & strings (André). Airs variés for clarinet & violin with orchestra or string quartet. Nonet for wind & strings, dedicated to Prince Karl Egon III of Fürstenberg (1840. Ms. – BrBC). "Thro' the Fields mid' Flowrets", Alpenlied op.167 for soprano & clarinet (Wessel 1857 – LBL).

Bibliography:

SCHLEDER, Hermann – "Andreas Späth." MGG.

SPIESS. Two brothers of this name were clarinettists in 1802 in the court orchestra at Brunswick, where in 1804 they performed a double concerto. From about 1809 to 1812 they played in the court orchestra at Kassel.

SPINA, Guglielmo. 1823-1893, Rome. Italian. He was a fine teacher at the St Cecilia Academy in Rome.

SPINDLER. English. He played with Platt in the orchestra for the Theatre Royal, Edinburgh. They had a Benefit on 24th May 1827 at which they performed a Scottish Air with Variations for 2 clarinets.

SPITZ, Peter Dominik. In 1781 and 1782 he was second clarinet in the court orchestra of the Elector of Trevès, at Coblenz-Ehrenbreitstein.

SPONHEIMER, H. Conrad. At the opening of the Paris Conservatoire in 1795 he was made a professor of the second class for solfège. From 1800 to 1802 he taught the clarinet and in 1801 was a member of the committee called to discuss Lefèvre's tutor.

Work: Concerto op.8 in F (Gombart 1803).

(B–H). **SPRINGER.** He was well-esteemed as a clarinet and basset-horn player and as a composer. It is possible he was the son of Vincent Springer. He was first employed in the court orchestra at Stuttgart. From there in 1835 he visited Mannheim, where they said his playing had much dexterity but that his tone was hard in the loud passages. By 1836 he had moved to Frankfurt a. M. to become a member of the theatre orchestra and remained there until 1834 or later.

His concerts, all for Frankfurt's Museum Society unless otherwise stated, included the following: . 1835 – concert at Mannheim. 1836 – 5th February, unspecified concertante. 1837 – 24th February, Concertino by Peter von Winter. 1838 – 12th January, variations for basset-horn (probably his own). 1839 – Mozart's Quintet K581 and a "concertino" by Crusell at Frankfurt, though not for the Museum Society. 1841 – 22nd January, his own Fantasie for clarinet. 5th February, his own variations for clarinet, also the clarinet obligato to his own composition "Der Hirten Winterlied" with Herr (?) Jungman. 1842 – 18th February his own variations for basset-horn. 1843 – his own variations for basset-horn at Hamburg; they praised the composition as well as his playing. March, a "very good" basset-horn concerto at Weimar, in a concert with military band.

Works: Fantasie. Variations. "Der Hirten Winterlied" for voice and clarinet. Variations for basset-horn.

(B–H). **SPRINGER, Vincent.** Jung-Bunzlau (near Prague), 1760-? Czech. See OV. He was the son of a music director, whom Mooser thinks may have been Dominik Springer. Dominik was music director, violinist and composer at the St Petersburg Court from 1760 to 1772. From 1783 to 1796 he was a commissionaire at the Imperial Theatre in Prague. Vincent learnt the clarinet from David, probably in St Petersburg. In the 1770s he learnt the basset-horn in Hungary, and by 1781 was back in St Petersburg. Early in 1782 he performed with David in Berlin and they then went on to Lübeck. In November Springer introduced the basset-horn to Hamburg and played a concerto on it there in December. In 1783 Dworschak joined Springer and David for a tour of Germany. It is possible that Springer then went back to Prague, for David went off on his own. In 1785 they were together again in Vienna. As they had fallen on hard times the freemasons of Vienna organised concerts in October and December to raise funds for them. The following year they found employment with Baron Hochberg and lived on his estate at Plogwitz in Silesia. Here they taught the Krause brothers to play clarinet and basset-horn. Springer visited Berlin in 1787 and then Leipzig where, on 17th December, he was joined by David and the cellist Möller for a performance at the Gewandhaus of a work for 2 basset-horns and cello. On 3rd January 1788, again at the Gewandhaus, Springer played a basset-horn obligato in a Scena by Reichardt, for Mme Schicht. From 1788 to 1792 he was a member of the Bentheim-Steinfürt Court. During the summer of 1790 he travelled with David and Dworschak through Germany, northern Italy and Holland. In the summers of 1789 and 1791 the trio performed at the Vauxhall Gardens in London. On 1st April 1791 Springer and Dworschak performed a concertante for 2 basset-horns at a Haydn-Salomon concert in the Hanover Square Rooms. At some time during 1791 Springer was at Amsterdam.

By 1793 he had settled in Amsterdam as a teacher and numbered amongst his pupils Christiani. He married the daughter of Joseph Schmitt, a well-known bookseller and publisher in the town. Schmitt had been a Cistercian monk, but came out of the order, married a rich Dutch lady and set up his business. On Springer's marrying his daughter he handed the shop over to his son-in-law. Springer carried on until, a few years later, troubles under French occupation forced him to close the shop down. (It was reopened some time later under the management of J.J. Hummel). The family fled, losing most of their possessions. Father Schmitt became theatre director at Frankfurt, but Springer was unable to find permanent employment. He travelled about through Germany and in 1801 was in Italy before finally, according to Schilling, buying a small property in Bohemia. Steiner of Vienna published some marches and other pieces for military band by Springer. The basset-horn he used was in G, with 7 keys and a diatonic extension.

STAAB, Adalbert. Langenberg, 22 Aug 1813-? In 1830 he toured through Germany and Switzerland as a soloist. He then settled for a while at Düsseldorf, where he came into contact with Mendelssohn. In 1836 he had become a music teacher at Unna in Westphalia. By 1851 he was a music director at Hamm and had given up the clarinet.

STAATS, C.L. American. He was solo clarinet in Sousa's band in 1892, the year of its first tour. He directed the Bostonia Sextet Club.

(B–H). **STADLER, Antonius.** Vienna, 4 Nov 1791-? Austrian. He was the son of Anton Stadler and became first basset-horn player at the Theater an der Wien.

(B–H). **STADLER, Anton (Paul).** Bruck-on-Leitha, 28 June 1753-1812 June 15, Vienna. Austrian. See OV. He was the brother of Johann Stadler. Much new information has come to light on the Stadler family, a great deal of it due to the researches of Karl Maria Pisarowitz. The parents of Anton and Johann were of Hungarian-Jewish stock, the father Joseph (Döllersheim, 7 Mar 1719-c.1781 or 2) being a musician and cobbler, the mother Sophie (1723-1790 June 4, Vienna) a midwife. They were married in 1743 at Vienna and their first son Leopold Lorenz was born in 1745. After this they led a wandering life, coming in 1753 to the small castle-town of Bruck on the south-eastern side of Vienna, and here Anton was born. By 1755 they were back in Vienna for the birth of Johann. At some time they also had a daughter Josepha who died when she was fourteen. The assumption that Therese Stadler was a daughter of this marriage is incorrect.

The brothers received their initial musical training from their father and in the 1770s became musician-servants to Count Dimitri Galitsin, Russian Ambassador at Vienna. From 1779 they were employed on a freelance basis at the Imperial Court. In 1781 they sought better employment and on 6th November wrote to Ignatz von Beecké, music director at Wallerstein, offering themselves as clarinet, basset-horn, oboe, violin and viola players. They wrote also on behalf of other musicians, who were then out of work through the disbandment of Count Pálffy's music. One of these was Griesbacher (q.v.), with whom they were prepared to play an assortment of duets and trios. The letter, quoted by Saam, says they can obtain a recommendation from their patroness, the Countess of Thün. The Emperor Joseph II, getting wind of this, took quick action to secure them for himself and on 8th February 1782 an Imperial Court document was drawn up which read: "The two Stadler brothers, who play the clarinet, are appointed to the court orchestra, because they are quite often necessary, and otherwise they might find employment elsewhere or even travel." They were no sooner installed than new clarinets in C were bought for them at a cost of 102 gulden 24 kreutzer each. These had *pièces de rechange* to turn them into B flat instruments when required.

After his visit to Russia in 1794 Anton Stadler travelled to Hamburg with the violinist Jakob Scheller. Scheller was a drunkard and had had to sell his violin to meet his debts. At each town they came to it was necessary to borrow an instrument in order that he could play for his supper. Scheller was a companion after Stadler's own heart and, although he had considerable talent, preferred to lark it on his fiddle, loosening the bow and imitating an old woman, a bassoon, etc.. Stadler gave concerts at Hamburg on 29th November and 20th December 1794, Scheller taking part in the second. He advertised himself as "Chamber Musician to the King of Prussia" and announced that he would perform on his extended clarinet. Leopold Kozeluch, Mozart's successor at the Imperial Court in Vienna, wrote a Concerto in E flat (VNB) for Stadler's clarinet.

Elizabeth Stadler was not Anton's wife, as Deutsch assumed, but his sister-in-law. Anton married, as "gentleman's musician", Francisca Bichler (Pichler) on 12th October 1780. They lived first with his brother at no.1248 Schottenbastei and then moved in 1785 to no.1126 Bürgerspital. Between the years 1781 and 1791 Francisca bore him eight children, two only surviving infancy. Anton's mother acted as midwife on two occasions. There seems little doubt that the children succumbed to acute under-nourishment, for their dissolute father was always short of money. The two who survived were Michael-Joannes, whose god-father was Michael Puchberg, and who was apprenticed to an instrument maker, and Antonius (q.v.) who became a basset-horn player at the Theater an der Wein.

When Anton drew up his "Musick Plan" for Count Festetics on 10th July 1800 he was to all appearances a reformed character. This was an illusion and the following year he left his wife and went off with their maid-servant, Friederika Kabel. He took Friederika to live in the Landstrasse suburb, and here he died in 1812 of consumption. He left no will and only the following effects: I iron-coloured cloth "Kaput", 2 pairs of boots, 1 pair of shoes, 2 round hats, I cloth cap, 3 old shirts, 4 cloth bags, I writing desk and some music.

Works: 3 Caprices for solo clarinet, dedicated to Count John Charles Esterházy of Galántha (Cappi. Diabelli. Haslinger. Magazin de l'imprimerie chimique – VGM). 10 Variations on the air "Müsst ma nix in übel nehma" for solo clarinet (Traeg 1810. Diabelli). Variations sur différens Thêmes favoris (Cappi. Witzendorf). 12 Ländlerische Tänze for 2 clarinets (Cappi). 6 Progressive duettinos (Haslinger). 18 Trios for basset-horns (VGM). Partitas for 6 wind instruments.

Bibliography:

CROLL, Gerhard & BIRSAK, Kurt – "Anton Stadlers 'Bassett-klarinette', und das 'Stadler-Quintett' KV581." OM. 1/1969.

HESS, Ernst – "Die ursprüngliche Gestalt des Klarinettenkonzertes KV622." MJB. 1967.

KROLL, Oskar – "Mozarts Klarinettist." DO. 15/1932.

MAYNARD, William – "Anton Stadler: Composer." WW. January 1968.

PISAROWITZ, Karl Maria – " 'Müasst ma nix in übel aufnehma . . .' Beitragsversuche zu einer Gebrüder-Stadler-Biographie." MISM. February 1971.

(B–H). **STADLER, Johann (Nepomuk Franz).** Vienna, 6 May 1755-1804 May 2, Vienna. Austrian. See OV. He was the brother of Anton Stadler. At the end of May 1783 he married Elizabeth Grittner and during the next seventeen years she bore him seven girls and four boys. During the last years of Johann's life he and his family moved from lodging to lodging in direst poverty. Elizabeth was brought to court for debt in 1799 and Johann in 1801. Finally Johann succumbed to typhus in 1804 and died in hospital. Elizabeth died in 1811, aged only 49 and possessed of a mere 219 gulden 55 kreutzer. Three children survived their parents: Barbara (1790-1867?); Johann (1796-?), apprenticed to the cloth trade; and Magdalena, (1800-?).

Bibliography:

PISAROWITZ, Karl Maria – " 'Müasst ma nix in übel aufnehma . . .' Beitragsversuche zu einer Gebrüder-Stadler-Biographie." MISM. February 1971.

STAPS, Jean M.F. Born at Ebersdorf – died Brussels? His beautiful tone won him compliments from Mendelssohn, Lindpaintner and Spohr. He played for a short time in the court orchestras at Greiz, Weimar, Eisenach and Wiesbaden. Although Spohr tried to persuade him to join his orchestra at one stage Staps went to live in Belgium in 1833. In 1834 he was solo clarinet for the Regiment of Guides and in 1836 became their assistant conductor. He conducted the Brussels Wind Society and in 1850 was made assistant music director to the King. His daughter Amélie became a well-known pianist.

(B–H). **STARK, Robert.** Klingenthal, 19 Sept 1847-1922 Oct 29, Würzburg. German. He was a fine teacher and performer on the clarinet, using an instrument of the Baermann type with modifications. He learnt the clarinet at the age of five from his father, who was an instrument-maker, and later studied various brass instruments. Before he was fourteen he had become a bugler in the band of a Saxon infantry brigade and fought with them in the war of 1866. From October 1868 to April 1869 he had an intensive spell of clarinet instruction under Friedrich Lauterbach at the Dresden Conservatoire and then made this his main instrument. After fighting in the 1870/1871 war he came out of the army and joined the orchestra at Chemnitz under Müller-Berghaus. The latter engaged him in 1873 for the Wiesbaden orchestra. In 1881 Stark was appointed teacher of clarinet, basset-horn, piano and ensemble music at the Royal Music School in Würzburg. Here he wrote most of his great study works and he also organised a large clarinet ensemble. Between 1881 and 1885 he was often engaged for concerts at Meiningen and at Bayreuth, where he probably played with Mühlfeld. In 1904 he was made a Royal Professor at Würzburg. He retired in 1919 and gave a farewell concert on 6th October in which he performed a Brahms sonata with his daughter Ella and the Mozart Quintet K581 with the Schörg Quartet.

Works: Concerto op.4 in E flat (Schmidt). Concerto op.13 in F (Schmidt – LRCM). Concerto op.50 in D minor (Schmidt). Canzone op.41 (Fischer). Lyric Pieces op.19 (Schmidt). Romanze op.1 (Schmidt). Sonata in E flat, 4 Grössere Duette (Schmidt). Sonata in G minor for 2 clarinets & basset-horn (Schmidt). Serenade op.55 in E flat for 2 clarinets, basset-horn & bass clarinet (Schmidt).

Concertante op.44 for wind quintet (Oertel). Präludium & Rondino for 3 basset-horns. Grosse theoretisch-praktische Clarinett-Schule op.49 (Schmidt 1892) – this includes instruction for basset-horn and bass clarinet; it was awarded a prize at the Chicago Exhibition of 1893. Der hohe Schule des Clarinett-Spiels op.51 (Schmidt 1900). Die Kunst der Transposition ops.28 & 29 (Fischer. Rahter).

Bibliography:

KROLL, Oskar – "Robert Stark." DMMZ. 29th October 1932.

STAUTZ, Karl. ?-1844 German. He played in the Hesse-Darmstadt court orchestra from 1817 to 1830. He taught the clarinet to Ludwig III, then heir apparent, and was decorated with the Order of Ludwig, second class. He also played the flute, violin and cello.

STAVELOT. From 1802 he was first clarinet for the Société du Concert at Neuchâtel.

(B–H). **STEFFENS, Friedrich.** Soest or Werden, 6 Dec 1803-1849 Feb 3, Detmold. He was first a clarinettist and non-commissioned officer in a military band at Münster. In 1824 he was engaged as principal clarinet in the court orchestra and the Leopold-Corps at Detmold. He experimented with the tone quality of the basset-horn and travelled considerably to gather information from other players. After a long illness he was forced to give up the clarinet for the violin, though at his death he was still designated court clarinettist.

Bibliography:

MÜLLER-DOMBOIS, Richard – *Die Fürstlich Lippische Hofkapelle.* Regensburg 1972.

STEINER, F.W. German. He was clarinettist to Baron Albert de Rothschild in Vienna. On 5th January 1892 he gave the first Vienna performance of Brahms' Quintet op.115 with the Rosé Quartet.

STIASSNY, Hans. ?-1891 Feb 28, Vienna. He was engaged for the Vienna Philharmonic Orchestra in 1884.

STIÉVENARD, E.H. French. He was a pupil under Rose at the Paris Conservatoire, gaining First Prize in 1894. He was playing at the Opéra Comique in 1918.

STÖTZER (STÖLZER). German. He was a clarinettist and then music director to the court orchestra at Coburg from about

1800 to 1818. He gave the following solo performances at Leipzig: 1800 – 13th May, concerto by Westerhoff; they said he possessed "a pleasant tone with truly great dexterity and precision." 1818 – 19th April, concerto by Späth. Stötzer was the dedicatee of Späth's 2nd Potpourri. A violinist and music director of the same name mentioned at Coburg in 1835 and 1841 was probably a son.

Works: Concerto in E flat (Breitkopf & Härtel 1785/7). Adagio in B flat (Breitkopf & Härtel 1785/7).

STOHWASSER. German. He took up residence in England and in 1819 played Weber's Concertino at the Reading Festival. In 1825 he succeeded Willman as professor of clarinet at the Royal Academy of Music, London.

STONE. He flourished as a clarinettist at Boston, Massachusetts from 1793. He also played the flute and oboe.

STRADTMANN, Ludwig Friedrich Carl. Oldenburg 29 Sept 1855-? German. He became second clarinet in the Leipzig Gewandhaus Orchestra in 1881.

STÜBER, Joseph. Oberhasselbach, 3 Oct 1766-1837 Jan 12, Ludwigslust. Austrian. He went to Ludwigslust in 1798 and entered the Royal Guards. From 1808 he was second clarinet in the Mecklenburg-Schwerin court orchestra, retiring from this in 1829.

SÜSSMILCH. German. He was second clarinet in the orchestra at Hamburg in 1846.

SUNDELIN, August. c.1785-1842 Sept 6, Berlin. He is chiefly known for his didactic works on orchestration. He also made some experiments with combination clarinets. In 1804 he became a member of the court opera orchestra at Berlin and in 1827 was made a Chamber Musician. He had to give up playing in 1829 because of a throat ailment and was given a pension for his twenty five years service. For a short time in 1830 he was music director at the theatre in Königsberg. In 1832 his brother Karl, who was a professor of medicine at Berlin, wrote *Aerzlichen Rathgeber für Musiktreibende* (Medical Advice for Professional Musicians) "from the accounts of the Royal pensioned chamber musician August Sundelin." The book contains useful, at times alarming, information and offers remedies for complaints. August became editor of the newspaper *Der Deutsch und sein Vaterland* in 1833.

SWOBODA, August. 1787-1856 May 17, Prague. Czech. He was the nephew of Farník and became his pupil. For many years, from about 1805, he played second clarinet to his uncle in Count Johann Pachta's orchestra and at the Strahov Monastery Church, where they won warm applause. Later he became director of an infantry band and about 1826 went to live in Vienna as a music teacher. Here he had several didactic works published which made a considerable stir. In old age he returned to Prague. He may be the father of Franz Swoboda.

SWOBODA, Franz. Born at Prague. Czech. He was probably the son of August Swoboda. From 1828 to 1834 he was a pupil under Farník at the Prague Conservatoire and played at the following puplic concerts of the Conservatoire: 1833 – 15th March, Müller's Concertante with Anton Sykora, another of Farník's pupils. 1834 – Polonaise (from the Andante & Polonaise?) by Tausch.

SYRINEK (SIŘINEK), Adalbert. Born at Prague. Czech. He was a pupil under Pisařovic at the Prague Conservatoire from 1858 to 1864. At a Conservatoire concert on 25th March 1863 he performed the first movement of Späth's Symphonie Concertante with Wenzel Kozel, another of Pisařovic's pupils. He became principal clarinet in the Vienna Philharmonic Orchestra and a member of the court orchestra from 1879 until he was pensioned in 1904. On 17th December 1891 he performed Brahms' Trio op.114 with the composer and Ferdinand Hellmesberger, in the Hellmesberger Concerts.

TADRA, Wenzel. Weltrup, 1828-1853 Jan 6, Hanover. Czech. He was second clarinet in the court orchestra at Hanover from 15th August 1852 until his untimely death on the following 6th January.

TAMM, K.M. (G?). German. He is probably the "Tanne" whom Mendel lists as a famous clarinet player. He played in the Berlin court opera orchestra from 1818 until 1858 when he received a pension. He also taught at the Friedrich Charitable Institute, where Bolsius was his pupil. In July 1818 he took part in a quartet for flute, clarinet, bassoon & horn by Mengal in a concert at the Royal York Lodge. In November of the same year he played an Adagio & Polonaise for 2 clarinets by Krommer with Pfaffe. In 1844 he visited Dresden and made the acquaintance of Kotte.

TAUSCH. German. He was the father of the pianist

Julius Tausch (born Dessau 1827). It is not known if they were related to the famous Tausch family. Tausch father was a Chamber Musician in the Dessau court orchestra from 1822 to about 1849. In 1822 he performed a concerto by Krommer at Dessau and in 1838 Weber's Concertino at Wittenberg. In 1841 he and his daughter, who was a contralto, performed at the Dessau Subscription Concerts.

(B–H). **TAUSCH, Franz (Wilhelm).** Heidelberg, 26 Dec 1762-1817 Feb 9, Berlin. German. See OV. Whilst under the patronage of the Queen Mother at Berlin, Tausch had a Benefit on 9th February 1793 which was a brilliant occasion and established him firmly in the forefront of the city's musical life. Much new information on the compositions of Tausch has come to light, a great deal of it due to the researches of Peter Clinch. Clinch deduces that Tausch used a 5-key clarinet, because of the almost total avoidance of c'sharp in his compositions. He also thinks that Tausch played with the reed underneath, because the wide leaps and many fast repeated notes in his compositions, together with his reputedly "soft, caressing tone and stylish delivery" could not have been achieved the other way about. If the assumption is correct, then Tausch was one of the first to use this method and would undoubtedly have passed it on to his pupils, who included both Heinrich Baermann and Crusell.

Works: Concerto in E flat (Hummel 1796. André. Ms. copy in LBL, Ms. solo part in UUB, Ms. orchestral parts in PrNM). Concerto op.7 in E flat (c.1796-1806. André. Schlesinger c.1810-1817. Ms. copies – BDS, MarPKS). Second Concerto for 2 clarinets op.26, dedicated by the composer's widow to Friedrich Willhelm III (Schlesinger c.1818 – BDS, BIM, EiKEM, VNB). Concerto op.27 in B flat for 2 clarinets, dedicated to His Imperial Majesty the Grand Duke Alexander of all the Russias (By 1797. Hummel 1800 – MuUB, copy lacking first solo part in LRCM. Schlesinger). Andante (Adagio) & Polonaise in B flat, dedicated to Count Henry LXIII of Reuss-Plaen (see Quartet in B flat) (c.1807-1810. Peters 1818 – BDS, SKMA, VGM). 3 Duos (Schlesinger). 6 Duos (Kühn, Dunker & Humbolt. Werckmeisten 1805). 12 Waltzes for 2 clarinets (Brietkopf & Härtel 1807). 12 Duos from Himmel's *Fauchon* (Bureau des arts et d'industrie, Leipzig 1813). Duet for horn & clarinet (see Crusell article). 3 Duos op.21 for clarinet & bassoon (Schlesinger 1812 – BIM, TBMAM). Trios for 2 clarinets & bassoon. Very Easy Quartet op.30 in B flat (probably a very early work. Schott c.1820/1 – EiKEM, SpPLM). Quartet in B flat, dedicated to Prince Henry LXIII of Reuss-Plaen (André 1820 – FSU, LRAM, MiBC, SKMA, WLC). 13 Pieces op.22 for 2 clarinets, horn & bassoon in 2 suites, dedicated to Count Charles de Brühl (Bochsa Père c.1814/16. Schlesinger. Haslinger. Tausch used an Adagio from this for the slow movement of his op.26). Trios for 3 basset-horns. 6 Quartets op.5 for 2 basset-horns, 2 bassoons & 2 horns ad lib, dedicated to Captain von Bredow (By 1797. Dunker & Humbolt. Werckmeisten 1805 – CSL, ZAM. Captain von Bredow was a well-known patron of music, amateur bassoonist and composer of a Concertino for basset-horn).

Bibliography:

Report. BMZ. 1793, ps.7 & 194.

CLINCH, Peter – "Concerto no.3 in E flat for Clarinet & Orchestra by Franz Tausch – An Annotated Performing Edition with Historical Commentary." Master's thesis, University of Western Australia 1973.

KÖHLER, Karl-Heinz – "Franz Tausch." MGG.

(B–H). **TAUSCH, Friedrich Wilhelm.** Berlin, 1790-1845 Apr 29, Berlin. German. See OV. He was the son of Franz Tausch. He used his influence with Meyerbeer to get the salaries of all the Berlin court orchestra raised in 1843. Writing from his home at no.40 Jerusalem Street on 14th November he thanks Meyerbeer profusely for achieving this, saying that in his own case, as he had played first clarinet for twenty five years without a rise, he feels fully justified. Unfortunately Tausch did not live long to benefit from the rise. In June 1844 he was thrown from his horse, broke his collarbone and was unable to play at Court for three months. The following April he died from consumption. Like his father, Friedrich Wilhelm was a remarkably fine teacher and numbered amongst his pupils Karl Eichhorst and August Schubert. The following works were dedicated to him: Ludwig Blum's Concertino op.123 and Lindpaintner's Concertino op.41.

F.W. Tausch's principal concerts, all at Berlin unless otherwise stated, were as follows: 1804 – 19th February, Winter's Concertante for violin, clarinet, basset-horn & bassoon, in which he played basset-horn and his father the clarinet. 1805 – 20th July, a double concerto with Georg Reinhardt. 21st December, a double concerto by and with his father. 1806 – 30th March, a solo concerto. 1807 – 12th November, Trios for 3 basset-horns by and with his father and Georg Reinhardt. 21st December, a double concerto by and with his father. 1810 – 2nd April, his father's Adagio & Rondo alla Polacca (Andante & Polonaise) – AMZ's report on this says that his tone was clear and round, his delivery sure and ready – and a double concerto by his father with F.A. Bliesener. 1811 – 29th November, a concerto by Lefèvre. 1812 – 6th January, a double concerto by and with his father, which earned exceptional applause. 1814 – 17th December, Beethoven's Wind Quintet. 20th December, a concerto by Spohr. 1815 – 26th February, a concerto by his father. 26th November, a concerto, "with beautiful tone." 1817 – 13th October, in the Saale der Stadt Paris, his father's Adagio & Rondo. 1818 – 11th February in the Saale der Loge Royal-York, a concerto for flute & clarinet by Friedrich Ludwig Seidel with Johann Wilhelm Gabrielsky. 27th November, a concerto and variations (probably op.20) by Heinrich Baermann. 1819 – February, a concerto. 1827 – a double concerto with his pupil Eichhorst. 1829 – at the Halle Festival, a double concertino by A. Müller (this is probably an error for "F." – Friedrich – Müller) with Pfaffe, which was well received. 1830 – Weber's Concertino. 1831 – Rondo by Joseph Panny, in a concert given by the composer.

(B–H). **TAUSCH, Jacob.** ?-1803 Nov 23, Munich. German. See OV. He was the father of Franz and Joseph Tausch. He also played the violin. He belonged to a very musical family at Heidelberg. His father was also called Jacob and played the violin, viola, bass and drums in the orchestra at the catholic church. Jacob senior was employed first in 1740 without pay, but in 1746 received a salary. In 1757 he deserted his wife and family of seven and went "to foreign parts." In 1758 his son Jacob was appointed "second wind player" in the church orchestra, the "first wind player" being an uncle. The following year, because of his father's continued absence, Jacob junior was given an increased salary of 15 florins. His great moment came in 1764 when the Elector Carl Theodor visited Heidelberg and heard him play the clarinet. As a result, he was engaged the following year for the court orchestra at Mannheim. In 1777 he moved with the Elector's Court to Munich and remained there until he retired from the orchestra about 1787.

Bibliography:

STEIN, Fritz – *Geschichte des Musikwesens in Heidelberg bis zum Ende des 18. Jährhunderts.* Heidelberg 1921.

TAUSCH, Joseph. Heidelberg, 25 Dec 1763-? German. See OV. He was the younger brother of Franz Tausch. He became a member of the Munich court orchestra in 1779 and when Franz left in 1789 he took his place as first clarinet. He is probably the "Johann Tausch" whom Bihrle records as playing for the Subscription Concerts in 1811 and 1812. He was a fine teacher, his pupils Georg Werle and Schönche becoming members of the court orchestra. Like his brother, Joseph became excessively stout.

TAUT. German. He was a town musician at Nuremberg, where he first performed as a clarinet soloist in 1820. In 1823 he played Variations by Baron de Boyneburgk. A younger Taut who played the horn at Nuremberg was probably either a brother or son.

(B–H). **TEIMER.** Mendel lists him as a well-known basset-horn player.

THEMSCHE, Louis van. Meirelbeke, 9 June 1786-1847 Jan 5, Ghent. Belgian. He fought with a French military band in the Spanish, German and Russian campaigns. Later he became music director for the 17th division of the Dutch army garrisoned at Ghent and in 1831 for the 4th regiment of the line. He became first clarinet at the Grand Theatre. When Ghent Conservatoire was opened in 1835 Themsche was made clarinet professor, with a salary of 400 francs. He held the post until his death.

THIELEMANN. He played in the Stockholm court orchestra from 1786 until about 1802.

THOMAS, Cadwallader. 15 Nov 1838-1899 Mar 1. English. He was a remarkably fine clarinettist in the Coldstream Guards, becoming bandmaster for them from 1880 to 1896, when he received a pension. He was known outside the army as well and at the time he joined the Royal Society of Musicians in 1863, was playing in the stage band at Drury Lane.

THOMAS, Frances. ?-1925 Nov 7. English. She may have been the daughter of Cadwallader Thomas. She was a pupil under Lazarus at the Royal Academy of Music. It was still considered somewhat improper for a woman to appear in the orchestra at that institution and she was not allowed to play at rehearsals unless Lazarus himself was present. She played second to him in the Crystal Palace Orchestra and first, with a Miss Pamphion on second, in the English Ladies Orchestra. As a soloist she acquired a reputation for good tone and execution, and from 1878 she often played at concerts in London and Birmingham. On 25th February 1879 she played Weber's Concertino and Beethoven's Septet in Hampstead.

THURSTON, Frederick (John). Lichfield, 21 Sept 1901-1953 Dec 12, London. English. See OV. Elizabeth Maconchy dedicated her Concertino of 1945 to him.

Recordings not listed in OV:

Brahms – Sonata op.120, no.2. Decca G-25722.
Ferguson, Howard – Octet op.4. Decca K 1095/6/7.
Galuppi/Craxton – Largo & Allegro Giocoso. Decca 25728.

Work: The Clarinet (Hawkes 1939).

Writings:

"Clarinet Tone." WYB. 1940/1.
"The Orchestra looks at the Audience." PMM. 1/1946.
"The Clarinet and its Music." PMM. 6/1948.
Clarinet Technique. London 1956.

Bibliography:

REES, C.B. – "Personality Corner." PMM. 6/1948.

TIRRY (TYRI), Anton. 1757-? Hungarian. He learnt the clarinet from Michael Quallenberg at Mannheim about 1772 to 1777. In 1778 he performed in Italy with great success. In 1780 he returned through Germany to Vienna and became Chamber Musician and first clarinet to Prince Anton Grassalkovics. On 20th October 1785 he performed at the Leipzig Gewandhaus. In 1787 he went on an extended tour through Germany. He spent some time in Princess Elizabeth's Hauskapelle at Freiburg in Breisgau and then became Chamber Musician to the Duke of Würtemberg at Stuttgart. In 1792 he performed at Berlin and was warmly applauded. By 1798 he had moved to St Petersburg and was still there in 1800.

TOMASZEWSKI. Polish. He was well-known as a clarinettist in the eighteenth century.

TOULOUSE, M. de. French. He gave a concert at the Leipzig Gewandhaus on 8th March 1796, playing a concerto by "Michel" (Yost).

TOURNEUR, Georges. 1872-? Belgian. After gaining a First Prize at the Brussels Conservatoire he held the post of solo clarinet for the Brussels Popular Concerts, the Ysaye Concerts and at the Monnaie Theatre. He then went to Liège to play for the New Concerts and became clarinet professor at the Liège Royal Conservatoire. Later he became a conductor in Hainault.

Works: 2 Concertos.

TRETBACH (TRETBAR?). German. He was probably the father of F. Tretbar. He played in the Brunswick orchestra under Spohr, who composed a concert-piece in the form of a Recit.& Adagio for him about 1804 to 5. The only known performance of the work was by C. Mahr, a pupil of Hermstedt's, in 1821. Spohr utilized it for his violin concerto op.28.

TRETBAR, F. German. He was probably a son of the above. Schumann described him as an excellent player. Tretbar became a pupil of Wilhelm Barth at Leipzig about 1820 and from 1823 until 1829 was a member of the Leipzig orchestra. He then became a Chamber Musician at Brunswick, where he acquired a reputation as one of the best clarinettists of his day. He remained at the Brunswick Court for the rest of his life, although by 1865 he had stepped down to second clarinet.

His solo concerts, at Leipzig unless otherwise stated, included the following: 1823 – 3rd April, unspecified solos. 1824 – 26th February, Spohr's First Concerto. 1825 – 10th February, unspecified solos. 21st November, a concertino by Henrich Baermann. 1826 – 9th February, unspecified solos. 29th October at Berlin, Lindpaintner's Concerto. 1827 – 11th January, Rondo by Lindpaintner. 29th September, Concerto by Lindpaintner. 1828 – Lindpaintner's Concerto. 1829 – 2nd April, a concerto by Spohr. 29th September, a concerto by Iwan Müller. 20th November for the Frankfurt Museum Society, Iwan Müller's Concertino. Solos at Magdeburg. Compositions by Iwan Müller and Lindpaintner at Bremen. 1834 – September at the Weimar Court, Concertino by Lindpaintner and Variations by Berr, "with extraordinary ease, strength and sweetness." 1835 – 12th June for the Elbe Festival at Dessau, Concertino by Lindpaintner. 20th & 23rd October, solos at the Halle Festival. 1837 – concert at Lübeck. 1838 – at Hamburg, Variations for clarinet & cello by Sebastian Lee, with the composer. 1839 – at Brunswick, Fantasie by Klein (Thomas?). 1840 – 1st January at the Gewandhaus in a concert which he shared with Elisa Meerti, Maurer's Concertino and Klein's Fantasie; the audience gave Tretbar a great welcome back and he was hailed as the best clarinettist in Germany. In the Royal College of Music, London, is a letter from Mendelssohn negotiating with Tretbar over the date of this concert and saying he is looking forward to hearing his "magnificent talent" again.

TRIEBEL. He was a member of the theatre orchestra at Frankfurt a. M. in 1863.

TRIPP. English. At the Drury Lane Miscellaneous Concerts on 5th March he played the obligato for Mozart's "Parto!" and in 1832 that for Bishop's "The Ray of Hope can cheer the Heart."

TROPIANSKI, Konstanty. Wilna, 1820-1877, Warsaw (?). Polish. In the 1840s he toured Italy, France, England and Germany as a virtuoso on clarinet and violin. In 1850 he returned to Warsaw and became very popular as a clarinettist. He then went to Moscow, where he performed as soloist and also conducted the Aljabĕv Orchestra. Later he travelled to Siberia and organised concerts in Tobolsk, Jrkutsk and Kiachta. In 1860 he returned once more to Warsaw.

Works: Pieces for voice, clarinet & violin.

TROU (TROUE). French. He was the only clarinettist at the Cirque Olympique at Paris in 1824 and 1825. In 1827 and 1828 he was second clarinet at the Odéon and living at no.3 rue Marmousets. During the following two years the Odéon dispensed with the normal theatre orchestra and employed a basically wind band. The players consisted of 1 violin, 11 clarinets, 2 flutes, 5 horns, 2 trumpets, 3 trombones, 4 bassoons, 2 serpents, 3 double-basses, 1 big drum, harp, kettle-drum, and triangle. The list of clarinettists was as follows: Derevel, Trou, Blin, Marmurier, Guil (probably Guyot?), Hustinoy, Lecerf, Cassignol, Kroolle, Mercier and Bertrand.

TROYER, Count Ferdinand. Brno, 1 Feb 1780-1851 July 23, Vienna. Austrian. See OV. On 2nd March 1817 he played the obligato to Mozart's "Parto!" for the Vienna Philharmonic Society at the Large Ridotto Room. His "sensitive, extremely tender handling" of the instrument was commented on.

TULY, Francesco. Italian. He was first clarinet at the Teatro la Pergola in Florence from 1791 to 1795.

TURBAN, Charles (Paul). Strasbourg, 3 Oct 1845-1905, Paris. French. He learnt the clarinet from Klosé at the Paris Conservatoire, gaining a Second Prize in 1864 and a First Prize in 1865. He was solo clarinet at the Théâtre du Gymnase, Théâtre Italien and the Opéra (from 1868). When Taffanel founded the Société des Instruments à Vent in 1879 Turban and Grisez were the clarinettists. Turban also played for the Société des Concerts from 1892 to 1897, with Mimart as his second. He was a professor from 1888 to 1905 at the Conservatoire, where Hamelin was his most famous pupil. The following Conservatoire contest pieces were dedicated to him: Reynaldo Hahn's Sarabande et Thême Varié (1903) and Arthur Coquard's Mélodie et Scherzetto op.68 (1904). Other works dedicated to him were Theodore Gouvy's Sonata and Klosé's

6th Air Varié.

TURGIS. He was first clarinet at the Ambigu Comique in Paris in 1821 and 1822.

TYLER, George. 22 Oct 1835-1878. English. He played in the orchestras for the Philharmonic Society and the Royal Italian Opera (Haymarket), also at the Argyll Rooms. On 16th March 1868 he played the obligato to Mozart's "Parto!" for Natalie Carola at a Philharmonic Society concert. He used simple system ebonite clarinets made in 1862 by Fieldhouse. These had extra keys for forked b flat and forked f'. The tube was in one piece. Tyler was taken ill at rehearsals for the Danreuther/Wagner concerts of 1877 and died, still a young man, the following year. The *Musical Directory* spoke of his death as "an almost irreparable loss." His widow sold his instruments to Julian Egerton, who used them until his own death in 1945 and they are now in the ERC. Tyler joined the Royal Society of Musicians in 1862 and was then living at no.62 Pratt Street, Camden Town. Antony Lamotte (conductor of the dance orchestra at the Argyll Rooms) dedicated a "Grand Irish Fantasia" to Tyler.

Work: Instruction Book (listed in J.G. Brown's *Biographical Dictionary* of 1886, under "G. Tytler").

VAGNY (VAGUI, WAGNY), Pierre Ange. He held positions at Bouvinnes and in the court orchestra at Berlin before settling at Bückeburg, where in 1796 he became music director. He also composed and played the violin.

VALETTE (VALLET), Antoine Nicolas. Saint-Dié, 16 Jan 1787-1865 Aug 24, Metz. French. He was a clarinettist in the theatre orchestra and a member of the Philharmonic Society at Metz. In 1834 he performed a concerto by Berr at Strasbourg.

VAN ACKERE, Constant. Ménin, 1823-? Belgian. In 1837 he studied at the Ghent Conservatoire, probably under Themsche, and in 1840 went to the Brussels Conservatoire to study with Blaes. At some time he also had lessons from Valentin Bender. From 1841 to 1846 he performed as a soloist and after this turned to musical criticism, at which he became well-known. On the death of his father, he gave up criticism to take over the family notary business.

VAN BUGGENHOUT, Emile. Brussels, 1825-? Belgian. He was a pupil at the Brussels Conservatoire, where he won First Prize in 1841. He was solo clarinet for the Royal Wind Band during the reign of Leopold I. In 1852 he began publishing the music journal *Le Metronome.* In 1856 he composed a cantata for the twenty-fifth anniversary of Belgian independence, which earned him a Grand Gold Medal from the King. Later Van Buggenhout moved to Luxembourg. He conducted the Arlon Philharmonic Society and was vice-president of music societies for the province. He composed for wind instruments.

VANDENBOGAERDE, F.L. Ghent, 1832-? Belgian. He studied first at Ghent Conservatoire from 1846 to 1851, gaining a First Prize in the latter year. He then went to the Brussels Conservatoire to study with Blaes and became a laureate here also. He joined Jullien's orchestra and in 1855 was in Scotland and Ireland. From 1856 he was music master of the 9th regiment of the line. He also conducted several orchestras.

Work: Concertino (Lafleur – LBL).

VAN der FINCK, Joannes Christiaan. Amsterdam, 22nd Feb 1828-1902 Mar 14, Amsterdam. Dutch. He was the son of a well-known Amsterdam musician, Christiaan v. d. Finck, who taught him to play the clarinet and piano. At a later stage he had lessons from Christiani. From 1847 to 1852 he was solo clarinet in J.E. Stumpff's orchestra. He also played for the Italian and German theatres and the French Opera. Quite early he became orchestral director of the Eruditio-Musica Sunday Concerts and this led to a distinguished career as conductor. In 1858 he was made assistant director of the Cecilia Society concerts. After he became principal director in 1864 he brought them to a high degree of prosperity.

(B–H). **VANDERHAGEN, Amand (Jean François Joseph).** Antwerp, 1753-1822 July, Paris. Belgian, of German parentage. He is best known for his instructional books on clarinet, flute and oboe. He was the son of an organist and at ten became a choirboy in Antwerp cathedral. He was then sent to Brussels to learn wind instruments from his uncle, A. Vanderhagen, who was principal oboe in Prince Charles of Lorraine's orchestra. Van Malder, another member of this orchestra, taught him composition. By 1783 Vanderhagen had moved to Paris and become first clarinet in the French Guard. Through the auspices of the Prince of Guéméné, he was made conductor of this band in 1788. At the Revolution the band was dissolved but he was invited by Sarrette, with forty four other instrumentalists, to form the band of the National Guard. This became Directoire Guards, then Consular Guards, and by the time the name had been changed again to Imperial Guards he was their assistant conductor. Napoleon honoured Vanderhagen with the Legion of Honour for his services in the Prussian Campaign of 1806/7. At the break-up of the Empire Vanderhagen left the army and became first clarinet at the Théâtre Français, with Péchignier as second. In 1818 he moved down to second, with Hugray on first, and retained this position until he died. His address in 1821 and 1822 was no.23 rue du Dragon.

Vanderhagen's *Méthode nouvelle et raisonnée pour la clarinette* was written for the five-keyed clarinet, played with the reed on top, and was the first tutor to go into technical processes in any detail. There are sections on embouchure, reeds, tone quality and ornaments, all well set out. The music consists of simple duets in which the parts are of equal difficulty. Vanderhagen finishes with a recommendation to the pupil to progress to the duets of Michel (Yost) where he will find "everything that it is possible to do on the clarinet." The tutor was popular and appeared in several pirated and very inaccurate editions. About 1800 Naderman published a new edition and included some "petits airs" to distinguish it from these pirated editions. Pleyel published an entirely different *Nouvelle Méthode,* also about 1800. Vanderhagen's final effort was a tutor for the twelve-keyed clarinet. This was published posthumously by Pleyel in 1827.

Works: Concerto no.1. Concerto no.2. Concerto no.3 in B flat (Pleyel). Andante d'Haydn varié (Janet & Cotelle). 13 Variations (Haslinger). Airs et Duos de Primrose for 2 clarinets (Leduc 1798). Receuils d'ariettes choisies bks.1 & 2 for 2 clarinets (Boüin c.1783 – LBL). 6 Duos op.13 for clarinet & bassoon (Sieber – BrBC). (Whistling lists numerous other solos and duos). Méthode nouvelle et raisonnée pour la clarinette (Boyer & Lemenu 1785 – PBN. Naderman c.1800). Nouvelle Méthode (Pleyel c.1800). Nouvelle Méthode pour la clarinette moderne à douze clefs (Pleyel 1827 – PBN, WLC).

VANDERPLANCKEN, Corneille. Brussels, 23 Oct 1772-1849 Feb 9, Brussels. Belgian. He was a virtuoso on the clarinet and violin.

Work: Concerto (Ms.)

VAUPEL, Jean. He was first clarinet in both the court orchestra and the Leopold-Corps at Detmold from 1872 to 1876. In 1875 he performed the slow movement from Mozart's Concerto, and in 1876 Weber's Concertino. In later years he was employed in the court orchestra at Sondershausen.

VAUTH (VAUT, BAUTH). German. He played in the court orchestra at Kassel from about 1835 to 1850. His solo performances included the following: 1835 – 27th March, a double concerto by Krommer with Heisterhagen. 1837 – Lindpaintner's Concertante for wind. 1839 – 15th November, Schindelmeisser's Symphonie Concertante for 4 clarinets with Heisterhagen, Lesser and Schultheis. 1845 – Lindpaintner's Concertante for wind.

VENZL, Heinrich. From 1851 to 1863 he played in the Vienna Philharmonic Orchestra. He then went to Munich where until 1881 he played in the orchestra for the Subscription Concerts, appearing with them as a soloist.

VERLEN. He was a member of the court orchestra at Wallerstein in 1791. From 1792 to 1802 he belonged to the music establishment of Prince Schwarzenberg at Vienna.

VERNEY, R. 1880-? French. He was a pupil of Rose at the Paris Conservatoire, gaining a First Prize in 1898. He became solo clarinet of the Garde Républicaine and featured in some recordings made by them about 1912.

VIERSNICKEL (VIERNICKEL, FIRNICKEL), Anton (Philipp). German. He learnt from Meissner, as did his brother Joseph and was solo clarinet in the wind band at Würzburg.

(B–H). **VIERSNICKEL (VIERNICKEL, FIRNICKEL), Joseph.** Würzburg, May 1782-? German. It was said he had a beautiful tone and splendid technique. Like his brother Anton he learnt from the great teacher Meissner. He played clarinet and basset-horn in the court orchestra at Würzburg from 1801 to 1814.

VILMAR. On 29th March 1835 he performed Lindpaintner's Concerto at Fulda. It is possible that he was one of the four players in Schindelmeisser's Symphonie Concertante which was performed the same year at Fulda, on 13th February.

VIONNE. French. He was the clarinettist for the Société moderne d'Instruments à Vent of Paris when it was founded in 1895.

VOCK, Anton. ?-1885 Dec 8, Vienna. He played in the Vienna Philharmonic Orchestra from 1851 until he was pensioned in 1879.

VOGT, Emil. German. He was probably a brother of the oboist Gustav Vogt. He became a member of the town orchestra at Danzig. In 1833 he played variations by Berr at the Marienburg Festival.

Works: Air de Joseph varié (Janet). Airs variés (Janet). Solo du Carnival de Venise varié (Janet).

VOISIN, Louis. French. From 1793 to 1795 he taught at the Institut National de Musique in Paris. Then until 18th July 1796 he was a member of the Conservatoire staff.

VOLLMAR, August. 1792-? German. He also played flute and violin. He fought in the wars of 1813 and 1814. From 1823 to 1843 he was second clarinet in the court orchestra at Detmold.

VOLODIN, Alexander Vladimirovich. 1897-1966. Russian. He was a pupil of Rozanov in Moscow. In 1924 he joined the Persimfans Orchestra. Two years later, as the result of a competition, he won a post in the Bolshoi Theatre Orchestra. In 1935 he won First Prize at the Second All-Union Music Competition, held in Leningrad. He taught at the Moscow Conservatoire from 1937 until his death and his name is inscribed on their Honours Board. In 1956 he was made an Honoured Artist of the RDFSR.

WACHTELBRENNER. He was first clarinet in the court orchestra at Copenhagen in 1806.

WACHTER (WACHTRES). In spite of serious rivals, his performances for the Concert Spirituel were exceptionally well received. It was considered amazing that he could play so well on "an instrument so ungrateful as the clarinet" and his powers of expression sent audiences into ecstasies. There were some who criticized him for bad taste, but others commended him for purity and beauty of tone, the quality being compared to that of the armonica. (Shades of Willman!) His performances for the society were as follows: 1782 – 2nd February, concerto by Punto. 6th April, unspecified concerto. 1786 – 24th December, his own concerto. 25th December, his own concerto and one by the Chevalier de Saint-Georges. 1787 – 2nd February, a "new" concerto by Saint-Georges. 30th March, a "new" concerto by himself. 1790 – 28th March, Symphonie Concertante for 2 clarinets by Solère, with the composer.

Works: 2 Concertos.

WACK. 1733-? German. He was first clarinet from 1755 to about 1786 for the Thurn and Taxis court orchestra at Regensburg. Wolfgang Wack was probably his son.

WACK, Wolfgang. Regensburg. 1758-1811 or later. German. He was probably a son of the above. Wolfgang learnt from Joseph Schierll, another Regensburg clarinettist, and with Schierll's son he appears in the court lists at Esterház for 1783, as second clarinet. In 1784 they both moved back to Regensburg to take up similar appointments there. Wack moved up to first clarinet, probably on the death of Schierll in 1797, and was still in this post when the Thurn and Taxis orchestra was disbanded in 1806. He lived on at Regensburg until 1811 or later.

WADSWORTH. ?-1895, Manchester. English. He played in the Hallé Orchestra at Manchester from 1885 to 1895. T. Wadsworth was probably his son.

WADSWORTH, T. English. He was probably a son of the above. From 1897 to 1900 he was third clarinet in the Hallé Orchestra at Manchester and then stepped up to second, which he played until 1929.

WAGNER. German. He was employed for the Schaumberg-Lippe Court at Bückeburg and taught Lellmann there in 1811.

WAGNER, Carl. He played for the Munich Subscription Concerts from 1892 to 1911 or later, and was also a court Chamber Musician.

WAGNER, Friedrich. ?-1849. German. In 1808 he became a member of the court orchestra at Darmstadt and was still in it as Chamber Musician in 1823. He may be the "Wagner" who performed in the Beethoven Septet at Coburg in 1847.

WAGNER, Wilhelm. German. He was employed in the orchestra at Mainz from 1774 to 1784.

Works: Duets, bks.1 & 2 (Sieber 1798).

WAGNER, Wilhelm. German. He was living at Munich about 1830. In 1833 he undertook a tour to Italy, which included a most successful concert at Bologna's large theatre on 18th June. From 1837 to 1851 he lived in St Petersburg as first clarinet for the German Opera. When Blaes visited St Petersburg on his second tour, in 1847, he found a formidable rival in Wagner. Blaes received scant audiences, whereas Wagner drew large ones, and it was said that Wagner's tone was bigger and fuller, that his playing was more animated. Wagner's playing of the Adagio from Mozart's Concerto was reported to be extraordinarily beautiful. In 1851 he went to live in Vienna. He became a member of the Tonkünstler-verein, and gave a concert for them on 22nd January 1852.

Work: Divertissement brillant op.5 (Ms. – VGM. Kistner).

WALBRÜL, Johann. German. He also played bass clarinet and violin. In 1855 he was a Chamber Musician at the Weimar Court.

WALCH, Anton. He played for the Munich Subscription Concerts from 1900 to 1911 or later and taught at the Royal Music School. He was a Chamber Musician in the court orchestra.

WALTER, Albert. Coblenz, ?-? German. When a young man he went to Paris and entered the orchestra of the Théâtre Montansier as second clarinet, becoming first in 1798. He was in the first clarinets for the Consular Guards from their formation and later became assistant conductor for the riflemen of the Imperial Guard. At the Restoration he lost the appointment and thereafter earned a living composing and making arrangements for various publishing firms.

Works: Symphonie Concertante for 2 clarinets (Pleyel). Walzes for solo clarinet, 2 bks. (Pleyel). Airs variés for 2 clarinets (Pleyel). 3 Potpourries for 2 clarinets (Pleyel). Variations for clarinet & violin (Hug). 6 Quartets op.27 (Pleyel).

WALTHER, Johann Georg. German. He played

clarinet, oboe and viola at the Brandenburg-Ansbach Court from 1770 to 1796 or later. He was also copyist for the Court.

WASMUTIUS, Bernhard. Born at Kralowitz. Czech. He played for several years in Prague and then in 1808 became clarinettist for the orchestra at Passau cathedral.

WASSILIEFF. Russian. He was a pupil of Blaes in St Petersburg. In 1842 he was a member of the Empress's Horse Guards. On 20th March 1847 he played a double concerto by Vollweiller with his teacher at the Imperial Theatre.

WEBER, Henri. ?-1876 June 20, Ghent. He taught at Ghent Conservatoire from 1870 until his death.

WEICHSEL, Carl. Freiburg-in-Saxony, ?-1811, London? German. See OV. He also played the oboe. By 1757 he was established in London and was probably the "Mr Wrexell" who was engaged as oboist for the Covent Garden season of 1760/1. His usual fee was 5 shillings a night, but when Arne's *Thomas and Sally* was performed he played clarinet and the fee was raised to ten shillings and sixpence. He became a member of the Royal Society of Musicians in 1761. During the next few years he found regular employment at the King's Theatre, but was freed if required to play clarinet at Covent Garden. On 19th February 1763 he played clarinet at the Kings Theatre for the first performance of J.C. Bach's *Orione ossia Diana Vendicata.* He played at the Three Choirs Festival at Gloucester in 1763 and again in 1770. He also played as a civilian in the band of a foot guard regiment.

In 1765 Weichsel married Mlle Weirmann, a singer at Covent Garden. She had been the mistress of the Duke de Nivernois, the French Ambassador, and then of the Irish singer Robert Owenson, who fathered her daughter Elizabeth (see OV), born in the autumn of 1765. The Weichsels had a son Charles, born in 1766, who became a well-known violinist.

WEISE, I & II. Probably brothers, they were in the Weimar court orchestra in 1909.

WEISSGÄRBER. German. He was a clarinettist and then Kapellmeister at the Court of Anhalt-Cöthen. In 1833 he appeared as a soloist at the National Theatre in Prague, and played obligatos for Sophie Heinefetter.

WEISSMÜLLER (WEITZMÜLLER). He was the son of a bassoon player at Fulda, where in 1829 he played Maurer's Concertante for 2 clarinets with Kukro. Later he and his father moved to Fribourg and became teachers. They both played in the orchestra for the Swiss Music Festival at Fribourg on 24th August 1843. The son performed a concerto by Spohr, surmounting its difficulties with ease.

WELLER, Friedrich. Wörlitz, 1786-1870 May 30, Zerbst. German. He learnt the clarinet from the town musician at Wörlitz. In 1809 he joined a Prussian light infantry regiment. In 1814 he transferred to the 2nd regiment of Guards at Berlin and with this fought in the French Campaign. On the regiment's return to Berlin he was made conductor of the band. He gave summer concerts in the Mewes Flower Garden which attracted large audiences because he had the unique idea of securing all the latest symphonies and operas, arranging them for band and performing them in this setting before their appearance elsewhere. Weber's *Oberon* was heard here before it was produced on the Berlin stage. Weller also composed for military band. He was awarded the Military Order in 1838 and retired in 1844. His son Franz (Berlin, 5 Aug 1815-1860 July 15, Stockholm) became a clarinettist in his father's regiment in 1834.

WENCZLICŽEK (VENCLÍCĚK). Czech. For several years from 1796 he played in the German Opera at the Prague Theatre.

WENDEROTH. German. At Kassel in 1841 he took part in Schindelmeisser's Symphonie Concertante for 4 clarinets with Bättenhausen, Curth and Kollmann.

WENKEL. German. He played in the court orchestra at Sondershausen in 1847.

WERLE, Georg. German. He was related to Sebastian Werle and appears in orchestral lists of the Munich Court in 1824 and 1827.

WERLE, Sebastian. German. He was related to Georg Werle and was a member of the Munich court orchestra from 1805 to 1845, performing Winter's Concerto with them in 1813. He also played for the Subscription Concerts from 1811 to 1851. His teacher was Joseph Tausch.

WIEBEL, Hermann. German. He played second clarinet to Mühlfeld in the court orchestra at Meiningen. On Mühlfeld's death in 1907 he became first clarinet and was made a Chamber Musician. His first appearance as soloist with the orchestra was on 31st January 1909.

WIENEN, Mikolaj. Polish. He was clarinet professor at the Warsaw Conservatoire in the 1820s.

WIEPRECHT, Wilhelm (Friedrich). Aschersleben, 10 Aug 1802-1872 Aug 4, Berlin. German. He is well-known as a reformer of Prussian military bands. His father taught him to play the clarinet and other instruments. In 1819 Wieprecht went to Dresden as a violinist. In 1821 he played at his home town with Hermstedt, who gave him an introduction to Wilhelm Barth at Leipzig. He may have had further clarinet lessons from Barth, and certainly played at musical gatherings in Barth's large house. No post being available for him on the clarinet, he played the violin for some time in the Leipzig theatre and concert orchestras before going to Berlin in 1824 to become a Chamber Musician at the Court there. His real interest was with wind instruments and he became involved with the music of the Royal Guard, eventually attaining the post of inspector of German military bands. In 1839 he invented the bathyphon, a type of contra-bass clarinet, which was used with success in the bands. When Sax produced his *Clarinette-bourdon* Wieprecht accused him of imitation and an acrid dispute followed. In 1845 a meeting was arranged between the protagonists, with Liszt and others arbitrating. Wieprecht was humiliated and made to retract his words, but on return to his home ground he continued to vilify Sax in the press.

Works: Concerto (Logier). Fantasia. Schweizer Variations (Logier).

Bibliography:

HAMANN, Heinz Wolfgang – "Wilhelm Wieprecht." MGG.
KALKBRENNER, August – *Wilhelm Wieprecht.* Berlin 1882.

WIESNER, Paul. German. He succeeded Julius Berger in the court orchestra at Schwerin.

(B–H). **WILLIAMS, Joseph.** Hereford, 1795-1875 April, London. English. See OV. He also played the violin and piano. His talents were not appreciated in his native Hereford and by the autumn of 1829 he had moved to London with a position as first clarinet at the King's Theatre. When Queen Victoria came to the throne in 1837 he was made leader of her private band. Early in 1840 he became second clarinet in the Philharmonic Society's orchestra and after Willman died, later the same year, he was made first clarinet. He excelled as an obligato player and the majority of his solo performances for the Philharmonic Society were in this capacity. He later became a director of the Society, and retired in 1862. The instrument he used had 12 keys, with a ring key on the right hand joint. He played with the reed on top and in his tutor gives instructions for the placing of it one sixteenth of an inch from the tip of the mouthpiece. James Waterson dedicated his Andante & Rondo for 2 clarinets to Williams.

He played at the following concerts, all those from 1840 onwards being for the Philharmonic Society: 1819 – his own concerto for the Hereford Festival. 1820 – 23rd February for the Concerts of Ancient Music at Drury Lane, Paer's "Una voce al cor mi parla." 1828 – September at Hereford, Guglielmi's "Gratias agimus." 1829 – 19th October at Bristol's Theatre Royal, a Fantasia. 1840 – 25th May, Mozart's "Parto!" for Caradori-Allan. 1841 – 19th April, Paer's "Una voce al cor mi parla" for Caradori-Allan. 16th May, Beethoven's Septet. 17th May, Mozart's "Non più di fiori" for Elisa Meerti. 1843 – 8th May, Mozart's "Non più di fiori" for Emma Albertazzi. 1844 – 2nd April, Cherubini's "Ave Maria" for Elizabeth Rainforth. 1845 – 31st March, Mozart's "Non più di fiori" for Emma Albertazzi. 1846 – 18th May, ditto for Louisa Bassano. 1850 – 3rd June, Cherubini's "Ave Maria" for Sims Reeves. 25th June, Mozart's Trio K498. 1852 – 19th April, Mozart's "Parto!" for Jeanne Castellan. 1853 – 18th April, Mozart's Serenade K388, with Lazarus on second clarinet. 1855 – 30th April, Spohr's Nonet. 11th June, Cherubini's "Ave Maria" for Clara Novello. 1858 – 21st June, Mozart's "Parto!" for Louisa Payne. 1861 – 27th May, Mozart's "Non più di fiori" for Miss Lascelles. 1862 – 10th March, Mozart's "Parto!" for Mme Guerrabella.

Works: Concerto. Pensées fugitives (Schott 1855 – LRAM). Boosey's Universal Tutor (Boosey 1857 – LBL).

(B–H). **WILLMAN, Thomas Lindsay.** London?, 1784-1840 Nov 28, London. English, of German descent. See OV. He also played the bass clarinet. In the list of Willman's performances which follows it will be seen that the majority were of obligatos and chamber works, rather than concertos. Although there were many fine virtuosi about, woodwind concertos were not popular and when he ventured to play Baermann's Fantasia for the Philharmonic Society on 19th

May 1823, the *Harmonicon* of June voiced its disapproval in the following manner: "Mr Willman is the most delicate and finished clarinet player we have ever heard; but a clarinet concerto is quite out of its place at these concerts, which, at their first institution, professed not to admit performances of this nature." Baermann had got away with it when he played the Fantasia for the Society in 1819 and Willman saw no reason why he should not also have a chance to shine in it. He disregarded the report and performed the Fantasia on two more occasions. Again he flouted public opinion in pioneering concertos by Mozart, Spohr and Weber, but got little support. Nonetheless, as Mendelssohn wrote to Baermann, Willman was "all in all" to his English audiences and singers fell over themselves to procure his services. George Hogarth wrote in the *Musical World* that "he peculiarly excels in playing obligato accompaniments . . . . . and those who have listened with delight to *Gratias agimus, Parto, Non più di fiori* sung by one of our first vocalists, and accompanied by him, cannot but have remarked the exquisite skill with which he develops the beauties of his own instrument, while, at the same time, he strengthens instead of impairing, the expression and effect of the voice." Clarinettists of the present day accept engagements with a singer, knowing that the key of the original will be adhered to. Not so the obligato player of the nineteenth century and "J.P.", writing in the *Harmonicon* of 1830, tells us that although "Gratias agimus tibi" may be written in the key of E flat, Mary Ann Paton preferred to sing it in F and Catalani insisted on either D or E, caring not a whit that the whole orchestra as well as the clarinettist had to transpose!

Willman's concerts for the Philharmonic Society were as follows: 1817 – 24th February, Beethoven's Septet. 1818 – 30th March, ditto. 13th April, Beethoven's Wind Quintet. 9th June, Mozart's "Parto!" for Eliza Salmon. 1819 – 24th May, Beethoven's Septet. 7th June, Beethoven's Wind Quintet. 8th June, Mozart's Wind Quintet. 1820 – 6th March, Sacchini's "Lieta quest 'alma amanti" for Eliza Salmon. 24th April, basset-horn obligato to Mozart's "Non più di fiori" for Miss Goodall. 19th June, Spohr's Nonet. 1821 – 12th March, Mozart's "Parto!" for Violante Camporese. 9th April, Beethoven's Septet. 28th May, Septet (Ms.) by C.R.N. Bochsa. 1822 – 13th May, Mozart's "Parto!" for Camporese and Beethoven's Septet. 27th May, Mozart's "Non più di fiori" for Camporese. 1823 – 5th May, Paer's "Una voce al cor mi parla" for Catherine Stephens. 19th May, Baermann's Fantasia. 2nd June, Mozart's "Parto!" for Camporese. 1824 – 8th March, quintet by Reicha. 1825 – 21st March, ditto. 11th April, Paer's "Una voce al cor mi parla" for Catherine Stephens. 9th May, Beethoven's Septet. 1826 – 13th March, Crusell's Concertante. 17th April, Mozart's "Parto!" for Caradori-Allan. 1827 – 5th March, Mozart's "Parto!" for Catherine Stephens and Baermann's Fantasia. 2nd April, Beethoven's Septet. 1828 – 10th March, Mozart's "Parto!" for Caradori-Allan. 1829 – 9th March, Onslow's Sextet. 23rd March, Küffner's Introduction & Thème Varié. 25th May, Mozart's "Non più di fiori" for Mme Wranizkij. 1830 – 19th April, Mozart's Serenade K388. 17th May, Mozart's "Non più di fiori" for Malibran. 14th June, Hummel's Septet. 1831 – 21st February, ditto. 7th March, Mozart's Serenade K388. 21st March, Beer's Adagio & Air (with variations). 6th June, Onslow's Sextet. 1832 – 12th March, Neukomm's Septet. 9th April, Baermann's Fantasia. 30th April, Mozart's "Non più di fiori" for Mme de Mério. 18th June, Mozart's "Parto!" for Schröder-Devrient and Neukomm's Septet. 1833 – 25th February, Spohr concerto. 15th April, Grand Septet (Ms) by Moscheles. 10th June, Mozart's "Non più di fiori" for Malibran. 1834 – 17th March, Spohr's Nonet. 19th May, Neukomm's Septet. 1835 – 6th April, Mozart's Quintet K581. 27th April, Neukomm's Septet. 1836 – 7th March, a concerto by Weber. 11th April, bass clarinet obligato to Neukomm's "Make haste, O God" for Mrs Alfred Shaw. 9th May, Mozart's "Non più di fiori" for Malibran. 23rd May, Neukomm's Septet. 1837 – 3rd April, Adagio & Allegro (from the First Concerto) by Weber. 1st May, Mozart's "Non più di fiori" for Mrs Wood (*née* Mary Ann Paton). 1838 – 5th March, Mozart's "Parto!" for Clelia Placci and Mozart's Concerto. 1839 – 22nd April, Spohr's Octet. 3rd June, Mozart's "Parto!" for Dorus-Gras.

His concerts for the New Musical Fund were as follows: 1821 – 3rd May, C.R.N. Bochsa's "New Trio" (Ms.) with the composer playing the harp and Puzzi the horn. 1823 – 1st May, Paer's "Una voce al cor mi parla" for Miss Goodall. 1824 – 20th May, Guglielmi's "Gratias agimus" for Catalani. 1834 – 25th April, Neukomm's Concertante Sextet. 1837 – 21st April, Guglielmi's "Gratias agimus" for Charlotte Birch. 1839 – Panseron's "Tyrol, my Fatherland" for Miss Cawthorn. 1840 – 10th June, Cherubini's "Ave Maria" for Emily Woodyatt.

Miscellaneous performances: 1819 – 1st June, Sacchini's "Lieta quest 'alma amanti" for Eliza Salmon. October at Edinburgh, Guglielmi's "Gratias agimus". 1820 – at Birmingham, ditto. 1821 – 1st March at the Mansion House, C.R.N. Bochsa's Trio for clarinet, horn & harp. 2nd May at the Guildhall, Guglielmi's "Gratias agimus" for Henriette Sontag. 1822 – for Reading Festival; Paer's "Una voce al cor mi parla"; 28th August, Sacchini's "Lieta quest 'alma amanti" for Eliza Salmon; 30th August, unspecified concerto. 1823 – September at York, Mozart's "Parto!" for Eliza Salmon. 1824 – Guglielmi's

"Gratias agimus" for Catalani. 1826 – Carafa's "Va lusingando" for Alberico Curioni. 16th June at Moorfields Chapel, Mozart's *Requiem* with Powell and other members of the Philharmonic Society for the memorial service to Weber. 1827 – November at Cambridge, a basset-horn concerto. 1828 – 29th February & 28th March at Covent Garden, Guglielmi's "Gratias agimus." 1829 – 30th January at Drury Lane, ditto. 13th March at Covent Garden, Küffner's Introduction & Swiss Air with Variations. 2nd April at the Guidhall, Guglielmi's "Gratias agimus" for Henriette Sontag and Mozart's "Parto!" for Violante Camporese. 1833 – 18th June at Oxford, "Fantasia" (op.12?) by Crusell. 1836 – at Norwich, Beer's Fantasia. 28th April at the Mansion House, Karl Bochsa's Fantasia for basset-horn, and Panseron's "Tyrol, my Fatherland" for Clara Novello. 1837 – at Birmingham: 19th September, Mozart's "Non più di fiori" for Clara Novello; 20th September, Guglielmi's "Gratias agimus" for Giulia Grisi; 22nd September, Guglielmi's "Ave Maria" for Giulia Grisi.

Works: Air & Variations (D'Almaine 1847). A Complete Instruction Book for the Clarinet, dedicated to Robert Wiss (Goulding D'Almaine & Co. 1826 – LBL).

WINTER. A player of this name held positions at the Munich Court in 1803, and at the Théâtre de la Gaité at Paris in 1830.

WIPPERT (WIPERT), L. German. He played at a concert given by Mme Schick at Berlin in 1804. Later he became a member of the theatre orchestra at Frankfurt a. M., where he performed a concerto by Krommer in 1809 and an unspecified Polonaise in 1811.

Work: 3 Duets (1808).

WISSE (WEISSE). Johann Anton. ?-1830. German. He was known as "the famous Bis." In 1795 he settled at Lisbon with an appointment as first clarinet at the San Carlos Theatre. Some authorities state that this was the first time a clarinettist had been employed there, but the information is incorrect, for in 1793 Ignacio Canongia was the theatre's first clarinet. On 15th December 1795 Wisse performed a solo at the New Assembly. He remained active as a performer until 1799 and then entered the Brotherhood of Saint Cecilia. He taught one of Portugal's most famous clarinettists, Avelino Canongia.

WITT. German. He and his brother, a bassoon and horn player, were members of the orchestra at Königsberg in 1809.

WITTSTADT, Bernhard. He played at the Munich Subscription Concerts from 1869 to 1893.

WLACH, Leopold. Vienna, 9 Sept 1902-1956 May 7, Vienna. Austrian. The high reputation of Viennese wind playing in the 1930s and 1940s was due in great part to the influence on interpretation by Wlach. His tone was extremely beautiful and he had superb control of dynamics. He studied clarinet at the Vienna Conservatoire with Bartolomey and Viktor Polatschek. In 1926 he toured the world with an instrumental group, during which time he received many offers of employment. In 1928 he became a member of the Vienna Philharmonic and Staatsoper orchestras. When Polatschek resigned as first clarinet in the Philharmonic in 1930 to go to Boston, Wlach took his place. In the same year Wlach became a teacher at the Conservatoire, where he trained many fine pupils, including Alfred Boskovsky. He was a founder-member of the Vienna Octet, who were all members of the Philharmonic Orchestra. Under his leadership this group achieved world-wide fame. The Philharmonic Orchestra awarded him their crown in 1953 in recognition of his twenty five years service. Wlach excelled in playing Mozart and in 1954 the Vienna Mozart Society conferred on him its Medal. He did a great deal to popularise the two beautiful quintets by Franz Schmidt and for this the Schmidt Society gave him honorary membership.

Recordings:

Brahms – 2 Sonatas op.120. Westminster 9023.
Brahms – Trio op.114. Westminster 9017.
Brahms – Quintet op.115. Westminster 9016.
Glinka – Trio Pathétique. Westminster WL 50-19.
Mozart – Concerto K622. Westminster 18287.
Mozart – Quintet K581. Westminster 18269.
Pfitzner – Sextet op.55. Favorit Klassik FK 50135.
Schmidt – Quintet in A major. Preisser 3066. (This was completed by Alfred Prinz, owing to the death of Wlach during recording).
Schumann – Märchenerzählungen. Westminster 18494.

WOHLLEBE, C.Z. German. He was blind and learnt from Forckert (q.v.) at Dresden's Royal Blind Institute. With his teacher he performed Iwan Müller's double concerto at the Leipzig Subscription Concerts on 28th November 1833. In Dresden's Harmonie Hall on 27th February 1837 he gave a Grand Concert with the support of the royal court orchestra at which he performed a "Grand Rondo" (probably the Rondo brillant op.45) by Lindpaintner and a double concerto in E flat by Dagobert Fischer, both with Forckert. He is reported to have played with assurance and a beautiful tone.

WOLF (WOLFF), Franz Xaver. German. He was a clarinettist in the Royal Prussian Hohenlohe Regiment in 1797.

Works: Concerto. 6 Duets for clarinet & violin. 4 Quartets. 3 Quintets for 2 clarinets, 2 horns & bassoon (Holäufer). 2 Serenades op.1 for 2 clarinets, 2 horns & 2 bassoons (André 1795).

WOLF, Johann Kaspar. 1 Jan 1775-1811 Apr 17, Wallerstein. German. About 1810 he was engaged for the Öttingen -Wallerstein Court.

WOLFE (WOLF, WOLFF), A. German. He is probably the "Wolff" who performed a concerto at the Concert Spirituel on 28th May 1778. In 1786 he settled at Baltimore, U.S.A., where he became well-known as a soloist. Sonneck records numerous performances given by him in Philadelphia and New York, as well as Baltimore. Wolfe shared a benefit with Dubois on 26th April 1799, when they played a "Medley Trio for clarinet, violin and lute," Dangel playing the violin and Dubois the lute. Later the same year Wolfe performed a Rondo by Michel (Yost).

WOLFF. German. He was a clarinet teacher as well as performer at Breslau and was probably brother to Franz Wolff, Breslau's music director. His concerts included the following: 1837/8 season – concertos by Heinrich Baermann and Reissiger. 1838/9 – compositions by Crusell and Gerke. 1839/40 – compositions by Spohr and Crusell. 1840/41 concertos by Heinrich Baermann and Crusell.

WÜSTENHAGEN. German. He was a clarinettist in a wind band at Bernburg and appeared there as soloist in 1833 and 1834.

WUILLE, M. Antwerp, 1822-? Belgian. He also played bass clarinet and saxophone. His father was a German who settled in Antwerp as an instrument maker. Wuille learnt the clarinet from Valentin Bender, played in the band of the Guides and was then soloist in the private band of the King of the Belgians, before leaving the country of his birth to seek his fortune elsewhere. In 1852 he came to England and introduced Müller clarinets, made by Mahillon and Albert, in a series of very successful recitals. His phrasing and technique were good and he had a soft pleasing tone, especially on high notes. On 2nd June 1852 he performed for Ella's Musical Union

Breslau, den 26ᵗ Nov: 1795.

Hochwohlgebohrner Herr.

Die 6 Exemplar von meinen Serenaten habe durch Herrn Leuckard mit Vergnügen erhalten. wenig sie dieselben bey Ihnen eben so stark gesucht möchten werden als sie hier [illegible] gefunden.

Herr Leuckard klagte über Mangel an Violin Trio's, etc, und [illegible] würden heraus und werden sehr stark gesucht; so trugen Herr Leuckard mir an welche zu machen: ich sagte ja, will diesen Winter welche machen wann mir Herr André wenigstens vor jedes Stück einen Dukaten accordiert: also hängt es nun von Ihnen gänzlich ab.

Ich habe bereits ein Concert vor die Clarinett mit ganzem Orchester welches ich [illegible] [illegible] [illegible] [illegible] zu machen, 6 Duetten vor eine Clarinett und eine Violin — 3 Quartetts vor zwei Violin Alt und Cello 4 Dito vor eine Clarinett. Violin Alt und Cello fertig; wären Ihnen von diesen etwas gefällig, so kann ich Ihnen das Concert vor 9 — die 6 Duetten vor 6 — und jedes Quadro vor 4 [illegible] überlassen.

Jetzt habe ich einige Aufzüge aus den Weibern und der Müllerin in Arbeit welche ich vor 8 blasende Instrumenten arangiere.

Bin mit Hochachtung

Euer Hochedelgeb:

ergebener Diener

F: X: Wolf.

Den Brief von Herrn Leuckard habe richtig abgegeben.

6. Letter from Franz Xaver Wolf to the publisher André, Breslau 26th November 1795. *(Deutsche Staatsbibliothek, Berlin/DDR).*

concerts. The *Musical World* said he played the clarinet "with a rich tone and good execution" and that "the room was thronged". His programme included a clarinet solo by one of the Baermanns, a bass clarinet obligato to Frank Mori's "The Last Farewell" for Susan Sunderland, and a Fantasia of his own composition "upon the saxophone, one of the most remarkable instruments of M. Sax's invention, with which the audience were particularly pleased." Jullien engaged Wuille for his 1852 summer season at the Surrey Gardens and for the winter promenades at Drury Lane. The following year Wuille went with Jullien on his mammoth American tour, when he was billed as "The Belgian Lazarus." He was still playing for Jullien in 1856 but left England some time later and after a short sojourn in Paris settled at Strasbourg as a teacher at the Conservatoire. As "Professor Wuille from Strasbourg" he performed on the clarinet at Baden-Baden on 26th July 1865. He married a pianist.

YOST, Michel. Paris, 1754-1786 July 5, Paris. French. See OV. Yost taught both Rathé and Solère, as did Beer. His playing was characterised by brilliant colouring of the sound, great volubility and faithful adherence to expression. His popularity as a soloist at the Concert Spirituel will be seen by the following list of performances he gave for the society: 1781 – 2nd February, Symphonie Concertante for clarinet, horn, harp & piano by Maréchal, with the composer playing the piano. 26th March, concerto by himself. 6th April, Maréchal's Symphonie Concertante. 11th April, "new" concerto by himself. 15th April, "new" Symphonie Concertante by Maréchal. 17th April, his own concerto. 22nd April, his own "new" concerto. 24th May, unspecified concerto. 14th June, ditto. 15th August, concerto by Vogel (i.e. one of the concertos Vogel wrote in collaboration with Yost). 8th September, ditto. 1st November, unspecified concerto. 24th December, ditto. 1783 – 25th March, a "new" concerto by Vogel (Yost/Vogel). 13th, 16th(?), 18th, 20th, 21st April, ditto. 22nd April, concerto by himself. 27th April, 8th & 19th June, 15th August, 8th September, unspecified concerto. 8th & 25th December, concerto by himself. 1784 – 25th March, 4th April, unspecified concerto. 7th & 12th April, concerto by Vogel (Yost/Vogel). 16th April, unspecified concerto. 1786 – 5th April, his own concerto. 9th April, his own "new" concerto. 14th, 16th & 23rd April, 4th June, his own concerto.

Works, generally published under the name of "Michel (J)": Concerto no.1 (Sieber 1782 – PBN). Concerto no.2 in B flat (Sieber 1782 – PBN). Concerto no.3 in B flat (Sieber 1782 – PBN. Ms. copy – DrSL). Concerto no.4. Concerto no.5 in E flat (Ms.

copies – LBL, RTTH). Concerto no.6. Concerto no.7 (Imbault 1783). Concerto no.8 in B flat (Imbault 1785 – WLC). Concertos nos.9, 10, 11 & 12, all in B flat (Pleyel 1807 to 1809 – LBL, no.11 entitled "de Michel et Vogel." Ms. copy of no.12 – DrSL). Concerto no.13. Concerto no.14 in E flat (Pleyel 1807 to 1809 – LBL, entitled "de Michel et Vogel." Cochet – VNB). Duo Concertante for 2 clarinets (Ms. – VGM). 12 Grand Solos or Studies, 4 bks. (Chanel). Airs variés avec A ou B (Sieber). Duos ops.1, 2, 3, 4, 7 (Naderman). 6 Duos op.5 (Imbault – BoLM). 6 Duos op.6 (Broderip & Wilkinson c.1800 – LBL). 6 Duos op.10 (Frey c.1798. Sieber c.1798. Simrock – BoLM). 6 Favorite duets op.12 (J. Kohler c.1800 – LBL). Duos extraits de ses Concertos par Vanderhagen (Pleyel). 6 Duos op.8 for clarinet & violin (Boyer c.1800 – WLC. Frey). 6 Duos op.9 for clarinet & violin (Sieber c.1786. Boyer c.1800 – WLC). 3 Trios for flute, clarinet & bassoon (Viguerie – VGM). 3 Trios for 2 clarinets & cello (Viguerie – VGM). 3 Trios for clarinet, violin & cello (Viguerie – VGM). Airs variés for clarinet, viola & cello (Sieber). 5 Quartets, with Vogel (Frey. Sieber c.1798). 6 Quartets, with Vogel, ops.1, 2, 3, 4, & 5 (Decombe – PBN. Carel – 1 only, BrBC). Méthode de clarinette (Leduc).

YUSTE Moreno, Miguel. Alcalá del Valle, June 1870-1947 Apr 8, Madrid. Spanish. He was a great virtuoso and teacher, making big reforms in the course of clarinet study at the Madrid Conservatoire. At the age of eight he was orphaned and taken to Madrid where he entered the Asylum of San Bernardino and began to study music with José Chacón. In 1883 he became a pupil under González at the Madrid Conservatoire. At the age of fifteen he was made first clarinet in the Royal Corps of Halberdiers and at seventeen won First Prize at the Conservatoire. He played first clarinet at the opera in the Buen Retiro Gardens and in 1890 at the Theatre Royal and for the Society of Concerts (National Orchestra). Subsequently he played for the Society of Chamber Music and the Madrid Symphony Orchestra. He was also first clarinet and assistant conductor of the municipal band of Madrid.

Yuste was clarinet professor at the Madrid Conservatoire from 1910 to 1940. He drew up a systematic curriculum for a six-year course of study which was based on works from the Romero and Klosé tutors. General studies were drawn from the works of Carl Baermann, Buteux, Krakamp, Kroepsch, Magnani, Marasco, Stark and Wiedemann. Also included were staccato studies by Aumont, the Gambaro caprices and all the Paris Conservatoire test pieces. Yuste lived at the following addresses: 1910 – no.6 calle Cara Baga. 1911 – no.4 calle Ramales. Later – no. 19 calle Doctor Cárceles and no.28 calle Buen Suceso.

He composed over a hundred clarinet pieces, including the following: Caprices Pittoresque. Intermezzo & Ballade. Legend, Andante & Rondo. Solo de Concurso op.39 (Union Musical Espanola). Vibraciones del Alma op.45 (Harmonia 1953).

ZACH. German. In 1814 he was second clarinet in the court orchestra at Kremsmünster. When Mikesch was called on to play oboe, Zach played first clarinet.

(B–H). **ZANGENBERG, I.C.** German. He played in the band of the 2nd Hanoverian infantry regiment at Osnabrück from about 1799 to 1810. On 5th December 1799 he performed a clarinet concerto by Démar and on 3rd February 1803 an unspecified basset-horn concerto. He was also a dancing master.

ZENKER (ZÄNKER). He performed a clarinet concerto by Triebensee at the Augarten in Vienna in July 1805. His playing was well reviewed and he was described as a dilettante, so may have been a student at the time. He became first clarinet in the wind band at Sondershausen and played solos with them during the summer of 1823 at a concert in Nordhausen, which was conducted by Hermstedt. He was probably the brother of a trumpeter of the same name in the band.

ZIMMERMANN, F.K. German. He studied clarinet under Carl Baermann at the Munich Conservatoire and then went to Russia. From 1872 he taught at the Moscow Conservatoire and was the leading teacher in Russia at the end of the century. He adopted Russian citizenship in 1876. He was a highly cultured man and fluent in several languages.

ZUCKERMAN, I.V. 1885-1963. He was a pupil under Friedrich and then Bellison at the Moscow Conservatoire. He served an apprenticeship in the Moscow Philharmonic Orchestra and later became first clarinet in the USSR State Orchestra.

ZWICKER. German. In 1836 he was employed in the orchestra at Naumburg.

Epilogue

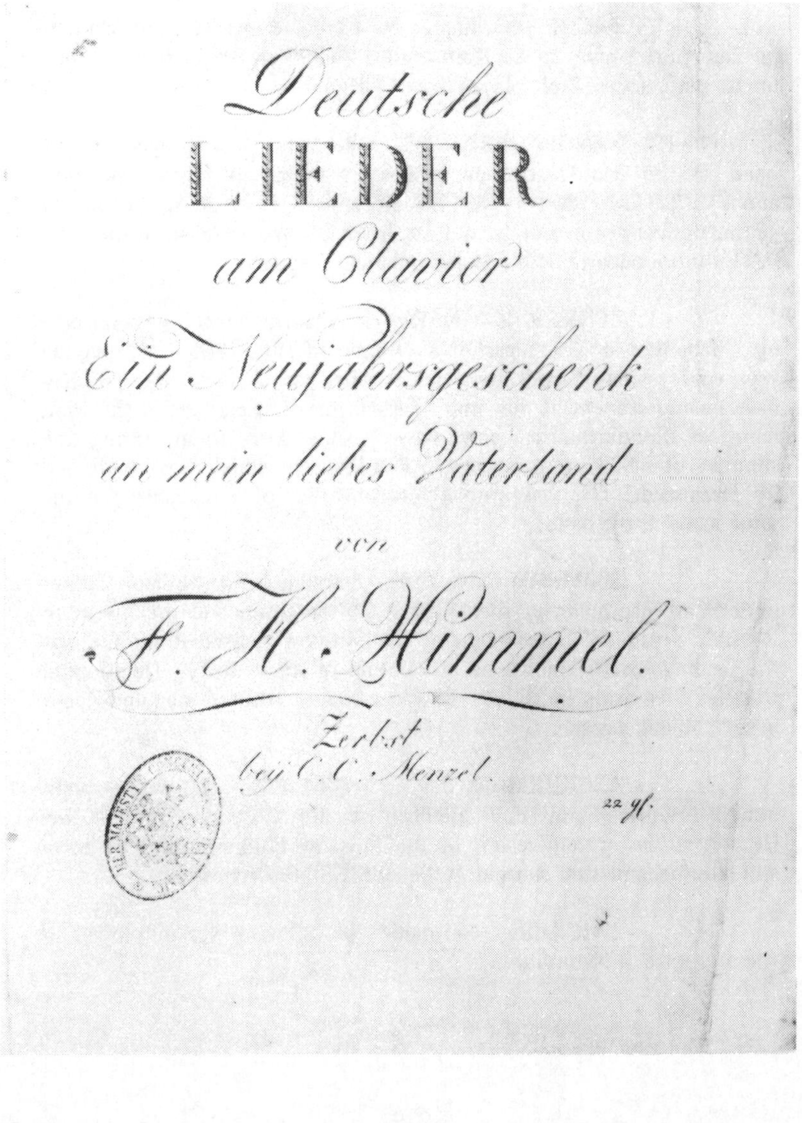

Deutsche
LIEDER
am Clavier
Ein Neujahrsgeschenk
an mein liebes Vaterland
von
F. H. Himmel.
Zerbst
bey C. C. Menzel.
22 gl.

(Royal College of Music, London)

DER ARME SPIELMANN AN SEINE CLARINETTE.

1. O töne sanft und inniglich
Geliebte Clarinette!
Was hätt'ich, Armer wenn ich dich
Zu meinem Trost nicht hätte:

2. Die mich als Knab ergötzt, als Mann
Begleitet unter Waffen,
Du wirst gewisslich mir fortan
Mein täglich Brodt verschaffen!

3. Lies ich als Knab am Wiederhall
Der Felsen dich ertönen
Dann sammelten zu deinem Schall
Sich Hirt und Hirtenschönen!

4. Geworben, in die neue Welt
Zu ziehn mit tapfern Hessen,
Konnt ich bey Märschen und im Zelt
Doch deiner nicht vergessen.

5. Durch frohen Ton erhieltest du
Uns frisch bey sauern Gangen
Und in der Kantonnirung Ruh
Spielt ich dich zu Gesängen.

6. Als einst der Feind uns überfiel
Drang ich durch Pulvernebel
Und rettete beym Angstgewühl
Nur dich und meinen Säbel.

7. Verwundet und gefangen lies
Man dich mir und zu milden
Gefühlen stimmt ich, wenn ich blies
Die Herzen selbst den Wilden.

8. Sie legten sich rund um den Kreis
Sie horchten mir zu Stunden
Und gaben mir von ihrem Reis
Und heiten meine Wunden.

9. Und gaben sonder Ranzion
Mich frey – bald drauf wards Friede!
Entlassen ohne Pension
Bettl'ich als Invalide.

10. Auch jezt noch kann dein Zauberklang
Manch wildes Herz erweichen
Von Armen ärndt ich Lohn und Dank –
Zuweilen auch von Reichen.

11. Zu Morgenseegen, Nachtmusik,
Zu Tanz und Hochzeitschmäusen
Sollst du mit mir in Leid und Gluck
Bis einst ich sterbe reisen!

12. Dann säusle meiner Treu zum Lohn,
Statt Sang und Todtenmette
Um meinen Hügel noch dein Ton,
Geliebte Clarinette!

v. Nostiz u. Jänckendorff

THE POOR MUSICIAN TO HIS CLARINET.

1. Oh softly sound and ardently,
Beloved Clarinet!
What hadst a poor man if not thee
To be his boon associate:

2. In boyhood you delighted me,
In manhood went with me to war
And now you'll surely furnish me
With daily bread for evermore.

3. When as a boy I made you sound
And echo through the mountains,
Then gathered close from all around
The shepherds and their maidens.

4. Conscripted, in the new world sent
To exercise with Hessians stout,
While on the march and in my tent
You never were laid up, miss'd out.

5. With rousing sounds you gave us zest
On dreary days campaigning
And when in camp we had some rest
I played you then for singing.

6. One day the foe surprised us,
I fought through smoke and powder
To rescue midst the exodus
Yourself and then my sabre.

7. Imprisoned, I lay wounded
And you were giv'n to cheer me.
Lo, as I played it melted
Those savage hearts to hear thee.

8. They lay encircled round me,
For hours on end my playing heard
And from their rice some offered me,
My injuries they deftly cured.

9. They gave me special benison –
Peace shortly came and I was freed!
Discharged without a pension
I had to beg, an invalid.

10. Likewise e'en now your magic ring
Ferocious hearts can soften.
Poor men rewards and thanks will bring –
Tho' rich men give less often.

11. At morning prayer or evensong,
At masquerade or wedding gay,
In joy and sorrow you belong
With me until I die one day.

12. Then 'stead of chant and requiem mass,
Above my grave sing softly yet
In tribute to my faithfulness,
Beloved Clarinet!

With apologies to Nostiz & Jänckendorff

Locations

This list is compiled from information occurring in both the original and present volumes. It includes every player mentioned who is known to have been employed at a town for a year or more, with dates of his employment where known. An asterisk before a single date means this is the only date known and the employment could have extended either side. An asterisk before a first date indicates the employment could have begun earlier, and similarly a question mark after a second date, that it could have continued longer. The reader wishing to find players employed at a court with a series-name should consult under the final name of the series, for this generally was the town at which the court was established. Exceptions to this rule, with the name of the town in parenthesis, are as follows: Mecklenburg-Schwerin (Ludwigslust, as well as Schwerin itself), Mecklenburg-Strelitz (Neu-Strelitz), Schaumberg-Lippe (Bückeburg), Thurn & Taxis (Regensburg).

AACHEN		
Town wind band:	Huppertz	+1816
	Knops	+1816
AMORBACH		
Court:	Neuparth	+1806 to 1807?
	Bauer, A.	+ 1839
AMSTERDAM		
Court:	Rauscher	1807 to ?
	Christiani	+1813 to 1850
	Kleine, J.W.	? to ?
Cecilia Concerts:	Kleine, J.W.	
Felix Meritis Society:	Christiani	+1805 to 1845
	Kleine, J.C.	1815 to 1832
	Planke jun.	+1815 to 1817
	Planke sen.	+ 1817
	Kleine, J.W.	1832 to ?
Park Orchestra:	Kleine, J.W.	
Stumpff Orchestra:	Van der Finck	1847 to 1852
Opera:	Kleine, H.	? to 1798
	Christiani	1801 to 1840
	Kleine, J.C.	? to ?
French Opera:	Faubel, Ph.	
	Van der Finck	
German Theatre:	Van der Finck	
Grand Theatre:	Renard, J.	1885 to ?
Italian Theatre:	Van der Finck	
ANSBACH		
Court:	Schatz	1763 to 1785
	Ruff	1770 to 1779
	Seel	1770 to 1786
	Walther	1770 to 1796?

	Schwärzer	1786 to 1796?
ANTWERP		
Opera:	Moysard	
	Printz	
Cathedral:	Eeckhound	1773 to 1780?
AREZZO		
Appointment unknown:	Pollastri	+1835
ASCHAFFENBURG		
Court:	Faubel, J.	1811 to 1813
Military music:	Fauble sen.	+1801 to 1816
BADEN-BADEN		
Court:	Reusch	1771
Theatre Orchestra:	Sobeck	1849 to 1851
BALTIMORE		
Appointment unknown:	Wolfe	+1786 to 1799
	Dubois	+1798 to 1799
BELFAST		
Radio Orchestra:	Gomez, F.	1931 to 1938
Teaching:	Owens	+1801
BERLIN		
Court:	Fasch	1767 to ?
	Schramm, J.C.	1767 to ?
	David	1780
	Tausch, F.	1789 to 1817
	Beer	1792 to 1811
	Jäger	1810 to 1823?
	Tausch F.W.	1815 to 1845
	Belke	? to ?
	Pfaffe	+1817 to 1833?
	Schubert, A.	1830 to 1870?
	Gareis, A.	1834 to 1859
	Becker, K.F.W.	+1837 to 1886

		Gareis, G.	1841 to 1846
		Dettmann	+1860
		Pohl	1860 to 1886?
		Schmidt	+1885
		Huth	+1886
		Essberger	? to ?
	Royal Theatre:	Kühn	1787 to 1799
		Kuntz	1787 to 1799
		Sundelin	1804 to 1829
		Bliesener, F.	1805 to 1823
		Lindner	1814 to 1817
		Schick	1818 to 1859
		Tamm	1818 to 1858
		Nehrlich	1827 to 1849
		Schindelmeisser	1830 to 1833
		Schubert, O.	1878 to 1903?
	Bilse Orchestra:	Schubert, O.	1875 to 1878
		Bolland	+1880 to 1886
		Menz	+1880 to 1885
	Engel Orchestra:	Pohl	+1851
	Philharmonic Orchestra:	Oehler	1882 to 1888
	High School:	Hostié	1824 to 1834
		Schubert, O.	1892 to 1903?
	Appointment unknown:	Ebert	+1822 to 1825
BERNBURG			
	Wind band:	Wüstenhagen	+1833 to 1834
BOLOGNA			
	Teatro Communale:	Avoni	1797 to 1826
	Conservatorio:	DeMajo	+1800
		Avoni	1812 to ?
		Bianchini	
		Liverani	
		Maccagni	

BONN

Court:	Baum	+1783
	Meuser	+1783 to 1790?
	Pachmeier	+1789 to 1790?
Count Belderbusch:	Moock	+1783
	Pachmeier	+1783
Appointment unknown:	Romberg, G.	1792 to ?

BORDEAUX

Theatre:	Jandot	+1822
	Postula	1856 to ?
Conservatoire:	Postula	1861 to ?

BOSTON (Massachusetts)

Philharmonic Society:	Granger, Th.	1810 to ?
	Schaffer, L.	1810 to ?
Symphony Orchestra:	Selmer, A.	+1895
	Hamelin	1926 to 1930
	Polatschek	1930 to ?
Appointment unknown:	Granger, F.	+1793
	Stone	1793 to ?
	Schaffer, F.	+1796 to 1798

BREMEN

Town orchestra:	Rakemann sen.	+1807 to 1823
	Helfrich	+1821 to 1834
	Rakemann, C.	+1834 to 1842
Hanseatic Music Corps:	Klingenberg	+1819 to 1821
	Helfrich	1821 to 1834?

BRESLAU

Prince-Bishop:	Berner	1797 to 1805
	Schnabel	+1800 to 1819
	Langer	+1819
	Metzler	1826 to 1833?
Count Hoym:	Krause, J.	1794 to 1805
	Krause, K.	1794 to 1811

BRUNSWICK		
Court:	Dossenbach	+1771
	Hesse, J.W.	1784 to 1795
	Spiess bros.	+1802 to 1804
	Tretbach	+1804 to 1829
	Rasch	+1819 to 1827
	Herrig	1826 to 1848
	Tretbar, F.	1829 to 1865
	Gruner	1840 to 1855
	Bachmann, ?	1865 to ?
BRUSSELS		
Court:	Godecharle	? to ?
	Broue	? to ?
	Bachmann, G.	? to 1842
	Blaes	1845 to 1871?
	Wuille	? to ?
Royal Wind Band:	Bachmann, G.	? to 1838
	Sax	1838 to 1842
	Van Buggenhout	? to ?
Théâtre de la Monnaie:	Eeckhound	+1780 to ?
	Franck	
	Lambelée	
	Poncelet	
	Tourneur	
Conservatoire:	Bachmann, G.	1832 to 1842
	Lambelée	1844 to 1871
	Blaes	1842 to 1872
	Poncelet	1871 to 1903
	Hannon	1901 to 1906
	Bageard	1906 to 1911
BUDAPEST		
Hungarian National Theatre:	Reinel	1852 to ?
BÜCKEBURG		
Schaumberg-Lippe Court:	Vagny	+1795 to 1799?

	Wagner, ?	+1811
	Bargheer	1828 to 1855
	Müller, I.	+1846 to 1854

BUENOS AIRES

Academy of Instrumental Music:	Prada	1810 to ?

CAMBRIDGE

Appointment unknown:	Hellendael	+1789

CARLSRUHE

Court:	Klipfele	1772 to 1775
	Kustner	1772 to 1775
	Reusch	1772 to 1775
	Eigler	+1775
	Dahlinger	1785 to ?
	Erhardt	+1793
	Schall	+1793
	Schmittbauer	+1793
	Kleine, D.	1 815 to 1837
	Schleicher	1819 to 1822
	Roth,?	+1867
	Klupp	+1911

CHAMBÉRY

Conservatoire:	De Groot	+1847 to 1854
Philharmonic Society's School:	De Groot	+1847 to 1854

CHARLESTON

City Theatre:	Foucard	1796 to 1799

CHEMNITZ

Town Orchestra:	Stark	1871 to 1873

CHICAGO

Symphony Orchestra:	Schreurs	1891 to 1921

COBLENZ

Court:	Meder, K.	+1759
	Meder, V.	? to ?

		Gumpelshamer	1769 to 1772
		Langenbeck	+1769
		Klee	1773 to 1794
		Spitz	+1781 to 1782?
		Beckau	1783 to 1792
		Ehlen	? to ?
		Röder	+1814
COBURG			
	Saxe-Coburg Court:	Stötzer	1800 to 1818
		Greding	+1827
		Müller, I	+1827
CÖTHEN			
	Anhalt-Cöthen Court:	Weissgärber	1833
COLOGNE			
	Cathedral:	Götzscher	+1785
		Klein, J.H.	+1785
		Pfeffel	+1822 to 1830?
COPENHAGEN			
	Court:	Füssel	+1806
		Krag	+1806
		Wachtelbrenner	+1806
		Petersen	1832 to ?
CÓRDOBA			
	Cathedral:	Prada	1806 to 1810?
CRACOW			
	Orchestra:	Krzyzanowski	+1821
DANZIG			
	Orchestra:	Vogt	+1833
		Krause, ?	+1885
DARMSTADT			
	Hesse-Darmstadt Court:	Sartorius	+1780
		Schüler	1780 to 1814
		Habermehl	1790 to 1807
		Back	1795 to 1816
		Dickerhof	1795 to 1805

		Niebergall	1795 to 1826
		Anton, L.	1804 to 1842
		Wagner, F.	1808 to 1849
		Haller	1810 to 1858
		Backofen, H.	1811 to 1839
		Scherzer	1812 to 1834
		Anton, F.	1813 to 1850
		Reinhardt, G.	+1814
		Bögel	1815 to 1823
		Schnittspahn	1816 to 1852
		Stautz	1817 to 1830
		Banger	1819 to ?
		Crispin	1819 to 1854
		Kircheis	1819 to 1856
		Ruch	1819 to 1840
		Reitz, A.	1820 to 1837
		Reitz, ?	+1850
DESSAU			
	Anhalt-Dessau Court:	Ermel	1798 to ?
		Barth, W.	? to 1802
		Rauschschindel	+1805 to 1849?
		Lindner	1817 to 1827
		Tausch, ?	1822 to 1849?
		Lorenz	+1823 to 1849?
		Grützmacher	+1832 to 1862
		Amelang	+1849
		Buch	+1849
DETMOLD			
	Lippe-Detmold Court:	Neumann, H.	1823 to 1824
		Vollmar	1823 to 1843
		Steffens	1824 to 1849
		Richter	1843 to 1876
		Meier	1849 to 1871
		Ehrlich	1871 to 1872
		Vaupel	1872 to 1876
	Leopold Corps:	Neumann, H.	1823 to 1829
		Neumann, Ph.	1823 to ?
		Steffens	1824 to ?

DONAUESCHINGEN			
	Fürstenburg Court:	Heller, A.	? to ?
		Heller, E.	? to ?
		Braun	+1792
		Kopp	+1792
		Schrenk	+1850 to 1851?
DRESDEN			
	Court:	Roth, J.T.	1794 to 1823
		Roth, K.G.	1794 to 1828
		Gäbler, Chr.	1813 to 1823
		Kotte	1817 to 1849?
		Lauterbach, J.G.	1817 to 1824?
		Lauterbach, F.W.	+1824 to 1849
		Forckert	1833 to 1874
		Dominik	1840 to 1849
		Reinel	+1848 to 1852
		Kötzschau	1857 to 1890
		Kaiser, J.	+1875 to 1885?
		Demnitz	1875 to 1890?
		Nöthlich	+1880 to 1925?
		Gabler, M.	1881 to 1906?
		Lange	1890 to 1925?
		Schneider, G.	1890 to ?
		Richter	+1925
	Conservatoire:	Kotte	? to 1857
		Forckert	? to ?
		Lauterbach, F.W.	1857 to 1875
		Demnitz	1875 to 1890?
	Blind Institute:	Forckert	1830s
		Kotte	1840s
DUBLIN			
	Dublin Theatre:	Willman	1805 to 1816?
	Hawkins Street Theatre:	Barton	+1824
DURLACH			
	Court:	Reusch	1730 to 1771
		Hengel	1760s

EDINBURGH

Theatre Royal:	Platt	+1827
	Spindler	+1827

ERFURT

32nd regiment Prussian infantry	Landgraf	1837 to 1840
Appointment unknown:	Peger	1840 to 1843

ERLANGEN

Appointment unknown:	Möhrenschlager	+1847

ESTERHÁZ

Court:	Griesbacher	1776 to 1778
	Schierll jun.	+1783
	Wack, W.	+1783

FLORENCE

Royal Theatre:	Senft	+1795
Teatro Cocomero:	Poggiali	1800 to ?
Teatro degli Intrepidi:	Poggiali	1793 to 1798
Teatro la Pergola:	Tuly	1791 to 1795
Santa Croce:	Senft	+1778
	Corman	+1788
Conservatorio:	Bimboni	
	Nocentini	

FRANKFURT a. M.

Theatre Orchestra:	Mayer	+1788 to 1797
	Ludwig	1800 to 1804
	Baumgärtner	+1804 to 1817
	Hoffmann, J.G.	1804 to 1806
	Wippert	+1809 to 1811
	Hoffmann, J.G.	1812 to 1814
	Reinhardt, G.	1814 to 1821
	De Groot	1818 to 1821
	Bretschneider	1821 to 1834

		Faubel, Ph.	1821 to 1829
		?Funk	+1832 to 1835?
		Mehner	1836 to 1861
		Springer, ?	1836 to 1843
		Triebel	+1863
		?Abel	+1872 to 1874?
	Teaching:	Neumann	+1800
FREIBURG			
	Princess Elizabeth:	Czerny	1780s
		Kirstein	1780s
		Matauschek	1780s
		Tirry	1780s
FRIBOURG			
	Teaching:	Weissmüller	+1843
FULDA			
	Court:	Rihl	+1800
		André	+1824 to 1834
		?Hamburger	+1835 to 1845
	Military band:	André	+1834
		Hamburger	+1834
GENEVA			
	Appointment unknown:	Sabon	+1841 to 1843
GENOA			
	Paganini Institute:	Giampieri	1922 to ?
GHENT			
	Casino Concerts:	Haute	
	Grand Theatre:	Themsche	
		Franck	1840 to 1843
		Haute	1844 to ?
	Conservatoire:	Themsche	1835 to 1847
		Haute	1847 to 1870
		Weber	1870 to 1876
		Gracht	1876 to ?

GÖTTINGEN

Jacobi's Orchestra:	Meinberg	? to 1823
	Hebestreit	+1828
	Müller, ?	+1828

GOTHA

Saxe-Gotha Court:	Backofen, H.	1804 to 1806
Saxe-Coburg-Gotha Court:	Müller, I	+1841 to 1844?
	Rulf	+1841

HAGUE, the

Court:	De Groot	1826 to 1830
	Faubel, Ph.	1830 to 1854?
	Becht	+1839 to ?
	Wuille	1850s
Prince William V:	Kleine, H.	
Diligentia Concerts:	Becht	+1850 to 1900?
French Theatre:	Kleine, H.	? to ?
	Kleine, J.C.	? to ?
	De Groot	? to 1818
	De Groot	1821 to 1823
	De Groot	1826 to 1830
	Becht	+1850 to 1900?
Royal Music School:	De Groot	1826 to 1830
	Faubel, Ph.	1830 to 1852
	Becht	1852 to ?

HALLE

Theatre Orchestra:	Grosse	1838 to 1843?
	Oehler	1877?

HAMBURG

City theatre orchestra:	Dufour	+1789 to 1807?
	Bultos	+1795
	Krause, K.J?	+1795
	Hartmann, C.	+1801 to 1832
	Gross	+1807
	Jodry	+1818

	Kaiser	+1818
	Schramm, C.W.	+1841 to 1846?
	Süssmilch	+1846
	Hofmann	? to 1889
Laube Orchestra:	Oehler	1881 to 1882
Appointment unknown:	Herzog	1830s & 1840s
HANOVER		
Court:	Barbandt	1735 to 1752
	Seeman, G.W.	1818 to 1850
	Albes	1821 to 1844
	Hellwig	1825 to 1829
	Seeman, A.	1841 to 1850
	Meyer, H.	1844 to 1851
	Beate	1850 to 1884
	Sachse	1850 to 1888
	Sobeck	1851 to 1901
	Tadra	1852 to 1853
	Feller	1853 to 1884
	Kellner	1884 to 1886
	Menz	1885 to 1925
	Bolland	1886 to 1926
	Hofmann, R.	1889 to 1922
	Gabler, E.	1901 to 1944
HAVANA		
Italian Opera:	Broca, P.	1836
HEINICHEN		
Town musician:	Amme	+1833
HILDBURGHAUSEN		
Court:	Gugel	+1802
	Mahr	+1819 to 1821
HOLSTEIN		
Count Röder:	Krause, K.	1789 to 1794
KASSEL		
Court:	Nolte	+1809 to 1812

		Spiess bros.	+1809 to 1812
		André	+1823
		Ruprecht	+1823
		Bänder, C.	1823 to 1846
		De Groot	1823 to 1826
		Deichert	1829 to 1846
		Neff	1830s to 1866
		Heisterhagen	+1835 to 1839
		Vauth	+1835 to 1850
		Bänder, F.	+1836 to 1850
		Griesel	+1836 to 1839
		Lesser	+1838 to 1839
		Schultheis	+1838 to 1866
		Bättenhausen	+1839 to 1841
		Curth	+1839 to 1841
		Holzapfel	+1843 to 1848
		Bührmann	+1844 to 1848
		Hamburger	+1850
		Schaub	+1866
		Klotzsch	+1885
		Lohmann	+1905
		Richter, A?	+1905
		Schnurbusch	+1905
KÖNIGSBERG			
	Theatre orchestra:	Czermack	+1809 to 1815
		Witt	+1809
		Hostié	1812 to 1824
		Köttlitz	1840 to ?
KREMSMÜNSTER			
	Court:	Gründlinger	1802 to 1812
		Hollnsteiner	+1814
		Kolbe	+1814
		Mikesch	+1814
		Zach	+1814
LEIPZIG			
	Euterpe Society:	Kunze	+1832 to 1833
		Rosenkranz	+1832 to 1834
		Lopitzsch	+1833 to 1847

Gewandhaus Orchestra:	Haberland	1784 to 1806
	Hübler	1784 to 1792
	Hunger	1788 to 1800
	Maurer, G.	1792 to 1813
	Berger	1798 to 1807
	Barth, W.	1802 to 1829
	Claus	1803 to 1811
	Heinze, F.	1811 to 1850
	Mejo	1814 to 1821
	Tretbar, F.	1823 to 1829
	Drobisch	1829 to 1837
	Heinze, G.	1837 to 1844
	Landgraf	1840 to 1884
	Albrecht	1850 to 1863
	Gentzsch	1863 to 1885
	Bauer, E.	1881 to ?
	Stradtmann	1881 to ?
	Heyneck	? to 1902
Conservatoire:	Gentzsch	
Town musician:	Maurer, G.	+1792 to 1813
	Barth, W.	1814 to 1849?
Appointment unknown:	Mehner	1831 to 1835

LENINGRAD (See St Petersburg)

LIÈGE

Theatre:	Massaert	? to ?
	Postula	? to 1846?
Athénée:	Postula	? to 1846?
Conservatoire:	Massaert	1827 to 1862
	Hasenier	? to ?
	Tourneur	? to ?

LINZ

Theatre orchestra:	Barth, J.	? to ?

LISBON

Court:	Canongia, J.A.	+1816 to 1842

LOCATIONS

San Carlos Theatre:	Canongia, I.	1793 to ?
	Wisse	1795 to 1799
	Neuparth	+1815 to 1817
	Canongia, J.A.	1821 to 1842
	Campos	1824 to 1850?
Conservatoire (Patriachal Seminary):	Canongia, J.A.	1821 to 1842
Appointment unknown:	Odalde	+1822 to 1824

LÖWENSTEIN

Court:	Neuparth	1804 to 1806

LONDON

Court:	Kramer	1803 to 1834
	Eisert	+1805 to 1837
	Egerton, W.	1837 to 1869
	Williams	1837 to ?
	Clinton, G.	1867 to 1900
	Egerton, J. (I)	1870 to 1910
	Egerton, P.	+1898 to 1902
6th & 7th Dukes of Devonshire:	Lazarus	
8th Duke of Devonshire:	Langenus	
Philharmonic Society:	Kramer	1813 to 1817?
	Mahon, W.	1813 to 1816
	Oliver	+1813 to ?
	Willman	1817 to 1839
	Powell	+1826 to 1837
	Binfield	? to 1840?
	Williams	1840 to 1862
	Lazarus	1841 to 1872
	Tyler	+1868
	Clinton, G.	1873 to ?
	Egerton, J. (II)	? to ?
	Egerton, P.	1899 to 1902
Sacred Harmonic Society:	Willman	1833 to 1840
	Lazarus	1838 to ?

Crystal Palace Concerts:	Lazarus	
	Thomas, F.	
	Papé	1855 to 1874
	Clinton, G	1874 to ?
Richter Concerts:	Egerton, J. (I)	1879 to 1897?
	Augarde, G.	1881 to 1887
BBC Symphony Orchestra:	Thurston	1930 to 1946
English Ladies Orchestra:	Thomas, F.	? to ?
London Symphony Orchestra:	Anderson	1904 to 1943
	Augarde, A.	1904 to 1916
	Gomez, M.	1904 to 1915
	Egerton, P.	1904
	Mills, O.	1905 to 1913
	Augarde, E.	1913 to 1933
	Draper, M.	1919 to 1923
	Draper, M.	1930 to 1948
Queen's Hall Orchestra:	Gomez, F.	1894 to ?
	Gomez, M.	1894 to ?
	Fawcett, Ch.	? to 1910?
	Langenus	1905 to 1910
Carl Rosa Company:	Gomez, F.	
	Gomez, M.	
Covent Garden:	Mahon, J.	+1794 to 1812?
	Mahon, W.	+1794 to 1812?
	Hopkins, E.S.G.	1812 to 1838?
	Hopkins, G.	+1812 to 1829
	Willman	1829 to 1840?
	Egerton, W.	+1838
	Lazarus	
	Maycock	+1857 to 1892
	Gomez, F.	
	Gomez, M.	
	Draper, H.	
	Anderson	

Drury Lane:	Müller, I.	1815 to 1820
	Kleine, J.W.	? to 1847
	Maycock	1857 to 1892
Haymarket Theatre:	Willman	+1816 to 1840
	Williams	1829 to ?
	Lazarus	1840 to 1883
	Pollard	+1859
	Tyler	? to ?
Coldstream Guards:	Eley	1785 to 1816
	Egerton, W.	1815 to 1835
	Willman	1816 to 1825
	Lazarus	1829 to 1838
	Maycock	+1842 to ?
	Pollard	+1859 to 1866
	Thomas, C.	+1863 to 1896
	Egerton, J. (I)	? to ?
	Egerton, P.	? to ?
	Egerton, J. (II)	? to ?
Grenadier Guards:	Schott, A.	1844 to 1856
Scots Guards:	Hopkins, E.	1797 to 1838
Guildhall School of Music:	Draper, Ch.	1895 to 1940
Kneller Hall:	Lazarus	1858 to 1894
	Egerton, J. (I)	1889 to 1910
	Clinton, G.	1905 to 1913
Royal Academy of Music:	Kramer	1823 to 1825
	Willman	1823 to 1825
	Stohwasser	1825 to ?
	Lazarus	1854 to 1894
	Clinton, G.	1900 to 1913
	Augarde, E.	1913 to 1923
	Draper, H.	1923 to 1934
	Anderson	1941 to 1951
Royal College of Music:	Lazarus	1882 to 1894
	Egerton, J. (I)	1894 to 1910
	Thurston	1930 to 1953

	Trinity College of Music:	Lazarus	1881 to 1892
		Clinton, G.	1892 to 1912
		Draper, Ch.	1915 to 1937
LUCCA			
	Court:	Casali	1818 to 1839
		Lucchesi	1818 to 1839
		Pellegrini, A.	+1822 to 1823?
		Pellegrini, D.	+1822 to 1823?
LUDWIGSLUST			
	Mecklenburg-Schwerin Court:	Mainzer	1792 to 1795
		Hammerl	1795 to 1825?
		Stüber	1808 to 1829
	Life Guards:	Stüber	1798 to 1808?
		Selike	+1812 to 1819?
LÜBECK			
	National Theatre:	Hesse	+1814
	Town musician:	Schulze	1790 to 1797?
		Derlien	1859 to 1867?
LYONS			
	Grand Theatre:	Mocker	1790 to 1822?
MADRID			
	Court:	Schindtler	? to 1823
		Jardin, Magin	? to 1858
		Broca, P.	1816 to 1836
		Martinez, J.A.	? to ?
		Broca, R.	1836 to 1849
		Romero	1844 to 1867
		Romero	1875 to ?
		González	? to ?
		San Miguel	? to ?
	Royal Corps of Halberdiers:	Broca, P.	1816 to ?
		Romero	1833 to ?
		San Miguel	? to ?

	Yuste	1885 to ?
	Gomez, A.F.	? to ?
Society of Chamber Music:	Yuste	
Society of Concerts (National Orchestra):	González	
	Yuste	1890 to ?
	Parra	
Philharmonic Orchestra:	Gomez, A.F.	
	Parra	
Symphony Orchestra:	San Miguel	
	Yuste	
Itlaian Theatre:	Carlos	+1799
Opera, Buen Retiro Gardens:	Yuste	
Royal Theatre:	González	
	Yuste	1880 to ?
Teatro del Principe (Spanish Theatre):	Juliá	+1806
	Broca, P.	1818 to 1836
	Broca, R.	1836 to 1849
Variety Theatre:	González	1865 to ?
Municipal Band:	Yuste	
Conservatoire:	Broca, P.	1829 to 1836
	Jardin, Magin	1829 to 1857
	Broca, R.	1839 to 1849
	Romero	1849 to 1876
	Rodriguez	1876 to ?
	Fischer, E.	? to 1883
	González	1883 to 1909
	Yuste	1909 to 1940
	Gomez, A.F.	1943 to 1950
	Parra	1950 to 1971

MAGDEBURG		
Theatre Orchestra:	Schuberth	1804 to 1833
	Feldt	+1824 to 1828
	Kühne	+1824 to 1825
MAINZ		
Court:	Harburger	1774 to 1803
	Wagner, W.	1774 to 1784
	Becker, A.J.	1788 to 1802?
	Scribanek	+1791
Duke of Bretzenheim:	Hammerl	1790s
MANCHESTER		
Gentlemen's Concerts:	Grosse	1851 to 1858
Hallé Orchestra:	Cortesi	1858 to 1860
	Grosse	1858 to 1886
	Pollard	1861 to 1862
	Gladney	1862 to 1892
	Wadsworth, ?	1885 to 1895
	Hoffmann, A.	1887 to 1897
	Norton, F.	1893 to 1900
	Mills, E.	1897 to 1919
	Wadsworth, T.	1897 to 1929
	Norton, H.	1899 to 1900
	Douglas	1900 to 1906
	Brough	1901 to 1915
	Slade	1906 to 1916
	Mortimer	1917 to 1937
	Slade	1919 to 1937
MANNHEIM		
Court:	Hampel	1758/9 to 1777
	Quallenberg	1758/9 to 1777
	Tausch, Jacob	1765 to 1777
	Tausch, F.	1770 to 1777
	Habert	1793 to ?
	Mayer, J.	1793 to ?
	Ahl	+1813 to 1815
	Eichorn	+1824 to 1831
	Gassner	+1824 to 1831
	Röhrig	1834 to ?

MÉAUX			
	Conservatoire:	Rose	1900 to 1902
MEININGEN			
	Saxe-Meiningen Court:	Goepfert	1793 to 1818
		Härtel	+1811
		Fischer, M.	1817 to 1854?
		Haushälter	1827 to 1863?
		Langlotz	1827 to 1866?
		Reif	1855 to 1879
		Schwarze	1867 to 1888
		Mühlfeld	1873 to 1907
		Preller	1888 to ?
		Wiebel	+1907 to 1909?
METZ			
	Theatre orchestra:	Chardon	
		Valette	
MILAN			
	La Scala:	Bassi	? to ?
		Carulli	1820s & 1830s
		Cavallini	+1835 to 1852
		Orsi	+1878 to 1889
		Blonk-Steiner	1914 to 1918
	Conservatorio:	Adami, G	1808 to 1815
		Carulli	1817 to 1873
		Cavallini	1870 to 1874?
		Orsi	1873 to ?
		Bove	? to ?
		Blonk-Steiner	1915 to ?
		Giampieri	? to ?
MINNEAPOLIS			
	Symphony Orchestra:	Schmidt, R.O.	1910s & 1920s
MODENA			
	Court:	Cuboni	+1825
		Petz	+1825
MONACO			
	Court:	Roeser	+1763 to 1770

MONTEVIDEO

Casa de Comedias:	Ferrán	

MOSCOW

Persimfans Orchestra:	Volodin	1924 to 1926
Symphony Orchestra:	Bellison	1905 to 1914
USSR State Symphony Orchestra:	Zuckerman	
	Shtark	
Bolshoi Theatre:	Friedrich	
	Rozanov	
	Bessmertnov	
	Nikolaevsky	
	Alexandrov	
	Maiorov	
	Volodin	1926 to ?
Italian Opera:	Farnari	+1824
Opera:	Bellison	1905 to 1914
Shatsky Opera Studio:	Semenov	
Conservatoire:	Zimmerman	1872 to ?
	Friedrich	1890s to ?
	Rozanov	1916 to 1937
	Semenov	1920s to ?
	Volodin	1937 to 1966
Gnesinykh Music Teacher's Institute:	Alexandrov	
	Shtark	

MÜHLHAUSEN

Town musician:	Schollmeyer	+1833

MÜNSTER

Court:	Romberg	? to 1784

MUNICH

Court:	Hampel	1778 to ?
	Quallenberg	1778 to ?
	Tausch, Jacob	1778 to 1787?
	Tausch, F.	1778 to 1789
	Tausch, Joseph	1779 to 1806
	Dimmler	1796 to 1829?
	Ruppert	+1800
	Winter	+1803
	Werle, S.	1805 to 1845
	Hoffmann, J.G.	1806 to 1812
	Baermann, H.	1807 to 1847
	Mainzer	1807 to 1827
	Schönche	1811 to 1845
	Schülein	1812 to 1866
	Faubel, J.	1818 to 1864
	Schott, A.	1819 to 1824?
	Held	1824 to 1864
	Werle, G.	+1824 to 1827?
	Klein, Th.	+1826 to 1828
	Baermann, C.	1832 to 1880
	Reitmayer (I)	1839 to 1864
	Venzl	1864 to ?
	Meyer, H.	1866 to ?
	Hartmann, F.	? to ?
	Wagner, C.	? to ?
	Walch	? to ?
Subscription Concerts (Akademie):	Baermann, H.	1811 to 1843
	Dimmler	1811 to 1829
	Schönche	1811 to 1849
	Tausch, Joseph	1811 to 1812
	Werle, S.	1811 to 1851
	Faubel, J.	1818 to 1865
	Held	1818 to 1874
	Schott, A.	1821 to 1829(7?)
	Schülein	1821 to 1863
	Reitmayer (I)	1823 to 1881
	Baermann, C.	1828 to 1880
	Venzl	1863 to 1881
	Hartmann, F.	1869 to 1899
	Wittstadt	1869 to 1893
	Hefele	1881 to 1882

	Fischer, K.	1882 to 1911?
	Marx	1886 to 1907
	Wagner, C.	1892 to 1911?
	Knirsch	1894 to 1911?
	Walch	1900 to 1911?
	Wagner, J.	1910 to ?
Royal Music School:	Baermann, C.	+1864 to 1882
	Walch	? to ?
Appointment unknown:	Lutz	? to 1837

NANTES

Teaching:	Rebeyrol	1834 to ?

NAPLES

Court:	Sebastiani	
San Carlo Orchestra:	Sebastiani	
Conservatorio della Pietá de' Turchini:	Fetter	1794 to 1801
	Brattoli	1795 to 1802
	Cataneo	1797 to 1801?
	Sedelmayer	1801 to 1805
	Rupp	1805 to 1807
Real Conservatorio:	Sebastiani	
	Labanchi	

NAUMBURG

Orchestra:	Zwicker	+1836

NEUCHÂTEL

Société du Concert:	Benoît	1785 to 1787
	Denis	1786 to 1787
	Kastus	1790 to 1802
	Stavelot	1802 to ?
Royal Cavalry:	Benoît	1785 to 1787
	Denis	1786 to 1787

NEU-RUPPIN		
Military Music:	Pollmächer	1836 to 1841
NEU-STRELITZ		
Mecklenburg-Strelitz Court:	Mainzer	1795 to 1807
NEW YORK		
NBC Symphony Orchestra:	Duques	+1937 to 1954?
Philharmonic Orchestra:	Goeller	+1842
	Groenevelt	+1842
	Drewes	+1892
	Reinecke	+1892
	Selmer, A.	+1900
	Chiaffarelli	+1917
	Christman	+1917
	Bellison	1921 to 1948
Symphony Orchestra:	Langenus	1910 to 1923
	Duques	+1923 to 1933?
Juilliard School of Music:	Duques	1923 to 1963
NICE		
Symphony Orchestra:	Oehler	+1879
NUREMBERG		
Town orchestra:	Backofen, H.	1794 to 1804
	Backofen, G.	1803 to 1822?
	Taut	+1820 to 1823
	Saud	+1822
ÖHRINGEN		
Hohenlohe-Öhringen Court:	Bauer, A.	
OFFENBACH		
Herr Bernhard:	Mangold	1798 to 1800?
OLDENBURG		
Court:	Koehn	+1845

OSNABRÜCK			
	2nd Hanoverian infantry regiment:	Zangenberg	+1799 to 1810?
OUDENARDE			
	Société des Beaux-Arts:	Postula	1847 to 1855?
	Conservatoire:	Postula	1847 to 1855?
OXFORD			
	Music Room:	Mahon, J.	1772 to 1800
		Mahon, W.	1774 to ?
PARIS			
	Court:	Hayenschinck	+1785 to 1789
		Solère	1785 to 1789
		Duvernoy	1804 to 1824?
		Lefèvre, X.	1804 to 1829
		Solère	1804 to 1816
		Dacosta	1805 to 1842?
		Berr	1832 to 1838
	Prince Louis François of Conti:	Duport	1760s
		Flieger	1763 to ?
		Procksch, G.	1763 to 1771
	Prince Louis François Joseph of Conti:	Biche	+1785
	Prince of Lambesc:	Beer	1778 to 1779
		Beer	1781 to 1782
	Prince of Rohan:	Meissner	1766 to 1769?
	Duke of Orleans:	Beer	1767 to 1777
		Solère	1778 to 1785
	Duke of Montmorency:	Hostié	+1788
	Marquis of Brancas:	Meissner	1769 to 1776?
	La Pouplinière:	Flieger	+1750 to 1762
		Procksch, G.	+1750 to 1762

Colonne Concerts:	Lefèbvre, H.	? to 1925
Concert Spirituel:	(Kermazin	1750?)
	Flieger	1755
	Procksch, G.	1755
	Reiffer	1763 to 1785?
	Meissner	1767 to 1775
	Klein	1775
	Yost	1777 to 1785
	Wolf	1778
	Rathé	1780
	Solère	1782 to 1788
	Wachter	1782 to 1786
	Ernest	1785 to 1791
	Barbay	1786 to 1787
	Hostié	1786
	Lefèvre, X.	1787 to 1791
	Chelard	1790 to 1791
Concerts de la rue de Cléry:	Lefèvre, X.	? to ?
Concerts Populaires:	Auroux	1861 to 1863
	Grisez	1861 to 1863
Concerts Symphoniques Touche:	Cahuzac	
Société des Concerts:	Boufil	1828 to ?
	Buteux	1828 to 1833?
	Dacosta	1828 to 1842?
	Frion	1828 to ?
	Klosé	1832 to 1848
	Leroy	1849 to 1859?
	Rose	1857 to 1872
	Grisez	+1879
	Mimart	1892 to 1897
	Turban	1892 to 1897
Société des Instruments à vent:	Grisez	+1879
	Turban	+1879

Société moderne d'Instruments à vent:	Vionne	1895 to ?
	Guyot, J.	+1913
Société Philharmonique:	Lamour	1850
	Perez	1850
Orchestre Lamoureux:	Selmer, A.	+1885
	Selmer, H.	+1885
	Lefèbvre, H.	? to 1925
	Paradis	? to ?
Orchestre National:	Hamelin	1934 to 1951
Opéra (Académie Royale de Musique):	Reiffer	1749, 1751 & 2
	Schiefer	1749, 1751 & 2
	Flieger	1753
	Procksch, G.	1753
	Meissner	+1769
	Procksch, G.	1771 to 1775
	Assmann	1773 to 1774
	Ernest	1773 to ?
	Scharf	1773 to ?
	Abrahame	1788 to 1790
	Lefèvre, X.	1791 to 1817
	Chelard	? to 1802
	Solère	1802 to 1816
	Dacosta	1817 to 1842
	Lefèvre, L.	+1818 to 1824
	Péchignier	1818 to 1840
	Buteux	1825 to 1843?
	Mohr	+1843 to 1848
	Leroy	+1857
	Rose	1857 to 1891
	Mayeur	1860 to ?
	Turban	1868 to ?
	Bretonneau	? to ?
	Paradis	1891 to 1934
	Lefèbvre, H.	? to 1925
	Cahuzac	1901 to 1920

Opéra Buffa (Société Olympique):	Buteux	1819 to 1821
Opéra Comique (Théâtre de Monsieur, Théâtre Feydau, Comédie Italienne):	Duvernoy	1790 to 1824
	Solère	1790 to 1802
	Dacosta	1802 to 1807
	Boufil	1807 to 1830
	Janssen	1814 to 1835
	Hugot, A.	1824 to 1833
	Frion	1831 to 1833
	Grisez	? to ?
	Selmer, A.	+1885
	Selmer, H.	+1885
	Périer	+1918
	Stiévenard	+1918
Ambigu Comique:	Poulain	1821 to 1822
	Turgis	1821 to 1822
	Mohr	1823
	Delamotte	1824 to 1825
	Peinte	1826 to 1827
	Frion	1828
	Guyot	1828
Cirque Olympique:	Regnault	1821
	Clausé	1822 to 1823
	Trou	1824 to 1825
Cité:	Albesby	+1795
Colonne:	Cahuzac	
Délassements Comiques:	Abrahame	1790 to 1805?
Folies Dramatiques:	Dufour	1831 to 1833
Français (Comédie Française):	Péchignier	1815 to 1818

	Vanderhagen	1815 to 1822
	Hugray	1818 to 1830
	Maré jun.	1822 to 1830
	Scudo	+1844
Gaité:	Bazin	1821 to 1825
	Crépin	1821
	Hugot, A.	1822 to 1823
	Georges	1824 to 1825
	Neveu	1827 to 1829
	Guyot	1827
	Winter	1830
Gymnase:	Turban	
Italien (Opéra Italien):	Dacosta	1807 to 1817
	Gambaro	1816 to 1828
	Buteux	1821 to 1825
	Berr	1825 to 1838
	Loudelle	1828 to 1830
	Klosé	1836 to 1844?
	Müller, I.	1838 to 1841
	Turban	? to ?
	Beletti	+1860
Lyrique:	Gaveaux	+1798
Molière:	Dacosta	1798 to 1802
Montansier:	Walter	+1798
Nouveautés:	Delamotte	1827 to 1829
	Dufour	1827 to 1828
	Egger	1829
Odéon (Second Théâtre Francais):	Dufour	1821 to 1825
	Plater	+1821
	Mocker	+1824 to 1827
	Mohr	1827 to 1828
	Trou	1827 to 1830
Palais Royal:	Georges	1831 to 1833

LOCATIONS

Panorama Dramatique:	Félix	1821
	Maré jun.	1821
	Delamotte	1822
Porte St Martin:	Clermont	1822 to 1826
	Hugot, P.	1823 to 1829
	Lauel	1827
	Caldes	1828 to 1829
Renaissance:	De Groot	1838 to 1840
République:	Lefèvre, X.	+1799
S.A.R. Madame (Gymnase Dramatique):	Klett	1821 to 1825
	Maré sen.	1821 to 1825
	Laurent	1826
	Loudelle	1826
	Bazin	1827 to 1829
	Georges	1827 to 1829
Spectacles de Curiosités:	Mocker	1829
Variétés:	Conrad	1821 to 1827
	Gallet	1821 to 1827
	Clermont	1828 to 1833
	Desvignes	1828 to 1830
	François	1831 to 1833
Vaudeville:	Legendre	1821 to 1822
	Leriche	1821 to 1822
	Bergevel	1823 to 1829
	Berr	1823
	Guyot	1824
	Scruder	1827 to 1828
	Danais	1829
Ventadour:	Franck	? to ?
Life Guards:	Meissner	1767 to 1775
French Guards:	Vanderhagen	1783 to 1789
	Lefèvre, L.	1784 to 1789
	Méric	? to ?

National Guard (I):	Fuchs	+1789 to 1795
	Lefèvre, L.	1789 to 1795
	Lefèvre, X.	1789 to 1795
	Méric	1789 to 1795
	Solère	1789 to 1795
	Vanderhagen	1789 to 1795
	Duvernoy	1790 to ?
	Hostié	? to 1794
	Blasius	1793 to 1795
	Chelard	1793 to 1795
	Legendre	1793 to 1795
Directoire Guard:	Vanderhagen	1795 to 1799
	Dacosta	1798 to 1799
Consular Guard:	Dacosta	1799 to 1804
	Lefèvre, L.	1799 to 1802
	Vanderhagen	1799 to 1804
	Walter	1799 to 1804
Imperial Guard:	Dacosta	1804 to 1814
	Vanderhagen	1804 to 1814
	Walter	1804 to ?
National Guard(II):	Lefèvre, L.	1814 to 1827
	Lefèvre, L.	1830 to 1831
Republican Guard:	Selmer, H.	+1880
	Paradis	1882 to 1909
	Lefèbvre, H.	
	Jeanjean	
	Verney	
Conservatoire:	Assmann	1795 to 1802
	Chelard	1795 to 1802
	Duvernoy	1795
	Fuchs	1795 to 1800
	Lefèvre, L.	1795 to 1802
	Lefèvre, X.	1795 to 1824
	Leriche	1795 to 1800
	Méric	1795 to 1802

Location	Name	Dates
	Solère	1795 to 1802
	Voisin	1795 to 1796
	Duvernoy	1800 to 1816
	Legendre	1800 to 1802
	Lefèvre, L.	1824 to 1832
	Berr	1831 to 1838
	Lamour	1835 to 1840
	Klosé	1838 to 1868
	Leroy	1869 to 1880
	Rose	1876 to 1900
	Turban	1888 to 1905
	Mimart	1905 to 1923
	Périer	1923 to 1949
Institut National (École Gratuite):	Lefèvre, L.	1789 to 1795
	Méric	1789 to 1795
	Duvernoy	1790 to 1795
	Assmann	1793 to 1795
	Chelard	1793 to 1795
	Fuchs	1793 to 1795
	Legendre	1793 to 1795
	Solère	1793 to 1795
	Voisin	1793 to 1795
PASSAU		
Cathedral:	Wasmutius	1788 to 1808
PHILADELPHIA		
Philadelphia Orchestra:	McLane	1943 to ?
Curtis Institute:	McLane	? to ?
Appointment unknown:	Gautier	+1795 to 1796
PLOGWITZ		
Baron Hochberg:	David	1786 to 1789
	Springer, V.	1786 to 1787
PORT-AU-PRINCE		
Comédie:	Barbier	1779
	Louis	1780s

POTSDAM

Philharmonic Society:	Meinberg	+1839 to 1841
Royal Guard:	Meinberg	1823 to 1844?
Royal Military School:	Beer	1792 to 1811
	Meinberg	1849 to ?

PRAGUE

Count Hartig:	Grimm	? to 1778
Count Johann Pachta:	Farník	1799 to 1838
	Swoboda, A.	+1805 to ?
Archbishop Pržichowský:	Heller, A.	pre 1799
	Heller, E.	pre 1799
National Theatre:	Nejebse	+1793
	Wenczliczek	1796 to ?
	Farník	1807 to 1834
	Blatt	+1820 to 1843?
	Pisařovic	1834 to 1881
1st Imperial Artillery Regiment:	Lang	+1780 to 1808
Conservatoire:	Farník	1811 to 1838
	Blatt	1820 to 1843
	Pisařovic	1843 to 1881
	Reitmayer (II)	1881 to ?
Blind Institute:	Farník	? to ?
	Schönberger	+1824
Appointment unknown:	Ernst	+1844 to 1846

PRESSBURG (BRATISLAVA)

Prince Albert:	Schröder	1760s
Prince Joseph Bathyány:	Bum	1781 to 1783
	Lotz	1781 to 1783
Theatre:	Fournier	1764 to ?

	Dietrich	+1821 to ?

REGENSBURG (RATISBON)

Thurn & Taxis Court:	Engel	1755 to 1781?
	Wack, ?	1755 to 1786?
	Hampel	? to 1758?
	Quallenberg	? to 1758?
	Schierll sen.	+1769 to 1786?
	Rottweil	+1769 to 1787
	Schierll jun.	1784 to 1797
	Wack, W.	1784 to 1806
	Sänger	? to 1806

RIGA

Town theatre:	Kellner	? to 1884
	Förster, W.	1885 to ?

RIO DE JANEIRO

Court:	Silva	+1807 to 1824?
	Campos	1817 to 1824
Italian Theatre:	Silva	+1807 to 1824?

ROME

Queen Margherita:	Magnani	
Opera Society:	Maccagnani	+1839
Augusteo Orchestra:	Blonk-Steiner	1905 to 1912
	Luberti	1913 to 1919
Buenos Aires Colon:	Blonk-Steiner	1909 to 1910
Costanzi Theatre:	Blonk-Steiner	1901 to 1905?
	Luberti	1919 to ?
St Cecilia Academy:	Spina	? to ?
	Magnani	1888 to 1921
	Blonk-Steiner	1903 to 1913
	Luberti	1913 to ?

ROTTERDAM

Appointment unknown:	Rooms	+1823 to 1825

RUDOLSTADT		
Court:	Müller, F.	1803 to 1854
	Dorn	1811 to ?
	Flittner	1811 to ?
ST PETERSBURG (LENINGRAD)		
Court:	Lankammer	1763 to 1787
	Ladunke	1764 to 1800?
	Schiller	1776 to 1787
	Brunner	1779 to 1826?
	Grimm	1779 to 1831
	Beer	1782 to 1792
	Müller, I.	1800 to 1807
	Frisch	1814
	Bänder, C.	+1815 to 1822
	Bänder, L.	+1815 to 1822
	Schäfer	+1840 to 1845?
	Cavallini	1852 to 1867
Imperial Opera:	Bolm	+1900
	Bellison	+1915
Imperial Military Instructor:	Blaes	1842 to 1843
Romano Castle:	Nuder	+1820
Philharmonic Orchestra:	Gensler	
German Opera:	Addner	+1837
	Wagner, W.	1837 to 1851?
Kirov Theatre:	Brekker	
Conservatoire:	Cavallini	1862 to 1870
	Nidman	1868 to 1901
	Brekker	1897 to 1926
	Gensler	1937 to 1966?
Theatre School:	Mannstein	+1789 to 1794
Appointment unknown:	David	1781 to 1782
	Springer, V.	1781 to 1782

	Tirry	+1798 to 1800
	Schlosser father & son	+1838 to 1840

SANTO DOMINGO

Orchestra:	Hastie	+1798
Théâtre du Cap:	Henri	+1782

SCHLEIZ

Court:	Reithardt	+1810 to 1816
	Krause, ?	+1849

SCHWEDT

Margrave of Brandenburg-Schwedt:	Mainzer	1785 to 1792

SCHWERIN

Mecklenburg-Schwerin Court:	Eichhorst	+1830
	Lappe	+1841 to 1847?
	Demnitz	1868 to 1875
	Berger, J.	+1883
	Marhefka	1883 to 1924
	Schwemer	+1883
	Wiesner	? to ?
Town musician:	Hartig	+1819

SEVILLE

Teaching:	Palatin	+1870

SIGMARINGEN

Hohenzollern-Sigmaringen Court:	Schleicher	1812 to 1814

SONDERSHAUSEN

Schwarzburg-Sondershausen Court:	Hermstedt	1801 to 1839
	Bendleb	1828 to 1835
	Kellerman	+1846
	Wenkel	+1847
	Vaupel	1877 to ?

Wind band:	Hermstedt	1802 to 1828?
	Heinrici	+1805
	Zenker	+1823

STEINFÜRT

Bentheim-Steinfürt Court:	Hesse, W.	+1783
	Holmann	+1783
	Springer, V.	1788 to 1792
	David	1790 to 1792
	Nagel	1793 to ?
	Boehmer	+1812

STOCKHOLM

Court:	Gelhaar	1785 to 1793
	Thielemann	1786 to 1802?
	Crusell	1793 to 1833
	Schatt	1802 to 1820
	Addner	+1828 to 1836
	Köbel	1834 to 1871
	Sjöberg	1851 to 1885?
	Ehrenreich	1853 to 1866
	Kjellberg	1871 to 1890
	Palmblad	1879 to ?
	Hessler, G.E.	1894 to 1921?
Theatre:	Müller, J.G.	+1822
Conservatoire:	Ehrenreich	1858 to 1864
	Sjöberg	1867 to 1885?
	Kjellberg	1886 to 1904
	Hessler, G.E.	1904 to 1921?

STRASBOURG

Prince of Rohan:	Meissner	+1766
Theatre:	Betz	+1814 to 1818
	Jundt	+1822
	Kern	+1822
	De Groot	1831 to 1832
	Boymond	+1835 to 1846

Garrison band:	Kieseler	+1830
Conservatoire:	Wuille	1860s

STUTTGART

Duke of Würtemberg:	Tirry	+1788 to 1793
King of Würtemberg:	Bofinger	+1806
	Schwegler	+1806
	Reinhardt, F.	+1815 to 1823
	Scheffauer	1815 to 1828
	Reinhardt, G.	1821 to 1838?
	Hollenstein	+1823
	Beerhalter	1828 to 1852
	Springer, ?	+1835
	Schneider	? to 1860
	Meyer, H.	+1851 to 1866

TURIN

Court:	Merlatti	+1823
Theatre:	Merlatti	+1816

VENICE

La Fenice:	Cimetta	+1823 to 1824
	Cavallini	1830
Liceo:	Marasco	? to ?
	Magnani	+1878 to 1888

VIENNA

Court:	Stadler, A.	1779 to 1796
	Stadler, J.	1779 to 1804
	Klein, G.	1796 to 1832
	Purebel	1807 to 1838
	Friedlowsky, J.	1832 to 1859
	Klein, Th.	1838 to 1867?
	Friedlowsky, A.	1859 to 1867
	Giller	+1859 to ?
	Lengerke	? to ?
	Schmidl	? to ?
	Schöfmann	? to ?
	Bartolomey	+1890 to 1920

Court Opera (Burgtheater, Kärntnerthortheater):	Rüttinger, Ch.	+1807 to 1817?
	Dobyhal	1810 to 1824?
	Pauer	1823 to ?
	Rüttinger, J.	+1823 to 1837
	Friedlowsky, A.	+1824 to 1859
	Klein, Th.	1828 to ?
	Petschacher	+1860
	Bartolomey	1890 to ?
Prince Esterházy:	Horník	pre 1817
Prince Anton Grassalkovics:	Tirry	1781 to 1787
	Griesbacher	1796
Prince de Rohan:	Lotz	1772 to 1774?
Prince Schwarzenberg:	Oliva	+1787 to 1789?
	Verlen	1792 to 1802
Princess Poniatowsky:	Czerny	1770s
	Matauschek	1770s
	Oliva	1770s
Count Johann (?) Esterházy:	Lotz	+1774
Count Dimitri Galitsin:	Stadler, A.	1770s
	Stadler, J.	1770s
Count Liechtenstein:	Bähr	1795 to 1819?
	Sedlak	+1818 to ?
Count Pálffy:	Griesbacher	1778 to 1781
Baron Albert de Rothschild:	Steiner	+1891
Philharmonic Orchestra:	Klein, Th.	1828 to 1881
	Dobyhal	? to ?
	Agner	1830 to 1874
	Kania	+1836 to 1849
	Philipp	? to 1851?
	Friedlowsky, J.	? to ?

	Venzl	1851 to 1863
	Vock	1851 to 1879
	Otter	1862 to 1892
	Giller	1863 to 1884
	Lengerke	1870 to 1885
	Syrinek	1879 to 1904
	Stiassny	1884 to ?
	Schöfmann	1885 to 1910?
	Schmidl	1885 to 1910?
	Bartolomey	1892 to 1920
	Behrens	1903 to 1910?
	Schida	1907 to 1910?
	Polatschek	? to 1930
Carltheater:	Blümel	1896 to ?
Leopoldstadt Theater:	Dobyhal	1794 to 1800
Theater an der Wien:	Friedlowsky, J.	1802 to ?
	Stadler, A. jun.	+1810 to ?
	Beuschel	1834 to ?
Conservatoire:	Friedlowsky, J.	1821 to 1847
	Friedlowsky, A.	1835 to 1875
	Klein, Th.	1851 to 1881
	Otter	1881 to 1898
	Bartolomey	1898 to 1920
	Polatschek	1921 to 1930
Appointment unknown:	Salieri	+1832 to 1834

WALLERSTEIN

Öttingen-Wallerstein Court:	Fürst	+1778
	Link, X.	1780 to 1825
	Bähr	1787 to 1794
	Verlen	+1791 to 1792
	Hiebetsch	+1810
	Wolf, J.K.	+1810 to 1811
	Link, J.A.	? to ?

WARSAW

Court:	Donat	+1780
	Nizinski	+1819

Theatre:	Philipp	+1851
Conservatoire:	Wienen	+1821
	Sobolenski	1865 to 1903
Appointment unknown:	Tropianski	1850s
WEIDE		
Municipal orchestra:	Oehler	+1875
WEILBURG		
Nassau-Weilburg Court:	Habert	1789 to 1792
	Mayer	1789 to 1792
WEIMAR		
Court:	Edling	+1770 to 1786
	Schlömilch	+1802 to 1826
	Agthe	1821 to 1855
	Franke	1823 to 1833?
	Kohlschmidt	+1855
	Saul	+1855
	Walbrül	+1855
	Hinze	+1909
	Weisse I	+1909
	Weisse II	+1909
WIESBADEN		
Court theatre:	Reinhardt, G.	+1810
	Schmidt, Th.	1815 to 1865?
	Röhrig ?	+1841
	Stark	1873 to 1881
WÜRZBURG		
Court:	Blum	1760 to 1790
	Hessler, M.	1760 to 1807
	Meissner	1776 to 1806
	Küffner	1797 to 1802
	Viersnickel, J.	1801 to 1814
	Küffner	1805 to 1815
Military band:	Viersnickel, A.	? to ?

Royal Music School:	Stark	1881 to 1919

ZURICH

Appointment unknown:	Schleicher	1805 to 1809
	Allegra	1910s & 1920s

ZWEIBRÜCKEN

Nassau-Weilburg Court:	Habert	1763 to 1789

Compositions

This list is compiled from information occurring in both the original and present volumes. It includes all performances mentioned in the narrative where the composer of the work and date of performance are known. The order of compositions is that used for works lists in the articles.

AHL

Variations: J.G.G. Hoffman 1812.

ANDRÉ, C.L.J?

"Benedictus" with obligati for clarinet, horn, violin & cello: E. Hopkins 1827.

ARNE, Dr Thomas

"Not unto us" for soprano & 2 clarinets: J. & W. Mahon 1773.

BACKOFEN, Heinrich.

Quintet op.9 for basset-horn & strings: (H. Backofen 1802)?

BÄNDER, Heinrich

Introduction & Rondo: C. Bänder 1845.

BÄNDER, Ludwig

Concerto for 2 clarinets: C. & L. Bänder 1818.

Variations on Tyrolean & Swiss Songs for 2 clarinets: C. & L. Bänder 1818, 1820, 1821.

BAERMANN, Carl

Concerto in C minor: C. Baermann 1839.

Concerto militaire: C. Baermann 1839.

"Newest" concerto: C. Baermann 1837.

Divertissement op.2: Neff 1845.

Ein Abend auf dem Berg: C. Baermann 1843.

Gnomenklänge: Busoni 1882.

Mélancholie: J. Egerton (I) 1900.

Phantasiegebilde: Kotte 1843.

Rondo (op.36?): C. Baermann 1843.

Variations on an original theme (op.8?): C. Baermann 1843.

Variations (op.8?): G. Gareis 1843. Sobeck 1848.

Fantasie (Duo in E flat) for 2 clarinets: C. & H. Baermann 1838 (2), 1839.

BAERMANN, Heinrich

Concerto op.28 in D minor: Ott-Imhoff 1826.

Concerto (Concertino) in C minor: H. Baermann 1820.

Concerto: F.W. Tausch 1818. H. Baermann 1820, 1821, 1822, 1833. J. Faubel 1828. Hermann 1833. Wolff 1837, 1840.

Concertino: H. Baermann 1818. Pauer 1822. Feldt 1825. F. Tretbar 1825. Pisařovic 1830. Zettel 1832. Lesser

1838. Lutz 1841.

Divertissement: H. Baermann 1839.

Fantasia op.26: H. Baermann 1819. Willman 1823, 1827, 1832.

Introduction & Variations: Ebert 1822. Pfaffe 1824.

Polonaise (Introduction & Polonaise op.25?): H. Baermann 1822.

Recit.-Introduction & Variations in E flat: H. Baermann 1818(2). Dacosta 1818.

Variations: H. Baermann 1817, 1818, 1821. F.W. Tausch 1818. Mejo 1819. Pfaffe 1820. Pauer 1822. Kotte 1823. Rooms 1825. Ph. Faubel 1826. A. Schott 1827. Budinsky 1829. Preis 1832. Pisařovic 1836. Meyer 1838.

Quintet op.23: H. Baermann 1819.

Composition: A. Schott 1847.

BATTA, Joseph
Fantasia: Blaes 1846.

BEER, Joseph
Concerto: Beer 1777, 1779(2), 1781, 1807, 1808, 1809. K. Krause 1811(2).

Adagio & Air with Variations: Willman 1831. Mehner 1835.

Fantasia: Willman 1836.

Royal French hunting song: Beer 1785.

Quintet for clarinet, horn & 3 viola d'amour: Beer 1785.

BEERHALTER, Aloysius
"Der Kritikaster" for basset-horn: Beerhalter 1832.

"Im Kühlen Keller" for basset-horn: Beerhalter 1830, 1831, 1832.

Variations for basset-horn: C. Baermann 1831, 1833, 1834.

BEETHOVEN, Ludwig van
Trio op.11: Hermstedt 1841. Lazarus 1852. Mühlfeld 1895.

Quintet op.16: Bähr 1797, 1798. Crusell 1812(2). F.W. Tausch 1814. Willman 1818, 1819. Ebert 1825. Nehrlich 1835. A. Schubert 1839. Mehner 1844, 1851.

Sextet op.71: Bähr 1805. Fr. Wagner 1847.

Septet op.20: Bähr 1800. Crusell 1805(2), 1806, 1807, 1813, 1814, 1818. Kramer 1813. I. Müller 1816. Willman 1817, 1818, 1819, 1821, 1822, 1825, 1827. Bretschneider 1822. J. Friedlowsky 1825. Kotte 1835, 1842, 1847. F. Heinze 1837. F. Bänder 1839. A. Schubert 1839. L. Bliesener 1840. Williams 1841. Blaes 1842, 1845. Auroux 1862, 1863. Lazarus 1878. F. Thomas 1879. J. Egerton(1) 1891, 1892(2).

BELLOLI, Agostino
Sextet for wind: Carulli 1816.

BENDER, Valentin
Concertino no.2: J. Egerton(1) 1879.

BENUCCI (of Amsterdam)
Concerto: Christiani 1817.

Variations: Christiani 1816.

BERANGER, ?
Concerto: Beranger 1793.

BEREZOWSKY, Nicolay
Sextet for clarinet, strings & piano: Cahuzac 1927.

BERGER, Wilhelm
Trio op.94: Mühlfeld 1906.

BERLIOZ, Hector
"Chant Sacré" for clarinet, bass clarinet, bass saxophone, trumpet, soprano & alto saxhorns: Leperd, Duprez &

Sax 1844.

BERR, Frédéric

Concerto: Valette 1834. Boymond 1835. Leroy 1849.

10th Air varié: Klosé 1837.

Variations on the Polonaise from Bellini's *I Puritani*: Boymond 1839.

Variations: Kieseler 1830. Vogt 1833. F. Tretbar 1834. Pisařovic 1843. Boymond 1846.

Solo: Leroy 1853, 1855.

BERWALD, Franz? (AMZ says August)

Septet: Crusell 1818, 1819.

BISHOP, Sir Henry

"Lo, here the gentle lark" for clarinet & flute: Lazarus 1843, 1844.

"The Ray of Hope" for soprano & clarinet: E. Hopkins 1820. Tripp 1832.

BLAES, Joseph

"Ranz des vaches d'Appenzell" by Meyerbeer arranged for soprano & clarinet: Blaes 1847.

BLASIUS, Matthieu Frédéric

Concerto: Massaert 1808.

BLATT, Thaddäus

Variations on a Theme from Rossini's *Barber of Seville*: Blatt 1827.

Variations: Blatt 1828. Addner 1834.

BOCHSA, Charles R.N.

Variations for clarinet & harp: I. Müller 1819.

Nocturne for clarinet, violin & harp: Kotte 1835.

Trio for clarinet, horn & harp: Willman 1821(2). Ph. Faubel 1828. Bretschneider 1831.

Septet: Willman 1821.

BOCHSA, Karl

Concertante for flute & clarinet: Willman 1836.

Quartet: I. Müller 1815.

"Cease your funning", Fantasia for basset-horn: Willman 1836(2), 1840.

BOEHMER, Johann Sebastian

Concerto: Christiani 1817.

Concerto for basset-horn: Boehmer 1812.

BÖHMER Karl

Variations op.17: Nehrlich 1835.

BÖSINGER, ?

Concerto: Baumgärtner 1815.

BOYNEBURGK, Baron de

Introduction & Variations on a Theme of Weigl: Taut 1823.

BRAHMS, Johannes

Sonata op.120, no.1: Mühlfeld 1895(11). J. Egerton(1) 1900.

Sonata op.120, no.2: Mühlfeld 1895(12).

Sonata: Stark 1919.

Trio op.114: Mühlfeld 1891(2), 1892(3), 1893, 1894, 1895(2). Syrinek 1891. Cahuzac 1921.

Quintet op.115: Mühlfeld 1891(2), 1892(4), 1893, 1894, 1895(3). F.W. Steiner 1892. G. Clinton 1892. J. Egerton(1) 1892, 1898.

BRAUN, Wilhelm
Concertino: Hostié 1822.

BRENDLER, Johann Franz
Concerto: J.G. Lauterbach 1809.

BRETSCHNEIDER, ?
Variations: Bretschneider 1823.

BUSONI, Ferruccio
Concertino op.48: H. Draper 1921. Essberger 1921.

CAMBINI, Giovanni Giuseppe
Symphonie Concertante for violin, cello, clarinet & bassoon: Romberg 1785(4).

CANDEILLE, Amélie Julie
Symphonie Concertante for clarinet, bassoon & horn: Solère 1786.

CANONGIA, José Avelino
Concerto in G minor: J.A. Canongia 1820.

Concerto: J.A. Canongia 1822. De Groot 1824.

Fantasie with Variations: J.A. Canongia 1820.

Introduction & Thême varié: J.A. Canongia 1821, 1822.

Nocturne: J.A. Canongia 1820.

Variations in G after Rode: J.A. Canongia 1820. Odalde 1824.

CARAFA, Michele Enrico
"Va lusingando" for tenor & clarinet: Willman 1826.

CARTELLIERI, Casimir
Concerto: W. Farník 1807. Czermack 1810. Blatt 1816. Hostié 1817.

Concerto for 2 clarinets: A. & J. Stadler 1797.

CAVALLINI, Ernesto
Casta Diva: Busoni 1882.

Fantasia on Verdi's *Il Trovatore*: Busoni 1882.

Fantasia: Cavallini 1842(2), 1845.

Scherzo from Verdi's *Don Pasquale*: Busoni 1882.

CAVOS, Catterino
Aria for soprano, chorus & clarinet: ?Bänder 1816, 1817.

CHERUBINI, Luigi
"Ave Maria" for soprano & clarinet: Willman 1837, 1840. Sabon 1843. Williams 1844, 1850, 1855. Mehner 1850. Lazarus 1875. G. Clinton 1877.

"Ave Maria" for soprano & basset-horn: G. Reinhardt 1833.

COLERIDGE-TAYLOR, Samuel
Sonata in F minor: Ch. Draper 1893.

Quintet op.10: Anderson 1895. Ch. Draper 1906.

COPLAND, Aaron
Concerto: McLane 1950.

CRAMER, Franz
Concerto in E flat: H. Baermann 1813.

Adagio & Rondo for clarinet & bassoon: H. Baermann 1812.

CRAMER, John Baptist
Concerto: Ph. Faubel 1821. (Jundt 1822)?

(Concertino: Bolsius 1825)?

Variations: Schülein 1818.

CRÉMONT, Pierre
Concerto: Massaert 1808.

Adagio & Rondo: Hostié 1823.

CRUSELL, Bernhard
Concerto op.1: Crusell 1807, 1813. F. Heinze 1823, 1828.

Adagio & Rondo (from op.1): Crusell 1815. Ott-Imhoff 1820. F. Heinze 1830.

Adagio (from op.1): G. Heinze 1843.

Concerto op.5: W. Barth 1812. F. Heinze 1819, 1826. Schönberger 1824.

Andante Pastorale (from op.5): Addner 1834. G. Heinze 1840.

Rondo (from op.1 or op.5): Crusell 1814. J. Friedlowsky 1818.

Adagio (Andante?) & Polacca (from op.11?): Crusell 1815.

Concerto: Crusell 1805, 1808, 1815(2), 1817, 1819. Hostié 1812. C. Bänder 1816, 1817. Christiani 1816. G. Reinhardt 1816. W. Barth 1818, 1821. Hermstedt 1818. Troyer 1818. Mahr 1819. G. Backofen 1820. Agthe 1821. F. Heinze 1821. Lorenz 1823. Ebert 1825. Haushälter 1826. Helfrich 1828. Schultheis 1838. ? Springer 1839. Wolff 1841.

Introduction & Variations op.12: Crusell 1804(3), 1805(2), 1807, 1808, 1812, 1813. Willman 1833.

Symphonie Concertante op.3: Crusell 1808, 1813, 1814(2), 1817. W. Barth 1816. Mahr 1819. Schlömilch 1823. Ott-Imhoff 1824. Willman 1826.

Trio for clarinet, horn & bassoon: Crusell 1814. Köbel 1828?

Aria for soprano & clarinet: Crusell 1814, 1815.

Compositions: Helfrich 1823. Rooms 1823. Wolff 1838, 1839.

DANZI, Franz

Concertino: J.C. Kleine 1819.

Concerto (Concertino?) for 2 clarinets: C. & L. Bänder 1820, 1821.

Symphonie Concertante for flute & clarinet: Feldt 1824, 1825.

Symphonie Concertante for clarinet & bassoon: Feldt 1826.

Potpourri: Crusell 1816, 1819. Schleicher 1821?, 1822. Kühne 1824. Eichhorn 1831.

Variations: Jundt 1822.

Compositions: Rooms 1823.

DAVID, Ferdinand
Concerto: Landgraf 1855, 1857.

Introduction & Variations on Schubert's *Sehnsuchts-Waltzer*: G. Heinze 1838, 1840. Nehrlich 1839. Richter 1851. Grosse 1860.

DEBUSSY, Claude
Ier Rhapsodie: Mimart 1911. Cahuzac 1925.

DÉMAR, Sébastian
Concerto: Zangenberg 1799.

DESHAYES, Prosper Didier
Concerto: Solère 1783.

DESTOUCHES, Franz Seraph von
Concerto: Schlömilch 1803.

Variations for basset-horn: Schlömilch 1803.

DEVIENNE, François
Symphonie Concertante op.25 for 2 clarinets: Solère & Hayenschinck 1787, 1788.

Symphonie Concertante for clarinet & bassoon: X. Lefèvre 1787, 1788, 1789? Rehm 1802.

Symphonie Concertante for flute, clarinet & bassoon: X Lefèvre 1787. A. Stadler 1789.

DOTZAUER, Friedrich
Concertino: Langlotz 1831.

DRESCHER, ?
Phantasie for basset-horn: Drescher 1863.

DUBOIS, William
Concerto: Dubois 1795(2), 1798(2).

DÜRING, Gustav
Concerto for clarinet & bassoon: J.G.G. Hoffmann 1813. Bretschneider 1826.

Symphonie Concertante for 7 clarinets, wind orchestra & Turkish Music: J.G.G. Hoffmann 1813.

DUVERNOY, Charles
Concerto: J.G.G. Hoffmann 1812.

EBERWEIN, Max
Concerto no.1: Hermstedt 1817.

Concerto no.2: Hermstedt 1818(2).

Concertino: Hermstedt 1819, 1820?, 1821. Feldt 1824.

Adagio & Variations: Hermstedt 1818, 1821.

"Wie die Nacht mit heiligem Beben" for soprano & clarinet: G. Heinze 1839.

"Sehnsucht der Liebe" for soprano, chorus & clarinet: Hermstedt 1818.

EGGERT, Joachim Nicolo
Sextet: Crusell 1807.

FASANO, Tommaso
Concerto: Fasano 1842.

FAUBEL, Joseph
Andante & Variations (6 Variations on a Theme in C?):

J. Faubel 1830. Budinsky 1831.

Composition: J. Faubel 1834.

FISCHEL, Adolph
Concerto: Rehage 1830.

FISCHER, Dagobert
Concerto for 2 clarinets: Forckert & Wohllebe 1837.

FLORIO, G.
Duet for 2 sopranos, clarinet & 2 guitars: J.G.G. Hoffman 1804.

FLOTOW, Friedrich von
Serenade from *Allessandro Stradella*: Pisařovic 1846.

FOUCARD, ?
Concerto: Foucard 1793.

FRANKE, Sylvain
Variations & Rondo on a Theme from Auber's *La Muette de Portici*: Agthe 1833.

FREEDLAND, Garry
Variations op.33 by Weber arranged for basset-horn & orchestra: F. Gomez 1903.

FREY, M.
Composition: Gassner 1831.

FÜRSTENAU, Anton
Reminiscences of *Euryanthe* for flute, clarinet, cor anglais, bassoon & orchestra: Kotte 1846.

GADE, Niels
Fantasiestücke: Lazarus 1892. J. Egerton(1) 1931.

GÄHRICH, Wenzel
Concertino: A? Gareis 1842.

Concertante for 2 clarinets: A. & G. Gareis 1841, 1842. 1843(2).

Rondo & Variations for 2 clarinets: A. & G. Gareis 1841.

GAMBARO, Giovanni Batista
Thême varié: Ott-Imhoff 1822. Manuel Jardin 1833.

GARNER, Horatio
Concerto: Garner 1791.

GAUTIER, ?
Concerto: Gautier 1795, 1796, 1802.

GEORG, J.G.
Potpourri op.2 on Themes from Weber's *Der Freischütz*: (J. Friedlowsky 1816, 1817)? Feldt 1824, 1825. Preis 1832. (F.A. Richter 1851)?

GERKE, Otto
Fantasie: Landgraf 1849.

Potpourri on Themes from Spohr's *Jessonda* and *Zemire*: Rehage 1830. F. Heinze 1838.

Variations op.4 on a Romance from Spohr's *Zemire*: Bretschneider 1823.

Composition: Wolff 1839.

GIRSCHNER, Christian
"Un amante sventurato" for soprano & clarinet: Blaes 1845.

GOEPFERT, Karl Andreas
Concerto: Schleicher 1822.

Concertino: Schleicher 1815.

GOSSEC, François
"O Salutaris" for 2 cor anglais & basset-horn: Betz 1818.

GRENSER, Johann Friedrich
Concerto: Crusell 1797, 1808.

Adagio & Rondo: Crusell 1803, 1804, 1805(2), 1807.

GRUTSCH, Franz
Adagio & Rondo: Th. Klein 1833.

Potpourri: Th. Klein 1835.

GUGLIELMI, Pietro Alessandro
"Gratias agimus tibi" for soprano & clarinet: J. Mahon 1814. J. Friedlowsky 1818. Klingenberg 1819. Willman 1819, 1821, 1823, 1824(2), 1828(3), 1829(2), 1837(2), 1838. W. Egerton 1822. E. Hopkins 1827. Lazarus 1858.

GUGLIELMI, Pietro Carlo
Aria from *Paolo e Virginia* for tenor & clarinet: T. Roth 1818.

GYROWETZ, Adalbert
Concertante for oboe, clarinet, horn & bassoon: Beuschel 1833.

HALM, Anton
Variations: J. Friedlowksy 1818.

HANSSENS, Charles
Concerto: Blaes 1843.

Concertino: Blaes 1841, 1846.

HEINZE, Gustav
Adagio (from Concerto): G. Heinze 1842.

HENRI, ?
Concerto: Henri 1794.

HINDEMITH, Paul
Concerto: Cahuzac 1957.

HOSTIÉ, J.
Concerto: Hostié 1787.

HOFMEISTER, Franz Anton?
Concerto for basset-horn: Rehm 1799(2), 1802.

HUMMEL, Johann Nepomuk
Septet: Bretschneider 1822. Willman 1830, 1831. G. Clinton 1892.

Aria for soprano & clarinet: Horník 1817.

INDY, Vincent d'
Trio op.29: Cahuzac 1921.

JADIN, Louis Emmanuel
Symphonie Concertante for 2 clarinets: Solère & Hayenschinck 1788.

Symphonie Concertante for clarinet, horn & bassoon: Crusell 1805.

JANSA, Leopold
Concerto: Schleicher 1834(2).

Concerto for clarinet & cello: Schleicher 1840.

JENNER, Gustav
Sonata op.5: Mühlfeld 1901.

KAHN, Robert
Trio for clarinet, cello & piano: Mühlfeld 1905.

KALLIWODA, Johannes
Introduction & Variations: G. Heinze 1844.

KAUFMANN, Friedrich
Slumber Song of the Mute for clarinet & harmonichord: Kotte 1835.

KHAYLL, Alois
Duo Concertante for flute & clarinet: A. Friedlowsky 1835.

KLEIN, Thomas
Air varié op.1: Th. Klein 1829.

Divertissement op.2: Th. Klein 1829.

Fantasie: F. Tretbar 1839, 1840.

KLEISNER, ?
Concerto: Baumgärtner 1815.

KLOSÉ, Hyacinthe Eléonore
Composition: Klosé 1844, 1848.

KOCH, Bernard
Military Concerto: J.C. Kleine 1825.

KRÄHMER, Ernst
Concerto for oboe & clarinet: Schleicher 1822, 1823, 1833, 1834(2).

Variations: Schleicher 1823.

KREHL, Stephan
Quintet op.19: Mühlfeld 1901.

KREUTZER, Conradin
Divertissement: Schleicher 1840.

Variations: Ott-Imhoff 1822.

KROMMER, Franz
Concerto op.36: W. Barth 1805.

Concerto op.52: W. Barth 1804, 1805, 1806.

Concerto: F.A. Bliesener 1804. J.G.G. Hoffmann 1804. Crusell 1806, 1807(2), 1808, 1819. W. Barth 1808. Wippert 1809. Schönche 1814. Sedlak 1819. De Groot 1820. ?Tausch 1822.

Concertino: Odalde 1824.

Concerto op.35 for 2 clarinets: W. Barth & G. Maurer 1804. F.A. Bliesener & G. Reinhardt 1804. J. & K. Krause 1804(2). W. Barth & Claus 1807.
Concerto op.91 for 2 clarinets: W. Barth & F. Heinze 1815.

Concerto for 2 clarinets: Crusell (and Schatt?) 1805, 1806, 1815. Betz & pupil 1815. J.C. Kleine & Planke jun. 1815. Planke sen. & jun. 1817. Hermstedt & J.C. Kleine 1819(3). Christiani & pupil 1820. A. & J. Friedlowsky 1821. De Groot & G. Reinhardt 1821. C. Bänder & Egling 1823. Christiani & J.C. Kleine

1823. Ph. Faubel & Bretschneider 1825. Feldt & Kühne 1825. Pfaffe & Berendt 1825. C. & F. Bänder 1835. Heisterhagen & Vauth 1835.

Adagio & Polonaise for 2 clarinets: C. & L. Bänder 1818. Tamm & Pfaffe 1818.

Quintet: Bretschneider 1821.

KÜFFNER, Josef

Introduction & Thême varié: Willman 1829(2).

KUMMER, Friedrich August

Concerto: Kotte 1834.

Concertino: Kotte 1837.

Concerto for 2 clarinets: Kotte & F.W. Lauterbach 1838.

Adagio & Polacca: Kotte 1837.

Divertimento on Weber's *Der Freischütz*: Pisařovic 1831.

Fantasie on Themes from Bellini's *Capulets & Montagues*: Kotte 1837, 1839.

KUMMER, Gaspard

Potpourri op.11: Feldt 1824.

Variations op.45 for basset-horn. Chr. Rüttinger 1817?

LACHNER, Franz

"Das Waldvöglein" for soprano & clarinet: Addner 1834.

LACOMBE, Louis

Adagio & Rondo: Kotte 1838, 1839.

LALO, Édouard

Aubade: G. Clinton 1892.

LAZARUS, Henry

Fantasia on *I Puritani*: Lazarus 1861.

LEBRUN, Ludwig August

Concerto: Crusell 1802, 1803(2), 1804, 1807.

LEE, Sebastian

Variations for clarinet & cello: F. Tretbar 1838.

LEFÈVRE, Xavier.

Concerto: X. Lefèvre 1787, 1788(2), 1789(2), 1790. Gautier 1795, 1796. F.W. Tausch 1811. Damse 1815.

Symphonie Concertante for clarinet & bassoon. X. Lefèvre 1790, 1805.

LIEBAU, Friedrich Wilhelm

Song for soprano & clarinet: Hermstedt 1841.

LIMMER, J. Franz

Polonaise: Limmer 1828.

Rondo: Limmer 1827.

LINDNER, Friedrich?

Phantasiestück: H. Meyer 1865.

LINPAINTNER, Peter von

Concerto: Schick 1819. G. Reinhardt 1823. Agthe 1825. Christiani 1825. F. Tretbar 1826, 1827, 1828. Feldt 1828. Vilmar 1835.

Concertino op.19: Feldt 1824. Hostié 1824.

Concertino: De Groot 1825. Blatt 1827. F. Tretbar 1834, 1835. Landgraf 1841. A. Gareis 1843.

Polonaise: G. Reinhardt 1826.

Rondo brillant op.45: F. Tretbar 1827. Forckert 1837. Holzapfel 1848.

Concertante for wind: Hostié 1824. F. Heinze 1828. C. Bänder 1830. G. Reinhardt 1830, 1833. Th. Klein 1833. Kunze 1833. Vauth 1837, 1845.

Composition: F. Tretbar 1829.

MACFARREN, Sir George

"Pack Clouds Away" for soprano & clarinet: Lazarus 1881.

MAHON, John

Concerto: J. Mahon 1772, 1773(2), 1774, 1775, 1776, 1797?

Variations on "The Wanton God" from Arne's *Comus*: J. Mahon 1775.

"Hope thou cheerful Ray of Light" for soprano & clarinet: J. Mahon 1796.

MANGOLD, Wilhelm

Quintet for wind: Reitz 1837.

MARÉCHAL, ?

Symphonie Concertante for clarinet, horn, harp & piano: Yost 1781(3).

MAURER, Ludwig

Concerto op.57: Röhrig 1834, 1835. Bührmann 1844.

Concertino op.64: G. Reinhardt 1832. G.W. Seeman 1829, 1833(2). Ott-Imhoff 1834. A? Gareis 1837. Agthe 1839. F. Tretbar 1840.

Symphonie Concertante for 2 clarinets: Kukro & Weissmüller 1829.

Variations: De Groot 1821.

MAYER, Johann?

Concertante for 9 wind: J. Mahon & Oliver 1810.

MAHR, Simon

Aria for tenor & clarinet: Sedlak 1818.

MEJO, August Wilhelm

Concertino: Mejo 1820.

MENDELSSOHN-BARTHOLDY, Felix
Concerstück op.113. H. & C. Baermann 1833(3), 1838. M. & F. Gomez 1904.

Concertstück op.114: H. & C. Baermann 1833(3), 1838.

Concertstück: Lazarus & Maycock? 1868

MENGAL, Martin Joseph
Quartet for flute, clarinet, bassoon & horn: Tamm 1818.

MESS (MEES), D.
Concerto for 2 clarinets: C. & L. Bänder 1816, 1817.

Rondo for 2 clarinets: C. & L. Bänder 1820.

METHFESSEL, Albert
Concerto: Hermstedt 1815, 1819.

Variations on "Leb wohl, mein Bräutschen schön": Hermstedt 1814.

MEYER, Carl Heinrich
Concerto: Claus 1811.

MEYERBEER, Giacomo
Quintet: H. Baermann 1813.

"Gli Amori di Teolinda" for soprano, clarinet & chorus: H. Baermann 1817.

MOLIQUE, Bernhard
Concerto: Th. Klein 1827. Beerhalter 1829, 1834. Lazarus 1851.

Concertino: Th. Klein 1841.

MORI, Frank
"The Last Farewell" for soprano & bass clarinet: Wuille 1852.

MOSCHELES, Ignaz
Variations: I. Müller 1809.

Grand Septet for clarinet, horn, strings & piano: Willman 1833.

MOZART, Wolfgang Amadeus

Concerto K622: A. Stadler 1791. Crusell 1802, 1804. Hermstedt 1809, 1814. Barth 1815, 1821. Feldt 1823. C. Rakemann 1836. W. Farník 1837. A. Friedlowsky 1837. Willman 1838. C. Baermann 1843. Landgraf 1853. Grosse 1855. Mühlfeld 1891. Cahuzac 1931(2), 1933(2), 1934(3), 1955.

Adagio (from K622): Kotte 1842, 1846. W. Wagner 1847. Landgraf 1870. Vaupel 1875.

Symphonie Concertante K app.9: Baumgärtner 1813. G. Clinton 1887. Reitmayer(II) 1891. M. Gomez 1903.

Variations on Gretry's "March of the Samnites": Beer 1808, 1809.

Trio K.498: Crusell 1806. F. Müller 1827. Williams 1850. Mühlfeld 1894.

Quintet K581: A. Stadler 1789. Baumgärtner 1805. Crusell 1805(?), 1807(?). Hermstedt 1808, 1840(3), 1841. J. Friedlowsky 1816, 1827. Ph. Faubel 1822, 1829. Feldt 1824. Willman 1835, 1836, 1840. ?Springer 1839. G. Heinze 1841. Blaes 1842. C. Baermann 1843. Lazarus 1852. Mehner 1861. Auroux 1862. H. Meyer 1864. Mühlfeld 1891, 1895. Ch. Draper 1893. Stark 1919. Cahuzac 1924, 1928(2).

Wind Quintet K452: A. Stadler 1784. Rüttinger sen. 1817. Willman 1819. Bretschneider 1829. Mehner 1839. A. Schubert 1839. Abel 1872, 1874.

Serenade K388: Willman & Powell 1830, 1831. Williams & Lazarus 1853. Lazarus & J. Egerton(I) 1880(2).

"Parto!" for soprano & clarinet: A. Stadler 1791. K. Krause 1804. W. Barth 1807. Czermack 1810. Betz 1814. Hermstedt 1815, 1819, 1833. T. Roth 1815. Crusell 1817, 1819(2). Troyer 1817. Willman 1818, 1821, 1822, 1823(2), 1826, 1827(2), 1828, 1832, 1838(2),

1839. Hostié 1819. F. Reinhardt 1819. Jäger 1820. J.M. Maurer 1821. Schleicher 1822. J. Friedlowsky 1825. Blatt 1827. Beerhalter 1828. Limmer 1828. Tripp 1828. Kotte 1832. Bretschneider 1833. Schollmeyer 1833. F. Heinze 1834. F. Bänder 1839, 1841. Williams 1840, 1852, 1858, 1862. Lappe 1841. A. Schubert 1842. Th. Klein 1843. Blaes 1846. G. Clinton 1892, 1899.

"Non più di fiori" for soprano & basset-horn: A. Stadler 1791. F. Tausch 1802. T. Roth 1815. F. Reinhardt 1819. Willman 1820, 1822, 1829, 1830, 1832, 1833, 1836, 1837(2). Schalk 1823. Agthe 1841. Williams 1841, 1843, 1845, 1846, 1861. Lazarus 1861, 1874. Marhefka 1895. F. Gomez 1903.

"Al desio, di chi t'adora" K577 for soprano & 2 basset-horns: A. Stadler (& J. Stadler)? 1798. Schalk & Rakemann sen. 1823. I. Müller (& W. Barth)? 1825.

Requiem: Leffler & Munro 1801. Hartmann & Jodry 1818. Willman & Powell 1826.

MÜLLER, F.

Rondo: J. C. Kleine 1815.

MÜLLER, Friedrich

Concerto op.10: F. Heinze 1818.

Concerto: J.C. Kleine 1817.

Concertino: Friedrich Müller 1824.

Concertino for 2 clarinets: F.W. Tausch & Pfaffe 1829. F. Heinze & Rosenkranz 1834.

MÜLLER, Georg

Concertino op.7: Mehner 1832.

MÜLLER, Iwan

Concerto no.1: I. Müller 1810.

Concerto no.3: Odalde 1822. I. Müller 1826.

Concerto no.4: I. Müller 1823.

Concerto no.6: I. Müller 1825, 1826.

Concerto no.7: I. Müller 1829.

Concerto: C. Bänder 1819, 1829. Ebert 1822. F. Tretbar 1829. Mehner 1830.

Concertino no.2: I. Müller 1826.

Concertino: G. Reinhardt 1829. F. Tretbar 1829. Lopitzsch 1834. C. Bänder 1835.

Concertino capriccioso: Kotte 1842.

Symphonie Concertante op.23 for 2 clarinets: Budinsky & Pisařovic 1831. Amme & Kunze 1833. Forckert & Wohllebe 1833. F. Swoboda & Sykora 1833. J. Faubel & Ott-Imhoff 1834. C. & F. Bänder 1836. Ernst & Griesel 1836. Bättenhausen & Curth 1839. Nehrlich & K.F.W. Becker 1845.

Beethoven's "Adelaide": I. Müller 1826, 1829. Schleicher 1833. Kotte 1837(2), 1839. Hentschel 1848.

Cavatina "Una voce poco fà" from Rossini's *Barber of Seville*: I. Müller 1826.

Fantasie on a Theme of Rossini: I. Müller 1825. G.W. Seeman 1833.

Fantasie op.58: I. Müller 1829.

Fantasie: I. Müller 1817.

Siciliano: I. Müller 1826.

Variations on an original (new) Theme: I. Müller 1825, 1826.

Variations on a Russian Folksong: I. Müller 1809.

Variations op.69 on Carafa's "O cara memoria": I. Müller 1826.

Variations: G.W. Seeman 1829.

Quartet no.1: I. Müller 1816.

Compositions: Helfrich 1823. Rooms 1823. F. Tretbar 1829. Meinberg 1839. Bauer 1840.

MÜLLER, Theodor

Concerto for clarinet & horn: Agthe 1826.

MÜLLER-BENDER, Mme.

(Introduction, Adagio &) Variations: G. Reinhardt 1819. J.A. Canongia 1820.

NETZER, Joseph

"Die Loreley" for tenor & bass voices & clarinet: A.? Gareis 1843.

NEUKOMM, Chevalier

Concertante Sextet: Willman 1834.

Concertante Septet: Willman 1830, 1832(2), 1834, 1835,1836.

"Make haste, O God" for contralto voice & bass clarinet: Willman 1836.

NEUMANN, Heinrich

Composition: Meier 1850.

NICCOLINI, Giuseppe

Aria for soprano & clarinet: Sedlak 1818.

NOHR, Friedrich

Potpourri: Langlotz 1831.

Rondo brillant for 2 clarinets: F. Heinze & Rosenkranz 1832.

Potpourri op.3 for wind quintet: F. Heinze 1831, 1834. Rosenkranz 1834.

OBERTHÜR, Charles
Lieder ohne Worte: Th. Schmidt 1859.

ONSLOW, George
Sextet: Willman 1829, 1831. Pisařovic 1844.

OXENSTIERNA, ?
Prologue for clarinet & violin: Crusell 1805.

OZI, Étienne
Symphonie Concertante for clarinet & bassoon: Solère 1786.

PACINI, Giovanni
Aria for soprano & clarinet: J. Faubel 1832.

PAER, Ferdinando
"Una voce al cor mi parla" for soprano & clarinet: H. Baermann 1814. Hesse 1814. Crusell 1815. J. Friedlowsky 1818. Hermstedt 1819. Williams 1820, 1841. Willman 1820(2), 1822, 1823(2), 1825. J.M. Maurer 1829. De Groot 1832. C. Rakemann 1836. Pisařovic 1842.

Duet from *Sargino* for soprano & contralto voices & clarinet: H. Baermann 1814, 1818. J.M. Maurer 1829. De Groot 1832.

PAISIELLO, Giovanni
Aria for soprano(?) with clarinet & bassoon: Hübler 1789.

PANNY, Joseph
Rondo: F.W. Tausch 1831.

PANSERON, Auguste
"Tyrol, my Fatherland" for soprano & clarinet: Willman 1836, 1839. Bowley 1840.

PECHATZECK, Franz
Polacca: Feldt 1824.

PETIT, A.S.
Evocations for bass clarinet: F. Gomez 1904.

PIERNÉ, Gabriel
Canzonet: J. Egerton(I) 1931.

PITT, Percy
Concertino op.22: M. Gomez 1897.

PLEYEL, Ignaz
Concerto: Foucard 1799. Massaert 1808.

Symphonie Concertante for 2 clarinets: Dubois & Beranger 1798. Dubois & ? 1799.

POISSL, Baron
Aria from *Der Wettkamf zu Olympia* for soprano & clarinet: H. Baermann 1815.

Aria for soprano & clarinet: H. Baermann 1813, 1814.

"Se in liberta pot" for soprano & clarinet: W. Barth 1818.

PRÄGER, Heinrich
Variations: Jundt 1822.

PROCH, Heinrich
"Schweizer Heimweh" op.38 for soprano & basset-horn: Beerhalter 1844.

PROKSCH, Joseph
Concerto: Proksch 1817.

Variations: Proksch 1817.

PUNTO, Giovanni
Concerto: Wachter 1782.

PUY, J.B.E. du
Concerto: Crusell 1814.

Adagio & Rondo: Crusell 1813, 1814, 1819.

Variations: Crusell 1798.

RABL, Walther

Quartet op.1: Mühlfeld 1897.

RATHÉ, ?
Concerto: Rathé 1780(2), 1782(2).

REICHA, Anton
Wind Quintets: Boufil 1818, 1819. J.A. Canongia 1822. Kotte 1824. Willman 1824, 1825, 1838. Leroy 1856, 1857. Lazarus 1892.

REICHARDT, Johann Friedrich
Scena for soprano(?) & basset-horn: V. Springer 1788.

Vocal duet with clarinet & bassoon: Crusell 1802.

REIF, Wilhelm.
Concerto: Mühlfeld 1885.

REINHARDT, Georg
Variations: G. Reinhardt 1814?, 1816, 1818.

REISSIGER, Karl
Concertino (concerto) op.63: J. Faubel 1825. F. Heinze 1832. Wolff 1838. G. Heinze 1839. Pisařovic 1840. Landgraf 1845. Holzapfel 1847.

1st Fantasie: Grosse 1858?, 1872.

2nd Fantasie op.180, "L'Attente et l'Arrivée": G. Heinze 1840. Mraz 1862.

Fantasie: Goudswaard 1842. Holzapfel 1843. Landgraf 1846. Sobeck 1849.

Introduction (Adagio) & Variations: Kotte 1842. Landgraf 1846.

Adagio (from the above?): J. Faubel 1832.

Composition: J. Faubel 1834. Mehner 1854.

REULING, Wilhelm
Wind Quintet: Th. Klein 1835.

RIES, Ferdinand
Octet op.128: I. Müller 1816.

RIGHINI, Vincenzo
Aria for soprano(?) with clarinet & bassoon: Crusell 1804.

RIMSKY-KORSAKOV, Nikolay
Wind Quintet: J. Guyot 1913.

RIOTTE, Philipp
Concerto op.36: I. Müller 1809(2). J. Friedlowsky 1817.

Concerto: J.G.G. Hoffman 1804. H. Baermann 1818(2), 1820, 1821. Kotte 1824. G. Reinhardt 1830.

Concertino: H. Baermann 1819.

Variations: J. Friedlowsky 1818. Kröpsch 1826.

Aria for soprano & clarinet: H. Baermann 1813.

RÖHRIG, ?
Concerto: Mehner 1847.

Concertino: Mehner 1848.

ROMBERG, Andreas
Quintet op.57: G. Reinhardt 1821.

ROSSINI, Gioachino
Fantasie: Addner 1834.

Air with Variations for 2 clarinets: Gambaro & F. Berr 1825.

ROTH, Karl Gottlob
Concerto: J.T. Roth 1800.

RUMMEL, Christian
Concertino op.58: Neff 1845.

Fantasie op.77 on Beethoven's "Ah perfido": Kotte 1841.

Potpourri on themes from Meyerbeer's *Robert the Devil:*

Mehner 1840.

Composition: A. Schubert 1841.

SACCHINI, Antonio

"Lieta quest' alma amanti" for soprano & clarinet: Willman 1819, 1820, 1822.

SAINT-GEORGES, Chevalier de

Concerto: Solère 1782(2), 1783(2). Wachter 1786, 1787.

SAINT-SÄENS, Camille

Tarantelle op.51 for flute & clarinet: Leroy 1851.

SAXE-MEININGEN, Princess Marie of

Romanza: Mühlfeld 1892.

SCHAFFER, Francis

Concerto: F. Schaffer 1798. F. Granger 1801. Hart 1820.

SCHALK, Franz

Polonaise of Beethoven for basset-horn: Schalk 1823, 1825.

Polonaise of Meyerbeer for basset-horn: Schalk 1821.

Potpourri for basset-horn: Schalk 1825, 1831.

Reminiscences of Switzerland (Swiss Round-Dance) for basset-horn: Schalk 1823, 1825(2), 1831, 1834.

Variations on a Theme from Rossini's *Cenerentola* for basset-horn: Schalk 1821, 1823, 1824, 1825, 1829, 1831, 1832?, 1834.

SCHINDELMEISSER, Louis

Concerto op.1: Schindelmeisser 1833.

Symphonie Concertante (Concertstück) op.2 for 4 clarinets: Schindelmeisser, Mehner Mey(er), Rosenkranz 1832. Schindelmeisser, (André, Hamburger, Vilmar)? 1835. Heisterhagen, Lesser, Schultheis, Vauth 1839. Bättenhausen, Curth, Kollman, Wenderoth 1841.

SCHLEICHER, Caroline
Variations: Schleicher 1822(2).

SCHMIDT, Aloys
Concerto: Bretschneider 1833.

SCHNABEL, Joseph
Variations: K. Krause 1811(2).

SCHNEIDER, Friedrich
Concerto: I. Müller 1809. W. Barth 1810, 1817.

SCHNEIDER, G. Abraham
Concerto: J.C. Kleine 1815(2), 1817. F. Heinze 1815, 1818, 1824. Christiani 1817.

Concerto for clarinet & bassoon: Hammerl 1806. F.A. Bliesener 1814.

Obligato in Adagio of bassoon concerto: Pfaffe 1822.

Concerto for basset-horn: Schalk 1823.

SCHNYDER von WARTENSEE, Xaver
"Der Friede" for vocal quartet, clarinet & piano: G. Reinhardt 1821. Mehner 1837.

SCHUBERT, Franz
Octet op.166: Troyer 1824. G. Klein 1827. H. Meyer 1864. Lazarus 1878, 1881.

"Der Hirt auf dem Felsen" for soprano & clarinet: Nehrlich 1833. Mehner 1848. Landgraf 1869.

SCHUMANN, Robert
Phantasiestücke: Mühlfeld 1894, 1895.

Märchenerzählungen: Lazarus 1876.

SEBASTIANI, Ferdinando
Concerto: Sebastiani 1828.
Variations on a Theme of Rossini: Sebastiani 1828.

SEIDEL, Friedrich Ludwig
Concerto for flute & clarinet: F.W. Tausch 1818.

SEYFRIED, Ignace von
Concertante for 5 wind: J. Friedlowsky 1819.

Aria for soprano(?) & clarinet: J. Friedlowsky 1819.

SKAPELSEN, ?
Duet for horn & clarinet: Crusell 1806.

SOBECK, Jan
Concerto: Sobeck 1858.

SOLÈRE, Étienne
Concerto: Solère 1783, 1785(3), 1787.

Symphonie Concertante for 2 clarinets: Wachter & Solère 1790.

SPÄTH, André
Concerto: Stötzer 1818.

Concertino: Hamburger 1835.

Concerstück: Neff 1845.

Symphonie Concertante op.103 for 2 clarinets: G. Bachmann & Blaes 1836. Kozel & Syrinek 1863 (1st mvt only).

Potpourri: Gassner 1831.

Scène chantante sur deux airs suisses op.113: G. Reinhardt 1829, 1831.

Potpourri for 2 clarinets: (A. & J. Friedlowsky 1821)? F.W. & J.G. Lauterbach 1824. F. Bänder & Griesel 1839.

Compositions: Helfrich 1823. G. Reinhardt 1829. Späth 1831, 1832.

SPAGNOLETTI, Paolo
Concertante for violin & wind quintet: Kramer 1815.

SPOHR, Ludwig

Concerto no.1: Hermstedt 1809(2), 1812(2), 1814, 1819(3), 1821, 1822, 1824, 1828. Feldt 1824, 1825. F. Tretbar 1824. Ott-Imhoff 1825. Koehn 1845. G. Clinton 1876.

Concerto no.2: Hermstedt 1810(3), 1811(2), 1812(3), 1825.

Concerto no.3: Hermstedt 1821(4), 1834, 1840. M. Gomez 1904 (2nd mvt only).

Concerto no.4: Hermstedt 1829, 1834.

Concerto (no.1 or no.2; nos.3 & 4 were not published until much later): Hermstedt 1811, 1814(2), 1815, 1816, 1818. F.W. Tausch 1814. C. Bänder 1823. Lorenz 1823. F. Tretbar 1829. Lopitzsch 1833. Willman 1833. G. Reinhardt 1834. A. Freidlowsky 1836. Sabon 1841. Weissmüller 1843. Kellerman 1846.

Adagio: F. Heinze 1834.

"Alruna" Variations: Hermstedt 1810(2).

Fantasie & Variations op.81 on a Theme of Danzi: Hermstedt 1815.

Potpourri op.80 on two Themes from Winter's *Opferfest*: Hermstedt 1811, 1812(2), 1814(2), 1815, 1816(2), 1819.

Recit. & Adagio: Mahr 1821.

Variations on an Alpine Song: Blatt 1817, 1820.

Variations: Hermstedt 1811, 1812, 1815, 1818, 1820(2), 1821, 1832.

Variations from the Nocturne op.34 arranged for clarinet & strings by Hermstedt: Hermstedt 1817.

Wind quintet op.52: Hermstedt 1816. W. Barth 1821. Boufil 1821. A. Schubert 1839. Pisařovic 1841. Lazarus 1844.

Octet op.32: J. Friedlowsky 1814. G. Reinhardt 1833. Willman 1839. Neff 1846.

Nonet op.31: Boufil 1820. Willman 1820(2), 1834. Reitz 1837. Williams 1855. Th. Schmidt 1859. Lazarus 1877. G. Clinton 1892.

Aria from *Der Zweikampf mit der Geliebten* for soprano & clarinet: Hermstedt 1811, 1815, 1816. Hostié 1824.

Six German Songs op.103: G.W. Seeman 1838. G. Heinz 1839 (no.2 only). Mehner 1839. Hermstedt 1840, 1841 (2 songs only). Pisařovic 1840 (no.5 only). C. Bänder 1841 (2 songs only). Hentschel 1848 (2 songs only). J. Egerton(I) 1884 (no.2 only). G. Clinton, 1885 (no.2 only).

Compositions: Helfrich 1823. Wolff 1839.

SPRINGER, ?

Fantasie: ?Springer 1841.

Variations: ?Springer 1841.

"Der Hirten Winterlied" for voice & clarinet: ?Springer 1841.

Variations for basset-horn: ?Springer 1838?,1842, 1843.

STADLER, Anton

Partitas for wind: A. & J. Stadler 1785.

STAMITZ, Karl

Concerto no.1: Beer 1772.

Concerto: Beer 1771, 1772. Pinot 1795.

STANFORD, Sir Charles

Concerto: Ch. Draper 1904. Thurston 1922.

STARZER, Joseph
Concerto for 2 clarinets: A. & J. Stadler 1780.

STENBORG, Carl
Aria for soprano(?) with clarinet & bassoon: Crusell 1808.

STERCKEL, Abbé J.F.X?
Concerto: Meissner 1780.

STRAVINSKY, Igor
Three Pieces: Allegra 1919. Cahuzac 1923, 1928, 1933.

STUMF, Johann Christian?
Concerto: J.C. Kleine 1817.

STUNZ, Hartmann
Concerto no.1: J. Faubel 1834.

Concerto: F. Hartmann 1858.

Adagio & Rondo: J. Faubel 1837.

SÜSSMAYR, Franz
Aria from *Der Retter in Gefahr* for soprano & clarinet: A. Stadler 1797.

TÄGLICHSBECK, Thomas
Composition: Agthe 1842.

TAUSCH, Franz
Concerto: Crusell 1798, 1799. F.W. Tausch 1815.

Concerto for 2 clarinets: Baumgärtner & J.G.G. Hoffmann 1805. F. & F.W. Tausch 1805, 1807, 1812. W. Barth & Claus 1809. F.A. Bliesener & F.W. Tausch 1810. Baumgärtner & Schecker 1814. Jundt & Kern 1822. Bretschneider & Ph. Faubel 1825.

Andante & Polonaise (Adagio & Rondo alla Polacca): F.W. Tausch 1810, 1817. Blatt 1820, 1824. Schleicher 1822. F. Swoboda 1834 (Polonaise only).

Duet for horn & clarinet: Crusell 1802(?), 1805, 1807.

Trios for 3 basset-horns: F. Tausch, F.W. Tausch & G. Reinhardt 1807.

TITL, Anton Emil
"Der Sennin Heimweh" for soprano & clarinet: Pisařovic 1843.

TRIEBENSEE, Joseph
Concerto: Zenker 1805.

VANDERHAGEN, Amand
Concerto: Labatut 1799.

VOGT, Emil
Compositions: Bauer 1840.

VOLLWEILER, Carl
Concertino: Schlosser 1840.

Concerto for 2 clarinets: Blaes & Wassilieff 1847.

WACHTER, ?
Concerto no.1: Wachter 1786(2).

Concerto no.2(?): Wachter 1787.

WALTHEW, Richard
Trio for clarinet, violin & piano. G. Clinton 1898.

"The Song of Love & Death" for soprano & clarinet: G. Clinton 1898.

WEBER, Carl Maria von
Concerto no.1: H. Baermann 1811(4), 1812(2), 1827(2), 1831, 1834. Feldt 1824(2). Ott-Imhoff 1824, 1826. F. Heinze 1825. Lutz 1827, 1841. Agthe 1832, 1834. G. Heinze 1838. Neff 1848. Reitmayer(II) 1881. Mühlfeld 1895.

Adagio & Rondo (Allegro) from Concerto no.1: H. Baermann 1813, 1820, 1820 (Adagio only), 1821, 1827. F. Heinze 1830, 1836, 1837. Willman 1837. (G. Gareis 1839)? Nehrlich 1839. Peger 1842 (Rondo only). Landgraf

1844 (Rondo only), 1848. Kotte 1846 (Adagio only). Blaes 1853.

Concerto no.2: H. Baermann 1811, 1812, 1813. Hermstedt 1815(2). Kotte 1823. Feldt 1824(3). Galilei 1824. Agthe 1833(2).

Romanza, Recit. & Polacca from Concerto no.2: Cahuzac 1934.

Concerto: H. Baermann 1812, 1813. G. Reinhardt 1815, 1834. A. Schott 1816. F. Heinze 1823. J. Lauterbach 1824. Schick 1825. J. Faubel 1827. Ph. Faubel 1829. Schindelmeisser 1831. Willman 1836. Hentschel 1848. Derlien 1859. Rose 1862. Mühlfeld 1891.

Concertino: H. Baermann 1811. Schulze 1815. Hostié 1819. F. Reinhardt 1819. Stohwasser 1819. F. Heinze 1821, 1829, 1834, 1835, 1836. Schleicher 1822. Bretschneider 1823. Bolsius 1824. Schönberger 1824. Feldt 1825. Herzog 1825. F.W. Tausch 1830. Th. Klein 1833. Agthe 1834. Kotte 1835, 1846. Pollmächer 1836. ?Tausch 1838. Peger 1840, 1842. G. Heinze 1841. Landgraf 1844, 1848. Hamburger 1845. Mehner 1856. G. Clinton 1876. Vaupel 1876. F. Thomas 1879. Mühfeld 1886, 1892. Ch. Draper 1945.

Variations op.33: H. Baermann 1811, 1812(2). Hermstedt 1816, 1828, 1841. F.A. Bliesener 1817. Schick 1818? Kotte 1835. C. Rakemann 1836. A. Schubert 1839, 1843. (See under FREEDLAND, Garry).

Grand Duo op.48: H. Baermann 1815 (2nd & 3rd mvts only), 1833, 1836. Kotte 1824, 1837(2). Blaes 1836, 1841(2), 1845. Willman 1838. A. Schubert 1839. Nehrlich 1844. G? Gareis 1845. Mehner 1861. Grosse 1868. Mühfeld 1892.

Quintet op.34: H. Baermann 1815. Blaes 1841, 1842(3) 1845.

Phantasie from Quintet: Schick 1816, 1818? Schindelmeisser 1833.

"Se il mio ben" for 2 contraltos with clarinet, horn & strings: H. Baermann 1811.

Compositions: Addner 1827. Meier 1851.

WESTENHOLZ, Friedrich
Concerto for flute & clarinet: Hostié 1819.

WESTENHOLZ, Wilhelm Franz
Concerto: Rauchschindel 1805.

WESTERHOFF, C.W.
Concerto op.7: Rauchschindel 1805.

Concerto: Stötzer 1800.

Variations: Baumgärtner 1811.

WIEPRECHT, Wilhelm
Fantasia: Meier 1849.

Schweizer Variations: Kotte 1834, 1839.

Composition: Meinberg 1837.

WILLIAMS, Joseph
Concerto: Williams 1819.

WILMS, J.W.
Concerto op.40: Christiani 1816. J.C. Kleine 1817.

Allegro (from Concerto): Pauer 1821.

WINTER, Peter von
Concerto: Crusell 1799, 1800(2), 1804, 1806, 1807(3), 1808, 1813, 1817, 1818. W. Barth 1807. S. Werle 1813. Frisch 1814. Baumgärtner 1817.

Concertino: ?Springer 1837.

Concerto for clarinet & cello: H. Baermann 1808.

Symphonie Concertante op.11 for clarinet, basset-horn, bassoon & violin: Beer & F. Tausch 1802. F. & F.W. Tausch 1804.

Symphonie Concertante for clarinet, bassoon, horn, 2 violins & cello: Crusell 1819.

Aria for soprano(?) & clarinet: Crusell 1802.

WITT, Friedrich

Concerto: Bähr 1794, 1796, 1803. J.G.G. Hoffmann 1805, 1813. J.C. Kleine 1812.

Concertante: Odalde 1824.

WITTEK, Anton

Trio for flute, clarinet & horn: Sonnenberg 1847.

WOLF, ?

Symphonie Concertante for clarinet, bassoon & horn: X. Lefèvre 1789.

YOST, Michel.

Concerto: Yost 1781(6), 1783(9), 1784(2), 1786(6). X. Lefèvre 1783, 1784, 1785(2), 1788(2). Graziosi 1786. Barbay 1787. Hostié 1787. de Toulouse 1796. Crusell 1797. Dubois 1798.

Rondo (from Concerto?): Wolfe 1799.

Duet for clarinet & violin: Dubois 1799.

Quartet: Hartmann 1792.

ZAHLBERG, ?

Duo: H. Meyer 1864.

Bibliography

For further titles see OV

Almanach des Spectacles. Paris 1822 to 1834.

BARY, Helene de – *Museum. Geschichte der Museumsgesellschaft zu Frankfurt a. M.* Frankfurt 1937.

BATLEY, Thomas – *Sir Charles Hallé's Concerts in Manchester.* Manchester 1896.

BERGMANS, C. – *Le Conservatoire royal de Musique de Gand.* Ghent 1901.

BERNSDORF, Eduard & SCHLADEBACH, Jules – *Universal Lexikon der Tonkunst.* Offenbach 1856-1865.

BIHRLE, Heinrich – *Die Musikalische Akademie München 1811-1911.* Munich 1911.

BÖSKEN, Franz – *Musikgeschichte der Stadt Osnabrück.* Regensburg 1937.

BRANBERGER, Jan – *Das Konservatorium für Musik in Prag.* Prague 1911.

BRESCIUS, Hans von – *Die Königl. Sächs. musikalische Kapelle von Reissiger bis Schuch (1826-1898).* Dresden 1898.

CARINGI, Joseph J. – *The Clarinet Contest Solos of the Paris Conservatory.* University Microfilms, 1963.

CARSE, Adam – *The Life of Jullien.* Cambridge 1951.

DANDELOT, Arthur – *La Société des concerts du conservatoire de 1828 à 1897.* Paris 1898.

DLABACZ, Bohumil Jan – *Allgemeines historisches Künstlerlexikon für Böhmen.* Prague 1815.

EBERST, Anton – *Klarnet od A do Z.* Cracow 1970.

ERRANTE, F. Gerard – *A Selective Clarinet Bibliography.* New York 1973.

ESTOCK, Joseph J. – *A Biographical Dictionary of Clarinetists born before 1800.* Unviersity Microfilms 1972.

FÜRSTENAU, Moritz – *Beitrage zur Geschichte der Königl. Sächs. musikalischen Kapelle.* Dresden 1849.

FÜRSTENAU, Moritz – *Das Dresdener Konservatorium.* Dresden 1881.

GILBERT, Richard – *The Clarinetists' Solo Repertoire. A Discography.* New York 1972. *The Clarinetists' Discography II.* New York 1975.

GREGOIR, Édouard G.J. – *Biographie des Artistes-Musiciens Neerlandais.* Antwerp 1864.

GREGOIR, Édouard G.J. – *Galérie biographique des Artistes-Musiciens Belges du XVIIIe et du XIXe Siècle.* Brussels 1862.

HOPKINSON, Cecil – *A Dictionary of Parisian Music Publishers, 1700-1950.* London 1954.

KAUL, Oskar – *Geschichte der Würzburger Hofmusik im 18. Jahrhundert.* Würzburg 1924.

LANGWILL, Lyndsay G. – *An Index of musical Wind-Instrument Makers.* 4th edition. Edinburgh 1974.

LEDEBUR, Carl von – *Tonkünstler-Lexicon Berlins.* Berlin 1860/61.

LEIBROCK, Adolf – "Die herzoglich braunschweigische Hofkapelle." *(Braunschweigisches Magazin).* Brunswick 1865/6.

LEMACHER, Heinrich – *Zur Geschichte der Musik am Hofe zu Nassau-Weilburg.* Bonn 1910.

LETZER, J.H. – *Muzikaal Nederland 1850-1910.* Utrecht 1913.

LIPOWSKY, Felix Joseph – *Baierisches Musiklexikon.* Munich 1811.

METTENLEITER, Dominik M. – *Musikgeschichte der Stadt Regensburg.* Regensburg 1866.

MÜHLFELD, Christian – *Die Herzogl. Hofkapelle in Meiningen.* Meiningen 1910.

MÜLLER-DOMBOIS, Richard – *Die Fürstliche Lippische Hofkapelle.* Regensburg 1972.

Musikalische Almanach. Leipzig 1782 to 1784.

NORLIND, Tobias – *Allmänt Musiklexikon.* Stockholm 1916.

NORLIND, Tobias – *Kungl. Hovkapellets historia.* Stockholm 1921.

PERGER, Richard von – *Denkschrift zur Feier des fünfzigjährigen ununterbrochenen Bestandes der Philharmonischen Konzerts in Wien 1860-1910.* Vienna & Leipzig 1910.

PIERRE, Constant – *Histoire du Concert Spirituel 1725-1790.* Paris 1975.

PIERRE, Constant – *Le Conservatoire national de muisque et de déclamation.* Paris 1900.

POUND, Gomer – *A Study of Clarinet Solo Concerto Literature composed before 1850.* University Microfilms 1965.

SAAM, Josef – *Das Bassetthorn.* Mainz 1971.

SALDONI, Baltasar – *Efemérides de músicos espagñoles.* Madrid 1860.

SCHIEDERMAIR, Ludwig – *Der junge Beethoven.* Leipzig 1925.

SCHMIDT, Günther – *Die Musik am Hofe der Markgrafen von Brandenburg-Anspach.* Kassel & Basle 1956.

SCHNEIDER, Ludwig – *Geschichte der Oper und des königl. Opernhauses in Berlin.* Berlin 1852.

SCHREWE, Hans & SCHMIDT, Friedrich – *Das Niedersächsische Staatsorchester Hannover.* Hanover 1971.

SITTARD, Josef – *Geschichte des Musik-und Concertwesens in Hamburg und Altona.* Altona & Leipzig 1890.

STEIN, Fritz – *Geschichte des Musikwesens in Heidelberg bis zum Ende des 18. Jahrhunderts.* Heidelberg 1921.

STIEHL, Carl – *Lübeckisches Tonkünstler-Lexikon.* Leipzig 1887.

STIEHL, Carl – *Musikgeschichte der Stadt Lübeck.* Lübeck 1891.

THOMAS, Georg Sebastian – *Die Grossherzogliche Hofkapelle in Darmstadt.* Darmstadt 1859.

TITUS, Robert – *The Solo Music for the Clarinet in the Eighteenth Century.* University Microfilms 1952.

VALENTIN, Caroline – *Theater und Musik am Leiningenschen Hofe.* Würzburg 1921.

WALTER, Friedrich – *Geschichte des Theaters und der Musik am kurpfälzischen Hofe.* Leipzig 1898.

WARNER, Thomas E. – *An annotated Bibliography of Woodwind Instruction Books, 1600-1830.* Detroit Studies in Music Bibliography 1967.

WOLLRABE, Ludwig – *Chronologie sämtl. Hamburger Bühnen usw..* Hamburg 1847.

Index

AACHEN, 32, 101, 220
Abano, 61
Abel, 23
Abrahame, 23
Adam, Adolphe, 43
Adami, Giuseppe, 24
Adami, Vinatier, 24
Addner, Anders, 24, 75
Adelsheim, Baron, 149
Agner, Karl, 24
Agthe, Johann A., 24-25, 185
Ahl, 25
Akerhjelm, Baron Gustave d', 77
Albert, Eugène, 157-158
Albert, Prince, 233
Albertazzi, Emma, 270
Albes, Karl W., 25
Albesby, 25
Albrecht, Julius B., 25
Alexandrov, A.M., 25-26
Allegra, Edmondo, 26
Alt, 26
Altay, 46
Altenburg, 134
Ambrosi, Carl, 26
Amburg, 29
Amelang, 26
Amme, 26, 150
Amorbach, 42, 186
Amsterdam, 56, 64, 71, 89, 99, 101, 118, 126, 138, 139, 196, 210, 245, 261; Cecilia Society Concerts, 261; Eruditio-Musica Sunday Concerts, 261; Felix Meritis Society, 196, 231
Amtmann, Prosper, 136
Anderson, George, 26, 158
André, 26, 225
André, Johann, Fig 6
André-Bloch, 193
Angoulême, Duchess d', 79
Ansbach, 29, 235
Anschütz-Capitain, Elise, 174
Anton, Friedrich, 26-27
Anton, Ludwig, 27
Antwerp, 230, 231, 275; Cathedral, 261; Royal Wind Society, 48, 186, 199
Aragon, 209
Arban, Baptiste, 218
Arditi, Luigi, 155
Arezzo, 62, 197; Philharmonic Society, 197
Arias, Pedro, 135
Arne, Dr Thomas, 267
Arnold, Mme, 134
Aschaffenburg, 98
Assmann, Guillaume E., 27
Augarde, August, 27
Augarde, Edward, 27
Augarde, Edwarde, 27
Augarde, Gustave, 27
Augsburg, 45, 175; Subscription Concerts, 228
Aumont, (Henri R?), 278
Auroux, 27-28
Austria, Archduke Rudolph of, 200
Austria, Emperor Franz I of, 205
Austria, Emperor Joseph II of, 247
Austria, Empress of, 226
Austria, Grand Duchess Sophie of, 226
Austria, Grand Duke Anton of, 226
Austria, Grand Duke Franz of, 226
Austria, Princess Leopoldina of, 65, 186, 193
Avé-Lallement, Louis J.G.E.S., 28
Avoni, Petronio, 28

BACH, JOHANN C., 267
Bach, J.S., 61
Bachmann, Franz?, 28
Bachmann, Georges Chr., Plate I; 28-29, 62, 217
Back, N., 29
Backofen, Ernst, 29
Backofen, Gottfried, 29, 51
Backofen, Heinrich, Plate I; 15, 29-31, 51
Backofen, Heinrich (son of the above), 30
Bad Liebenstein, 204
Baden, 198, 226
Baden, Elector of, 74
Baden-Baden, 189, 277
Bähr, Josef, 16, 31, 171, 175, 236
Bänder, August, 34
Bänder, Charlotte (*née* Rambach), 32-34
Bänder, Conrad, 15, 16, 31-34, 82, 182
Bänder, F., 34, 117
Bänder, Heinrich, 34
Bänder, Johann H., 31, 33
Bänder, Ludwig, 15, 16, 31-35, 182
Baermann, Barbara, 35
Baermann, Carl, 35-37, 99, 143, 159, 188, 204, 278, 279

Baermann, Carl (son of the above), 36
Baermann, Heinrich, 16, 17, 31, 32, 33, 35-38, 66, 79, 98, 99, 125, 128, 134, 143, 145, 149, 153, 164, 185, 192, 205, 213, 231, 253, 270, 271
Bättenhausen, 38-39, 78, 142, 268
Bageard, Alphonse, 39, 197
Baillie, Isobel, 88
Baillot, Pierre, Plate 5
Baissière, François, 39
Baissières-Faber, 39
Balabio, Mme Fanny de Capitain D'Arzago de, 69
Balfe, Michael, 119, 171
Baltimore, 275; Starck's Long Room, 49, 90
Banger, Adam, 39
Barat, J.E., 193
Barbandt, Barthold, 39
Barbandt, Carl, 39
Barbay, 40
Barbier, 40
Barcelona, 64, 69
Bargheer, 40, 182
Bargheer, Carl, 40
Barnard, 40
Barret, Apollon, Plate 18; 155
Barth, Joseph, 40, 237
Barth Wilhelm L., 15, 40-41, 71, 125, 171, 176, 258, 269
Barth, Wilhelm (son of the above), 41
Bartolomey, Franz, Plate2; 41-42, 274
Bartolomey, Mathias, 41
Barton, 42
Barton, James, 42
Basle, 64, 166; Music Society, 190
Bass clarinet, 28-29, 62-63, 80, 90, 91, 157
Bass clarinet makers: Orsi, 189; Sax 216-217
Bass clarinet players, 25, 27, 28, 34, 35, 62, 78, 82, 89, 91, 103, 115, 142, 171, 178, 181, 187, 217, 218, 266, 270, 275
Bassano, Louisa, 270
Basse, Emma, 45
Basset-clarinet, 165, 247
Basset-horn, 29, 42, 81, 113, 165, 220, 246, 250
Basset-horn makers: Griesbacher, 117; Hesse, 129; Key, 156; Lotz, 165; Pask, 156-157; Selmer, 239
Basset-horn players, number of, 16
Bassi, Luigi, 42
Bathyány, Prince Joseph, 60, 165
Bauer, Adolf, 42
Bauer, E., 42
Bauersachs, Carl, 42
Baum, Joan, 42
Baumann, Friedrich, 155, 156
Baumgärtner, Joseph, 43, 131, 223
Bavaria, Elector Carl Theodor of, 122, 255
Bayreuth, 29, 207, 249; Festival, 170
Bazin, 43, 113
Beate, Hermann, 43
Becht, Carel J., 43, 100
Beckau, Joseph, 43
Becker, Anton J., 43-44
Becker, Karl F.W., 44, 186
Beecham, Sir Thomas, 88
Beecké, Ignaz von, 247
Beer, Joseph, 16, 44, 50, 92, 98, 164, 202, 223, 231, 232, 241, 277
Beerhalter, Aloysius, Plate 2; 15, 44-45
Beethoven, Ludwig van, 17, 36, 151, 171, 176
Behrens, Franz, 45
Belderbusch, Count, 179
Beletti, 45
Belfast, 190
Belgium, King Leopold I of, 170, 261, 275
Belgium, King Leopold II of, 232
Belke, M.F., 45
Bellini, Vincenzo, 67
Bellison, Simeon, Plate 4; 15, 45-47, 105, 279
Belloli, Agostino, 67
Bender, Adam, 15, 47
Bender, Constantin, 15, 47
Bender, Herman, 47
Bender, Jakob, 15, 16, 47-48, 186
Bender, Mme, 48
Bender, Valentin, Plate 4; 15, 16, 47-48, 184, 216, 260, 275
Bendleb, Karl, 48-49
Bendleb, Siegfried, 48
Benedikt, Julius, 145
Benoît, Christofle, 49
Beranger, 49, 90, 166
Berendt, 49, 195
Berezin, Anatoly V., 49, 112
Bergamo Philharmonic Society, 69
Berger, 49
Berger, David, 49
Berger, Julius, 49, 269
Bergevel, 49
Bériot, Charles de, 237
Berlin, 32, 35, 49, 54, 57, 62, 66, 74, 81, 92, 96, 110, 111, 113, 114, 116, 133, 134, 164, 177, 180, 185, 191, 195, 205, 206, 220-225, 233, 235, 245, 251, 253-255, 257, 258, 268, 273; Academy of Singing, 110, 111; Bliesener Institute, 54-55; Deutsche Staatsbibliothek, 226; Friedrich Charitable Institute, 57; High School for Music, 133, 225; Kroll Theatre, 196; Kullak Conservatoire 233; Mewes Flower Garden, 268; Opera House, 24, 145, 149, 150, 233; Philharmonic Orchestra, 188; Royal Theatre Hall, 66, 205, 220, 221, 225, 237; Royal York Lodge, 252, 255; Russian Hotel, 221; Stadt Paris Hall, 54, 223, 255; Subscription Concerts, 99
Berlioz, Hector, 24, 36, 140, 151, 155, 163, 193, 217, 218, 237
Bermann, Moritz, 53
Bernburg, 275; Wind band, 275
Bernburg, Prince of, 129
Berne, 32, 42; Society of New Music, 64
Berner, Friedrich W., 49
Bernhard (merchant), 169
Berr, Frédéric, Plates 5 & 6; 49-50, 58, 81, 108, 119, 141, 166, 173, 238
Berr, Phillipe, 50-51, 52
Berra, Marco, 222
Bertini (flautist), 82
Bertrand, 259
Bessmertnov, P.S., 51
Bethlehem, Pa., 207
Betz, 51
Beuschel, 51
Bianchini, Francesco, 51, 167
Biarritz, 189
Biberach, 226
Biche, 51
Bičistě, Josef, 51
Bié, Paul, 209
Bilbao, 64
Billington, Elizabeth, 189, 267
Bimboni, Giovacchino, 51

Bimboni, Giovanni, 51
Binfield, 51
Birch, Charlotte, 272
Birckmann, H., 29, 51
Birmingham, 256, 272, 273
Bischoff, Carl, 30
Bishop, Anna, 159
Bismarck, Prince Otto von, 233
Blaes, Joseph, Plate 7; 28, 34, 36, 52, 116, 260, 261, 266, 267
Blaha (oboist), 146
Blancou, V., 51, 52
Blaschke, 52
Blasius, Frédéric, Plate 8; 15, 52-53, 57
Blasius, Jean M., 52
Blatt, Thaddäus, 53-54, 97, 98, 192, 195
Blève, 54
Bliesener, Ernst, 54
Bliesener, Frederich A., 54, 92, 205, 254
Bliesener, Louis, 54-55
Blin, 259
Blizzard, John, 55, 156
Bloch, Kalman, Plates 3 & 4
Blonk-Steiner, Carlo, 55
Blonk-Steiner, Umberto, 55, 167
Blümel, Franz, 55
Blum, Carl, 37
Blum, Ludwig, 254
Blum, Stephen, 55
Bochsa, Charles R.N., 55, 272
Bochsa, Karl, 55-56, 242
Bögel, Christian, 56
Böhme (town musician), 143
Böhme, K.F., 75
Boehmer, Johann S., 56
Boehmer, Karl, 56, 143, 185
Bofinger, 56
Bohemian Quartet, 234
Bohrer brothers, 32
Boieldieu, François, 109
Boisdeffre, René de, 117
Bolland, Hermann, 56
Bolm, Carl, 56
Bologna, 61, 66, 181, 220; Accademia Filarmonica, 61, 181, 182; Conservatorio, 167; Large theatre, 266
Bolsius, 57, 252
Bona, Pietro, 69
Bonade, Daniel, 159
Bonn, 36, 208
Bordeaux, 78, 79; Theatre, 78
Borsdorf, A.E., 115
Boscavy, Monsieur, 184
Boskovsky, Alfred, 274
Boston, Mass., 103, 116, 219, 220, 233, 239, 251; Boylston Hall, 122, 219; Freement Theatre, 231; New England Conservatory, 116, 172; Philharmonic Orchestra, 26; Philharmonic Society, 116, 220
Boufil, Jacques J., 15, 53, 57, 160
Bourgoing, Baron Jean F. de, 74
Bournonville, Armand, 193
Boutruy, K.I., 57, 141
Bouvinnes, 260
Bove, S., 57
Bowley, 57-58
Boymond, 58
Boyneburgk, Baron Friedrich von, 58
Brahms, Johannes, 17, 63, 233, 252
Brain, Aubrey, Plate II
Brancas, Marquis of, 175
Brandel, Genséric, 77
Brandis, Herr, 186
Brandsteller, Mme, 236
Brattoli, Giacinto, 58
Braun, Johann B., 58
Braun, Moritz, 175
Bredow, Captain von, 254
Breitkopf & Härtel, 30
Brekker, Vasily F., 58, 112
Bremen, 127, 140, 220, 221, 258; Cathedral, 140; Orchestra, 201, 202; Trade Hall, 127
Breslau, 126, 147, 177, 229, 275
Bretonneau, 58
Bretschneider, 58-59, 100
Bretzenheim, Duke of, 122
Brexendorff, Mlle, 36
Brissler (pianist), 111
Bristol Theatre Royal, 270
Broca, Pedro, 59, 170
Broca, Ramón, 59
Broeu, Jean F. de, 60
Bronice, A., 161
Brough, L., 60
Bruchsal, 175
Bruck, 246
Brühl, Count Charles de, 254
Brünn, 200
Brunner, Georg, 60
Brunswick, 187, 244, 258
Brunswick, Duke of, 129
Brussels, 28, 109, 216, 217, 231, 260-262; Church of the Augustins, 28; Conservatoire, 39, 103, 116, 122, 151, 152, 232, 260, 261; Instrumental Museum, 219; Palais des Beaux-Arts, 64; Popular Concerts, 257; Royal School of Singing, 216; Royal Wind Band, 28, 217, 249; Ysaye Concerts, 257
Bryant, Lillian, 89
Brymer, Jack, 155
Buch, 60
Buch, Antoine, 161
Buchwieser, Catharine, 131
Buck, Sir Percy, 94
Budapest Quartet, 172
Budinsky, Franz, 60, 97, 196
Bückeburg, 162, 163, 182, 260
Bührmann, 60
Bülow, Hans von, 42, 204
Bünau, Henrietta, 126
Buenos Aires, 198; Academy of Instrumental Music, 198
Buffet, Louis-Auguste, 80
Buffet-Crampon, 163
Bultos, 60
Bum, Michael, 60
Bundy, George, 238
Busch Quartet, 172
Buschinsky (flautist), 101
Busi, Alessandro, 167
Busoni, Anna, 61
Busoni, Ferdinando, Plates 8 & 9; 15, 60-62
Busoni, Ferruccio, 26, 60-61
Busse, 62
Busser, Henri, 193
Buteux, Claude F., 62-63, 92, 120, 160, 209, 217, 278

CAHUZAC, LOUIS, Plate 9; 15, 63-65, 210

Calcutta, 149
Caldes, 65
Calvist, Enrique, 65, 116
Cambridge, 127, 273
Campbell, Robert, 65
Camporese, Violante, 271, 273
Campos, Gaspar, 65, 192
Candeille, Amélie J., 242
Cannabich, Christian, 105
Cano, 68
Canongia, Ignacio, 65-66, 273
Canongia, J. Avelino, 15, 65-67, 73, 273
Canongia, Joaquin I., 66, 67
Cantu (bassoonist), 67
Canzi, Catherine, 45
Caradori-Allan, Maria, 270, 271
Carafa, Michele, 141
Cardiff, 88
Carlos, 67
Carlsruhe, 74, 128, 175, 180, 226, 235; Grand Ducal Theatre, 228
Carola, Natalie, 260
Cartellieri, Emilia, 133
Carulli, Benedetto, 67, 68, 189
Casa, Giuseppe, 28
Casali, Domenico, 67
Casagli, Mme, 76
Caspari (singer), 174
Cassignol, 259
Castellan, Jeanne, 270
Castronovo, Lorenzo, 67
Catalani, Angelica, 140, 271, 272, 273
Cataneo, Tomaso, 68
Catel, Charles S., 90
Cavallini, Ernesto, Plate10; 15, 60, 67-69, 119, 150
Cavallini, Eugenio, 68
Cawthorn, Miss, 272
Celinicke (bandmaster), 239
Chacón, José, 278
Chalumeau (Shalamo), 16, 70, 212
Chambéry, 119
Champmartin, M. de, 110
Chappell, S. Arthur, 157-158
Chardon, David, 70
Chardon, Jean, 70
"Charles", Mr, 16, 70, 104, 210
Charleston, 103, 150
Chatelet, 119
Chatenet, M. de, 92
Chelard, André, 70, 241
Chelard, Hippolyté, 70
Chemnitz, 176
Cherubini, Luigi, 90, 206
Chiaffarelli, A., 70
Christiani, Cornelia H.A., 71
Christiani, Philippe, 70-71, 139, 196, 245, 261
Christman, H., 71
Christoph, Wilhelm, 71
Cimetta, 71
Clappé, Arthur, 155
Clarinet d'amour, 180
Clarinet ensembles: Bellison, Plate 3; 47; Poncelet, 197; Renard, 207; Stark, 249
Clarinet makers & systems: Albert, 89, 157-158, 233, 275; Bachmann, 28; Backofen, 30, 187, 205, 207, 229; Baermann, 188, 249; Barret, 72; Boehm 26, 50, 52, 87-89, 165, 170, 197, 209, 233; Bühner & Keller, 231; Buffet, 13, 158, 159, 210; Buffet-Crampon, 72, 158, 170; Clinton-Boehm, 72; Clinton-Combination, 72; Fauelhaber, 100; Fieldhouse, 156, 157, 260; Full-Boehm, 115; Grenser, 75; Griesbacher, 117; Key, 55, 156, 157; Lefèvre, 54; Lotz, 165; Mahillon, 275; Martel, 87, 88; Müller, 28, 40, 52, 63, 80, 92, 107, 108, 181-182, 212, 216, 275; Oehler, 46, 188; Orsi, 189; Romero, 209, 210; Sax, 216; Simple, 197, 209; Vinatieri, 62
Clarke, Hamilton, 155
Claus, 41
Clausé, 72
Clausthal, 42, 71
Clerisseau, 119
Clermont, 72, 113
Clinton, Arthur, 72
Clinton, George, 27, 72
Clinton, James, 72
Coburg, 243, 251, 266
Coburg, Prince of, 243
Cole, Plate 18
Coleridge-Taylor, Samuel, 87
Collinet (flageolet player), 112
Cologne, 186, 220, 234
Comettant, Oscar, 219
Como, 243
Compagnon, 73-74, 154
Compositions for clarinet, relative popularity of, 17
Conrad, 73
Conroy, James, 158
Constance, 148
Conti, Prince Louis François of, 200
Conti, Prince Louis François Joseph of, 51
Contrabass clarinet, 58, 90, 217, 269
Contrabass clarinet players, 34, 58
Contra-basset-horn, 197
Conway Band, 229
Copenhagen, 111
Copland, Aaron, 172
Coquard, Arthur, 259
Cor anglais, 24-25
Corfe, Joseph, 168
Corman, Giuseppe, 73
Cortesi, 73
Cramayel, 162
Crémont, Pierre, 73
Crépin, Théodore N.C., 73, 160
Crispin, 73
Croner, Antonio J., 67, 73
Croydon Public Hall, 87
Cruciano, 73-74
Crusell, Anna S., 74
Crusell, Bernhard, 17, 24, 40, 74-77, 95, 112, 127 137, 142, 160, 184, 185, 222, 253
Crusell, Sofia, 75
Cuboni, Raimund, 77, 194
Cuenca, 59
Curioni, Alberico, 273
Curth, 39, 77-78, 142, 268
Czermack, Abundius, 78
Czerny, Kaspar, 78, 113, 170, 189

DACOSTA, ISAAC, 15, 50, 62, 73, 78-81, 90, 108, 110, 160, 217
Dacosta, Mme, 79, 80, 217
Dahlinger, 81
Damrosch, Walter, 152
Damse, Jósef, 81
Damse, Therese, 81
Danaïs, 81

Dangel (violinist), 275
Dantan, Jean P., 50
Danzi, Franz, 139, 226
Danzig, 168
Darmstadt, 166, 169, 206, 226
Dauprat, Louis, 57
Dautremer, M., 193
David, Anton, 15, 81-82, 92, 146, 147, 165, 245
David, Ferdinand, 24, 126
Dazzi, 82
Debussy, Claude, 63, 178
Deichert, 34, 82, 185
Delamotte, Gabriel E., 82-83, 179
Demajo, Babini, 83
Demnitz, Friedrich, Fig.I; 83, 170
Demnitz, Mme Julie, 83
Denis, 83
Deprez (banker), 161
Derby, 198
Derevel, 259
Derlien, Gotthard H.A., 83
Derska, Johann, 34
Dessau, 164, 165, 253; Elbe Festival, 258; Subscription Concerts, 165, 253
Dessau, Prince of, 40
Destouches, Franz, 228
Desvignes, Hippolyté, 83
Detmold, 174, 186, 207, 263
Dettmann, Friedrich E., 83
Devienne, François, 161
Devonshire, Spencer Compton Cavendish, 8th Duke of, 152
Diabelli & Co., 86, 87
Dickerhof, E., 83
Dietrich, 83
Dillingen, 175
Dimmler, Anton, 86
Dimmler, Franz, 86
Dittersdorf, Karl Ditters von, 103
Doberan, 122
Dobyhal, Franz, 86
Dobyhal, Josef, 86
Doizi, Monsieur, 182
Domanzi, 176
Dominik, August, 86
Donat, 86
Donizetti, Gaetano, 62-63, 67, 217
Doppler, Josef, 86-87
Dorn, 87
Dorn (merchant), 224
Dorn, Heinrich, 203, 224, 225
Dorus, Vincent, 163
Dorus-Gras, Julie, 272
Dossenbach, 87
Double sounds, 16, 185
Douglas, F., 87
Dover, Duke of York's School, 55

Draper, Haydn, Plate II; 88-89, 100
Draper, Mendelssohn, Plate II; 88-89
Draper, Paul, 88
Draper, William, 87
Dreiklufts, 89, 138, 210
Drescher, 89
Dresden, 35, 66, 96, 100, 102, 126, 143, 145-146, 150, 154, 175, 177, 180, 201, 201-211, 233, 252, 269; Conservatoire, 83, 107, 146, 152, 170, 249; Harmonie Saale, 98, 145, 274; Poland Hotel, 145, 212; Public Quartet Concerts, 143; Royal Blind Institute, 128, 274
Drewes, F., 89
Drobisch, Johann G.T., 89
Dublin, 70
Dubois, William, 49, 89-90, 275
Dubourg, L. Aimé, 56
Düring, Gustav, 59, 131
Düsseldorf, 246
Dufaut & Dubois, 55
Dufour, 90
Dufresne (trumpet player), 218
Dulken, Violanda, 99
Dumas, 80, 90, 217
Duport, Charles, 91
Duport, Jean P., 91
Duprez, E., 91, 217, 218
Duprez, Gilbert, 91
Duques, Augustin, 91
Duverné, François G.A., 218
Duvernoy, Antoine, 92
Duvernoy, Charles, Plate II; Fig 2; 15, 57, 62, 91-92, 160, 194
Duvernoy, Charles (son of the above), 92
Duvernoy, Frédéric, 161
Duvernoy, Henri, 92
Dworschack, Franz, 81, 82, 92, 245

EBERT, CARL, 54, 92, 94
Eberwein, Max, 180
Echotone, 32, 220, 222
Edinburgh, 232, 272; Theatre Royal, 196, 244
Edling, Johann, 94
Eeckhound, Pierre J. van, 94
Egerton, Gustavus R., 95
Egerton, Julian (I), 87, 88, 94-95, 260
Egerton, Julian (II), 94
Egerton, Percy, 94-95
Egerton, William, Plate 12; 94, 95
Egerton, William (son of the above), 95
Egger, 95
Egling, 33, 95
Egypt, Viceroy of, 48
Ehlen, Johann G., 95
Ehrenreich, Carl, Plate 12; 75, 95
Ehrlich Max, 95
Eichhorn, 95
Eichhorst, Karl, 96, 254, 255
Eigler, Melchior, 96
Eisenach, 249
Eisert, 96
Eisert, Johann, 145
Eley, Christopher, 96
Elliot, Carlotta, 94
Emminger (tenor), 196
Empoli, 61
Engel, Engelhard, 96
England, King George III of, 96
England, Queen Victoria of, 94, 95, 96, 270
Erfurt, 142, 151, 174, 193; Theatre, 173
Erhardt, Jakob, 96
Erlangen, 29
Erlau, 200
Ermel, 96
Ernest, 70, 97
Ernst, 97, 117, 222
Eschmann, Carl, 190
Essberger, Carl, 97
Estabel, M., 50
Esterház, 224

Esterházy, Count John Charles, 165, 248
Esterházy, Prince, 132
Esterházy, Prince Nicolaus, 224

FABIAN, J.A., 75
Fabiani, Gaetano, 61
Farnari, 97
Farník, Gustav, 53, 97
Farník, Wenzel, 15, 60, 97-98, 195, 200, 252
Farrobo, Count, 66
Fasano, Tommaso, 98
Fasch, 98
Faubel, A?, 98
Faubel, Joseph, Plate 13; 15, 38, 98-100, 190
Faubel, Philipp, 15, 43, 59, 98-100
Fauelhaber, Emmanuel, 100
Fawcett, Charlesworth, 100
Fawcett, Mendelssohn, 100
Feldt, 101, 149
Felix, 101
Feller, Immanuel, 101-102
Ferrán, Louis, 102
Fessy, Alexandre Ch., 50, 119, 159
Festetics, Count Georg, 248
Fetter, Giuseppe, 102
Fink, Charlotte, 145
Fioravanti, Vincenzo, 236
Fischel, Adolph, 203
Fischer, Dagobert, 103
Fischer, Enrique, 102
Fischer, Konrad, 102
Fischer, Michael, 102
Fischhof, Joseph, 228
Fitzpatrick, Horace, 70
Flath brothers, 102
Fleury, Abraham, 79
Flieger, Simon, 102, 199-200
Flittner, 102-103, 180, 212
Florence, 68; Conservatoire, 113
Florio (flautist), 130
Flotow, Friedrich von, 196
Förster, Karl, 103, 143
Förster, Wilhelm, 103
Forckert, Johann G., 103, 142, 143, 274
Foucard, 103
Fournier, 103
France, Emperor Napoleon I of, 57, 90, 91, 186 241, 262
France, Emperor Napoleon III of, 218
France, King Charles X of, 39, 108
France, King Louis XVI of, 124, 141
Franchetti-Walzel, Mme, 202
Franck, Frédéric, 103
François, 103-104
Franke, Sylvain, 104
Frankfurt, 16, 23, 30, 31, 33, 43, 55, 64, 98-100, 118, 130-131, 171, 175, 177, 179, 186, 205, 220, 223, 231, 235, 244, 273; Museum Concerts, 23, 32, 58-59, 98, 100, 107, 118, 173-174, 181, 205-206, 208, 221, 226, 231, 234, 244-245; Theatre, 23, 31, 45
Frankfurt, Grand Duke of, 98
Freiburg, 186; Festival, 215
Freiburg, Princess Elizabeth of, 137, 171, 257
Freudenfeld, August, 15, 70, 104, 210
Frey, M., 111
Fribourg, 268; Swiss Music Festival, 268
Frickler, 104, 124
Friedlowsky, Anton, Plate 13; 104, 105, 138
Friedlowsky, daughters of, 105
Friedlowsky, Joseph, 104-105, 138, 186
Friedrich, Joseph, 46, 105, 187, 279
Friedrichs, Mme, 145
Frion, 105
Frion, C.L., 105,
Frisch, Joseph, 105
Frischner, Franz, 87
Fröhlich, Josef, 230
Frohleiten, 62
Fuchs, Georg, 105-106
Fürst, Elisabeth, 125
Fürst, Michael, 106
Fürstenau, Moritz, 143
Fürstenberg, Prince Carl Alois of, 127
Fürstenberg, Prince Karl Egon III of, 232, 243
Füssel, Carl G., 107
Fulda, 225, 263, 268
Funk, 107

GABLER, EGON, 107
Gabler, Maximilian, Plate 14; 107
Gabrielsky, Johann W., 255
Gade, Niels, 194
Gäbler, Christoph, 107
Gänrich, Wenzel, 225
Galilei, 107
Galitsin, Count Dimitri, 246
Gallay, Jacques F., Plate 5
Gallet, 107
Gambaro, Auguste, 109
Gambaro, Giovanni B., 15, 50, 107-110, 166, 178, 179, 278
Gambaro, Vincenzo, 108-110
Gambaro ainé, 108-109
Gambaro ainé, Mme, 108, 109
Ganz, Francisca, 185
Garcia, Pauline, 237
Gareis, Albert, 110-111
Gareis, Gustav, 110-111
Garner, Horatio, 111
Gasseau, 111
Gassner, 111
Gaubert, Philippe, 178
Gautier, 112
Gaveaux, Guillaume, 112
Gaveaux, Pierre, 112
Gaveaux, Simon, 112
Gelhaar, Carl S., 112
Geneva, 215
Gennaro, Marcel, 193
Genoa, 66, 68
Gensler, Vladimir I., 49, 112
Gentzsch, Traugott, 112
George, Lorenz, 113
George, Mme, 132
Georges, 113
Gerlach, G.G., 75
Germain, M., 39
Germany, Emperor Wilhelm II of, 241
Ghent, 256; Casino Concerts, 124; Conservatoire, 116, 260, 261
Giampieri, Alamiro, 113
Giller, Josef, 113
Girardin, Alex., 92
Gladney, J., 113
Glasgow, 231
Glinka, Michael, 75, 181
Glöggl, Joseph, 78, 113, 171, 189

Gloucester Festival, 267
Godecharle, 113
Godfrey, Charles, 197
Goeller, 113
Goepfert, Karl, Plate 14; 114-115, 175, 212
Görlitz, 201
Göteborg, 179
Göttingen, 174; Jacobi's orchestra, 124
Götzscher, Anton, 115
Golestan, Stan, 193
Gomez, Aurelio F., 115
Gomez, Francisco, 88, 115, 210, 239
Gomez, Manuel, 87, 115, 191, 210
González, Manuel, 65, 102, 115-116, 209, 278
Goodall, Miss, 271, 272
Goossens, Leon, Plate II
Gorizia, 61, 62
Gossec, François, 51, 74
Gotha, 29, 30, 185, 203, 204
Gotthard, 66
Goudswaard, David, 116
Gounod, Charles, 210
Gouvy, Theodore, 259
Gracht, Arthur J. van der, 116
Granger, Frederick, 116
Granger, Thomas, 116, 220, 239
Granval, C. de, 117
Grassalkovics, Prince Anton, 257
Graupner, Gottlieb, 116
Graz, 61, 147, 198, 200
Graziosi, 116
Greding, 116, 181
Greifswald, 28
Greiz, 249
Grenser, Heinrich, 75
Griesbacher, Raymund, 117, 247
Griesel, 34, 97, 117
Grimm, Joseph, 117
Grisez, Léon, 27, 117, 141, 259
Grisi, Giulia, 273
Groenveldt, T.W., 117
Groot, Adolphe de, 119
Groot, David de, 15, 16, 33, 50, 69, 100, 117-119, 182, 205, 206
Groot, Henri de (father of David), 118
Groot, Henri de (son of David), 119
Groot, Jules de, 119
Gross, 119
Grosse, Friedrich W., 119-120
Grove, Sir George, 68
Grovlez, Gabriel, 178
Gruber, G.W., 29
Gründlinger, 120
Grünfeld (pianist), 41
Grützmacher, 120
Grützmacher, Friedrich, 120
Grützmacher, Leopold, 120
Gruner, F., 120
Grutsch, Franz, 138
Guéméné, Prince of, 261
Guerrabella, Mme, 270
Gugel, 120
Guillou, Joseph, 57
Gumpelshamer, Sigismund A., 120
Guyot, 120, 259
Guyot, Jean F., 121

HAASE, LOUIS, 145
Habeneck, 35, 217
Haberland, Johann Chr. F., 121
Habermehl, Georg M., 121
Habert, J.M., 121
Habgood, Thomas, 121, 192
Haeffner, Johann Chr. F., 74
Härtel, 121
Hagen, F.C., 182
Hague, the, 43, 118, 119; Toonkunst Society, 43
Hahn, Reynaldo, 259
Haidner (bassoonist), 122
Halberstadt, 187; Festival, 180
Halbreiter, Mlle, 99
Halévy, Fromental, 217
Halir Quartet, 234
Halle, 30, 119; Festival, 195, 255, 258
Hallé, Sir Charles, 119-120, 180
Haller, Max, 121
Halm, Anton, 105
Hamann (pianist), 221
Hamburg, 24, 35, 36, 60, 74, 81, 87, 90, 123, 126, 129, 135, 153, 177, 181, 208, 221, 234, 236, 244, 245, 247, 258; Apollo Hall, 123, 237; City Theatre, 90; Festival, 232; Philharmonic Society, 237
Hamburger, 121-122, 225
Hamelin, Gaston, 122, 172, 173, 193, 259
Hammerl, Cornelius, 122
Hampel, Johannes, 105, 122, 201
Hampstead, 256
Hanmann, Charlotte von, 211
Hannon, David, 122, 197
Hanover, 126
Hansen, Lambertus J., 71
Hanssens, Charles, 124
Harburger, Johann, 122
Harlas, Helene, 37
Hart, 122-123, 219
Hartig, 123
Hartig, Count, 117
Hartig, Count Ludwig, 123
Hartmann, Albert, Plate 18
Hartmann, Carl, 123, 135, 236
Hartmann, Ferdinand, 123
Hartmann, Herr von, 147
Harty, Sir Hamilton, 88
Hasenier, Georges, 123
Haslang, Count, 39
Haslinger, Tobias, 226
Hasse, Johann, 212
Hastie, 123
Haushälter, Karl W.E., 124
Hausmann, Robert, 180
Haute, Isidore F. van den, 124
Havre, le, 54, 231
Hawkes & Co., 87
Hawkins, Sterling, 173
Haydn, Joseph, 167, 207
Hayenschinck, 124, 242
Heap, Charles S., 155
Hebestreit, 124
Hefele, Joseph, 124
Heidelberg, 255
Heilbronn, 102
Heinefetter, Sabine, 25
Heinefetter, Sophie, 267
Heinichen, 26
Heinike, Mme, 54
Heinnitz, John, 104, 124
Heinrici, Georg F., 124

Heinrici, Wilhelm, 124
Heinroth, Dr, 174
Heinze, Ferdinand, 15, 40, 41, 125-126, 211
Heinze, Gustav, Plate 15; 15, 125-127, 143, 151
Heisterhagen, 127, 164, 234, 263
Held, Karl, 127
Helfrich, 127, 202
Heliopolis, 55
Hellendael, Peter, 127
Hellendael, Peter (violinist), 127
Heller, Anton, 127
Heller, Eustach, 127-128
Hellier, Sir Samuel, 70
Hellmesberger, Ferdinand, 252
Hellmesberger Quartet, 86
Hellwig, 128
Hengel, Jacob, 128
Henri, 128
Henry, 128
Henry, Antoine, 57
Henry, Bonaventura, 128
Hentschel, Johann, 128, 143
Hereford, 269, 270; Festival, 270
Hermann, 128
Hermberg, 128
Hermstedt, Simon, 16, 41, 66, 101, 124, 128-129, 136, 139, 168, 174, 184, 185, 205, 258, 269, 279
Herrig, 129
Herrnhut, 201
Herz, Heinrich, Plate 5
Herzog, August, 129
Hesse, 129
Hesse, Grand Duke Ludwig III of, 250
Hesse, Grand Duke Ludwig X of, 205
Hesse, Johann G. Chr., 129
Hesse, Wilhelm, 129
Hesse-Philippsthal-Bergfeld, Prince of, 31
Hessler, Gustaf, Plate 15; 129-130
Hessler, Martin, 130, 175
Hetsch (town musician), 45
Heurteur, Mme, 105
Heyneck, Edmund, 130
Hiebetsch, Carl E., 130
Hildburghausen, 29, 168
Himmel, Friedrich H., Fig 7
Hindemith, Paul, 64
Hinze, 130
Hochberg, Baron, 82, 146, 147, 245
Höchst, 175
Hoffman(n), 130
Hoffmann, A., 130
Hoffmann, Johann G.G., 43, 130-131
Hofmann (violinist), 118
Hofmann, Richard, 131
Hohenlohe-Öhringen, Prince of, 42
Holbrooke, Joseph, 88
Holland, King Louis Bonaparte of, 203
Hollenstein, Michael, 131
Hollnsteiner, 131
Holmann, U., 131
Holmès, Augusta, 131, 141, 210
Holzapfel, 131
Honegger, Arthur, 63
Hopkins, Edward, 131-132
Hopkins, Edward (horn player), 131-132
Hopkins, George, 131-132
Horn (clarinettist), 132
Horník, 132
Horník, Caroline, 132
Horník, Johanna, 132
Hosterwitz, 211
Hostié, J., 132-133, 171, 225
Hoym, Count, 147
Hublard, 197
Hubler, Carl F., 133
Hughes, Samuel, Plate 18
Hugot, Adolphe, 133, 160
Hugot, Antoine, 133, 161
Hugot, Pierre, 133-134, 160
Hugray, 134, 262
Hummel, Friedrich, 38, 134
Hummel, J.J., 246
Hummel, Johann N., 117, 118, 229
Hummel, Tobias, 134
Hungary, King Francis I of, 226
Hungary, Queen of, 226
Hunger, Johann H., 134
Hurka, Friedrich, 74
Husk, William, 155
Hustinoy, 159
Huth, 134

INDY, VINCENT D', 64
Italy, Queen Margherita of, 167
Itjen, 134
Ivon, Carlo, 67

JACOBI (town musician), 124, 174
Jäger, Christian, 134
Jahnel, Louise, 196
James, E.F., 115
Janaček, Leoš, Plate II
Jandot, 134
Janssen, César, 134-135, 160
Jardin, Jerónimo, 135
Jardin, Josephine, 135
Jardin, Magin, 59, 135
Jardin, Manuel, 135
Jeanjean, Paul, 135, 210
Jeckl, Mlle, 164
Jena, 25, 151, 193, 234
Joachim Quartet, 234
Jodry, 123, 135, 136
Jülich, Mlle, 129
Juliá, Manuel, 135
Jullien, Louis A., 154-155, 171, 243, 277; Orchestra, 95, 119, 134, 140, 154-155, 197, 242, 261
Jundt, 135, 137
Jundt, Mlle A., 135
Jung-Bunzlau, 200
Jungman (singer), 244

KABEL, FRIEDERIKA, 248
Kahn, Robert, 180
Kainz, Mariana, 220
Kaiser, 136
Kaiser, Julius, 136, 170
Kalkbrenner, Friedrich, Plate 5
Kania, Johann, 136
Karlsbad, 152, 237
Kassel, 34, 118, 126, 128, 142, 181, 185, 204, 220, 221-222, 234, 263; Court theatre, 34; Euterpe Society, 33, 95; Subscription Concerts, 34, 60, 82, 131, 141, 164, 185
Kassel, Elector of, 221
Kassel, Electress of, 221
Kastner, Jean G., 217, 218

Kastus, Anthoine J., 136
Kaszuba, Pawel, 136
Katzung (bassoonist), 203
Kauer, Ferdinand, 136
Kaufmann, Friedrich, 145
Kaye, Milton, 173
Kellermann, Thilo, 129, 136
Kellman, 75
Kellner, Joseph, 136
Kempten, 150
Kermazin, Franc de, 136
Kern, A., 135, 137
Key, George, 38
Key, Thomas, 156
Khachaturian, Aram, 46
Khayll, Alois, 104
Kieseler, 137
Kiev, 226
Kindgren, 75
Kircheis, 137
Kirn, 172
Kirstein, 78, 137
Kjellberg, Johan, Plate 16; 137, 240
Klee, Johann, 137
Klein, 137, 204
Klein, Georg, 137-138
Klein, Johann H., 138
Klein, Thomas, Plate 16; 86, 138
Kleine, Christoph, 15, 71, 89, 138-139, 196
Klein, Dietrich, 15, 139
Klein, Heinrich, 15, 139
Klein, Jacob, Plate 17; 15, 139-140
Kleine, Johann W., 139
Kleine, Wilhelm G., 138
Kleinhaus, 140, 175
Klett, 140
Klingenberg, 127, 140
Klipfele, Georg, 140
Klosé, Hyacinthe E., 57, 110, 117, 131, 140-141 163, 172, 192, 210, 218, 238, 239, 259
Kloss, Karl, 185
Klotzsch, 141
Knecht, Justin, 226
Knirsch, Emil, 141
Knittel, Mme, 141-142
Knoch, 142
Knoll, Mme von, 206
Knorre, Auguste, 132
Koch, Bernard, 139
Koch, Heinrich, 180
Köbel, Carl, 75, 142
Koehn, 142
Königsberg, 34, 78, 101, 129, 132-133, 168, 171, 172, 203, 221, 222, 223, 224, 225; Kronen Lodge, 33; Theatre, 101, 251
Köttlitz, 142
Kötzschau, Hermann, 142, 143
Kohlschmidt, Leopold, 142
Kolbe, 142
Kolisch Quartet, 172
Kollmann, 39, 78, 142, 268
Komorn, 200
Kopp, Franz J., 142
Kotte, Johann, Plate 17; Fig 3; 15, 36, 103, 126, 128, 142-146, 154, 177, 252
Kozel, Wenzel, 252
Kozeluch, Johann A., 200
Kozeluch, Leopold, 247
Krähmer, Ernst, Fig 5; 199, 226, 228, 237
Krähmer, Ernst (son of the above), 228
Krag, 146
Krakamp, E., 278
Kramer, Christian, 146
Kranklin, Fig 3
Kratkh, Mlle, 173
Kratky, Nanette, 24
Krause, 146
Krause (bassoonist), 101
Krause, Johann G., 82, 146-147, 245
Krause, Karl J., 82, 147-148, 245
Krebs (town musician), 143
Kremsmünster, 177
Kreutzer, Conradin, 148
Kreutzer, Marie, 148
Kröpsch, Fritz, 148, 164, 278
Kroll, François, 149
Krommer, Franz, 17, 40, 77, 118
Kroolle, 259
Krzyzanowski, 149
Küffner, Josef, 37, 149, 216, 230-231
Kühn, Friedrich W., 149, 150
Kühne, 101, 149
Kugelmann, M., 61
Kuhlan, 149
Kukro, 150, 268
Kummer, Friedrich A., 143, 145
Kuntz, 149, 150
Kunze, K., 26, 150
Kustner, Ludwig, 150

LABANCHI, GAETANO, 69, 150
Labatat, 150
Lacher, Joseph, 150
Lacombe, Louis, 145
Ladunke, Theodor, 150
Lafleur ainé, 109
Lahou, Jean F.J., 216
Laibach, 61
Lake Ontario, 231
Lambelée, Gabriel, 151
Lambelée-Alhaiza, Aline, 151
Lambesc, Prince of, 44
Lamotte, Antony, 260
Lamour, Charles G., 151
Landgraf, Bernhard, 15, 112, 151-152
Lang, 152
Lange, Aloysia, 131
Lange, Hermann, 152
Langenbeck, Johann G., 152
Langenus, Gustave, 15, 152-153, 197
Langer, Dominik, 153
Langlotz, Karl A., 153
Lankammer, Christoph B., 73, 153
Laon National Guard, 238
Laparra, Raoul, 193
Lappe, Philipp, 153-154
Larsonneur (violinist), 192
Lascelles, Miss, 270
Lauel, 154
Laun, 100
Laurent, 154
Laurent (oboist), 179
Lausanne, 221, 222, 243; Festival, 190
Lauterbach, Friedrich, 145, 154, 249
Lauterbach, Johann G., 143, 154
Layer, Antoine, 154
Lazarus, Henry, Plates 18-20; 26, 55, 68, 94, 154-159, 171, 198, 256, 270, 277; instrument

collection, 156-158
Lecerf, 159, 259
Lecerf, B.A.A., 159
Lecerf, E.F., 159
Lee, Sebastian, 258
Leeds Festival, 88, 178
Lefèbvre, Henri, 159-160, 210
Lefèbvre, Pierre, 160
Lefèvre, François, 54, 62, 209
Lefèvre, Louis, 79, 160, 192
Lefèvre, Xavier, 57, 62, 70, 73, 74, 78, 110, 133, 135, 160-162, 192, 203, 241
Leffler, 162, 184
Legendre, August A., 162
Legendre, Mme, 162
Leghorn, 61, 68
Leipzig, 32, 35, 40, 41, 56, 62, 82, 105, 107, 125, 126, 128, 134, 136, 137, 151-152, 165, 171, 173, 176, 177, 191, 202, 212, 225, 251, 258, 269; Beygang Museum, 56; Euterpe Society, 125, 126, 150, 165, 210; Gewandhaus Concerts, 30, 71, 111, 120, 145, 154, 164, 173, 181, 185, 228, 245, 257, 258; Gewandhaus Orchestra, 151, 177; Poland Hotel, 202; Subscription Concerts, 103, 126, 177, 211, 237, 274; Theatre Hall, 220
Lellmann Georg, 162-163, 182, 265
Lener Quartet, 88, 89
Lengerke, Karl von, 163
Leningrad (see St Petersburg)
Leoben, 62
Leperd, 218
Leriche, Mathias, 163, 194
Leroy, Adolphe, Plate 21; 163, 238-239
Leroy, Léon, 141, 163
Lesser, 127, 164, 234, 263
Lesueur, Jean, 241
Liechtenstein, Count, 236
Liège, 170; Cathedral, 198; Conservatoire, 198, New Concerts, 257; Spa, 198; Société d'Émulation, 170; Wind orchestra, 198
Ligature, 188
Lilienfeld, 26
Lima, 89
Limmer, Franz, 164
Lind, Jenny, 44, 185, 240
Lindner, Friedrich, 164, 177
Lindner, Roderich A., 164
Lindpaintner, Peter von, 17, 37, 38, 249, 254
Link, Joseph A., 38, 164
Link, Sebastian, 164
Link, Xavier, 164
Linz, 78, 113, 170, 188
Lisbon, 64, 66, 179, 186, 187, 188, 273; Brotherhood of St Cecilia, 65, 273; New Assembly, 273; San Carlos Theatre, 66; Subscription Concerts, 188
Liszt, Franz, 34, 229, 269
Litaize, Gaston, 194
Liugin (trumpet player), 82
Liverani, Domenico, 165, 167
Löschorn (pianist), 185
Löwenburg, 82
Loewenhielm, Count Gustave of, 77
Löwenstein, Prince of, 186
Logier system, 201
Lohmann, 165
London, 45, 58, 64, 66, 88, 96, 188, 189, 230, 231 239, 240, 256, 267, 270; Adelphi Theatre, 95; Aeolian Hall, 89; Argyll Rooms, 260; BBC Military Band, 26; Beecham Opera Company, 26; Clarinettists' Society, 72; Coldstream Guards, 156, 171; Covent Garden, 94, 119, 155, 157, 158, 162, 167, 184, 242, 267, 273; Dannreuther/ Wagner Concerts, 260; Drury Lane, 119, 256, 258, 270, 273, 277; English Opera House, 134; Exeter Hall, 159; Grenadier Guards, 27; Guildhall, 272, 273; Hanover Square Rooms, 92, 123, 232, 235, 245; Haymarket (Her Majesty's, King's) Theatre, 39, 119, 121, 192, 267; Hickford's Room, 15, 39, 104, 210; LSO Wind Quintet, 115; Mansion House, 198, 272, 273; Marylebone Gardens, 104, 124; Moorfields Chapel, 198, 273; Musical Union, 275; New Musical Fund, 37, 272-273; Philharmonic Society, 68, 69, 72, 116, 159, 184, 198, 260, 270-273; Queen's Hall, 94; Richter Concerts, 27; Royal Academy of Music, 27, 94, 256; Royal College of Music, 26, 87, 88, 258; Royal Italian Opera, 159; Royal Military Asylum, 55; Royal Society of Musicians, 27, 95, 96, 124, 171, 178, 189, 192, 197, 256, 260, 267; St James's Hall, 94, 159; Stationers Hall, 70; Surrey Gardens, 140, 243, 277; Swan Tavern, 70; Vauxhall Gardens, 82, 92, 132, 245; Winterton House, 242
London Wind Quintet, 88-89
Lopitzsch, 165
Lorenz, 165
Lorraine, Prince Charles of, 261
Lotz, Theodor, 165-166
Loudelle, 50, 166
Louis, 166
Louis (horn player), 199-200
Louis Musical Instrument Co., 88
Luberti, Carlo, 166, 167
Lucchesi, Giuseppe, 166
Lucerne Festival, 64, 215
Luchon, 63
Ludwig, L., 166
Ludwigslust, 251
Lübeck, 28, 32, 35, 56, 81, 83, 123, 128, 154, 168, 181, 220, 234, 245, 258
Lullier, 49, 166
Lutz, Eduard, 166
Luxembourg, 261
Lyons, 178

MAASTRICHT, 202
Maccagnani, 166-167
Maccagni, Clemente, 51, 167
Mackenzie, Sir Alexander, 27
Maconchy, Elizabeth, 256
Madras, 149
Madrid, 59, 209, 278; Asylum of San Bernardino, 278; Conservatoire, 59, 115, 135, 209, 278; Wind Instrument Chamber Music Society, 215
Magdeburg, 30, 101, 107, 149, 181, 221, 222, 234, 258; Friendship Society, 101; Harmonie Concerts, 101, 149; Lodge Subscription Concerts, 101
Magnani, Aurelio, 51, 55, 165, 166, 167, 278
Mahillon, Charles, 28
Mahon, Catherine, 168
Mahon, John, 131, 167-168, 189
Mahon, Sarah, 167
Mahon, William, 131, 167-168
Mahr, C., 129, 168, 258
Maintzer, Franz, 168
Mainz, 175, 232
Mainzer, Friedrich, 168, 169

Maiorov, I.N., 169
Malibran, Maria, 272
Malsch, William, 115
Manchester, 180, 198, 231, 232; Hallé Orchestra, 180
Mandel, Carl, Plate 18
Mangold, August D., 169
Mangold, Johann W., 169
Mann, T.E., Plate 18
Mannheim, 102, 105, 123, 172, 175, 181, 208, 213, 229, 232, 244, 257
Mannstein, Karl, 169
Marasco, Giuseppe, 169, 278
Marchetti, Mme, 40
Maré junior, 169-170
Maré senior, 169
Marechal (composer), 277
Marhefka, Franz, Fig 1; 83, 136, 170
Marienburg Festival, 264
Marmurier, 259
Marschner, Heinrich, 126
Marseilles, 82, 119
Martelli, Henri, 194
Martin, Plate 18
Martin, M., 57
Martinez, Andréas, 59, 170
Martinez, Juan A., 170
Marx, Michael, 170
Maschek, Vincent, 25
Massaert, Jean P., 170, 198
Massenet, Jules, 210
Matauschek, Johann, 78, 113, 170-171, 189
Mauermann, 53
Maugüé, J.M.L., 193
Maurer, Alois, 138
Maurer, Edward, 133, 171
Maurer, Gottlob, 40, 41, 171
Maurer, J.M., 171
Maycock, John, Plate 22; 159, 171
Mayer, 171-172
Mayer, Charles, 146, 172
Mayer, Jakob, 121, 171
Mayer, Mme (*née* Lévêque), 172
Mayer, Wilhelm, 61
Mayeur, Louis, 141, 172
Mazellier, Jules, 193
Mazzoleni, Pietro, 172
McLane, Ralph, Plate 22; 122, 172-173
Mecklenburg-Schwerin, Grand Duke Friedrich Franz I of, 238
Mecklenburg-Schwerin, Grand Duke Friedrich Franz IV of, 170
Meder, Konrad, 173
Meder, Valentin, 173
Meerti, Elisa, 126, 258, 270
Mehner, F., 173-174, 177, 211, 225
Méhul, Étienne, 90
Meier, Wilhelm, 174
Meinberg, Johann G., 174
Meiningen, 124, 134, 153, 180, 203, 204, 249, 269
Meissner, Philipp, 15, 31, 114, 130, 140, 174-175, 199, 205, 263
Mejo, Wilhelm, 176
Mendelssohn-Bartholdy, Felix, 79, 126, 145, 159, 246, 249, 258, 271
Menter (cellist), 99
Menz, Robert, 176
Mercadante, Giacinto, 176, 236
Mercadante, Saverio, 68, 69, 176
Mercier, 259
Méric, Jean, 176
Mério, Mme de, 272
Merlatti, 176
Merseburg, 30, 150
Mess, D., 32
Messager, André, 63
Metrowsky, Count, 152
Metz, 70; Philharmonic Society, 260
Metzler, 177
Meuser, Christian, 177
Meyer, Carl H., 71, 72
Meyer, Eduard, 143, 173, 177, 211, 225
Meyer, Hermann, 177
Meyerbeer, Giacomo, 35, 36, 37, 62, 80, 91, 99, 254
Meyerbeer, Minna, 35
Miedzny, Stefan, 177
Mikesch, 177, 279
Milan, 55, 61, 62, 69, 98, 181, 189, 220; Canobbiana Theatre, 68; Conservatorio, 67, 68, 69, 189
Milanollo, Teresa, 240
Milde, Rosa A. von, 25
Milhaud, Darius, 63
Mills, Edward, 177-178, 197
Mills, O., 178
Mimart, P.A., 178
Mimart, Prospér, Plate 23; 15, 178, 259
Mitau, 33
Mittag, August, 237
Mocker (father), 178
Mocker (son?), 178
Modena & Parma, Duchess Maria of, 69
Möhrenschlager, 178-179
Möller, Carl Wilhelm, 82, 245
Möseler, Heinrich, 36
Möser, Karl, 225, 233
Mohr, (horn player), 210
Mohr, J., 110, 179
Molendo, Mlle, 128
Molter, Johann M., 207
Monaco, 189
Monaco, Prince of, 208
Montbrun, Raymond G., 194
Montevideo, 190; Casa de Comedias, 190
Montmorency, Duke of, 132
Moock, 179, 190
Morelli, 179
Morges, 243
Mortimer, Harry, 179
Moscheles, Ignaz, 57, 118, 123
Moscow, 172, 188, 259, 264; Aljabĕv Orchestra, 259; Conservatoire, 25, 46, 187, 212, 239, 240, 279
Moscow Quintet, 46
Mouthpiece, 129, 155, 188, 239
Moutton, Balthaz, 162
Moysard, Michel, 179
Mozart, Franz, 132
Mozart, Wolfgang A., 17, 26, 27, 40, 43, 65, 82, 98, 99, 114, 120, 151, 206, 247, 266, 271, 274
Mraz, Josef F., 179
Mühlfeld, Richard, 16, 180, 204, 249, 269
Mühlhausen, 230; Jacobite Church, 230
Müller, 180
Müller, Carl?, 180, 203
Müller, F., 139
Müller, Friedrich, 15, 103, 180-181, 212
Müller, Iwan, Plate 21; Fig 4; 17, 31, 32, 34, 40, 48, 92, 107, 116, 119, 127, 141, 163, 181-184,

194
Müller, Johann G.G., 184
Müller, Wilhelmine, 78
Müller-Bender, Mme, 66, 181, 206
Müller-Berghaus, 188, 249
Münster, 208, 250
Münster, Bishop of, 208
Munich, 30, 32, 37, 99, 130, 134, 166, 175, 204, 220, 222, 231, 234, 263, 266, 268; Conservatoire, 279; Isarthor Theatre, 37; Museum Society, 66, 99; Subscription Concerts, 230, 231, 234, 268
Munro, 162, 184
Murchie, Robert, Plate II; 89

NAARDEN, BATTLE OF, 71
Naderman, harp by, 30
Nagel, Heinrich, 184-185
Nancy, 61
Nantes, 66, 203
Naples, 214; Real Conservatorio, 236
Naples, King of, 236
Nason, Georg, 16, 185
Nassau, Duke Christian IV of, 121
Nassau, Duke Friedrich Wilhelm of, 121, 172, 214
Naumann, Johann, 212
Naumburg, 229, 279
Neff, A., 185, 188, 204
Nehrlich, Wilhelm, 25, 44, 185-186
Nejebse, 186
Neresheim, 45
Netherlands, King William I of the, 118, 139
Netherlands, King William II of the, 218
Netzer, Joseph, 145
Neuchâtel, 99, 101, 136, 243
Neukomm, Chevalier, 192
Neumann, Heinrich, 186
Neumann, Philipp, 186
Neumann-Sesse, Mme, 41
Neuparth, Eduard, 186-187, 192
Neu-Ruppin, 197
Neveu, 187
Neveu, Maurice, 187
New Orleans, 134
New Ross, 65
New York, 46, 90, 112, 172, 232, 233, 238, 275; Chamber Music Society, 152; City Hall, 47, 232; Philharmonic Orchestra, 47
Nice, 119, 188
Nidman, Karl, 187
Niebergall, Georg, 30, 187
Nielsen, Carl, 190
Nikolaevsky, F.O., 187
Nivernois, Duke of, 267
Nizinski, André, 187
Nocentini, Domenico, 187
Nöthlich, Wilhelm, 187
Nohr, Friedrich, 153
Nolte, 187
Nordhausen, 279
Norton, F., 187
Norton, Haydn, 187-188
Norwich, 273
Nottingham, 94
Novara, 61
Novello, Clara, 270, 273
Nuder, 188
Nuremberg, 29, 30, 51, 138, 256
Nuth, Mlle, 78

OBERTHÜR, CHARLES, 155, 232
Odalde, Thiago de Deos, 188
Oederan, 176
Oehler, Oskar, 15, 185, 188
Oeiras, 66
Öttingen-Wallerstein, Prince Kraft of, 31
Ogínski, Count Michael, 153, 188, 200
Oldenburg, Grand Duke of, 142, 214
Oliva, František, 78, 113, 170, 188-189
Oliver, James A., 189
Oliver, Richard, 189
Olmütz, 200
Orange, Prince of, 118
Orange, Prince William V of, 139
Orlamünda, 180
Orleans, Duke of, 241, 242
Orsi, Romeo, 67, 189-190
Ortega, Hermenegildo, 190
Ortega, Tiburcio, 190
Osnabrück, 180, 185, 203, 279; St. Mary's Church, 203
Otter, Franz, Plate 24; 190
Ott-Imhoff, C., 99, 190
Owens, Joseph, 190
Owenson, Robert, 267
Oxenvad, Aage, 190
Oxford, 173; Commemoration Concerts, 167
Ozi, Étienne, 242

PACHMEIER, JOSEPH, 179, 190-191
Pachta, Count Johann, 97, 252
Paderborn, 186
Paganini, Nicolo, Plate 5; 45, 68, 119, 222
Palatin, Antonio, 191
Pálffy, Count, 247
Palmblad, Karl J., 191
Pamphion, Miss, 256
Panny, Joseph, 255
Papé, Carl, 191
Paradies, Maria von, 200
Paradis, Henri, Plate 25; 191, 210
Paradis, Mme, 191
Pardubitz, 200
Parès, C.I., 191
Parès, Eugène, 191
Parès, Gabriel, 191
Parès, Philippe, 191
Paris, 16, 32, 42, 44, 52, 55, 61, 66, 74, 90, 98, 99, 107-109, 118, 119, 128, 137, 163, 172, 175, 181, 189, 192, 194, 195, 198, 199, 200, 206, 217-219, 229, 230, 231, 232, 236, 241, 261-262, 266, 277; Académie des Beaux-Arts, 68; Colonne Concerts, 64; Concert Spirituel, 44, 132, 136, 137, 161, 166, 175, 200, 202, 204, 208, 242, 264-265, 275, 277; Concert de la Loge Olympique, 161; Concerts Dandelot, 121; Conservatoire, 35, 52, 57, 62, 63, 73, 74, 78, 82, 83, 90, 91, 109, 117, 121, 122, 133, 135, 149, 151, 159, 163, 172, 178, 187, 191, 192, 193, 194, 203, 210, 217, 218, 219, 238, 250, 259, 263, 278; Garde Républicaine, 191, 263; Hôtel des Fermes, 192; Ridotto Room, 79; Salle Herz, 91, 218, 236; Salle Laffitte, 181; Salle Saint-Jean de L'Hôtel-de-Ville, 80; Société des Concerts, 35, 52, 57, 68, 99, 141, 163, 210; Société d'Études Mozartiennes, 64; Théâtre Favart, 32, 57; Théâtre Italien, 74, 231; Odéon wind band, 259;

Opéra, 35, 63, 199, 200, 204, 217, 224
Parke, James, 207
Parkinson, Jeremiah, 92
Parma, 68, 221
Parma, Duke of, 222
Parma, Grand Duchess of, 222
Parma & Plaisance, Archduchess of, 222
Parra, Leocadio, 191
Pask, John, 157-158
Passy, 199
Paton, Mary A. (Mrs Wood), 271, 272
Patti, Adelina, 158
Pauer, Franz, 53, 191-192
Paulus, I.G., 141, 192
Payne, Louisa, 270
Pearson, Hugh, 121, 192
Péchignier, Gabriel, 134, 160, 192, 262
Pedal clarinet, 197
Pedrizzi, 192
Pedro, Emperor of Brazil & King of Portugal, 65, 192-193
Peger, 193
Peinte, Antoine, 193
Pellegrini, Antonio, 193
Pellegrini, Donato, 193
Perez, 193
Périer, Auguste, 122, 193
Perret (bassoonist), 161
Persch, General, 147
Pesth, 69, 200
Peters, C.F., 40, 75
Petersen, Mozart, Plate 25; 194
Petit, Charles, 194
Petit, Marie P., 92, 194
Petschacher, Friedrich, 194
Petz, Martin, 194
Pezzana, 194
Pfaffe, August, 49, 194-195, 252, 255
Pfeffel, Konrad, 195
Pfeilsticker, Nicolas, 195
Pforzheim, 228; Guesthouse of the Knights, 228; Theatre, 228
Phasey, Alfred J., Plate 18
Philadelphia, 90, 103, 128, 130, 166, 275; Oeller Hotel, 49
Philipp, Joseph, 195
Pièces de rechange, 247
Pierné, Paul, 193
Pinot, 195
Pisařovic, Julius, 15, 60, 97, 195-196, 204, 206, 240, 252
Pistor, Betty, 34
Placci, Clelia, 272
Planke junior, 139, 196
Planke senior, 70, 196
Plater, 196
Platt, E., 196, 244
Poggiali, Gaetano, 196
Pohl, Julius, 196
Polatschek, Viktor, 197, 274
Pollard, Charlotte (*née* Godfrey), 197
Pollard, William, 197
Pollastri, 197
Pollmächer, 197
Poncelet, Gustav, 39, 122, 152, 177, 197, 232
Poniatowsky, Princess, 78, 113, 170, 189
Port-au-Prince, 166
Porteau, 172
Portmann, Johann Th., 121
Portsmouth, U.S.A., 111
Portugal, King Ferdinando II of, 67
Portugal, King João VI of, 65
Portugal, King Pedro IV of (see Pedro)
Portugal, Marcos, 192
Postula, Hypolite, 170, 198
Potocki, Prince Vincenz, 175
Potsdam, 147, 174, 233; Philharmonic Society, 174; Theatre, 111, 233
Pott, August?, 221
Poulain, 198
Pouplinière, Jean le Riche de la, 199-200
Powell, Philip, 198, 273
Powolny, Anton, 198
Prada, Victor de la, 198
Prague, 26, 117, 123, 129, 134, 136, 145, 152, 200, 201, 220, 221, 222, 245, 252, 267; Blind Institute, 97, 200, 230; Conservatoire, 28, 53, 60, 97, 179, 192, 195, 204, 206, 224, 240, 252; Dauscha Hall, 24; Imperial Theatre, 245; National Theatre, 152, 225, 267; Order of Charitable Brothers, 78; St Franz Monastery, 97; Strahov Monastery, 252; University, 78
Pratt, Alfred, 88
Preis, 198
Preller, Louis, 199
Prentano, Baron, 199, 226
Pressburg (Bratislava), 83, 165, 200
Printz, Jean, 199
Printz, Jean (son of the above), 199
Prinz, Alfred, 274
Procksch, Gaspard, 15, 102, 199-200
Prokofiev, Sergey, 46
Proksch, Joseph, Plate 26; 97, 200-201
Providence, 231, 239
Prudent, Emile, 119
Prussia, Dowager Queen of, 253
Prussia, King Friedrich Wilhelm II of, 98, 232
Prussia, King Friedrich Wilhelm III of, 114, 201, 253
Prussia, King Friedrich Wilhelm IV of, 71, 218
Pržichowský, Archbishop, 127
Puchberg, Michael, 247
Purebel, Josef, 201
Puttick & Simpson, 156
Puy, J.B.E. du, 74
Puzzi, Giovanni, 79, 272

QUABEC, 231
Quallenberg, Michael, 105, 122, 201, 257
Quesada, General Vincente, 59

RAAB, 200
Rabboni, Giuseppe, 67, 68
Radziwill, Count Karol, 201
Rainforth, Elizabeth, 270
Raiter, D.I., 58
Rakemann senior, 127, 201-202, 220
Rakemann, C., 202
Rakemann, Louis, 202
Rameau, Jean Ph., 102, 199, 200, 204, 224
Rasch, 202
Rathé, 202, 277
Rathgen, Adam, 124
Rauchschindel, 202
Raupach, Hermann F., 150
Rauscher, Jacob, 202-203
Ravel, Maurice, 63
Reading Festival, 251, 272
Rebeyrol, Pierre, 203

Rechtenbach, Christian T., 203
Recoaro, 61
Reed, 46, 62, 98, 125, 239, 253, 262, 270
Reeves, Sims, 270
Regensburg (Ratisbon), 45, 89, 265
Reger, Max, 233
Regnault, 203
Rehage, 203
Rehm, Johann G., 180, 203
Reibnitz, Baron Ludwig G. Chr., 203
Reich, Mlle, 59
Reicha, Anton, 163, 203
Reif, Wilhelm, 204
Reiffer, Francois, 137, 204, 224
Reinecke, Karl, 151
Reinecke, R., 204
Reinel, Albin, 195, 204-205
Reinhardt, F., 100, 205
Reinhardt, Georg, 15, 16, 30, 54, 118, 175, 205-206, 254
Reissiger, Karl, 126, 143
Reithardt, Heinrich A., 206
Reitmayer, Franz (I), 206
Reitmayer, Franz (II), 195, 206, 224
Reitz (son of the following?), 206
Reitz, Adolf, 30, 206
Renard, Charles, 207
Renard, Jean J. Th., 207
Reuling, Wilhelm, 138
Reusch, Johann, 207
Reuss-Plaen, Count (Prince) Henry LXIII of, 253
Richardson, Joseph, 154-155
Richmond-Wells, 16
Richter, Arthur, 207
Richter, Friedrich A., 207
Ricksecker, John, 207
Ricordi, Giovanni, 69
Ricordi, Giulio, 190
Ricordi of New York, 109
Rieger (harpist), 200
Rietz, Julius, 196
Riga, 33, 132, 148
Rihl, 207
Rimini, 192
Rinsum, C. van, 182
Rio de Janeiro, 65, 186, 192
Riotte, Philipp, 243
Ritter (violinist), 213
Rivier, Jean, 63
Rode, Pierre, 66, 78
Rodolphe, Jean J., 162
Rodriguez, Teodoro, 102, 208
Röder, Count, 146, 147
Röder, Philipp J., 208
Röhrig, 208
Roeser, Valentin, 208
Rohan, Prince of, 165, 175
Rollers, 134-135
Romberg, Andreas, 208
Romberg, Anton, 208
Romberg, Balthasser, 208
Romberg, Bernhard, 34, 208
Romberg, Gerhard, 208
Romberg, Therese, 209
Rome, 64, 73, 181; Adriano Theatre, 55; Argentine Theatre, 181; Costanzi Theatre, 55; Opera Society, 166-167; Philharmonic Society, 69; Pichetti Hall, 55; St Cecilia Academy, 55, 64, 166; Verdi Hall, 55
Romero, Antonio, Plate 26; 15, 115, 208, 209-210
Rooms, 89, 210
Rose, Cyrille, Plate 27; 15, 63, 131, 135, 141, 159, 172, 178, 191, 210, 238, 239, 250, 263
Rosé Quartet, 234, 250
Rosenburg, Francis, 15, 70, 104, 210
Rosenhain, Jacob, 35
Rosenkranz, 125, 173, 177, 211, 225
Rossach, 243
Rossini, Gioachino, 67, 68, 86, 108, 165, 236
Rostock, 101, 136; Lodge Concerts, 101
Roth, 211
Roth Carl F., 211-212
Roth, Gottlob, 15, 211-212
Roth, Traugott, 15, 102, 103, 180, 211-212
Rothschild, Baron Albert, 250
Rothschild, Baron Solomon?, 226
Rotterdam, 118; Subscription Concerts, 210
Rottweil, 212
Roussel, Albert, 63
Rozanov, Sergei V., 25, 169, 212, 239, 240, 264
Rubinstein, Anton, 69
Ruch, Justus, 213
Rudall Carte & Co., 88
Rudolstadt, 180, 212
Rüttinger, Christof, 213
Rüttinger, Johann, 213
Ruff, Johann C., 213
Rulf, 213
Rumburg, 136
Rummel, Christian, 15, 213-214, 230
Rummel, Joseph, 214
Rummel, Josephine, 214
Rupp, Michele, 214
Ruppert, Stephen, 215
Rupplin, Mlle von, 215
Ruprecht, 215
Russia, Emperor Alexander I of, 30, 77, 253
Russian Zionist Organisation, 46
Russianoff, Leon, Plate 3
Ruzicka (viola player), 41
Ryan, Pat, 179

SABON, 215
Sachse, Ferdinand, 215
Sänger, 215
Safonoff, Wassily, 46
St Petersburg, 16, 32, 33, 34, 44, 49, 66, 69, 73, 78, 81, 92, 101, 112, 153, 172, 177, 182, 219, 220, 221, 228, 232, 245, 257, 266, 267; All-Union Musical Competition, 240, 264; Conservatoire, 69; Empress's Horse Guards, 267; Imperial Theatre, 267
Saint-Gall, 64
Saint-Georges, Chevalier, 242
Saint-Nicolas Wind Society, 48
Saint-Saëns, Camille, 163, 173
Salamanca, 209
Salieri, Anton, 215
Salieri, Girolamo, 215
Salisbury, 167, 168; Assembly Rooms, 168; St Thomas' Church, 168
Salitre, 66
Salmon, Eliza, 168, 271, 272
Salzburg, 64, 99, 128, 134
Samuel, Harold, 88
San Miguel, Mariano, 215
San Sebastian, 64
Santa Cruz, 193

Santo Domingo, 195
Santolini, Dionilla, 73
Sarmiento, Pedro, 135
Sarrette, Bernard, 262
Sartorius, Georg K., 215-216
Saud, 216
Sauerbrey (town musician), 45
Saul, Ernst C. Chr., 216
Saunders, John, 87
Savinelli, Angelo, 67
Sax, Adolphe, Plate 28; 15, 28-29, 48, 62-63, 80, 109, 141, 216-219, 236, 239, 269; saxophones by, 157, 217-218
Sax, Charles J., 216
Saxe-Coburg-Gotha, Duke Ernst II of, 37, 240, 241
Saxe-Gotha, Hereditary Princess of, 31
Saxe-Gotha, Prince August of, 29, 30
Saxe-Meiningen, Duke Bernhard of, 204
Saxhorn, 218
Saxhorn players, 218
Saxony, King Friedrich August of, 212
Saxophone, 157, 165, 191, 216-218, 236, 277
Saxophone players, 73, 116, 141, 157, 165, 172, 177, 178, 189, 197, 218, 275
Saxotromba, 218
Scaramelli, Joseph, 136
Schäfer, 219
Schaffer, Francis, 16, 123, 219-220
Schaffer, Louis, 116, 219-220
Schalk, Franz, 16, 202, 220-222
Schall, Christian, 222
Scharf, 97, 222
Schatt, Johann Chr., 76, 77, 222
Schatz, Johann F., 222-223
Schaub, 223
Schaumberg-Lippe, Prince Georg Wilhelm of, 182
Schecker, 43, 223
Scheelith (oboist), 107
Scheffauer, 223
Scheller, Jakob, 247
Schenker, 199, 200
Scherzer, Georg, 223
Schicht, Mme, 133, 245
Schick, Ernst, 223
Schick, Friedrich, 223-224
Schick, Julie, 223
Schick, Margarete, 223, 273
Schida, Richard, 206, 224
Schiefer, Jean, 204, 224
Schierll, Joseph (I), 224, 265
Schierll, Joseph (II), 224, 265
Schiller, Christoph, 224
Schimon, Adolph, 35
Schindelmeisser, Fanny, 224-225
Schindelmeisser, Herr, 224
Schindelmeisser, Louis, Plate 28; 15, 133, 173, 211, 224-226
Schindtler, Francisco, 226
Schirolli, Giuseppe, 67
Schlegel, Mme (*née* Gareis), 111
Schleicher, Caroline, Fig 5; 199, 226-228
Schleicher, Franz J., 226
Schleicher, Sophie, 226
Schlömilch, 228
Schlosser, father & son, 228
Schmidl, Alois, 228
Schmidt, 228
Schmidt, Franz, 274
Schmidt, Mme, 230
Schmidt, R., 228-229
Schmidt, Roy, 229
Schmidt, Th., 30, 229
Schmitt, Joseph, 245-246
Schmittbauer, August, 229
Schnabel, A., 229
Schnabel, Joseph, 229
Schnabel, Julius, 229
Schnabel, Karl, 229
Schnabel, Michael, 153, 229
Schneider, 229
Schneider, Friedrich, 180
Schneider, Gustav, 229
Schnittspahn, J., 230
Schnurbusch, 230
Schoberlechner, Franz, 148
Schöfmann, Karl, 230
Schönberger, Isidor, 230
Schönche, Wilhelm, 230, 255
Schörg Quartet, 249
Schollmeyer, 230
Schott, Adam, 38, 44, 214, 230-232
Schott, Bernhard, 44, 230, 232
Schott, Franziska (*née* Rummel), 214, 230
Schott, Peter, 214, 230
Schott, Therese (*née* Ziegler), 231
Schott-Söhne, B., 108, 230-232
Schramm, C.W., 232
Schramm, Johann Chr., 232
Schrenk, 232
Schreurs, Joseph, 153, 197, 232-233
Schröder, Bonaventura, 233
Schröder-Devrient, Wilhelmine, 145, 154, 272
Schröter, C.F., 127
Schubert, August, 233, 254
Schubert, Franz, 86, 87, 138, 237
Schubert, Oskar, Plate 29; 233-234
Schubert, Ottilie, 238
Schuberth, Carl, 234
Schuberth, Friedrich, 234
Schuberth, Gottlob, 234
Schuberth, Julius, 234
Schuberth, Ludwig, 234
Schülein, Ludwig, 234
Schüler, G., 234
Schüler, Johann P., 234
Schultheis, 127, 164, 234, 263
Schultze, Hedwig, 111
Shulz, Adolph, 233
Schulze, Michael, Chr., 234
Schumann, Robert, 258
Schumann-Heink, Ernestine, 170
Schuppenzigh, Ignaz, 148
Schuster, Joseph, 212
Schwärzer, Georg, P., 234
Schwartz, Andreas, G., 133, 235
Schwartz, Christoph G., 54, 195, 235
Schwartze, Gottlob, 235
Schwarzburg-Rudolstadt, Prince of, 180
Schwarzenberg, Prince, 189, 263
Schwegler, 235
Schwegler, Johann D., 235
Schwemer, 235
Schwenke, C.F.G., 123, 236
Schwenke, Johann F., 123, 236
Schwerin, 170
Schwetzingen, 175
Scribanek, Johann, 236
Scruder, 236

Scudo, Pietro, 236
Sebastiani, Ferdinando, 236
Sedelmayer, Ferdinando, 236
Sedlak, Anna, 237
Sedlak, Wenzel, 236-237
Sedlatzek, Johann, 237
Seel, Johann H., 237
Seeman, Adolf, 237
Seeman, Gottfried, W., 237-238
Seeman, H., 207
Seidl, Anton, 188
Seipst, Peter, 124
Selike, 238
Selmer, Alexandre, Plate 29; 15, 172, 210, 238
Selmer, Charles, 238
Selmer, Emil, 238
Selmer, Frédéric, 15, 50, 141, 238
Selmer, Henri, Plate 29; 15, 163, 210, 238-239
Selmer, Jean J., 49, 238
Semenov, A.G., 239
Senft, Luigi, 239
Seven Years War, 235
Seville, 191
Seydelmann, Friedrich, 212
Shaw, Oliver, 239
Shaw, Mrs Alfred, 272
Shtark, A.L., 240
Siebert, Franz, 101
Siebert, Mme, 101
Silva, 240
Simonet, François, 161, 162
Simrock, Nikolaus, 182
Sjöberg, Frans, 240
Slade, G., 240
Smart, Miss E.J., 58
Smart, Sir George, 96, 199, 221-222
Smith, Alex, 207
Smith, Robert, 207
Smolensk, 46, 75
Snel, Joseph, 52
Snelling (bassoon), Plate 18
Snoeck, César, 219
Sobeck, Jan, 15, 195, 240-241
Sobolewski, Michael, 241
Solère, Étienne, 15, 124, 241-242, 265, 277
Sondershausen, 48, 168, 174, 279
Sondershausen, Duke Gunther I of, 49, 242
Sondershausen, Princess of, 206
Sonnenberg, 242-243
Sontag, Henriette, 35, 118, 272, 273
Sousa Band, 229, 246
South Carolina, 90
Spa, 116
Spadina, Antonio, 243
Späth, Andreas, 127, 243, 251
Spain, King Amadeo of, 209
Spain, King Joseph Bonaparte of, 214
Spiccato, 16, 219-220
Spiess brothers, 244
Spina, C.A., 86
Spina, Guglielmo, 244
Spindler, 196, 244
Spitz, Peter D., 244
Spohr, Dorette (*née* Scheidler), 30
Spohr, Louis, 16, 17, 30, 33, 34, 43, 57, 67, 117, 118, 126, 127, 142, 145, 168, 180, 185, 212, 221, 222, 237, 249, 257-258, 271
Spohr, Marianne, 238
Sponheimer, Conrad, 244
Spontini, Gasparo, 32
Springer, 15, 244-245
Springer, Dominik, 245
Springer, Mme (*née* Schmitt), 245-246
Springer, Vincent, 15, 70, 81-82, 92, 146, 147, 165, 244
Squire, W.H., 88
Staab, Adalbert, 246
Staats, C.L., 246
Stadler, Anton, 43, 82, 138, 165, 246-248
Stadler, Antonius, 246, 247
Stadler, Barbara, 248
Stadler, Elizabeth (*née* Grittner), 247, 248
Stadler, Francisca (*née* Bichler), 247-248
Stadler, Johann, 138, 246-249
Stadler, Johann (son of the above), 248
Stadler, Joseph, 246
Stadler, Josepha, 246
Stadler, Leopold L., 246
Stadler, Magdalena, 248
Stadler, Michael J., 247
Stadler, Sophie, 246, 247
Stadler, Therese, 246
Stamitz, Johann, 102, 200, 204, 224
Stamitz, Karl, 44
Staps, Amélie, 249
Staps, Jean, 229, 249
Stark, Ella, 249
Stark, Robert, Plate 30; 15, 154, 249-250, 278
Stautz, Karl, 250
Stavelot, 250
Steffani, Karolina, 177
Steffens, Friedrich, 174, 250
Stegemüller, Mlle, 34
Steinbach, Fritz, 180
Steiner, F.W., 250
Steinert, Mme (*née* Backofen), 29
Steinfürt, 56
Stephens, Catherine, 132, 171, 172
Stettin Theatre, 195
Stiassny, Hans, 250
Stiévenard, E.H., 210, 250
Stockholm, 74-77, 221, 222, 234; Conservatoire, 95, 129, 137, 191; Music Society, 234; Royal Academy of Music, 130, 137, 142
Stöckl-Heinefetter, Maria, 138
Stötzer, 250-251
Stohwasser, 251
Stone, 251
Stradivarius Quartet, 172
Stradtmann, Ludwig F.C., 251
Stralsund, 223, 224
Strasbourg, 32, 42, 45, 51, 58, 81, 91, 118, 119, 135, 137, 171, 175, 181, 232, 260, 277
Straus, Anna, 151
Strauss, Johann, 41
Strauss, Richard, 204
Stravinsky, Igor, 63, 64
Stüber, Joseph, 251
Stunz, Hartmann, 99
Stuttgart, 32, 44, 45, 61, 99, 138, 177, 205, 206, 226, 235
Stuyvesant Quartet, 172
Süssmilch, 251
Sullivan, Thomas, Plate 18
Sundelin, August, 251
Sundelin, Karl, 251
Sunderland, Susan, 277
Sweden, King Gustavus Adolphus of, 74

Sweden & Norway, Prince Oscar of, 77
Swoboda, August, 97, 252
Swoboda, Franz, 97, 252
Sykora, Anton, 252
Syrinek, Adalbert, 195, 252

TADRA, WENZEL, 252
Täglichsbeck, Thomas, 25, 99
Taffanel, Paul, 259
Tamm, K.M., 36, 57, 195, 252
Tanner, Catherine (*née* Mahon), 168
Tanner, Joseph, 168
Taubert, Wilhelm, 185
Tausch, 252-253
Tausch, Franz, 17, 54, 55, 74, 195, 205, 223, 253-255
Tausch, Friedrich W., Plate 30; 36, 54, 96, 195, 205, 233, 254-255
Tausch, Jacob, 255
Tausch, Jacob (son of the above), 255
Tausch, Joseph, 230, 255, 269
Tausch, Julius, 253
Tausch, Mlle, 253
Tausch, Mme (*née* von Hammer), 253
Taut, 256
Teimer, 256
Teplitz, 201
Thalberg, Sigismond, 228
Themsche, Louis van, 256, 260
Therrien, Elzier, 172
Thielemann, 112, 256
Thomas, Ambroise, 157
Thomas, Cadwallader, Plate 31; 256
Thomas, Frances, 256
Thomas, Theodore, 232
Thün, Countess of, 247
Thurston, Frederick, 256-257
Tietze, Ludwig, 87
Tinholt, H., 184
Tirry, Anton, 78, 201, 257
Tomaszewski, 257
Toulouse Conservatoire, 63
Toulouse, M. de, 257
Tourneur, Georges, 257
Tretbach, 168, 257-258
Tretbar, F., 15, 40, 257-258
Triebel, 258
Trieste, 61, 68
Tripp, 258
Trolle-Bonde, Count Gustave de, 74, 77
Tropianski, Konstanty, 259
Trou, 259
Troyer, Count Ferdinand, 87, 259
Tuczech, Mlle, 233
Tübingen, 45
Türnau, 200
Tulou, Jean L., Plate 5; 79
Tuly, Francesco, 259
Turban, Charles, 122, 141, 259-260
Turcoing, 163
Turgis, 260
Turin, 24, 66, 68
Turkey, 43
Turlonia, Duke Alessandro, 73
Tuscany, Grand Duke Ferdinand of, 149
Tutors: Baermann, 46, 153, 234; Berr, 72, 178, 209, Klosé, 46, 113, 117, 278; Lefèvre, 42, 47, 63, 67, 92, 113, 189, 196, 209, 241, 244; Magnani, 167; Müller, 107, 182, 209; Romero, 209, 278; Rozanov, 212, 239; Williams, 270; Willman, 198
Tyler, George, Plate 31; 260

UNNA, 246
Utrecht, 56

VACCAI, NICOLA, 194
Vagny, Pierre A., 260
Valette, Antoine N., 260
Van Ackere, Constant, 260
Van Buggenhout, Emile, 261
Vandenbogaerde, F.L., 52, 261
Van der Finck, Christiaan, 261
Van der Finck, Joannes Chr., 71, 261
Van der Gracht, 52
Vanderhagen, A., 261
Vanderhagen, Amand, 15, 134, 192, 261-262, 278
Vanderplancken, Corneille, 262
Van Malder, 261
Vannini, 172
Vantroba, P.P., 58
Vaupel, Jean, 263
Vauth, 127, 164, 234, 263
Venice, 42, 61, 64, 194
Venzl, Heinrich, 263
Verdi, Giuseppe, 68, 150, 189
Verhey, Theodor, 180
Verlen, 263
Verney, R., 210, 263
Versailles, 53, 90
Vibrato, 46, 173, 193
Vichy, 189
Vídni, 189
Vienna, 62, 68, 69, 82, 99, 104, 105, 114, 123, 132, 136, 145, 147, 148, 165, 171, 188, 189, 200, 201, 205, 209, 226, 235, 236, 243, 245, 246-248, 252, 257, 266, 274; Augarten, 98, 279; Conservatoire, 51, 55, 113, 129, 148, 163, 164, 197, 198, 228, 230, 274; County Hall, 237; Gesellschaft der Musikfreunde, 199, 226; Hellmesberger Concerts, 252; Kärntnerthortheater, 136, 138, 148, 220; Konzertverein, 197; Large Ridotto Room, 138, 259; Mozart Society, 274; Philharmonic Orchestra, 138, 274; Red Hedgehog, 138, 213; Roman Emperor's Room, 213; St Michael's Church, 199; Schmidt Society, 274; Schuppenzigh Subscription Concerts, 105; Small Ridotto Room, 33, 148, 215; Summer Palace, 236, 237; Tonkünstlersocietät, 33, 104, 138, 165, 190, 194, 201, 213, 233, 266; University, 200
Vienna Octet, 274
Viersnickel, Anton, 175, 263
Viersnickel, Joseph, 175, 263
Vilmar, 225, 263,
Vilworde Royal Wind Society, 47
Vincennes, 187
Vio, Lisette, 105
Vionne, 264
Vock, Anton, 264
Vogel, Johann, 277-278
Vogler, Abbé, 213
Vogt, Emil, 264
Vogt, Gustav, Plate 5; 57, 206, 264
Voisin, Louis, 264
Vollmar, August, 264
Volodin, Alexander V., 264
Vriès, (Indian), 219

WACHTELBRENNER, 264
Wachter, 242, 264-265
Wack, 265
Wack, Wolfgang, 224, 265
Wadsworth, 265
Wadsworth, T., 265
Wäselia, Mlle, 76, 77
Wagner, 162, 265
Wagner (Kapellmeister), 213
Wagner, Carl, 265
Wagner, Friedrich, 265-266
Wagner, Richard, 143, 213, 225, 234
Wagner, Wilhelm, 266
Wagner, Wilhelm (of Mainz), 266
Walbrül, Johann, 266
Walch, Anton, 266
Walckiers, Eugène, 163
Wallerstein, 164, 175, 247
Walter, Albert, 266
Walter, J. Georg, 243
Walther, Johann G., 266-267
Walthew, Richard, 94
Wander von Grünwald, Mlle, 196
Warsaw, 44, 92, 259; Institute for the Poor, 187; Theatre, 105
Wasmutius, Bernhard, 267
Wassilieff, 267
Waterloo, Battle of, 55, 132, 214
Waterson, James, 155, 270
Webbe, Samuel, 39
Weber, Carl M. von, 17, 24, 29, 35, 37, 49, 129, 132, 143, 145, 149, 185, 198, 201, 210, 211, 268, 270, 273
Weber, Caroline, 211
Weber, David, Plate 3
Weber, Henri, 116, 267
Weichsel, Carl, 267
Weichsel, Charles, 267
Weichsel, Mme (*née* Weirmann), 267
Weilburg, 172
Weimar, 25, 35, 58, 66, 98, 104, 128, 134, 154, 185, 198, 204, 221, 222, 228, 233, 237, 244, 249, 258
Weise I & II, 267
Weissgärber, 267
Weissmuller, 150, 268
Weixelbaum, Georg, 37
Weller, Franz, 268
Weller, Friedrich, 268
Wenczliczek, 268
Wenderoth, 39, 78, 142, 268
Wenkel, 268
Werle, Georg, 255, 268
Werle, Sebastian, 268-269
Westphalia, King of, 31
Wetterström, 75
Whitehouse, Caroline B., 152
Widor, Charles, 210
Wiebel, Hermann, 269
Wiedemann. L., 278
Wienen, Mikolaj, 269
Wieprecht, Wilhelm, 40, 145, 217, 269
Wiesbaden, 52, 205, 214, 229, 249
Wiesner, Paul, 269
Williams, Joseph, 15, 159, 269-270
Willman, Thomas, L., 51, 95, 96, 132, 146, 198, 251, 264, 270-273
Winchester, 168
Winding, August, 194
Winter, 273
Winter, Peter von, 17
Winterthur, 190
Wippert, L., 273
Wiss, Robert, 273
Wisse, Johann A., 66, 273
Witt, 273
Wittek, Anton, 243
Wittenberg, 253
Wittstadt, Bernhard, 274
Wlach, Leopold, Plate 32; 15, 41, 197, 274
Wörlitz, 268
Wohllebe, C.Z., 103, 274-275
Wolf, Franz X., Fig 6; 275
Wolf, Johann K., 275
Wolfe, A., 90, 275
Wolff, 275
Wolff, Franz, 275
Wood, Daniel, 115
Wood, Fred, Plate II
Wood, Mrs (see Paton, Mary A.)
Wood, Sir Henry, 100
Woodyatt, Emily, 272
Wranizkij, Mme, 272
Würtemberg, Duke of, 257
Würtemberg, King of, 205
Würzburg, 31, 149, 175, 205, 213, 231, 263; Music Institute, 230; Wind band, 263
Würzburg, Prince Adam Friedrich of, 175
Wüstenhagen, 275
Wuille, M., 48, 243, 275, 277
Wustemann (flautist), 243

YORK, 272
Yost, Michel, 162, 175, 199, 202, 241, 262, 277-278
Ypres, 163
Yuste, Miguel, Plate 32; 15, 116, 278-279

ZACH, 279
Zangenberg, I.C., 279
Zeiss, Carl, Plate 18
Zenker, 279
Zimmermann, F.K., 105, 279
Zimro, 46
Zittau, 134, 201
Zomp, Mme, 53
Zuckerman, I.V., 105, 279
Zurich, 26, 64, 66, 99, 148, 190, 220, 221, 232; Large concert hall, 33; Music Society, 190
Zweibrücken, 105, 180
Zwicker, 279